THE BROKER

R. DARRYL FISHER

THE
BROKER

INTRODUCTION BY

DENTON A. COOLEY, M.D.

QUILL
Q
PRESS

THE BROKER is published by
QUILL PRESS, LLC
2911 NW 122nd
Oklahoma City, Oklahoma 73120

Library of Congress Cataloging-in-Publication Data

Fisher, R. Darryl
The Broker / R. Darryl Fisher—1st Edition
96-67800
CIP

ISBN 0-9651404-0-7

First Edition.

All characters in this book are fictitious, and any resemblance to actual persons,
living or dead, is purely coincidental.

For my parents—especially for Dad who
was a printer by trade and a reader by heart.

ACKNOWLEDGMENT

I am indebted to numerous individuals for their encouragement and helpfulness in the creation of this story and the fictional people who live in it. But especially to my wife, Orpha Lou. If it were not for her, THE BROKER would not have been possible. She has provided the daily encouragement and enthusiasm for this novel as well as for the living of all our days together.

The editing skill of our daughter, Laura, showed her dad that writing is more than telling a story, and in so doing we learned more about each other. The pragmatic advice of our son, Eric, led THE BROKER from the typed manuscript to the published page.

Without the example and advice of Margaret and Ted Ritter, this novel would not have progressed beyond a dream. Margaret, an accomplished and experienced writer, nurtured dormant writing passions in me years ago. I am grateful to Ted for the hours of patient sharing of his knowledge of the art and craft of fiction. Sandra Gluckman provided the initial stimulus to place my fictional ideas into words on paper. Russ and Fionnuala Gurley gave of their youthful exuberance, confidence, and talents in so many ways. Claudia Hisle's and Christi Holman's microscopic review of the text was extraordinarily helpful. And Skippy O'Neal's management skills, unflagging energy, and support made this writing effort, as well as so many other projects, possible. I appreciate all the support as well as the heritage I share with these individuals, arising from our beginnings in Ada, Oklahoma.

I am indebted to a host of special friends across the country who offered their special talents, insights, and experiences to me, listening to the story, criticizing the drafts, and giving their moral support over the years of the writing of THE BROKER: Bob and Pat Pipkin of Woodside, California; Bill and Judy Sloan of Seal Beach, California; Judy Stover of Boston; Heard and Alice Faye Broadrick, Cathy Devine, and Coe London of Oklahoma City; Jack and Adri Peacock of El Paso; Mack and Carolyn Holmes of Los Angeles.

Nancy Coffey of the Jay Garon-Brooke literary agency of New York City and Jerry Van Cook of Oklahoma City provided their editing skills that honed the manuscript into a novel. Tony Lugafet kept our computers alive and well during the countless rewrites of the manuscript.

Any success I share with all of my friends. Any mistakes are exclusively mine.

For the thousands of heart transplant surgeons around the world who have served their patients and their profession with selfless dedication since the beginning of human cardiac transplantation in the late sixties, I dedicate this novel. By their individual efforts, cardiac transplantation has eliminated suffering and prolonged life for past and future generations.

I am especially grateful to Dr. Denton Cooley of Houston for his advice and assistance with this novel but more importantly for his support of my surgical career over the years. He is truly an internationally recognized cardiovascular surgeon whose achievements and accomplishments serve as a benchmark against which other surgeons are and will be measured. I am honored to share with him our heritage of the Johns Hopkins Hospital surgical training program in Baltimore, Maryland.

For all those patients around the world who are still waiting for an organ donor, I hope that the message of THE BROKER will influence at least one more person to step forward and make the decision for organ donation—the ultimate gift of life.

This novel is an imaginary creation rooted in a metropolitan medical center, like the many hospitals where I have spent years as a cardiovascular surgeon. However, the characters and events are entirely fictional. References to persons, organizations, places, or events are illusory.

INTRODUCTION

T HROUGHOUT THE AGES, the heart has been regarded not
only as the center of physical life but also as the seat of human
thought, will, and wisdom. In many cultures, the heart even sig-
nified divine presence and was considered symbolically as food for the
gods. The ancient Aztecs took this idea to a particularly cruel extreme. In
a sacrificial ritual, they actually tore the hearts from living prisoners, offering the organs as gifts to placate their gods, who demanded a steady diet
of hearts to keep the universe in order.

What makes THE BROKER so compelling is the plausibility of its
premise. The sale (and sometimes theft) of organs is already a reality in certain areas of the world. In India, donor kidneys can be bought, a practice
that has been documented in the British medical literature. Organ pur-
chases are also said to occur in some South American countries, the Philip-
pines, Egypt, and even Great Britain. In China, prisoners have supposedly
been used as organ donors for the wealthy—their executions timed to
coincide with the need for their organs. From other countries, including
the United States, have come unsubstantiated reports of organs for sale to
the highest bidder, organs that have been obtained through kidnappings
and murders—not unlike the black market constructed by Tenoch.

That fact could so closely mirror fiction testifies to the desperate shortage of donor organs that exists today. Although efforts have been made to
educate the public about organ donation, the number of donor organs
available for transplant annually has remained fairly constant. In the last
eight years, the number of heart donors in the United States has increased
by only 100 each year, while the number of patients waiting on the trans-

plant list has more than doubled. In 1994, about 1,000 patients died while waiting for a donor heart. Another 60,000 never made it to the waiting list. The number of organs procured by the current system simply fails to meet the present demand.

To increase the supply of donor organs, some have suggested offering financial incentives or "rewarded gifting" to families of organ donors. Suggested incentives include paying a lump sum to the donor's family, reimbursing the family for funeral expenses, deferring estate taxes, and setting up donor insurance or a "futures market," whereby an individual agrees in advance to donate organs, with payment to his beneficiaries or his estate taking place only after donation. Others have suggested that donors or their families should at least receive commendation from the President or other top-level government official. All of these suggestions, however, have met with fierce opposition.

Opponents of financial incentives argue that altruistic donation needs only to be better promoted to become more effective. According to such opponents, potential dangers of financial incentives for donors include brokering of organs for profit, taking advantage of the poor to benefit the rich, and coercing of families to donate for the "wrong" reasons (financial rather than altruistic). At the very least, altruistic donation could be compromised by introducing market principles to organ procurement. A recent Gallup survey found that such a system may, indeed, prove to be ineffective. In that survey, offering financial incentives made a difference to less than 20% of respondents, and incentives decreased the number of altruistic donations, indicating that capitalistic principles may not be applicable to organ donation.

To offer financial incentives for donating organs in the United States, the current ban on "payment for organs" would have to be repealed and some controls implemented. Reversing this ban without implementing controls could transform our world from a place where the sanctity of the human body is held in great esteem to a place where body parts are treated as commodities for sale to the highest bidder. With THE BROKER, Darryl Fisher gives his readers a chilling glimpse into just such a world. In reading this book, I ask the reader to consider the circumstances that have made a black market of organs an all too real possibility. Donating an organ for any reason is the ultimate gift—the gift of life. It is a gift everyone should consider giving.

Denton A. Cooley, M.D.
President and Surgeon-in-Chief
Texas Heart Institute
Houston, Texas

THE BROKER

ONE

A WAVE OF evening rain darkened the sky and wrapped the ambulance as it screamed toward Dallas Metropolitan Hospital, parting the Harry Hines Boulevard traffic off its bow. The thick lenses of the driver's glasses flashed reflections of the van's interior as he leaned forward against the steering wheel, straining to see the dark roadway between the lashing windshield wipers. The knuckles of his fingers blanched white, like carved ivory claws on the steering wheel, as he fought the buffeting winds blowing directly across the three southbound lanes. Headlights of cars in front of the screaming van marked the roadside like channel marker buoys. The rotating roof beacon blew surreal scarlet reflections on the pools of water collected in low spots on the road surface. A black limousine, like an oversized dinghy, hugged the rear bumper of the careening ambulance as the pair raced each other toward the hospital.

A stalled pickup truck blocked the middle of a flooded intersection. The ambulance's right front fender caught the truck's tailgate as the ambulance fishtailed through the intersection, spraying shards of headlight glass across the intersection when the driver fought the bucking van back into the roadway. "You son of a bitch," screamed the ambulance driver as the ambulance swerved back to the center lane.

In the boxlike enclosure of the rear of the swaying van, a pale, unconscious middle-aged man, his dark skin a bleached brown, lay on the stainless steel gurney cleated to the floor. The wind abruptly caterwauled around the emergency medical van, like a sailboat in rough sea, pitching the medical technician against the side of the boxy rear enclosure of the emergency van. Holding onto the chrome overhead bar, the paramedic frantically readjusted adhesive electrode pads, the size of half dollars, on the smooth hairless chest of the man.

"Get Dr. Baldwin on the horn," the technician shouted through the window opening in the bulkhead separating the driver from the rear of the van. "This guy's going down the tubes . . . I can't get any blood pressure."

"I couldn't raise the ER five minutes ago when we left the funeral home," the driver shouted back over his right shoulder.

"See if the ER is receiving the electrocardiogram signal we're transmitting from this guy," the young technician said, punching his index finger at the lighted control buttons of the EKG machine above the gurney.

The driver keyed the handheld microphone while he held the accelerator to the floor. "562 to Metro ER," he said, releasing the microphone and looking into the rear view mirror. "That goddamn limousine is running right up my ass."

"Come in, 562," the radio squawked back immediately.

"Why the hell didn't you answer my first call?" the ambulance driver shouted. "Code 9. We're bringing in a fifty-five-year-old man. Looks like he's had a heart attack. No blood pressure. Unconscious. Do you read the EKG?"

The radio hissed in static until a crackling voice from the radio speaker finally sounded above the roar of the siren, "Slow, erratic idioventricular heart rhythm. About twenty beats per minute."

"That's how I read it," shouted the sweaty technician. His forehead lined itself in concentration, and his cinched mouth focused on the radio speaker in the bulkhead. He wiped the dripping sweat from his forehead on the long shirt sleeve of his white duck uniform. A sour smell, the combination of expensive men's cologne, the fruity sweet aroma of champagne, and the awful stench of vomit, saturated the close air of the van. Yellow stains of vomit particles pockmarked the shiny satin lapels of the portly man's black tuxedo jacket. He lay immobile like a recumbent brown Buddha. A half inch of clear vinyl tubing protruded through his thin bluish lips. A neat mustache circled the upper half of the endotracheal tube.

As the paramedic squeezed a black balloon ventilator bag attached to the tube jutting from the man's mouth, the man's glistening nut-brown chest heaved against his ruffled tuxedo shirt that had been ripped open to the waist. A gold link chain noosed the comatose man's neck. A filigreed cross attached to the chain dangled onto the sheet under the man's fleshy neck. "What's your ETA?" squawked the radio speakerphone.

"Eight minutes," the driver said, his eyes never leaving the rain-splashed windshield.

"Stand by. Let me find Dr. Baldwin," the voice from the radio speaker crackled back.

―

The Saturday evening traffic of patients through the Emergency Room of the Dallas Metropolitan Hospital had gridlocked just before six o'clock on the rainy Memorial Day weekend. This Saturday evening was no different from the seventy-four years of Saturday nights in the Metro Hospital ER before it.

The parade of suffering humanity through the Metropolitan Hospital Emergency Room doors had included two heart attacks, one fatal drowning, two cocaine overdoses, a hypertensive nosebleed, two domestic shootings, four upper respiratory infections, two kidney infections, and one case of gonorrhea. The relentless onslaught of illness and injury reduced each of the hospital supplicants to faceless diagnostic groups in competition with each other for attention. There was no time for names, just diagnoses attached to a body. A fractured forearm in room four; the finger laceration in room two; the gastroenteritis in six.

A three day holiday weekend invariably filled the Emergency Room, because little other medical care was available in central Dallas from Friday evening until Tuesday morning when the hospital clinics reopened. The hospital Emergency Room served its public with the efficiency of a fastfood restaurant and just about the same degree of familiarity. This Saturday evening's surge of patients overflowed the crowded Metropolitan Hospital reception area, already crammed wall-to-wall with the afternoon's holdovers of family members and friends of the holiday weekend victims.

The overhead intercom in the Emergency Room barked an exasperated telephone operator's search every thirty seconds for a doctor, a laboratory technician, a nurse, or a patient's family. The fourteen curtained treatment cubicles surrounding the open central triage area each contained a waiting diagnosis . . . a diagnosis of injury, illness, or abuse, each separated into holding pens awaiting treatment.

Trauma Room One in the center of the ER receiving area bore its own battle scars. The scuffed white terrazzo stone floor absorbed the fluorescent light, mixing it with indelible stains of blood, spilled antiseptic fluids, and other effluvium of the traffic of a generation of patients from the homeless to the highest elected officials of the country, each seeking relief from pain and death. The triage area, like the center of a bull ring, awaited the dance of life and death often decided in seconds and minutes, the outcome in each case shaped by the training and skill of the emergency team.

Less than a dozen steps from the concrete ambulance receiving dock of the Metro ER, the blue canvas curtains inside Trauma Room One enclosed the tiled room like a circus tent. In its center was a hospital gurney, the focal point of misery and suffering in Trauma Room One. This Saturday evening the gurney held a black teenager, moaning incoherently, naked except for ragged filthy Levis. His arms and legs squirmed at heavy cloth restraints binding them to the table. A half dozen bags of intravenous fluids, a video monitor displaying an erratic electronic heart tracing, and an array of aluminum coned surgical lights hung from the ceiling around the gurney. Three emergency room nurses flitted about the gurney like hummingbirds.

Dr. Cassandra Baldwin draped her long white lab coat on the end of one of the equipment chains dangling from the ceiling and stepped up to the left side of the gurney. Her gray surgical scrub shirt and pants concealed her trim figure as she leaned forward to study the two-inch gaping hole in the boy's chest just beneath his left nipple.

"What's this knife fighter's blood pressure?" Dr. Baldwin asked Louise Wilcox, the evening ER supervisor, a pear-shaped woman filling out her glistening white nurse's uniform.

"I get fifty, systolic," Wilcox said, bending over the young man and again pumping up the blood pressure cuff wrapped about the teenager's arm.

"Fifty?" Dr. Baldwin said. Her steady voice gave no hint of the urgency of the man's deteriorating blood pressure. She quickly placed her long fingers ensheathed in latex gloves on either side of the two-inch gash and probed the wound with her fingertips. Her slender index finger disappeared into the wound.

A uniformed Dallas policeman stepped out of the corner of the curtained cubicle and stood beside Dr. Baldwin as she concentrated on the tactile sensation of her fingertips. The policeman touched her arm. Startled, Cassy turned her head but still kept her index finger in the stab wound.

In the policeman's hand was a fifteen-inch stiletto switchblade knife. Fully opened, its seven-inch stainless steel blade glistened in the glare of the overhead surgical lights. "Here's the frog sticker that his buddy shived him with, Doc."

"His blood pressure has bottomed out!" Louise Wilcox called out in a loud voice, worriedly looking up across the boy's sweaty chest at Dr. Baldwin. The teenager's writhing and moaning quieted suddenly, and the boy became a motionless form on the gurney, as if his engine had sputtered to a stop.

Cassy pulled her finger out of the gash, blood dripping from her glove. "Oh hell, this kid has been stabbed in the heart. He's tamponading. Stat page Dr. Welsh. Call the OR and tell them to post an emergency thoracotomy for a stab wound of the heart."

A stray lock of chestnut hair brushed her forehead above her dark brown eyes. Dr. Baldwin flipped the wave of hair back in place with a jerk of her head. "Get me a pericardiocentesis tray. I've got to suck the blood out of the pericardial space with a syringe and needle."

Cassy then quickly inserted a polyvinyl chest tube, the size of a garden hose, directly into the stab wound until about a foot of the tube disappeared into the depth of the stab hole. Instantly, a gush of dark blood appeared in the clear tube and filled the gallon plastic jug on the floor beside the gurney with nearly two pints of blood that had pooled in the teenager's chest cavity.

The young nurse studied the video monitor hanging above the gurney displaying a glowing dot flowing across the screen. "Dr. Baldwin, his heart beat is slowing down."

"Forget the needle. Get the emergency thoracotomy tray now. I've got to open this kid's chest. He's going out on me."

"Yes, Doctor," the nurse said and disappeared through the opening in the blue canvas curtain.

Louise Wilcox moved to the head of the gurney, giving up her attempts to hear a blood pressure. Holding the boy's pale black face in her hands, she wiped the clammy sweat from his forehead and closed eyelids. The boy lay still as if asleep.

"Dr. Baldwin, he's quit breathing."

"Where in the hell is the anesthesiology resident? Didn't you page him when this kid hit the triage? This boy needs to be intubated. Somebody is going to have to breathe him."

"Dr. Bradley hasn't answered his page. Nobody knows where he is," the nurse said, shrugging her shoulders.

"Then give me the damn endotracheal tube. I'll intubate his trachea while I'm waiting on the surgical instruments." Dr. Baldwin stepped to the front of the gurney and lifted the boy's chin upward, extending his neck like a curved swan's neck. With her gloved fingers she pried apart his slack jaw and quickly inserted a tongue depressor into his mouth. There was no gag reflex even as Dr. Baldwin lifted his slack tongue up. The lighted bulb at the end of the metal blade illuminated the back of the boy's throat.

The blood pooling around the boy's heart in the pericardial sac was choking off the heart's contraction, shutting down his blood pressure and interfering with the central function of the heart . . . to pump blood. Without effective blood circulation and oxygen flow, the boy had already slipped into unconsciousness and was just moments away from death.

Dr. Baldwin insinuated a clear polyvinyl tube down the boy's throat and flipped the tip of it through the dark opening between his vocal cords. There was still no gag reflex, even with the tube jammed into the larynx. The boy lay lifeless.

"Breathe him," Dr. Baldwin said as she connected the plastic fittings of the endotracheal to the black ventilating balloon and handed the football-shaped bag to Louise Wilcox. With both hands the head nurse squeezed the black balloon like kneading dough, forcing air into the boy's lungs. His chest rose and fell with each squeeze.

The upward spikes of the glowing electrocardiogram dot on the video monitor slowed, each spike accompanied by a chirp until the electronic sounds of the heart tolled like a clock. Dr. Baldwin stepped quickly to the left side of the gurney and felt the edges of the laceration that closed around the chest tube she had inserted to drain the collected blood in the boy's chest. The edges of the skin parted around the tube exposing the blood-tinged yellow fat of the subcutaneous tissue. With each squeeze of the black breathing bag, frothy bloody foam spewed out the stab opening and ran down the tube.

The third nurse leaned over the boy's right arm, pumping on the blood pressure cuff and listening to the stethoscope pressed like tongs in her ears. She shook her head sadly. "No blood pressure."

"Where are the thoracotomy instruments? I've got to cut open this kid's chest and drain off the pericardial collection of blood that's pressing his heart."

At that moment the curtains of Trauma Room One opened. A breathless nurse crashed a green cloth wrapped tray onto the fire-engine red resuscitation cart, a converted Sears tool chest that had been pushed up to the foot of the gurney.

"Throw some Betadine around the stab wound," Dr. Baldwin said as she shrugged a green disposable surgeon's gown over her gray scrub clothes. The nurse slopped a brown iodine soaked surgical pad over the boy's chest. An instant later Dr. Baldwin fanned sterile cloth towels around the stab wound.

Turning back to the resuscitation cart, Dr. Baldwin grabbed a scalpel from the instrument tray. With a swift movement of her hand she slashed the stab wound into a six-inch curved incision angling under the boy's breast up toward his left armpit. With more strength than delicacy, Dr. Baldwin plunged her right hand bluntly through the rib space, parting the chest muscles until her hand entered the chest cavity.

"Keep ventilating him, Louise," Dr. Baldwin said calmly. Her icy reserve and dispassionate calm took over for the anxiety that wired the three nurses together.

The fingers of her right hand felt familiar territory inside the boy's left chest. With her index finger she traced the track of the long knife that had plunged into the boy's chest. The pericardial sac containing the barely beating heart bulged like a tense balloon filled with blood. Each feeble contraction of the boy's heart spewed more blood from the stab wound of the heart's ventricular chamber, increasing the pressure within the pericardium on the heart.

"His pericardium is so tense, I can't even feel his heart beating."

"He's not got any blood pressure. The EKG shows his heart rate is twenty. Hurry!" Louise Wilcox said.

"I know," Dr. Baldwin said easily. "Give me a second." Her left hand reached behind her and grabbed the surgical retractor from the instrument tray. With her right hand still plunged up to her wrist in the boy's chest, Dr. Baldwin slipped the ratcheted surgical retractor into the wound until the prongs of the retractor grabbed the cut edges of the thoracotomy incision. Twisting the gear mechanism of the retractor, she pried open the incision beneath the nipple until she could see into the dark depth of the boy's chest. Still there was no response from the lifeless boy.

"I can see his pericardium now," she said. The pink spongy lung edge lapped like a flashing tongue into the wound with each inflation of Louise Wilcox's balloon bag.

"He's going out. The EKG is flat-lined," Louise shouted.

"Easy, Louise," Dr. Baldwin said evenly. A sheen of perspiration appeared on her forehead. The base of her chestnut hair hung wet below her sharply angled jaw.

With chromed dissecting scissors longer than her left hand, Dr. Baldwin inserted the scissors' tips deep in the incision. She snipped the tense pericardial sac. A geyser of dark black blood shot forth from the pericardial space like a burst water balloon. The dark oily blood spilled out of the incision onto the gurney.

"The heart's in standstill," she said as she wormed her right palm into the space around the heart and folded her fingers over the organ, firmly squeezing the heart like a hollow rubber ball. "Let me give his heart a squeeze."

The flaccid heart muscle in her hand immediately filled with blood once the pressure of the blood collecting around it had been relieved. "I can feel the heart refilling . . . there . . . it's beginning to contract again. Yes. Yes. We've got a beat."

At that moment two doctors dressed in gray surgical scrub clothes slipped through the privacy curtains of Trauma Room One. "Welcome, Doctors," Cassy said smiling. "Come join the party. It's the Saturday night session of the knife and gun club of central Dallas."

"Sorry I'm late," one of the doctors said. "My beeper batteries are down." Louise handed the black balloon bag to him with a disbelieving smirk.

At that moment the black teenager started to writhe. The restored circulation from his returning heart beat had begun to revive his brain's function. Cassy pulled her hand from the incision, trailing driblets of blood onto the gurney sheets.

"What happened?" Dr. Welsh, the surgery resident, a burly black-haired man asked.

"Stab wound of the left ventricle. Acute tamponade. He nearly arrested. I had to open his chest," Dr. Baldwin said, stripping off the blood-soaked surgical gown and gloves. "Will you take over from here? I've still got a house full of patients waiting to see me."

"Sure, Dr. Baldwin. We'll take him up to the OR, wash him out, and close his chest back up. Did you see any active bleeding?"

"I don't think so. But I know you'll take a good look. I think the stiletto blade must have nicked the tip of the ventricle."

—

At the far end of the ER, beyond the Trauma Rooms, Dr. Baldwin stopped in front of a treatment cubicle and jerked a metal clipboard from the door rack. She arched her low back against the metal frame of the cubicle door, trying to stretch out the dull ache that had settled there after the strenuous effort of the emergency surgery to open the teenager's chest and massage life back into his heart. Her back muscles recoiled in aching bands.

This Saturday had been a grueling marathon, cubicle to cubicle. The weariness of the past twelve hours of emergency duty were etched in the dark fatigue shadows under her eyes. A fine trace of wrinkles netted corners of her deep brown eyes. Except for these subtle changes of near exhaustion, she was as attractively groomed, even in a surgical scrub blouse and baggy pants, as when she reported for her holiday duty as Director of Emergency Room Services at Metro Hospital twelve hours earlier. Her alert eyes scanned the medical record in her hand, absorbing chunks of the patient's data.

She quickly flipped the pages on the aluminum clipboard. Just another half hour and I am out of here, she thought. Then a warm bath and into some real clothes for a change. She smiled to herself and stretched her arms together in front of her in a brief isometric relaxing exercise, unconsciously adjusting the white laboratory coat that hung to her knees over the surgeon's scrub shirt and pants that concealed her slender body.

"Gracie. What is this?" Dr. Baldwin asked the nursing aide, a short, round woman with skin as dark and shiny as oiled mahogany. A red, green and yellow striped turban wound around the woman's head, covering her hair completely. Gracie's turban always concealed her hair; no one had ever seen her without it. It was even rumored among the generations of ER staff that Gracie might have no hair at all.

"This baby has had a fever and runny nose for three days. Now the mother brings the kid into my Emergency Room at six-thirty on Saturday night. Damn, this is not an Emergency Room. I'm running an infirmary sick call for central Dallas," Dr. Baldwin said and shook her head. "I'm the pediatrician, obstetrician, drug counselor, psychiatrist, heart surgeon, and every other kind of doctor rolled into one for the holiday weekend!"

"This mama's only a child," the black woman said in a soft lilting blend of French and English that seasoned her native Haitian dialect. "She doesn't know how to take care of her baby."

"Gracie, you can find some good in everyone," Dr. Baldwin said, the corners of her eyes wrinkling with her smile.

Gracie's soft expressive black face held her years so well that no one knew her exact age. Dr. Baldwin had an idea that Gracie must be close to sixty. For thirty-five years, eight years longer than anyone else, Gracie had worked in the Metropolitan Hospital Emergency Room, beginning the week after she had arrived in Dallas fresh from Haiti. She remained a benign mystery to everyone. Her Haitian name, unpronounceable to most Texans, had given way to the nickname, Gracie, a derivative of the hymn, *Amazing Grace,* that Gracie hummed throughout her work shifts.

Dr. Baldwin parted the cloth curtain of the treatment cubicle. A pregnant teenage Hispanic mother cradled a screaming infant in her arms. Dried scales of mucus crusted the baby's nose. "Buenas noches, Señorina," Dr. Baldwin said. Continuing in fluent Spanish, she asked the mother-child, "How long has your baby been sick?"

"Dos días. Tres días," the mother said, shrugging and rocking the screaming infant in her bony brown arms.

"Let me see what's wrong with you," Dr. Baldwin said in Spanish. She took the squirming and protesting baby from the mother's arms and laid the infant on the examining table. She listened to the baby's chest with her stethoscope and quickly peeked into the infant's mouth and ears with her flashlight.

"Otitis media," Dr. Baldwin said to Gracie who was trying to hold the screaming infant on the examining table so that Dr. Baldwin could see into the infant's ear. "Let's do a throat culture. I want to start her on antibiotics."

"I think I can find some pediatric penicillin liquid in the cabinet," Gracie said, handing the wiggling baby to the doctor. Gracie slipped out of the treatment cubicle, humming the hymn. Dr. Baldwin cradled the infant in the crook of her left arm and whispered gently to the baby. Moments later the crying stopped, and the infant slept.

"Señorina, your baby has an ear infection. I want you to give her this medicine Gracie will give you and bring her back here on Tuesday evening. I'll check your baby for you then," Dr. Baldwin said.

At that moment the pale blue heavy cotton curtain shuttering the cubicle swept open under the abrupt hand of Louise Wilcox. "I've been looking for you, Dr. Baldwin," Louise said, her mouth puckering into a peevish twist.

For the past fifteen months, beginning with Dr. Baldwin's appointment as Director of Emergency Services, the relationship of the two women a generation apart had frozen into a chilly professionalism, and this evening shift was like every other working day between them . . . intense.

"Big problem for you, Dr. Baldwin," Louise said in her usual twitting tone. A haughty correctness underlay Louise's heavily starched white nurse's uniform. Louise wore her white uniform like a protective armor plate, insulating her from contact with patients as well as her co-workers and Dr. Baldwin. "The EMS van just radioed in. They've got a heart attack who's dying on them. They'll be here in eight minutes."

"Not another one. That's the third heart attack today," Dr. Baldwin sighed and placed the sleeping infant in the teenage mother's arms. "You know the dosage of the penicillin, Gracie. Be sure the mother knows how to give it to her baby." Gracie nodded. Dr. Baldwin slipped around the curtain behind Louise Wilcox.

Moments later, the nursing supervisor and Dr. Baldwin leaned forward over the communication radio console in the supervisor's office near the front entry of the Emergency Room. The speaker buzzed with static, nearly obscuring the emergency medical technician's voice transmitted from the ambulance. "We're not doing much good," his disembodied voice crackled. "Have you got his EKG tracing that we're sending?"

"Yes. It looks like slow sinus bradycardia," Dr. Baldwin said. The deflections of the green phosphorescent electrocardiogram dot traced slowly on the monitor, positioned like a television screen above the radio. The digital computer recorded the heart rate at thirty-two beats per minute. A strip of electrocardiogram paper unreeled from the machine into a jumbled heap on the floor.

"Can't get much of a blood pressure either," the radio voice said.

"Give him four-tenths of atropine and start an isuprel drip," Dr. Baldwin said, hoping that the combination of cardiovascular drug stimulants might increase the heart rate and also boost his blood pressure.

"Four-tenths atropine and an isuprel drip. Will do," the technician said, repeating the medical order formally. "We should be in the driveway in five minutes."

"I'll be waiting," Dr. Baldwin said, straightening her low back up from the radio console and stretching unconsciously until her fingertips nearly touched the ceiling. Dr. Baldwin looked down at Louise, a full head shorter than Dr. Baldwin's five foot eight-inches. "Get the resuscitation crash cart, Miss Wilcox. I'll need three nurses ready when this heart attack hits the door. I'm going to my office to make a phone call."

⸺

Dr. Cassandra Marta Baldwin's ER office was a patient cubicle in the back hallway of the Emergency Room, a space that she had commandeered thirteen months earlier when she had accepted the Director's position. The windowless room was barely large enough for a drab gray metal desk and the cracked leather couch that she had been given by a retiring psychiatrist. Her desktop was cluttered with patient charts in separate manila folders.

Medical journals still sheathed in their plastic mailers stood in piles in each of the corners. Cassy flopped on the couch, the running shoes on her feet hanging off the end, and dialed her home phone number. She slipped off her Nikes and walked her bare feet up the cool plastered concrete wall of the room, feeling the day's pressure drain from her legs and feet. With her feet pushed as high up against the wall as she could reach, the scrub pants fell around her knees exposing her slender pale legs.

The single framed photograph in the room hanging on the pale yellow plastered wall was just at the tip of her toes—a picture of the President of the United States shaking Dr. Baldwin's hand in the Rose Garden of the White House. It was inscribed, 'To an outstanding American and international surgeon. For Cassy.' The President in his flourishing scrawl had signed his name across the bottom of the eight-by-ten inch color photograph.

On the eleventh ring, her home phone was answered. "Dr. Baldwin's residence," a heavily accented Spanish voice said.

"Lupita, Buenas noches. I'm going to be late again. Maybe midnight."

"Sí, Señora."

"May I speak to Alex?" Cassy asked in Spanish.

"He's in the swimming pool," her housekeeper responded in Spanish.

"And you're inside the house?" Dr. Baldwin asked. Lupita did not respond.

"Is he in the pool?" Dr. Baldwin asked. "It's storming. You know better than to let Alex swim in the rain." Her tone left no doubt that Cassy had had many similar conversations with her son's nanny.

"No, Señora," Lupita said in her typical non sequitur that always exasperated Dr. Baldwin.

"Lupita, I want to talk to my son. Go get him now," Dr. Baldwin said, reverting into English. "Bring Alex to the telephone, and be sure he stays out of the pool when it's raining. You know he's not to be in the pool after dark."

Cassy rubbed her forehead, trying to dissipate the headache that had begun just above her eyebrows. She cradled the silent phone against her left ear and stared at the white acoustical tile ceiling, studying the arrangements of tiny holes in each ceiling tile. Her fingertips nervously brushed at the thick forelock of deep brown hair that dangled over her left eye. She heard her seven-year-old son's familiar footsteps running toward the phone just as she spotted a single strand of gray hair shining like an incandescent filament in her dark hair that lay on the sofa about her slender neck.

"Hi, Mom," Alex's voice shouted into her ear as she jerked the offending gray hair strand out by its root. "When will you be home?"

"That's why I'm calling, Alex. I'll be late again tonight."

"Oh, Mom. What about the pizza you promised?"

"I'll bring some pizza when I come home. I'll wake you up when I get in. We'll watch the late show on television. Is that a deal?"

"Okay." His disappointment was transparent. "What about tomorrow?"

"I haven't forgotten, soldier. It's your eighth birthday."

The door to Dr. Baldwin's office suddenly vibrated open under insistent pounding. Louise's head popped into the room. "It's here. Come quick or not at all," Louise said, dropping into her usual impersonal description of an incoming patient.

"Alex, Mom's got to run. See you tonight. Love and kisses," Cassy said.

Her bare feet found her running shoes. She stuffed the tail of the loosely fitting V-neck surgical scrub tunic under the drawstring of the matching gray scrub pants. She slammed the office door behind her. Shrugging into her knee length white coat, she ran down the hallway to the triage area in the central area of the ER. As she rounded the corner into the receiving area, a frenzy of nurses and technicians blocked her view. All she could at first see were the black patent leather shoes of a man lying on the rolling stretcher in the center of the Trauma Room One. She pushed herself between a nurse and an emergency medical technician to stand at the head of the gurney. Instantly the three nurses and two technicians looked to her, awaiting her orders.

"Where did you pick this man up?" Cassy asked the emergency medical technician.

In the minute before Cassy had arrived at the unconscious man's side, the three nurses had descended on him as soon as the gurney had stopped rolling. In less than a minute the man's tuxedo was cut away and intravenous tubing fed into large veins at the bend of each elbow. Cassy's eyes scanned the activity, registering and recording her impressions of the man's condition, as the electronic vital sign monitoring modules were calibrated and attached to the unconscious man. Connecting monitor wires were slapped on the chest, arms, and legs.

"It was just like a scene from a movie, Dr. Baldwin," the ambulance paramedic said. "We got this 911 call to the Park Haven Funeral Home. Just like the movies, an ambulance run to a funeral home in the middle of the cemetery on a dark rainy night. . . ."

"Roger. Just give me the clinical details about this man."

"Yes, ma'am. Joey pulled the ambulance up to the front of this marble palace. It looks like a mausoleum."

Cassy listened to the paramedic's rambling description, sifting and sorting the useful information, discarding the rest, and already beginning to formulate an emergency room treatment plan for the unconscious man.

The middle-aged Hispanic, his face sweaty and pale beneath smooth coffee-colored skin, lay limp and unresponsive. An endotracheal breathing tube protruded from the man's mouth like an oversize transparent drinking straw. His chest rose and fell mechanically in timing with the technician's squeeze of the black Ambu balloon breathing bag.

"It was just like that old movie, *Citizen Kane* . . . you know the big house scene. The guards hustled us into an office bigger than my house. There this guy was, all laid out in a tuxedo."

As much as Cassy wanted to cut short the paramedic's inappropriate chatter, she held back. The impressions of a person at the scene often give the clue to the diagnosis for an emergency room patient, especially an unconscious one, and Cassy wanted the first impression unfiltered.

"Where was he, Roger? Try to be more specific," Cassy said as she shined her penlight into the unconscious man's eyes testing for a constriction of the pupillary opening in response to the bright light. There was none. The eye openings were wide, black voids. "The pupils are fixed and dilated. Has he got a blood pressure?" Dr. Baldwin asked the nurse at her side without looking up from her examination of the interior of the unconscious man's eyeball.

"The isuprel and atropine we gave on the way here helped a little. Bumped his pressure up to sixty," the young paramedic spoke up.

The nurse pumped up the blood pressure cuff on the man's bare arm. She listened through her stethoscope, frowning and shaking her head. "I think I hear his blood pressure at forty."

"Get a dopamine drip started. Bolus him with a gram of intravenous calcium. We've got to get his blood pressure up even more," Cassy said, her mind racing, already beginning to treat the man without being fully certain of a working diagnosis. "If he doesn't respond quickly, we're going to lose him right here."

"What did he look like when you found him, Roger?" she asked. Her stethoscope rose and fell in time with Louise Wilcox's squeezing the football-sized breathing bag that inflated the man's lungs.

"He was laid out in front of a huge desk."

"Had he been eating?" Cassy asked.

"He might have eaten. There was a gold plate of tacos and two glasses of champagne."

"You didn't see any food in his mouth or throat when you inserted the endotracheal tube? He might have choked on a piece of food that he aspirated into his windpipe."

"No, ma'am, I put the tube in myself. Right there on the office floor. Clear airway. Nothing in his throat. He just wasn't breathing."

"Did he ever respond? Did he say anything? Did he move at all?"

"No, ma'am. All I could get out of the Mexican man who was in the office with him was that one minute this guy is eating his fancy tacos and sipping champagne . . . then the guy stops talking, gets real pale, his eyes roll up, and bang . . . he falls over. That Mexican man insisted that we bring this guy to Metro even though St. Joseph's Hospital was a lot closer to the funeral home."

The ambulance driver looked up at Cassy, his eyes enlarged by the lenses of his glasses. "The Mexican's limousine followed my ambulance all the way here, never more than fifty feet behind us." Cassy spread her patient's eyelids apart while she peered again into the interior of the man's eyeball through her handheld ophthalmoscope. "Eye grounds look fine. No hemorrhages or edema. I'm worried that he had brain injury from lack of oxygen before you arrived," she said, looking up at the video monitor display of the man's vital signs.

"I started CPR as soon as we got there," Roger said. "He must not have been out long. Not more than seven or eight minutes."

"Any family here?" Dr. Baldwin asked.

"I'll check with the receptionist to see if anybody has showed up," Gracie said.

"Begin an epinephrine drip if the dopamine doesn't get his pressure above one hundred," Cassy said. "He'll need a Foley bladder catheter. Draw the usual blood studies . . . chemistries, blood gases, and also get a toxicology blood screen for drugs and alcohol. And I want a stat twelve-lead electrocardiogram and a quick set of cardiac enzymes on the first blood sample." Her formally mechanical voice of oral instructions belied her racing thoughts. What is wrong with this man? Why is he unconscious?

"What do you think happened?" the paramedic asked Dr. Baldwin as he continued to squeeze the black ventilating balloon bag with both hands, inflating the unconscious man's chest every four seconds.

"Most likely, he's had a massive heart attack. If I can't stabilize him in the next hour, he won't make it out of the ER alive," Cassy said, leaning across the man's chest to listen through her stethoscope to the air rushing like wind in and out of the man's lungs.

The Emergency Room receptionist caught Cassy's arm. "Dr. Baldwin, there's a Mexican man out in the waiting room asking about this guy."

"Who is this fellow anyway?" Cassy asked the receptionist, nodding toward the unconscious man.

"Jeorg Marquez. He owns the biggest funeral home in Texas. It's the big one in the cemetery in North Dallas."

"Looks like he might have need of his own services," the young paramedic said, smiling at his remark.

"Roger, that's not funny," Dr. Baldwin snapped. "I have to find out this man's medical history. Work on getting his blood pressure up with the dopamine while I go talk to the man that came with him."

Cassy walked into the waiting room filled with patients and families in every chair, mostly Hispanic and blacks, all wearing tired and worn expressions like their clothes. Standing above and apart from the others was a distinguished Hispanic man in a white dinner jacket. "Señor, I am Dr. Baldwin. I am treating your associate."

"Doctora, I am Tenoch." His anthracite black hair lay neatly clipped above an unwrinkled, flawless angular face. A long sleeve, casual black silk shirt hung perfectly over his bare muscular chest that was exposed to the open third button.

"How can I be of assistance, Doctora? Jeorg is far more than a business associate. He is like my brother."

"Tell me precisely what happened," Cassy said.

"Certainly, Doctora," Señor Tenoch said. His expensive men's cologne

breezed against Cassy's face. "Jeorg and I were celebrating our new business partnership in his funeral business. After champagne cocktails in his
office at the Park Haven Funeral Home, we were planning to go to my
home in Highland Park for dinner."

"Was Señor Marquez drunk?"

"Absolutely not. One champagne cocktail. He was thinking clearly.
Jeorg was certainly not inebriated," Señor Tenoch said, a gentle sternness
in his voice.

"Go on."

"We were sipping champagne and eating our tapas when Jeorg complained of being dizzy and light-headed. Suddenly his eyes rolled back,
and he fell to the floor."

"Yes. What next?"

"I rolled him over and spread him out on the floor. He wasn't
breathing."

"Was he conscious?"

"He never said anything. I pulled his eyes open and slapped his face.
He seemed to be trying to tell me something," Tenoch said, gesturing
with his palms. "No, I am sorry, I shouldn't say that. It was nothing. He
was unconscious." He paused a moment searching Cassy's face with his
probing eyes. "How is he now?"

"Not good. Unconscious. His blood pressure is barely obtainable. I believe he has had a massive heart attack and possibly severe brain damage."

"And your prognosis, Doctora?"

Cassy thrust her hands into her pockets, aware of the muscled Hispanic
man, dressed in a dark navy suit, flanking Tenoch. A bodyguard? Cassy
wondered as she avoided his question by asking, "Does Señor Marquez
have a wife . . . family?"

"Señora Marquez and their family are in Mexico City," Tenoch said.
"I will certainly contact her immediately."

"Dr. Baldwin, I need you stat," Louise Wilcox shouted through the
waiting room doors. The implication of the nurse's summons was clear to
everyone in the crowded room.

Cassy turned and ran back into Trauma Room One to find the paramedic straddling Marquez's gurney and pumping the dying man's chest
in a series of stiff-armed, once-every-second punches. "His heart just
stopped," Roger panted. "Complete cardiac arrest. No heartbeat at all.
Flat-lined," he said frantically.

"Keep massaging him," Cassy said to Roger. "Get the external pacemaker." One nurse quickly slapped four circular adhesive pads to the
man's chest, above and below the left nipple, as the electronic pacemaker

console was wheeled up to the stretcher. "Pace his heart at seventy beats per minute, full voltage," Cassy ordered.

"Pacer is on," the nurse said, flipping the switch.

"Come on. Come on," Cassy muttered, adjusting the control knobs of the pacemaker to increase its output. "Nothing. The pacemaker won't stimulate the heart. Complete arrest. No beat." Roger's brutal pounding of the chest with his stiff-armed massage continued, marking each passing second, while the nurse squeezed the black respirator bag between every fourth chest compression by Roger's hands.

Cassy's attempts to restore the man's heartbeat with closed chest massage and intravenous injections of cardiac stimulants assumed a ritualistic death dance. Finally at seven forty-five p.m., after a frantic hour of CPR and with a last glance at the flat-lined machines, Cassy called an end to the effort. A quiet collective sigh of relief and dejection rippled the CPR team.

"Let's call the time of death 19:45," Cassy said. Turning to head nurse, Louise Wilcox, she said, "I'll talk to his friend now, Louise. Get the man in the private waiting room. I don't want to tell him in front of all the gawkers in the waiting room that his friend just died."

Roger stripped off the adhesive pacemaker electrodes and pulled the intravenous and endotracheal tubes from the man's body. Then he covered the body with a clean white sheet.

Cassy returned to her cubbyhole office and fell exhausted onto the couch. It was fifteen minutes before the hospital telephone operator could find and connect her to the Dallas Medical Examiner on call for the holiday weekend.

When the coroner answered, Cassy introduced herself and listened to a young man's voice, "Dr. Sam Heron here, I'm the new kid on the block. This is my second week with the Medical Examiner's office." Cassy then described the events of Jeorg Marquez's treatment.

"Sounds like a straightforward heart attack to me," the assistant ME said. "Any history of heart disease?"

"Not that I know. I agree it sounds like a massive myocardial infarct," Cassy said. "But I'm puzzled by the death. The slow heart beat. The way the heart just stood still in asystole. I couldn't get any contraction out of it with the cardiac pacemaker. I don't know. It's a curious way for a heart attack to kill. I would have expected to see more electrocardiographic changes than a slow heart rate. This guy just apparently faded out. Then his heart slowed to a standstill. I've never seen a heart attack kill somebody that way."

"What did the cardiac enzyme blood test show?" the ME asked.

"We haven't got the results back. The blood sample was drawn as soon as he hit the triage area," Cassy said.

"Any sign of heart failure? Did you hear any heart murmurs?" the ME asked.

"No. Nothing. His heart just seemed to run out of steam," Cassy said.

"Oh, hell," the medical examiner said. "With no history of heart disease and your uncertainty about the cause of death, I don't have any choice except to perform an autopsy to see if I can figure out what killed the poor bastard."

"I'll bet your autopsy will show that a heart attack killed him," Dr. Baldwin said. "I just can't prove it with the data I have from the ER."

"You never know. A heart attack that kills so quickly may not leave us much to see at autopsy," the ME said. "I'll let you know what our postmortem shows. I'll send the ME's van for the body right now."

"I ought to warn you that this man is well known in Dallas. I'm letting my hospital public relations guys handle it from here."

"Who is he?"

"Jeorg Marquez," Cassy said.

"Jesus. The funeral home owner. I see him on TV all the time hawking his funeral services like a used car salesman."

"You got it right. That's him. Send me a copy of your autopsy report when it's done," Dr. Baldwin closed the conversation and replaced the receiver.

For the next several minutes she lay on her couch. Death was the hardest part of being a physician for her. Even the anonymity and transient nature of ER patients did not relieve Cassy of the anguish of a death in her ER. Hardly anyone died without leaving grieving family and friends. And for Cassy, death of her patients always left her saddened.

As she walked toward her meeting with Marquez's friend, Cassy passed the curtained triage area containing the blanketed body of Jeorg Marquez, the familiar sadness of death surrounded her like a shroud. The triage area was deserted again except for the body and Gracie. The short, black-skinned woman stood near the covered head of the man, her eyes closed and her lips moving silently. She rested her hand on the man's head covered by a white sheet. Every Metro Hospital ER death received Gracie's unspoken, reverent incantations. The rite rarely took more than a minute. The staff never interrupted Gracie's solemn moment with the draped bodies before they were dispatched from the ER.

"What shall I do with the body?" Louise asked Cassy.

"Take it to the morgue. The Dallas ME said their van would be right over, but you know how long that can be. It will probably be later this evening before they pick it up."

the last sixteen hours. At that moment the overhead speakers blared,
"Code Blue to the Morgue." Again the overhead speakers in the Emergency Room blared an excited female announcer's voice, "Code Blue to
the Morgue."

"Is that a sick joke? A cardiac arrest in the morgue," Cassy asked as she
continued to read the patient's chart, ignoring the repeating Code Blue
announcement.

"I've never heard the Code Blue team called to the Morgue," Gracie
said.

"You don't suppose one of the lab techs or housekeeping orderlies
fainted or had a heart attack?" Dr. Baldwin asked without looking up
from the chart.

The agitated receptionist's voice from the overhead speaker interrupted. "Dr. Baldwin, you're needed in the Morgue. The intern on the
Code Blue team called to say he needs you right now. Marquez is not
dead!"

"What?" Dr. Baldwin said, not believing the words but responding to
the emergency call without thinking. "Gracie, grab the emergency tackle
box and get one of the orderlies to bring a tank of oxygen to the
Morgue." Cassy leaped down the two flights of concrete stairs in the back
hallway and raced through the double doors of the basement Morgue.
A knot of curious hospital workers, nurses, orderlies, and technicians
clumped inside the hallway door to the Morgue. She wedged through
the crowd until she reached the white porcelain-lipped autopsy table. In
the chilled room, the surgical intern caught Cassy's astonished look and
shook his head grimly at the nude body of Marquez breathing spasmodi-
cally every few seconds.

"Charles was mopping the room," Dr. Evans, the intern, said wearily,
rubbing a two-day stubble of heavy beard covering his pale jaw.

"Yes, ma'am. I seen the sheet move," the wizened black janitor said.
"I run out of the Morgue right then to get help." His head shook in a
Parkinsonian tremor. His gnarled hands gripped the mop handle that he
had grabbed as soon as he returned to the Morgue.

"I was the first to get here after Charles called the operator," the intern
said, pulling the sheet completely off Marquez's body and feeling for a
groin pulse. "He's got a thready pulse." Then he shined a penlight at
Marquez's eye. "Eye pupils are slightly reactive."

"Let's get him back up to the ER," Dr. Baldwin said to Gracie who
had followed her through the crowd into the Morgue. Gracie stood
transfixed against the wall. "Now!"

Fifteen minutes later Marquez again lay naked on the white sheeted ER table in the Trauma Room One, once more connected to IV's. Monitoring wires and tubes protruded from every orifice of his body. And once again Marquez was the center of attention of nearly a dozen ER personnel hovering over him, adjusting IV's, fiddling with monitors and nervously busying themselves at the side of their revived patient.

"It's amazing. I've never seen anything like this," Louise said, listening for Marquez's blood pressure with her stethoscope as she pumped up the cuff around his arm with the rubber bulb held in her hand. "His vital signs are near normal."

"Señor Marquez, can you hear me?" Cassy shouted in the man's ear in Spanish. He nodded almost imperceptibly. A beginning tear formed at the corner of each of his eyes.

"Louise, contact that Mexican man. His business card is in my coat pocket hanging on that IV pole," Cassy said, nodding toward the six-foot pole holding the intravenous solutions bottles. "Don't tell him why or what happened. Say I need to talk to him immediately about Señor Marquez. Tell him it's an emergency, and he should return to the ER right now."

"Do you want me to call anyone else?"

"Not yet. I'll call the ME and the hospital medical director myself. Let me know when Señor Tenoch arrives," Dr. Baldwin replied, suddenly remembering the man's name.

—

The nurses and technicians continued to swarm around Marquez's body, restarting intravenous tubes, inserting a bladder catheter, adjusting the respirator—all with the practiced skill of hurried rote tasks. When Cassy finished examining the patient and writing out a page of orders for Marquez's immediate care, she left Trauma Room One with instructions to call her immediately if Marquez's condition changed. Back in her office she paged the on-call Assistant Medical Examiner for Dallas again.

"Dr. Herron, this is Dr. Baldwin in the Metropolitan ER again," Cassy said, pulling herself up to a sitting position on her office couch and hugging her knees.

"Surely not another ME case tonight," the pathologist said.

"No, not another. It's the case I talked to you about earlier this evening."

"Oh yeah, the heart attack. My boys should be arriving there with the ME van to pick up the body about now. It's been a busy night for them."

"They won't need to come," Cassy said.

"What? I'm planning an autopsy tomorrow morning. I thought we had agreed on that?"

"It's not necessary," Cassy said. "Marquez is now alive."

"Didn't you pronounce him dead . . . over three hours ago?"

"Yes. I did, but he woke up, or came back from the dead in our morgue."

"My god," the assistant ME said, letting out a whistle that echoed down the telephone line. "The family must think you're Jesus Christ . . . or the worst doctor in the Western hemisphere."

"Thanks a lot," Dr. Baldwin said.

"Well, good luck. Let me know if your man eventually needs the ME's services."

Cassy took a deep breath as she dialed the number for Dr. Walter Simmons, Medical Director for Dallas Metropolitan Hospital.

The doctor answered the telephone on the eighth ring at his home. "Evening, Dr. Baldwin," his resonant bass voice poured through the telephone. "How may I be of service?"

"I want you to know about an unusual patient situation in the Emergency Room tonight," Cassy said, tentatively and defensively.

"Why are you calling me?"

"A fifty-five-year-old man was brought in here about three hours ago after collapsing at a meeting with a business associate. I tried everything but couldn't resuscitate him. I pronounced him dead at 19:45 and notified the ME of an unexplained ER death. Even though I thought the man had died of a myocardial infarction, the ME and I felt we ought to get a postmortem . . . just to protect the hospital if any question should ever be raised about the cause of death."

"Why are you calling me about some poor bastard that died of a heart attack in the ER?" Dr. Simmons asked.

"He's not dead now. He woke up in the morgue about ten-thirty . . . ," Cassy continued.

"Woke up . . . alive?"

"Yes. Alive and improving. I've got him back up here in Trauma One. Looks as if he's going to live. He's responsive. His vitals are improving."

"For god's sake, Cassy. How could that happen? What did you miss?"

"I didn't miss a damn thing. He was dead at 19:45. Flat-lined EKG. I've got the EKG strips to prove it."

There was a long pause. "Who the hell is this patient? Some alcoholic bum or homeless drunk, I hope."

"Jeorg Marquez, the funeral home owner," Dr. Baldwin said.

"Goddamn. Anyone who watches television has seen that son of a bitch. This is going to be a public relations nightmare. I'll be right down."

"I've already called his business associate, Señor Tenoch. He's on his way back to the Emergency Room."

"Señor Tenoch? My god. I'm on my way."

"I'll be in the ER when you get here, Walter."

———

Dr. Evans, the intern, smiled through his fatigue-lined face when Cassy stepped to the side of Marquez's gurney. "I've never seen anything like this guy. He's Lazarus for sure. Back from the dead."

Cassy could only shake her head, not returning the intern's smile or his enthusiasm. She leaned over the gurney to open Marquez's eyelids with her right index finger and thumb. When her fingers touched the dark pouch under the man's left eye, both his eyes blinked open, gazing directly into her eyes. For a frozen moment, their eyes locked on each other. Then the fear in Marquez's eyes took over. He darted his eyes in quick feral movements around the ceiling.

"Have you found anything abnormal on your neurologic exam?"

"Not really. He moves all his extremities. Responds to his name. No pathologic reflexes," the intern said. "Obviously he can't talk with the tube in his windpipe." The young doctor wiggled the breathing tube that protruded from Marquez's mouth, causing a spasm of gagging and coughing. "His gag reflex is great, and he's breathing on his own. We ought to be able to remove the endotracheal tube from his throat soon. I think this guy's going to make it. What the hell do you think happened?"

"I wish I knew. My diagnosis earlier this evening was a massive, fatal myocardial infarction."

"Obviously not fatal," the intern said, flushing at his rude comment and immediately averting his eyes back to Marquez.

"And most likely not a heart attack either," Cassy said, studying the strip of electrocardiogram paper that slithered from the monitor into snarled coils on the tile floor. "His electrocardiogram is normal."

"He's waking up in front of us. What do we do with him now?"

"Move him up to the Intensive Care Unit," Cassy said. "He's going to need close attention tonight. Since we don't know what happened, he might well fade out on us again unless we figure out what the hell is going on and treat him for it."

"I'll stay with him in the ICU tonight," the intern said. "Who will be the attending physician while he's in the ICU?"

"I will," Cassy said. She turned away and began writing in the physician orders section of the chart held in the metal clipboard.

"Dr. Baldwin, that Mexican man is here," Louise Wilcox said as she appeared in the doorway. "I don't envy you. How're you going to explain Marquez coming back from the dead?" she asked, contempt underscoring her words.

"I'll just tell him like it happened," Cassy said curtly, handing Louise the clipboard chart.

———

Cassy grasped the cool knob of the gray steel door leading into the windowless Consolation Room and breathed deeply twice before letting herself into the beige, closet-size room. Señor Tenoch, flanked by the same Hispanic guard, stood quietly in the center of the room. The single overhead light bathed his head in a halo. He stepped forward to greet her and extended his hand in a gracious Spanish greeting.

"Mucho gusto, Dr. Baldwin. Why did you call me back?"

"Señor Marquez is alive," Cassy said simply. She could think of no appropriate preamble or any way to soften the impact of her words.

"What?"

"Señor Tenoch, I am sorry . . . I'm sure he was dead, Señor," Cassy began, brushing her dark hair back from her forehead.

"Do not be sorry. But how could this happen?"

"He had complete cardiac standstill in my ER. No pulse, nothing. Fixed and dilated pupils. Then he revived three hours later."

"Where?"

"In the morgue."

"How unfortunate," Tenoch said.

"I believe that he will be all right. He's recovering quickly."

"The incident will be quite a problem for you and for the hospital," Señor Tenoch said. "How shall the hospital respond to this situation?"

"Respond to this situation? What are you saying? I've notified Dr. Simmons, the hospital director. He's on his way here."

"Maybe you do not realize, Dr. Baldwin," Señor Tenoch said. "Not many know that my personal foundation provides the major funding for a variety of research and many patient care activities at this hospital. All of my gifts have been anonymous over the years."

"No, I did not know."

"I have seen no reason to publicize my philanthropy," Tenoch continued quietly. "But now the hospital should spare no expense for my friend. Call in every medical specialist."

"He will be admitted to our Medical Intensive Care Unit. I will be his attending physician, Señor Tenoch. Let me decide what specialty physicians are necessary to call in."

"Would it be wise for you to continue treating Marquez? The press will certainly. . . ."

"My treatment of Señor Marquez was not negligent, Señor."

"I am sorry. I didn't mean to imply that."

"Señor, he was dead when I declared him dead at 19:45. Now please excuse me. I must get back to my patient."

—

The news of Señor Marquez's resurrection telegraphed itself through the hospital grapevine. Within the hour television reporters, camera crews, and newspaper reporters flooded the hospital lobby and crowded into the waiting room of the ER.

Dr. Walter Simmons, Medical Director of the Dallas Metropolitan Hospital, parked his maroon Maserati Quatraporte in the ambulance zone of the receiving dock of the Emergency Room. His luxuriant, blow-dried silver hair sagged slightly under the rain as he jumped the two steps to the shelter of the ER receiving dock.

"Hi, Doc," one of the security guards waved to him as he strode through the ER entrance just missing the automatic sliding glass doors as they hissed open.

Dr. Simmons walked quickly into the central triage area of the ER, saluting a greeting to two more hospital guards standing outside Trauma Room One. He was a resplendent figure in a vested charcoal pinstripe. Droplets of rain sparkled on the full head of perfectly cut hair. Cassy knew Simmons had arrived in the ER before she even heard or saw him. His characteristic olfactory signature of mouthwash, cigarettes, expensive cologne, and bourbon whisky announced his arrival.

"Good evening, Dr. Baldwin," Dr. Simmons said as he walked just behind her and to the side of Marquez who was lying semiconscious on the gurney. Simmons' fumed mixture wafted over her causing her head to flinch away.

"What's going on?"

"Señor Marquez is improving," Dr. Baldwin said. "We're not doing much except watching. I'm giving him some intravenous fluids, and I have dosed him with a bolus of steroids."

"There must be a dozen reporters out there," Dr. Simmons said, throwing his head in the direction of the entrance. He barely glanced at Marquez who suddenly began to thrash wildly against the cloth restraints that tied his feet and arms to the stainless steel railing of the gurney. "Have you talked to any of them?"

"No, I've been in here with Marquez except when I talked to Señor Tenoch."

"Where is Tenoch?" Simmons asked.

"He's in the Consolation Room," Cassy said.

"He's a solid player," Dr. Simmons said, as if that comment were supreme praise. "Tenoch has been responsible for over ten million dollars in charitable donations to the hospital in the past four years."

"He wants me off the Marquez case," Dr. Baldwin said.

"That's an understandable reaction, Cassy, under the circumstances," Dr. Simmons said. Cassy met his crooked smile with a frozen stare. "Tenoch is trying to protect the hospital's image."

"Walter! Taking me off the roster as Marquez's attending physician is just like telling everyone at this hospital and in Dallas that I made a mistake and sent a live patient to the morgue!"

"Well . . . Marquez is alive, isn't he?" Simmons asked. "Looks like a serious clinical error to me."

"This man was dead at 19:45," Cassy shot back.

"Take me to Señor Tenoch," Simmons said, ignoring her.

"Don't you want to examine Marquez first?"

"Why should I? I'm sure you are doing whatever is necessary," Simmons said smiling. "It's more important that I see Tenoch."

They left the ER together through a side door and took the back hallway, entering the private Consolation Room away from the main ER, out of sight of the reporters. Tenoch's bodyguard stood in front of the door to the small room and nodded to Cassy as they approached from the back hallway. When they opened the door, Tenoch looked up pleasantly from one of the worn tweed stuffed chairs that filled the room.

"Señor Tenoch, I came as quickly as I heard," Dr. Simmons announced. Cassy stood in the doorway, her mind racing to make clinical sense of this resurrection. "Rest assured, Marquez will receive the finest care. I am taking personal charge of his medical treatment. There is much for me to do to ensure his full recovery," Dr. Simmons said. "If you have no objection, I would like to make an announcement to the press. It seems as if the media has already learned of Señor Marquez's resurrection."

"That will be fine, Walter. But for the good of the hospital's image, you must deemphasize the unusual nature of his death," Tenoch said.

"Leave it to me," Simmons said. "Everything will be taken care of. Now let me return to your friend."

When Cassy and Walter Simmons stepped into the hallway, she pulled Simmons around the corner into the deserted rear hallway out of the sight of Tenoch's guard. "Thanks for the support, Walter," Cassy said. "Why not just tell Tenoch that I sent Marquez to the morgue while he was still alive?" Cassy began in icy sarcasm as the two of them walked back through the deserted rear hallway toward Trauma One.

"Cassy, tomorrow morning every dumb schmuck in central Texas as well as in the United States is going to read his paper and watch his television and learn about your fuck-up at the Metropolitan Hospital in Dallas."

"The man was dead, I tell you," Cassy lashed back.

"Bullshit. You missed the diagnosis. You sent a live man to the morgue."

"For god's sake, Walter. Do you think I can't tell when someone is dead?"

"Apparently not, and that's what Joe Schmuck will think when he hears the story. The only way I can protect the reputation of this hospital is to suspend you."

"You have got to be kidding, Walter. At least wait until we do a complete investigation and find out what's wrong with Marquez. You can't do this to me."

"I am quite within my authority," Simmons said as he opened the rear hallway door. "Read the medical staff bylaws. I am summarily suspending you for the good of the hospital and to protect the health and safety of its patients."

"You can't . . . ," Cassy said, starting after him. "You owe me one."

"What is it that you don't understand?" Dr. Simmons turned to face her. "You're fired."

"Walter, you owe me one," Cassy repeated. "I saved your ass three weeks ago. I stuck my neck out for you and buried your blood alcohol report in the ER medical records that night."

"Why, Cassy, I have no idea what you're talking about," he said, looking at her full in the face, barely twelve inches from her nose.

Cassy did not flinch. "You and I are the only ones who know you were legally drunk when you drove your car over the retaining wall at the Anatole Hotel," Cassy said. "If I hadn't forged a fictitious name onto the blood alcohol report that showed you were roaring drunk, you'd be suspended as Medical Director. Everyone would know that you're drinking again."

"My advice to you is to forget that whole incident." He paused and laid his manicured fingers on her shoulders. "Cassy, I won't sit still for blackmail. If you don't leave the hospital in the next five minutes, I will call the security guard."

"Walter, I covered for you that Saturday night. Just support me until I can figure out what happened to Marquez. That's all I ask. I know he was dead at 19:45 when I sent him to the Morgue."

"Get out of my hospital and don't set foot in here again without my permission. And if you say anything about that Saturday night three weeks ago, I'll sue you for defamation of my reputation as a surgeon."

"You drunk son of a bitch," Cassy whispered when Dr. Simmons disappeared into the ER, leaving Cassy on the threshold of the rear door of the ER.

THREE

INSIDE THE rear corridor of the ER, Cassy stood stunned and bonded to the tile floor after Dr. Simmons slammed the hallway door behind him. "That bastard. I should have known he'd come after me!" Cassy said as she stared at the door. "That bastard!" she said even louder, her voice echoing in the empty tiled hallway. She turned and ran out through the ER emergency exit door.

The hospital's silhouette outlined itself against the black sky behind Cassy as she walked quickly under the covered walkway around the ER wing of the hospital building. The lighted pedestrian parkway arched across the boulevard between the hospital and the parking garage. Rather than risk an embarrassing encounter with the hospital staff by reentering the hospital to use the covered pedestrian crosswalk, Cassy ran against the red light across the six lanes of traffic. A Dominos Pizza delivery car skidded to a stop on the rain wet hospital driveway as Cassy reached the far curb.

The rain stung her face as she ran for the cover of the overhanging entrance to the multistory parking garage. The wash of rain drenched her white coat, soaking immediately through to the gray surgical scrubs underneath. Her chest heaved and her throat burned from the exertion of the hundred yard dash. Never another cigarette she told herself, breathing deeply trying to slow her racing heart beat.

"That bastard," Cassy muttered again. She stalked up the ramp of the parking garage to the second level and her forest green Range Rover. As soon as she had buckled her seat belt, she fumbled in the glove compartment until she found a leather pouch with a half pack of Marlboro cigarettes. Lighting a crumpled stale cigarette, Cassy inhaled deeply and felt the familiar nicotine rush.

The engine caught immediately. She slammed into reverse gear and pushed the accelerator abruptly. Both rear tires squealed backward. The right rear bumper cracked into a Mercedes sedan in the adjacent parking slot. Cassy hesitated a moment and looked around the deserted parking garage. Then she eased the Range Rover forward and down the ramp into the slick street, checking in her rear mirror to be sure the parking garage remained empty.

The rain enveloped her into the secure cocoon of her car. The tears began as she drove. Cassy Baldwin would never allow any of her medical colleagues to witness this overt display of emotion, but in the solitude of the car, her usual controlled demeanor broke down. Among the medical students and house staff she was known as the Iron Lady, a recognition of her gracious, but firm, control even under the most stressful surgical conditions. The rain and the tears blinded her so that she had to pull into the McDonald's parking lot and sit in the car to wait for the summer storm to pass. The rain eventually slowed to a steady chatter on the windshield. She lit her second cigarette.

On nights like this one when she was tired and frustrated, words her father had told her the day that she entered medical school echoed in her mind: *Don't ever let them see you cry* he had whispered in her ear as he put her on the plane in Mexico City seventeen years ago. For the most part she had been able to live by his admonition. Even after her parents' deaths and her divorce, she had suppressed her tears. The Iron Lady would not be broken.

But tonight it was just too much . . . the ER death and the failed resuscitation . . . the suspension . . . the fender bender. Her tears gradually dried up as the rain eased enough for her to drive home. Cassy flipped the cigarette over the edge of the window and eased her car back onto Harry Hines Boulevard. The glowing ember of the cigarette stub was extinguished by the rain before it hit the pavement.

———

She stopped the car at the brick entry post in front of her home in Dallas' posh University Park suburb and punched her five digit security code, C-A-S-S-Y, into the keypad embedded in a brass intercom plate of the brick pillar. The bar gate slid to the side over the decorative stone paving, more like a prison gate opening into its yard rather than into a lushly landscaped estate surrounded by a vine-covered six-foot brick wall. She eased the Range Rover up the long curved drive of her two-story Tudor mansion.

The dark roofed driveway in front of her house was empty as Cassy parked the car under the porte cochere. The rain had stopped a half hour before in University Park, leaving the air scented with a fresh washed cleanness. She breathed deeply several times, wanting to clear her lungs of the cigarette smoke before entering her house.

Using the same code, C-A-S-S-Y, she tapped the keypad next to the front door. The red blinking security alarm light turned a continuous green. She inserted her door key, clicking open the triple locking mechanism of the metal reinforced door. The smell of popcorn greeted Cassy when she pushed open the door into the luxurious foyer that extended to a bronzed skylight two floors above. She rearmed the alarm after she closed the door behind her. The red bulb winked at her.

The light of a flickering television floated down the hallway from the family room adjacent to the country kitchen. This casual, open family room was Cassy's favorite place in the huge house. Here she and her son spent much of their time together in this large informally decorated room.

Cassy draped her rain-soaked white lab coat over the coat tree in the hallway just as a German shepherd bounced down the staircase and embraced Cassy with his front paws grabbing at her wet scrub blouse.

"Get down, Charlie," Cassy whispered. "You know better than to put your feet on me." She rubbed his ears. The dog's tail wagged in delight. With the dog trailing in her footsteps, Cassy tiptoed into the family room.

Lupita, her Hispanic housekeeper-nanny, snored softly in the soft leather chair in the family room, her feet propped on the ottoman. The dubbed Spanish voice from the movie on the Mexico City television station caught her ear. Tom Cruise speaking Spanish just didn't seem right. A half eaten bowl of popcorn teetered on her ample lap. Her throat rattled loose phlegm with each inspiration that pouted out her flabby neck.

Quietly Cassy opened the white birch cabinet above the kitchen telephone, and from behind the telephone books she pulled an unopened package of Marlboro cigarettes. Her cigarette smoking was an on-again off-again struggle. For most days she never craved the cigarettes, but she did need another one now. Lupita awakened when Cassy slumped into the overstuffed leather chair next to her and lit the cigarette.

"Señora, it is one o'clock," Lupita said in Spanish, pushing a yawn back into her mouth. "You work too much."

"It's not my choice."

"Your son misses his mother. You don't come home until after he's asleep."

"Has he been asleep long?"

"Ten o'clock. He wanted to wait up for you. The last three nights you've missed his bedtime," Lupita said.

Cassy leaned back on the sofa. I do not need Lupita's recriminations now, Cassy thought. Not tonight.

"You need to spend more time with your son. Maybe he wouldn't act so sad," Lupita said. "He's not been happy since Mr. Spence moved out. I'm worried about my Alex."

"Alex is not sad! He's a quiet, intelligent young man," Cassy said, fidgeting with the burning cigarette.

"Why didn't he eat his supper? I fix a good tamale. He does not eat," Lupita said as she heaved her bulk out of the overstuffed leather sofa.

"Oh, no!" Cassy groaned. "I forgot to bring his pizza home! I promised Alex I would bring a pizza home tonight."

"He not hungry . . . my tamale is good," Lupita said sullenly and poured the popcorn hulls down the disposal.

"I'm going to make him a pizza right now."

"Let him sleep, Señora."

"I promised him pizza. I'm going to keep my word." Cassy jumped out of the chair and dropped her burning cigarette into the sink garbage disposal, running water down the drain as the disposal roared. The un-popped corn hulls rattled in the disposal like steel bearings. "What have you put in the disposal?" Cassy shouted over the screech.

Lupita hunched her shoulders indifferently. Cassy shut off the deafening roar of the disposal. "Leave Alex be," Lupita said. "He needs his rest."

"He can sleep late tomorrow morning," Cassy said defiantly. "I'm going to have some quality time with my son. I don't care if it is one o'clock in the morning."

"He needs to sleep," Lupita said. "His father has planned a big birthday party tomorrow for Alex. Mr. Spence will be here to take his son to Six Flags early tomorrow morning."

"He's my son, too. And I'll decide what's best for him. If I want to eat pizza with my son at one a.m., I'll eat pizza with him," Cassy said, a harshness creeping into her voice.

"Buenas noches," Lupita said, shrugged her shoulders deeply and disappeared into the dark hallway, shaking her head.

Cassy lit another cigarette and sighed. She's a crabby leftover from my marriage, just like this huge house, the Range Rover, the furniture. All my baggage. I don't need her to remind me of that part of my life, and I sure as hell don't need her to tell me how to raise my son.

Lupita's service to the Spence family had begun when Scott Spence was about Alex's age, and his wealthy parents needed a full-time nanny to look after their only child. They had found Lupita through a long defunct nanny agency. Lupita moved in with the Spence family, leaving her nine brothers and sisters in a tiny Mexican village on the Mexican-Texas border. Lupita had outlasted Scott Spence's mother and father. Now she was growing old and cranky in less than graceful retirement with Cassy and Alex, more as a family retainer than as an employee.

Upstairs Cassy inched her son's bedroom door open. A rectangular shaft of hallway light fell through the doorway onto Alex's sleeping face in the lower bed of his bunk beds. *The Adventures of Huck Finn* lay open on the floor at her son's bedside. Cassy tiptoed to the bed, nearly stumbling into it when she stepped on the flashlight lying on the floor next to his bed. She kneeled at his bedside and gently brushed his dark hair off his forehead. The sheets were scrambled at his feet. Sweat ringed the neck of his Texas Rangers' pajamas despite the coolness of the room. For several minutes she knelt there, watching his quiet innocent sleep. Then she leaned across his face and touched her lips to his forehead. "Night, night, my man."

Alex's eyes popped open, startled. "Oh, Mom. Why are you so late?" Alex asked groggily.

"Had to take care of the Emergency Room until my relief got there. The doctor was late. The tornado over in the panhandle. . . ."

"Did you bring my pizza?" Alex interrupted.

"I forgot, but I'll make you one right now if you're hungry," Cassy said, rubbing her long fingers through her son's brown hair, a dark chestnut color that perfectly matched hers.

"That's all right. I'm not hungry anyway," Alex said and rolled up on his elbow in the bed.

"You're always hungry," Cassy said, pulling him upright and hugging him. "Let Mom make us a pizza. It will be my special birthday treat for you. Do you know that you are now eight years old? It's nearly one-seventeen." She studied her Piaget watch and showed its face to Alex. "Eight years ago about this moment at the Metro Hospital, you came into this world."

"Can I have a chocolate shake, too?" Alex asked, not interested in the precise description of his age or the place of his birth.

"Sure," Cassy said, standing full upright and laying her arms across the top bunk as she looked down at her son in the shadow of the light from the hallway.

Alex flipped on his headboard reading lamp and leaped from the bed into the hallway in a half dozen jumping steps. The dog loped behind him down the curving staircase. Cassy plodded after them.

A half hour later the smell of mozzarella and pepperoni wafted through the house as Cassy pulled a steaming fifteen-inch pizza from the oven. After cutting it into quarters with a circular rolling pizza knife, she set half of the bubbling slab in front of Alex. With a quarter of the pizza folded in her hand, Cassy nibbled at its hot edges and walked around the kitchen counter to reach the glasses for the chocolate milk shake that Alex had concocted in the blender. Alex pulled the frosted metal mixing can from the blender and let the thick, dark chocolate milk shake ooze into the glasses.

"Did your father call today?" Cassy asked nonchalantly.

"Umha," Alex mumbled around and through the pizza.

"Don't talk with your mouth full," Cassy said mechanically and without thinking, just like she had chided him for his table manners since he was two years old. She smiled at herself realizing that these motherly warnings erupted from her despite her attempt to treat Alex as an equal in their world.

Alex nodded and swallowed the pizza down with a gulp of the chocolate shake, overlaying his tomato mustache with a chocolate coating. Cassy reached across the bar top counter and wiped his upper lip clean with a paper napkin.

"He's taking me to Six Flags," Alex said.

"Did he say when?" The visiting arrangements with Alex's father had been an uneasy accommodation for the past three years. Although the custody arrangements of their divorce settlement gave Alex to his father every other weekend and for six weeks each summer, Alex had only stayed overnight with his father twice during the past six months. The apparent lack of interest of Alex's father in his son tormented Cassy, but she admitted only to herself that she liked the extra time with her son.

"Do we still have a date for your birthday party tomorrow evening after you see your dad?" Cassy asked. Alex nodded vigorously, pushing another edge of the pizza into his mouth. "Do you want to invite Peter and Mark over for birthday cake and ice cream, or maybe some of the other boys from your class?"

"No. Just you and me."

"All right then," Cassy said. "I'll be home all day tomorrow. As soon as you get back from Six Flags with your father, we'll do whatever you want."

After they finished the pizza, Cassy tucked Alex back into bed and for several minutes read to him from *Huck Finn* until his eyes drooped closed. The bedtime reading ritual had been a part of their lives since Alex was a few weeks old. Cassy had never missed a night except when she was out of town or when she had to stay late at the hospital. Some evenings it was only a paragraph from the classics, but most nights Alex listened intently, following the words, as Cassy read a variety of stories ranging from *Winnie the Pooh* to Jack London's *Call of the Wild*.

Cassy leaned her head under the top bunk and kissed her sleeping son's forehead, tender euphoria replacing her anger and anxiety of the evening at the ER. She returned the book to the nightstand and picked up his baseball, his mitt, and his Texas Rangers' cap from the floor.

As soon as she turned off the room lights, a sprouting kaleidoscope of color bloomed from Alex's Macintosh computer in the corner of the room and cascaded a snowstorm of colors on the windows of his room. The screen saver light of his computer was Alex's night light. He would not sleep without it. She gazed at her son's head for a moment, then turned and walked through the doorway. The door closed quietly behind her. Cassy retraced her steps through the house, turning off lights, checking the locks, and once again rearming the intrusion alarm at the front door and the patio doors.

———

Cassy returned to the kitchen and quickly stacked the dishes in the sink. Then she poured herself a glass of chardonnay from an open bottle of Robert Mondavi in the refrigerator door and carried the wine glass around the kitchen island into the family room where she collapsed into the soft leather cushions of the sofa.

Sipping at the wine, she stretched the length of the sofa and took the telephone from the end table. She punched a single button to speed dial the home telephone number of Dr. Betty Freeman in the Dallas suburb of Plano.

A gruff, moist voice declared before the second ring, "Dr. Freeman," as if it were in the middle of the afternoon rather than two-thirty in the morning.

"Hi, Betty. I didn't wake you?"

"Oh hell no. You know a lot of women my age only sleep in four hour shifts," the gruff voice melted into a cozy hoarseness. "This is my best time."

Cassy sipped again at her wine and unconsciously smoothed her fingers down the legs of her wrinkled scrub trousers as she kicked off her running shoes.

"I need to talk."

"Fire away." Dr. Freeman's intake of breath was caught by the telephone connection. Cassy knew her friend had lit a cigarette, and she also lit herself a cigarette, prompted by her friend's inhaling. For the next several minutes she detailed the apparent death and resurrection of Jeorg Marquez.

"You're not the first doctor who has made a wrong call."

"Wrong call is a euphemism. I'm the dumb ER Director who can't tell when somebody's dead. At least that's the way Walter Simmons described it when he suspended me tonight."

"That's just like the pompous ass. Let me see what we can find out at the Coroner's Office."

"Can you do that?"

Dr. Freeman snorted. "I'm the Deputy Coroner, aren't I? I believe that we can find some rational explanation for your man waking up in the morgue."

Cassy shook her head without thinking and ground out the cigarette. Her neck had begun to tighten as she sat slouched in the sofa with her bare feet propped on the edge of the walnut coffee table. "I know Marquez was dead when I pronounced him dead. But he's alive now. If I can't figure it out, my professional reputation is in the toilet . . . at least in Dallas. I'll not be able to live this down."

"Come see me at the Coroner's Office Tuesday morning. Monday's the Memorial Day holiday," Betty said, and the two women said their goodbyes.

Cassy refilled her wine glass for the third time, finishing off the bottle of Mondavi chardonnay. Carrying the wine glass in one hand and her running shoes in the other, she padded quietly to the bathroom adjoining her bedroom. She dropped her gray scrub pants to the floor and stepped out of them while she shrugged the shirt over her head, then filled the tub with hot water. After sprinkling bubble bath oil in the water, she lighted four sandalwood scented candles about the edge of the tub. Then she flipped off the bathroom lights and slipped into the hot, scented bubbly water, letting her body submerge up to her chin.

Cassy leaned her head against a Turkish towel folded under her neck as she stretched her legs up through the water to rest her feet against the cool wall tile. She felt the length of her body float up from the bottom of the enormous sunken tub. The tenseness of her shoulders and back muscles gradually eased. In a way, her nightly bubble baths washed away the day's suffering she saw in the hospital. She always felt cleansed afterwards, physically and emotionally.

With her left foot lifted from the bubbly water, she twisted the faucet to ease in a trickle of hot water. "Just one more cigarette," she said, groping to reach into the pocket of her blue terry cloth robe draped on the brass towel rack. An opened box of Marlboros fell to the tile floor. The burning tip of the cigarette flared in the dark bathroom as she sucked full breaths of the smoke. The evening's events began to fade from her mind as drowsiness slipped upon her consciousness. Finally, Cassy sipped the last of the wine and pitched the cigarette into the toilet bowl. The ember of the cigarette arced in the dark room before hissing and rolling in the water of the toilet.

The tight muscles in her wide shoulders still pulled at her stiff neck despite the steamy warmth, and she could feel the tension bunching her neck muscles again. Rolling her head from side to side, her fingers massaged the nape of her neck under the dark hair that swirled around her slender neck. The taut bands of muscles slowly released.

She blinked the tears that filled her eyes and placed a folded moist terry wash cloth across her forehead. In the darkness beneath the warm wet washcloth, thoughts burst through her drowsiness like the multicolor cascade of her son's computer screen. What am I going to do? Suspended without pay. Walter Simmons. That bastard. How am I going to support Alex and me?

The throbbing ache just above both eyes pounded under the cold washcloth. The muscles in her neck stretched like guy wires to her shoulders. Cassy ran more hot water until it lapped the rim of the sunken tub. She stretched herself the length of the tub, arching her back in the warm water lifting her buttocks off the bottom of the tub. But her anxiety floated as free as her body. Time was measured by the temperature of the hot water. Cassy buoyed in the tub until the water cooled again. She blinked the tears back from her eyes and climbed out, wrapping herself in the fluffy terry robe. As the dying candles shimmered the steamy room into shadow, Cassy lit another cigarette.

She turned on the ring of cosmetic make-up lights about the bathroom mirror and wrinkled her nose as she wiped away the moisture from her face. Her skin was creamy and perfectly smooth. After studying her face a moment, she lathered on moisturizing cream, letting the Turkish robe drop at her feet. She looked at her naked body in the full length mirror on the opposite wall and then turned sideways to inspect her profile. Not too bad, she thought . . . for a thirty-eight-year-old mother.

"Another few pounds and you'll be at your ideal weight," Cassy said to her mirror's image and smiled into a wide grin that stopped short of a laugh. That was before the half pizza she thought. She pulled on a pair of white bikini underwear and slipped into an oversized T-shirt with a Texas Rangers' logo, a Mother's Day gift from her son.

Returning to her bedroom, Cassy flopped the bed covers down on her king-size bed—another legacy from her divorce—and climbed into the side of the bed nearest the window, overlooking the elaborate patio and pool beyond. She lay staring at the ceiling. Sleep would not come. Her last thought before sleep did overtake her conscious mind was her own inner voice—'Let's call the time of death 19:45.'

FOUR

MORNING LIGHT leaked around the wood shutters covering Cassy's bedroom windows. The numbers 6:08 glowed red on the bedside clock in the darkness. Her bedside telephone rang a single time. Cassy had it to her ear before the second ring. "Dr. Baldwin," her groggy voice croaked.

"Good morning. It's Trent," said Dr. Trent Hendricks, Chief of Surgery at the Metro Hospital and the senior cardiovascular surgeon on the hospital staff. "I'm sorry to wake you so early on Sunday."

"Trent, what's wrong? It's six a.m."

"I need your help. There's a twelve-year-old girl who needs a heart transplant this morning," Trent said.

"Are you serious? Why me? You taught me how to do heart transplants, remember? You surely don't need me to show you how to do a heart transplant," Cassy said. Trent Hendricks, a decade older than Cassy, had been her surgical teacher and mentor throughout her years of surgical residency and cardiac surgery fellowship at the Dallas Metropolitan Hospital. In the six years that followed, when she and Trent were the faculty surgeons at Metro, their respect of each others surgical abilities and judgment had ripened.

"Yes. I remember. And you're still the best. And I need the best for this kid." Until last year when she retired from cardiac surgery, Cassy had established herself as a talented and gifted surgeon, particularly skilled in the complex heart surgery of infants and children. The Dallas community considered her its answer to Houston's famed heart surgeons, DeBakey and Cooley.

"What's so special about this case? You know I've not done any heart surgery in a year."

"Any other surgeon I'd trust is out of town. It's the holiday weekend, remember?"

"Can't this heart transplant wait until one of them gets back . . . ?"

"No. I'm in Mexico City right now. I'll be leaving in thirty minutes with a donor heart that I just harvested."

"Mexico City?" Cassy asked, rolling upright in bed and swinging her bare feet to the carpet. "You're procuring a donor heart in Mexico City, and you're bringing it back into the United States. You want me to transplant it? Trent, I can't believe. . . ."

"I'll be at the Metro Hospital in two hours. The jet is standing by ready to fly me back to DFW airport. I need your help, Cass. This is a very special case. The recipient is a twelve-year-old girl who's been waiting for a heart for nearly a year."

"But why are you in Mexico City?" Cassy interrupted.

"It's a very special situation. This girl's been in and out of the hospital this past year . . . almost died on several occasions with severe heart failure."

"Since when did Mexico and the United States begin an organ sharing program?" Cassy asked. "You're bringing a donor heart into this country from Mexico City? I've never heard of that . . . you know what problems I encountered in setting up the heart surgery program for the Mexican children to come to Dallas. How did you manage to get approval to procure a donor heart in Mexico City?"

"It's a long story, and I had a lot of help. I obtained a special exemption for this recipient," Trent interrupted. "A compassionate exemption from the Metro Hospital and the transplant organizations in the United States to look for a donor heart in Mexico for this particular patient."

"Somebody must have had a lot of clout," Cassy said as she stood up at her bedside and opened the plantation shutters of the bank of windows overlooking the pool. "I've never heard of anyone bringing a donor organ across the border except for those crazy stories in the tabloid magazines about organs being bought and sold in other countries."

"This donor was a young teenage girl in Mexico City, brain dead after a head injury in an auto accident," Trent Hendricks said impatiently. "Cass, I've got to be on my way. Can you help me?"

"Give me more details about the case, Trent." The German shepherd sitting at the foot of the bed looked up at Cassy, flopping his tail as if this might be the morning for one of Cassy's two mile dawn walks.

"She's the sweetest twelve year old you will ever meet . . . huge blue eyes, blonde hair," Trent said. "Her heart has failed to the point that she won't live another month."

Cassy paused. "Trent, I'd recognize a father's description of his daughter anytime." Her voice softened. She stood at the bedside stretching her back. "I knew she was sick last year. But I had no idea. So, that's how you managed the exemption to find a donor heart in Mexico City. The patient is your daughter."

A silence between them drifted momentarily. "You're the best surgeon with kids, Cassy. Heather needs a surgeon with your special talent. As Heather's father, I need you to be there."

"But I don't have cardiac surgical privileges at the Metro Hospital any longer, Trent. Walter Simmons suspended me from the medical staff last night." Cassy quickly explained the clinical course and revival of Jeorg Marquez but omitted the three-week-old incident with Dr. Simmons' blood alcohol report.

"I can take care of Walter Simmons. He won't object to your being Heather's surgeon, I assure you."

"Okay, I'll be there. Tell me when."

"It's about a ninety minute flight from Mexico City to DFW and then less than a half hour helicopter ride to the Metro Hospital OR. I should be there just after eight."

———

At seven-thirty that morning, Cassy pushed through the double doors of the Main Operating Room at the Dallas Metropolitan Hospital. The chilled, dank air of the tiled corridors shivered her as the pneumatic doors of the OR swooshed closed behind her, isolating her in the deserted surgical corridor. A faint Bach concerto drifted down the hallway from the direction of the cardiovascular surgical suite at the far end of the corridor.

Nothing had changed in the year that she'd been gone. The pungent smells of surgical soaps and the intoxicating sweet aroma of stray anesthetic vapor hung like a familiar miasma in the empty corridor stretching the length of the fourth floor of the Metro Hospital. But on this Sunday morning, the operating room was strangely quiet, a startling contrast to the usual hectic activity on a weekday morning.

Cassy shoved the double-swing doors aside and peeked into the chilled Heart Surgery OR. The Bach concerto flooded the room from speakers mounted in the four corners of the spacious operating room, easily twice the size of a regular operating room. An anesthesia console dwarfed a short skeletal man almost hidden by its collection of tubes, canisters, dials, and video scope monitors all compactly arranged on a rolling metal platform.

"Good morning, Akihito." The man turned from his console. A surgical mask and hood covered his small head, revealing only his dark eyes. His almond shaped eyes brightened into a crinkled squint.

"Welcome home, Cassandra," Dr. Akihito Tanaka, Chief of Anesthesiology at the Metro, said, bowing slightly in a traditional Japanese greeting.

"It's wonderful to see you again. How's your wife?" Cassy asked.

"Fine. Fine." Akihito said, bowing again.

"And your two daughters?"

"They're both at Stanford, freshman and sophomore premedical students."

"Planning to do cardiac anesthesia like their father?" Cassy asked.

"Who knows," he said, shrugging his head in a gesture that Cassy assumed was the Japanese equivalent of any parent's concern and love for their children. Cassy donned a surgical mask and hood and pulled off the lab coat she had worn over her fresh scrub clothes, then stepped into the OR.

The chirping of the electrocardiogram monitor at one hundred forty beats per minute penetrated the Bach concerto like a cricket in the evening. The brushed aluminum inverted cones of the four surgical lights like metal umbrellas hovered over the operating table. Cassy stopped at the head of the table insinuating herself between Dr. Tanaka and a young girl's head that protruded from the mound of blankets. The darting turquoise green eyes of the young girl lying on the operating table jumped from one person to another around the operating room. "Hi, hon," Cassy said, laying her hand on the girl's cool forehead. "I'll bet you're chilly."

Heather's head nodded once. Her eyes continued flitting about, watching the bustling surgical technician, a tall slender woman concealed behind a surgical mask, gown, and hood as she spread sterile green sheets on flat tables. Then the technician piled mounds of stainless steel surgical instruments in an orderly array like setting an elaborate dining table.

"You must be Heather Hendricks," Cassy said. Heather's blonde head bobbed up and down twice, but she said nothing. Her flat facial expression did not budge.

"I have a son who is a little younger than you." Heather's roving eyes stopped for a moment and stared at Cassy, inquiring a bit. Cassy continued, "He's eight years old today. How old are you?"

"Twelve," came her whispered voice. The mound of white thermal blankets hid Heather's emaciated body. Only after the anesthesiologist folded back the blankets to expose Heather's chest so he could position his stethoscope did Cassy see the young girl's frail bony rib cage. Her yellowish skin and the jaundiced white sclerae of her eyeballs showed the telltale signs of severe heart failure. A frown pointed Heather's lips downward. Her eyes returned to roving the room as Cassy pulled the blankets back up to cover Heather's scrawny chest.

"Who are you?" Heather asked in a barely audible whisper.

"I'm Dr. Baldwin. We've met before at your daddy's Christmas parties," Cassy said, leaning her head down directly over the young girl's face.

"Are you my daddy's friend?"

"He's a very good friend," Cassy smiled.

"Where's my daddy?" she asked. "I'm scared."

"He'll be here soon, hon."

"Am I going to die?" Heather asked, focusing her gaze on Cassy's eyes. A conical blue paper-mache surgical mask covered Cassy's nose and mouth and prevented the young girl from seeing Cassy's frown.

"No. You're going to feel much better. Your heart is about worn out, and I'm going to replace that tired old heart with the new one your dad is bringing home for you."

"Mom died," the girl said without warning.

"Yes, I know, dear," Cassy said, expertly fielding the stray question without changing the expression in her eyes or the tone of her voice.

"Will I see her if I die?"

"You're not going to die. You're going to get well and take care of your daddy."

"Will you stay with me?" Heather asked.

"Of course, I will," Cassy said and reached under the thermal blankets to find her hand. Heather's entire thin hand fit the palm of Cassy's. "Now you just close your eyes a bit. Dr. Tanaka is going to give you a little medicine to make you drowsy." The anesthesiologist looked over his mask at Cassy, his eyes frowning.

"Where's Trent?" Dr. Tanaka asked.

"He's on his way from Mexico City," Cassy said, turning away from Heather but still keeping her fingers on Heather's forehead. "I want to wait until Trent gets here with the donor heart before we anesthetize her." Heather's eyes closed and she slipped into the first stage of anesthesia immediately after Dr. Tanaka flushed a tiny dose of sedative through the intravenous tubing. Cassy released the girl's hand and tucked it under the blanket. She slept soundly following the sedation but roused when Cassy took her fingers off her forehead.

"I'll be with you until your dad gets here," Cassy said, holding Heather's forehead for several minutes more until Heather no longer opened her eyes when she lifted her fingers away.

The door lock to the Female Surgeons' Locker Room clicked open after Cassy punched in her four digit code. Strange what I remember after a year away from the OR, she thought when the four digit sequence popped into her consciousness. Her hand twisted the cold steel doorknob.

At the lavatory, she splashed cold water into her face and held her hands steady. Her long, slender fingers were absolutely motionless. Cassy patted her face gently with a terry cloth towel stamped with Property of Metropolitan Hospital in large block lettering. What did I do to deserve this? she asked herself. It's hard enough operating on these sick kids' hearts without being expected to transplant your best friend's daughter. How can I possibly live with myself if Trent's daughter dies?

But for Cassy the emotional turmoil of operating on the highest risk patients was worth it. The satisfaction of correcting a complex malformation of an infant's heart or of restoring a damaged adult heart to renewed life was a sensual experience that few knew, and perhaps could be appreciated only by another professional who was maximally challenged by the professional creativity required of him—or her. Cassy knew that she was among the best in her profession—not hubris but simply an acknowledgement of her self-confidence in her surgical talent.

Despite this well-deserved confidence in her own ability, the fear of failure with her friend and mentor's daughter would not leave her. The cardiac surgical procedures were not always under her complete control. The end result was not always predictable. Fate? Luck? Accidents? God's will? Death was an ever-present specter in every heart transplant procedure. She could not put down her apprehension about the transplant procedure.

The roiling gurgle in her stomach brought a foul acid into the back of her throat. She leaned forward to splash more cold water into her face. When she bent her head to the sink, bitter, frothy straw-colored fluid scorched her throat and lips as she vomited into the lavatory. Droplets of yellow stomach contents spilled onto her gray blouse.

At that moment the surgical nurse rapped on the locker room door. "Dr. Baldwin, the donor heart's here. Dr. Tanaka wants to know if he can sleep the patient."

A moment's hesitation later, Cassy called to the nurse, "Not just yet. I want to examine the donor heart first." She rinsed the frothy yellow liquid down the sink and splashed more cold water into her face. After changing into a clean gray scrub blouse, she tied on a fresh surgical mask and pulled her wavy chestnut hair away from her neck and tucked it under a green bouffant gauze paper hood and for a moment was able to set aside the foreboding.

Inside the Heart Surgery OR Trent Hendricks greeted her with a ferocious hug. "Cassy, there's no way I can thank you for this . . . on such short notice. I'm sorry. The donor in Mexico City just became available. Poor kid. Thirteen-year-old girl hit by a car. Severe head injury. Massive brain damage."

Trent Hendricks' appearance stunned her. He seems to have aged five years, she thought. His eyes were all she could see above his surgical mask—red veined whites behind hooded and puffy heavy lids with dark black pouches beneath each eye.

"It's great to see you," Cassy said, returning Dr. Hendricks' embrace. "You know we don't always have to meet in the operating room." She squeezed his forearm and pulled him by the hand out of the surgical suite.

"Trent, let's go into the surgeons' lounge. Fill me in on the details of Heather's course the last few months. I need to review her most recent cardiac catheterization data."

The main OR lounge was empty, but the low coffee table between the two well-worn leather sofas contained a plate of salami, ham, cheeses, and a variety of sliced breads, bagels, muffins, and sliced oranges. "Have you eaten breakfast?" Cassy asked, pointing to the food laden table in the corner of the deserted lounge.

The buffet meal for the transplant team began as a necessity in the early days of heart transplantation when an operation might require more than twelve hours, and the surgeons and OR nurses needed to be on duty through their usual mealtimes. The surgical team then could take turns eating the buffet meal in the OR lounge while their counterparts carried on the lengthy procedure. Despite improved heart transplantation techniques reducing operating time to about three hours, the tradition of the free transplantation meal continued. The surgical team was superstitious enough not to break tradition.

"I'm starved," Trent Hendricks said as he lifted a slice of Mozzarella cheese into his mouth. Cassy poured two cups of steaming coffee and rested her hand on his arm as he reached for a piece of Swiss cheese.

"Are you all right, Trent?" Cassy asked. "It must have been a long night."

"It's been a longer year," Trent said, sipping the steaming black coffee while chewing on the Swiss cheese. "Heather's been living in the hospital for the past six months," Trent said. He grimaced and swallowed another sip of coffee. "She would come home for a few days, but each time she bounced back into the hospital in worse condition."

"Are you taking care of yourself?" Cassy asked.

"I'm fine. Don't worry about me. Hell, I've already set up a trust fund to take care of Heather if anything should happen to me."

"That's not what I meant," Cassy said. "You look exhausted."

"Hell, I've just been to Mexico City and back and harvested the donor heart for my daughter. Superman would be worn out after a night like that," he said, draining the steaming coffee and chewing on a raisin bagel. "Let's get on with her transplant, Cass." He stood up and pitched the Styrofoam cup into the wastebasket.

Not moving from the sofa, Cassy said, "Not so fast. I need to know more about Heather as well as about the donor heart you just brought back before I sign on to do the transplant."

"What do you want to know?" Trent asked as he stood directly in front of her. "Heather has terminal idiopathic cardiomyopathy. Unusual at her age but the diagnosis is absolutely certain. Ejection fraction of her heart is eleven percent. Hell, you know that she ought to be ejecting at least fifty percent of her heart volume with each beat. I don't see how she's still alive. Neither does her pediatric cardiologist. Her heart is just a nonfunctioning bag of blood."

"She's shown no improvement on medical treatment?" Cassy asked.

"No improvement at all on maximum drug therapy. She's going straight down the slide. Here's her medical record for just the past three months," Trent said and picked up a stack of bound papers twelve inches thick from a bookcase in the corner of the room. Carrying it back to Cassy, he pitched it on the sofa next to her. "Read it yourself. She's been in the hospital four times this month. I've only had her home a total of six days all during May. I had to have nurses around the clock with her for those six days when she was at home."

Cassy flipped through the voluminous record, stopping to read a notation or a report that caught her eye. Soon she looked up to see Trent studying her with the anguish of a parent in his eyes. "Has there been no available heart donor until now?" she asked, closing the volume and placing it on the table next to the tray of bagels.

"None. Not until last night in Mexico City, and I sure wasn't going to let this one get away. She's been right at the top of the nationwide priority transplant list in this country for six months. But there have been no donors her size. Thought we had a donor a couple of times in the past six months, once in Louisiana and once in Florida, but the damn family refused to consent to organ donation." Anger riffled his voice.

"Let's get on with it, Cassy. She's going to die unless we use this heart. What other choice is there? I've watched Heather die a little bit every day for the past year. She's been slipping away from me right in front of my eyes despite everything we've tried! Have you seen her?"

"Yes. Just a moment ago," Cassy said softly after letting his anger subside. "I agree that a heart transplant is her only chance of surviving."

"Then will you tell Dr. Tanaka to put her to sleep so that we can get on with the transplant?"

"Not yet," Cassy said. "A couple of more things I have to ask about."

"Goddamn, Cass. We don't have all day. It's been over three hours since I harvested that heart. Even with my new harvesting and cardiac preservation techniques, the donor heart cannot stay suspended out of the donor's body for more than six hours before transplanting it into the recipient."

"I want to inspect the donor heart myself," Cassy said patiently.

"Jesus Christ. I procured it myself. I cut it out of the Mexican kid. I ought to know if it's a good donor heart or not. Goddamn, Cass. Go look at the fucking heart yourself if it will satisfy you. It's in the ice chest."

"All right," Cassy said, calmly replacing her half-empty coffee cup on the buffet table and leaving the surgeons' lounge.

Cassy lifted her surgical mask to cover her mouth and nose and re-entered the cold OR. Trent followed silently in her footsteps into the room. Heather lay sleeping quietly under the roll of blankets. Dr. Tanaka flashed a thumb's up sign to them as they entered the room.

Trent picked up a heavy dark blue paper folder off the Igloo picnic cooler that sat unobtrusively in the corner of the room. Except for the red lettering, HUMAN ORGANS FOR TRANSPLANT—RUSH, the ice chest looked like it had been purchased off the shelf at the local Target department store, as it had been.

Cassy opened the dark blue folder containing a dozen crisp white sheets of heavy bond paper. "It's a clinical summary of the donor," Trent said, flipping quickly through the papers and handing each to Cassy.

After reading several pages, Cassy said, "I'm impressed. I've never seen such neat and precise summaries."

"The heart is from a thirteen-year-old Mexican girl who was run over by a truck in Mexico City. Massive head injury but her heart functioned perfectly until I harvested it three hours ago," Trent said. He checked his watch and stared at Cassy. "The papers look all right to you?"

Cassy continued to read through the sheaf of papers, slowly and thoroughly. "Everything appears in order. The Medical Director of the Instituto de Medico signed the death certificate," she said. Holding one paper up, Cassy said, "And the detailed neurologic assessment confirming the donor's brain death . . . everything appears to be in order."

"Then let's get on with the transplant," Trent said. "We're wasting time."

"No, just a few minutes more," Cassy said, still studying the papers in the blue folder. "The organ donation consent forms are all in order . . . signed by the mother and father." Cassy looked up at Trent who had begun to pace the edge of the room.

"For god's sake, Cass, what more information do you possibly need to know. Sleep Heather and stop wasting time."

"Not yet, Trent. Just let me examine the heart before Akihito anesthetizes Heather. I can tell a lot by just looking at the donor heart and touching it."

"Whatever you say," Trent said, impatience roughening his voice.

Back inside the OR, Cassy nodded to the surgical nurse who pushed the Igloo picnic cooler toward a table draped with sterile green sheets. Cassy readjusted her surgical cap and mask and entered the scrub sink alcove just beyond the OR door. She scrubbed her hands and arms in the warm, sudsy iodinated water for five minutes. After drying her hands on the sterile towel the nurse handed her, Cassy wiggled into the surgical gown held up for her by the nurse. Then latex surgical gloves were snapped onto Cassy's outstretched hands by the surgical nurse.

"All right, let me see the heart," Cassy said, holding her gloved hands cupped together toward the nurse. Opening the Igloo picnic cooler, the nurse lifted a giant plastic refrigerator bag out of the icy slush water filling the ice chest. A second bag inside the outer transparent plastic bag contained the still heart, a fist-sized mass of red muscle hibernating in frigid stillness. The nurse removed the outer bag and plopped the inner transparent sterile plastic bag containing the donor heart into Cassy's cupped hands.

Cassy snipped away the drawstring of the inner bag and pulled out the cold, motionless muscle, the size of her clenched fist. She placed the heart into a sterile basin filled with more icy slush. "The heart looks like it will be a good size match. Looks normal on the exterior," Cassy said. Hunching over the basin, she stroked the tiny coronary arteries and veins that lay collapsed like separate lengths of spaghetti tubing on the heart's surface.

The cold, smooth surface of a donor heart in suspended animation condition always surprised Cassy—so different from the first time she had touched a live human heart. It was Trent Hendricks who had taken her hand at the operating table when she was a third-year medical student and placed her fingertips on the warm vibrant contractile heart of a fifty-three-year-old man undergoing coronary artery bypass surgery. It was that simple touch of the human heart that had decided her career choice. And life had never been the same for Cassy since then—since touching the essence of physical life.

The apparent lifelessness of the cold, flaccid heart that Cassy held cupped in her palms contradicted the life forces that were temporarily suspended in the biochemistry of the muscle tissue. The donor's heart lay collapsed and deflated in her hands, devoid of all contractility and seemingly devoid of life. But its lifeless appearance was a magic trick performed by the surgeon harvesting the actively beating heart from the brain dead donor.

This period of suspended animation of the donor heart was a pharmacologic trick that induced the beating heart into stillness and preserved the high energy biochemical stores within the heart muscle until it could be reimplanted into the waiting recipient. Cassy knew for certain that Trent, the moment before he excised this heart from the Mexico City teenager, had induced a temporary state of suspended animation in the heart from the Mexico City teenager by instilling a special mixture of drugs and chemicals directly into the donor heart's blood circulation, stilling and suspending the heart instantly.

Turning the heart over back and forth between her cupped palms, Cassy studied the cold, pale red muscle through the transected ends of the great vessels, exiting and entering the heart. Like looking into the neck of a delicate vase, Cassy could inspect the diaphanous tissue of the heart valves deep inside the heart chambers. Cassy looked up from the stainless steel basin and found Trent watching her examine the heart. "I'm still not sure, Trent. The heart looks good. But how can I be sure it was procured properly and preserved adequately?"

"Trust me on this," Trent said. "I procured it using my new Hiberna cardiac preservation protocol."

"Hiberna preservation protocol? What is that?" Cassy asked, looking up at him. The surgical mask did not hide her skeptical expression.

"My laboratory research. For the past two or three years I've been refining the technique of suspending the metabolism of the heart donor. The Hiberna solution is the best pharmacologic method of suspending the heart's animation that I've discovered. This donor heart will perform like a normal heart once you suture it in place."

"Which pharmaceutical company supplies the Hiberna solution?"

"None," Trent said. "It's my own mixture. I formulate it myself in my research lab."

"What's in it?" Cassy asked.

"It's a special group of nonprotein heterocyclic quinazolines."

"What the hell is that?" Cassy said, replacing the heart in the icy water slush in the metal basin.

"Cassy, we don't have time for me to lecture you on the pharmacology of my cardiac preservation techniques. We have to get on with the transplant. We have to use this donor heart now."

"If the heart doesn't start pumping immediately after it's in place, I won't get Heather off the operating table. She'll die."

"I know that gamble as well as anyone," Trent said.

Cassy looked at the sleeping child on the surgical table. "Okay," Cassy finally said, her words barely audible behind her mask.

"You can go ahead and sleep her, Akihito," Trent said, nodding to the anesthesiologist. "We're ready to cut."

"No, wait!" Cassy said to Dr. Tanaka who stood with a syringe of amber fluid ready to inject the anesthetic drugs into the intravenous tubing leading to a vein in Heather's arm.

"What the hell . . . ," Trent said.

"Trent, I want a word with you . . . outside," Cassy interrupted, pulling off her surgical gown and throwing her latex surgical gloves into a rolling metal bucket parked in the corner of the OR.

"What now?" Trent said, his eyes dumbfounded and angry above the surgical mask.

"Let's talk a moment in the hallway," Cassy said. She steered Trent through the double-swing door into the deserted corridor where they'd be out of earshot. "You can't come in my operating room during Heather's surgery," Cassy said, pulling her mask down around her neck like a kerchief. Trent's face glowered at her. He unconsciously moved forward to within a few inches of her face.

"I'll not only be in the room. I'm helping you do the surgery," Trent hissed, the pink spider veins on his cheeks vibrating. "I'm scrubbing in on my daughter's transplant. Cassy, you and I are the best transplant team in the world."

"Trent, it's best for Heather if I do her transplant with the chief resident in surgery helping me and not you as my assistant," Cassy said, touching his bare forearm. "You can't be Heather's father and her surgeon. You should wait in the lounge. It's impossible for you to have any surgical objectivity under these circumstances."

"Please, Cass. I need to be there for her."

"No. You know that it's no good. You can't be objective. Your surgical judgment would be biased. You're her father. Come on," she said, pulling him toward the surgeons' lounge door a dozen steps down the empty hall corridor. "You need some rest. I'll take good care of her," she said softly and tugged his arm.

Cassy opened the surgeons' lounge door. "Wait here," she said. Trent collapsed into the sofa. Cassy hoped he would remain there unmoved until she returned to the lounge after the surgery.

Cassy walked back to the OR and stuck her head through the door. "Go ahead and sleep her, Dr. Tanaka. I'm scrubbing my hands." The anesthesiologist nodded silently and with his thumb pressed the plunger of the syringe, sending amber fluid through the intravenous tube into Heather's blood stream. Moments later, she was anesthetized. Dr. Tanaka expertly slipped an endotracheal tube into Heather's mouth, attaching the half-inch diameter tubing to the mechanical ventilator of his anesthesia console.

While Cassy scrubbed her hands and arms again, the surgical nurse painted Heather's chest with the same brown iodinated surgical soap that Cassy was using to scrub her hands. As soon as the soapy 'prep' was completed, she draped heavy green surgical sheeting over Heather's frail naked body, covering it completely except for a square of bare skin left exposed between her nipples.

"Everyone ready?" asked Cassy. Gowned and gloved, she looked around at the team of nurses and doctors on either side of the table. "Scalpel." She took a deep breath then and drew the scalpel blade from the base of Heather's neck to her upper abdomen. The jaundiced skin separated like a furrow cut into a virgin field, exposing the whiteness of the breast bone in the depth of the incision. Dark blood welled up from the cut edges of the yellowish pink tissues.

Cassy hunched forward over the open chest incision, spreading the kerf in the breast bone apart with a stainless steel retractor. The bisected breast bone separated under Cassy's ratcheting of the mechanical retractor revealing Heather's massively swollen heart.

Only a rare word passed between Cassy and the senior Metro surgical resident and the two junior surgical residents as their hands worked together in smooth synchrony to attach Heather's failing heart to the heart-lung machine. Two gloved and gowned nurses clustered around the four surgeons, passing instruments back and forth into Cassy's hands. The choreography of hand movements was a polished ballet performance. Words were unnecessary. The nurses anticipated her needs and placed the appropriate instruments in her hand as soon as Cassy opened her palm.

Within fifteen minutes Heather's heart was attached to the heart-lung machine, a cabinet-size collection of pumps, tubes, and canisters that purred quietly at the side of the operating table. The machine oxygenated Heather's blood while it pulsed through the tubing outside Heather's body. The space-age machine, in essence, replaced her body's blood circulation by returning oxygenated blood back into her body while Cassy cut away the diseased heart and stitched in the donor heart.

"Her heart is huge and barely pumping," Cassy said. "I don't see how she lasted this long." Cassy quickly severed the blood vessels anchoring the heart into the chest and pulled Heather's bulky damaged heart out of the incision, much like delivering the head of an infant through a Cesarean incision. The heart popped between the stainless steel edges of the retractor with a soft plop.

Once Heather's heart had been removed, a gaping void in the center of her chest seemed to mock the surgical team. The surgeons and nurses stared in awe and respect at the vacant space where Heather's heart had once been. Nature abhors a void. Each person in the room realized the missing heart in Heather's chest cavity to be the ultimate void of Nature.

"Let's get her new heart hooked up," Cassy said to the scrub nurse, a trace of urgency slipping beyond her cool surgical control. "Let me have the donor heart." Taking the cold, flaccid heart from the nurse, Cassy positioned it in the vacancy in Heather's chest cavity. Then she meticulously placed the gossamer strands of sutures necessary to attach the cuff remnants of Heather's old heart to the tissues of the heart of the dead Mexican girl. Time wore on, but Cassy was mindless to its passage. By the end of the third hour, she had placed and tied the last of a thousand sutures. The new heart lay perfectly positioned—still, quiet, cold, and suspended.

"The size match is perfect," Cassy said, standing full upright and bringing her shoulders square as she tried to squeeze out the dull pain that had settled between her shoulder blades.

"Two hours, fifty-two minutes," the senior resident said.

"Not too bad for a surgeon that's been out of the OR for a year," Cassy said. The self-congratulation she allowed herself was more a tension-releasing comment than self-praise. "Let's see if we can jump start this donor heart and start it beating."

"Begin rewarming her," Cassy said to the heart-lung machine operator as she gently lifted the donor heart up, massaging the four chambers of the donor heart to remove bubbles of air entrapped in the heart chambers during the transplantation. The technician rotated the control knob on the heart-lung machine's heat exchanger, beginning to rewarm Heather's chilled body from its eighty-five degrees Fahrenheit to a normal body temperature, by warming her blood passing through the circuits of the heart-lung machine.

"Dr. Hendricks has really made a discovery with the Hiberna mixture," said the senior resident, a burly man wearing surgical magnifying loupe glasses. "It may not even be necessary to lower the patient's body temperature during heart operations in the near future because the Hiberna mixture is so effective at suspending the body's metabolism and preserving the donor heart's functions. It's just like the donor heart has been hibernating and wakes up from a cold winter's sleep, ready to go."

"Trent's got a lot of lecturing to do for me to get up to speed on his new metabolic methods and organ preservation techniques," Cassy said.

Smiling understandingly with his eyes, Dr. Tanaka tilted his head across the sheet-draped screen that separated him from the sterile surgical field and brought himself into the conversation between Cassy and the resident doctors. "The new heart looks like it is a perfect size match," Tanaka said, looking directly at the newly implanted donor heart. The anesthesia console behind Tanaka stood like a futuristic electronic robot holding a panoply of drugs, bottles, and syringes on its flat cabinet surface.

"It fits her chest well," Cassy said as she released the main surgical clamp allowing the new heart to fill with blood from the heart-lung machine. She carefully inspected the neat rows of blue synthetic stitching that joined the donor heart into Heather's chest. "I don't see any blood leaks or spurters."

"Very nice job," the anesthesiologist said. "I've missed your meticulous surgical needlepoint this year. You make surgery seem a work of art."

"Thanks, Akihito. You're very kind," Cassy said, winking affectionately at him. "This is the part of the transplant operation I hate. Waiting to see if the new donor heart is going to begin beating or not!" She stepped back from the table a half a step and brought her arms together in a few isometric exercises to wring the tension from her hands and forearms.

"Don't worry about the donor heart resuming a beat," Dr. Tanaka said. "Dr. Hendricks' new Hiberna protocol that he's perfected this past year is amazing."

"I've never had the opportunity to see Trent's new donor preservation technique used before this operation."

"The donor heart will begin with a normal beat in just a few minutes," Dr. Tanaka said. The surgical team huddled over the incision, staring at the newly-implanted heart lying quiet in Heather's chest while her body's circulation was supported by the oxygenating pump of the heart-lung machine. "The heart preservation technique that Trent has discovered is a major improvement over our older metabolic suspension methods," the anesthesiologist said.

"If the Hiberna mixture preserves the donor heart for transplants as well as you say it does, Trent deserves all the awards he'll receive for this discovery," Cassy said. "This kind of preservation technique could help solve the shortage of organs for transplant."

"I've never seen the Hiberna solution fail to preserve a donor heart perfectly," the anesthesiologist said.

"Look. The new heart has already started to beat," Cassy said, the excitement of her voice breaking through her usual surgical coolness. "My god, it's already beating like a normal heart. It has the snap and vigor of a supernormal heart. What has Trent put into the Hiberna solution?"

"Trent won't say. He's already applied for a patent on the drug mixture," the anesthesiologist said. "He should be a very wealthy man if the patent is granted."

"Whatever is in that Hiberna mixture, it's working like a charm. This heart's ready to fly on her own circulation," Cassy said and turned to the technician operating the heart-lung machine. "She's ready to come off the heart-lung machine. Turn off the pump."

———

Later in the morning, Cassy and Trent stood at the foot of Heather's bed in the cardiac intensive care unit as two young nurses fluttered about the motionless figure of Heather lying tethered to the the bed with an array of IV and drainage tubes. Each of the nurses was a composed whirlwind of activity as intravenous drip rates were adjusted, blood samples were drawn, chest x-rays were made, lung ventilator machines were adjusted, and blood pressures were recorded. A network of wires connected Heather's body to monitoring machines as if the electronic devices were energizing her still anesthetized body.

"She looks great," Trent said, beaming like a new father.

"Heather's going to be fine," Cassy said. "She'll wake up from the anesthetic in about an hour. I'll bet that she will want to see her dad right then."

"Thanks, Cassy," Trent said, turning his head quickly as if to look in the direction of the video monitor monitor display of Heather's vital signs but not before Cassy spotted his glistening eyes.

"I'll buy you a cup of coffee," Cassy said. "Then you can come back to her bedside so you'll be here when she wakes up."

"I do need a cup," Trent said.

In the lounge Trent poured coffee into two Styrofoam cups on the low table in front of the sofa. When Cassy started to sit down in the leather lounge chair next to the table, Trent pulled her to him, holding her close. "Thanks, Cass," he said, his voice cracking.

"Heather's going to be fine," Cassy said, repeating her earlier words and kissing his cheek. Then she pulled back from him and settled into the chair. Trent sat opposite her on the sofa and sipped the black coffee. Cassy studied her friend's general appearance. Fatigue etched his face into droopy wrinkles. Her mentor's slow, deliberate body movements were those of an exhausted man. Cassy realized that Trent had pushed himself to the point of near collapse for his daughter's life.

"I can't possibly thank you, Cass," Trent said. "How will I ever return the favor?"

He paused a few seconds and looked up again at her, kindly engaging her brown eyes. "Would you think about coming back to the heart surgery team? We do make a great team."

"I don't think so right now," Cassy said. "My son needs me more than I'm able to be with him."

"Is he any better this past year?"

"Some. The stuttering is improving. He's no longer so withdrawn. The psychiatrist says he's making a lot of improvement and getting adjusted to my divorce."

"My god, that's three years ago."

"I know . . . I know," Cassy said, sighing and nodding her head.

"Perhaps we could work out some practice arrangement where you could spend even more time with Alex than you have for him with your job running the ER."

"Walter Simmons wouldn't sit still for it," she said, draining the last of her coffee. "Besides, I don't have an ER job anymore."

"Let me speak to Walter again. He didn't refuse me when I asked him about your performing Heather's transplant."

"It won't do any good. Simmons has his own agenda for me, and it doesn't include the Metro Hospital."

"Don't be so certain, Cass. Walter can be persuaded," Trent said. "I need your help. All those children with congenital heart defects from Mexico are still coming here for their heart surgery through the Am-Mex Foundation you set up. Frankly, I'm overwhelmed, trying to operate on all those kids and do everything else I'm supposed to do. You've got to come back, Cass. You just can't walk away from all those Mexican kids."

"I don't know . . . ," Cassy hesitated. "Maybe when Alex is better."

"I wish you would reconsider," Trent said, holding her gaze. "I can't go on like this. I'm going to have to have to send the Mexican kids back. I doubt that I can find a hospital that will take them."

"Is the money a problem for the kids?"

"We're really running low. But, I believe I can find another source of funds if you'll agree to come back. I'm sure you could raise a lot more money for your Am-Mex surgical program if you would just come back to surgery."

"Okay. We'll talk more about it but not today though," Cassy said and stood in front of Trent as she lifted his hand up. "You go be with Heather while she's waking up from the anesthetic."

"Do you suppose . . . ," he said, hesitating as he stood up. "Would you consider having dinner with me this evening? Sort of a celebration, per-haps." His hand tightened on hers.

Cassy covered his hand with her other hand. "Not right now. You need to be with Heather. She needs you."

"Soon then," Trent said.

"Sure," Cassy said, kissing his cheek lightly. "I've got to scoot home now and get Alex ready for his birthday party with his father. Go be with your daughter."

FIVE

T HE LATE morning heat had already penetrated the overhanging
cover of elm branches that shaded the sweeping front yard leading up to her five bedroom two-story Tudor house when Cassy
rolled the Range Rover under the porte cochere. Charlie jumped against
the glass storm door, barking his greeting, and shot out the door the
moment Cassy opened it. The dog ran a frenzied circuit of the yard, retrieved the morning paper and returned to the driveway following a
winding path known only to his senses. He dropped the log-size Sunday
newspaper at Cassy's feet.

"Good dog, Charlie," Cassy said, rubbing the dog's long muscular
neck and bunching his tan brown coat under her fingers. His bushy tail
curved down his powerful hindquarters and flapped as Cassy kneeled beside him.

A dull fatigue pushed her shoulders down as she bent over the dog to
scratch Charlie's ear. He immediately rolled over on his back, a playful
signal to Cassy that he wanted her to rub his stomach.

"Enough, Charlie. You are one spoiled animal," she said and walked
into her house. "Where is everyone?" Cassy called into the quiet.

"Lupita?" she shouted up the curved stairwell that formed the rear wall
of the open foyer.

The Hispanic woman appeared at the top of the stairwell. "Buenos
días, Señora."

At that moment, Alex darted around his nanny and bounded down the
stairwell. A Texas Rangers' baseball cap sat low on his head. A new Texas

Rangers' T-shirt flapped over his short pants. "Hi, Mom. See my new outfit Dad sent."

"You look like a Rangers' pitcher," Cassy said, catching him in her arms as he lunged at her from the third step. "Look what else," Alex said, tugging her by the hand into the family room.

Ribbons, crumpled wrapping paper, and cardboard boxes spilled around the dining table. A baseball pitcher's glove, a dozen different computer games, another junior size Texas Rangers' uniform, and more presents cluttered the table. Every birthday and major holiday Scott Spence Jr. showered his son with gifts, an obvious overcompensation for the little time he spent with him.

Alex pulled a black fiberglass roller blade boot from a cardboard box under the table. "Mom, can I skate tonight when I get back from Six Flags?"

"Maybe," Cassy said and pushed her hand into the boot of the roller blade.

"Lupita wouldn't let me use them. She said that you would think they're too dangerous." Lupita turned toward the kitchen sink, ignoring the conversation.

"Well, maybe tomorrow," Cassy said. "I'll go skating with you but only in the driveway. Not the street."

Charlie suddenly leaped from the room toward the foyer, growling and barking.

"Stop it. Charlie," she commanded the dog as she ran the length of the hallway after him.

"Hello, Cass," Scott Spence Jr. said, smiling behind the protection of the glass door. "Charlie seems to have forgotten who's responsible for his presence in this house. Maybe I should have found him another home as part of our divorce settlement."

"No. Charlie just doesn't like strangers, and you've become a stranger in this house," Cassy replied, firmly gripping Charlie's collar. Scott Spence Jr. ducked his head, reflexively bending his six-foot four-inch frame through the door.

"Where's Alex?"

"He's in the family room making an inventory of all the loot you sent over," Cassy said, not surprised that her ex-husband missed the sarcasm in her tone.

"Happy birthday, Son," Spence said when he walked into the family room.

"D-Dad," Alex said and dropped the roller blade boot as his father lifted him from the floor in a bear hug.

"Ready for our day, Ranger?"

"Scott, I would like to see you out back a minute before you leave," Cassy said, opening the patio door to the pool area.

"Mom, Dad and I have to go to Six Flags," Alex shouted over his father's shoulder as Scott Spence walked about the family room with his son held up to his chest.

"Your dad and I need to talk a few moments. Maybe you could try installing one of your new computer games on your Macintosh. We won't be long."

As soon as the two were outside in the afternoon oven of Texas sun, Cassy slid the patio door forcibly shut and faced off with her ex-husband. Maybe it was the long morning operating on Heather Hendricks. Maybe it was the left over anxiety from the confrontation with Dr. Walter Simmons. Whatever the combination of events of the past eighteen hours, her emotional reserves were nearly empty. Her ex-husband presented a convenient and logical target to transfer her anxiety. "Scott, why don't you spend more time with Alex?"

"My dear Cassy, it's Alex's eighth birthday. I am here and intend to enjoy my son today despite your carping."

"Can't you see what you're doing to our son? Can't you even hear his stuttering?"

"There's nothing wrong with my son," Spence said as he looked across the top of Cassy's head into the house where Alex sat at the table in the family room, rubbing Charlie's neck.

"My god. The moment you come around, he starts stuttering. He never stutters when he's alone with me."

"It's not my fault that he stutters," Spence said.

"Oh no. Nothing is ever your fault. Alex's psychiatrist says his stuttering is all stress related. With no thanks to you, Alex has made a lot of progress in the past few months. At least he's not stuttering at home."

"He sure stuttered this morning," Scott Spence said.

"Yes, when you blew in here. You'd make me stutter."

"Cassy, that's not fair. I love my son."

"You only want to be with Alex because he might get you a few thousand extra votes from the mothers in Texas," Cassy said. "You and your damned gubernatorial campaign."

"Alex knows I love him. Maybe you don't know, but my son does."

"I hope he knows," Cassy said, looking towards Alex inside the family room. He waved back at his mother through the glass patio door, gesturing for them to come back in.

"At least give me the benefit of your doubts," he said coolly.

"Don't think of using Alex as a political tool, or I'll see to it that you kiss off your political ambitions forever," Cassy said, pausing. "You know what I can and will do."

"Back off, Cassy. I know it's not been a good weekend for you . . . not after last night."

"What do you know about last night?"

Spence pulled out a newspaper clipping from the interior pocket of his tan linen blazer. "Here. You made the front page."

DEAD MAN RETURNS TO LIFE
AT METROPOLITAN HOSPITAL

by Daniel Lopez, Staff Writer of The Dallas Morning News

A Dallas man is alive after being declared legally dead by a doctor at Dallas Metropolitan Hospital Saturday evening. Jeorg Marquez, 55-year-old Park Haven Funeral Home owner, was stricken by an apparent heart attack in his office at his funeral home in North Dallas at approximately 7:30 last evening. He was rushed to the Metro Hospital Emergency Room where he was declared dead by Dr. Cassandra Baldwin, Director of Emergency Services at the hospital. Nearly three hours later, Marquez revived in the hospital morgue and was discovered by the night janitor.

Cassy scanned the rest of the article and continued reading the clipping, searching for her name. In the last paragraph of the article, the reporter concluded, 'Dr. Baldwin, attending physician for Marquez, did not return phone calls to the ER.'

"At least the newspaper didn't publish my picture," Cassy said.

"But the reporter tied you to me as my ex-wife," Scott Spence Jr. said. "That is indeed a political bombshell for my campaign. Everyone in Texas will ask how could a man be pronounced dead and then three hours later come back to life. It won't help my campaign to be linked by a former marriage to a doctor who would make such a dumb ass mistake."

"Well, excuse me," Cassy said, her sarcasm again eluding her ex-husband.

"The obvious deduction is that Marquez wasn't dead when the doctor said he was," Scott said. "The public will rightfully ask how could Scott Spence Jr. have ever married anyone so damned incompetent."

"You bastard," Cassy said. She wilted into a wrought iron chair under the patio umbrella. Her face flushed scarlet from her anger as well as from the ninety-one degree noonday brightness. "Marquez was dead! I damn well know a dead man when I see one," Cassy ground out. "Must you always be so abusive?"

"Your ego needs deflating periodically," Spence said calmly.

"Scott, can't you for once be sympathetic? Just a little," Cassy said.

"Alex and I are going to need your help. What the newspaper article didn't say was that I was suspended last night."

"Over this misdiagnosis of death?"

"Yes," Cassy said, avoiding her ex-husband's glare.

"Suspended? As in fired?" he said, picking the newspaper clipping up from the patio where it had fallen from Cassy's hand.

"Yes. Suspended without pay means just that. No money. Nada."

"My god. Who's responsible for that decision at the Metro Hospital?"

"Dr. Walter Simmons, the hospital Medical Director."

"Does it have anything to do with Walter Simmons and Señor Tenoch being buddies?" Spence asked grimly.

"How do you know that?" Cassy asked.

"Every good politician has his sources of information in the community, Cassy. I'm surprised you don't know who Señor Tenoch is. He's only the wealthiest man in Texas."

"But what does that have to do with me?"

"Don't be so naive, Cassy. Follow the money. All disputes are invariably about money, my dear, and there will be the answer to Simmons' firing you so abruptly."

"No, I can't believe that," Cassy said.

"Well, it's really your problem, not mine. You'll have to deal with Simmons yourself."

"But . . . I'm going to need some help to find a way to support Alex and myself. You do recall that you have not paid any child support or alimony since our divorce."

"You refused alimony and child support."

"I didn't want your money when I could earn a living for Alex and me," Cassy said.

"Arrogant would be a better way to describe your attitude about the money I offered," Spence said.

"Maybe, but Alex and I are going to need your financial help until I can get this mess straightened out," Cassy continued. "I don't have a job. An ex-heart surgeon, fired emergency room director may have more than a little problem finding a job in Dallas, especially after the way I was terminated from the Metro Hospital by Simmons."

"Haven't you put any money aside?"

"Are you serious?" Cassy asked. "The mortgage on this house, private school, psychiatric counseling for Alex and for me, Lupita. . . . How could I save money?"

"You should have taken my child support," Spence said.

"I'm asking you for some help now. Do you want me to beg for it?" Cassy asked. "Call it a loan if you want. But I can't keep Alex and me going beyond next month without money from somewhere. It's been hand-to-mouth for us since I quit my surgical practice last year."

"I told you that you were making a dumb mistake, walking away from that high-income surgical practice."

"Alex needed me to spend more time with him. The ER job gave me a predictable life and more time to be with our son when he needed me. And it has helped. He's settled down a lot even if I couldn't spend as much time as I wanted with him," Cassy said. "The psychiatrist is pleased with his progress in the past twelve months."

"Is the psychiatrist pleased with your progress?"

"Thanks, Scott, for your concern about my welfare," Cassy said sarcastically. "I've always appreciated your tender concern about my emotional well-being."

"I wish I could give you and Alex some financial help, but right now I've committed every cent to my election campaign. I'm living like you . . . hand-to-mouth."

"Then it's time for us to get into our rainy day fund," Cassy said.

"You know I can't get into that money . . . not just now," Scott said, shaking his head.

"Well, I need some of that three million dollars. You promised me my share. . . ."

"Cassy, for god's sake! I'm in the middle of my campaign for governor. My financial records for the last five years were just released. I didn't disclose the Cayman account."

"That's your problem. Not mine," Cassy said.

"You know I can't let that information become public knowledge." Scott's face began to flush. A sheen of sweat shone on his forehead.

"Your political supporters would find a secret offshore bank account with three million dollars embarrassing to say the least." Cassy bore into Scott with her eyes. "I imagine that the disclosure of our little secret slush fund would kill any political future you might ever hope for."

"You'll have to wait until after the election in November, and I'll figure a way into that money for us then. But not now. It's just not possible."

"I can't wait. I'm already behind on the mortgage. My bank account is overdrawn."

"You never could manage money," Scott said with disgust.

"Just give me my share of the three million dollars that you stashed in the Caymans. Then I will leave you alone."

"I can't, Cassy. We didn't pay income tax on the money."

"What! You said you'd take care of all of that with our accountants. I remember asking you," Cassy said, a look of shock crossing her face.

"Don't be naive, my dear. I took care of it all right. You're the only other person who knows about this account. Remember our vacation at Grand Cayman to celebrate the sale of our company? I took three million in cash with us on that trip and deposited it in a numbered account in a Cayman bank. Nice and tax free."

"You didn't pay income tax for us on the three million dollars from the sale of CompuTeen?" she asked, shaking her head wearily and rubbing her eyes.

"We didn't report the three million dollars in income to the IRS," Spence said.

"For god's sake, Scott. Your falsification of our tax return could wind you up in jail as well as cost you the governor's race." Cassy's voice was panicked.

"Remember, you signed our joint tax return form that year," Scott said. "What happens to the gander will happen to the goose."

"I signed our tax return like every other year. You know I relied on you to take care of the bookkeeping for us," Cassy said.

"I did take care of us. That's why I stashed the money in a Cayman bank."

"Well it's time I took my half. I'll even pay the income taxes and penalties, if necessary."

"That's not possible right now, not with the election coming up. Give me a few days, and I'll think of something."

"I need my half now," Cassy said.

"Be patient, dear. You have no choice really. I'm the only one with the number of the account. I'll give you what I want. When I want."

"I can't wait. I have to have some money now."

"You'll have to wait until after the election. I'm sorry," Scott said and stood up. He pulled out his billfold from his dark silk trousers and extracted three one hundred dollar bills. "Will this help for now?"

"Don't patronize me. Just figure out a way for me to have some of that money that's in the Cayman account," Cassy said. "And I want Alex back here by eight o'clock."

"Maybe you'd like for me to find you a job," Spence said as he walked across the patio towards the family room door. "When I'm governor, I'll see to it that you get a good job. Until then, you can find work all by yourself."

Scott Spence Jr. disappeared through the open patio door. Cassy heard his booming baritone voice from inside the house, "Alex, let's go, birthday boy."

Cassy closed her eyes and leaned forward, resting her forehead against the glass patio door. God, how did this happen? she sighed to herself. Divorced, fired, broke, and now a resurrected patient, she thought. A minute later Lupita's voice scratched its way into Cassy's depression. "What is it, Lupita?" Cassy said, moving her face away from the patio door to look through the glass at Lupita standing in the family room.

"I'm leaving for the day, Señora."

"Have a nice day," Cassy said and moved back from the glass door. A smudged spot at eye level on the glass marked the spot were Cassy's head had rested.

"Señora, there was a telephone call for you this morning," Lupita said. The maid brought her face close to the glass door and raised her voice. "Gracie. Her telephone number I took. You call . . . today. Say it important," Lupita said in broken English.

"All right," Cassy said, wishing that Lupita would leave quickly. The front door banged shut behind the nanny. Only then did Cassy reach to open the patio door to enter the cool stillness of the family room. After pausing a moment at the refrigerator door, Cassy looked absently inside the refrigerator, barren except for a skimmed milk carton, leftover pizza, a worn-out head of lettuce, a couple of spongy tomatoes, and a half-filled carton of orange juice.

"Why can't I have a housekeeper who can shop and cook? For god's sake, what I need is a wife!" she said aloud to herself as she closed the refrigerator. Unconsciously glancing at the digital clock on the micro-wave oven, Cassy opened the refrigerator again and removed an un-opened bottle of Mondavi chardonnay. "I know, it's early afternoon, but I owe myself a glass of wine," she said to the empty kitchen and poured the wine into a water glass. The cold wine frosted the side of the glass. Cassy studied the pale yellow liquid and then drained half the glass in a single gulp.

Cassy piddled through the making of a tuna and tomato sandwich on a sourdough baguette loaf that she defrosted in the microwave. Juggling the wine and sandwich in one hand and the Sunday paper in the other, she squeezed through the opening in the sliding glass patio door and settled into the poolside lounge chair under the shade of the umbrella.

With the newspaper balanced on her knee, she gnawed at the sandwich while she reread the front page article about the Marquez resurrection. I know this man was dead, she thought. No pulse; no blood pressure; no respiration; flat-lined EKG tracing. What more could I have done to de-termine he was dead? Then she remembered that she had not checked the toxicology and drug screen results on Marquez's blood sample from Saturday night. Walter Simmons had ejected her from the hospital before she had the chance to call the laboratory.

Cassy dialed the portable phone she kept on the poolside table. A mo-ment later she was connected with the laboratory supervisor at Metropolitan Hospital. "Agnes, this is Dr. Baldwin. Would you check the toxicology screen on a patient from the Emergency Room last night . . . a Jeorg Marquez?"

"Oh yeah. The Lazarus patient," she said. "All the poison screens were negative. Clear as a newborn baby."

"Thank you, Agnes," Cassy said formally and started to hang up the telephone.

"What happened to that man?" Agnes interrupted before Cassy had replaced the phone. "You're the second person who's called about the tox screen this morning."

"Who else called?" Cassy asked, startled by the interest in the toxicology report. She sat up on the chaise lounge. The newspaper fell from her lap to the patio deck.

"Dr. Walter Simmons," the technician said, and quickly asked, "What happened to Marquez Saturday night?"

"I don't know," Cassy said. "But let me hear if you see any abnormal lab results on Marquez." Cassy sat lost in her puzzled mind for several minutes before pulling herself out of the chaise lounge.

She returned to the kitchen and refilled the glass of wine before changing into her two-piece swimming suit. Back at the poolside she settled onto the chaise lounge and lathered suntan oil all over herself. Then she unsnapped the halter piece of her suit and rolled face down in the chaise lounge in the afternoon sun. The warmth on her back lulled her into drowsiness.

The persisting chirping intrusion of the portable phone called her back from the edge of her consciousness to a reluctant wakefulness. By the ninth warble Cassy grabbed the portable phone off the poolside table and held the receiver against her ear as she lay on the chaise.

Cassy immediately recognized the Haitian accent. "Dr. Baldwin. You must leave town. It is dangerous. Do not go to the hospital." The quick frightened voice of Gracie screeched down the line.

"Gracie, what are you talking about? Calm down. Where are you? Why did you run away from the ER last night?"

"The man is a zombie," Gracie said. Her voice trembled as if she were being shaken.

"What?" Cassy asked, lifting her head off the chaise cushion.

"Marquez is a zombie. He's come back from the dead. The spirits possess him."

"Gracie, that's absurd."

"I have seen the zombie men when I was a little girl in Haiti. The spirits will come for me. He is the living dead."

"Calm down," Cassy said. "Let's meet and talk about this."

"No. I leave until the zombie is gone." The vacant noise of the disconnected line buzzed in Cassy's ear. Oh god, thought Cassy. I simply can't deal with Gracie and her Haitian superstitions right now. Finishing off the rest of the wine that had warmed in the glass under the afternoon sun, Cassy slid the portable phone under the lounge and draped her arms over the edge as the sun scorched the bare skin of her back and legs.

Charlie snored softly in the shade of the patio table umbrella. A warmth suffused her face. A slick, silky peel of perspiration encased her body. The combination of the midday heat, the fatigue of the weekend, and the two glasses of wine shoved her conscious mind into a dull, thoughtless emptiness. Her breathing became slow and steady as she lay face down on the soft cushion of the chaise lounge chair. The film of glistening perspiration condensed on her body. Gravity coalesced the sweat into tiny streams down the creases of her body as the unfiltered blazing sun stood still in the afternoon sky.

—

Multicolored gauzes floated before Cassy's eyes for what seemed a forever period of time, obscuring all mental images except for the rainbow swirls of fabric. As she struggled to see through the undulating colors, her mind recognized as an objective conclusion that her eyelids were closed and that her visual images were the patterns of the interior of her closed eyelids.

Her eyelids would not open. Repetitively, she commanded her eyes to open, but all she could see was the waving reddish gray of the back side of her closed eyelids. As hard as she struggled to open her eyes, they remained closed as if the lids had been sealed with crazy glue.

The sun's heat seared her back as though she were under a flame broiler. She tried to wiggle her toes and fingers, but nothing happened. Her fingers and toes were disconnected from her mind. The connections of her brain with her extremities were severed as if the wiring had been snipped.

Where in the hell am I? she tried to ask but her lips would not move. Her tongue was paralyzed and lay slack in her mouth. Then the organ music began softly in her mind. What was the melody? The notes coalesced and separated, ebbed and swelled, until she recognized the hymn, *Amazing Grace*. The organ music filled her mind with the chords of the old hymn until the mind churning church music obliterated her futile attempts at moving her body.

Cassy lay motionless under the white-hot afternoon sun, her mind filled by the words of *Amazing Grace, how sweet the sound*. At last her dream thinking jerked away the metal gauze revealing flashing images, like a

television screen out of control scanning through channels without pausing, until her mind picture stopped on the image of a sanctuary in an ancient cathedral.

The organ music faded in her mind to be replaced by a man's rich baritone voice broadcasting words through her brain. What did he say? Cassy
tried to sort the sounds of the man's voice into words. Whose voice? Was
it Trent Hendricks? No, that baritone voice could only be Dr. Walter
Simmons' voice without the whiskey roughness. What did Simmons say?
Cassy strained at recognizing the words. The voice clarified into *Friends
of Cassandra Marta Baldwin-Spence, we are gathered today not to mourn the
death of Cassy but to celebrate her life.*

Cassy managed to command her eyes open so that she now looked
down on an open casket from a vantage point near the lofty arched ceiling of the nave of an enormous cathedral. Shadows obscured the face of
the young woman in the casket. So this must be the out-of-body death
experience she casually told herself, as if her transcendence into death was
quite a commonplace occurrence.

The cathedral was filled with mourners. Cassy recognized all their
faces. She floated above her friends, teachers, and former patients. There
were her mother and dad in the first pew. Then she recognized herself as
the woman lying in the open casket on the black marble bier in front of
the first pew. Her body looked to be resting, apparently asleep in a high
collared, white silk dress that blended against the light blue satin upholstery of the bronze and walnut casket. My god, Cassy thought, I really am
dead. How curious to be attending my own funeral. Not many people
have such good fortune, her dreaming subconscious told her.

On the raised pulpit above the casket, Dr. Walter Simmons, covered
in a white cleric's collar and a black robe, smiled at the mourners.
*Cassy was a loving mother, compassionate physician, skilled surgeon, devoted
daughter. . . .* His voice faded as the organ music of *Amazing Grace* over-
rode his eulogy. Hovering above the congregation, Cassy could see everyone stand up. Her mother and dad hobbled toward the open casket. Alex,
dressed in his Texas Rangers' T-shirt and baseball hat, followed her elderly parents toward the open casket. The multicolored gauze closed
once again over her eyes, obliterating the image of the sanctuary. Colors
swirled and danced on a gray field in her mind.

She felt Alex's hand touch her cheek. Her face ignited under his small
fingers. Tears formed in the corner of her eyes. Her father's lips touched
her other cheek, and his voice whispered into her ear. *Be tough, kid. Don't
ever let them see you cry.*

The variegated gauze solidified into a dense black cloth over her eyes as
the casket lid closed. All sound ceased when the casket top squeezed shut

into a hermetic seal. Cassy soon felt the casket trundling on a rolling bier. Then she was lifted upward. Later, a car engine transmitted its vibrations to the casket. The sensation of motion began once again. Finally the motion stopped. She felt herself being lifted again. Muffled voices filled the coffin. She thought for a moment she heard Alex's cry.

Then she felt the sensation of her body being lowered. She tried to scream, but her faint cry was only a chirp. With great effort her leaden hands reached the lining of the lid of the casket. Then she felt the pebbles strike the top of the casket and heard clearly in her mind *Ashes to ashes and dust to dust. No,* she screamed inside her head. She clawed at the upholstery of the coffin, ripping the satin lining.

"No!" she screamed and rolled upright on the chaise into the blazing afternoon sun. For several moments she looked about in a panic, gradually focusing on the familiar—the sleeping dog, the glistening pool, the hot patio bricks. Cassy's face dripped in sweat. She heaved herself upright and sat huddled on the end of the chaise lounge, shivering in the white heat of the Texas sun. She thrust her trembling fingers in front of her face. Then she grabbed a cigarette and filled her lungs with quick deep breaths of the tobacco smoke until her quivering had slowed to a tremor. What the hell is happening to me?

"I've got to find out what's going on, or I'm going to lose my mind," Cassy said to the empty patio. "What the hell happened to you, Jeorg Marquez? Tell me what happened." She emphatically ground the cigarette out in the soil of the poolside planter and ran for the protected refuge of the shower in her bedroom.

SIX

SUNDAY AFTERNOON was usually a quiet time in the visiting and patient care cycle of the Dallas Metropolitan Intensive Care Unit. Cassy hoped by going to the hospital at this hour that she would avoid anyone involved in the Marquez incident, especially Dr. Walter Simmons.

The heavily starched long white laboratory coat hung like a cardboard tube over Cassy's crisp short sleeve white blouse and olive chinos. She blended unnoticed with the other white-coated hospital personnel as if she were invisible in the hallway. The stethoscope draped over her neck signaled her physician's authority more clearly than an military epaulet.

She pushed through the swinging double doors into the ICU and strode directly into the hub of the circular sixteen bed Medical Intensive Care. "I'll bet you're here to see Marquez," the duty nurse said.

"How's the patient?" Cassy said as she reached for the chart in the revolving lazy susan file of charts.

"Let me get Joannie. She's been looking after him since early this morning."

Cassy leaned onto the standup writing counter enclosing the nurses' station and scanned the handwritten medical history and doctors' notes contained in the metal clipboard binder. None of the physicians who had seen Marquez in the fifteen hours he had been in the ICU had come up with an explanation for the patient's revival in the morgue. Cassy counted at least a dozen possible diagnoses for Marquez's sudden death, each offered by a different physician, the speculation ranging from a silent heart attack to an allergic food reaction to epilepsy. Cassy did notice the subtle shades and innuendos of the doctors' written phrases. Without directly accusing Cassy of declaring Marquez dead when he, in fact, was not dead, each of the physicians ever so subtly raised the possibility of a mistaken diagnosis of death.

The reserved civility of written comments in Marquez's record would be replaced by blazing derision Monday morning in the Doctors' Lounge. She could already imagine the mocking and ridicule—the Saturday night fiasco, Baldwin's Blunder, Cassy's Castoff.

"We're calling him Lazarus." Joan Markison, a diminutive, attractive ICU nurse dressed in loose fitting surgical scrubs, interrupted Cassy's thoughts.

"Oh, hi, Joannie," Cassy said, looking up from her concentration on the medical record. The pungent scent of Georgio Red perfume swept over Cassy.

"Good to have you back here in the ICU. You've been away too long."

"How's Señor Marquez today?" Cassy said carefully as she returned to Marquez's chart, the drifting fragrance of Joan Markison's Georgio enveloping her like a cloud.

"Well, he's acting like he's asleep . . . he's having a hard time waking up," the nurse replied. "He hasn't said much, mumbling occasionally in Spanish. All the x-ray and lab results are normal."

"Let me try to talk to him," Cassy said, replacing the chart. "Maybe he'll understand me if I talk to him in Spanish."

"That's not a good idea. Dr. Simmons told the Nursing Service, 'No Visitors for Marquez,' and he said he meant no one. Besides that you're not even Marquez's attending physician."

"Five minutes is all I need," Cassy said. "What's to hurt? I just want to ask him a few questions."

"It won't do you any good. Marquez is not talking to anyone," Joan said. "He's lying in bed, rolled up like a baby."

"I've got to talk to him," Cassy said.

The nurse shook her head again even more vigorously and looked nervously about the ICU. "I can't let you, Dr. Baldwin. I could lose my job. You shouldn't even be in the hospital."

"Joannie, I'm going in for just five minutes," Cassy said, looking to the nurse for approval. Not finding it, she turned and headed towards Marquez's cubicle.

"Dr. Baldwin . . . ," the nurse anxiously called after her, but Cassy had already slipped through the curtain.

Except for the muffled metronome beat of the EKG monitor, silence filled the cubicle. Cassy paused at the foot of the bed. Marquez lay immobile, the bed covers crisply tucked around him in mitered corners. His dark, virtually black, eyes stared unblinking at the ceiling. A transparent vinyl bag filled with one liter of clear saline and dextrose solution hung on a six-foot stainless steel rod and dripped a precise spherical drop of liquid each second into a single intravenous tubing that snaked under the top of the bed sheet.

Cassy approached the right side of the bed. "Buenas noches, Señor Marquez," Cassy said. The man lay as still as a pink corpse. With a quick flick of her index finger she poked at Marquez's unblinking eyes, stopping her finger just short of touching the staring right eyeball. His eyelids snapped shut in a reflex protective snap and stayed closed. Cassy then clapped her hands near Marquez's right ear. His eyes popped open again into the same fixed ceiling stare, looking like dead fish eyes. "I'm sorry about last night," Cassy said in Spanish. "I don't know what happened to you yet, but I will find out. Can you tell me about last night?"

Marquez continued staring at the ceiling. After a minute, Cassy tried communicating again with the mute. This time she picked up Señor Marquez's soft limp hand hoping to reach to him in a primitive touching form of human communication, much as she often did with infants in the Emergency Room. She felt the buffed sheen of his manicured fingernails.

Cassy held Marquez's hand, saying nothing, while she watched his easy breathing. His black goggle-eyes stared at the fixed point on the white ceiling. Marquez's round pudgy face was smooth, expertly shaved. His black hair lay slicked above a hair line that continued the smooth brown complexion of his forehead in two parallel tongues leaving a widow's peak of black hair. A flash of recognition creased the man's face when Cassy put her hand under his chin and turned his face toward her. His eyes fixed on her face, but Cassy could not see behind his flat eyes.

"Habla me, Señor. Talk to me," Cassy said. "I want to help you. I know that you hear me. I know that you can see. Talk to me." After a long pause, Marquez's stubby fingers progressively tightened around Cassy's hand until his fist clenched her fingers.

"Estoy muerto. Estoy muerto . . . I am dead."

"No, you are alive," Cassy said as she pulled a chair closer to his bedside and sat. The man's hand clutched her fingers. She could see the terror in his eyes as they flitted wildly about the room.

"Sí, I am dead," the man said again in Spanish. "You said, 'Let's call the time of death 19:45.' I am dead."

Cassy paused, stunned at his perfect memory of her death pronouncement in the Emergency Room the previous night. After a moment she asked, "What did you see or feel when you heard me say that?"

"I could not move. I was weak."

"When did you first feel the weakness?"

"When I fell off the chair in my office. Next I remember the Emergency Room. The light you shined in my eyes, but I just couldn't move."

"What happened after then?"

"You said, 'Let's call the time of death 19:45'."

"What next?"

"I was not sure where I was. All I could see when I finally opened my eyes was the white sheet. Estoy muerto."

"But you are not dead. It is Sunday afternoon. Eighteen hours after you were in the Emergency Room. You are not dead."

"Señora, you are most kind to me," Marquez said and turned his face toward Cassy fixing her eyes on his dark, unwavering gaze. "Leave me now. I am dead."

"No, you are alive. You can hear, see, think, and feel," Cassy persisted.

"Señora, usted es muy amable. You are most kind," Marquez repeated and pulled his face away from her. "Dejame ya! Leave me now. Estoy muerto."

"You are not dead. You have come back . . . if you ever were away," Cassy said, conceding to herself for the first time that perhaps Marquez had not been dead when she pronounced him dead at seven forty-five Saturday evening.

"No, Señora. You must go now. He has killed me just like he said he would," Marquez said so softly that Cassy could barely hear. "He will kill everyone around me."

"Killed you? Who are you talking about? Who killed you?"

Marquez's head rolled over on his pillow, and his gaze narrowed to the same fixed focal point on the ceiling. "He did," Marquez said in a guttural voice before closing his eyes and rolling his head away from Cassy.

The curtain to the cubicle abruptly snapped aside. "Dr. Baldwin, you have an urgent telephone call from Dr. Simmons," Joan Markison said formally.

Cassy held Marquez's hand for another moment. "Gracias, Señor Marquez. I'm glad you're feeling better. I will be back to see you as soon as I take this phone call." When she laid his hand down, there was absolutely no response.

At the nurse's station she picked up the telephone from the counter top writing desk. "What the hell are you doing in my hospital?" Dr. Simmons' voice asked even before Cassy finished her hello. Joan Markison stood with her arms akimbo on her hips, watching Cassy's facial expression. "You have no authority to be interviewing Marquez."

"But Walter. . . ."

"Get the hell out . . . you've caused enough trouble already. You have no business at the Metro Hospital. Please leave now and put Joan back on the phone."

Cassy turned to face the nurse who stood with a disapproving frown inside the protective circle of the nurses' station.

"Thanks, Joannie," Cassy said sarcastically, handing the telephone receiver to her. "I'll return the favor sometime."

———

Vivaldi's *Four Seasons* filled the Range Rover with soothing runs of violins. Cassy turned up the volume until the car vibrated with the reverberations of the violins playing with and against each other in delicate harmony and crashing contrasts. Despite the soothing effect of the music in the cool isolation of her car, she drove mindlessly along the familiar route home. She could not put down the riddle of Marquez. He was the dissonant out-of-tune violin in a Vivaldi symphony orchestra. His was the sour note in her career that had blemished her life's performance.

Marquez's precise recollection of her statement, 'Let's call the time of death 19:45', caused the hair on the nape of her neck to stand. Her probing scientific mind kept asking why? Why? Why? He was dead I am absolutely sure. She tried to reinforce her conviction and wished she felt as sure about her diagnosis of death as before she had visited Marquez. Now she was not certain. Her rational mind could not ignore Marquez's perfect recall of the moment of his death . . . or more precisely the hour after his heart stopped and the moment after Cassy abandoned the CPR.

By the time she pulled under the porte cochere, the Vivaldi tape was finished, and she had smoked her third cigarette. The early evening air had already started to relieve the afternoon's heat. Cassy fumbled for the house keys and tapped in her code on the intrusion alarm. Charlie barked his welcome. The moment the heavy wooden double door closed behind her, Cassy heard the telephone ring. She ran to the family room and grabbed the wall phone.

"Hi, Cassy," Trent Hendricks said. "You sound disappointed that it's me."

"No. No. Alex is spending the day with his father. I thought you might be him calling in. I'm always a little antsy when he's away . . . especially with his father."

"Sorry. It's just me," Trent said, chuckling into the phone.

"He's supposed to be home by eight o'clock, but Scott usually brings him home early. He doesn't have the patience for a whole day with his son."

"Well, Alex has two more hours before his mother's curfew."

She flipped a cigarette from the carton of Marlboros and lit it with a gold lighter she fished out of the cabinet drawer. "He'll be home very soon. How's Heather?"

"She's why I called. I've some great news about Heather. She's recovering so rapidly that we've taken her off the respirator. She's wanting Blue Bell ice cream for dinner!"

"God, Trent. That's wonderful."

"It is. I can see that I have my daughter back. I want to thank you for her life."

"That's not necessary," Cassy said, taking a deep smoke filled pull on the cigarette.

"I have to say this. And I hope you'll accept it in the spirit of friendship . . . ," Trent began.

"Why do I think I'm not going to like what you're about to say?" she interrupted.

"Cassy, you're wasting your talents in the ER when you can save lives like Heather's in the Heart Surgery OR," Trent began again. "I hope that you'll consider coming back to heart surgery at the Metro Hospital."

"Ah, Trent, I'm not welcome at Metro any longer. Walter Simmons just told me again to stay out of the hospital."

"Give Walter a few days. He'll cool off."

"I'm not so sure," Cassy said.

"Forget Simmons. I'll take care of him when the time comes, Cassy," Trent said. "Let's talk about more pleasant subjects. If you're free tomorrow, I would like to drop off a thank you gift. Maybe we could talk some more about your long term career plans."

"Sure, anytime. Alex and I will be here all Memorial Day. It's his birthday celebration," Cassy said. "We're planning to take it easy by the pool all day. But I don't think my career prospects are all that interesting at Metro or anywhere else right now."

"Come on, Cassy. Let up. You're the best heart surgeon in Dallas," Trent said seriously. "How about eleven tomorrow morning?"

Cassy hung up the phone slowly and stood for several minutes with her hand on the receiver, seemingly still connected to Trent but lost in her mind's rerun of the events of the past twenty-four hours. Indecision and uncertainty fell over her, leaving a physical malaise like the beginning of the flu.

For the next hour Cassy prowled restlessly through the huge empty house, Charlie at her side. The bank of windows overlooking the patio framed her custom-designed work station and desk on the exterior wall of her bedroom. The answering machine on the edge of the desk blinked its red message signal. She tossed her clothes onto the cushioned reading chair in the corner of her bedroom. Standing in front of the desk in her underwear, she pushed the machine's play button. A moment later the machine's recorder played back.

"This is Debbie Wilkins. I'm Gracie's daughter." Cassy immediately recognized the pattern of Gracie's Haitian accented lilting speech in her daughter's voice. The maternal imprint of Gracie's speech rhythms identified her daughter as clearly as her name. For an instant Cassy wondered whether Alex's voice bore the same resemblance to her speech cadences and inflections. She knew that she would listen for her own influence in her son's voice as soon as he returned from his day visit with his father.

The soft Texas-tinged, Haitian-accented voice continued, "Mama told me to call you. She trusts you. Call me as soon as possible." The voice left two telephone numbers. Cassy dialed the first number. As soon as the soft frightened voice answered, Cassy identified herself.

"What's the matter with Gracie? Is she hurt?" Cassy asked. "What has she done?"

"She is frantic, running all over everywhere," her daughter said, the anxiety crowding the softness from her voice.

"Where is she?" Cassy asked.

"I don't know, Doctor, Mama is so scared," the woman said. "I've never seen her like this before. She wanted me to warn you that there is evil in the hospital. . . ."

"That's crazy talk. Is it the Saturday night incident that has spooked her?" Cassy asked.

"It's the man returning from the dead. Mama saw zombies when she was a little girl in Haiti. Mama believes that the spirits in the zombie man are loose in the hospital."

"Gracie needs to see a psychiatrist," Cassy said flatly. "Has she ever been this way before?"

"Never! Mama said that you must leave the hospital. There is evil there."

Oh hell, Cassy thought. Gracie has flipped out.

"How can I reach Gracie? I have to talk her out of this crazy idea," Cassy said.

"She wouldn't tell me where she was going to hide, but Mama promised to call me every day. I'll tell her that you want to talk to her."

"Tell her to call me at home or come see me at my home," Cassy said. "I won't be back in the hospital for a while."

"I'll tell Mama," Gracie's daughter said. "She'll be glad that you are not at the hospital."

"Thanks," Cassy said, dropping the phone into its cradle and pulling on an oversized Texas Rangers' T-shirt that hung to her upper thighs. She walked back to the kitchen and poured a full glass of white wine from the Mondavi bottle that she had opened that morning. Then she settled into the end of the leather sofa, resting her legs and feet on the sofa. With her second glass of chilled wine she fixed a plate of cheddar cheese and a handful of crackers. She knew that there would be no dinner.

After rereading the front page article of the *Sunday Dallas News* again, Cassy noticed a sidebar column on the definition and declaration of death. In the second paragraph of the article, the science and medicine reporter for the *Dallas News* quoted an ER physician from a Dallas community hospital: 'Reliable criteria for the declaration of death permit physicians to diagnose death with certainty. These criteria include complete and continuous absence of consciousness, no reaction to external stimuli, lack of respirations, and total absence of electrocardiographic and electroencephalographic activity.'

In the next paragraph, the reporter struck a reassuring note: 'There is little to fear of being closed in a morgue before death is unequivocal and irreversible. Established criteria of death virtually eliminate the likelihood of an erroneous declaration of death.'

"All right, wise guy," Cassy said aloud. "If Marquez was without blood pressure, pulse, consciousness, respirations, or reaction, why wasn't he dead? Or if he was dead, why and how did he return to life?"

'Let's call the time of death 19:45', Marquez's precise recall of her words declaring him dead haunted her. No, he couldn't be dead and remember so clearly her precise phrasing, she conceded.

She also knew that unless she could provide a believable explanation for Marquez's apparent death and revival, Simmons would be certain that she'd never return to the Metro Hospital.

The newspaper article concluded with questions: 'Did the attending physician make a mistake and was Señor Marquez not dead, or was Marquez dead by accepted clinical criteria only to revive in the Morgue of Metropolitan Hospital? Or is there a yet unexplained valid reason for Marquez's resurrection?' In frustration Cassy tossed the newspaper to the floor of the family room and stretched her body the length of the sofa, propping the end pillow under her head.

Just as Cassy dozed off, Charlie jumped up abruptly and barked, shattering the stillness and bringing Cassy wide awake. The click of the front door opening took the dog out of the family room at a full run.

"Hi, Mom!" Charlie's barking stopped at the sound of Alex's voice in the foyer. Cassy walked in her bare feet to the foyer just in time to see a black limousine roll through the wrought iron gates at the end of the driveway.

"Alex, you're an hour early. Where's your father?" Cassy asked.

"He had to go, Mom. Said to tell you he was sorry he had to bring me home early."

"I'm glad to see you," Cassy said, hugging her son. "Have you eaten?"

"Four hot dogs, a giant huge pretzel, and three cokes."

"Is that all?" Cassy asked, a mother's smile wrinkling her face.

"Two ice creams."

"Sounds like you had a great time. What's in your black bag?"

Alex leaped to the floor and began pulling souvenirs from a Texas Rangers' canvas bag. Rangers' pennants, baseball caps, souvenir programs, T-shirts. Another two hundred fifty dollars of overcompensation, thought Cassy.

"Let's get you cleaned up," Cassy said, as she rubbed her son's dark ruffled hair.

"Do I have to?"

"Yes, and shampoo your hair."

"Oh, Mom," Alex said and trudged up the foyer stairway, dragging his afternoon's booty as if weighted under an impossible burden.

—

The evening passed quietly. Cassy had muted the telephone after the first newspaper reporter had called for her reaction to the Marquez incident. Messages piled up on the answering machine—reporters from all three networks, the *New York Times*, the *Chicago Tribune*, and *The Los Angeles Times* as well as the *Enquirer* and a half dozen other newspapers. She returned none of their calls.

"It's time for bed, big boy," Cassy said as she stood in the doorway of her son's room. Alex had spent the rest of the evening in his room, hunched before the Macintosh videoscreen, installing each of the new computer video games his father had given him for his birthday.

"Let's pick up *Huck Finn* where we left off."

Alex shut down his Macintosh, leaving the screen display flashing its cascade of colored light. After he climbed into the lower berth of his bunk bed, Cassy pulled the padded captain's chair near the head of his bed.

"Let's see where we were," she said, flipping the pages. "We missed last night, but on Friday night Huck and Jim were. . . ."

Alex squirmed beneath the sheet and interrupted his mother. "Mom, why did you and Dad get a divorce?"

"We just weren't happy living together," Cassy said, knowing that the truth could never be a wrong answer with her son. "It was best for all three of us."

"Do you still love Daddy?"

"In a way, maybe," Cassy said, not knowing how to answer—uncertain herself about the complex mixture of emotions for the man who was the father of her son. "But not in the way that married people love each other."

"How?"

"I'll always be your mother and your father will always be your father. But the three of us can't live together. Do you understand?" Cassy asked softly.

"No," Alex said.

"We'll talk some more about it tomorrow," Cassy said, recognizing that sometimes the truth was not a good enough answer. "But for right now, let's find Huck and Jim."

"Can we stay up to watch the late movie on HBO? Today's my birthday."

"We'll see," she said and began reading. Ten minutes later, Alex's eyes drifted shut. Cassy inserted the bookmarker and switched off the reading light. Alex rolled slightly to the side when Cassy kissed his forehead. His lids twitched but did not open.

"Good night, my man." Cassy left the bedroom door ajar. Charlie bounced down the staircase just ahead of her.

SEVEN

AMAZING GRACE, *How sweet the sound.* The woman's warm vibrant voice floated through Cassy's mind as she slept. The frigid breeze from the air-conditioning vents chilled the tomb-like silence of her bedroom. Cassy had been sleeping fitfully just below the edge of consciousness for the four hours since midnight. She searched for the woman, but the sound of her voice surrounded her completely. The source of the singing eluded her, yet the sound enveloped her like a white sparkling fog. Was it Gracie's voice?

Amazing Grace, that saved a wretch like me. I once was lost but now am found. . . . The rich, mellifluous feminine voice refrained the ancient hymn in Cassy's subconscious mind. The multicolored gauze that blinded her in the afternoon swirled again through her dreaming mind, blocking out all visual images.

Cassy strained to see through the gauze. Rolling red clouds replaced her vision. She struggled to open her eyes. When she tried to bring her hands up to her eyes to pry her lids apart, her forearms would not respond to her brain's command. Her hands, pressed by their own weight into the sheets, lay paralyzed at her side. Her arms, legs, and entire body felt weighted as if she were trying to run under water. Cassy again willed her extremities to move. They would not budge. Her toes and fingers would not even curl. Her arms and legs remained frozen in a viscous liquid.

Her sensory impressions magnified themselves in her immobilized body. The tiny movement of the sheet across her thighs felt like a whipping canvas sailcloth under the tornadic roar of the air conditioner breeze.

Cassy's silent screams pierced her mind, but the bedroom was as quiet as a burial vault.

It was then that she felt something broad and wet flick against her cheek. A fetid breath puffed into her nostrils. Still she could not move. The singer's soothing melodious voice soared in her mind. *Amazing Grace, how sweet the sound. . . .* The rough moist slab grated her left cheek again. She struggled to turn her head away from the rancid breath, but her body would not respond to her brain's command. The bioelectric signals to the voluntary muscle groups in her body went unacknowledged. She lay motionless. Screams of terror filled her head.

Time had no meaning until her head exploded when Charlie barked into her left ear and licked her cheek again, startling Cassy awake. She bolted upright in bed, tearing at the sheets that lashed her legs to the bed in a scrambled tangle. Her body felt broiled. Sweat bathed her face. Her dark hair hung wet at its roots and clung to her neck.

After fumbling with the lamp switch, the room blazed in light. "Jesus," she muttered aloud as her eyes squinted into the brilliance of the bedside lamp. The German shepherd looked at her, puzzled. His long tongue flopped and unfurled itself below his lower jaw. The red LED dial on the bedside radio glowed 4:15.

Charlie nuzzled her bare legs as she swung them to the floor and tested her steadiness. The soles of her feet tingled when she stood on the plush pile carpet. Her sweat-drenched Texas Rangers' T-shirt clung like a wet bathing suit to her skin. Cassy pulled it over her head and stepped out of her panties. She stumbled groggily toward the bathroom, touching the wall for balance and support.

The dog looked at her quizzically as she steadied herself on the lavatory in front of the bathroom mirror. "How did you know I needed to wake up?" she asked the dog who sat on his haunches, watching Cassy as she leaned nude toward the mirror. "My god, that nightmare was so real I knew I was dead. Maybe that's how Marquez felt." Cassy leaned further into the mirror, her face an inch from the glass surface, studying the fatigue lines in her face.

"I'll never get back to sleep now, Charlie." She closed the heavy, clear glass shower door behind her and adjusted the water controls. Charlie coiled himself onto the bath mat and closed his eyes.

Cassy stood under the stinging water hammers of the steaming shower until the blistering streams shimmered her skin a bright red where the pulsating jets struck her back. The sweet pain of the hot shower steamed away her dream confusion. Her rational mind slowly came into focus. The steam filled the tiled shower with a white mist so thick she couldn't see. Cassy turned off the shower and leaned backward, pressing the small of her back against the tiles. Breathing slowly and deeply, Cassy filled her lungs with the warm moist air until all the steam faded from the shower and her skin prickled into goose flesh. After slipping into her soft terry cloth robe, she toweled her hair into a turban and padded quietly through the dark hallway into the kitchen to make her morning coffee.

The roar of the coffee grinder erupted through the kitchen before Cassy could throw a kitchen towel around the machine to muffle the noise. "Shit. Why can't they make a quiet coffee grinder," Cassy said to the empty kitchen. She flipped off the grinder switch and listened to the predawn silence recapture the house.

The hot water streamed through the freshly ground coffee in the machine releasing the rich, thick aroma of brewing coffee. As she waited for the coffee to drip through, Cassy lit a cigarette. This is my one and only cigarette for the entire day, she promised herself. She placed the nearly full package in the pocket of her robe.

The morning newspaper usually was a low priority item in Cassy's day. But this morning the front page would be a barometer of the community's interest in the second day of the Marquez resurrection. Before the coffee had finished brewing, she walked to the foyer with the dog following her bare feet. She hoped that yesterday's news would be old news today and that some gruesome event might have captured the interest of the reporters. Maybe then the media would leave her alone, an unlikely prospect she knew.

The German shepherd shot through the crack in the oak door, banging Cassy's left leg as she released the dead bolts and opened the front door. Their game of newspaper retrieval required Charlie to explore the yard for an additional ten minutes after dropping the paper at her feet. Then he would return to the patio door where he could see Cassy reading the morning newspaper.

Cassy sank into the family room sofa with a second cup of coffee and another cigarette, slipping off the protective plastic sleeve of the Dallas newspaper. Thank god for small favors, Cassy thought, seeing that the article was at least below the front page fold.

METROPOLITAN HOSPITAL
EMERGENCY ROOM DIRECTOR FIRED
Erroneous Diagnosis of Death Cited.

by Gloria Ortega, Staff Writer of The Dallas Morning News.

Dr. Cassandra Marta Baldwin-Spence, director of the Emergency Services Department at the Metropolitan Hospital, was suspended from her position Saturday night. "Dr. Baldwin-Spence has been relieved of all duties and responsibilities at this hospital pending further investigation into the circumstances surrounding her diagnosis and treatment of Jeorg Marquez," announced Dr. Walter Simmons, Medical Director of the Metropolitan Hospital, in a prepared statement released Sunday morning.

Marquez, 55, became ill Saturday evening during a business meeting with H. Tenoch, President of Aztec Enterprises, a private conglomerate of Dallas-based import-export companies. After being rushed to the Emergency Room of the Dallas Metropolitan Hospital, Marquez was declared dead by Dr. Baldwin at 7:45 Saturday evening.

Three hours later Marquez awoke in the morgue of the Metro hospital and gained the attention of Charles Knight, housekeeping orderly, by shaking the morgue sheet covering his body. Marquez remains in the Intensive Care Unit of Metropolitan Hospital where his condition is listed as fair. Hospital officials could not be reached for further comment on a possible explanation for Dr. Baldwin-Spence's apparently erroneous declaration of death.

Dr. Baldwin-Spence, 38, retired from a distinguished but abbreviated career as a heart surgeon at Metro Hospital last year. During her six years' tenure on the Metro Hospital cardiovascular surgical staff she was credited with establishing the Am-Mex Children's Foundation, a nonprofit organization that has allowed lifesaving heart operations to be performed on hundreds of children brought from Mexico to Dallas for the complex heart surgeries that she performed.

The Presidential Medal was awarded to Dr. Baldwin-Spence in a Rose Garden ceremony four years ago. Two years ago she received the Governor's Humanitarian of the Year Award for her successful efforts at establishing the international heart surgical program with Mexico.

Dr. Baldwin-Spence was married to Scott Alexander Spence Jr., Republican gubernatorial candidate, until their divorce three years ago. Mr. Spence was away from the city and could not be reached for comment.

Cassy laid the newspaper on the counter top and sipped the freshly brewed coffee. Saturday night flashed through her mind again. The green dot tracing the flat, luminescent line on the television monitor was as clear in her mind as when she saw it Saturday night. She was absolutely certain that there was no respiration, no pulse, and a flat-lined EKG.

Cassy threw the front section of the newspaper across the room. "What the hell am I going to do?" she asked herself aloud. "Who'll hire a doctor who can't recognize when a patient is dead or alive? I have to find an explanation."

Cassy pulled herself upward and let Charlie in the patio door. He ran directly to the kitchen, searching his empty dish at the end of the cabinet for his breakfast. The dog's breakfast reward was the second half of the newspaper retrieval ritual. Cassy emptied a can of dog food in one bowl, dry pellets into a second, and filled the third one with water. "Boy, you're a lot of trouble," she said to him in a conversational voice. He caught her stare and held it in his eyes. She smiled and rubbed his head as he gulped the dog food. "At least you believe in me."

After refilling her coffee cup and lighting another Marlboro, Cassy went out onto the patio and settled onto a chaise lounge beside the pool. Stars dotted the cloudless remnant of the lingering night sky. The eastern sky was fringed with half-light. The predawn air hung in suffocating stillness over the patio in contrast to the frigid dehydrated climate within the house. Cassy stretched her legs to reach the edge of the water. The pungent odor of chlorine hovered over the pool and erupted upward to her nostrils.

Cassy lolled her hand on the dog's head as he sat beside her on the deck. All I have left is you and Alex, Cassy thought. Marriage, job, profession, happiness, fulfillment—all gone.

The night sky fused into an orange ball on the horizon. Tendrils of sunlight grew through the trees surrounding the perimeter of the yard as Cassy sat for a long time and bobbed her feet in the water, trying to work through the dilemma of Marquez. The weekend had become a watershed moment for her and Alex. It was a crisp black and white point in her life. I can either roll over and leave Dallas, or I can find out what the hell happened, she thought. If I can demonstrate conclusively that I did not make the near fatal mistake with Marquez and that I acted like a reasonable doctor, maybe I can come through this with my reputation intact.

With the tenacity that had brought her through years of medical training and bedside patient care, Cassy set the problem before her mind as if it were a difficult clinical problem that required her solution just like the other diagnostic questions for the thousands of patients before Marquez. First, define the known and then articulate the unknown. Defining the parameters of the illness or injury was the first step to any diagnosis. What do I know for sure about Marquez? Cassy asked herself.

Cassy rolled the events backward in her mind until she stopped about an hour before 19:45 Saturday. The CPR replayed before her eyes as though she were reliving the event. Cassy saw in her mind the video monitor with its green phosphorescent flat line. When she called him dead at seven forty-five that evening, she knew that he had no detectable blood pressure, no pulse, and no respiration. He had fixed and dilated pupils. His EKG tracing was flat. By all the usual criteria for death he was dead, just as dead as every patient she had pronounced dead since she was an intern. But Marquez remembered her saying, 'Let's call the time of death 19:45'. And Marquez told her that he could hear and feel but could not move. So he was obviously not dead. Or was he?

What am I missing? Cassy asked herself. I know he was alive three hours later, but I don't know for sure if he was dead at 19:45. Why did he die and revive? Why did I think he was dead? Or was he so near death that all the usual indicators of death showed him to be dead? She had no answer. The edge of the sun reached over the trees when Cassy finally hoisted herself off the pool chair. It was time to begin the research.

Cassy enjoyed the ambience of her home office. She often thought she preferred the desk and computer work station in her bedroom office more than any other part of the house with the exception of the family room. She and her ex-husband had purchased the huge home years before when Scott's CompuTeen computer software company was generating extravagant profits. Cassy had remodeled the master suite to accommodate a work station overlooking the pool and patio through a bank of sliding glass windows. Beneath the windows, the built-in cabinetry contained Cassy's personal computer, flanked on either side by tightly filled shelves of medical books and custom-made file cabinets.

During those early years of marriage, her husband had badgered her into computer literacy. In contrast to Alex whose computer skills appeared instinctive, Cassy had struggled with a variety of software programs until she was now comfortable at the computer. It was during this time that she had taught herself to type, using a self-instruction computer game. Her surgeon's nimble dexterity quickly allowed her to become a rapid and accurate typist.

Cassy placed the fresh steaming coffee mug on the pullout shelf, an arm's length away from the glowing computer screen. Moments later her personal computer was connected via modem into the computer bank at the National Library of Medicine in Washington, D.C. She expeditiously narrowed the descriptors of her computer search and punched in the computer keystroke commands, looking for recent case reports and articles under the broad descriptive headings of Resuscitation and Death. A few minutes later, her printer spewed forth summaries of articles and case reports from the world's medical literature under the computer rubric, CLINICAL DEATH. Abruptly the printer whine stopped as quickly as it had started.

Cassy looked to the computer screen and found an error code flashing on the video monitor. "Shit, what do I do now?" she asked. Concentrating on trying to rid the screen of the error and start the printer using several keyboard computer commands, Cassy did not hear the clicking of the bedroom door knob. Alex, dressed in his Rangers' T-shirt, walked across the room to stand beside his mother.

"What the hell is wrong with the printer?" Cassy asked the machine, banging her fist on the hard plastic cover.

Alex tapped her left shoulder at the same moment and said, "The printer's out of paper."

Cassy jumped as if she had been touched with an electrical current. "My god, Alex. Don't sneak up on me like that. I'm going to put a bell on you so I can hear you come in."

"I'm sorry, Mom. Let me fill up the printer with paper." Efficiently he stacked blank sheets into the paper tray, tapped the keyboard twice, and fiddled with the computer mouse. Cassy had no idea what her son had done until the laser printer whined into life. The green light on the computer console blinked. Printed paper spewed from the machine. The whirring in the interior of the laser printer continued, as more sheets spilled onto the pile of documents.

"Help me print up the rest of these reports," Cassy said, pulling her son close to her. The morning sun gradually lightened Cassy's bedroom as she and Alex printed forty-three articles from the medical literature data banks at the National Library of Medicine.

She scanned the titles of the articles when the printer spit each of them out, stopping to read the titles of several of the articles. "The futuristic potential of resuscitation from clinical death, the physiologic limits to the reversibility of clinical death, and clinical death and reanimatology. I have a day's reading for our afternoon by the pool."

With the stack of papers in her hand she laid them in forty-three separate piles around the room and on the unmade bed while Alex stapled the articles together. "Did you sleep well?" Cassy asked, tousling her son's dark hair, as the two finished stacking the stapled medical literature reprints into a neat pile.

"I guess so. I didn't have any nightmares last night," Alex said proudly.

"That's great. How long has it been since you had a bad dream? Two months?" Cassy asked. Alex shrugged indifferently. Cassy placed the pile of papers in Alex's outstretched arms and hands. "How about breakfast?"

"I'm hungry for pizza," Alex said as he walked to the door with the papers held on both outstretched arms.

"Do you always want pizza?" Cassy asked. Alex nodded his head without smiling.

"Okay. We'll have the leftover pizza for your birthday breakfast."

"Mom, we ate all the pizza."

"We're still celebrating your birthday. If you want pizza for breakfast, we'll have pizza. Then we'll go for a swim."

A frown of concentration creased Alex's face. "I want to go to Six Flags."

"But you and your father were at Six Flags yesterday."

"I want to go today with you."

"All right. It's your birthday party. How about Joey and David? You want to ask your friends to go with us?"

"Nope. Just you and me," Alex said.

"All right. Let's have pizza now and then go for a swim. Dr. Hendricks said he'll be by this morning. Then we'll see about Six Flags later this afternoon." Cassy shut down the computer and turned to her son. "You could ask Joey and David to come for a swim," Cassy said again.

"I don't want to ask them," Alex said as he left the bedroom. Cassy looked at the empty doorway, uncertain. She never quite knew what was going on in her son's mind or who, if any, were his school friends.

—

The glare of morning sun bounced off the pool, sparkling the droplets of suntan oil on Cassy's skin. She slathered more oil on her arms and legs and in between the narrow fabric strips of her two-piece fuchsia bikini. A wide-brimmed straw hat rode low over her eyes. Her dark hair hid under it. She adjusted her oversized sunglasses after smearing more oil on her face.

During the past two hours she had worked her way through most of the stack of medical articles and placed them on the wrought iron table next to her lounge chair. Intermittently, as she read, she watched Alex jump off the pool board.

"Mom, watch me," Alex shouted, jumping from the diving board in a cannonball splash, scattering spray onto Cassy's legs and dousing the article she was reading.

"Jump to the other side," Cassy said, looking up from the wet pages of the article. "You're getting me all wet."

The portable phone by Cassy's chair chirped. Her son pulled himself over the edge of the pool, alerted by a familiar interruption to his time with his mother. Alex frowned at the phone as Cassy reached for it. "I'm not going anywhere today without you, my man," she assured him before answering the portable phone.

Cassy listened for the moment, then said, "Hi, Trent. Sure. Alex and I are out by the pool. Come on around back. Just punch the letters of my name into the keypad. The gate will automatically open." Cassy clicked off the telephone. "Dr. Hendricks is calling from his car phone. He'll be by in a few minutes." Alex jumped again from the board, flaunting his lack of interest in his mother's visitor.

"Is he a friend of Dad's?" Alex asked when his head surfaced in the pool.

"No, he's my friend. I worked with him. He's a heart surgeon."

"Oh," Alex said and mounted the diving board without looking back at Cassy. After bouncing on the board several times, he jumped into a flip. His face and head cleared the end of the board by less than an inch.

Moments later Cassy looked over the top of her sunglasses and laid her papers aside when Trent walked around the corner of the house, carrying a plastic grocery sack in one hand while his other hand was tucked behind his back.

"Hello, cowboy," she said and rose quickly from the chaise lounge to cross the hot smooth tile in her bare feet. "Where's your horse?"

Hendrick's ruddy face reddened into a flush that accentuated the spider web of veins over each cheek. His tapered western style shirt hugged his trim torso and was tucked neatly into starched Wrangler jeans. The soft pebbled texture of his tan cowboy boots fairly screamed the cost of the expensive ostrich leather.

"Give me a break, will ya? The one day I get out of my Brooks Brothers pinstriped uniform, you give me a hard time," he said, tossing his pearl gray felt cowboy hat onto the patio table. Darkly tinted horn-rim sunglasses hid his eyes.

"I'm sorry," Cassy said, laughing and grabbing his hard muscular forearm. A gold Rolex watch matched the gold chain bracelet on his right arm. She started to hug him in a friendly greeting until she realized her skin was soaked in suntan lotion.

"You look great . . . for a mother," Trent said, teasing Cassy with an elevator move of his eyes from her toes slowly upward to the chestnut hair shoved under her wide-brimmed straw hat. She grabbed the suntan bottle and playfully squirted it toward him, narrowly missing his pants leg with the stream of oil.

"Have a seat," Cassy said. She swirled a white beach towel about her hips and sat on the end of the chaise lounge. She gestured for Trent to sit opposite her. Before he sat down he pulled a bouquet of a dozen long stem red roses wrapped in tissue paper from behind his back where he had hidden them from her view.

"Trent, they're beautiful." She buried her oiled face in the flowers. "Where did you find these on a holiday morning?"

"I've my contacts in this city," he said, grinning widely and showing perfectly capped teeth. His closely cropped flat top was mostly iron gray. Flecks of red were scattered in with the gray hair like iron filings.

"You're very kind, and I appreciate you," Cassy said and stood up, nearly matching Trent's height and looking directly into his eyes, she kissed his cheek.

"Thanks for everything yesterday," Trent said. "Heather looks great this morning. Her new heart is functioning like a normal heart."

"I'm pleased for Heather, but also for you. I know it's been a long year for you," Cassy said.

"Thanks, Cass," he said just as a shower of pool water from another Alex cannonball caught his boots. "Maybe you ought to introduce me to your son. Remember, it's been a couple of years since I last saw him."

"Alex, come here a minute. I want you to shake hands with Dr. Hendricks."

Alex jumped into the water, again sending a splash toward them. Then he slithered over the concrete lip at the edge of the pool. Trent pitched a red and white striped cardboard box the size of a coffee can to Alex. He caught the box easily with his wet hands.

"T-Thanks," Alex said and ripped away the paper. The shreds of wrapping paper and ribbon floated onto the surface of the pool.

"I-It's a baseball," Alex said, studying the box.

"Look inside. It's a special one," Trent said. Alex ripped off the top of the box and pulled out a gleaming baseball, the color of polished ivory.

"A-Autographs," Alex said excitedly.

"See the names?" Trent asked. "All the Texas Rangers autographed it."

"W-Wow," Alex said, studying each of the names like a jeweler inspecting a gem stone. "W-Wow," he said again, stuttering so fiercely that the word sounded like a bark.

"I wouldn't play with that baseball," Trent said, pulling another ball from the plastic grocery bag. "Try this one."

Alex handed the autographed ball to Cassy and stepped back a few steps, motioning for Trent to throw the other ball to him.

Trent shook his head. "I think you need a glove," Trent said and pulled a tan leather pitcher's glove from the grocery bag and tossed the glove to Alex. Slipping it on his left hand, Alex pounded his fist into the mitt and said, "T-Throw it t-to m-me." Trent lobbed a slow high ball. Alex caught the ball with an athletic grace that reminded Cassy of his father. He fired the ball back to Trent in a fast level sidearm throw.

"I-I'll g-go out farther," Alex said, running around the deep end of the pool. Cassy lounged on the chaise, watching the younger and the older boy pitching the ball across the pool, each throw in a bit higher arc. Each a test of the other player's throwing arm and catching ability.

"My god, your boy's got an arm on him. He'll be ready for the Rangers soon."

"Shouldn't you be wearing a glove?" Cassy asked when Trent caught the high arced ball that Alex threw across the pool. "A surgeon with a broken finger is not much use."

"Not to worry. I was the third baseman for the Texas Aggies years ago," Trent said, pitching the ball low and straight across the pool. Alex caught it one-handed in his new glove.

"Give me another high one," Trent said with an exaggerated look into the sun. Alex flung the ball higher than the elm tree at the edge of the yard. The ball fell toward Trent like a spent rocket several degrees off target.

"Head's up, Mom," Alex screamed across the pool without any trace of stutter. Cassy looked skyward again, holding her arm bent at the elbow to shade out the fiery disc of the afternoon sun from her vision. She saw only the brilliance of the sun. Her sight of the baseball hurtling out of the sky toward her was obliterated by the blinding brightness of the sun. Trent stumbled over the wrought iron table, knocking the portable phone to the deck and scattering the pile of computer reports over the wet surface of the tiled pool deck in his attempt to catch the ball before it struck Cassy.

Crack! The ball sounded as if it had been hit by a wooden bat rather than Cassy's left forearm.

"Goddamn," screamed Trent. "Cass, are you all right?" Cassy pulled her left forearm back and could see a red circular bruising blotch spreading beneath the fleshy surface of her forearm even before the jolt of pain seized her whole left arm and shoulder.

"Is it broken?" Trent asked, hovering over her.

"No, I don't think so," Cassy said and rubbed her forearm that was quickly puffing with swelling.

"Let me see," he said and took her forearm in both his soft hands, more the hands of a rancher than a surgeon. They moved with the delicate touch of a concert violinist as he moved and rotated her forearm and bent her elbow. "Looks all right." With a light gentleness, his fingers expertly palpated the muscle groups about the forearm, his hands dwelling on her forearm a fraction longer than Cassy thought clinically necessary. The excruciating pain under the contact point vanished with his tender massage. She felt a warmth beyond the noonday heat spreading outward from her arm.

"Let's get an ice pack on that," Trent said, pulling her up with her right arm until she was easily upright off the lounge chair.

"M-Mom, I'm s-sorry. I-I didn't mean to . . . ," Alex said, his first stutter in direct conversation with Cassy in months.

Inside the kitchen Trent took charge while Cassy sat in her towel and swimsuit at the kitchen table. It's really not that bad, a minor contusion, she thought. Trent obviously enjoyed making her comfortable, breaking ice cubes into a plastic baggie and molding it as an ice pack to the front of her forearm. "Better?" he asked.

"Much better," she said. "But how am I going to pay your fee, Doctor?"

"How about lunch?" Trent asked. "That would more than cover my fee."

"I'm afraid my cupboard is bare," Cassy said.

"Alex and I'll go out for some carryout. What about it, Alex?"

"P–Pizza for m–me."

"All right, birthday boy," Cassy said. "Run and change out of your bathing suit." She laughed at her son's enthusiasm as he ran for his room.

⸺

Nearly two hours later, Trent and Alex burst through the front door, their arms stacked with Dominos pizza boxes, grocery bags, two six-packs of long-neck Lone Star beer, and three plastic bags from the Sports House.

Cassy smiled at the two boys, separated by a generation, and felt the flush of happiness for her son in the company of an adult male. In the time since the two had left on the shopping expedition, Cassy had showered, shampooed, and changed into a carefully selected casual outfit. The white sleeveless cotton ribbed top over her white twill shorts accented her long torso. The reddening glow of her face and cheeks from the morning's poolside sun accentuated her naturally tawny skin. She noticed the approving look that Trent unknowingly sent her way as he set the pizza boxes on the kitchen island.

"How's the forearm?" Trent asked and took her arm in both his hands, inspecting the bruise.

"All well, Doctor, but I'm starved," she said. The aroma of the pepperoni pizzas filled the kitchen and reminded Cassy she hadn't eaten since the day before.

"Give me five minutes and I'll lay it all out . . . pizza, salad, beer," Trent said. "You do want a beer to begin? Not a light beer either!"

"Why not?" Cassy said. Trent popped the caps from two Lone Star long necks and handed her a cold bottle. "All right, boys, are you going to show Mom what's in the sack from the Sports House?" Cassy asked.

"Just a couple things for Alex to wear to the game this evening," Trent said, pulling a Texas Rangers' baseball cap from the bag.

Cassy looked at the two of them with a mock suspicious glance, rolling her eyes. "Another Rangers' cap for your collection?"

"Alex and I want to take you to the Rangers-Kansas City game this afternoon," Trent said and pulled a Rangers' logo T-shirt from the sack. "Here's a Rangers' T-shirt for Mom, too."

"Can we, Mom?" Alex asked. "Please."

"What about Six Flags?"

"No. I want to go to the Rangers' game," Alex said without a stutter.

"Sure, sounds like fun," Cassy said as she took the T-shirt from Trent and held it up in front of her.

Trent slapped the six-inch slabs of pizza onto plates and dealt them across the table like playing cards. Alex finished off his second slice of pizza before Trent had begun to eat. After Cassy and Trent had each eaten three slices and Alex had finished five, Cassy turned to her son. "If you're finished eating, go take a shower and get dressed," Cassy said. "I need to talk some medical business with Dr. Hendricks. Then we'll go to the game." After her son had left the kitchen, Cassy turned to Trent and said, "Did you read the newspaper this morning?"

"Yes, as well as yesterday," Trent said without meeting her gaze. "The media are having a great time with the Marquez incident. I heard the announcer on the car radio on the way over here calling our hospital the Hospital of the Grateful Dead. The morning disc jockeys were even dedicating songs to Dr. Dracula at Metropolitan Hospital."

"Were there any other jokes about me?"

"Afraid so," Trent said, looking into the box for another pizza slice.

"Well?" she said, waiting.

"The doctors' lounge is full of comedians. You know lots of stand up comic doctors."

"Who?"

"I'm not going to say who the doctor comics were. Your knowing would serve no purpose," Trent said and bit off the tip of a triangle of pizza.

"Tell me the funny one-liners then. I need a good laugh."

"You sure you want to hear?" Trent asked.

Cassy nodded and sipped at her beer.

"Did you hear the one about Bring 'em back alive Baldwin . . . or how about Dr. Oral Roberts Baldwin . . . or the Great 'Baldwini'?"

Cassy sat silent, a thin-lipped frown on her face. She sipped her beer again and said, "That's not funny."

"Did I say it was funny?" Trent asked.

"No," Cassy said. "But I'll bet the boys in the Doctors' Lounge got a big hoot out of it this morning." Cassy looked across the litter of pizza fragments and slowly shook her head in frustration. "Trent, I'm not going to be able to practice medicine again in this city, or maybe not anywhere, unless I can find some plausible explanation for what went on with Marquez on Saturday night. I'm being laughed right out of Dallas."

"I don't know how you'll ever prove whether it was you or Marquez who had the seizure Saturday night. Just leave it alone. It'll blow over like a West Texas rainstorm."

"I can't. I have to know what happened. I've started researching the question already this morning," Cassy said. She pointed at the stack of medical articles she had left on the kitchen counter. "I haven't gone through all these articles yet, but several possible explanations are starting to gel. I ought to have a tenable theory soon."

"Cass, I don't mean to be tacky, but isn't it quite possible you simply made a mistake?" Trent asked.

"No way, Trent," Cassy said. "By all clinical criteria, Marquez was dead at 19:45."

"What about Marquez today?" Trent asked. "Have you heard any more details about him? Is he still improving?"

"Yes. I saw Marquez in the ICU last night," Cassy said as she cleared the plates from the kitchen table.

"I thought you were persona non grata at the hospital? Simmons told you to stay away from the hospital," Trent said.

"For sure, I am now. One of the nurses called Simmons while I was in the ICU with Marquez. When I got on the phone, I thought Walter was going to have a stroke. He was screaming at me to get out of the hospital and never come back!"

"Walter does have a short fuse," Trent said. "Go on. Tell me what you have learned about Marquez."

"He's the most bizarre case I've ever seen. Last evening he was damn near catatonic . . . rigid, staring at the ceiling, mute. But I got him to talk to me."

"How?"

"How do I know? I sat by his bed with him, held his hand, talked to him in Spanish," Cassy said. "After a little while he finally began to talk."

"Who wouldn't talk to you after that dose of feminine charm?"

"Whatever it was, it worked," Cassy said. "He told me exactly what I said when I pronounced him dead. He repeated my exact words. He recalled my words better than I remembered them."

"Shouldn't it be fairly obvious to you then . . . if he can quote the words of your declaration of his death . . . then he wasn't dead when you thought he was dead?"

"Yes," Cassy said. "I will concede he was not brain dead at 19:45."

"Did he say anything else?" Trent asked.

"Estoy muerto," Cassy said.

"What the hell does that mean?"

"That's Spanish for 'I am dead'," Cassy said.

"Sounds to me like that Mexican is crazy," Trent said and opened his third long-neck Lone Star beer.

Cassy ignored the comment and shook her head when Trent offered her another beer. "Marquez also said 'He killed me like he said he would'."

"These near-death experiences can be quite disturbing, even hallucinogenic," Trent said, taking a long swallow from the bottle. "You've seen patients go crazy and delusional for days after heart surgery. Sounds like Marquez is out of his gourd."

"I'm suspicious that someone is trying to kill Marquez," Cassy said. "I believe what he said. I don't think Marquez is crazy. I wonder whether I should go to the police about it."

"That's ridiculous. You're trying to justify your mistake about calling him dead by concocting some sinister plot to kill Marquez," Trent said, taking the rest of the beer in one swallow. "What proof do you have?"

"Listen to the patient, you've always told me. You always say 'Listen to the patient and he will tell you his diagnosis'," Cassy said. "I listened to Marquez. He told me that someone is trying to kill him. That's my diagnosis. Someone is trying to kill Señor Marquez. I have to believe him."

"The man's crazy. After being shut up in our hospital morgue for three hours and given up for dead, I'd be crazy, too."

"He's lucid and rational," Cassy said. "His recall of the events in the ER is quite coherent. Except for this idea of someone trying to kill him, there are no other suggestions of paranoia."

"Marquez sounds paranoid and delusional to me. If you believe him, I will have to wonder whether you're also paranoid," Trent said, opening another beer. "For god's sake, you're trying to rationalize your mistake so that you don't have to eat a piece of crow pie."

"I didn't make a mistake Saturday night. Marquez was clinically dead," Cassy said, pausing to look out the window in the direction of the pool and trying to control her rising anger at Trent's skepticism. "At least he had no signs of life at 19:45, Saturday night."

"Was he dead or not dead?" Trent asked. "It's one or the other, up or down."

"Hell, I don't know," Cassy said. "He had every indication of being dead . . . no pulse, no electrocardiographic activity, no physical reaction, no breathing, no heart beat."

"Well, if he was as dead as you think he was . . . ," Trent interrupted. "How do you explain his remembering your declaration of his death with such clear recall?"

"I can't," Cassy said.

"When a person's brain dies, he can't have recall," Trent said. "The brain is silent. The brain is dead. Those stories of people floating over their bodies and other bizarre near-death tales always require functioning brain cells. It's fundamental; you can't remember without a functioning brain. It's grade school simple. Sure, the near-death event might distort a victim's perception of reality, but your Señor Marquez sure as hell wasn't dead if he can quote you declaring him dead at 19:45."

"You sound like one of my medical school professors," Cassy said coldly. Trent's patronizing lecture grated her. She tried to keep her face as neutral as possible.

"I was your professor if you still remember those days. It sounds to me like your guy was paralyzed but not dead. You're just going to have to admit that he wasn't as dead as you thought he was."

"Trent, I've got to find out what happened Saturday night. There has to be an explanation that will salvage what's left of my professional reputation in this city. My career depends on my finding out what went wrong with Marquez."

Trent said quietly, "You're trying to concoct some explanation for Marquez to explain away your momentary lapse. You're just going to have to admit that you made a mistake. Doctors are not perfect. We all make mistakes. You were tired, worn out, at the end of a long day in the ER. It's understandable. Marquez must not have been dead when you pronounced him dead. There's nothing more you can do now. Put it behind you and get on with your career."

"What's left of my career," Cassy said dejectedly.

"Cassy, take my advice. Go along to get along."

"I can't . . . I won't," she interrupted.

"At least put it aside for the rest of the day," Trent said, opening another beer. "How long have you been working on this today?" He gestured with the neck of the beer bottle at the pile of scientific papers lying haphazardly on the kitchen counter.

"Since four-thirty," Cassy said. "I couldn't sleep."

Cassy picked up the jumbled pile of computer printouts from the end of the counter where she had dumped them. "There must be an explanation in here. Look here at this article." She then quoted from sentences in the article. "Hypothermia is a well-known cause of a mistaken diagnosis of death. Cold drowning victims occasionally revive when they are rewarmed."

"And what was Marquez's body temperature in the ER?" Trent asked.

"Ninety-eight point six degrees. Normal." Cassy paused and stared at Trent. "But I just use hypothermia as an example. Drugs, poisons, allergic anaphylactic reactions . . . all can cause near-death responses."

"Cassy . . . Cassy. Listen to me. Don't push on this. Forget about the Saturday Marquez incident. Everyone else will forget it, too. Keep poking at it, and this whole mess will fester up like a skin boil." Trent reached to touch her hand.

"But Trent, I didn't make a mistake. The man was dead, or at least he had all the clinical indications of death," she said and pulled her hand away from him.

There has to be an answer, thought Cassy. Maybe it was some anaphylactic reaction, like an allergy to something. Maybe Marquez reacted to a drug. That could explain the revival in the morgue as his body metabolized whatever it was that caused him to lose all his vital signs. "Or a poison," Cassy said as she finished her convoluted thought processes out loud.

"Are you now saying Marquez was poisoned?" Trent asked. "Cassy, you're begging for trouble if you start making accusations about poisons. What were the results of the blood screens for drugs and poisons?"

"Negative. He was clean. No drugs. No poisons could be traced by the lab," Cassy said.

"It's difficult to make a case for a poisoning with a negative toxicology screening," Trent said, a trace of condescension in his voice.

"I'm not the only one who thinks something bizarre happened to Marquez in the ER Saturday night," Cassy said.

Trent's eyebrows flinched upward. "And who might that other person be?"

"Gracie. She's a nursing assistant in the ER who has been there for years. She's originally from Haiti. . . ."

"I know Gracie. Everybody knows Gracie. Most people think Gracie is a little touched in the head," Trent said with a smile and tapped the side of his head with his index finger. "Don't tell me that Gracie thinks Marquez is a zombie back from the dead."

Cassy nodded slowly, leaning forward across the kitchen island and resting her elbows on its wood surface. "Her daughter called me to tell me that Gracie is hiding because she's afraid of the evil spirits at the hospital. Gracie is convinced that Marquez is a zombie, the walking dead who have revived from the grave to terrorize the villages in Haiti. Gracie thinks she saw them when she was a little girl in Haiti . . . and again last night in the ER."

"Jesus Christ, Cass. Don't talk to anybody about Haitian zombies, please. Here in Texas, zombie talk will get you locked up in a psychiatric unit," Trent said, pitching the empty beer bottle into the trash compactor.

"At least I'm not the only person who thinks something bizarre happened," Cassy said, wiping down the kitchen table with vigorous long strokes of a moist cloth.

"Bizarre. Yeah," Trent said. "I'll agree to that. You blew the diagnosis and declared him dead."

"If I blew the diagnosis, then what is the diagnosis?" Cassy asked.

Trent inspected her closely. "I don't have a diagnosis for Marquez either, Cass. Strange things happen all the time in hospitals. You know of bizarre and unexplained events with patients all the time. People die for no apparent reason. Other people get well from incurable diseases. Who knows what the hell happened to Marquez? But let it pass. Leave it alone and get on with your life. For chrissake, Cassy, have you lost touch with reality? Don't you realize how crazy all this talk sounds? If you want to talk about your theories explaining Marquez's resurrection, promise me not to talk to anyone but me."

"Okay. I promise," she said, knowing that Trent's advice was the appropriate course.

Trent nodded slowly and leaned back in the kitchen chair. "I just might be able to cool Walter Simmons off if you'll just be quiet for a change. Then maybe you might be able to work at the Metropolitan Hospital again if you'll just forget about this Marquez business. Maybe we could even be a team again," he said and laid his hand on her right forearm.

Cassy pulled her arm back. Trent's grip tightened and prevented her withdrawal. Trent leaned across the table toward Cassy just as the kitchen door opened.

"I'm ready," Alex said as he walked into the kitchen bouncing the new baseball into his new leather mitt. Trent tilted his head away from Alex and whispered almost threateningly to Cassy, "Don't say any more about any of this Marquez business to anyone. Keep your mouth shut, and this mess will disappear. Trust me on that."

EIGHT

———•———

MEMORIAL DAY traffic on I-30 between Dallas and Fort Worth crawled like lines of ants toward a sugar castle on the distant prairie. The red brick Ranger Ballpark in Arlington soared on the horizon like a medieval coliseum, larger than any Roman forum. The green peaked turrets mounting the upper edge of the brick stadium resembled guard towers overseeing the flow of fans seeping into the entrances below to the Rangers-Kansas City baseball game.

Trent wheeled his Mercedes into the reserved parking lot immediately west of the stadium, and Alex and Cassy followed Trent's quick strides through the rushing current of baseball fans. After riding a private elevator up to the concourse level, he ushered them into a luxurious sky box suite large enough for two dozen baseball fans.

"W-Wow!" Alex said and ran to the glass wall fronting the interior of the stadium. "I-I-I'm o-on the f-first base line." The wall of glass gave a panoramic view of the infield. The Texas Ranger team hustled through its program of warm-up drills and exercises as the three stood in front of the glass window watching the choreography of the ball players. "C-Can I s-sit on the b-balcony?"

"Sure." Trent opened the door in the glass wall leading onto a private box of seats on the cantilevered balcony of the suite. Alex wiggled into the stadium seat, studying the players one level below. "Here's today's lineup," Trent said, handing him the day's program.

When Trent returned to the suite, Cassy asked, "Is this suite yours?"

"No, it belongs to a friend. The president and CEO of an import company has this suite. He's not much of a baseball fan, but he keeps it for his friends," Trent said smiling.

The interior wall of the lavishly appointed suite was dominated by a reproduction of the twelve-foot wide Aztec stone calendar that is the featured exhibit of the National Anthropological Museum in Mexico City. The grotesquely carved Sun god face in the center ring of the circular tan stone disc glared at Cassy. For a moment Cassy felt drawn to the stone calendar by the hypnotic gaze of the Sun god carving at its center.

"This must be a precise copy of the Aztec calendar stone," Cassy said, running her fingers around the concentric rings of bas relief carvings chiseled into the enormous disc.

"Don't ask me," Trent said. "I don't know anything about the Aztecs."

"Your friend must be quite a collector of Aztec antiquities," Cassy said. She reached to touch the face of the stone god in the center of the twelve-foot disc. "I've not seen anything like these carvings outside the National Museum of Anthropology in Mexico City."

"Yeah, he's an expert on Mexican art," Trent said as he stepped behind the tile-surfaced bar near the interior door of the suite. "He imports a lot of real stuff. How about a beer?" Cassy didn't seem to hear Trent. She concentrated on the carvings of the giant stone disc, her face only inches away from its surface.

"This Aztec stone calendar was never really a calendar but was a religious sculpture dedicated to the ancient Aztec Sun god," Cassy said. She moved around the room, her fingertips caressing the stone carvings and antiquities that were tastefully displayed throughout the suite.

"I don't know anything about all this old stuff, but the Mexicans do make a good beer," Trent said, lifting a Carta Blanca beer to his lips. "I didn't hear you name your poison."

Cassy turned to him with a quizzical look to see a wide grin. "Sorry for the attempt at humor. I didn't hear you say what beer you would like."

"Whatever you're having," Cassy said, continuing her slow circuit of the room until she stood in front of a sculptured statue of a life-size stone figure resembling a deformed man with exaggerated ears and a jutting jaw. Shiny ebony stones filled the eye sockets, giving the grotesque stone face an ominous otherworldly presence.

Trent opened the glass fronted wall cabinet containing a climate-controlled wine cellar and took another beer from the refrigerator below. "Alex, do you want a Coke?" Trent shouted the length of the suite.

"Y-Yes," Alex yelled back from his box seat on the outside balcony, his eyes never leaving the infield. Trent filled the Mexican pottery on the side tables with peanuts and pretzels, then reached for the soft drink in the refrigerator.

"Here you are," Trent said, passing the beer to Cassy. He opened the glass door onto the balcony seating and handed the soft drink can to Alex. "Alex, let me know when the game starts. I want to talk some more business to your mother for a few minutes."

"S-Sure," Alex said.

Plush leather chairs and a matching sofa grouped in the center of the room were arranged around a tan stone table made from a hard textured rock similar to the Aztec calendar. The sides of the stone table danced in bas relief figure carvings of Aztec warriors. Cassy and Trent sat down opposite each other in the low slung Mexican sofas. The stone monolith that served as a coffee table filled the space between them. Alex turned and waved excitedly to his mother through the glass walls of the suite.

"The baseball game is a great birthday idea for Alex," Cassy said, sipping at her beer.

"Next time we come to the Rangers' game, we'll bring Heather with us," Trent said. "Thanks to you."

"I wouldn't have thought that your daughter was a baseball fan."

"Without a son, what's a dad to do?" Trent asked, looking away toward Alex beyond the glass wall and to the stadium that had nearly filled with people. "She's not quite the fan that Alex seems to be, but close." The door chime of the suite interrupted Trent. He lifted himself out of the low chair. "Come on in," Trent shouted through the closed door.

A college-age Hispanic dressed in a Rangers' T-shirt, identical to Alex's shirt, wheeled a rolling table covered with a white tablecloth into the room. Trent motioned the waiter toward the stone monolith table centered between them.

"Shall I open the suite door, sir?" the waiter asked. "The game is just about to begin."

"Sure," Trent said. When the waiter slid the glass wall aside, the roar of the crowd flooded the room. The young man quickly transferred the plates covered with silver-plated warming domes to the stone table. Trent finished his beer and poured himself a straight bourbon from the bar as the waiter finished the meal services.

"Thank you, sir. Enjoy the game," he said as Trent slipped him a twenty dollar bill.

"Let's eat," Trent called to Alex in the front row of the two rows of 'Ranger Green' bleacher seats on the private balcony. "Hamburgers and hot dogs. Take your pick."

"C-Can I eat out here? The g-game is ready to start." At that moment, the music of the Star Spangled Banner rose from the infield. Alex stood still on the balcony with his hand placed over his heart. As soon as the singer finished the anthem, Alex rushed into the suite. A moment later he was back on the balcony, a hot dog in one hand and a Coke can clutched in the other.

Trent sipped his bourbon and nibbled on a French fry until Cassy asked, "Who is your friend who has this sky box? I'd like to write him a note to tell him how much Alex and I appreciated his kindness today."

"Señor Tenoch," Trent said and took a bite from his hamburger.

"Tenoch? The friend of Marquez?" Cassy asked, putting her beer down and staring at Trent. "You've got to be kidding." She could feel the dry constriction in her throat. The desire for a cigarette was overpowering. "Is this some of your weird sense of humor? Inviting Alex and me to be the guests of Marquez's friend?"

"Not at all," Trent said, draining off the bourbon from his glass in one swallow. "He's been very generous to me with his support of my cardiovascular research laboratory."

"Why is it I never heard of Tenoch before Saturday night, and I've worked with you for nine years?" Cassy asked.

"Tenoch wanted his donations to my research program to remain anonymous. He's supported my cardiovascular research laboratory with nearly four million dollars in the past four years."

"Is he married?" Cassy asked and instantly regretted the question.

"No. Never married as far as I know," Trent said. "But I don't think he's your type."

"Sorry I asked," Cassy said. She nibbled at the edge of the hamburger and looked beyond the doors to the play beginning in the infield. "What does he do to earn the kind of money it takes to have a sky box suite?"

"Import-export business here in Dallas. A lot of oil interests in Mexico. He's one of the largest shareholders in Pemex, the private Mexican oil company."

"How well do you know him?"

"I've met with him for lunch at least twice a month for the past four years to discuss my laboratory research with him."

"The Hiberna project?" Cassy asked.

"Yes. He's an amazingly quick study just like you. He's a curious and extremely intelligent man. You'd like him," Trent said. "Without any medical training he's able to understand the complex and sophisticated cardiac preservation experiments I've been conducting with the Hiberna protocol."

Alex appeared in the doorway with his empty plate, looking like a waif in search of a meal.

"What's the score?" Trent asked.

"O-One to n-nothing, Rangers. B-Bottom of the s-second."

"Another hot dog?" Trent asked. Alex nodded vigorously. Moments later, he was back outside, not having missed a pitch. The stadium lights were now more visible. The bank of floodlights mounted above the steepled green roof of the Ballpark illuminated the playing field with a sunlight intensity.

"Tenoch wants to talk to you," Trent said casually, finishing off his third bourbon and taking another bite of the hamburger.

Cassy stopped, her hamburger midway to her mouth. "You're joking, of course."

"Not at all," Trent said. "He called me last night and wants me to bring you for lunch at his home on Preston Avenue, day after tomorrow."

"Is that why you came to see me today? Did Tenoch put you up to this little baseball party?" Cassy asked. "And why have you waited all afternoon to spring Tenoch on me? Trying to soften me up before bringing up this crazy idea?"

"Jesus, Cass. Don't be so sensitive. I didn't want to mention him in front of Alex. You've been preoccupied all day long with your goddamn Marquez inquisition."

"Why does Tenoch want to have lunch with me?" Cassy asked. "What does he want from me?"

"I don't know. He just wanted me to invite you for lunch. Maybe he's grateful for your effort with Marquez."

"Don't be sarcastic," Cassy said, finally able to take a bite of the hamburger. "A meeting with Tenoch is not a good idea. I surely can't talk to him about Marquez. And he seems to know Walter Simmons quite well." She hesitated and then abruptly asked, "Walter Simmons hasn't been invited to the lunch, has he?"

"No," Trent said. "I doubt it." Standing unsteadily, Trent refilled his bourbon glass from the wet bar and returned to the table. "Another beer?" he asked. Cassy shook her head.

"What does Tenoch want from me?" Cassy asked again. "Surely you must have some idea."

"I'm not certain," Trent said. He looked out toward the playing field, avoiding her eyes.

"Yes, you do! I've always been able to tell when you're not telling me everything." Cassy finished off her Carta Blanca beer and walked across the suite to the wet bar for another beer.

"It could be an important conversation for you and Alex."

"What are you talking about?" Cassy said, settling back into her chair at the table.

"He wants you to move to Mexico City and head up a heart surgery program at the Instituto de Medico, the major cardiovascular medical center for Mexico."

"What has Tenoch got to do with the Instituto de Medico?"

"He's the largest contributor to the Instituto. He's richer than God. He gives a lot of his money away to good causes, especially medical programs. His import and export business has done quite well for him in Mexico City and Dallas, and he says that he wants to return some of his success to Mexico. That's really all I can tell you. Tenoch called me last night and asked me whether I thought you'd be interested in an opportunity like this."

"What did you tell him about me?"

"I said I couldn't speak for you, but I told him you were the best surgeon I knew. Tenoch is aware that you did the heart transplant on Heather."

"And that you procured the donor heart from the Instituto de Medico?"

"Oh, yes. He deserves the credit for obtaining the permission of the Mexican government so that we could extend our search for Heather's donor into Mexico."

"Still, why me?" Cassy asked. "What does he want from me?"

"He wants heart transplantation to be as readily available in Mexico as it is in the United States. He has an enormous commitment to Mexico and is very well connected there. It's a Mexican thing. I expect he wants to see whether your Mexican heritage is as strong as his."

"I don't want to live in Mexico City again or have Alex grow up there."

"Don't throw this opportunity away, Cass. It might be your best and only chance to get out from under this Marquez fiasco."

"Everything depends on Marquez, doesn't it?" Cassy asked.

"A lot depends on Marquez."

Cassy thought for several moments, saying nothing. Her mind whirled through the possibilities, the risks, and the benefits of meeting with Tenoch. Finally she said, "I'm sorry, Trent. I really shouldn't. It's better for me to decline right now rather than say no after a lot of discussion. I suspect Señor Tenoch has a monstrous ego. I don't wish to offend him, for your sake, by rejecting his offer."

"We all have giant egos. But as long as Señor Tenoch is funding my laboratory at the rate of a million dollars a year, I'll have lunch with him every day if he wishes."

"Would it embarrass you if I refused his lunch invitation?"

"Hell yes, Cass," Trent said. "Your saying no could piss him off so that he might hold up the funding of my research this year."

"All right then, I'll go with you to lunch at Tenoch's. But I'm going just for you. Not that I'm any way interested in what Tenoch might offer."

"I owe you another one," he said, lifting his bourbon glass in a salute. "Now that we've settled the Tenoch problem, let's help Alex win the game for the Rangers. Bring your hamburger. We'll sit outside with Alex."

They sat on the front row of the green balcony seats and balanced their drinks in the arm receptacles while they held their hamburgers in their hands. By the fifth inning, the Texas Rangers' relief pitcher struggled to hold the one-to-nothing margin, but he was in trouble with Kansas City Royals' runners on first and third. The Rangers' pitcher, on the three-and-two pitch, fired a fast ball catching the edge of the plate in the low strike zone. By Trent's judgment the pitch struck out the Kansas City left fielder, but the plate umpire thought otherwise and walked the Kansas City player, filling the bases for the Royals. "You blind man!" Trent jumped up, screaming and shaking his clinched fist at the umpire. "You're crazy. That was a strike!" Trent's face reddened. His nostrils flared.

Alex leaned to his mother and whispered, "What's wrong with Dr. Hendricks?"

"Nothing, son. He's just a baseball fan . . . a fanatic. He doesn't mean anything by it. We all change the way we look at things depending on where we are. Baseball fans are just more obvious about the way they see things."

The next Kansas City batter unleashed a liner to right center field, driving in two of the Royal runners and beginning the five-to-one defeat for the Texas Rangers. When the fifth run crossed the plate in the eighth inning, Trent slumped in his seat and shook his head. "Jesus, what a bunch of jerks the Rangers are. The Texas bums can't even beat the Royals at home. Let's get the hell out of here."

—

The mood in Trent's car on the drive back to Cassy's home in University Park was somber. Cassy tried a few upbeat remarks, but Trent was deflated by the Rangers' loss. Trent took out his disappointment on the car, whipping in and out of traffic. He wheeled his Mercedes up the circular drive in front of Cassy's home, causing Alex to slip to the right side of the back seat of the big sedan. After stopping abruptly under the the porte cochere, he turned off the engine and looked inquiringly toward Cassy.

"It's been a wonderful day. Thanks so much for everything," Cassy said, laying her left hand into the crook of his right elbow. She reached for the passenger door handle.

"May I come in, Cassy? I need to talk to you some more . . . ," Trent said. Cassy looked at him quizzically and glanced out the car window to see Alex disappear through the front door into the house. Charlie bolted through the door towards the car. "About me," he said, taking her hand.

"Trent, it's a bit late for this single mother. I try to have Alex in bed by nine-thirty, and then I read with him for a half hour."

"I don't mind waiting," Trent said.

Cassy looked at her watch. "It's eight-thirty now. It'll be nine-thirty before Alex is in bed and asleep."

"Really, it's no problem for me to wait. I need to talk."

"Tonight?"

"I don't mind waiting. I'll read your newspaper and watch a little TV," Trent persisted.

"Okay. Come in," Cassy said.

Once inside the foyer, she showed Trent to the study, a dark walnut paneled room with empty floor-to-ceiling bookshelves. At the far end of the corner room, a massive antique walnut desk faced luxurious wing backed burgundy leather chairs. Beneath the leaded glass windows overlooking the wide expanse of landscaped and lighted front yard, a matching burgundy sofa balanced the rest of the sterile vacant room. The faint scent of a winter fire lingered in the massive fireplace. Cassy adjusted the room lighting to a soft indirectness, blunting the harshness of the polished empty room.

"The bar's behind the door," she said, opening a closet filled with a fully stocked liquor cabinet and crystal glasses of various shapes, perfectly aligned behind a glass panel. "This was Scott's room. Help yourself to what he left," Cassy said. "I think there's some bourbon there, but all the wine's gone. Make yourself comfortable. I'll be back soon."

"Can I fix you a nightcap?" Trent called out as she turned the corner of the double doorway.

"The chardonnay in the kitchen refrigerator would be nice," she said over her shoulder as she started up the stairwell toward Alex's room.

After Cassy left the study, Trent mixed a double bourbon from Scott Spence's Maker's Mark bottle. He took the top half of his bourbon in one long swallow. A few minutes later Trent's glass contained only ice cubes. He refilled it to the rim. With the fresh glass of whiskey in his hand, he walked the perimeter of the room, his fingers touching and tracing the edges of the empty shelves, his heels squeaking on the hardwood pegged floor. From beyond the grand spiral staircase, muffled sounds of Alex's laughter floated down into the den from the second floor.

Trent's footfalls creaked on the polished hardwood floor as he explored the first floor hallway. He hesitated a moment at the partially opened door of Cassy's master bedroom before pushing it open. The dark room was lighted from the glowing swimming pool surface, filling the room with soft iridescent shadows. The scrambled covers over half the king-size bed outlined a hollow space in the bed nearest the window, the shape of Cassy's body. The other side of the king bed was untouched with the pillows still fluffed over the unfurled bedspread.

A flurry of paper scraps and scribbled notes, like leaves, covered the wood surface of the custom desk cabinetry beneath the windows. Trent flipped on the desk lamp next to Cassy's computer screen and scanned through the jumble of notes that littered the desktop. Cassy's random jottings were an incoherence of ideas, words, and sentence fragments in her tight cursive hand.

Trent peeked into her dressing room and ran his fingers along the edge of the antique chest in the corner. At an open drawer, he hesitated and looked inside. A disarray of underwear spilled over the edge of it. His hand paused on the edge of the walnut dresser as he stared into the drawer. Then he moved on.

In the kitchen, Trent found a wine glass in the cabinet and filled it with the chardonnay from the opened Mondavi bottle in the refrigerator door. He retrieved the morning newspaper from the kitchen cabinet top and returned to Scott Spence Jr.'s study. Trent fixed himself another bourbon and settled into the end of the burgundy leather sofa. The softness of the leather sofa cradled Trent. The article about Jeorg Marquez dominated the lower half of the front page. He read the article again. "Jesus, what a fucking mess!" he said. He quickly returned the front page section back into the stack of newspapers and shook out the sports section.

Alex's voice from the doorway of the study surprised Trent. He lowered the sports section that he had studied for most of the last hour. "G-Good night, D-Dr. H-Hendricks," Alex said from the doorway.

"Call me Trent, mister!" Trent said with mock sternness. Alex's face wrinkled at the tone. Trent's smile brought a quick, delighted laugh from Alex.

"Y-Yes, sir!" Alex said.

"Say goodnight to Trent then," Cassy said. She stood behind her son with both her hands on his shoulders. "It's way past your bedtime." Alex walked to the sofa, his pink face shiny under perfectly combed hair, nearly black from the wetness of his shampoo.

"G-Goodnight, T-Trent," Alex said. Trent stood up to shake the boy's hand. "T-Thanks for my b-birthday."

"I'm the one who needs to thank you for sharing your birthday and your mom with me." Alex looked puzzled and turned his head to find Cassy. "Your mother didn't tell you that she saved my daughter's life Sunday morning? I've a daughter four years older than you. Your mother did a heart transplant operation on her yesterday and saved her life."

"M-Mom d-did?" Alex asked. His eyes were proud.

Trent, still holding onto Alex's hand, leaned forward above Alex's head and kissed Cassy lightly on the cheek.

"That's very nice of you, Trent. Thanks," Cassy said, touching his arm that held Alex's hand.

"I would like to take you to another Rangers' game soon," Trent said, bending his face near Alex. "The next time we go, we'll pick a game that the Rangers will win."

"Can I?" Alex said, turning to his mother. "Can I? Please, Mom!"

"Sure, as long as it's not a school day."

"You've got a deal, Alex!" Trent said, impulsively hugging Alex to him.

"It's bedtime," Cassy said.

"Good night, Trent," Alex said and waved as he and Cassy disappeared around the doorway. Cassy noticed the easy, unstuttered words, the first time Alex had succeeded in saying a sentence without a stutter to someone other than her in nearly a year.

———

It was ten-thirty when Cassy returned to the study and flopped down on the sofa next to Trent and kicked off her tennis shoes. She accepted the crystal wine glass with the chardonnay. "Thanks for a wonderful day," Trent said, raising his freshly filled bourbon glass in a toast. "I hope you and Alex had as much fun as I did. He's a great kid."

"You're very kind to Alex," she said.

"You and he have given me the best day I've had since August twelfth last year," Trent said and turned his head aside. Cassy said nothing. A moment later Trent was at the bar, refilling his glass with whiskey.

When he returned to the sofa, he looked at Cassy intently before speaking. "Marilyn died on August twelfth. . . ."

"I know," Cassy said.

"Life is so damn arbitrary, Cass. One day, my wife is fine. The next day she starts to lose a word or two, and forty-eight hours later she's undergoing a craniotomy for an high grade astrocytoma brain tumor. You know the rest . . . irradiation. She was gone in ten weeks and five days from the day she first had the spell at dinner when she couldn't say 'pass the salad'."

"Remember what you told me to do?" Cassy asked. "Quit picking at it or it will fester up."

"I'm trying," Trent said. "But I'm having a hard time. I need someone like you to talk to. . . ."

"You've got to go forward," Cassy said.

"That's what I've been trying to do. The hospital has become my second home . . . sometimes my first home. I've been living mostly at work. With Heather in the hospital so often and the additional surgical load since you've been away this past year, I'm never at home."

Cassy could see a new glisten to the blood shot look of his eyes. She doubled her legs under her and leaned toward him to pick up his hand. "I'm sorry, Trent." Cassy felt the softness of the surgeon's fingertips and stroked the bristly reddish brown hairs on the back of his hand. She could feel the flush in her cheeks and the moistening in the pit of her palms. He intertwined his fingers with hers. Nothing was said for a long time.

"Are you all right?" she finally asked, searching his gaze that was fixed on the far wall. He slowly shook his head and sipped on the whiskey. "Tell me about it," Cassy said as she put her wineglass on the coffee table and laid her other hand on top of their two joined hands. "I'm sorry, Trent. I should have been more help to you. I've been preoccupied with my own problems . . . the divorce . . . looking after Alex . . . keeping up this place . . . and earning a living. I should have called you after the funeral. I thought about calling, but I was afraid of appearing pushy and forward . . . divorced women can be a bit oversensitive about calling recent widowers." Impulsively she leaned forward and kissed him on the cheek and squeezed his hand. "You're my friend. Forgive me?"

"It could have been so different. Marilyn could be alive today," Trent said.

"No self-recriminations, Trent. Remember what you told me this afternoon. Lay it down and let's go forward."

"Those last few weeks when Marilyn was alive were hard for the three of us. It seemed that was the time when Heather started to get worse. You remember, don't you, that Heather was in the ICU when her mother died. Heather was so sick that she couldn't go to her own mother's funeral."

"I remember. But yours and Heather's lives must go on."

"I need you back with me in the operating room," Trent said, swallowing deep from the whiskey. "I'm not sure I can go on with surgery much longer without your support or some other arrangement. . . ."

"I'm sorry, Trent, but there is no way I can even think about returning to the cardiac surgical practice right now. Yesterday with Heather was a special favor to both of you. But I have Alex to consider before everything else in my life."

"It's not the surgical practice . . . ," Trent said, pausing as if afraid to go on.

"I have to think of Alex first," Cassy said firmly. "You saw him today.

He's much better. Sure, he still stutters with everyone except me, but he's no longer withdrawn like he was a year ago."

"I know he needs you, Cass," Trent said. "I wouldn't ever ask you to do anything you weren't completely comfortable doing. That's not what I really need to talk about tonight. It's about Heather. I need some motherly advice." Cassy frowned uncertainly. Trent continued, "What am I going to do about her?"

"She's going to do well," Cassy said. "The new heart will function great. You'll notice an enormous improvement soon. My goodness, she'll be attracting the young boys soon. She's such a lovely girl."

"I know, Cass. What am I going to do? I'm afraid of being a single parent. She's got needs that go beyond what I can give her as a father . . . emotional things, you know. What a mother gives to her daughter."

"I understand," Cassy said, squeezing his hand between hers.

The glistening in Trent's eyes had watered into a droplet at the corner of each eye. The pouches under his eyes seemed to darken further like an approaching storm. Before speaking, Trent gnawed at his upper lip. "I'm going to have to give her up, Cass. She needs more than I can give. Marilyn's sister and her husband want Heather to live with them."

"You're fortunate to have family that care so much about both of you."

"They live in Houston. I wouldn't be able to see Heather but two or three times a month."

"Trent, I can't tell you what you should do," Cassy said. "You'll do what's best for Heather."

"I know, Cass. Just listening to me ramble on helps me deal with losing my daughter now that she's going to be well again. I have to admit to myself that Heather's living with my sister-in-law may be the best for Heather."

Cassy moved closer to him on the sofa and leaned her shoulder against his chest. He nudged her closer with his hand firmly on her shoulder until there was no room between them. They sat quietly holding hands for several minutes. Leisurely she rolled her bare legs out from under her and laid her head on his shoulder.

"You will make the right decision . . . for both you and Heather," Cassy said at last and turned her face toward him. "Anytime you need for me to listen, give me a call."

His large hand took her chin and moved her face gently to him.

"Thanks, Cass. You're just what the doctor ordered," he said, as his lips brushed a gentle kiss across her forehead. Cassy squeezed his hand and rubbed her neck on his shoulder. His large hand took the point of her chin and lifted it upward to him. His lips pressed against hers until his mouth covered hers. Cassy felt her heart pound. A warm tingling surged throughout her. His powerful arm rolled her shoulder inward to him holding her firmly against him.

"No, Trent," she said, squirming away from his arms and settling herself at the other end of the sofa. "Not now. We're good friends. Always have been. Let's leave it that way," she said, her words coming rapidly in torrents.

"Sorry, Cass," he said, standing up and walking toward the wet bar and placing his empty crystal glass on the bar.

"It's late. You need to be going. Tomorrow's a surgery day for you," Cassy said, standing up, and without thinking stroked the wrinkles out of her white shorts. "Let me walk you to the car."

Cassy reached through the open driver's window of the Mercedes and touched Trent's cheek. "I had a wonderful day, my friend," she said.

"Thanks Cass . . . for everything . . . and for Heather," Trent said, grasping her hand and slowly releasing it as the Mercedes glided down the driveway. Cassy stood in the driveway watching the red tail lamps of Trent's car disappear through the gate. The barred gate slid slowly back across the driveway. She returned to the house, set the deadbolt, and armed the security alarm.

NINE

JUST BEFORE ten the next morning Cassy eased her Range Rover into a parking spot designated for visitors in front of the entrance to the Forensic Sciences Building, a three-story glass and concrete box hidden behind the Dallas Metropolitan Hospital. Across the common driveway shared by the hospital and the coroner's building, the hospital emergency medical vans stood in readiness at the ER loading dock to retrieve the injured or sick.

Cassy stopped inside the front door of the Forensic Sciences Building and searched the glass-encased roster of names of the coroner's office until she found the Toxicology Section. As Director of the Emergency Room for the past year, death had been the outer bounds of her professional interest. Causes of death were rarely uncertain in ER patients. The fatal results of a gunshot wound or a crushed skull in an auto accident were of little anatomical interest to Cassy. The cause of death was clearly established to even a bystander. She had rarely been in the Dallas Forensic Sciences Building. Only then to visit her friend, Betty Freeman, for lunch or for some nonmedical reason. But Marquez's death and resurrection now obsessed her every conscious thought and brought her to the coroner's building this morning.

Cassy's reflection in the glass surface of the interior door caught her eye when she pushed through the inner door into the utilitarian lobby of the coroner's building. Pausing to check her appearance, she was pleased with her reflected image in the glass. Her business woman's uniform as she called any working attire other than surgical scrubs nicely shaped her slender torso. The softly textured Armani pants suit in muted beige patterns accentuated the fluid movements of her long stride as she pushed on through the inner glass doors into the Forensic Science Building. Her striking appearance in the stylish pants suit and the midheel lace-up pumps contrasted with her usual weekday morning uniform of gray surgical scrubs, a long white starched laboratory coat, and Nike running shoes. She smiled at her reflected image in the interior glass door and continued on into the building.

Cassy fidgeted in front of the elevator for nearly a minute, watching the unmoving lighted numbers above both closed elevator doors until her restlessness would not let her wait any longer. She took the three flights of stairs to the fourth floor. At the end of the tiled corridor, she knocked on the cream-painted metal door marked Betty Freeman, Ph.D., M.D., Chief of Toxicology. "Come on in, Cassy, it's open." The scratchy deep voice echoed as soon as Cassy knocked on the door. When the door swung open, an invisible fog of cigarette smoke collided with Cassy, causing her nose to wrinkle in an attempt to close out the stench.

A short plump woman, her hair a lifeless dull gray the color of her desktop, stood behind the steel institutional desk burdened with stacks of papers and medical journals. "Hi, Cassy. It's been too long since we've seen each other," the woman said, extending her short broad hand with sausage-shaped fingers. The dark yellow nicotine stain on the index and middle finger displayed for the world to see what Dr. Freeman's moist raspy voice announced eloquently. . . a three-pack-a-day smoker.

"What have you found out about Marquez?" Cassy asked, bypassing the usual chitchat that would have been socially required had Betty not been such a comfortable friend.

"I'm surprised you didn't call me back over the holiday . . . especially after I read what the reporters have done to you in the paper."

"The television news has had a good time, as well," Cassy said, not able to avoid staring at Dr. Freeman's face even though they were close friends. The initial look at Betty's facial features always startled Cassy. The protruding jaw, the prominent flat nose, and her puffy face set into a large head were almost grotesque. "Even the doctors are getting off some good one-liners in the doctor's lounge."

"Doctors can be terrible gossips . . . sometimes vicious," Dr. Freeman said in her gravelly hoarse voice. "Don't pay any attention to them."

For another moment, Betty's unusually protuberant jutting jaw and flat cheekbones distracted Cassy's concentration on the doctor's words. Cassy remembered twelve years ago, back to the first time she encountered Betty Freeman. Cassy was a junior surgical resident working on the

neurosurgery service of Dr. Walter Simmons. Betty was his patient at
Metro Hospital. Cassy as the tireless resident had eventually pieced all the
x-ray and laboratory information together until she was able to prove
Betty's diagnosis of acromegalic giantism in what had been a neurologic
diagnostic puzzle that had defied everyone until Cassy made the arcane
diagnosis.

"Are you smoking, or not, these days?" Dr. Freeman asked, shuffling
the open pack until a cigarette stuck from the end. "You deserve a cigarette. No apologies about smoking, dear. None of the customers of the
coroner that come in on the loading dock complains of my smoking.
It's only my co-workers that give me a hard time about my cigarettes. I
always tell them to take pleasure when you can get it. Life's too short,"
Dr. Freeman said. A cigarette burned its final third amid the heaped ashtray of crumpled, burnt butts. Dr. Freeman lit another, apparently unaware of the burning cigarette on the ashtray rim.

"You know I'm a closet smoker . . . more like a bathroom smoker,"
Cassy said, her face turning dark crimson beneath the tawny cream color
of her cheeks. "I don't smoke in public or around my son. Sometimes
I'm able to go for weeks without a cigarette," Cassy said, smiling sheep-
ishly. "I try not to smoke, but I'm not always successful. In fact, I'd like a
cigarette right now."

Betty tapped a cigarette from the end of the Marlboro package for her.

Cassy lit the cigarette with a gold lighter from her Fendi purse and felt
the satisfying rush begin to calm the anxiety she had felt in coming to see
her longtime friend. The professional embarrassment of the death and
resurrection of Marquez spilled over everything in Cassy's life.

From somewhere below the desk, Betty Freeman brought a spray can
of Lysol room deodorant and sprayed a fine mist throughout the room.
The cloying odor of the disinfectant spray combined with the stale cigarette smoke gagged Cassy. She thought she could hear the green plants in
the hanging pots in the two corner windows wilting and choking under
the Lysol mist floating throughout the room.

"That's for the smoke patrol," Betty Freeman said, returning the Lysol
can to the lower desk drawer. "This building is smoke free but not my
office. The Lysol is my camouflage. My nonsmoking co-workers can't
smell my cigarettes through the Lysol."

"I'm not sure which smell is worse, the old cigarettes or the Lysol,"
Cassy said and pulled deeply on the cigarette.

"At least, the nonsmokers will leave us alone for awhile," the pathologist said. "Now, you want to know what I have found out about the Marquez case since you called me Sunday." Her thick pouting lips parted into
a broad smile, pulling the coarse facial skin away from her teeth.

"I hope you've found out the reason that Marquez came back to life."

"I wish I knew. I checked the tox screen . . . had the blood study repeated and a portion of Marquez's serum held back from the Saturday night sample . . . everything's negative," the doctor said, fiddling with the single strand of faux pearls that hung outside her wrinkled white laboratory coat. Yellowing ocher splashes of reagents used in toxicology tests stained the front of her long white coat. The two friends were an odd pair, the disheveled Mutt looking across her desk at the elegant, slender Jeff.

"That's not much help. I had hoped that you might have found some evidence of poisoning. Walter Simmons is surely going to block any reinstatement of my Metro staff membership unless I can somehow show I didn't blow off the diagnosis of death in Marquez."

"Walter Simmons is such an asshole," Betty blurted. She heaved herself up from behind her desk. "He's nearly as bad as my ex-husband," Betty said and gestured to a dart board, large as a newspaper page, hung on the wall to the left of her desk. In the bullseye was a black and white photograph of a bald, middle-aged man. Dart holes eroded his face. A single feathered dart stuck between his eyes. "Simmons has never ever credited you with diagnosing my acromegaly twelve years ago."

"That's not important."

"Sure it is. Shows you what an ego jerk he is. Just like my ex-husband, marrying the younger woman."

"I'm sorry, Betty. I didn't mean . . . ," Cassy said, her voice trailing away. On the wall behind the desk was a posed picture of a young man and a ravishing brunette woman holding an infant. The dated clothes of the couple in the picture and the faded colors of the print told Cassy the photograph must be at least twenty-five years old. Cassy could not keep from staring at the picture. "The picture . . . I've never seen it before. Why do you have it out?"

"It's a reminder, I guess, that I was once an attractive young thing," she said, glancing wistfully over her shoulder at the photograph. "My pituitary tumor wrecked my face and made me look like I do today. The damned acromegaly destroyed my marriage. It's to remind me," the pathologist said indifferently.

"I'm sorry," Cassy said. "I didn't mean to stare at your picture."

"At least I survived Simmons' neurosurgery. I thought the Metro Hospital was rid of the bastard when he was forced out as Chief of Neurosurgery into the Medical Director's job four years ago."

"You know why he was forced out, don't you? The man's an alcoholic but won't admit it. He's my problem, Betty. Don't you get crosswise with him over me. . . ."

"I hear you, but that bastard can't touch me here in the coroner's office."

"Be careful. He's a political infighter. You know how vicious medical politics can get."

"Not to worry about me," Betty said, biting at an imaginary hangnail on her thumb. "I wish I had more to offer you in this Marquez incident."

"Couldn't Marquez have been poisoned? Some poison your toxicology tests might not detect . . . ?" Cassy asked hopefully. "That's why I'm here. You already know the clinical details from the Saturday night incident. I want your help in finding out who and what poisoned him."

"Whoa! What basis do you have for saying Marquez was poisoned?" Dr. Freeman asked. She sucked on the cigarette, rolling it in her thick lips.

"What other explanation is there? The man was clinically dead when I pronounced him. Then he revived three hours later in the morgue. It has to be a poisoning. I can't think of anything else to cause a body to respond in that manner."

"No, no, Cassy. That's where you're wrong. There are a lot of explanations for these morgue resurrections. It's much more common than you might think," the toxicologist said. "No hospital likes to publicize these return-from-the-dead episodes that occasionally happen even in the best of hospitals. Bad public relations for the hospital. Of course, also an enormous medicolegal liability. Hypothermia is, by far and away, the most common explanation for a supposedly dead person waking up in the morgue."

"I'm aware of the physiologic effects of cold on the human body but. . . ."

Betty ignored her protest and continued. "Last winter, we had a case not unlike your Señor Marquez. We called him the Fudgesicle man. You remember that bitter cold snap on New Year's Eve this year? An African-American gentleman, I believe that's the politically correct term here in Texas. Anyway this homeless guy fell asleep in an alley in downtown Dallas. Need I explain the origin of the name Fudgesicle? He was cold, stiff, and brown when the paramedics found him the next morning."

"And he revived in the Morgue when his body temperature rewarmed back to normal?" Cassy asked.

"You guessed it," Dr. Freeman said. "The African-American's story didn't make the papers like the two skiers in Utah did a couple of years ago when they got lost in a snowstorm and damn near froze to death."

"Yes, I remember that incident. The skiers were helicoptered to Salt Lake City and were saved by having their bodies rewarmed using the heart-lung machine like I use in surgery."

"That's right," Dr. Freeman said, lighting another cigarette off the burning end of the one she was smoking. "Same clinical situation last winter in Massachusetts with a kid who dropped through a frozen lake while ice skating," Dr. Freeman said, straining at the Marlboro. "Hell, Cassy, you're not the first physician who has been fooled into declaring someone dead who wasn't dead."

"No, but I must be the first doctor to make the front page of the *Dallas Sunday News*."

"Happens every winter up north. Some homeless person or alcoholic soaked bum falls into a snow bank and chills out. Then they're brought into the ER without any detectable signs of life . . . no blood pressure, no pulse, no breathing. After being declared dead by some unsuspecting emergency room doc, the corpse warms up in the morgue and starts screaming . . . 'I'm alive'."

"But . . . ," Cassy tried again. "Marquez wasn't cold. It's summer in Texas and hot as hell."

"Are you absolutely sure he wasn't hypothermic? Maybe Marquez was caught in the freezer at his funeral home. Did you take his rectal or ear temperature yourself?"

"No, but the ER nurse said it was ninety-eight point six degrees."

"I agree that it's not likely that Marquez was hypothermic," Dr. Freeman said. "When I first read about it in the Sunday paper I thought Marquez was just probably drunk. An alcoholic coma. Last month I read about some drunk Mexican in *The Enquirer*."

"*The Enquirer*?" Cassy laughed. "That's your resource for medical information?"

"Hell yes, honey," Dr. Freeman said. "I subscribe to it. I'm not one of your checkout stand readers at the grocery store. I read it cover to cover every week. I save the copies. I have a garage full of *Enquirers*. A month ago there was a story about this drunk Mexican who was damn near buried alive until he woke up in his coffin in the funeral home," she said, stopping in a paroxysm of a smoker's cough. "If a drunken binge could make that Mexican look dead drunk," she said, grinning at her play on words. "Then Marquez could have been another Mexican in an alcoholic coma."

"His drug, toxicology, and alcohol screens were all negative," Cassy said, stubbing her cigarette into the overloaded tray and shaking her head.

"You do point out a logical flaw to my theory of alcohol as the poisoning agent for Marquez," Dr. Freeman said, smiling broadly and rearing back in her desk chair. "I wish I could be more helpful. I've told the same thing to everyone who's called this morning about Marquez. I simply don't know what happened to him Saturday night."

"Who's called about Marquez but me?"

"Half a dozen reporters and Dr. Walter Simmons. I don't understand the interest in this case . . . must be their fascination with near-death episodes."

"I don't either, but I've already lost my job over it," Cassy said. "Unless I can find a rational explanation of what happened."

"You will be the living equivalent of a medical Polish joke," Dr. Freeman interrupted kindly with her understanding smile. "Don't expect a miracle answer here in the Toxicology Department. With negative drug and toxicology screens, I'm not sure I'm going to be much support to your poisoning theory."

"You still haven't answered my question, Betty. Is it possible that a drug or poison might have been present in Marquez and your blood toxicology screens didn't detect it?"

"Sure. Sure. But those poisons and drugs are awfully rare that don't show up on the routine tox screens."

"Then your negative routine toxicology screen does not eliminate the possibility of poisoning in Marquez?" Cassy asked.

"No, not at all. For example, my routine screen would not detect succinylcholine, the muscle relaxant used in surgery. It will paralyze a person quickly. I can't detect it on my toxicology tests because the body breaks it down into normal biochemical components very quickly."

"Any other possibilities?" Cassy asked hopefully.

"Yeah, maybe. Curare for one. It's that poison that some of the South American Indian tribes paint on the tips of their arrows to paralyze their animal and human targets."

"Sure, I'm familiar with curare," Cassy said. "It's also used every day in the OR to paralyze patients while they are anesthetized. Could you check Marquez's serum from Saturday night for breakdown products of these two drugs?" Cassy asked.

"Maybe," Dr. Freeman said. "But both those drugs would require an injection by someone with the knowledge and access to those drugs." The toxicologist paused to sip at her coffee. "Do you want some coffee?"

Cassy shook her head. "Any other poisons that you can think of that might produce the Marquez scenario?"

The doctor leaned back in her chair and propped her Birkenstock sandaled feet on the edge of her desk. "If Marquez were Japanese, I'd say poisoning could be a definite possibility. Puffer fish is quite a delicacy in Japan but eating it can be quickly lethal if the fish is not cleaned and prepared properly. The liver and ovaries of the puffer fish contain a powerful neuromuscular toxin. Unless the fish is meticulously prepared to eliminate the poison, eating the fish will cause a fatal paralysis."

"Marquez is not Japanese, and Dallas is not Tokyo," Cassy said, shrugging her indifference.

"I tried eating puffer fish once years ago in New York," Dr. Freeman continued, as if talking to herself.

"You ate a poisonous fish?" Cassy asked immediately. "On purpose?"

"Puffer fish is quite delicious. A light flavor that melts on your tongue. Don't criticize it until you've tried it, hon. The slight numbness of the tongue and the lips and the warm flushed all over feeling after eating the fish are probably due to traces of the poison, tetrodotoxin, that remain in the fish even after the best cleaning. Eating puffer fish is the next best thing to an orgasm." Dr. Freeman fumbled another cigarette from the open package on her desk.

"What?" Cassy asked, her face astonished at the woman's sexual allusion.

"The tiny amounts of residual tetrodotoxin, even in the properly cleaned puffer fish, induce a rush that is a lot like a sexual orgasm. Tetrodotoxin is a complex and potent poison, a non-peptidic neurotoxin. The symptoms can develop very quickly after eating the fish, especially if the tetrodotoxin dose is large. Tingling and prickly feelings in the face occur first. Numbness and paralysis of the whole body occur soon after eating the tainted fish. Difficult breathing, sweating, and low blood pressure also go along with the paralysis. Most victims are dead within hours after eating an improperly prepared puffer fish. But a fair number do revive after hours of total body paralysis, often after being given up for dead."

"Sounds like Marquez," Cassy said quickly.

"The tetrodotoxin does produce a rapid, total body paralysis, not unlike Marquez, I guess," Dr. Freeman said. "But like you said, Dallas is not Tokyo. I don't know where anybody would get hold of a puffer fish or tetrodotoxin in Texas."

"Suppose for a moment that the tetrodotoxin were available . . . ," Cassy said.

"But it's not commercially available. The only source of tetrodotoxin I know about is the puffer fish around Japan and some weird salamander on the west coast of the United States. I think maybe some other fishes in the tropical waters in the Caribbean might contain tetrodotoxin, I really don't know."

"If I wanted some tetrodotoxin, how could I get it?" Cassy asked.

Dr. Freeman shook her head. "Beats me. I'd probably do a Medline computer search through the National Library of Medicine in Washington D.C. See what research has been published on tetrodotoxin. Surely there will be some university groups interested in the toxicology of tetrodotoxin. It's still a big problem in Japan. Maybe two hundred Japanese die each year from this kind of poisoning. I've heard that in some of the coastal villages in Japan the bodies of suspected victims of puffer fish poisoning are laid beside their coffins for three full days before embalming or burial because of the fear of burying one of them alive."

"Zombies," Cassy said quickly. "Buried alive just like a zombie. One of the ER nurses thinks Marquez has become a zombie."

Dr. Freeman laughed uproariously. Then she fell into another spasm of coughing. "Those Haitian zombie stories just won't die," she said, finally able to talk. "About ten years ago an ecobiologist from Harvard thought he had discovered the biologic basis for the zombie's apparent return from the dead . . . he even made a movie about zombification. This scientist thought that the zombies were Haitian natives who had been fed a potion of drugs and poisons that included tetrodotoxin. He claims to have identified tetrodotoxin in some of the zombie powders that the voodoo priests use. I remember he even identified tetrodotoxin in some of the fish in the tropical waters around Haiti as well as in some reptiles on the island."

"Is it possible that the tetrodotoxin could induce a state of suspended animation for a day or two while the person is buried underground?"

"Nah," Dr. Freeman said, wrinkling her lips in disgust. "That scientist who came up with this crazy idea is so full of bullshit. The Harvard doctor's theory about a zombie potion containing tetrodotoxin hasn't been proved by any other scientist."

"Well then, what do you think happened to Marquez?" Cassy asked.

"I think you blew the diagnosis of death," Dr. Freeman said bluntly. "Marquez was never dead. Honey, after thirty-six years in this toxicology business, I'm here to tell you, dead is dead is dead."

"Do you know if the coroner's office might still have any more of Marquez's blood serum sample from Saturday night?"

"Should have. We freeze and save serum samples for Metro Hospital death cases for several months. I'll check to be sure."

"Could you test Marquez's serum from Saturday night for all those exotic poisons including tetrodotoxin?" Cassy asked.

"Do you realize what a laboratory project you're asking for? That's almost a week's work for one lab technician," Dr. Freeman said, shaking her head and stubbing out her cigarette. "What about the cost?"

"I'll pay for the tests myself," Cassy said. "A special request from me, but you'll have to keep the results off the coroner's records."

"Why are you so intent on this?"

"I have to clear my name, Betty. I'm thirty-eight years old. I'm a surgeon. I need my professional reputation back. I have a lot of years ahead of me."

"Is that all?"

"Someone tried to kill Marquez."

"How can you be certain? Who? Why?" Dr. Freeman asked calmly, leaning forward to rest her elbows on the cleared area in the center of her desk.

"I don't have any idea," Cassy said. "Sunday evening when I saw Marquez in the Intensive Care Unit he told me that someone tried to kill him."

"Cassy, have you gone to the police with this information?"

"Nobody would believe me. Not after I botched the diagnosis."

"You need to talk to a friend of mine. He's been with the Homicide Division of the Dallas Police Department for ten or twelve years. A real straight arrow. I've worked with him on a number of cases. His name's Kevin Knowland. Do you remember that arsenic case that was in all the papers?"

"No, I'm not going to the police. I'll just look paranoid," Cassy said and shifted in her seat.

"Come on. Let me call him." Dr. Freeman punched the intercom button on her telephone as she balanced the receiver against her prominent jaw and lit another Marlboro. "Jenny, get Kevin Knowland for me. I'll hold," she said into the receiver, as the cigarette bounced up and down between her lips. Less than a minute later her eyes wrinkled. A wide grin softened her face. "No, no, dear. I don't have time for you today." Her chuckle turned into laughter. "I want you to do me a personal favor. You need to talk to Dr. Cassy Baldwin. She's in my office now with a story that you should hear."

Dr. Freeman paused, listening to the receiver and rolled her eyes upward. "Behave yourself, and she might." Betty Freeman smiled and winked her left eye at Cassy. "But first listen to her story. Remember last year the case of the store owner who poisoned his wife with arsenic? Dr. Baldwin may be on to something similar. You need to talk to her." She listened for a moment. "Good. I'll send her over now. And behave yourself."

"I'm still not sure this is a good idea," Cassy said as she stood up.

"Cassy, either you report your conversation with Marquez to Kevin, or I will. I can't keep quiet. Neither can you with these suspicions of poisoning." Dr. Freeman stood up and Cassy reached forward to touch the toxicologist's forearm. "And if you don't go see Kevin, I won't run those exotic toxicology tests you want."

"Okay. Where is his office?" Cassy asked.

"Dallas Police Department."

"Where's that?"

"My, my, you have lead a sheltered life," Dr. Freeman said. "Main at Harwood. Go to the third floor of the building and ask for Lt. Knowland."

TEN

THE HOT NOONDAY air suffocated Cassy for a moment as she walked down the short flight of concrete steps outside the Forensic Sciences Building. Just as she turned to step into her car, the receiving dock of the Metro Hospital ER across the parking lot swung into her vision. From her position in the visitor's parking space, the rising cement driveway leading to the hospital ER across from the coroner's office shimmered with heat waves reflected by the sun's morning baking of the wide plateau of concrete.

At that moment a Metro Hospital van pulled into the loading ramp of the ER. Two paramedics flew out of the ambulance and quickly pulled a gurney with a sheet-swathed figure from the rear of the van. Cassy squinted against the brightness of the sun, trying to make out the faces of the two paramedics. The boyish face of Roger, the paramedic who brought Marquez into the ER Saturday night, was visible even across two hundred feet of glimmering heat waves. Cassy impulsively started to wave a greeting but stopped when she realized that Roger's attention was focused on his gurney patient, as it had been Saturday night with Marquez.

A nagging thought hummed at the periphery of her mind. She tried to pull it in. What was it that Roger kept saying Saturday night? Some silly irrelevance was all Cassy could remember. She stared across the parking lot again at the empty ambulance, its rear doors yawning wide open after the removal of the emergency patient. There she had Roger's comment in her mind . . . 'it was just like a movie scene,' he kept saying.

Roger's description of the funeral home scene flooded her mind as if by hypnotic recall. She could see Marquez lying stretched out on the floor of an enormous and lavishly appointed office. Cassy's mind filled in the details as if by brush stroke . . . dark hardwoods, massive desk, a panoramic window, soft lighting. What else did Roger say? The tacos and champagne he mentioned. What was it that Tenoch had described? He said that Marquez's eyes rolled up. He then collapsed to the floor. Something else Tenoch said, or didn't say, Cassy told herself. Then she remembered that Tenoch described Marquez as trying to say something but could not seem to make his words come out.

Her mind worried the fragments of data into a variety of diagnostic possibilities. Still she had no answers. The Marquez incident could only be explained by an exogenous source of poisoning, she concluded. Cassy examined that deduction and could find no other explanation for the Marquez scenario. Nothing else fit the medical facts. Any natural disease process that struck so suddenly would not allow such a prompt recovery, she told herself.

A well worn Shakespearean quote that she often used in her medical student lectures popped into her mind. 'Diseases desperate grown, by desperate appliance are relieved, or not at all.' She realized how well the aphorism fit the Marquez incident. If Marquez truly had a natural disease 'desperate grown' to the point that he appeared dead in the ER, then he would not be cured without a 'desperate appliance'. "Thank you, William Shakespeare," Cassy said out loud. Satisfied by her logic, she then opened the door of her Range Rover and settled herself into the leather seat.

. As she sat in the seat with her back pressed against the leather, she realized that her blouse was drenched in sweat to the inner lining of her Armani pants. The car's air conditioner cooled her quickly as she pulled onto Harry Hines Boulevard. "It has to be a poison," she said aloud to the car and punched the Vivaldi tape out of the car's stereo system. There's no other choice except a poison, she had now convinced herself. He must have been dosed with some drug or poison, either accidentally or intentionally. Then his body must have slowly metabolized the substance, whatever it was, while he lay in the morgue. As soon as his body metabolized and eliminated whatever it was, then Marquez woke up. Smiling for the first time all morning, Cassy pulled up to the intersection at Main and Harwood.

—

Cassy parked the Range Rover in the lot across Main Street from the stately three-story granite building that occupied the entire corner of

Main and Harwood in downtown Dallas. The classical square lines of the building and the columned entrances reminded her of the federal buildings in Washington D.C. along Constitution Avenue.

The uniformed Dallas police guards and metal detectors at the entrance signaled that this building was not for the idly curious. The policeman at the guard desk blocking the entry to the interior of the building sized Cassy up in a professional once-over glance. In response to Kevin Knowland's name, he sternly directed her around his sentry post desk to the elevators.

Just opposite the elevators, a line of disheveled men and women, their lives and clothes in dreary disarray, waited their turn at the cashier's window like a queue at a concession stand to make payment for bail bonds. The young man behind the single cashier's window eyed Cassy over the lowered head of a grizzled man counting wrinkled five and ten dollar bills. The stooped man dropped the crumpled bills into the metal drawer that slipped through the bulletproof protective glass panel and disappeared into the sealed cashier's booth.

The lineup of people awaiting their turn to bail a friend or family member out of jail reminded Cassy of the Metro ER . . . a line of humanity bending to an enforced process . . . at the jail and at the hospital . . . the men and women abandoning freedoms and submitting to a dehumanizing process. Cassy escaped into the elevator and sighed relief as the elevator doors closed on these individual cases of human misery.

When the elevator door reopened onto the third floor corridor, the stillness of the deserted corridor startled her. Stepping off the elevator, she searched for a sign for the Homicide Department. The yellow plastered walls were bare. The corridor reminded her of the high ceilinged hallways of her high school in Mexico City years ago. For no apparent reason Cassy turned right and walked past several closed doors, the frosted panes reminiscent of a fifty-year-old building. Her black kidskin leather pumps clattered on the tile flooring as she searched the deserted corridor for the Homicide Division.

The flow of the corridor led her to an open door at the end of the long hallway. A dozen gray desks filled the drab gray room beyond the doorway. The square space had the feel of an oversized college classroom. The desks were arranged in a precise geometrical slate of gray squares like a giant checkerboard. Shafts of sunlight fell into the room from the high silled, mullioned windows along the back wall. Behind about half the desks, serious young men talked on telephones or studied neat piles of papers. The room could have been a college class waiting for an instructor to appear. The common features of the half dozen men in the room were their age, clustered around thirty, and the presence of identical leather hip holsters containing identical Sig Sauer nine millimeter pistols. In most other ways they differed . . . race, physique, dress, all different.

Cork boards and slick white writing boards covered each wall. Hand-written lists of names scribbled on the wall-mounted writing slates were mixed with diagrams, doodles, and stick figures, decipherable only by the men at the desks. Scraps of paper, printed departmental memos, and wanted bulletins filled the cork boards until the tan cork texture was barely visible. A low murmur of conversation floated through the room, a mingling of male voices carrying on one-sided telephone conversations.

Cassy stood at the doorway to the squad room until finally a crewcut detective manning the desk nearest the door held a telephone away from his ear and looked expectantly at her. "Hi, you lost?" he asked pleasantly.

"Is this Homicide?" Cassy asked.

The young man pulled the telephone back to his mouth and without listening to the receiver barked into it, "Hold on." Then he laid the telephone on his plain gunmetal desktop and stood up to face her. The detective looked Cassy over professionally, taking her body measurements in inches, Cassy thought. She had the foreboding that the man was about to ask her if she might be free for dinner rather than offer directions to the Homicide Department.

"I'm Dr. Baldwin. I'm here to see Lt. Kevin Knowland," Cassy said quickly.

"I'm sorry," the young man said, his face registering real disappointment. "I'm Vernon Pierce, one of the detectives here. I thought you might be one of the lady lawyers who had strayed up here."

"No. Dr. Betty Freeman called Lt. Knowland. He's expecting me."

The murmured conversations in the room quieted. A half dozen pair of male eyes focused on Cassy. The sight of an attractive young woman visitor was an aberration on the third floor of the Homicide Department. "Lieutenant's office is through there," he said, pointing to the corner door at the back of the large room.

Cassy could feel the stares following her as the detective led her around the perimeter of the squad room to a secretary's anteroom just beyond the room. Through the open door, Cassy saw a muscular man leaning forward over a bare gray metal desk. In an instant she had sized up Kevin Knowland . . . blonde hair in a short trim cut, gray pinstripe suit, starched white long sleeve shirt, solid maroon tie, mid to late thirties . . . a few inches above Cassy's height. This man looks like a stockbroker, not a cop, thought Cassy. He waved her in, motioned her to a chair, and stood as he reached across the desk to shake her hand.

As the man took Cassy's hand in a quick firm pump, he continued talking into the telephone. "Roy, we could use your help on this one. Can you give me some front page exposure? We think this guy is holed up in Dallas somewhere. Maybe we'll get lucky and somebody will call us if you run his picture in your paper." Cassy felt the firmness of the man's hand enclose hers, his blue eyes locked onto her while he continued talking. Cassy noticed that there were no rings on either hand.

"How about a front page story with his picture? We want this son of a bitch. For chrissake, they buried his wife and three children down in El Paso today. You saw what he did to them with his shotgun." Knowland paused, listening. Finally he grinned widely, "Thanks, Roy. I owe you one."

He hung up the phone and waved Cassy to the metal chair in front of his desk. Sitting back in the swiveling bucket chair behind his desk, he said, "You must be Dr. Baldwin. Aren't you at the Metropolitan Hospital?" he asked.

"Yes, I'm the director of the Emergency Room at the Metro."

"I must be confusing you with another Dr. Baldwin. There's a Baldwin over there who's a heart surgeon. He operated on my cousin's baby three years ago."

"Yes. That's me. I've been away from heart surgery for over a year." The policeman looked puzzled. Cassy knew that this man could not leave such a vague response to his question unanswered. "I took some time off from my surgical practice so I could enjoy my son while he is still young. I'm a single mother . . . divorced. Taking the ER job was supposed to give me more time with my son. Somehow it's not worked out quite that way." She stopped talking abruptly, embarrassed that she had rambled on after such a simple question.

Cassy searched the bare walls of the office. The pale yellow institutional paint gave her no clue about this man or whether his question was more than an idle introductory statement. I've already forgotten what he asked me, she thought, realizing then how flustered she was about being in the Police Department. The lieutenant waited for Cassy to continue. She recognized his studied calm and obvious interest in the way she answered.

When Lt. Knowland did not speak, Cassy felt an urgency to fill the silent gap in their conversation. The lieutenant leaned back in his chair and smiled pleasantly until Cassy continued. "I was divorced and my seven-year-old son began having some adjustment difficulties." Cassy stopped and asked herself why am I telling him this? His steady cerulean blue eyes, clear as a cloudless sky, appraised her. She was unsettled by his calm, unflinching gaze that seemed to look inside her. "I-I'm sorry," Cassy said stuttering. "I d-didn't mean to get carried off on such a tangent."

Lt. Knowland leaned forward, resting his elbows on the desk top, vacant except for the console telephone. "That's all right," he said. "I enjoy listening to you much more than the usual folks I hear in this business. I'm sorry about your son. I didn't intend to pry into your personal life." His quiet presence commanded authority.

Cassy could barely keep from staring at his blue eyes that bloomed behind the lenses of the round metal frames of his glasses. She decided to reciprocate and waited for him to continue the conversation. The pause between them stretched for several seconds. Cassy sat quietly on the edge of the steel straight chair, a pleasant smile on her lips. He's quite attractive, she thought, now analyzing him beyond a first impression. It was the blue eyes that captivated her and seemed to draw her closer as the two sat facing each other silently across the empty desk top. Finally, the lieutenant spoke as his face broke into a wide grin, "You know the secret, don't you?"

"What secret?" Cassy said, returning his smile.

"The secret of the interview. It's the art of listening. So few people understand how effective a pause or silence can be to elicit information."

"Yes. I use it all the time with patients. There's an old adage in medicine . . . listen to the patient and he'll tell you his diagnosis."

Kevin Knowland tilted his head and smiled but said nothing. Again the silence stretched between them until he said, "You win. I spoke first." Cassy nodded and found herself laughing at the bantering exchange.

Kevin Knowland continued, "I use it all the time with homicide suspects. You'd be amazed at how many murder confessions I've heard just by waiting and listening."

He leaned backward in his chair with his fingers interlocked on the top of his head. She noticed a single framed diploma hanging on the wall behind him. "You are a good listener," he said.

The diploma engraving across the room looked familiar, but she could not quite make out the calligraphy. "Is that your degree from Southern Methodist University?" she asked. What do I find so appealing about this man? she asked herself. His self confidence? His friendly laughter? His strong and attractive presence? She almost did not catch his response.

"I spent the best part of a decade there, finishing with my Ph.D. seven years ago," he said, studying her.

"I'll bet we were on the SMU campus at the same time," Cassy said, leaning forward to look at the diploma. "I graduated from undergraduate school there, longer ago than I care to remember."

"I didn't spend a lot of time on campus," he said. "My degree is in abnormal psychology. My dissertation was on the development of the ego structure of the murderer. I doubt that our paths would have ever crossed."

"Why?" Cassy asked. For a long moment, Lt. Knowland said nothing, and Cassy waited. It was her turn to be the interviewer and wait the interviewee out.

"A Ph.D. in homicide?" Cassy asked finally, breaking the extended silence. It was evident that Kevin Knowland did not wish to discuss his career as a homicide investigator. He propped his chin into his hand and rested his elbow on the arm of the chair, peering at her. Cassy felt as if the man might read and interpret her thoughts, embarrassed that he could sense her attraction to him.

Cassy waited for him to say something until she could not tolerate the silence any longer. At last, she said, "I'm sorry, Betty Freeman urged me to come talk to you."

"I'm glad she did." Knowland smiled and brushed his short blonde hair across his head. He caught her again with his blue eyes and paused. "This is your first time in Homicide?"

"It's my first time in a police department, ever!"

"Congratulations!" he said. They both laughed again. "You've already achieved an accomplishment that eludes much of our society. Tell me. . . ." He left his words open ended inviting, almost requiring, a response.

"I'm not sure I should even be here," Cassy said. "Can this just be an informal chat?"

"Sure. It's eleven-thirty, maybe we could chat over lunch?" he asked. Cassy hesitated. She would enjoy lunch with this man, she knew. Any other time but not today. She had promised Alex to be home in the afternoon. She would not disappoint him again. Maybe the lieutenant would not be put off by her rejection.

"No . . . at least not today. I already have lunch plans," she said, then hesitated and added, "With my son. Perhaps another day."

"Sure, another time," he said, leaning backward in his chair again and added after a long pause, "soon." The easy grin reappeared. He waited for Cassy to begin. Now that she felt relaxed in the plain room with this man, Cassy completely put aside her initial reluctance to bring her suspicions to the police and quickly summarized the Marquez incident in a few sentences. She concluded her summary with an account of her bedside conversation with Marquez, quoting Marquez's statement that someone was going to kill him.

"'Estoy muerto' is another thing he said," Cassy said, as she finished reciting her presentation much in the manner of a medical student presentation. She balanced herself on the edge of her chair, gripping the edge of the desk for support. Despite the relaxed easy body language that Kevin projected throughout her short monologue, the retelling of the story had provoked the jittery anxiety again. Her throat ached for a cigarette.

"What does that mean?" Kevin Knowland asked.

"It's a Spanish phrase meaning 'I am dead.' I suppose that Marquez means that the person will succeed in killing him," Cassy said.

"Or possibly Marquez is delusional and thinks he really is dead," Lt. Knowland said.

"I didn't have enough time to find out what he really thought or what he was trying to tell me," Cassy said. "My impression was that the man was terrified that someone was going to kill him."

"This Marquez incident is beginning to sound a lot like a homicide case we had here in Dallas a couple of years ago. The doctors called us when they became suspicious after they couldn't diagnose a woman who was hospitalized with bizarre symptoms. They suspected poisoning but didn't know what kind. That's when I asked Betty to help us. She eventually came up with the proof that the woman's husband had poisoned her with arsenic."

"What happened to the wife?" Cassy asked.

"Unfortunately for her, we didn't figure the poisoning angle out in time. We eventually discovered that the husband had bought a lot of arsenic from a garden shop. One thing led to a dozen others. Now the bastard is in the the penitentiary for killing his wife."

"Tell me what I should do. I surely don't want to see Marquez dead if I can do something about it," Cassy said.

"These situations are always a bit touchy," Lt. Knowland said, shaking his head. "I don't want to jeopardize a formal investigation that we might have to undertake by acting prematurely on information that could be part of a confidential doctor-patient communication between you and Marquez."

Cassy felt the skin on the back of her neck dimple at the idea of a formal police investigation into the possibility of an attempted murder of Marquez. "I'm more concerned that if the police show up at the Metro Hospital and begin asking questions, the investigation will lead back to my conversation with Marquez," Cassy said. "And then I'll be in even more trouble with the hospital Medical Director than I am now."

"How so?" Kevin Knowland said and waited for Cassy to continue.

"I lost my position as Metro ER director over the Marquez incident. The Medical Director suspended me after my diagnosis of a death that wasn't." She flushed at her awkward choice of words.

"Now that you mention your suspension, I remember reading the newspaper over the holiday. . . ."

"I'm going to find out what happened with Marquez." Cassy stepped on his words. "I'm absolutely convinced he was poisoned. I'm going to find when and what and who. Dr. Freeman is conducting some sophisticated lab tests for exotic poisons on Marquez's blood that was saved from the night he died . . . or the night I thought he died."

"I'll see what I can find out about Marquez," Knowland said. "Whether or not someone would like to see him dead."

"Can you do it without involving me?" Cassy asked. "I've been hit hard enough already with this Marquez mess without provoking anyone unnecessarily."

"I'll do this informally without a report, if you'll return the favor by informally having lunch with me soon," he said.

"Okay. Now that I'm no longer employed, I'll be free for lunch most any day," Cassy said, standing up and extending her hand.

"Give me a couple of days. Something will turn up if Marquez isn't clean. If somebody wants him dead, the reasons should become clear," Kevin Knowland said. He shook her hand and walked her through the squad room.

The eyes of the same detectives followed her appreciatively to the hallway door.

ELEVEN

C ASSY'S BIG house was still and quiet when she poured her third cup of morning coffee and wandered onto the patio to sit near the pool. A nearness to water, whether the beach or the pool, almost always calmed her anxieties. Despite the relaxing quiet of the pool as the dawn sky lightened into morning, the uncertainty of her future smothered her. She pulled a deep lungful of the cigarette smoke, waiting for the familiar relaxation that smoking had always provided.

Dead is dead is dead, Betty Freeman's words haunted her. At last, she had conceded . . . maybe I did make a mistake. Maybe I was just tired and careless. After all it was a long day. I'd been seeing patients constantly since seven a.m. Maybe I just sloughed off a critical evaluation of Marquez's death and shipped him off to the Morgue when he wasn't even dead.

Until Saturday night, her life with Alex had been clearly marked by past and future signposts that guided her. In truth, theirs was a consciously armored life, protected by privilege, money, and status from the misfortunes that befall the lives of those less fortunate. But the storm that roared through her life this weekend had uprooted the signposts of their existence. Her perception of a stable life vanished with it. And this morning her uneasiness about her and Alex's future consumed her. Not only did she need to be next to a calm body of water, she needed another cigarette.

Just before noon, Trent Hendricks' voice rippled through the intercom, "Open the gate, Cass."

"Hi Trent. The security code is C-A-S-S-Y. You used it the other day. Punch my name," she shouted toward the wall-mounted intercom in the family room. Cassy wadded *The Dallas Morning News* into the trash compactor. There had been nothing in the paper again this morning. Maybe Trent is right, she thought. This whole mess will quiet down and go away if I just leave it alone.

"I'll drive up," Trent's voice came back through the intercom. "You ought to reprogram your security code. C-A-S-S-Y is not a very good choice for a burglar alarm."

"The obvious can be best hidden in plain sight," Cassy said, flipping the speaker off. She went upstairs and found Alex hunched over the computer video screen.

"I'll be back around three o'clock," she said and touched Alex's dark hair and kissed the top of his head. "See you, my man." Alex said nothing until Cassy was at the doorway.

"Where are you going?"

"I'm having lunch with Trent and a man from Mexico City."

"Why?" Alex asked. Cassy knew she should have anticipated Alex's curiosity and prepared him for the Mexico City possibility. She couldn't wait any longer. "He offered me a job in Mexico City."

"Would we move there?"

"We might move," Cassy said. "You could even attend the same school where I went when I was your age."

"I'd rather stay here," Alex said, matter-of-factly, not looking up from the computer screen.

"If I move to Mexico City, you would go with me," Cassy said.

"Could I live here with Dad?"

"No. I need you to go where I go."

"I like it right here," Alex said. "I don't want to move."

Cassy sighed. "Come on downstairs and say hello to Trent, honey."

"Okay, Mom. Sure," Alex said, grinning up at his mother at the mention of Trent.

She smiled in return, the discussion of moving to Mexico City over for now but far from settled.

Trent was leaning against his Mercedes, his arms folded against his chest, waiting none too patiently. A gray pinstripe suit draped his solid body smoothly.

"I like your suit," Cassy said, touching his coat lapel. "Sorry I'm late." She grabbed his arm in an affectionate squeeze.

"You look great today," Trent said.

"This is my businesswoman's outfit," she said, pulling back from him to model another one of her collection of Armani suits. The generous cut of the lightweight navy fabric emphasized the width of her shoulders and dropped smoothly to her narrow waist. The skirt hung just above her knee but was short enough to flatter her trim and attractive legs. She had added a gleaming strand of pearls that accentuated her slender neck. "I never get to wear these clothes in the hospital, just my scrub clothes every day."

"You look great. Like a real fashion model."

At that moment, Charlie bounded through the storm door that Alex held open.

"Hey, Alex." Trent waved at Alex and Charlie. The German shepherd barked playfully at Trent and sniffed at his pants legs. "How about a Rangers' game this weekend?" Trent asked, bending down so that his eyes were level with Alex's.

"S-Sure," Alex said, shaking Trent's hand vigorously.

"I'll check the schedule and call you soon. I'll look for the game that the Rangers are going to win this time." Trent rubbed Charlie's back. The dog rolled in the driveway with his imitation of a rollover trick. "I'm taking your mother to lunch now, Alex."

"T-Tell the m-man I-I don't w-want t-to m-move to Mexico City."

"Alex!" Cassy said, more sharply than she intended. "Don't start worrying about moving just yet."

Trent caught Cassy's eyes in a knowing and understanding way. He bent forward to whisper to Alex. "Yes, sir," Trent said softly. "Consider your message delivered to Señor Tenoch. Now don't you worry about moving. Your mom will take care of everything like she always does for you."

Cassy waved goodbye to Alex as the car rolled down the long driveway toward the gate. Alex and Charlie stood under the covered driveway until the car was out of sight and the security gate slid closed.

"Trent, you're easily becoming the number one man in my son's life. I thank you for your kindness to him . . . and to me," she said and touched her lips to his cheek leaving a faint red streak that she wiped away with her fingertips. "I appreciate you."

Trent eased the car onto Preston and turned off the CD player with its Willie Nelson recording. "I'm sorry I've caused us to be late," Cassy said.

"We've got plenty of time. Tenoch's Dallas home is only a few minutes away."

"You mean he has more than one home?" Cassy asked.

"Two that I know. The one here in Dallas and another home in Mexico City . . . a huge penthouse mansion atop the tallest building in Mexico City."

"I'm impressed," Cassy said with a flip shrug of her shoulder. Without a pause, she deliberately changed the subject, "How's Heather?" The thought of seeing Tenoch stirred her anxieties anew. She could feel her stomach already balled into a hard knot.

"Heather is doing great. Should be ready to come home in a few days."

"Have you decided to keep her at home with you or is she going to Houston with your sister-in-law?"

"It was a tough choice for me. You better than most can appreciate the dilemma of a single parent. Heather will go to my sister-in-law's home when she leaves the hospital. She'll stay there in Houston for awhile. We'll see how it all works out."

"She will be fine," Cassy said, touching his sleeve gently. "And so will you."

"How about you and the Marquez incident. Anything new?"

"Nothing yet. But I found a couple of more people who believe that my theory of poisoning may have some merit," Cassy said.

Trent turned his head to stare at her. His forehead furrowed into a frown before he returned his attention back to the traffic on Preston Avenue. "Who else have you been talking to?" Trent asked brusquely.

"I visited with Dr. Betty Freeman, the Chief of Toxicology at the Department of Forensic Sciences of the Dallas Coroner's Office. Betty is my longtime friend. She also thinks Marquez could have been poisoned. And so does Lt. Kevin Knowland, the head of the Homicide Division at the Dallas Police Department."

"Better be careful, Cassy. You sound just like a second-year medical student, thinking up the exotic rare diseases to explain commonplace symptoms. To a second-year medical student, a diaper rash is meningococcal sepsis. A common cold is tuberculosis. A wart is a melanoma. You're talking like a medical student, calling Marquez's heart attack a poisoning despite his negative drug and poison screening tests."

"I'm entitled to my opinion even if you don't happen to agree with me, Professor Hendricks," Cassy said sarcastically.

Trent's ruddy face flushed a deep red. "You hear hoof beats in Texas, you're always going to find horses." He took his hand from the steering wheel and shook his index finger at her. "You just ain't gonna find a herd of exotic zebras when you hear hoof beats here in Texas. A middle-aged man having a cardiac arrest in Texas is a heart attack and not some goddamn wild-eyed poisoning victim."

Cassy found herself struggling to control her seething anger at Trent's pedantic outburst. "Trent, you of all people should understand. I have to find out what happened," she said. "It's the only way to restore my reputation . . . and my confidence in my ability."

"Cass," Trent said, reaching across to touch her arm. She pulled away to stare straight ahead out the windshield. "I'm the man who has supported you professionally throughout your surgical career, ever since you were a medical student. Listen to me now. Leave this Marquez thing alone. A month from now it will be forgotten."

"I'm sorry, Trent. I don't mean to be an ingrate, but I need to figure some things out, if for no other reason but myself."

Trent pulled the Mercedes across Preston Avenue and braked the car next to a guard booth in front of ten-foot iron gates barring a brick pillared entrance. The white brick wall supporting the iron gate continued around the perimeter of the corner estate.

"Good afternoon, Dr. Hendricks," said the guard, a young Hispanic in a khaki uniform. The butt of a pistol peeked from the leather flap of his hip holster. The iron gates swung silently open. Trent followed the winding concrete driveway through the immaculately landscaped property.

"Tenoch bought this property a couple of years ago," Trent said. "Some estimates are that he paid twenty-three million for the house and grounds. I'll bet he's dropped another five into refurbishing it."

"Five million? Twenty-three million?" Cassy asked. "What does he do to earn that kind of money?" She shook her head, slowly taking in the lavish grounds as Trent steered the car through a tunnel of foliage and under a canopy of elms. The Mercedes emerged from the shade of the overhanging trees to confront a three-story white mansion, enormous even by Texas standards.

The white tile roof and gleaming white stone mansion shimmered in the hot noon sun like a mirage of a Mediterranean villa. The elaborate colonnaded porticos on the front and sides of the house sat bare and sterile. The huge house was devoid of all color but sparkled in its absolute whiteness. Massive alabaster double doors extended to the top of the two-story porch. A full size replica of a twelve-foot Aztec stone calendar was carved into the front of the white wooden doors. The carving was precisely bisected by the opening in the door.

"This is bigger than the White House," Cassy said as Trent parked the car at the foot of the massive stairway that swept up to the second level porch.

"I believe that was Tenoch's intent," Trent said. "The view from the rear veranda across Turtle Creek is breathtaking. We may be having lunch there. It's my favorite spot for Tenoch's lunches."

A tuxedoed Hispanic butler opened the massive white doors at the top of the stairs and gestured them up with a deferential bow. "Welcome to Señor Tenoch's home," the butler said in English. "He will be with you soon."

Trent and Cassy were escorted through a marble hallway covered by a woven carpet runner. Aztec patterns and designs Cassy recalled from her visits to the National Anthropology Museum in Mexico City embellished the edge of the plush carpet. The long hallway was cordoned by Aztec statuary every few feet on both sides of the carpet that ran the length of the gleaming hallway floor. A glass facade formed the rear wall of the hall and diffused the afternoon sun through tinted glass into the hall. Through the glass wall, Cassy saw a blue canvas four-post tent covering the rear veranda.

"You will await Señor Tenoch in here, please," the butler said, ushering them into a lavish drawing room filled with glass-enclosed museum displays of sculptures, stone carvings, and a variety of early Mexican antiquities.

"My god," Cassy said. "This is like the National Museum in Mexico City. Tenoch's collection is overwhelming. It must be priceless. How in the world did he collect all these pieces." She peered at a polished black stone vase with the head of a grotesque man-animal creature carved into its side.

"Do you like it?" Señor Tenoch's voice boomed from beyond the doorway. "It's an obsidian vase. Carved from volcanic glass. It was excavated from an archeological dig near Mexico City last year. Almost certainly it was in use at the time of Montezuma."

At the doorway, Tenoch's body was backlighted by the diffused sunlight in the entry hallway. The flawless dark brown skin of his face was framed by his perfectly placed anthracite hair. A long sleeve, white silk shirt covered his muscular chest. His high cheekbone structure offset a prominent but proportioned nose. His eyes shone, unblinking and dark. The pupillary opening of his eyes merged into the dark color of the iris, seeming to form a dense black hole in the center of an eyeball so white that it was virtually translucent.

"Trent. Buenos días. Dr. Baldwin, it is my pleasure to welcome you to my home. Mi casa es su casa," Tenoch said as he walked directly toward Cassy. "Thank you so much for your efforts on Saturday evening with Jeorg Marquez," Tenoch said, taking her hand in both his soft delicate hands in a clasp rather than a handshake. It was as if he had touched her with an electrical charge, her right arm tingled to the shoulder.

"You are most gracious, Señor Tenoch."

"Please, let's leave off the Señor," Tenoch said, smiling at Cassy.

"And what would you prefer?" Cassy smiled politely.

"Just call me Tenoch."

"You do not like your first name?"

"I have none."

"But your business card says H. Tenoch. What is the H?"

"Just Tenoch, if you will."

"Certainly. But please call me Cassy."

"It would be my pleasure. Cassandra Marta, is it not?" Tenoch asked. "An unusual combination of names . . . a classical Greek name and a Spanish name."

"Yes, my name is a compromise," Cassy said. "My father loved the Greek classics. Mother was the daughter of parents whose families go back to earliest Mexico."

"Yes, I know your heritage is the same as mine . . . Aztec," Tenoch said. "But are you aware of the heritage that the name Cassandra carries?"

"Oh, yes, my father loved the irony in Greek classics," Cassy laughed. "Cassandra was the prophetess who could see future events but no one would believe her warnings."

"Have you ever had that burden of future sight?" Tenoch asked, quite seriously.

"Oh no," Cassy laughed. "Sometimes I wish I could see the future."

"I sure as hell wouldn't want to see the future," Trent said. "Unless I could see the future of the stock market."

"And Marta translates from the Spanish as lady," Tenoch said, ignoring Trent's comment. "A most appropriate name for a lovely lady." He paused for a moment and then added, "Trent tells me that you were his best student and most skilled colleague."

"Thank you, Tenoch," Cassy said, her face coloring at the compliment.

"Shall we sit outside, my friends?" Tenoch nodded toward the veranda door. "May I offer you a drink?" Tenoch asked as the three waiters seated each of them at a table on the veranda under the enormous blue tent. The landscaped yard flowed for acres beyond the elevated veranda.

"Iced tea for me," Cassy said.

"I am afraid I only have ordinary tea to offer today. Whenever we are in Mexico City together you will taste my finest blends. I import them from Guatemala and Korea."

Cassy nodded. "American tea is just fine for me."

"Bloody Mary," Trent said to the waiter.

The butler returned with a gold tray and three crystal glasses. Tenoch accepted his crystal glass of water and nodded. "To a mutually satisfying relationship." They toasted each other, the touch of their glass rims producing a faint chime magnified under the enclosed four-poster canvas canopy. Refrigerated air wafted around the open tent from ductwork concealed behind banks of flowers, chilling the tent comfortably against the noon heat.

The black smooth stone in the simple gold ring on Tenoch's left index finger focused on Cassy as their two glasses touched across the table.

"After lunch, I will give you a tour of my Aztec collection, but now our meal is ready." He signaled his hand casually toward the veranda door. Three Hispanic waiters instantly appeared, each with a crystal bowl of gazpacho, a thick spicy tomato soup set in an outer crystal bowl of cracked ice.

"Enjoy," Tenoch said in Spanish, lifting a large spoonful to his mouth. After savoring the taste as if the soup were a fine wine, he turned to Cassy. "I am most impressed with you . . . beautiful woman, outstanding surgeon, caring mother, charming lady."

"I appreciate your compliments. For a moment I thought I was hearing my eulogy," Cassy said, blushing and trying to lighten the mood. Trent did not lift his head from his soup as he ate slowly. "Thank you again, Tenoch," Cassy said.

"My thoughts precisely, Tenoch," Trent said, lifting his head and smiling across at Cassy.

"You have roots in Mexico. That has great meaning for me, Cassy." Tenoch brushed by Trent's compliment.

"You've obviously done your homework about me," Cassy said. "I was an only child, born to my parents fairly late . . . both were in their late thirties when I came along."

"Your age now," Tenoch said, smiling pleasantly as he sipped at his mineral water.

"Yes, I hadn't thought of my parents in that way . . . Mother devoted herself to me, giving up a career as a dancer with the Ballet Folklorico de Mexico."

"I can see the dancer in you, Cassy, the way you move and hold yourself erect," Tenoch said.

Cassy blushed again and took a spoonful of the gazpacho before replying, "Oh yes, Mother had me in dancing class soon after I was walking."

"I've seen Cassy in action," Trent said. "Not on stage, but at the yearly hospital dinner dance. She could have been, or still could be, a dancer anywhere if that's what she wants."

"Dad was a career diplomat with the State Department. That's how Mother and Dad met . . . when he was assigned as Deputy Chief of Mission to the U.S. Embassy in Mexico City," Cassy said, wanting to shift the conversation away from herself.

"I am truly sorry about the death of your mother and father in the Mexico City earthquake of 1985."

"Their bodies were never recovered, buried under their collapsed apartment hotel," Cassy said. An uncomfortable pause filled the tent. "I only wish my parents could have known Alex."

"I'm sorry," Tenoch said gently and waited for a moment before continuing, "I admire the work you have done to establish the international children's foundation in their memory." Tenoch's thumb rolled the gold ring with the polished black stone around his index finger. "You have served your Aztec ancestors well."

"I told Tenoch about the Am-Mex Children's Foundation . . . how you set it up, organized it, raised all the money, and have operated on all those Mexican kid's hearts right here at the Metro."

"It's not just me. Many, many other people have contributed time, money, and their energy."

"But without you and your effort, nothing would have taken place. Those Mexican kids would never have had a chance," Trent said.

"Did Trent tell you about my ideas for you in Mexico City?"

"Yes, he described a few of the ideas you have for a heart surgery program in Mexico City. But I must tell you right up front that I could not consider leaving Dallas for Mexico City now."

"Perhaps the time has come for you to return to Mexico City," Trent said softly.

"My ex-husband has given me the same advice several times," Cassy said, a sarcastic tone slipping into her voice. She immediately regretted her unexpected harshness.

"Ah, yes, Scott Spence is a very capable man," Tenoch said. "Successful. Ambitious. No doubt Texas needs a man of his ability in the governor's house. Let us hope certain financial dealings related to the sale of his CompuTeen computer company do not become public information."

Cassy pulled the linen napkin to her lips like a veil. How did he find out about the sale of the company? she asked herself. My god, he surely doesn't know about the three million dollars.

As if reading her thoughts, Tenoch continued, "Certain monies related to the sale of your CompuTeen Company found their way to the Cayman Islands three years ago. There is also a splendid beach front home that goes with the bank account at the Caymanian Bank. Both can be traced directly to you and your ex-husband. It is a political bomb which could kill your ex-husband's political career."

"Señor Tenoch, my life is private and absolutely none of your business. I resent your snooping around in my life." Cassy turned to Trent. "What the hell is this luncheon all about? I came here as a favor to you. I feel like I'm at the Spanish Inquisition," Cassy said, glaring across the centerpiece of fresh roses on the elaborate table.

"Cassy, please . . . ," Trent said quietly.

"Perhaps you should consider my employment proposal before you become so overwrought, my dear," Tenoch said agreeably. "Your nine thousand dollar monthly mortgage on your million dollar home is two months overdue. The eighteen thousand dollar private school tuition for Alex's next term is overdue. Lupita, your nanny, costs you over twenty thousand dollars each year. There are the counseling fees for Alex's therapy sessions. My dear, you are nearly bankrupt. You have no job. Your ex-husband controls the Cayman account. Your financial options are quite limited."

Cassy pushed her chair from the table and leaned back, crossing her legs. She clasped her hands lightly on her knee and studied her navy suede pumps. The refrigerated air from the air conditioning units flooded the blue square canvas tent, uncomfortably chilling her. Cassy fought to order her thoughts and control her anger. "All right. Tenoch. What is this all about?" she asked, her eyes searching his face.

Tenoch smiled at her and turned to the doorway of the veranda, raising his eyebrow slightly. The butler appeared instantly at his side. "Bring us the 1990 chardonnay from my vineyard."

Silence filled the tent. Moments later, the butler returned with a chilled bottle of wine and expertly uncorked the bottle, filling the crystal glass in front of Tenoch with a small splash of the faintly yellow wine. Standing at Tenoch's side like a sommelier, he waited for Tenoch's smiling approval before filling all three glasses. Then he placed the wine in a gold pedestaled ice container. Tenoch lifted his glass and said, "I propose a toast."

Trent quickly raised his wine glass. Cassy reluctantly held hers up until the three crystal glasses tinged together. "To our destinies," Tenoch said and sipped very little from his glass. As he set the glass down, he steepled his hands under his chin and leaned forward toward Cassy.

"I did not intend any offense, Dr. Baldwin," Tenoch said pleasantly. "If I did offend you by my inquiries into your life, you have my apologies."

Cassy peered at the attractive man who studied her so intently. The gracious apology only slightly blunted her fury.

"Apology accepted," Cassy said stiffly. "Perhaps, you could begin again by answering my questions. What do you want from me? What do I possibly have to offer you?"

"Certainly, Cassy," Tenoch said. Cassy noticed that he had reverted again to her nickname. "But first, let me tell you about myself. I've inquired about your background, I will admit. It's only fair that you know about my private life. I'll sketch my life for you. I have nothing to hide. You see, I am a child of the Mexico City ghettos and slums. The poorest of the poor. I have no family. My mother is unknown. She must have not even known my father. In truth, I am an unknown. The Catholic sisters found me when I was only a few days old on the steps of their orphanage in Mexico City. I stayed with them until I was twelve."

"Were you not put up for adoption?" Cassy asked.

"Nobody wanted me. I was labeled as mentally retarded. I did not talk until I was six years old. I stayed at the orphanage until it burned when I was twelve years old. The cause of the fire was never known. The Catholic sisters never were able to rebuild it. Last year, over thirty years after the fire, I rebuilt the orphanage for them on the same street in Mexico City. It was a repayment of my debt to the Church for taking care of me for the first twelve years of my life," Tenoch said and smiled flatly. His black eyes focused on the distant sweep of his estate grounds. "My life in some ways began with the fire. I have lived on the street ever since. The street has educated me and rewarded my efforts. Today my private business enterprises would rank my personal financial worth among the Fortune 100 companies."

Cassy shifted uncomfortably in her chair.

"The secret of my success is to recognize talent and to recognize opportunities. In you I recognize talent . . . and beauty . . . and opportunity." Cassy did not allow her face to acknowledge the compliment.

"Medicine has rewarded me handsomely. I have made a great deal of money investing in the miracles of modern medicine before the treatments and new drugs became known as miracles." Cassy sipped nervously at her wine, drinking nearly half the glass in several small sips.

"I have had no formal education beyond what the good Catholic sisters taught me before the orphanage burned. Given the opportunity of a formal education, perhaps I might have become a doctor . . . perhaps a heart surgeon such as yourself."

"I can tell you, Cass, he's the quickest student of medicine I've ever known. He knows more medicine than most of our surgical residents," Trent said.

"Please, please . . . ," Tenoch said, waving his hand modestly. "Where you have used your talents to serve patients, I have used my talents to seize financial opportunities . . . to make a personal fortune."

"And you've been most generous in sharing your wealth, for example to the Metro Hospital and to the Instituto de Medico," Trent said.

Tenoch cut him off and spoke directly to Cassy, "I now recognize the commercial possibilities in human organ transplantation just as I have recognized other profit opportunities in medicine. Twenty-five thousand people are awaiting organs for transplantation in the United States, and most would be quite willing to pay a fee to facilitate the acquisition of the donor organ they need."

Tenoch stopped to sip at his crystal glass of water and smiled at Cassy. She sat stoic without responding. "Cassy, the shortage of organ donors is extreme. Here is a chance for us to do something in Mexico and in the

United States and around the world to help people who will die without an organ transplant. Working together we can solve that organ shortage."

"How do you plan to solve this organ shortage? You can't just open a market for organ shoppers to buy a heart, a kidney, or a cornea."

"The shortage of organs for transplantation is a function of supply and demand . . . just like any other commodity in the marketplace."

"But to buy and sell organs? It's completely unethical," Cassy said. "Surely you don't mean establishing a commercial market for human organs for transplantation."

"Most prefer the term 'rewarded gifting'," Trent broke into her words. "A reasonable payment to the donor or the bereaved family for an organ that will be used for transplantation."

Cassy sat perplexed at Trent's acknowledgement of outright compensation for a donor organ. She was momentarily unable to respond to the idea of commercializing organ donation. Finally she said to Trent, "You can't be serious. Paying for an organ?"

"Is it different from selling blood? Is it different from selling sperm or a human egg?" Tenoch asked, jumping ahead of Trent's response. "Tell me how it's different from a fee paid for an adoption?"

"Well, for one thing, our laws specifically prohibit buying and selling organs," Cassy said. "It's illegal."

"Who should judge whether a financial incentive for organ donation is illegal or immoral?" Tenoch asked.

"Organ donation is a social issue," Cassy said. "It's a moral question and a financial opportunity. Should our society allow its citizens to sell their own organs or the organs of their dead relatives just because they need the money someone might pay for those hearts, livers, corneas, or kidneys?" She looked toward Trent, searching his face for some support for her position in the philosophical debate. "Trent, I remember one of your medical school lectures on organ transplantation. You talked about the greatest gift . . . the gift of life that one bestows with organ donation . . . you compared it to giving birth. I remember you said it was the only way a man could give birth . . . to give life to another. Now you are agreeing with Tenoch that this gift should be rewarded? You're not being consistent."

Before Trent could respond Tenoch said, "You misunderstand my purpose in this international organ donation program. I will simply facilitate the availability of organs for transplantation. It is not buying and selling of organs. Of course, each person who receives an organ transplant will make a financial contribution to my foundation."

"What's the difference?" Cassy asked. "You're receiving money in return for the organ."

"That is the spirit of my plan, Cassy. Everyone who receives an organ from my program must contribute something, whether it is one dollar, one hundred pesos, or one million dollars. Each organ transaction will generate operational funds so that I can make the donor organs more readily available to all. From each according to his need, to each according to his ability," Tenoch said. A smile played on his lips.

"That Marxist comment is odd from you . . . the most successful capitalist in Texas and Mexico," Cassy said.

"You forget your history, Cassy," Tenoch said, smiling broadly. "Trotsky was a favorite son of Mexico and lived in Mexico after leaving Russia. In many ways, I am advocating certain socialist principles be applied in an egalitarian manner for organs for transplantation, so that all can receive the miracle of organ transplants in a timely and efficient manner."

"Everyone will have equal access to donor organs . . . no matter the patient's ability to pay?" Cassy asked. She twisted the stem of her wine glass and held Tenoch's steady gaze.

"Most certainly," Tenoch said. "The donor organs will be allotted based on need and not on the basis of the amount of the recipient's donation."

"Trent and I both know patients can often wait years for an organ," Cassy said.

"For many patients in need of a transplant organ, their underlying disease progresses to the point they are nearly dead . . . like Heather almost died," Trent said as he lifted his wine glass to his lips before continuing. "Many, many do die, waiting for an organ that never becomes available."

"Under my plan, each operation will provide a financial incentive for organ donation. The available supply of donor organs will undoubtedly increase due to this financial incentive," Tenoch said. "This shortage of donor organs will surely respond to the law of market economics. There will no longer be the long lists of sick people waiting in line for a precious few organs. Thousands of people a year in the United States will no longer die waiting for organs for transplantation."

"You've already seen how Tenoch's plan can work to find a donor organ and save a life," Trent said.

Cassy looked at Trent inquiringly. "I don't understand."

"Tenoch's network of contacts in Mexico City found Heather's donor within a week of the time they were alerted. Without Tenoch's effort, I'm certain Heather would have died."

"I . . . I had no idea that you were responsible for finding Heather's heart," Cassy said. "Was Heather the first patient in your plan of rewarded gifting?" She looked back and forth between the two men, her brow furrowing in concentration and confusion.

Tenoch nodded. "Our experience with Heather's donor heart showed me the way I could build upon that success and exploit this organ donor crisis for the benefit of everyone."

"You didn't tell me anything about a financial incentive for the dead girl's family," Cassy said, looking directly at Trent.

"I couldn't explain everything at the time because we only had a few hours. I was afraid you might not do Heather's transplant."

"You're right," Cassy sighed. "I might not have."

"I'm sorry, Cass. It was the only way I thought I could handle the situation. I needed you to do Heather's transplant. Heather had waited so long."

"What's done's done," Cassy said. "I'm glad that Heather's well. We will always mourn for an organ donor under any circumstance."

"Thank you, Cass," Trent said, reaching across the corner of the table to touch her forearm.

Looking back to Tenoch, Cassy asked, "If Heather was the first in what you call your rewarded gifting program, who then provided the financial donation to your organization for Heather's heart?"

"I did," Trent said.

"May I ask how much?" Cassy asked.

"Five hundred thousand dollars."

"Is that the standard fee for a donor heart?" Cassy asked, taken aback by the size of the donation.

"To each according to his need and from each according to his ability," Tenoch said. "Trent is well able to afford the half million dollars."

"And how much of the half million dollars went to the family of the donor?"

"Ten thousand dollars," Tenoch said. "The balance goes to benefit more recipients . . . so that more donors can be facilitated."

"I don't know," Cassy said, shaking her head slowly. "This plan of rewarded gifting for organ donation gives me a lot of ethical concerns. I'll need some time to sort through them."

"Cass, it's a practical solution to a desperate shortage of organs," Trent said. "Both of us have seen too many patients die waiting for an organ that never became available. I was not going to let Heather die. . . ."

"I understand your argument, Trent, but I've got to have some time. I really can't think through this ethical dilemma right now."

"My concept of an international organ procurement program will solve the donor organ shortage," Tenoch said.

"I understand your objective, Tenoch," Cassy said. "But I don't see what you want of me as far as this transplant program is concerned."

"Trent tells me that you are the finest transplant surgeon in the United States."

"You flatter me. I can name several more qualified surgeons," Cassy said.

"Trent's endorsement of you is the only recommendation necessary," Tenoch said. "I am prepared to recommend you for the position of Surgeon-in-Chief at the Instituto de Medico in Mexico City."

"Tenoch's recommendation is all that is necessary for you to be appointed," Trent added.

Without acknowledging Trent's recognition of his power at the Instituto, Tenoch continued, "You would have full authority for organ procurement and transplantation in my cooperative program between Mexico City and Dallas. You would be headquartered in Mexico City, and Trent will remain here in Dallas to coordinate the recipient program."

Cassy shook her head and frowned. "I'm not. . . ."

"Listen to him. You need this," Trent said, leaning forward across the table.

Tenoch relaxed in his chair and steepled his fingers again in front of his chest. "I am prepared to double your current salary, or should I say former salary . . . to pay off your home mortgage, to provide complete tuition benefits for your son, to supply an appropriate home in Mexico City comparable to my home here," Tenoch said. "The unpleasantness arising out of the Marquez incident will disappear. I will see to that immediately. And a signing bonus of two hundred fifty thousand dollars today."

"I need to think about it," Cassy said, immediately shaking her head. She was staggered by the proposal.

"What's to think?" Trent said, throwing his hands up. "Tenoch just solved all of your problems."

"But my son . . . ," Cassy started to answer. She knew Trent was right. All her problems would be solved by Tenoch. But her rational mind required more time to consider the implications of taking Alex to Mexico City to live, much less to sort through the new ethical framework the two men had thrust at her.

"You will have more time than ever before to spend with your son," Tenoch said. "You will have a full medical and surgical staff to support you in your surgical work. For transportation you would have my private jet at your command to travel anywhere in the world at any time, as well as a full-time chauffeur."

Cassy thought for a moment, averting her eyes. "No, gentlemen. I appreciate your interest in me," she said. "I am quite honored, but my answer has to be no. I simply cannot make this type of professional commitment that will take me away from my son and from our home in Dallas."

"Cassy, what are your alternatives?" Trent asked.

"Let me suggest this, Cassy," Tenoch said. "Give yourself some time to consider my proposal. I can understand how you might view this as a radical change in your life. Perhaps you simply need time. Come see for yourself. I would like for you to be my guest in Mexico City this weekend," Tenoch said. "I will introduce you to my Mexico City. You would then be better able to decide your future destiny."

Looking away toward the lushly landscaped back vista leading to a stream at the edge of the property, Cassy tried to interpret her own thoughts. Finally she sighed and looked back. "I..I will think about it. I..I must think about it."

Trent pushed his chair back from the table and looked at his gold Rolex. "Well, if I can add anything, let me know. I must get back to the hospital. I can drop you off on the way."

"But, Trent," Tenoch said. "We've not had the main course . . . a wonderful fresh salmon that I had flown in this morning from Chile."

"I'm sorry, Tenoch, I have a surgery at three o'clock."

"I can drop you off on my way," Trent said, looking toward Cassy, still at the table.

Tenoch interrupted Trent. "I would like to show you the rest of my Aztec collection, Cassy. We could enjoy the salmon together."

"I really must get home," she smiled, standing up. "My son is waiting."

Tenoch stood up and took her hand, firmly raising it to his lips and kissing the back of her hand. "Please consider my proposal. I would be honored if you were my guest in Mexico City this weekend."

Cassy pulled her hand back. "I'll consider it and call you if I should change my mind. But now I really can't think any more about your plan. But I appreciate your offer."

With a slight gesture of his head, Tenoch summoned a Hispanic man from his position by the veranda door. "Alex's gift," Tenoch said. The man Cassy remembered from the night at the ER pulled a heavy parchment envelope from his inside coat pocket and presented it to her. "Please thank your son for sharing you with me today," Tenoch said.

Cassy nodded her thank you. After a moment more of pleasantries, she and Trent left Tenoch on the veranda.

While Trent walked around the rear of his car in Tenoch's driveway after opening the passenger door for Cassy, she peeked into the envelope that Tenoch had given Alex. Inside was a baseball card sheathed in a clear plastic envelope.

TWELVE

"A LEX, I'M HOME," Cassy shouted up the stairwell. There was no response. "Alex. Are you upstairs?"

"He's in his room," Lupita said as she swung into the hallway, wiping her hands on a kitchen towel.

"Did he eat lunch?"

"No, Señora," Lupita said. "He hasn't been out of his room since you left at noon."

Cassy tossed her jacket onto the hall tree and ran up the staircase to her son's room. At the closed door she knocked. There was no answer. Cassy recognized the computer sounds of a video game.

"I know you're in there, Alex. Open the door." She stood waiting at the door. Moments later the lock clicked open. Cassy opened the door only to see her son retreating to the chair in front of his Macintosh video monitor. After several moments in the doorway, Cassy asked, "Do you want to invite some friends over for a swim?"

"No! I'm going to play the computer games Dad gave me for my birthday," Alex said without turning his head.

At that moment the ring of his bedroom telephone interrupted. "For you, Dr. Baldwin," the housekeeper called on the telephone intercom that sounded by Alex's bedside.

Cassy picked up the receiver of the phone set next to Alex's computer. She stood beside her son, watching him peck at the keyboard and manipulate the computer mouse controlling the humanoid figures on the video screen.

"Dr. Baldwin, this is Winston Hamilton at the First Fidelity Mortgage Company. I'm sorry to bother you at home, but we have become concerned by your lack of mortgage payments on your home for the past three months. Have you not received the overdue notices?"

"I'm sorry, Mr. Hamilton, I must have misplaced them," Cassy said, feeling a familiar aching throb begin just above her eyes.

"Our records indicate that you need to make three payments of nine thousand seven hundred and sixteen dollars to bring your amortization payment schedule up to date along with the late penalty charges." The banker paused, cleared his throat with a rumble that rolled down the telephone line, and then asked, "Is it correct that you are now unemployed?"

Cassy turned away from Alex and tried to direct her voice so that he could not hear her side of the conversation. "Mr. Hamilton, I will get those mortgage payments to you this week."

"That will be fine, Doctor. The total will be twenty-nine thousand one hundred and forty-eight dollars plus the late penalty charges. Can I expect you to bring the funds into the office tomorrow?"

"No, it will be Friday," Cassy said, knowing that she had no idea where she could get thirty thousand dollars by Friday except from Señor Tenoch.

"That will be fine. I will expect you here on Friday." Again the man paused to clear his throat as if embarrassed to continue. "By the way, our records indicate that you have a two hundred thousand dollar second mortgage on your home with an annual payment of forty thousand dollars plus accrued interest due on July first."

"You must be mistaken. There was a two hundred thousand dollar mortgage on my home. My ex-husband paid it off as part of our divorce settlement," Cassy said and tried to keep the truculence from her voice.

"I'm afraid not, Dr. Baldwin. Your ex-husband has indeed made regular annual payments on your second mortgage. But your property is still subject to both mortgages. I will expect your husband, or you, to forward a payment for this second mortgage later this month."

"I will speak to my ex-husband about the mortgage. This is the first time I've heard about it not being paid off."

"Very well, Dr. Baldwin." The banker once again cleared his throat. "I will look forward to seeing you on Friday." Cassy hung up the receiver and turned back to face her son. Alex no longer studied the computer screen but looked directly at her when she turned back to him.

"What did you mean when you said you'd get the mortgage payments?"

"It's nothing to worry about, Alex," Cassy said. "I just forgot to send in the money for our house payment to the mortgage company this month."

"The television said you didn't have a job," Alex said.

"I'll not be working at the Metro hospital for a while, but we'll be just fine."

"Why aren't you going to work at the hospital?" Alex asked, now looking back at his video monitor.

"I had an argument with one of the doctors at the hospital."

"What about?"

"It's a complicated situation with one of the patients. The hospital director thought I should stay away from the hospital for awhile."

"When are you going back to work at the hospital?"

"I don't know. I may not be able to go back to Metro."

"Where are you going to work?" Alex persisted.

"I wish I knew," Cassy said. "At lunch today, Señor Tenoch offered me a job as a transplant surgeon in Mexico City."

"Like you were for Dr. Hendricks' daughter?"

"Yes."

"Would we live in Mexico City?"

"Yes. You'd like it there. It's where I lived when I was your age."

"If you go to Mexico City, can I stay here and live with Dad?"

"Like I told you earlier, Alex, I need you to live with me."

"If I didn't live with you, it would save money."

"We've got plenty of money," Cassy said, catching a hardness in her voice.

"You told Dad that you needed money. I heard you and Dad talking about money out on the patio. If we don't have money, will we have to move from this house?"

"We're not going to move," Cassy said. "This is our home. We'll be staying here."

———

The fading evening light in the backyard pitched shadows against the glass patio door as Cassy and Alex settled into their places at the table in the dining nook of the kitchen. Lupita set a steaming plate of tamales between them. Charlie sat expectantly in the corner of the family room. The spicy smell of the pork-filled tamales aroused him, and he sat vigilant in hopes of a dropped scrap or an offered tidbit from the table. Alex hunched over the tamales, poking at the desiccated, yellow cornmeal covering. The kitchen phone rang. Cassy leaned away from the table to pick up the wall receiver and felt her stomach ball when she heard Walter Simmons on the other end.

"Good evening, Cassandra," he said. "I'm sorry to trouble you this evening." His voice was so unctuous and greasy she wanted to scream. "I apologize if I have disturbed your dinner hour." Simmons paused, and Cassy knew that he was sipping from his usual evening bourbon glass. Probably his fourth whiskey. Get on with it, she thought.

"Please go ahead. You're not interrupting," Cassy said, wanting to hear whatever bad news it was sure to be and get the shock over.

"Cassandra, today my office received three inquiries for confirmation of narcotic prescriptions you have written recently."

"Perhaps, I'm missing something, Walter. What concerns you about my prescription writing?"

"All three prescriptions were for large numbers of Demerol tablets," Simmons said. "Each of the pharmacists thought your narcotic prescriptions were unusual. Each prescription you wrote was for one hundred Demerol tablets. I'm as puzzled as the three pharmacists about these three narcotic prescriptions. What patient would ever need a hundred narcotic tablets to have around his house?"

"Walter, this is crazy. I never prescribe Demerol tablets for outpatients. I always use codeine or one of the newer synthetic narcotics."

"It appears that you have written prescriptions for at least three hundred Demerol tablets in the past seventy-two hours. Who knows how many more of these prescriptions are floating around out there in the Dallas pharmacies."

"If my name is on those Demerol prescriptions, it has been forged," Cassy said. She got up to pace around the kitchen as far as the telephone cord would extend.

"And of course, you would never have sold a written prescription for Demerol?"

Cassy waited several seconds, trying unsuccessfully to control her anger before exploding. "Walter are you accusing me of dealing in drugs . . . of selling Demerol prescriptions?"

"Each of the three pharmacists who called today has compared your signature on the prescription with a file copy of your signature that we faxed to them. The signatures look just like yours. Hell, I'm no handwriting expert, but the signatures are yours."

"They can't be my signature," Cassy said. "The signatures have to be forgeries. You know that I would never do something like that."

"I hope so, Cassandra. As Medical Director at the Metro Hospital, I have no choice except to report this incident to the Texas Board of Medical Licensure and the Drug Enforcement Administration."

"Walter, would you just hold off calling them until I have a chance to talk to the pharmacists myself. I'm sure that there is a mistake, or even an outright forgery of my signature."

"I've already made the phone calls. I had no choice. You are aware of the criminal penalties associated with selling prescriptions of narcotics? Perhaps you should consider retaining a criminal lawyer?"

She was dazed, unable to speak, and stood in the kitchen with the phone to her ear, unable to move.

"Good evening, Cassy." The telephone connection buzzed in her ear like the aftershock of a pistol when Dr. Simmons abruptly hung up.

She stood still, staring unseeing out the kitchen window and across the pool and patio. What the hell is going on? she asked herself.

The administrative nightmare Simmons had unleashed on her would consume her for days as she tried to prove that the signatures on the narcotics were forgeries. The burden of proving these prescriptions were forgeries had now, with no compassion, shifted to her as a result of Walter Simmons' telephone call to the licensing authorities. Cassy turned back to the table and saw Alex leaning across his plate, still noodling the tamale about, not eating.

"Who was that?" he asked when Cassy slowly replaced the telephone.

"That was Dr. Simmons . . . about some hospital business," Cassy said absently.

"Are you going back to the hospital tonight?" Alex asked, finally looking up from the tamale he had been playing with.

"No, not tonight," Cassy said, returning to her chair at the table. The tamales were cold. She got up immediately and took both plates to the microwave to reheat them.

"Lupita's tamales are disgusting. Do you want something besides tamales?"

"Pizza," he said quickly.

"That's all you ever want. You're going to turn into a pizza!" Cassy smiled at the look of elation on his face at the mention of pizza. "Let me see what I can do." Cassy rummaged through the Sub-Zero freezer, pulling a frozen pizza from the lowest shelf. Cassy unsheathed the frozen disc of dough from its plastic shrink-wrap while Alex scraped the rewarmed tamales into Charlie's food dish. The dog wagged his tail and sniffed at the plate in front of him, then licked the tamales once and looked up at Alex, seeming to shake his head.

"Charlie won't eat the tamales either," Alex said with a grotesque expression of disgust.

"I'm not surprised," Cassy said. "Pitch them down the sink drain and run the disposal."

The grinding roar of the garbage disposal soon blotted out all other sound in the room. The dog barked above the grinding noise and sniffed at the door to the patio. He began scratching at the sill of the sliding French door. "Charlie wants out," Cassy shouted above the grinding disposal. Alex flipped off the garbage disposal. The kitchen plunged into silence except for the frenzied barking of Charlie at the patio door.

"What's the matter, Charlie?" Alex asked, standing by the barking dog and looking through the patio door at the shadowy yard in the dusk of early evening.

"Alex, let him outside. He probably smells the Williamsons' cat prowling outside again." Alex tugged the sliding glass panel aside. The dog streaked through the door the instant it was far enough along the track to squeeze through. "Come help me doctor up this pizza."

Cassy handed Alex a fist-size block of Parmesan cheese and the battery operated cheese shredder as soon as he returned to the kitchen island. The frozen pizza lay on the table top like an icy hubcap. "We'll fix up this pizza and have a proper meal."

No sooner had Alex started to spray the sprinkles of freshly cut Parmesan cheese onto the top of the frozen pizza than the clamor of Charlie's ferocious growling and barking stayed Cassy's hand from arranging the pepperoni slices onto the pizza. Charlie's growling bay poured into the kitchen from beyond the pool. Cassy knew immediately that Charlie had found more than the Williamsons' cat.

"Let's see what Charlie has cornered," Cassy said, stepping across the threshold of the patio door.

When she and Alex were outside on the patio, it was easy to tell that the barking frenzy came from the walkway around the far corner of the house. Just then, a woman's terrified voice bounced off the tiled walkway. Cassy broke into a run for the corner of the house.

"My god, that sounds like Gracie," Cassy shouted, pulling Alex after her toward the sounds of barking and the woman's terrified screams. "Down, Charlie!" Cassy yelled as they rounded the corner to find the black woman cowering against the wooden gate.

"Dr. Baldwin, don't let him bite me," Gracie cried out the instant Cassy cleared the cedar bush at the corner of the house.

Cassy again commanded in her best dog obedience school voice, "Down, Charlie! Down." Charlie stood planted in an attack stance less than three feet from Gracie's legs. Frothy white saliva drooled over Charlie's bared teeth. His savage growl rumbled in the narrow walkway.

"Stop it, Charlie, she's our friend," Cassy said. She grabbed his thick leather collar. The dog's growl subsided to a low, guttural whimper. "Alex, take Charlie back into the house." Her son grabbed the dog's collar from her and led the dog back into the family room.

"Dr. Baldwin, I'm sorry," the black woman said. She lowered her arms and adjusted the sweaty red, green, and yellow striped turban on her head.

A floral caftan clung like a wet tent over her body. "I didn't know about your guard dog."

"Why didn't you call on the intercom from the front gate?" Cassy asked as she led the woman around the corner of the house toward the patio. "You could have rung the intercom and saved yourself all this grief."

"I didn't want anyone to see me but you."

"How did you get past the driveway gate?" Cassy asked.

"I climbed over the brick wall. It was easy. The vines made good hand-holds."

"Why don't you call me on the telephone the next time you want to visit. I'll open the gate or meet you somewhere."

"Yes, Doctor," Gracie said, wiping the film of sweat away from her glistening face with the hem of her caftan.

"Come inside where it's cool. I'll get you some iced tea," Cassy said. On the way into the house, Cassy resolved to have the security alarm service install a perimeter security alarm. If Gracie could climb over the wall so easily, anyone could.

Cassy filled two large glasses with fresh tea that she had just brewed and added a scoopful of ice to each. "Would you stay for dinner?" Cassy asked nonchalantly. "We're having pizza."

"No. I must go soon," Gracie said, looking nervously about the empty family room. Alex had taken Charlie to his room, and the sounds of the computer video games rattled in the distance. Gracie turned to Cassy, her trembling hands wiping away the sweat from her upper lip despite the refrigerated chill of the family room. "You must leave. Señor Marquez is dead."

"What are you talking about?" Cassy asked, startled by the statement of Marquez's death and wondering if Gracie had completely decompensated. "At lunch today I heard Marquez was fine. He is almost ready to leave the hospital. How can he be dead?"

"He was killed this evening," Gracie said, shaking her head and fidgeting with her turban.

"How?" Cassy asked and sank into the sofa.

Gracie's voice was agitated and panicky. "They say he jumped from his window. I know they threw him out the hospital window."

"Gracie. Stop. Slow down. You're confusing me," Cassy said.

"There are evil spirits at the hospital," Gracie said, her voice rapid and her breathing hard.

"When did he jump out the window?" Cassy asked, still skeptical.

"Two . . . three hours," Gracie said. "The spirits threw him out the window."

"How do you know he was thrown?"

"I know. There are evil spirits at the hospital," Gracie said and would say no more. She barely moved on the sofa. After a long while she drank all her iced tea quickly.

"I'm sure that we will eventually find a perfectly logical explanation for Marquez's resurrection on Saturday evening. He probably never was dead," Cassy said. Her mind raced ahead trying to connect the news of Marquez's death to the Saturday night incident.

"He was dead Saturday night," Gracie said flatly. "You and I both saw him dead. He was dead."

"But Marquez remembers me saying, 'Lets call the time of death 19:45'."

"The hougan caused it," the black woman said. Sweat poured from her face despite the coolness of the air-conditioned family room. Terror agitated her eyes.

"What? A hougan?"

"A voodoo priest," Gracie said, standing up abruptly.

"Gracie, let me get you some help," Cassy said.

"No. I must leave now."

"But let me drive you to the hospital. You need some attention. You're about to come apart."

"No," Gracie said. "I leave now. You and Alex must leave, too. It's dangerous to be near the hospital. There are evil spirits there."

Gracie started toward the patio door. Cassy caught her by the arm and stopped. "Please stay."

"No. I go. They must not find me, or I will die, too. Dr. Baldwin, take your son and leave before it's too late for you both." Gracie opened the sliding patio door and was most of the way through the door before Cassy was able to pull her back.

"If you must leave, come this way through the front door," Cassy said, escorting her to the entry foyer.

"Leave now. The evil spirits are loose," Gracie said. The black woman stood under the porte cochere like a terrified animal and grabbed Cassy's arm, mumbling several unintelligible words. Haitian words, thought Cassy until she made out the words, 'He is evil,' so clearly that Gracie could have shouted the words at her. Gracie broke away and ran down the long curving front driveway. Cassy punched in the security code on the keypad in the foyer to open the distant driveway gate for her. The last image Cassy had of Gracie was the flash of her floral caftan under the gatepost light as the woman turned at the end of the driveway, running down the street in the dying dusk.

Cassy stood in the foyer trying to calm herself. Marquez dead? Thrown from the window? The forged prescriptions for Demerol with her signature? She turned to see her son and Charlie standing at the top of the stairway.

"Is Marquez the man who died and came back to life?" Alex asked.

"How did you know?" Cassy asked.

"I heard what the woman said . . . he fell out the hospital window tonight and died." Looking up at her son, her shame was instant. I should have talked to Alex right after the Saturday incident, she told herself. If I want Alex to respond to me like an adult, then I'm going to have to treat him as an adult. But for god's sake, he's only eight years old.

"Alex, I'm sorry that I didn't tell you the whole story about Señor Marquez and what happened to him at the hospital on Saturday as well as tonight. But I'm still pretty upset about it all. Come on down. I'll tell you everything I know," Cassy said, looking up to the balcony railing where Alex and Charlie stood. "Come on down here. Let's talk." While the pizza finished cooking, she recounted the events of Saturday night including her idea about poisoning as a possible cause of Marquez's seeming death and revival.

"But why is he dead now?" Alex asked.

"Gracie says somebody threw him out the hospital window."

"Why did they throw him out the window?" Alex asked. The literalness of her son's mind always surprised her. He invariably jumped to the core of every conversation.

"I don't know if someone threw him or not. He could have been confused, afraid, or mentally disturbed."

"What did the woman mean when she said there are evil spirits there?" Alex asked. "Did she mean the devil?"

"You've been eavesdropping again, haven't you?"

Alex smiled and turned the oven light on, studying the baking pizza and ignoring her question. Cassy knew he would not forget his question about evil at the hospital. Cassy was not going to sidestep the question.

"Gracie is a nurse in the Emergency Room, hon. She's from Haiti and she's very superstitious. Gracie believes in a lot of strange things. Maybe she even sees ghosts sometimes."

"Like Halloween."

"Sort of. Yeah, like Halloween," Cassy said, hoping the explanation was enough for her son and wishing that the real answers would be that simple.

After eating the pepperoni pizza at the kitchen table, Cassy retreated to her desk in the bedroom and found Kevin Knowland by dialing the Homicide Department telephone operator.

"Hello, Dr. Baldwin. I was going to call you later this evening about some developments in the Marquez case." Cassy knew what his next words would be. "Señor Jeorg Marquez died this evening."

"I know," Cassy said. "He jumped or was thrown from his hospital room."

"How do you know about his death?" the lieutenant asked. "I'm standing at the scene right now, talking to you on my cellular telephone. We've not released his name or any information to the media yet."

"Gracie, the Haitian ER nurse from the Metro ER, came by to see me. She told me."

"She knows more than I do then," Kevin Knowland said. "Did she say who might have thrown this two hundred and fifty pound man out the fifth floor window?"

"No, but she's terrified and ran out of my house, telling me that my son and I are in danger from the evil spirits at the Metro Hospital."

"I don't think so," Kevin Knowland said, his sigh of aggravation audible through the scratchy cellular phone connection. "There's always a lot of hysteria after one of these dives. Right now, I don't know if it's suicide or murder. We're going to list the death as suicide for right now even though there was no suicide note and the hospital room wasn't locked."

"What does that mean?" Cassy asked.

"A suicide note is just that . . . a premortem statement of the dead person's intent to kill himself," Kevin said as if lecturing to a police recruits' class.

"What about the unlocked room?" Cassy asked, understanding the obvious importance of a suicide note but not able to pick up on the significance of an unlocked room.

"The fact that the room was not locked from the inside is obviously very important. The killer, if there is one, could have left the room after tossing Marquez out the window. But it would be near impossible for a murderer to lock the door from the inside and then leave the hospital room."

"Seems a fairly obvious distinction now that you explain it. What do you think really happened, lieutenant?"

"I don't know at this point. We're going to investigate this death in great detail. Every suicide gets a lot of our attention. Sometime soon you will need to give us a formal type statement about the conversation you had with Marquez Sunday night," Kevin Knowland said, evading her question. "What again was it he told you?"

"He told me that someone was trying to kill him," Cassy said.

"There was something else he said . . . ?" the lieutenant asked.

"Yes there was something else. . . ."

"Well . . . ?" the lieutenant asked and waited patiently.

Cassy finally said, "Estoy muerto . . . that's Spanish for 'I am dead'."

THIRTEEN

C ASSY NEVER dropped into deep sleep but woke every hour as if a lingering presence in her bedroom set off her internal biologic alarms. In the predawn silence of the frigid room she squirmed under the rumpled sheets just before the door to her bedroom creaked open. The beam of hallway light struck her face like a searchlight causing her to roll away from its brightness. Charlie lifted his head from his place at the foot of the king-size bed but did not move as a diminutive human form eased into the room. The dog's tail alerted upright and wagged at the sound of footsteps closing on the bed.

"Sh!" Alex said to the dog as he crept up to his mother's bedside. "Mom. Are you awake? Mom," he said and touched her face again.

Shaking her head and blinking her eyes, Cassy forced the fuzziness from her mind and recognized her son's form.

"Alex, what's wrong? What are you doing up at this hour?"

"I couldn't sleep."

"Another bad dream?"

Alex nodded.

"Sit up here, hon, and let's talk," Cassy said, patting the bed next to her as she pulled herself upright against the headboard.

Alex and the German shepherd leaped across her and onto the bed. The intensity of emotion she often felt for her only child overwhelmed her as she sat silently in the early morning quietness of the bedroom cradling him to her side.

The powerful feeling for her son was often triggered in ways she never understood but felt so potently—the smell of his hair, the touch of his hand, the voice that she knew better than her own, his brown eyes that danced with mischief, the feel of his arms in a hug. She knew every day of the past year that her decision to rearrange her professional life had not been a conscious decision but a decision that was born of her deeply felt bond with her son and her need to be with him at this time in his life and in her life.

The bedside clock radio alarm shattered the moment with the sounds of a familiar piano concerto filling the room. Cassy listened for a few moments trying to identify the composer but could not.

"It's time for me to get up," Cassy said, pinching her son's nose playfully. "You try to sleep for awhile. I'll make us breakfast." She slipped out of the bed. Charlie stretched at her side in anticipation of the ritual of his morning run for the newspaper. "What would you like?"

"Pizza," the boy said without hesitation.

"You're going to turn into a pizza. How about some hot chocolate and toast and jelly?" Cassy was not certain about Alex's fixation on pizza. This pizza preference which Cassy had at first worried might even be a form of an eating disorder had begun over a year ago. Alex's psychiatrist suggested that the pizza preference, as he euphemistically termed it, could be Alex's effort to exert some control over his life. Cassy realized that the theory did seem reasonable especially in the turmoil of the divorce. Certainly little else in Alex's life was under his control. At least he could choose what he would and would not eat. The doctor had reassured Cassy, but her motherly concern would not be denied when she realized Alex was eating pepperoni pizzas for almost every meal.

Alex lay sprawled in the king-size bed and did not acknowledge her counter-offer for breakfast.

"How about the hot chocolate and toast?" she asked again.

"Okay," Alex said reluctantly.

"Stay right here. I'll bring you breakfast in bed." Alex slid the sheet up about his neck. Cassy leaned down to kiss his forehead at the same time she pulled a robe over the SMU T-shirt that served as her nightgown.

Charlie followed her into the hallway leading to the entry foyer, then darted through the front door as soon as she twisted the dead bolt and cracked it open. The driveway was still wet from the fading night moisture and the early morning lawn sprinklers. The paw prints Charlie left on the wet tile brick driveway swerved like a coiled dotted line toward the security gate at the end of the driveway and back. Standing under the porte cochere where Charlie dropped the newspaper, she ripped the plastic sleeve off the rolled paper, looking for the article on Marquez's death.

Just under the front page center crease, a portrait of Marquez, dressed in a tuxedo, smiled at her. What did you know, Señor? thought Cassy as she read:

METRO HOSPITAL DEATH
SURVIVOR DIES IN FALL
Police List Suicide as Cause

by William Harris,
Staff Writer, The Dallas Morning News

Jeorg Marquez, 55, a patient at the Dallas Metropolitan Hospital, fell to his death last evening at approximately 6:00 p.m. from his fifth floor hospital room. Dallas Homicide officials have listed the cause of death as suicide. Marquez, owner of the Park Haven Funeral Home, survived an apparent near-death experience Saturday evening when he was declared dead in the Emergency Room of the Metropolitan Hospital, only to revive three hours later in the hospital's morgue.

Dr. Walter Simmons, Medical Director of Metropolitan Hospital, in a written statement released Wednesday evening said, "The tragic death of Jeorg Marquez saddens us all at Metropolitan Hospital. Our sympathy extends to his family and loved ones."

Dr. Cassandra Baldwin-Spence, the Metro ER physician who treated Marquez Saturday evening, could not be reached for comment. Dr. Baldwin-Spence was suspended from the Metro Hospital staff on Saturday evening following her erroneous diagnosis of Marquez's death. It is unknown whether the suicide was related to Saturday night's near-death experience. No hospital officials were available for comment. . . .

Dr. Baldwin-Spence retired from her position of Cardiac Surgeon at Metro Hospital last year. Sources close to the hospital administration attribute her withdrawal from cardiac surgery early in her career to personal and family reasons. She and Scott Spence Jr., Republican candidate for the Texas governorship in this fall's election, were divorced three years ago. Dr. Baldwin-Spence is best known for her international cardiac surgical program, the Am-Mex Children's Foundation, which has enabled hundreds of children from Mexico to undergo complex heart surgery at the Metro Hospital.

As Cassy folded the paper and looked up over the front yard, a black and white Dallas squad car rolled up and stopped outside the driveway gate. Charlie leaped from her side and raced in a frenzy of barking the two hundred feet to the gate. The uniformed policeman standing outside the metal bars of the gate beside his squad car ignored Charlie.

"What seems to be the trouble, officer?" Cassy asked as she approached the gate. "Charlie, down." She seized the dog's collar and pulled him away from the closed gate.

"Everything all right, Dr. Baldwin?"

"Just fine, officer," Cassy said as she reached through the bars of the gate to shake the officer's hand. "Why are you asking? What's happened?"

"Lt. Knowland told us to drive by here during the night. We've just been cruising by every hour or so, checking on your house. Everything's looked quiet."

"Why? He said nothing to me last night when I talked to him."

"I don't know, ma'am," the policeman said deferentially. "He just told us to make the squad car and ourselves a visible presence in your neighborhood."

"I appreciate your attention, officer. Everything is fine."

The policeman nodded and got back in the car. Cassy walked back up the driveway. Charlie scurried through the landscaped front yard, continuing his routine morning circuit around the yard.

Knowland must know more about Marquez's death than he is telling me, Cassy thought as she walked under the porte cochere. If he's ordering police surveillance of my home either I'm a suspect or I'm in real danger. Cassy closed the door behind herself and locked the triple bolt mechanism on the entry door, her mind racing into an unsettled anxiety.

She threw the front section of newspaper into the trash compactor, activating the masher mechanism. Cassy did not want Alex seeing Marquez's picture and reading the detailed description of the incident that was in the lengthy front-page article.

Cassy fixed hot chocolate, coffee, and sour dough toast with orange marmalade. It would be at least eight o'clock before Lupita left her room. Breakfast was not one of the meals that she deigned to fix for them. Cassy felt relieved not to have to see the woman at that early hour and was delighted to be alone with her son. She placed the sports section of the morning's newspaper on the wooden serving tray loaded with their breakfast and carried the tray to her bedroom down the first floor hallway.

Cassy smiled at her son, peacefully sleeping on her side of the king-size bed. Charlie curled himself on the opposite side of the bed, eyeing her as she moved into the room, hoping that Cassy had brought him breakfast in bed too. "Get off the bed, Charlie," Cassy said sharply. "You know better." Alex's eyes popped open at the sound of Cassy's stern voice. The dog dragged himself over the end of the bed with his tail tucked low.

Alex propped himself against the headboard as his mother shoved the tray between them and sat with her feet and legs crossed Indian style on the bed. The steaming cups of coffee and chocolate filled the room with a sweet, heady aroma. Charlie laid his head on the edge of the bed, a for-lorn look on his face, in search of a treat from the breakfast tray. Cassy spread the orange marmalade onto the thick pieces of toast while Alex hunched over the sports section of the newspaper, studying the baseball scores like an accountant. Charlie received a square of dry toast for his begging and gobbled it in one bite.

Cassy held the marmalade toast in her fingers and passed it to Alex. "Alex, we need to go on a vacation."

"Okay," he said, chewing on the toast and not taking his eyes off the paper.

"And I may have to go on a trip to Mexico City this weekend. Okay?" Cassy asked, testing her son's reaction to the idea of her being away from him for at least two nights.

Alex's dark eyes fixed on her. "Are we moving to Mexico City?"

"Not now," Cassy said. "But I have to think about the possibility that we might have to live somewhere besides Dallas for me to find a job." After handing Alex the last piece of toast, she slid the wooden serving tray to the end of the bed and went to the closet in her dressing room while Alex continued studying the sports section.

Above the clothes rack filled with her collection of tailored dresses and business suits, stacks of shoe boxes, three deep, filled the shelves. From beneath the end stack, Cassy slipped a faded leather album, its front cover tooled and embossed in a leather carving of an Aztec pictograph resembling a manlike serpent.

Cassy slid back in bed next to Alex who still was studying the sports section. "Let me show you the Mexico City I knew."

"I've seen that," Alex said, glancing up from the newspaper and showing no interest in the prospect of looking at family pictures again.

Cassy opened the album and for several minutes she flipped through the pages that compressed eighteen years of her life into an inch-thick photo album—the dance recitals, the senior class group picture, the girls' slumber parties, the snapshots of a teenage Cassy standing in front of a white-walled, orange-tiled-roof mansion—the remnants of a life past.

"Show me Grandmother and Granddad," Alex finally said as he pitched the sports page aside and peeked beneath the pages that Cassy studied. Alex's hand stopped her page turning and pointed to a picture of a seri-ous much younger Cassy standing before a lectern—a snapshot taken from the graduation audience of the preparatory school in Mexico City. "Is that you, Mom?"

"Twenty years ago. I was the valedictorian of my high school class in Mexico City." Cassy's hand hesitated on the page before turning.

"There they are," Alex said quickly as the page flipped to a picture of a middle-aged couple standing before the open door of the massive double entry of an impressive Mexican villa. Their smiles and waving hands were frozen in time nearly twenty years ago. Cassy remembered the picture well. It was the morning that she left Mexico City for Dallas to attend SMU.

Her parents were so alike in many ways—tall, physically attractive, intelligent, caring, and sensitive but differing in just as many ways. He was a scholar but an outgoing and gregarious man who thrived on the energy of the diplomatic affairs of the embassy. Her mother was quiet, nearly an introvert, but whose energy and personality bloomed on the dance floor.

Cassy knew she was a blend of the two, even down to the tawny coloring of her smooth skin. Her father's fairness had diluted her mother's smooth copper-bronze skin to produce the soft creamy coloring of Cassy's face. She was able to see the same coloring in Alex's complexion.

Cassy stared at the pictures. God, I miss them so much. Still after all these years. If only I could talk to them. Dad would know what to do and Mom would know just what to say to quiet my worries today.

"I don't want to go to Mexico City," Alex said abruptly and turned his attention back to his newspaper.

"There might not be any choice for us," Cassy said as she closed the album and stood up.

"I could live with Dad," Alex said without looking up from the newspaper.

Cassy clenched her teeth and slowly counted to five. The urge to retort with a quick cutting remark nearly overwhelmed her, but she knew she would immediately regret it. Cassy had fallen before to Alex's taunting with his not-so-subtle reminders of her failed marriage. She had resolved on several prior occasions not to let him bait her again. Without saying a word in response to Alex's verbal jab, Cassy picked up the serving tray and left the bedroom leaving Alex on her bed with the sports page.

It was just before eight o'clock when she settled onto the sofa in the family room with her third cup of coffee. The desire for a cigarette was close to overpowering as she worried through the realization of the police cruiser driving by her house every hour during the night and the implications for their safety it aroused. Finally she grabbed the phone and called Lt. Knowland.

"I didn't realize my son and I are under surveillance," Cassy said icily as soon as Kevin Knowland had identified himself. "Shouldn't you have the courtesy to tell me?"

"Hold on, Cassy," he said. She noticed for the first time that he had used her first name. "It's for your protection. . . . "

"Protection? What are my son and I being protected from?"

"I'm not sure," Knowland said and paused. When Cassy did not respond by picking up the conversation, Knowland continued. "This Marquez death is peculiar. I may be dealing with a homicide. If there's a killer out there, he might just be looking for someone else to kill."

"This morning's newspaper says the police are calling the death a suicide. Why are you so suspicious?"

"After fifteen years in this homicide business, I start picking up signals and hunches about cases. The Marquez dive bothers me. It doesn't take a forensic genius to start getting bad vibes. Think about it. A physician comes to the police with a bizarre story of a dead man reviving at the hospital. Then that same man is splattered on the sidewalk in front of the hospital. It could be a lot more than coincidence."

"That's hardly a basis for a murder investigation," Cassy said.

"Add to my suspicions the fact that there was no suicide note and that the door to the hospital room was not locked or barricaded from the inside. Someone could have easily slipped into Marquez's room and pitched him out the window . . . premeditated murder."

"Was there no sign of struggle in the room?" Cassy asked as she reached forward to bring the coffee mug to her lips.

"No. Except for the broken window, there was nothing out of place in his hospital room. The hospital room windows don't open wide enough to allow a person's body to go through. Marquez, or someone, threw a metal step stool through the glass window."

"I suppose none of the hospital staff saw or heard anything unusual?" Cassy asked.

"No. Nothing at all."

"I don't think you have anything, Lieutenant," Cassy said. Charlie sidled between the sofa and the coffee table, pushing himself under Cassy's bare feet until her foot rested on his back. Without thinking, she rubbed the arch of her foot slowly up and down the fur of his back as he lay wound in a spiral beneath her. "I believe Marquez could easily have become delusional and terrified and jumped to his death trying to escape the demons in his head," Cassy said.

"You've got your medical intuition. I've got my police hunch. We both know something is not right here, and for those reasons I'm concerned about you."

"You can't be serious."

"You may know something," the lieutenant said. "You might be the only one who heard Marquez say someone was trying to kill him. None of the other hospital personnel has told me that Marquez felt threatened by anyone."

Cassy refocused her mind from the anxiety that was mounting and tried to concentrate on Knowland's voice when she heard him say, ". . . did anyone else hear this conversation you had with Marquez when he told you someone was going to kill him?"

"No, just me. I was alone with him in the ICU at the time he told me."

"It's funny that he didn't talk to anyone except you about his fear of being killed," Knowland said. "Have you told anyone besides Betty Freeman and me?"

"No . . . ," Cassy said slowly. Then the chilling realization struck her. Kevin thinks someone might be stalking me; that's the reason for the squad car every hour. Why? Cassy asked herself. "But, you haven't explained to me why you think someone might want me dead," Cassy interrupted.

"I'm not sure that someone does want to kill you, but I can't be too careful. You might appear to know something that Marquez told no one else. For that reason alone you might be in danger."

"I don't like what I'm hearing. Are you saying that my son and I need to leave Dallas?"

"No. If I was certain of a killer, I would arrange to have you hidden away in protective custody. All I know for sure is that I have a puzzle. Something's not right. I can't piece it together yet. Until I do, I want to keep the police cruisers highly visible around your home. I would like to stop by your home later today and talk to you more about your last conversation with Marquez. Maybe there's something in that conversation you might remember."

"Sure. Anytime," Cassy said. "I should be home all day."

"Cassy, please keep your doors locked, and your security system turned on."

FOURTEEN

THE CONVERSATION with Kevin Knowland left Cassy with a raw anxiety. A cigarette became her overpowering need at that moment. But she would not bend to smoke in the family room. Picking up the portable phone, she shuffled a single cigarette from the open package above the kitchen sink and headed for the patio. When she reached the chaise lounge at the edge of the pool, she lit the cigarette, pulling the hot smoke along with the soft morning air deep into her lungs.

Before she finished half the cigarette, the portable phone chirped, signaling an incoming call to her unlisted telephone. She punched the listen button. It was Meagan Drake, her ex-husband's campaign manager. "Good morning, Dr. Baldwin, Scott would appreciate the opportunity of visiting with you this morning."

"Have him call me," Cassy said coldly.

"Would it be convenient for you to come to the campaign headquarters at eleven?" the woman asked, unperturbed by Cassy's coldness.

"Why?" Cassy asked. This was the first time since their divorce that her ex-husband had contacted her directly. All of their communication usually was through lawyers except the few times when Scott picked up their son for a visit.

"I don't know, Mrs. Baldwin, I believe it is of a personal nature."

Her curiosity overcame her pique at being summoned by her ex-husband. What personal nature business? Probably the Cayman rainy day account, she thought. "I suppose so. I'll be there," Cassy said and immediately regretted the decision. Whatever he wants it will have to do with money, she figured. She buried the cigarette butt beneath the soft soil in the planter.

⸺

Just before eleven o'clock, Cassy parked her Range Rover in front of a modernistic glass-sheathed cube building that housed the Spence for Governor campaign headquarters on its eighteenth floor. The announcer on the car radio began the hourly news summary. Cassy listened a moment before turning off the ignition. "Jeorg Marquez, the Lazarus man who returned from among the presumed dead in the Metropolitan Hospital morgue Saturday night, is now truly dead," the radio announcer intoned somberly. "Metro hospital officials announced the death of Jeorg Marquez last night from injuries when he apparently jumped from the window of his fifth-floor room at Metro Hospital. Marquez had been recovering from a near-death incident which one hospital source attributed to a profound allergy to shellfish Marquez had eaten Saturday evening." The announcer paused and continued, "In a related news release, Scott Spence Jr., leading gubernatorial candidate, expressed his sympathy to the Marquez family and urged a complete evaluation of the manner in which patients are declared dead in the emergency rooms of the state."

The radio report continued with a sound bite quote from Scott Spence Jr. as Cassy sat with her hand on the ignition key. "This type of mistaken diagnosis of an emergency room death must never happen again in Texas." Cassy's hands shook with rage as she listened to her ex-husband pontificate about the need for a governor's task force to investigate the declaration of death guidelines in the emergency rooms of Texas hospitals. Cassy started to turn off the ignition switch when she heard the announcer call her name, "Dr. Cassy Baldwin-Spence, the gubernatorial hopeful's ex-wife, was suspended from her position as Director of Emergency Services at the Metropolitan Hospital as a result of her mistaken diagnosis of Marquez's death Saturday evening."

"You son of a bitch," Cassy said, twisting the keys out of the ignition. "So that's why you wanted to see me this morning!"

Trembling with anger, she shoved her way through the double glass doors of the Spence for Governor campaign headquarters to confront an attractive young woman receptionist.

"Good morning, ma'am," the receptionist said, her pouting lipsticked lips widening into a friendly smile. "May I help you?"

"I'm here to see Mr. Spence," Cassy said. "I'm Cassy Baldwin."

"Oh, yes. Eleven o'clock." Turning to the telephone console centered on her desk, she picked up the receiver and whispered into it. "Meagan, Scott's ex-wife is here."

Moments later, a tall, lissome blonde appeared at a doorway behind the receptionist's desk as if she were walking the runway at a fashion show. "I'm Meagan Drake, campaign manager for Mr. Spence," the woman said, extending her hand.

It was one of those rare moments for Cassy when she immediately disliked someone. The unpleasant sensation of a greasy handshake rippled up Cassy's right arm.

"I'm Dr. Baldwin," Cassy said, choosing to use her professional title with this haughty woman rather than introducing herself simply as Cassy Baldwin as was her usual custom.

Megan Drake's outfit of a tailored red jacket trimmed in black over black straight skirt overpowered Cassy's conservative two-piece emerald green silk crepe. "Oh yes, I'm sorry. I didn't recognize you. You look so different, dressed up," Megan Drake said with a trace of disdain in her voice. "I was with Scott when we stopped by your home on Sunday afternoon to pick up his son."

"Alex is my son, too," Cassy said, her withering frown focused intently on Meagan Drake.

"Yes, certainly . . . ," the woman stammered, then immediately recovered her incandescent smile.

"The television promo we shot Sunday afternoon with your son and Scott . . . ," the woman said, " . . . for the campaign spot is super . . . pulls right at every parent's heart. Have you seen the television ad yet? Scott moved up five points in the polls since that television piece. We've been so busy these past few days. I'm just certain that Scott will be the next governor of Texas." The woman bubbled along, oblivious to the stern look on Cassy's face.

"Tell Scott I'm waiting," Cassy said coolly, finally able to connect to the woman's blue eyes. The woman, now agitated by Cassy's unspoken disapproval, turned abruptly and disappeared back through the inner office door.

The receptionist busied herself at her computer screen avoiding a look in Cassy's direction. Cassy moved about the empty reception room filled with chrome and glass in harshly modernistic styles.

At that moment, Meagan Drake reappeared through the door, still erect with the beauty and poise of a model. She had recovered her broad smile. "I'm trying to squeeze you in to see Scott, but you will have to wait. Three of his biggest political contributors flew up here unexpectedly this morning from Austin, Houston, and Kerrville to talk about his campaign strategy."

"You called me to meet him at eleven o'clock," Cassy said icily.

"Please come with me," Meagan Drake said solicitously. "You'll be more comfortable in Scott's conference room."

Nearly half an hour passed in the small windowless conference room. With each minute, Cassy's anger over Scott's exploitation of their son for his political ambitions surged even higher.

At eleven forty-five, Scott Spence Jr. reflexively ducked his head as he opened the door, even though his tall, muscular form cleared the door by at least two inches. The small room was immediately filled by Scott's presence. In a flash Cassy felt a twinge of the physical attraction that she had once known for this man.

"Appreciate your coming, Cass," he said nonchalantly and dropped his long frame into one of the cherrywood chairs at the matching circular table. With her arms folded over her chest, she leveled her eyes down at him, sprawled in the chair.

"You will not use our son again in any of your television ads for your damn political campaign."

"My dear, you are close to the edge . . . if you've not already gone off."

"No more TV ads. Don't push me, Scott. I mean it. I'll trash your campaign if you use our son as a political tool. . . ."

"Have you seen the ads?" he asked calmly.

"No."

"Did you ask Alex about them . . . maybe he liked being the center of attention with his dad."

"No, I haven't."

"Why don't you talk to your son before jumping up and down all over me."

"But . . . ," Cassy started to say more before checking herself. Her mind whirled. Maybe she was being unreasonable. Somehow she realized that her reaction to learning about the television ads was bound up in her failed relationship with Scott. With a sigh, Cassy relented, "All right. I will."

"My people . . . my campaign managers . . . are concerned about you. I'm getting some momentum going . . . we don't want to get whacked . . . this Marquez thing could be a problem . . . ," Scott continued in his characteristic broken sentence fragments.

"Concerned about me?" Cassy asked incredulously. "You've got to be kidding. I'm your ex-wife remember."

"That's just the point. Your problem with this Hispanic Marquez is getting way too much media coverage. Our focus groups tell us that my name is being unfavorably mentioned with yours in these news articles and the television reports. My campaign people are trying to figure a strategy so that we can put the right spin on this . . . turn your mess with Marquez into an opportunity . . . seize the initiative," he prattled in unconnected word groups.

"What do you expect me to do to control the curiosity of the media?" Cassy asked in the sarcastic tone that surfaced whenever she was stressed.

"I want to be sure you don't contradict some of my statements about the need for uniform declaration of death statutes for the emergency rooms in Texas."

"Scott, you are so full of shit."

"If you won't help me . . . at least don't get in my way on this Marquez thing . . . it might be worth a point or two in the polls if we play it right . . . better yet, maybe you could disappear for awhile . . . that way you wouldn't be talking to the media . . . take a vacation . . . out of the state for the summer. . . out of sight, out of the media's mind?"

"If the Marquez incident is what you invited me to discuss, I have nothing more to say." She reached for the doorknob.

"What are you and Alex going to do?" asked Scott Spence, startled by her seeming equanimity.

"You'll know my plans when they come together."

"Plans? From what I hear, you'd be lucky to get any kind of job in this state."

Cassy's anger surged again. For a moment she had the impulse to slap him. Controlling herself, she opened the door and turned to leave. "You son of a bitch," Cassy whispered.

"Play things my way, or you can just forget your share of our Cayman nest egg."

"You sleazy bastard! Don't you dare threaten me or Alex, or every voter in Texas will know about the Cayman account."

"My dear, you should weigh the implications of your position," Scott said calmly and in a completely formed sentence. "You do not have clean hands with the Cayman money. So don't start blowing the whistle on me, because you'll implicate yourself."

"I'll do whatever I have to do to protect Alex and me from you."

"Rest assured, Cassy, I will likewise protect myself . . . by whatever means necessary."

"Go to hell," Cassy said and slammed the conference room door behind her and strode past Meagan Drake who stood grim-faced behind the protection of the receptionist's desk.

FIFTEEN

D R. BALDWIN," Cassy said, her formal telephone greeting a re-flex response to the chirping of the phone in her Range Rover. Rarely were her cellular calls social. Almost always a call to her car telephone required a decision for one of her patients.

"Hi, Mom," Alex said, the brightness of his voice wiped the frown from Cassy's face. "When are you coming home?"

"I'll be there in a couple of hours. Have you had lunch yet?"

"No. Lupita fixed tamales again, and I didn't eat them."

"No way! She must have thought we liked her tamales so much last night that we ate them all rather than grinding them down the disposal," Cassy said, chuckling into the receiver. "What would you like to eat?" She knew the answer without asking the question.

"Pizza."

"Pizza it is. I'll stop at Dominos on the way home."

"Get a big combination with everything."

"Yes, sir," Cassy said and laughed again. It was one of those flashes of love for her son that she knew so well that left her with an undefined feeling of gratification of some inner need being met. She could never refuse her son.

In that moment the decision about the next turn in her life appeared in her mind. It was not a conscious, logical analysis that led her to a conclusion. Not a syllogistic argument with alternate premises and a deductive conclusion. But a course of action that appeared full blown, seemingly out of nowhere, but certainly emanating from the ferment of her mind during the past four days. She had arrived at her decision. She flipped her cellular phone open, thinking of the twisted knots her life had become in less than a week.

Punching the keypad on her cellular telephone for the information operator, she had no difficulty locating the telephone number. There was only one Tenoch listed in the Dallas telephone directory.

Moments later a man answered, "Aztec Companies."

Cassy identified herself as Dr. Cassandra Baldwin. She was asked to hold the connection. During the next several minutes while waiting on silent hold, thankfully without Muzak, Cassy parked the Range Rover in the visitors' space in front of the Dallas Forensic Sciences building.

"Good afternoon, Cassy. It is indeed a pleasure to hear your voice," Tenoch's voice materialized in her ear as Cassy sat in the parked car.

"Buenos días, Señor Tenoch," Cassy said, holding the cellular phone to her ear. "I've slept on your invitation for this weekend. I would be honored to travel to Mexico City to discuss the opportunity at the Instituto de Medico."

"Wonderful," Tenoch said. "I will make arrangements."

"Tenoch, I must insist that my trip to Mexico City does not mean that I've accepted your offer. I do not wish any misunderstanding. This visit will be just a preliminary get acquainted visit."

"Certainly. But you will not object if I attempt to interest you and to recruit you with the hospitality of Mexico?" Tenoch asked. Before Cassy could answer, he continued, "Shall we leave at nine tomorrow morning?"

Cassy agreed, and they exchanged goodbyes.

⸻

When Cassy walked through the door into Betty Freeman's office, the toxicologist looked up from her cluttered desk. "What took you so long?" The odor of burnt cigarettes and Lysol assaulted Cassy, again revolting her stomach but perversely whetting her desire for the nicotine rush. A brown paper bag and a Diet Pepsi can sat on the pullout shelf at the side of Betty's gunmetal gray desk.

"Would you like part of my homemade Reuben sandwich?" Betty Freeman asked as she reached into the brown paper bag. Circles of greasy moisture dotted the bag.

Cassy shook her head. "No thanks, Alex and I will be eating a pizza for lunch. I stopped by to ask a few questions. I didn't plan to disturb your lunch break."

"No bother." Dr. Freeman shook her head.

Betty's attention was focused on the interior of the brown paper sack. She stuck her oversized hand into the sack and pulled out an enormous sandwich of rye bread, sliced corned beef, and sauerkraut wrapped in a clear plastic wrapper. "The sauerkraut makes them a bit soggy after being in the paper bag all morning. They're still delicious even if the bread is soppy. Sure you don't want a bite?"

"Why not wait to put the sauerkraut on until just before you're ready to eat? That way the juice won't soak into the rye bread," Cassy said as she slipped into the chair in front of the desk.

Betty looked up from her sandwich, cocked an eyebrow, and said, "Doctor, you are a practical woman. You must be the Heloise of the Operating Room." Her wide grin pulled apart her thick lips. The droopy wet sandwich exuded juicy droplets when Dr. Freeman leaned forward, squeezing the sticky sandwich into her mouth. "This is absolutely delicious," she said. Her jaws ground away on the sandwich. She waved the sandwich toward Cassy, again offering to share it with her.

"I'll pass on the sandwich, but you don't mind if I smoke while you eat? I've had a bad morning with my ex-husband. I could use a cigarette."

"Sure. Light up. I'll join you," Dr. Freeman said, lighting a Marlboro between bites of the Reuben sandwich and pulling on the cigarette between mouthfuls of the sandwich.

"What has the fair-haired boy of the Texas Republican party done this time?"

"My ex-husband has been using Alex in the television advertisements for his governor's race."

"Oh, yes. I've just seen them. The one yesterday with Alex and his dad at Six Flags is a masterpiece."

Cassy's mouth twisted into a petulant frown. "I just found out an hour ago that Scott was using Alex in his political ads."

"So?" Betty Freeman concentrated on her sandwich, vigorously chewing on the corned beef. A strand of sauerkraut hung unnoticed on her prominent chin.

"Scott's using our son as a political tool to further his political ambitions," Cassy said and then sucked deep on another cigarette she had just lit. "He's not interested in Alex for who is is, but only in what Alex can do for him."

Betty stopped chewing and looked across the remaining half sandwich that she held in her spade-like hands. Then she put the soggy sandwich down onto the transparent plastic wrapper in the center of her desk. Her brow creased itself as a worried look replaced the natural smile she had been wearing while enjoying the Reuben. Silence hung in the room as Betty finished chewing and swallowed, washing down the mouthful with a gulp from the Diet Pepsi can.

"Cass," Betty said solemnly. "Why does the campaign ad with Alex bother you so much?"

"He . . . ," Cassy started to say.

Betty held up her hands stopping Cassy. "I've known you for a long time, and I've seen this anger with Scott building up in you even before the divorce. You're out of line on this. Hell, it's probably a good thing for Alex and his dad to have something they can do together for a change. You've been complaining to me that Scott doesn't spend as much time with Alex as you think he should." Betty folded her arms on the desk and leaned toward Cassy. "So?"

Cassy sat quietly, stunned by the realization that Betty's words were true and reluctantly admitted that her morning's response to Scott had been exaggerated by her lingering resentments of her ex-husband.

"So?" Betty repeated when Cassy sat unspeaking and unmoving for several moments.

"I just don't know, Betty. It's all so confusing right now. I'm trying to deal with everything that seems to be happening so quickly to Alex and to me. On the way over here, I called Señor Tenoch and accepted his invitation for a weekend visit to Mexico City to look over the possibilities of a job as Chief of Cardiac Surgery at the Instituto de Medico."

"Tenoch? Is he that rich Mexican businessman who lives in that mansion over on Preston?"

"Yes," Cassy said and then described for her the luncheon meeting discussion at Tenoch's home.

"Sounds like an opportunity that you ought to at least consider. Can I help out with Alex this weekend?"

"No. He'll be fine with Lupita. Trent Hendricks might take him to another Rangers' game. We all had a great time together at the Rangers' game on Memorial Day."

Betty raised her eyebrows a notch and smiled at Cassy as she picked up the rest of the Reuben sandwich. "I didn't realize you were a baseball fan."

"Stop it!" Cassy said, laughing as she bent forward to stub out her cigarette. "You're a hopeless matchmaker. Trent and I are just friends."

"Sure. Sure," Betty said and tore off another mouthful of the Reuben.

"Now that you've resolved, disapproved, and approved of my personal life," Cassy said as she leaned back with a sly grin. "Maybe you could tell me about Marquez. What did the autopsy show?"

"I'm surprised you weren't here early this morning," Dr. Freeman said.

"Last night Kevin told me it was suicide. He's not so sure this morning."

"I'll give you five-to-two odds that Marquez was tossed out the window," Dr. Freeman said. "I've never heard of a two hundred fifty pound man squeezing himself out a Metro hospital window. Marquez didn't leave a note, either. The swan divers almost always want someone to know why they took a header."

"You think Marquez was murdered too?"

"Mighty suspicious," Freeman said, pushing the rest of the sandwich across her lips.

"Even one of the ER nurses thinks Marquez was murdered," Cassy said as she savored the continuing rush of the nicotine. "I first found out that Marquez was dead from Gracie. . . ."

"Is she the Haitian nurse that thinks Marquez is the zombie?"

"Yes. Gracie is scared and claims that she knows for certain Marquez was thrown out the window."

"Sure. Just like she knows for certain Marquez is a zombie," Freeman said and inhaled deeply from a freshly lit Marlboro. "So why does she think that Marquez was murdered?"

Cassy shrugged. "I don't know. If she knows, she's not telling me. Gracie's absolutely terrified that she will be killed next. She's hiding somewhere in Dallas, but she slipped over the wall around my house last night to warn me that I'm in danger from the evil spirits."

"Warn you against evil spirits?"

"The evil spirits at the Metro Hospital," Cassy said.

"The nurse is a nut . . . ," Freeman declared.

"I tried to persuade her to let me get a psychiatrist for her, but she literally ran from the house," Cassy said. "I've not heard from her since."

"What about Gracie's family? Can they locate her?"

"I'm not certain. I've talked to Gracie's daughter. She won't tell me where Gracie is hiding," Cassy said.

"Well, there's at least four of us now that think Marquez was bumped off. Gracie, you, me and Kevin." Betty stuffed the sandwich wrapping in the brown sack, wadded it all together and tossed the paper ball across the room into the waste can in the corner.

"Did you find anything at his autopsy?"

"Not really. Our prosector couldn't find any sign of antemortem struggle on the body when he did the autopsy. It was a real crunch. Broke his neck. That's what killed him. Marquez had other injuries, too. Ruptured spleen, fractured ribs, fractured femur."

"Did you do toxicology screens on Marquez's body?" Cassy asked.

"Hell, yes," the doctor said, her Texas drawl muffled by a swallow of Diet Pepsi. "We ain't no amateurs in this business."

"Will you test Marquez's body tissues for all those exotic poisons you and I talked about?"

"Haven't, but might as well. I'll just add his postmortem blood and tissue samples to the Saturday night samples."

"When will you have some results?"

"About a week for those special tests."

"Do you think I could have a look at Marquez's body?"

"The autopsy has already been done. Marquez's body is gone. He's on his way back to Mexico City."

"Already? The man has been dead barely more than twelve hours. What's the rush?" Cassy asked.

"Marquez has a lot of friends. There were phone calls last night . . . from the mayor and one of the Texas senators . . . to the chief coroner," Dr. Freeman said. "It must be a cultural thing. Apparently the Mexicans like to get their dead in the ground pretty quick. No specific demands from anyone, just firm subtle pressure to get the body to Mexico City as soon as possible."

"Marquez must have had a lot of high-powered influence." Cassy stood up. "Let me know what the tests show as soon as you get them."

Betty nodded and after a moment's hesitation said, "I have a strange premonition . . . let me give you some more motherly advice, Cassy. Stay away from this Marquez mess."

Cassy felt a tenseness come over her as if she were bracing herself against a collision. "I can't. I have to find out what happened to him. I have to solve the puzzle."

SIXTEEN

—◁═▷—

IN THE LATE afternoon Cassy settled herself onto the chaise lounge near the deep end of the pool and pulled the wide-brimmed straw hat low over her eyes. The sheaf of medical articles on the subject of clinical death sat on the wrought iron table next to her lounge chair.

"Hey, Mom," Alex shouted and splashed the pool water with the flat of his hand sending a spray to her feet. "Come swim with me." Alex bounced in the shallow end of the pool. Charlie pranced at the edge of the pool with a baseball in his mouth.

"Not right now. I've still got some paper work to do."

"Come on," Alex yelled as he took the ball from Charlie's mouth and flung it into the far end of the yard, sending the dog scurrying after the ball.

"In a little while," Cassy said and began rereading the medical papers stacked beside her. Her mind was crowded every minute with the Marquez incident. She simply could think of nothing else. Some aspect of her encounter with Marquez always arose to block out other thoughts. At this moment her mind focused in short clips on the facts that she could verify. A fifty-five year old man. Rapid collapse of all vital functions. Progressive slowing of the heart rate to standstill. No response to all the usual resuscitative efforts. Revival and return of vital functions within three hours. Normothermic body temperature. No electrocardiographic sign of cardiac injury. No heart muscle damage as shown by normal blood enzyme studies. Mute catatonic state twenty-four hours later. Possible paranoid ideas about a death threat. Bizarre fragments of morbid ideation, thinking he was dead, 'Estoy muerto'. Possible post traumatic hallucinations. Possible profound depression and resulting suicide. Death from multiple internal injuries.

Cassy looked up from her brown study and glanced across the sun shimmering pool. Every time that Alex threw the ball into the far corner of the yard, Charlie raced to retrieve the ball and return it to the pool's edge, carefully laying it on the concrete coping. On Alex's last toss, the dog grabbed the ball in mid flight like a shortstop with a pop fly ball and ran a half circle about the pool. In his excitement to deliver the ball to Alex, Charlie jumped into the water and paddled to Alex standing in the center of the shallow end of the pool. After Alex took the ball, Charlie swam away and leaped up the submerged pool steps, his fur a wet shaggy mat. The dog vigorously shook himself dry, spraying water over the hot deck as his hair bristled up.

Alex caught his mother's amused look when Charlie ran through the yard rolling his wet fur in the dry hot grass. "Come swim with Charlie and me, Mom."

"Just five minutes more," Cassy said. Her mind was on the verge of applying the information she had gleaned from her medical literature search to the specific facts of the Marquez affair. Cassy wanted to try to organize her thoughts onto paper before the cool water of the pool might flush away a creative idea.

Cassy returned her thoughts to the Marquez conundrum. Why should a previously healthy fifty-five-year-old man collapse and apparently die within an hour only to revive three hours later? There must be a biologic explanation. She proceeded through a differential diagnosis, writing her ideas on the yellow legal pad that rested on her bare legs:

Diagnosis	Excluded by
Acute myocardial infarct	Normal cardiac enzymes and normal EKG
Diabetic/Insulin coma	Normal blood sugar
Drug overdose	Negative drug and toxicology screen
Stroke	Negative neurologic evaluation upon revival and normal CAT scan
Hypothermia	Normal body temperature
Poisoning	??

I'm missing something, Cassy thought and threw her pencil onto the pad in frustration. There has to be a physiologic explanation. I know what I saw—a flat-lined EKG, a nonresponsive man without pulse, respiration, or blood pressure. Goddamn it, the man was dead. But he revived three hours later and recalled her death pronouncement. What the hell happened? Cassy knew Betty Freeman must be correct. Marquez was not dead. She remembered the pathologist's hoarse, raspy voice, 'Dead is dead is dead'.

Cassy picked the yellow pad up and studied her list again. All right, she reasoned, let's accept that he was not dead when I pronounced him, but let's assume he was in a state of clinical death. Flipping through the copies of the scientific papers until she found the definition of clinical death, she reread it several times: 'that intermediate state through which life ends and death starts—a reversible death—a state of transition from life to irreversible biologic death—a continuous process of transition from the live to the lifeless state.'

"But I'm still back to the central question of what was the biologic basis for the collapse and revival?" Cassy asked aloud as she looked up to check on her son in the shallow end of the pool. The game of pitch and fetch continued. What then precipitated clinical death in Marquez? It surely wasn't a spontaneous event. The clinical death must have been provoked. But what could produce the suspended state? And why? Logic told her that the explanation had to be based in Marquez's reaction to a poison. Nothing else fits, she told herself. Whatever Marquez came into contact with induced a state of clinical death in the man, but instead of progressing to irreversible biological death, Marquez revived. Did his body metabolize or eliminate the substance, whatever it might have been, allowing his body to reverse the clinical death state?

Thwarted by the lack of a conclusion, Cassy threw the yellow legal pad back onto the patio. I just don't have enough information, she told herself. The diagnosis would be easy if I had the data. Just like any other clinical problem.

Cassy walked the length of the pool quickly, the brick surface hot under the afternoon sun, and slid herself into the cool water at the steps of shallow end of the pool. Alex swam up to her, staying submerged on the steps of the pool. The dog jumped into the pool and paddled toward them, inserting his head between them as all three sat on the underwater concrete steps in the shallow end of the pool.

"What are you going to do in Mexico?" Alex asked, holding his mouth just above the water as he floated off the steps.

"It's a business trip. I'll be touring the cardiovascular hospital in Mexico City and meeting some of the doctors."

"Do you suppose that Mr. Tenoch will give me another baseball card?"

"I wouldn't be surprised," Cassy said, splashing water onto her flushed face.

"Another Nolan Ryan card?"

"I wouldn't be surprised," Cassy said.

"I looked up the one he gave me yesterday in my baseball card catalog. It's worth sixteen hundred dollars," Alex said.

"No, you must be mistaken. Probably sixteen dollars."

"I could sell it wholesale to the dealer today for a thousand dollars. A Nolan Ryan rookie card sells for sixteen hundred dollars retail," Alex said as he stood up on the first step of the underwater stairs.

At that moment, Lupita opened the sliding glass door and looked across the patio without moving out of the air-conditioned interior of the house. "Señora, there is a policeman at the gate. He wants to talk to you," she shouted to Cassy.

"Did he say why?"

"No, Señora."

"Let him in," Cassy said and swam the length of the pool to the ladder at the deep end of the pool just as Lt. Knowland, dressed in a navy summer blazer, gray slacks and white shirt with a conservative striped tie, stepped through the patio door. Lupita stayed behind the partially open glass door of the cool family room. "Señora, the policeman say he knows you," Lupita shouted across the patio.

"Hello, Lieutenant," Cassy said. Charlie circled the detective barking and sniffing at the man's legs. Cassy climbed the steel ladder out of the deep end of the pool and grabbed a bath towel from the table next to her chaise lounge, wrapping the towel around her hips in a sarong fashion.

"Down, Charlie," Cassy said, shoving Charlie with her bare foot away from the lieutenant and motioning Lt. Knowland to the patio chair next to her. The German shepherd circled the table and continued to sniff at the lieutenant's black loafers.

"I imagine he smells my cat," Knowland said.

"You have a cat?"

"Himalayan Persian. One of the long hair pedigrees."

"Somehow I never imagined a homicide detective as a cat lover," Cassy laughed.

"I've had cats a long time. Keeps me company when I'm home."

"You live alone?"

"I'm a confirmed bachelor."

"Confirmed?"

"I guess I mean I don't have anyone in mind," Lt. Knowland said. He looked away toward Alex who at that moment leaped from the diving board.

"What did you stop by to ask me?" Cassy said. She fidgeted with the halter top of her two-piece bathing suit, unconsciously hitching it upward. "I'm sorry, I didn't offer you something to drink," Cassy said.

"Yes, iced tea would be nice."

When Cassy had gone through the patio door, Lieutenant Knowland's attention returned to the pool. "Hi, there," the detective said to Alex who now floated on a plastic pool raft, watching the detective. "I'm Kevin. What's your name?"

"Alex. Who are you?"

"I'm a policeman. Kevin Knowland is my name."

"You don't look like a policeman. Where's your uniform?"

"I don't wear a uniform."

"How can I know you're a policeman?"

"Here's my police badge to prove it." Alex paddled the float to the edge of the pool as Kevin dangled the leather badge case so that Alex could see his plastic embossed identification card.

"Do you have a gun?"

"Yes."

"Where is it?"

"Here," Lt. Knowland said, and pulled aside the flap of his coat to show a nine millimeter Sig Sauer pistol holstered on his left hip.

"Let me hold your gun."

"No. Can't do. I only take the pistol out to practice or when I have to use it."

Cassy returned with the two iced teas. "Lieutenant, I wish you wouldn't show your gun to my son," she said sharply.

"I'm sorry. I didn't think you would mind. Gun education is part of the children's education programs that the police department has begun to offer."

"I do not allow guns in my home."

"I'm required to carry my pistol when I'm on duty."

"Well, I guess you're not inside my home," Cassy said and handed an insulated glass of iced tea to him.

"Do you keep a gun in your home for protection?" Kevin asked.

"No."

"Can you even shoot a pistol?"

"Yes. My father taught me years ago," Cassy said. "But I still don't allow guns in my home."

"I can see that my gun education lecture won't be very effective with you," Kevin said, raising his hands in mock surrender. He drained the glass of iced tea in one long gulp.

"Would you like another glass?" Cassy asked.

"Not right now, but I'll take my jacket off, if you don't mind." He draped the blue blazer over the back of the wrought iron chair and rolled the sleeves of his long-sleeved white oxford shirt above his elbows. "This

Marquez case bothers me. A lot of it is not fitting together. I know I'm missing something here, and I'm thinking you may know more than you realize. I wanted to hear more about what Marquez told you Sunday night and what you think happened to him." The detective crunched an ice cube and continued. "Could Marquez's death and revival have been a botched attempt at a sophisticated murder? You said that you think he was poisoned."

"I'm not certain," Cassy said and shook her head. She squinted against the glare of late afternoon sun off the pool's surface and pulled her sunglasses down over her eyes. "Marquez had no signs of life when he left my Emergency Room for the first time. I really can't explain it without a poisoning. There seems to be no other biological explanation." She paused and looked in his direction, her eyes hidden behind the dark glasses. "What do you think happened?"

Kevin Knowland tilted the empty glass up to his lips. He caught another ice cube in his mouth before he answered. "After studying the hospital room and the broken window that Marquez went through, I'm suspicious that someone killed him. Of course, I can't prove it . . . yet."

"Maybe the first attempt was Saturday night? Whoever it was then returned to finish the job last night?" Cassy asked.

"I'm beginning to think that Saturday was indeed a murder attempt . . . ," the lieutenant said. "Especially now that you think he was not as dead as you thought he was Saturday evening."

"I'm less certain now that he was actually dead than I was Saturday night. He was apparently dead . . . maybe clinical death might be the most appropriate medical term for his condition Saturday night in the morgue," Cassy responded.

"What could cause him to appear dead when he wasn't?"

"The most likely explanation that I have come up with . . . and I've been thinking about hardly anything else since Saturday night . . . is that some substance, a poison, a drug, an allergen, could have been introduced into Marquez's body shortly before he collapsed at the funeral home office Saturday evening."

"How did the substance get into Marquez's body?"

"It must have been taken by mouth," Cassy said. "Any other route of administration, injection, inhaling, skin surface contact, Marquez would surely have recognized and tried to protect himself. My guess is that something was given to him in his food or drink, either intentionally to kill him or accidentally. Or perhaps his body reaction was a weird fluke to some substance that ordinarily is harmless."

"If someone slipped him a poison or a drug Saturday evening, it must have been Señor Tenoch or someone on his staff," the lieutenant said. "Marquez had spent the entire day at the funeral home."

Cassy paused a beat and looked aside. "You've been investigating Tenoch?"

"No, but I've just come from interviewing him over at his 'casa grande' over on Preston."

Cassy smiled at the lieutenant's subtle attempt at ethnic humor. "Why in the world do you think Señor Tenoch would want to poison Marquez?" Cassy asked.

"I didn't say that I suspected Tenoch," the detective said. "If there's a motive with Tenoch, I don't see it. He's extremely wealthy. Very successful importer from Mexico. He's into a variety of different businesses, stock investments, oil and gas companies. He's considered a wizard at picking successful medical companies and making a fortune investing in them early. Gives a lot of his money away. He's a big time philanthropist. He's certainly given lots of money to the Dallas Metropolitan Hospital." Kevin paused a moment, looking again toward Alex still floating on the pool raft. He turned back to Cassy almost as if reluctant to continue with the description of Tenoch's successes.

"Any family?" Cassy asked.

"No family I'm aware of. A parade of beautiful women but no steady woman."

"A confirmed bachelor, just like you," Cassy said. She hid a smile behind the rim of her iced tea glass. Kevin must have seen her eyes twinkle behind the sunglasses when she bent her head forward. He smiled in return.

"A bachelor like me. Yes, but I've not had Tenoch's parade of glamorous women." Knowland laughed and said, "I wish."

"Anything else about him besides the beautiful women?"

"The usual civil cases and litigation that go with being a successful business person," Lt. Knowland said. "If you mean does he have a criminal record, the answer is no."

"Are you aware that he's offered me a position as a heart surgeon in Mexico City? In the morning I'm going with him to Mexico City for the weekend."

"Yes. Tenoch told me. He was quite complimentary about you," the detective said and crunched the ice cube in his jaw. "Maybe it would even be a good idea for you to go out of town for a few days until this Marquez publicity blows itself away."

"You're the second person today who's told me I ought to leave town."

Knowland looked puzzled. "My ex-husband, Scott Spence Jr., wants me out of town. Says I'm hurting his campaign for governor."

"Yes, I'm aware of him."

"He said my notoriety as a result of the Marquez incident wasn't help-ing him."

"He didn't threaten you?"

"Not exactly," Cassy said. "Why do you ask?"

"No particular reason, just my detective's curiosity." He looked away one more time toward the pool before continuing. "I'll know a lot more about this Marquez case when you get back from Mexico City." He glided away from his question about her ex-husband.

"Do you think Alex and I could be in danger here in the house?"

"It's impossible for me to know. I'm not even sure that there has been a murder, but you're awfully close to the Marquez case. Maybe you know something you don't realize, or maybe someone thinks you know more than you actually do know. It's possible. . . ." He let the sentence die.

"What should I do?"

"Your burglar alarm is not much of a deterrent. The patrol cars are use-ful. But in my opinion you ought to have a gun. Believe me, I rarely ever advise anyone to keep a loaded gun in the house. But for the next few days, it might be worthwhile."

"Where can I buy one?"

"I have an extra one that I'll loan you. It's at my home," Kevin Know-land said and hesitated a moment before continuing. "I would even offer to fix an early supper for you, and Alex too."

"My goodness, a cat loving, bachelor, homicide lieutenant who cooks and who is interested in my safety," Cassy said. "You're full of surprises, Lt. Knowland. How can I refuse?"

"Please call me Kevin," he said.

SEVENTEEN

A GLOSSY SILVER-BLUE fur ball purred against Kevin Knowland's leg the instant he stepped across the threshold to his North Dallas condominium. Holding the door open with one hand, he scooped up the longhaired cat off the brick floor of the entryway to his home in the gated upscale residential complex.

"No you don't, Tosca," Kevin said as he held the cat up to his face. "You're not slipping out tonight."

"W-what kind of cat is he?" Alex asked. The cat's blue eyes set above a flat black nose peered intently at Alex. The cat clung to Kevin's blazer with all four paws.

"He's a she. A Himalayan Persian, a breed originally developed from crossing a Siamese and a Persian. Would you like to hold her?" Kevin asked. He pulled the cat carefully away from the fabric of his blazer.

"W-will she scratch?" Alex asked.

"She can't. I've had her claws tipped with plastic. She was sharpening her claws on my leather sofa. I didn't have the heart to have her declawed. I'm a softy, I guess."

Alex reached up to take the cat. The boy and cat looked at each other reluctantly. "She's a little shy with strangers at first." Alex hesitantly took Tosca from Kevin's hands, but the cat nestled easily onto Alex's shoulder as if they had known each other forever.

"Charlie will smell you tonight," Cassy said as she scratched the cat's luxuriant fur.

"W-what k-kind of name is Tosca?" Alex asked.

"It's an Italian opera. Tosca is the tragic heroine in the opera who loses her love and her life."

"Lieutenant, you are indeed a man for all seasons . . . ," Cassy said, shaking her head and laughing.

"Opera is one of my weaknesses," he said and hesitated. "I'd love to take you to the opera sometime."

"I'd love to go. I've never been."

"You've lived in Dallas and never been? It's wonderful. How about next Saturday? It just happens to be Verdi's *La Traviata*."

"Maybe. Let me see what happens in Mexico City. I can't see beyond this weekend."

"I'll get some tickets just in case. Now make yourself comfortable. Let me change clothes. Then I'll give you the grand tour." Kevin took the stairwell, two at a time, while Cassy and Alex wandered into the living room, a cozy corner with a beamed ceiling and glistening waxed hardwood floors. A grouping of carved handcrafted Southwestern chairs and sofas with tapestried upholstery gave the room an Arizona feel. The brick above the fireplace mantle was dominated by a G. Harvey print of weathered cowboys on equally weathered horses.

The built-in shelves, flanking the fireplace, were jammed with books of all types. Cassy scanned the titles, ranging from contemporary best-selling fiction to tomes detailing various Italian operas. Agatha Christie novels filled one section. Another row was filled with textbooks and treatises on abnormal psychology. The eclectic assortment of books showed signs of serious study—smudged edges, cracked bindings, even dog-eared pages. In the textbooks Cassy found underlining and marginal notes in a small, precise style that she assumed was Kevin's handwriting.

"Mother's the professional decorator," Kevin said as he returned to the living room. "She has a thing about Southwestern furniture. She and Dad live in Scottsdale. He's a retired anesthesiologist who has found a second career—playing golf."

"You have enough books for a used book store," Cassy said, running her fingers along the spines of the books.

"My hobby is books . . . all sizes, shapes, subjects, and ages," Kevin said. Now dressed in a dark blue knit shirt, baggy soft canvas trousers, and moccasins, he reminded Cassy of a Lands' End catalog picture.

"My ideal holiday is a whole day in a used book store. Last year I spent a week of my vacation exploring all the bookstores in Seattle." He pulled out a first edition Agatha Christie and lovingly held it in his hands for Cassy to inspect. Cassy took the book and gingerly opened it.

The metamorphosis from homicide chief to this relaxed, studious man left her puzzled—who was the real Kevin Knowland?

"Let me give you and Alex the grand tour," Kevin said and motioned them to follow him from the living room. The smaller of the two down-stairs bedrooms was filled with more books. In the center of the desk that occupied most of the room sat a Macintosh computer similar to Alex's.

"You might like to play with my Mac," Kevin said to Alex. "I've got a few games on the hard drive. How about Flight Simulator and Chuck Yeager's Jet Fighter Aerial Combat game?"

"Have you got a joystick or a mouse?"

"I've got a pilot's control," Kevin said. "Go ahead and fly it while I give your mother a present."

Leaving Alex in front of the Mac flying a MIG-2 in aerial combat, Cassy and Kevin turned toward the stairwell. Cassy noticed the other downstairs bedroom was also decorated in the Southwest motif in a severe sterile decorator's showroom atmosphere. "That's the guest room . . . another of Mom's interior decorating projects. She and Dad visit a couple of times a year and sleep there. It's the only time it's ever used."

"And you go to Scottsdale to play golf with your dad, I'll bet. Once a month?" Cassy asked.

"No," Kevin said ruefully. "I'm Dad's two biggest disappointments . . . I didn't become a doctor like him, and I don't like golf. I'm not sure which is a bigger disappointment."

As soon as they entered the upstairs master suite, Cassy was stunned by the contrast in decorating style—a stark modernistic room in a black and white scheme. A king-size bed. A Picasso print on the ceiling above the bed. A black cloth bed cover treatment. Chrome coat rack. A shiny white lacquered dresser and matching nightstand. An abstract neon tube light-ing was framed above the bed and served as a headboard. "As you can see, my mom's influence stops at the bedroom door."

Cassy stepped into the bedroom following the cat. "I'm impressed by your spotless house. I have a hard time keeping my bed made, and I have a full-time housekeeper."

"It's Thursday. My once-a-week housekeeper just left before we got here." Tosca jumped onto the bed. Cassy sat on the edge of the bed and idly coiled her fingers along the cat's ears causing a purring rumble from the cat.

"Before I fix our dinner, let me get the pistol business out of the way," Kevin said and disappeared into his bedroom closet. Moments later he returned with his hands around a maroon velvet parcel. "It's a Sig Sauer Model P 220 Automatic, one of the best nine millimeter pistols ever made," he said and handed the blue carbon steel revolver to Cassy. The checked walnut stock was slightly large for her hand, but she was able to grip her fingers completely around the cold surface. "Are you familiar with this type pistol? Think you can handle it?"

Cassy nodded. Kevin quickly showed her the loading mechanism and the safety. Then he slammed a full clip into the pistol. "Here are a dozen hollow point bullets. Keep one chambered and the safety on. Any questions?" She shook her head. "These are Black Talon bullets. They tear away more flesh than any other bullet of the same caliber."

Cassy weighed the pistol in her hand, feeling the cold roughness of the grip pressed against the softness of her palm. She pulled the pistol up to aim down the fixed barrel sight when she saw Alex standing in the doorway of the bedroom, holding the cat.

"Whose gun?" Alex asked, indifferently stroking the cat's neck.

"Kevin is loaning it to us."

"Why?" Alex asked.

"Because Kevin thinks it's a good idea."

Her answers seemed to satisfy Alex. He watched Cassy rewrap the pistol into the maroon velvet cloth before he turned back down the stairs to his computer game.

Kevin and Cassy went back to the living room, stopping by the bedroom office where Alex barely looked up from the computer screen. "He's a bright boy," Kevin whispered.

"His teachers have wanted to move him ahead in school," Cassy said. "I've refused. He's terribly bright, but he's still maturing no faster than a normal eight year old. Even if he does have a near-genius intelligence, he's still my little boy."

As soon as they settled onto the living room sofa, Kevin opened the door of the temperature and humidity controlled wine chest built above a wet bar cabinet in the corner of the room.

"How about a sampling of my new find?" Kevin asked, holding a bottle of wine in front of her like a sommelier. "I brought it back from my last tour of the Napa Valley. It's from a small vineyard near St. Helena."

Cassy leaned forward reading the label and then looked up at Kevin who bent forward brandishing the wine bottle. "And you're also a wine connoisseur?" she asked with mock amazement on her face.

"Not really, but I always bring a bottle back from my vacation trips." Kevin smiled and said nothing more as he deftly removed the cork. Sampling the first pour of the wine thoughtfully, he nodded and filled both glasses. He touched her glass with a dull clink.

"Do you go by yourself on these vacations?" Cassy asked.

"Usually. I just have to get away from Dallas and the homicide business every so often. I need some private time all by myself," he said. Then he disappeared in the kitchen and returned with a bowl of tortilla chips and Southwestern style salsa.

"How did you become involved in homicide investigation?" Cassy asked.

"Really wasn't a conscious decision. I just drifted into it. Dad wanted me in medical school, but I couldn't get past the chemistry. My mind just doesn't work that way . . . all those symbols and equations."

"How did you land in the police department?"

"I enjoyed the school experience . . . the academic environment . . . the books and libraries. I ended up with a Ph.D. in abnormal psychology after a lot of years."

"How did the Ph.D. get you into police work?"

"It was my doctoral thesis on the personality development of the pre-meditated murderer that first took me to the prisons. Eventually I wound up where I am, investigating murders," Kevin said. "The challenge of solving a murder is really a fascinating intellectual game, sifting information, assigning priorities, assembling the logical pieces . . . until there is an inescapable conclusion pointing to the murderer."

"You make homicide investigation sound so dispassionate . . . so devoid of emotion."

"I have to be dispassionate and shield myself from the horror of what I see men and women do to each other every day. If I didn't, I would soon lose my objectivity as an investigator . . . and the intentional death that I see every day could destroy my insides." Cassy realized then that Kevin had just dropped his protective shield to give her a peek into a world that he segregated so sharply from his private life.

"That's enough about me. How did you end up in heart surgery? A woman heart surgeon must be a very unusual combination." It was as if he raised his professional shield again, cutting off further inspection.

"No more so than a chief of homicide in a major metropolitan police department who is an opera buff and a pedigreed cat fancier," Cassy said.

"Point made," Kevin said and sipped from his wine. "I'm still fascinated about how you ended up in heart surgery," Kevin said, leaving the statement as an open-ended query. His interviewing techniques spilled onto his conversational style.

"You already know my background, I'm sure. Born and raised in Mexico City . . . only child . . . SMU graduate . . . medical school at UT . . . parents both dead . . . married to a highly successful computer engineer who made a fortune with his CompuTeen computer game company . . . a beautiful loving son . . . surgical training at the Metro Hospital here in Dallas . . . a failed marriage and all that goes with that . . . a successful surgical career until the Marquez incident." Cassy surprised herself again by how much of her personal life she so easily confided in this man she had known less than seventy-two hours.

"Most important of all, you have a son who loves you very much," Kevin said, refilling their wine glasses as they sat on the sofa.

"Sometimes I have to remind myself. I'm guilty of taking a lot for granted." Cassy sipped from her glass. "This wine is great," she said, intentionally steering the conversation to safer territory.

Kevin sat quietly, studying her. Cassy recognized his waiting manner of conversation. Even knowing that, the momentary lapse in the dialogue was too intense for her. She continued, "Kevin, you left out something when you told me about yourself. You're a man of charm and accomplishment. How have you come so far without. . . ."

"You're asking me why I've never married?" he interrupted.

Cassy flushed. "It's a reasonable question I think . . . a man of your charm and accomplishments."

"It's a reasonable question," Kevin said, nodding and touching her wine glass with his again.

"I'm sorry. I didn't mean to pry."

"No. No," Kevin said. "That's all right." Their eyes held each other across the wine glasses for several moments until Kevin raised his for a sip and said, "I only know that summer sang in me a little while, that sings in me no more."

"Are you answering my question?" Cassy asked.

"Edna St. Vincent Millay just answered your question for me." He sat on the sofa next to her, his eyes moving away from her. The cat continued her claim on the cushion between them.

"There's a sadness in you?" Cassy said, more as a question, inviting his answer only if he chose.

He sipped his wine again. "She was a long time ago. We were very much in love but realized our temperaments were so much different that living together was not possible."

" 'Tis better to have loved and lost, than never to have loved at all," Cassy said.

"Is it?" Kevin asked, sipping the wine and looking beyond the glass double door to the small walled patio beyond. "I'm not sure I agree with Tennyson." Kevin said nothing more, staring away thoughtfully and scratching Tosca's back, eliciting a purr. He was lost in a past that was closed to Cassy. Finally Kevin asked, "What about stir-fried vegetables and shrimp over rice? It's quick and easy."

"Sounds wonderful to me. Alex and I eat a lot of pizza. This will be a treat for both of us. Let me help." Kevin's relieved expression looked as if he welcomed the closure of the chink in the shield that allowed her a fleeting look into his innermost thoughts.

In the kitchen Kevin pulled on a serviceable canvas apron with the logo of the San Francisco Culinary Arts Institute and handed Cassy a matching one. "I don't believe you," Cassy said, laughing as she held the apron in front of the long blue denim dress that she had quickly changed into before they left her house in the late afternoon. "A trained gourmet cook. I know why you live in this gated compound with the guard at the front gate. It's to secure your home from attack by all the single women in Dallas."

"I wish," Kevin said as he began the preparation of the meal in an orderly and precise manner, lining up all the ingredients, then arranging them behind the appropriate utensil.

He assigned Cassy the salad preparation tasks. She was surprised when she opened the refrigerator to find it fully stocked with fresh salad greens, tomatoes, apples, orange juice, and milk.

Kevin noticed her expression. "The housekeeper does the shopping on Thursdays, too." He pulled the defrosted packages of shrimp and cut vegetables from the microwave and placed a battered oriental wok pan onto the gas burner of the stove. After pouring vegetable oil into the wok to heat, he placed the defrosted tiger shrimp onto the granite surface of the kitchen island, deftly peeling and deveining each shrimp under a steady stream of cold running water.

"Watching you peel and clean the shrimp reminds me about Betty Freeman's story of the puffer fish poisoning."

"The fugu fish."

"You know about puffer fish?"

"Sure. It's quite a delicacy. I've never tasted it. No one in Dallas that I know is qualified to prepare it. In Japan the chef must be licensed by the government to prepare the puffer fish. It's quite an art to clean the fish and remove all the poison without poisoning yourself or your guest who eats the fish."

"Betty told me about the paralysis that can occur promptly after eating the puffer fish. Sounds like a terrible way to die. The tetrodotoxin must be a powerful poison."

"Betty doesn't think Marquez ate a puffer fish?" Kevin asked.

"Hardly, but Marquez's paralysis was quite similar to the physiologic effects of eating an improperly prepared puffer fish."

"Is Betty checking Marquez's blood and tissue for the puffer fish poison?"

"She should know some results in a week," Cassy said, sniffing contentedly at the three plates she held while Kevin ladled the shrimp and stir-fried vegetables onto the rice. "This shrimp looks great."

"Alex, it's dinner time," Cassy called into the office. Simulated sounds of a jet airplane rolled down the hallway. A moment later Alex appeared in the kitchen, holding Tosca.

The dinner passed quickly. Cassy was surprised to see that it was nine o'clock as she helped Kevin clear away the dishes. Alex had returned to the bedroom office. Staccato sounds of gunfire and jet airplane engine noise once again erupted from the bedroom office.

"How about an espresso?"

"Sure. And I'm certain that you grind your own coffee."

"Certainly. A special Costa Rican blend that I . . . ," Kevin said just as the kitchen phone rang. He visibly stiffened. His face became grim and defensive when he brought the cordless phone to his ear. His expression degenerated further into a hardness that startled Cassy.

Kevin turned away from Cassy and carried the cordless telephone receiver into the living room. From the kitchen, Cassy heard his voice scream, "That scum bag. . . ." Even though the brick fireplace obscured her view of Kevin, she could feel his fury engulf the house like an arsonist's explosion. "He wants a chopper and a million dollars by midnight, or he's going to kill another one. . . . You tell that motherfucker to go to hell." Cassy's attention was riveted to the one-sided conversation and Kevin's accelerating furor.

As she stood before the open dishwasher with a plate in her hand, Kevin's angry commands stunned her. "Get the SWAT team for backup . . . I'll call the chief . . . I'm twenty minutes away." There was a long silence. Cassy turned toward the archway into the living room, expecting Kevin to appear.

Then Cassy heard Kevin's voice, so cold and menacing that she thought for an instant of grabbing Alex and running from the condominium. The rage that had rasped Kevin's voice at the first of the telephone conversation was now replaced by a possessed tranquility that chilled the nape of her neck. "No, there will be no negotiators . . . wait for me. I'll be there."

She faced Kevin when he returned to the kitchen and placed the telephone on the kitchen counter top. "What's happening?" Cassy asked, numbed by the transformation of the gentle man she had shared dinner with into this cold menacing presence.

"It's an emergency," he said as if he'd been called to the hospital for a friend's illness.

"Does this emergency have anything to do with Marquez or Alex and me? What's happening!" Cassy said and reached forward as he brushed past her, ignoring her completely.

"No. Nothing to do with you." Kevin's blank face registered no emotion. "I'll have a squad car take you home. I have to leave now." With that brusque dismissal, Kevin leaped the stairs to the master suite.

A couple of minutes later, he walked briskly down the stairwell, dressed once again in his blue blazer and gray pants, the uniform of the homicide chief. Cassy noticed his body was somehow different. Stronger, thicker, more powerful than she ever realized. She reached for him, but again he ignored her. As he moved past, her hand felt the rigidity of bullet-resistant ballistic nylon body armor under his freshly starched oxford shirt. The same conservative red striped tie he had worn earlier in the day was knotted in an exact half Windsor.

"Tell me what's happening!" Cassy shrieked.

"The man from El Paso . . . the one who killed his wife and children last week is barricaded in his parents' home in south Dallas. He's already killed his father tonight. He's threatening to kill his mother and two brothers unless the police meet his demands by midnight."

Kevin paused in the doorway, sadly looking at her, caught up in his world. "I must go. The squad car will be here for you in twenty minutes. Don't forget your present," he said and pointed to the velvet wrapped pistol on the counter top.

"Wait . . . wait. Do you think Alex will be all right while I'm in Mexico City this weekend?" Cassy asked.

"Should be," Kevin said. "If there's any danger, it's for you, not your son. You're the one who might be a target . . . not Alex. You'll be a lot safer in Mexico City and away from Dallas."

"Thanks for the reassurance," Cassy said sarcastically.

"I hope that you and Alex will come for dinner again." His mechanical expression devoid of emotion shivered Cassy. She shook herself, trying to rid the frigid rush that filled her. The front door closed behind Kevin, leaving Cassy and Alex alone in his home.

⸺

The black and white police squad car with Cassy and Alex sitting in the rear behind the rigid steel mesh grille separating the front and rear seat rolled up the long driveway to their home. Both of the uniformed officers were out of the car and opening the rear doors for them as soon as the car was parked under the covered driveway.

"We'll be by every hour tonight, Dr. Baldwin," the officer said.

Cassy thanked the officers and followed Alex into the house. The squad car did not roll down the driveway until the burglar alarm blinked red. Charlie danced around Alex, sniffing and barking at the imperceptible cat smells that his clothes spewed into the foyer. Alex and the dog raced up the stairs together.

When Cassy reached her bedroom, the answering machine blinked a single digit. Trent's recorded voice said, "Hi, Cass. It's nine-thirty. Calling with an update on Heather. She's doing great and will be coming home Sunday or Monday. Give me a call when you get in."

By the time Alex had showered and she had read part of a *Huck Finn* chapter to him, it was nearly eleven. Cassy hesitated to call Trent at that hour. She returned to her bedroom office and dialed his unlisted telephone number anyway. He answered on the first ring. "That's wonderful news about Heather. I'll come see her as soon as I get back from Mexico City," Cassy said after apologizing for the late call.

If Trent was curious about her whereabouts that evening, he did not ask, and Cassy was grateful for that. She had enough people, including two uniformed police officers, keeping her under surveillance. She didn't need Trent interrogating her.

"You've decided to take the Mexico City position with Tenoch?" Trent asked.

"No, I'm just going for a weekend. To meet some of the doctors. I want to tour the Instituto de Medico and visit my friend, Raul Garcia. He's the institute's Medical Director."

"This may be the opportunity of a lifetime for you," Trent said and paused a beat. "I would like to take Alex to the Rangers' game Saturday while you're gone. Okay with you?"

"He'd be delighted. It would take the sting out of my leaving him alone for the weekend."

"It'll do you good to be away."

"Yes. Too much has happened here in Dallas the last few days," Cassy sighed.

"Be careful," Trent said, his voice now serious and ominous.

"What's wrong?" Cassy asked, the change in his tone obvious. "Are you worried about something?"

"No. Nothing in particular, just be careful," Trent said.

"Don't worry. I'll be back Sunday."

"Be careful," she heard Trent say again. As she hung up the telephone the cautionary tone in his voice filled her with a foreboding. Or was she just imagining? No, she was not imagining. He had told her three times to be careful!

She juggled the velvet-wrapped gun in her hand and slid Kevin's pistol into the drawer of her bedside nightstand.

EIGHTEEN

"ALL RIGHT, DOG. I'll get up," Cassy groaned as she sat up and pulled her terry cloth robe over her T-shirt. Charlie's paws slid away from the bedside where moments earlier he had shaken her awake. His head popped up over the edge of her bed, his enormous eyes looking at her in the way that let Cassy know it was time for their morning newspaper retrieval ritual.

The thick morning air flowed into the cool foyer like molten wind as she opened the storm door at the front entrance. The chirping of unseen birds in the elm trees in the front yard quieted as Charlie circled the drive near the gate, grabbing the paper in his mouth. The dog raced back up the driveway with the rolled paper firmly gripped in his stout jaws just as a Dallas police cruiser eased slowly by the closed gate. The two uniformed officers waved to Cassy through the passenger window. Quickly she took the paper from Charlie and hurried back into the house, re-arming the burglar alarm after ramming the triple deadbolt mechanism locked.

By nine o'clock Cassy finished packing. Two overnight bags stood in front of the locked front door. While Cassy dawdled in the kitchen over a third cup of coffee, the kitchen intercom speaker buzzed. "Yes," she shouted in the direction of the wall speaker.

"Señora Baldwin, I am here to drive you to the airport," a Spanish accented voice came through the speaker. "May I assist you with your luggage?"

"Sí, por favor," Cassy said and pressed the button adjacent to the kitchen intercom to open the wrought iron driveway gate.

Lupita closed the dishwasher door noisily and picked up Cassy's coffee cup from the counter in front of her. "Lupita, where is Alex?" Cassy asked. The woman shrugged and began wiping the counter surface vigorously.

Cassy pressed the intercom switch to Alex's second-floor bedroom. "Alex, I've got to be going. Alex, are you there?" Cassy, after waiting several seconds for a response from her son, repeated into the intercom, "Alex?"

Cassy slipped her tapestried suit jacket over her cream-colored camisole and waited for a response from the intercom.

Lupita shook her head with a scowl. "Alex does not want you to leave without him."

"And how would you know what Alex wants?" Cassy asked, standing at the entryway of the family room.

"We talked at breakfast this morning while you were packing," Lupita said. "He cried a lot."

"And you waited until I'm walking out the door to tell me."

"You're his mother. What am I supposed to do with your son while you're in Mexico City?"

"For once . . . just once . . . you'll have to give more than you take around here." Cassy turned on her heeled pumps and left Lupita sulking by the dishwasher.

At the front door Cassy released the intrusion alarm and opened the double oak doors. Tenoch's gleaming black limousine idled in the brick circular drive in front of the house. She gestured to the chauffeur that she would be a moment.

With her hand on the knob to the closed door of Alex's bedroom, the resonant voice of Scott Spence Jr. jolted Cassy to a stop. "Ladies and gentleman, it is my honor to introduce the first and foremost woman in my life on the occasion of her selection as the Texas Humanitarian of the Year." His voice was drowned in a wash of applause that filled the bedroom and rattled the closed door.

"Oh, no," Cassy mumbled to herself. "Not this morning." Cassy twisted the doorknob and raised her voice to carry above the sound of the applause. "Alex, let me in." The clapping began to fade. Her son had chosen this moment to watch the videotape of the ceremony when she had received the Governor's Award for her service to the children of Mexico through the Am-Mex Children's Foundation. "Alex, open the door. I've got to be going. The car has come to take me to the airport."

Moments later, the lock clicked, but the door did not open. Cassy stood for several moments waiting for Alex to open the door until finally she pushed the door open. Alex, dressed in the denim jeans and Texas

Rangers' T-shirt he had worn the day before, sat huddled with his face two feet from the television screen. Scott Spence's handsome face was caught in profile by the camera as he turned to his left on the dais filled with formally dressed dignitaries. Cassy could not help but stare at her ex-husband's face. His highly placed cheek bones and angular facial features etched a star quality onto the videotape. He hasn't changed a bit in five years, thought Cassy. Still as handsome now as then.

"Alex, why are you watching that old videotape?" Cassy asked but knew why. "It's nine o'clock. I've got to be going." The videotape was Alex's weapon, the ultimate signal of his displeasure.

Then Cassy heard her husband's voice from five years earlier as the camera focused in a tight frame on her face, preserving for all time the tears glistening in her eyes. "Our three-year-old son, Alex, is as proud of his mother tonight as I am proud of Cassy. Believe me, Alex wanted to be here tonight." The crowd of fourteen hundred people laughed politely. Scott Spence continued with words that Cassy knew by heart, having heard them replayed by Alex many times since their divorce. "I present to you the love of my life. It is my privilege and honor to share this selfless and remarkable woman with you, with Texas, with this country, and with the world." The camera pulled back to show Scott Spence holding his hand outward to her as she stood up from her chair on the dais.

Cassy walked over to the television and punched the off button extinguishing the picture and touched her son's hair. She leaned forward to kiss the top of his head. The scent of Ivory shampoo momentarily flashed her mind to Alex's first few years and the nighttime baths and shampoos. A wrenching hurt in her heart arose over the memory of what was and what might have been, all revived by the videotape. Cassy leaned over her son's head, letting her arms drape over his shoulders. With her upside-down face inches from his, her eyes looked directly into his eyes, matching pairs.

"I don't want you to go to Mexico City," Alex said.

"But you'll have a good time here this weekend. Trent will take you to the Rangers' baseball game."

"Why can't I just stay with Dad?"

"Your father is a very busy man," Cassy said. "If your dad wants to win the governor's election, he has to work day and night."

"What am I going to do while you're gone besides the ball game?"

"You and Lupita will find something interesting and fun. You have all these new computer games your dad gave you," Cassy said. "I'll have all next week and probably more to be at home with you. We'll have a lot of time to do fun things together." Cassy straightened back up and leaned against the bunk beds. "I need to be going now. Help carry my suitcases to the car, my man."

Charlie bounced down the staircase ahead of them. Alex trailed Cassy down the winding stairway until they reached the foyer. "Look, Mom. A limo." Suddenly Alex's morose face turned bright. The moment Alex was out the door and running toward the open rear door of the car, Charlie leaped through the crack in the door, growling ferociously and baring his teeth at the Hispanic driver.

Alex jumped into the dark opening of the rear of the limousine. "Mom. There's a TV in here." When Alex disappeared into the rear seat of the limo, the Hispanic man moved toward the door much too quickly to satisfy Charlie. The dog leaped forward burying the man's forearm in his jaws like the morning newspaper.

"Down!" Cassy shouted. She frantically ran from the doorstep toward the rear of the limo just as Charlie wrestled the man to the driveway. Charlie's grip was like a steel animal trap slammed shut. The Hispanic driver beat the dog's head wildly with his free hand. "Stop!" Cassy shouted and struck Charlie's hind quarters twice before he finally released the driver. "Are you all right? Let me see."

The man stood up, brushed at his dark blue suit coat, and massaged his forearm through the sleeve. "I'm so sorry. He must have thought you were going to take Alex away." Cassy took the man's arm and pulled up the sleeve of his coat. A reddened ridge of bite marks scored the man's forearm. "You'll have a bruise but the skin is intact. Let me get an ice bag," Cassy said.

"No, Señora. It is not necessary," the man said, rolling the sleeve back down. "It is time to go. If you will permit me to take your bags."

"Alex, please help." The driver moved around Cassy, giving wide berth to Charlie who sat quietly next to Cassy, held by her firm grip on his collar. "You were with Señor Tenoch in the ER on Saturday?" Cassy asked as the man lifted the two bags into the trunk.

"Sí," the man said, turning to look at Cassy. "I am Señor Tenoch's assistant," he said, pride swelling his voice. "I am Alberto."

"I remember you from Saturday night as well as the luncheon." Alberto closed the trunk, then returned to the passenger door. Cassy slowly released her grip on Charlie.

"He doesn't like other animals or strangers," Cassy said.

"Sí, Señora. He is strong-willed . . . and handsome." Alberto held the rear door of the limo like a shield.

"Are we meeting Tenoch at the airport?" Cassy asked. Charlie stood beside Alex, quietly watching Cassy settle into the dim interior of the limousine's passenger compartment.

"No, Señora. He is already in Mexico City," Alberto said, his hand poised on the door handle. "Señor Tenoch has instructed me to convey his apologies that he will be unable to accompany you."

Alex leaned into the passenger seat, and Cassy kissed his cheek. "Tell Señor Tenoch that I want another baseball card," Alex said.

"We'll see. I'll bring you a present. Take care of Charlie. I love you," Cassy said as Alberto closed the rear door with a dull thud and quickly slid into the driver's seat. Her tears began when she looked through the rear window and waved at Alex as the limousine pulled away down the long driveway.

The limousine interior was accented in plush black leather and thick spongy carpeting. A gold ice bucket cradled a crystal pitcher of fresh orange juice. A carafe of coffee was secured to a table mounted in the foot well. A gold tray of Mexican breakfast pastries rested on the center bar of the facing seat.

"Good morning, Cassy," Tenoch's voice surrounded her from concealed speakers in the rear compartment. "I apologize for not being able to accompany you to Mexico City, but I had to return to Mexico City unexpectedly last night. My staff will ensure an enjoyable trip for you."

While Tenoch's voice filled the compartment, Cassy listened carefully, trying to determine whether he was speaking from a telephone somewhere or whether his voice was recorded.

"You will find a schedule of our activities in the notebook on the seat," the voice continued without waiting for her response.

Cassy picked up the supple black leather notebook and flipped it open to a neatly typed schedule of events, a day's tour guide. "We will have our first meeting with the doctors this afternoon at the Instituto. Then I have several other activities planned for you and me for tomorrow and Sunday."

"Fine," Cassy said. "This schedule looks interesting."

The voice rolled over her reply. "And Saturday evening I have arranged a fiesta in your honor with the U.S. Ambassador to Mexico, the mayor of Mexico City, and a few other influential Mexico City citizens. I will await your arrival with pleasure," Tenoch said, and then the speaker clicked into silence.

Twenty minutes later, the limousine slowed and momentarily stopped before passing through onto the concrete tarmac of the sprawling DFW Airport. Cassy glimpsed the lineup of small private jets standing in parade formation as the limousine rolled past their noses. The car stopped smoothly. The rear car door immediately swung open.

"Buenos días, Dr. Baldwin." An Hispanic man, dressed in a blue suit with small gold pilot wings on his left lapel, extended his hand to help her from the limousine. Her heels sank immediately into a red plush carpet that led to a mobile stairway rolled up to the forward cabin door of a Boeing 727. The gleaming aluminum sheen of the skin of the aircraft radiated the morning sun. The minimalist gold striping on the side of the aircraft converged onto a gold filigreed Aztec calender glowing on the upright tail assembly.

The blue-suited man introduced the flight crew. "I am Captain Carlos Menendez, your co-pilot is Hector Tomaso, your flight engineer is Luis Rodriguez . . . we are at your service." The two other blue suited men stood at attention at the foot of the staircase. "Your aircraft today is a Boeing 727, specially adapted for Tenoch's worldwide travel requirements."

"Am I the only passenger?" Cassy asked, looking around the deserted tarmac.

"Sí, Señora," the pilot said. "If you will allow me your passport, I will take care of the U.S. Customs formalities. Flight time to Mexico City will be ninety-eight minutes. The Aztec Corporation helicopter is standing by for your arrival. You should be with Señor Tenoch by eleven-thirty."

As soon as Cassy stepped over the threshold into the main cabin of the aircraft, she stopped, stunned by the opulence of the interior furnishings. It was as if she had stepped into the lavish living area of a Mexico City home she vaguely remembered from her childhood.

"May I familiarize you with the cabin and its safety features," Alberto said as he took Cassy's jacket. "I will serve as your flight steward today." Cassy tested the glove leather tufted sofa that swept the length of the forward half of the fuselage. A low table with gold accent strips was mounted between the sofa and the two oversized chairs along the opposite wall of the cabin.

Alberto gestured for Cassy to follow him on a tour of the interior. Just behind the frosted partition that separated the main cabin from the rear of the aircraft, a table surrounded by six cushioned leather chairs filled the dining section. A single setting of china and crystal stood before the end chair. A dozen red roses in a crystal vase fixed to the center of the table scented the main cabin.

"I'm overwhelmed," Cassy said. She rolled the linen table cloth between her thumb and index finger. "Does Señor Tenoch use the plane often?"

"It is a second home for him," Alberto said.

"What is beyond the wall?" Cassy asked, looking at the aft bulkhead. A miniaturized reproduction of the Aztec stone calendar formed the aft bulkhead wall beyond the dining room.

"That is Señor Tenoch's bedroom," Alberto said.

The aircraft shivered as the jet engines spun into a low rumble. Alberto led Cassy forward to the soft cushioned lounge chair on the right side of the main cabin. A muted chime sounded. Alberto cinched Cassy into the chair with a seat belt. "Captain Menendez has signaled that we are cleared for take off. Have you decided what you would like for brunch?"

"What do you suggest?"

"Anything the Señora wishes."

"You surprise me then."

"A mimosa champagne cocktail followed by my special light omelet? Nothing to overpower your appetite."

As the plane lifted up, Alberto appeared at her side, holding a crystal flute with the fresh orange juice champagne cocktail. "Here are the morning papers, *New York Times*, *Wall Street Journal*, *Dallas Morning News*. If you wish, I can adjust the television for you to a videotape of *CNN News*."

"That's not necessary, Alberto. Por favor. Usted es muy amable. You are most gracious."

The flat Texas country fell away beneath the plane as it rose steadily through patchy fluffs of gray clouds glowing like luminescent cotton balls under the sun in the east. The precise rectangular patterns of the cultivated fields grew smaller like a diminishing green and brown chess board until the plane leveled out. Cassy could barely distinguish the sections of the crosshatched earth more than seven miles below her. Cassy released her seat belt and touched the recessed button on the arm of her chair. Instantly Alberto stepped from the forward kitchen galley situated just behind the forward wall separating the flight crew from the main cabin. "Sí, Señora?" he said.

"I would like to freshen up before breakfast," Cassy said.

"Certainly." He nodded toward the rear of the cabin and lead her beyond the frosted glass partition. He opened the rear door with the Aztec sun calender embossed on it and gestured for Cassy to enter. Inside Tenoch's bedroom compartment occupying the rear third of the aircraft, a queen-size bed occupied the side wall. Alberto opened another door into a luxurious bathroom equipped with gold fixtures complete with a marble shower.

When Cassy returned to the front cabin, Alberto held the chair at the dining table for her. "Your breakfast is ready." The omelet was perfectly prepared . . . a fluffy, delicate melange of eggs, green and red pepper, eggs, and cheese. A second glass of the champagne cocktail left Cassy with a sleepy wooziness. She refused the offer of a third cocktail and settled into the soft lounge chair where she dozed until the slight downward tilt of the aircraft awakened her a half hour later.

As the plane descended into Mexico City, Cassy watched the sprawling city, in a cauldron of smoke and haze formed by a ring of mountains surrounding the city, enlarge to meet the descending 727. The wheels of the plane touched the runway so softly that Cassy was uncertain that the plane was on the ground until she heard and felt the thrust of the reversing jets.

The plane taxied to a stop in front of the Presidential hanger, the private terminal reserved for visiting dignitaries, guarded by a cyclone fence and Mexican military patrols. Alberto held her tapestried suit jacket as she slipped her arms in. "Señor Tenoch's helicopter will take you to his penthouse. I will take care of your baggage and the Mexican customs."

Cassy stepped out the forward door of the aircraft. The smoggy air immediately assaulted her nose and eyes as if she had been blasted by a hot air hose. The tan-gray sky laid over the city like a pall. She blinked rapidly, trying to flush out the stinging irritation that attacked the delicate membranes of her eyes and nose. By the time she had walked down the aircraft steps her chest heaved. She could feel her heart race.

About two hundred feet beyond the left wing of the 727, a Bell helicopter stood with its main rotor revolving slowly. A red carpet unfurled from the bottom of the stairwell to the open door of the six passenger helicopter. Two Mexican customs officials, dressed in heavily starched khaki uniforms, greeted Cassy at the foot of the portable stairwell. "Buenos días, Señora Baldwin. Welcome to Mexico City," the uniformed agent said. "Allow me to escort you to Señor Tenoch's helicopter." After Cassy had walked the two hundred feet to the helicopter, her head pounded with pain. She tried to conceal her breathlessness.

Just as she buckled her seat belt in the passenger compartment of the jet helicopter, the throbbing pulsation of the whirling jet rotor carried the helicopter into the dense layer of smoke and haze blanketing the city. Alberto sat opposite Cassy, rarely looking out the window.

Thirteen minutes later the chopper dropped gently onto the rooftop heliport of Tenoch's penthouse at the top of Mexico City's tallest building. As soon as the skids of the helicopter touched the rooftop, sixty-two floors above the city, the door opened. Another khaki uniformed guard greeted Cassy. She ducked under the turning rotor, stopping for a moment, to turn her body in a full circle to view the city stretching beyond her vision into the smoky haze.

"This way, please," the attendant said in unaccented English. A tremor of fright filled her as the height of the building flashed through her awareness. Her pulse still raced, and she felt just on the edge of air hunger. Her breathing came quick and deep. The horizon fluttered in the distance. She seemed at the summit of the unsteadiest point in her life.

"It is best not to look down, Señora," the young Hispanic said when he noticed her hesitation. "Are you all right?"

"I'm fine. It's been a while since I have been in Mexico City. I was trying to get my bearings," Cassy said.

"There is Chapultepec Park," the man said pointing to a green belt resembling New York's Central Park at the edge of the central city. He continued pointing with his extended arm as Cassy looked into the city. "The University is there. The Zócalo square in the center of town is just beyond us." A moment passed and Cassy's head began to clear. The guard seemed impatient and nervous by the delay. "Now we must go below. Señor Tenoch is waiting." He led her into the elevator at the edge of the roof. The car dropped them two floors and opened into a dark hardwood foyer where Tenoch stood.

"Cassy, I am delighted you are here," Tenoch said and took her right hand in both of his. The subtle pleasant fragrance of his cologne was a welcome change from the metallic odor of the city. His hands shook hers in a formal vigorous handshake.

"It is my pleasure to be back in our native city," Cassy said, noticing the words 'our native' provoked a wide smile from him.

Tenoch led her from the entry foyer into an enormous two story room. Groupings of black leather sofas and chairs were scattered on the dark hardwood floors. At the opposite end of the room, a magnificent dark marble staircase ascended to a balcony adorned with yet another stone replica of the Aztec sun calender. The two other walls of the cavernous room were curtains of tinted glass. When Cassy stood in the center of the room, a peculiar disoriented feeling came over her, as if looking into a cloud formation.

"The disorientation is momentary," Tenoch said, touching her elbow for support. Above them in the center of the cavernous room, a gold ball chandelier formed by tiny squares of Tiffany crystal glinted reflections of finely diffused light throughout the room. "You are now above everyone in Mexico City. My home is above all."

"It's incredible," Cassy said and turned her gaze back into the room, noticing an archway beneath the marble stairwell.

"It's my office and also the room for my Aztec collection," he said, taking her by the elbow. They walked together across the grand salon that reminded Cassy of an empty cathedral.

When they passed under the archway and into his office, Cassy felt her momentary spatial disorientation return as they stepped into the room. Glass walls on three sides surrounded them, again giving her the impression she was standing in a cloud. Tinted light filled the room with a celestial glow.

"My god," Cassy said as she looked around the room. "You have the National Anthropological Museum here." She touched a marble pedestal holding an intricately carved stone Aztec artifact resembling a serpent with humanoid features.

"I show this room only to my most trusted associates. Even Trent is unaware of it. There are some minor Mexican regulations about private ownership and export of Mexican antiquities." He smiled and waved his arms expansively to the edge of the room lined with glass display cases.

"My collection of artifacts details the history of the Aztec civilization in Mexico City from the establishment of Tenochtitlan in the fourteenth century until the arrival of that Spanish murderer, Cortez, in 1519." Tenoch lectured as he guided her among the display cases. The parabolic shape of the room pulled the light into the room, but it seemed immediately absorbed by the dark hardwood floors.

They stopped at a rounded tan stone stool with slanted sides embellished in bas relief carvings. "Do you recognize this?" Tenoch asked and Cassy shook her head.

"Oh, yes," Cassy said quickly. "It's just like the stone table you have between the sofas in your sky box at the Texas Ranger stadium."

Tenoch smiled. "You are most observant." Cassy ran her fingers over the cold granular surface of the gray stone.

"The table in my sky box is an exact copy of this original sacrificial stone."

Cassy looked at him quizzically.

"You are not familiar with the Aztec ceremonial rite of human sacrifice?" Tenoch asked.

"Yes," Cassy said quietly. "It is not a part of my Mexican heritage that makes me proud. Those human sacrifices were a barbaric and savage ceremony . . . a civilization gone crazy. This stone was part of that . . . ?" Cassy could not finish the question. She pulled her hand away from the flat surface of the stone.

"The stone has seen blood," Tenoch said. "It is an actual ceremonial pedestal on which human sacrifices were stretched as their hearts were removed for presentation to the Aztec gods."

"It's a barbaric period in the history of Mexico. I'm ashamed of my heritage for such human cruelty."

"Cassy, you misunderstand our ancestors," Tenoch said kindly. He ran his palm across the granular flat surface of the low stone pedestal. "The Aztec sacrificial rite is barbaric only to those who do not understand."

"How can you justify the savagery of removing a beating heart from another human?"

"Is it any different from utilizing heart donors for human heart transplantation in the last half of the twentieth century?" Tenoch asked, smiling pleasantly as he moved her away from the stone and continued his guided tour of his Aztec antiquities.

"But heart transplantation serves a humanitarian and noble purpose."

"The hearts of the human sacrifices were necessary in the theosophy of the Aztec culture to ensure that the sun would return each day. What more noble and humanitarian purpose than for the Aztecs to present human hearts to their gods who were the personification of the energy of the sun in their culture?"

"Except . . . ," Cassy tried to interrupt, but Tenoch continued in an agreeable tone as if they were discussing flowers or wine or ancient artwork.

"How is heart transplantation today any different?" Tenoch asked but didn't wait for her answer. "The Aztec sacrifice preserved sun and life, just as you preserve individual life in today's society with a heart transplant."

"You have conjured up an unusual analogy," Cassy replied. "Even if one accepted that the goal of removal of the heart in the Aztec society was humanitarian in the sense that it appeased an accepted god of their civilization, you overlook a critical difference in your comparison. The Aztec sacrificial victims were alive and healthy. Today's heart donor is brain-dead."

"But, Cassy, the sacrificial victims in the Aztec ceremony were dead in the Aztec social structure. As socially dead as today's brain-dead donor."

Cassy said nothing and looked away, realizing that it was pointless to continue debating Tenoch. He moved her along to a glass-fronted display case and opened the glass door to remove a twelve-inch stone dagger. A carved grotesque humanoid figure adorned its handle. "This is an Aztec sacrificial knife made from the volcanic glass found around Mexico City."

The double-edged sharpness of the cobbled blackish green blade felt like a scalpel under Cassy's thumb. "My goodness, it still has its edge. Where did you get this?" Cassy asked.

"The ceremonial knife was recovered from the Pyramid of the Sun at Teotihuacan. A few years ago a burial tomb and sacrificial chamber were discovered in the center of the pyramid. None outside my anthropology group realizes that subterranean tunnels exist in this pyramid. This knife was found in the central chamber of the Pyramid of the Sun during an archeological study that I have financed. My archeology group presented this sacrificial knife to me in gratitude for my funding the research mission at Teotihuacan."

"This knife has been used for human sacrifice?" Cassy asked, holding the sculpted knife at arm's length.

"Of course, my dear," Tenoch said lightly, dismissing the discussion. "Come let us have a nice lunch. Then we can begin our afternoon's business." Tenoch turned to Alberto who had silently stationed himself at the office entryway. "Place Dr. Baldwin's luggage in my guest room."

Cassy stopped and turned. "Tenoch, I'm afraid there is a misunderstanding. I assumed that I would be staying at one of the hotels in Mexico City."

"You do not wish to stay here?" His look was puzzled and affronted.

"Your hospitality overwhelms me, but I must insist on a hotel," Cassy said, having recovered her composure now that they had moved out of his office and into the grand salon once again.

"Very well," Tenoch said and turned to Alberto who stood just behind Tenoch. "The Presidential Suite at the Camino Real."

"Come, we will have our lunch now," Tenoch continued. A gracious smile once again returned to his face.

While they were in Tenoch's office, a single circular table had been set up in the center of the grand salon directly beneath the gold chandelier globe that hung from the ceiling beams of the two-story room. Tenoch pulled Cassy's chair out for her and seated her directly across from him at the small circular table. Two place settings of gold dishes and a lavish display of gold knives and forks adorned the glistening white linen tablecloth.

As soon as Tenoch seated himself, Vivaldi's *Four Seasons* floated through the room with a sound so real that Cassy felt as if she were seated in the orchestra. "Vivaldi is one of your favorites," Tenoch said as a simple statement of fact. Cassy smiled in return, wondering how and why Tenoch had searched out her favorite music.

The meal was simple but exquisite. A broiled fresh tuna flaked over a bed of crisp garden greens followed a tangy gazpacho soup. During the meal, the conversation was casual and desultory. Tenoch's mention of Alberto fascinated her. Perhaps it was the affectionate tone he used when speaking of Alberto. "I am pleased that you enjoyed your brunch on the airplane," he said. "Alberto is my talented chef. This lunch is also his creation. He oversees my kitchen as well as being my personal assistant."

"Has he worked for you long?" Cassy asked.

"Twenty years. Since I adopted him from the same orphanage where I lived," Tenoch said. For an instant Cassy sensed the pride of a father.

"You are most generous with your successes," Cassy said.

"I hope to share my successes with you," he said pleasantly, pulling her chair back for her. "Shall we now begin our tour of the Instituto de Medico?"

NINETEEN

C ASSY LEANED forward to peer out the side window of Tenoch's helicopter as the chopper tilted into a gradual circling pattern to land at the Instituto de Medico. Tenoch sat across from Cassy, completely uninterested in the changing views below. His attention focused on Cassy.

The complex of medical buildings, arranged like a modern college campus, grew quickly in size as the chopper descended to the landing pad that was ringed by a dozen white-coated figures like miniature soldiers standing at attention. The tiny figures telescoped into life-size figures as Tenoch's helicopter hovered to a touchdown perfectly centered on the crimson crossbars painted in the center of the white concrete landing pad.

When the main rotor blades slowed to a freely spinning idle, Cassy followed Tenoch down the steps of the passenger compartment. The thick hot air smothered her as she stepped onto the landing pad. The heat of the concrete flowed through the soles of her pumps as if they were paper. Alberto remained a moment in the helicopter until Tenoch and Cassy had walked quickly, heads down, under the slowly revolving rotor to reach the white-coated figures assembled in a horseshoe formation at the edge of the concrete landing square. He then followed them down the steps, carrying Tenoch's hand-tooled leather briefcase.

A distinguished, white-coated, balding Hispanic man broke from the apex of the group and approached Tenoch. "Señor Tenoch, you honor us by your presence." Sweat glistened on the man's brown bald head in a patina of miniature water droplets as he pumped Tenoch's hand. "I am an admirer of your beautiful honored guest." The doctor released Tenoch's handshake and turned to Cassy, opening his arms in a wide expansive greeting.

"Raul," Cassy said loudly over the diminishing whine of the chopper's jet engine. "I'm delighted to see you, as always, my dear friend." Raul Garcia took both Cassy's hands, pulling her toward him and kissing her cheek. "You have done so much for Mexico." He beamed at her and then turned to face Tenoch. "Dr. Baldwin is the best. . . ."

"The best at everything, of course, my friend. That is why I am recruiting her to return to Mexico City. It is her destiny."

The spinning rotor blades stopped. The noise of the chopper's engine cleared. The hot afternoon wind whirled around the concrete landing pad. The horseshoe formation of hospital personnel closed around Cassy and Tenoch like a white wreath. For several minutes Dr. Garcia introduced both of them to each of the hospital workers as visiting dignitaries to the Instituto. A young Mexican woman, dressed in hospital whites with cameras and lenses clipped to a Sam Browne belt, circled the group, darting in and out of the white wreath for quick flash pictures.

Dr. Garcia introduced Cassy to the Chief of Nursing Services, a heavyset Hispanic matron in a traditional nurses' uniform complete with starched white cap. The woman took Cassy's right hand in both of hers and said in Spanish, "Dr. Baldwin, we are so pleased that you came to the Instituto. We have many who need heart transplants. Seven have come to see you today."

At that moment, a young woman in a short white coat insinuated herself through the crowds and whispered in Dr. Raul Garcia's ear. His jovial expression turned grim.

"My apologies, Señor Tenoch," Dr. Garcia said, nervously rolling the papers he held in his hands into a tube. "We must delay our tour. Dr. Hendricks is calling for Dr. Baldwin."

"What did Trent want?" Cassy asked, immediately tensed by the thought that Alex had been hurt. Her stomach gurgled and knotted at the thought of an accident.

"An emergency situation has arisen in Dallas. Dr. Hendricks wishes Dr. Baldwin to call him as soon as possible," Dr. Garcia said. Cassy's legs weakened, and she leaned against the tile wall of the hospital corridor for support before moving down the hallway with Dr. Garcia and Tenoch.

Dr. Garcia opened the door to his modest office and ushered them past the secretary. He seated himself behind a small wooden desk only after Cassy and Tenoch were seated in straight wooden chairs opposite him.

"What is the emergency in Dallas?" asked Cassy, finally able to bring herself to form the words to inquire about Alex. "It's not my son, is it?"

"No, no, not at all," Dr. Garcia said soothingly. "We have a heart donor at the Instituto who is suitable for one of Dr. Hendricks' patients in Texas." The cramping in her abdomen disappeared. "A potential donor arrived at the Instituto late last night. Trent wants you to evaluate the donor and to harvest the heart for him, if possible." The telephone rang. He passed it to Cassy without answering.

"Trent, what's up?" Cassy said abruptly without a greeting.

"We have an opportunity to save the life of one of my patients who's dying here at the Metro. Dr. Garcia has a heart for him," Trent said. "I know we can't locate a donor here in this country quick enough for my patient. He's not going to last more than a few hours without a new heart. Another success like Heather will really help us get under way with Tenoch's plan of an international donor program."

"Who's your recipient?"

"A forty-two-year-old man in cardiogenic shock from a heart attack yesterday. We've got him on maximum life support—drugs, pumps, the usual drill," Trent said briskly.

"What's the donor situation you've come up with here in Mexico City?" Cassy asked, unaware of her own depersonalization of the donor as a patient.

"As luck would have it, a twenty-seven-year-old Hispanic came through Garcia's ER early this morning. The donor is an excellent match for my recipient. Raul tells me that his donor was declared brain-dead early this morning."

"Trauma?" Cassy asked matter-of-factly.

"No. Cerebral hemorrhage. Garcia says we need to move quick . . . the donor's heart rate is slowing and the blood pressure dropping. We need to get the heart out and suspended using my Hiberna mixture right now, or it won't be any good for a transplant. Could you snatch the heart? We ought to be able to transplant my man here in Dallas with it three hours from now if you hurry. God knows it's his only chance."

"How are we going to get the heart through Customs and into the United States?"

"Don't worry about that," Trent said. "Walter Simmons has already taken care of the administrative details."

"Walter?"

"Despite your differences with Walter, he's a helluva good administrator. He took care of the governmental exemptions we needed with a few phone calls. He's pretty well connected in the politics of these things, especially after the success with Heather."

"I'll get back to you in fifteen minutes just as soon as I look the donor over," Cassy said abruptly and hung up on Trent. The cooperation of

Walter Simmons took her aback. Maybe I'm reading Walter wrong, Cassy thought. Then her mind shifted into a medical mode. She knew what the next few minutes required. Time was ebbing for the donor heart—and the waiting recipient in Dallas.

"Dr. Garcia, where's the donor?" Cassy asked, standing up from the uncomfortable wooden chair.

Minutes later Dr. Garcia escorted Cassy into the ICU, state-of-the art unit comparable to that of the Metro. Cassy scanned through the donor's medical record. The clinical summary was neatly presented in clear hand-written Spanish: A twenty-seven-year-old man fell unconscious at a bar in Mexico City at one a.m. In the ER of the Instituto de Medico, he was diagnosed as suffering from an 'intracerebral hemorrhage.' Throughout the night, the donor showed no signs of any brain activity. The Instituto staff neurologist declared brain death an hour ago. His written opinion was countersigned by two other staff physicians.

"It's a tragedy, a young man's life extinguished in its prime by a brain hemorrhage," Cassy said, snapping the hinged metal clipboard closed.

Cassy studied the Hispanic man. He lay as still as a cadaver except for the mechanical movement of his chest. Each stroke of the ventilator bellows inflated and deflated his lungs. Cassy's emotional detachment see-sawed from her objectively clinical assessment of the heart contained in the brain-dead man to her unavoidable reflection on the human tragedy before her—a healthy life snuffed in its prime.

It took Cassy only a few seconds to determine that the man's vital signs were marginal and the trend worsening. "His heart's not going to last much longer." She continued her thinking out loud while she and Raul studied the video monitor together. "The slow heart rate and low blood pressure are not good signs. I've got to explant the heart as quickly as possible and suspend its metabolism before it shuts down completely and becomes worthless," she said.

Cassy studied the man's retinal eye fields through an ophthalmoscope. "Normal appearance of the ophthalmic arteries and veins. No swelling of the optic nerve. The eye reflexes are absent. His pupils are dilated and not reactive to light," she said and then ticked off the criteria of brain death. The man's arms and legs fell flaccid at his side when Cassy picked them up and released each. Cassy detached the tubing in the man's windpipe from the ventilator bellows that delivered oxygen to the lungs. The man lay completely motionless without any effort to breathe even after a full minute away from the life-sustaining artificial ventilation of his lungs.

"His brain is dead, Dr. Baldwin," Dr. Garcia said, reproaching her for her implicit questioning of his diagnosis of brain death.

"I just need to be certain . . . ," Cassy said without elaborating on her Saturday night experience with Marquez.

"The electroencephalogram shows no brain wave activity," Garcia said tactfully. His impatience with her showed in his fixed expression.

Cassy paused for a moment and then asked, "Is the Operating Room ready?"

"It will require fifteen minutes to take him to the OR and prep him," Garcia said.

"The consent from the family?" Cassy asked.

"All completed," Garcia said, nodding impatiently.

"Let me call Trent back so that he can coordinate the surgery of his recipient at Metro Hospital," Cassy said. She slowly moved away from the young Hispanic donor. "Who's going to fly the heart to Dallas?"

"Señor Tenoch will provide his aircraft," Dr. Garcia said as the two of them left the ICU. They turned down the shiny tile-lined corridor leading to his office. No sooner had they entered the office again than the secretary's voice on the intercom announced, "I have Dr. Hendricks on the line."

"I should have the heart out and in my hands in twenty-five minutes," Cassy said when she picked up the receiver. "It looks good except the heart rate is slowing and the blood pressure is falling."

"You need to get that damned heart now," Trent said. "Or it will be too late."

"The heart will be at Metro in less than three hours," she said.

"Go for it, Cass," Trent said. "I'll be ready to sew the heart into the recipient as soon as it arrives here."

Dr. Garcia hurried Tenoch and Cassy to the operating room, showing Cassy into the Nurses' Locker Room where she quickly changed into surgical scrub clothes. When she arrived in the OR, Dr. Garcia and Tenoch, each in scrub pajamas, stood beside the naked torso of a muscular man on the table.

The operating suite comforted Cassy. Her familiarity with its surroundings reassured her—the chilled room, the faint sweetness of the mixture of antiseptic solutions, and the human form on the operating table requiring her skills.

"Dr. Baldwin, I'm Dr. Fernandez," the anesthesiologist hidden behind a surgical mask and hood at the head of the OR said.

"How's the donor?" Cassy asked.

"You may wish to expedite your harvest," the anesthesiologist said in formal Spanish. "The heart rate has slowed. His blood pressure is down in the seventies. I've been trying to keep his pressure up since he arrived in the OR. I've turned up the dopamine drip, but his blood pressure is still sagging."

"Don't let it go lower," Cassy said.

"Sí, Doctora," the anesthesiologist said. "What is it you wish me to do?" His cool reserved tone defined the cultural and gender differences between them. The anesthesiologist's response tacitly challenged Cassy to take charge if she thought she could handle the maintenance of the donor's vital signs better than he.

Accepting his implied challenge of her skill, Cassy said, "Give a two hundred fifty milliliter bolus of Plasmalyte. We can't let the pressure fall much more or the heart won't function after we transplant it. If that amount of intravenous fluid doesn't bring up the blood pressure, then begin an intravenous calcium infusion."

"I suggest you facilitate the procurement," the anesthesiologist said stiffly.

"Prep him," Cassy said. Quickly two masked and hooded nurses painted the unconscious donor's chest with a mahogany coat of iodinated antiseptic solution. Moving efficiently and rapidly, the nurses folded sterile towels and sheets about the body leaving a bare opening over the front of his chest.

After slipping into the sterile surgical gown and gloves held by one of the two gowned surgical technicians, Cassy picked up the scalpel and drew a full thickness incision down the midline of the chest, exposing the glistening white breast bone beneath the filleted yellow fatty tissues and pectoral muscles. Dark red blood oozed out of the incision and was quickly blotted away with gauze cloths by the surgical technician. Cassy then zipped open the one-inch thick breast bone with a smooth motion of a battery powered saber saw. The heart lay beating, slow and strong, encased in its pericardial sac just beneath the cut edges of the breast bone.

"Blood pressure's falling," the anesthesiologist announced, a trace of panic in his heavily accented English.

"Bolus him with a dose of neosynephrine. I'll have this heart out in a couple of minutes." Moving hurriedly now, Cassy grabbed the sterile syringe containing a blood-thinning anticoagulant and plunged the needle into the aorta, the main artery of the heart, emptying the blood thinner directly into the young man's blood stream.

Cassy next took a second syringe filled with a potassium-rich saline solution. Pressing the plunger of the syringe, her fingers injected an ounce of clear yellow cardioplegic fluid also directly into the aorta. Instantly, the heart stood still, stopped as if stunned, as it indeed had been by the potassium ions that rendered the heart muscle temporarily paralyzed.

The technician slapped the dissecting scissors into Cassy's hand. She slashed the major blood vessels entering and leaving the now quiet heart, severing the heart's connection to the chest. Cassy then pulled the heart out of the gaping chest, the residual blood pouring out of the cut ends of the arteries and veins. With the heart held over the surgical field, Cassy tipped it over and over, draining the residual blood from the heart's chambers like pouring a thick red fluid from a round vase.

With the empty quiet heart held reverently in her hands, she turned to a long rectangular, sterile table and laid the limp organ into a stainless steel basin of icy slush. Cassy looked up to see Tenoch's dark eyes above his surgical mask peering at the heart. He said several words that Cassy could not understand.

"I'm sorry I didn't hear you."

"Thus he giveth the sun to drink," Tenoch said, leaning over so that his head nearly touched her ear and whispering softly so that none of the OR personnel could hear him. She looked up to meet his dark penetrating gaze. A shudder rocked her mind.

"It's an Aztec prayer," Tenoch said quietly. The flatness of his expression and the jumbled words sent a passing shiver of uncertainty over her. After a moment that seemed an eternity, her worry faded in the pressure of examining and preparing the donor heart for shipment. Cassy looked back at the heart to continue the preparation of the donor heart for transport. Cassy cupped it in one hand and rinsed it thoroughly in the icy slush. Then she slipped the chilled muscular organ into two sterile plastic bags, one inside the other. When she looked up again, Tenoch was no longer in the OR.

Dr. Garcia stepped forward with the insulated Igloo ice chest. "The helicopter is ready to take the heart to the Presidential hanger," he said.

"Who's meeting the plane in Dallas?" Cassy asked.

"The Metro Hospital emergency van will pick up the heart at DFW," Dr. Garcia said as he handed the ice chest to Alberto who stood in the hallway just outside the OR.

Cassy returned to the body to begin the surgical closure of the chest, suturing shut the void where the man's heart had beaten until moments before. "My staff will dispose of the body," Dr. Garcia said touching Cassy's gowned arm. "Please . . . shall we have our coffee in my office?"

Cassy retreated into the deserted Nurses' Lounge and changed quickly out of the surgical scrub clothes. Cassy was grateful for the solitude while she tried to sort through Tenoch's appearance at the donor harvesting. Why had Tenoch appeared at the donor procurement? What was his whispered comment? What was it that he had said? Then she remembered. 'Thus he giveth the sun to drink.'

Cassy reapplied a touch of lipstick and hesitated in front of the mirror as she studied her lips. She asked her mirror's image, "What was Tenoch doing in there?" Shaking her head and leaving the question unanswered in the silence of the Nurses' Lounge, Cassy found her way in the connecting tile hospital corridors back to the Medical Director's office.

⸺

Seated around the coffee table in Dr. Garcia's office, the Instituto Director poured thick, heavily aromatic Mexican coffee for himself. Tenoch and Cassy declined. Alberto, seated at the edge of the room in a straight chair with Tenoch's briefcase at his side, shook his head when Garcia offered him coffee.

"Raul, I have seen again our opportunity . . . life has been given," Tenoch said.

"Yes, it is satisfying, my friend. To provide the gift of life to a fellow human being," Dr. Garcia said, sipping his coffee.

"I wish to reward someone for this gift of life. Is that the correct term, Cassy, rewarded gifting?" Tenoch asked.

"Yes, it is one of the ideas you, Trent, and I discussed at lunch this week," Cassy said.

Tenoch nodded to Alberto who moved quickly from his chair and opened the leather briefcase, displaying its contents like a salesman's satchel. Cassy gasped, and Garcia sucked in his breath when he looked into the case. Packets of wrinkled and worn hundred dollar bills were neatly stacked, precisely filling the briefcase.

"I wish to reward the family of this donor for their gift of life," Tenoch said, lifting his index finger with the obsidian ring in a signal to Alberto who removed a neatly-bound ten thousand dollar packet of bills and presented it to Dr. Garcia.

"Oh, no," Garcia said. "The family does not expect anything, Tenoch. You do not need to do this . . . ," Garcia said, his hands trembling.

"No, Raul. This is rewarded gifting. It is the crux of my vision for the solution to the shortage of transplant organs. The family has made a gift of the heart. I wish to reward them from my heart," Tenoch said. "Over twenty-five thousand people await a transplant organ in the United States. Many of them will die before obtaining a suitable donor organ. We solved the shortage of transplantation organs for one person in Dallas today. You working with me . . . and Dr. Baldwin . . . can solve this terrible problem of donor organ shortages for many more in the future. It is our destiny, my friend."

"I could not accept this money for the man's family," the Medical Director said. "You cannot buy organs."

"I am not paying for the heart," Tenoch said sharply, reverting to Spanish. "This man's family gave the heart of their loved one so that one man in Texas might live. I am simply rewarding their selfless gift. The man's family deserves no less. Give it to them."

Dr. Garcia studied the packet of one hundred dollar bills encased by a single tan paper ribbon. The ten thousand dollars represented to the family of a Mexican worker—five, ten, maybe fifteen years' wages. He looked up at Tenoch. "We are a poor country," Garcia said. "Your generosity to this family is an act of mercy."

Tenoch gestured again with his hand in a signal that passed so quickly that Cassy did not see the exact movement. Alberto opened the briefcase again and stacked ten more packets of one hundred dollar bills on the table in front of Dr. Garcia. Again the Medical Director sucked in his breath, gasping and pulling back as if in fear of the money stacked before him.

"I do not understand," Dr. Garcia said in Spanish.

"One hundred thousand dollars for you and your staff. Use the funds as you wish to build success for my vision of an international donor program," Tenoch said, standing up in a move that foreclosed any further discussion. "It is now time for us to depart, my friend," he said, grasping Garcia's hand firmly. "We have done well today. Our friend, Marquez, would be proud."

"Gracias, Tenoch. Gracias, gracias," Garcia said, staring transfixed at the packets of bills piled on his desk.

The rotor blades of the chopper rotated slowly in anticipation of Tenoch's departure as Tenoch and Cassy, trailed by the retinue of hospital workers, reached the helipad. A red carpet extended from the edge of the concrete pad to the stairwell of the chopper. Tenoch stopped on the carpet and shook Garcia's hand again. The hospital Medical Director then leaned forward to kiss Cassy's cheek. Over the increasing roar of the rotors the doctor said, "We need your help, Cassy. Please return to Mexico City. Many need your skills." Tenoch gently pulled her toward the chopper. She waved to Dr. Garcia as they passed under the downdraft.

Moments later, the chopper lifted above the medical complex. Cassy sat quietly next to Tenoch as the chopper accelerated upward. The ring of burned-out volcanic mountains cradled the smoke and haze that filled the high, swampy basin on which the Aztecs had built their city. The chopper quickly disappeared into the haze.

—

Twenty-six hundred feet below Tenoch's helicopter as it knifed through the dense polluted air lay a shapeless ocean of shacks and hovels, cobbled together so densely that the slums lapped like waves at the tops of the low hills of Mexico City. This ciudad perdida, or lost city, was home for a large fragment of Mexico City's dense population of twenty million inhabitants who called this urban hell their home.

The mud-crusted pathway in front of one of the single room adobe shacks was filled with unsmiling brown-skinned children darting around brown rainwater puddles. Some carried open pails of turbid drinking water from the single common water faucet that served several dozen hovels strung haphazardly around the source of life-sustaining water. Seated in the shade of one of the cardboard and wood huts a blind elderly Mexican man, his eyes sunken orbs, unaware of the encircling children about him, jabbered to himself when the roar of Tenoch's helicopter passed overhead.

Inside one of the huts Juan Torres, a compact muscular Hispanic, barely more than a teenager, sat on the dirt floor of the one-room shanty in front of a low table sipping at tequila from a shot glass. Jaquita, his wife, stirred boiling red beans on the makeshift tin charcoal grille in the corner of the hut. In the opposite corner covered with pieces of ragged cloth sheets, two brown babies slept side by side in a makeshift crib of cardboard boxes.

"I have no more milk for the babies," Jaquita said. Her sallow brown adolescent face already showed the wrinkles of an old woman. "Mama's cow was stolen last night."

"We won't need your mama's cow anymore. We will be moving to a fine apartment in the city soon." Juan's hand closed about the tequila bottle, pouring himself another shotful from the pint bottle. "I will make more than ten dollars a day in tips with my new job driving the taxi."

"But you have to pay rent on your uncle's taxi."

Juan Torres' acne-pocked face scowled. "The taxi job is our way out of here. Uncle Ernesto will rent me his taxi every night. I will take the Americanos from the fancy hotels to the airport. They will give me big tips. I will make many more pesos than selling belts and purses on the Paseo de la Reforma."

Jaquita stirred the simmering beans and sat down slowly in front of him on a low stool. Reaching up to his face, her soiled fingers touched his acne-scarred cheek just above his bushy black moustache. "We have to get out of here. Our babies must have a better life," she said.

TWENTY

T HE HELICOPTER descended slowly out of the smoky cloud deck suspended like a bell jar over Mexico City and hovered over the landing pad adjacent to the Camino Real Hotel. The pilot set the chopper down as gently as if Cassy had lowered herself into a cushioned chair. Two of Tenoch's men stood at the perimeter of the landing pad and ran forward, ducking under the rotor blades when the door of the compartment dropped open.

The hot metallic taste of the thick haze caused Cassy to swallow twice before her feet touched the carpet. The throbbing frontal headache assaulted her again. Rising against the surrounding jumble of buildings in central Mexico City, Tenoch's building on the city's skyline jutted above all others. Cassy could not even see Tenoch's distant penthouse through the smog layer. The pinnacle of the tallest building in Mexico City disappeared as if thrust up into a dark cloud.

Standing under the slowly revolving rotors, Tenoch pulled Cassy near and asked into her ear above the continuing whine of the jet engines, "Would dinner at nine be agreeable?"

Cassy nodded her head, not even trying to make herself heard above the roar of the chopper. Tenoch brushed his lips against her cheek as he pulled back and smiled at her. Cassy was bewildered by the touch of his lips on her cheek. Then he was gone before she had a chance to ask more about the dinner plans. Tenoch's helicopter whipped the air as it ascended straight over the hotel before angling toward Tenoch's penthouse building in the dense smog.

The two guards escorted her to the private elevator enclosure. When the elevator door opened on the penthouse level of the hotel, a dignified Hispanic dressed in a perfectly fitted pinstripe suit with a red lapel carnation and a matching fluffy red pocket square identified himself as the hotel manager. He bowed slightly from his head as he opened the heavy double doors opposite the elevator. "Welcome to the Presidential suite," he said, waving his arm in a flourish. The glass wall of the two-level room commanded a sweeping panorama of the city. In the distant smog, Cassy identified Tenoch's building rising above all until shrouded by the smoke and haze.

"Rosa is your suite attendant. She will see to your every wish," the manager said, introducing a matronly woman dressed in a black uniform with a white lace pinafore apron. The expansive living room of the hotel suite would easily accommodate a reception party for a hundred guests. "The bedroom suites are upstairs," he said, nodding at the grand staircase.

"Gracias, Señor," Cassy said. "I'm sure I will be most comfortable here."

As the manager was leaving, another maid in an identical uniform appeared in the hallway, pushing a cart carrying an arrangement of two dozen roses, a chilled magnum of Cristal champagne, and a silver tray of luscious strawberries, each perfectly symmetrical and each identical as though cloned.

"Señora, I will be available for you anytime," Rosa said. "Just press the call buttons." She pointed to a recessed button on the low table in front of a grouping of sofa and chairs and to other buttons at hidden locations around the spacious room.

After the manager, the two guards, and Rosa departed, Cassy dropped into the chair. Fatigue settled on her shoulders and weighted her into the soft comfort of the overstuffed leather. The unsettled feeling left over from Tenoch's presence at the donor harvesting in the Instituto OR would not leave. Nor would the tightness of her throat and parched sensation of her mouth leave. She lit a cigarette she pulled from the fresh pack in her purse. After inhaling deeply once and then again, the constricted feeling in her throat slackened.

The champagne washed away the lingering bitter taste from her rooftop exposure to the Mexico City smog.

Her fingers hesitated over the perfect strawberries mounded into an exact quadrangular pyramid, not wanting to disturb its symmetric beauty. Then she picked the strawberry from the apex of the pyramid of berries. A pool of creamy tan sauce floated the strawberries. Cassy swiped the tip of the berry into the sauce before bringing it to her mouth. The soft ripe berry and the tangy sweetness of the sauce were so delicious that she ate four more of the sauce-dipped berries before she collapsed into the soft leather chair again.

As she sprawled in the low chair, guilt descended upon her. With the blurred rush of the heart procurement in the afternoon and in the hypnotizing presence of Tenoch, she had not thought about her son. She grabbed the telephone on the table next to her chair. Instantly a man's voice said, "Yes, Dr. Baldwin."

"I wish to call my home in Dallas."

Seconds later the telephone at her home rang.

Lupita answered her home phone after several rings. In Spanish, Cassy asked, "Is everything fine? Have I had any messages?"

"Sí, Señora. Alex is in his room," Lupita answered immediately with her usual non sequitur that required Cassy to ask again.

"Any problems? Any messages?"

"Tres. Lt. Knowland call. Gracie woman called but leave no message. Dr. Simmons called . . . he wants you Monday."

"Okay. Write the telephone number of my hotel down but do not give it to anyone. Understand? Escriba, por favor." Cassy slowly gave the number of the hotel to Lupita.

"Sí, Señora," Lupita said and repeated the digits including the country and city code numbers.

"Call me if you need anything."

"The reporters were here last night. They ask me where you were. I told them you were in Mexico City," Lupita said in her offhanded way of delivering important information.

"What reporters?" Cassy asked, repressing the urge to jump at Lupita's passive-aggressive response.

"The television cameras and the bright lights, right here yesterday. They say that Señor Marquez was murdered."

"What were the reporters doing at my home?"

"I do not know, Señora."

"What did you tell them?"

"I told them you were in Mexico City."

"Anything else?"

"Lt. Knowland wants you to call."

"You gave me that message. What does he want?" Cassy asked impatiently.

"No, he call twice. Say it urgent that you call him."

"Okay. But don't give my telephone number in Mexico City to anyone except Dr. Hendricks. You are not to talk to anyone, especially re-porters. Understood?" Cassy asked.

"Sí, Señora."

"Now, call Alex to the phone," Cassy said, the anger like a rasp in her voice.

The phone clicked into a vacant hum. Cassy could not be sure whether Lupita might have hung up on her and would later blame a bad connec-tion. She sipped at her champagne and inhaled again from her second cigarette. She stopped looking at her watch after another sixty seconds passed. Finally the line clicked alive. Alex's voice filled her with a satisfy-ing warmth.

"Hi, Mom. Where are you?" Alex asked. Her son's voice told her that he was fine. The petulance from the morning had disappeared.

"I'm in Mexico City in my hotel room," Cassy said. "What are you doing?" Cassy asked.

"I'm into my computer," Alex said.

"I miss you," Cassy said.

"Miss you, too," Alex said automatically. "When are you coming home?"

"I'll be home Sunday," Cassy said. "Has Trent called about the Rang-ers' game this weekend?"

"Yeah. We're going Sunday. The Rangers are playing the Detroit Tigers."

"You'll have a good time. I may even be home before you are on Sunday."

"Okay," Alex said. The conversation then fell flat.

Finally Cassy said, "I'll call you tomorrow." It was one of those times with Alex when she knew he was no longer talkative for reasons only he knew. No amount of coaxing by her would provoke further conversation from him .

"Okay."

"I love you, Alex," Cassy said. She heard the phone click.

After replacing the telephone, Cassy stood at the window wall of the suite and stared into the smoky gray clouds of haze lying so low over the city that the sun blurred into an incandescent presence. She lit another cigarette. The click of a door startled her. Rosa appeared in the doorway and rolled another white-linen-covered serving cart into the living area. Another silver canister of long stem red roses stood in the center of the rolling table.

"Is there anything else you wish, Señora?"

"No. Thank you." The maid disappeared back into the kitchen.

Cassy paced the suite, still amazed at its vast size and the panoramic view of Mexico City and Chapultepec Park through its wall of windows.

She stopped at the window, drawn there as if to the edge of a high cliff, and looked again in the direction of Tenoch's building. The dense smog layer had lifted slightly, and from her hotel window she could now look up into the heart of Mexico City to glimpse Tenoch's penthouse perched like a glittering glass cage atop the tallest skyscraper in Mexico City.

Cassy stubbed out her cigarette after inhaling a deep lungful of smoke. The jittery, shaky feeling and racing heart beat now replaced the satisfying relaxation of her first cigarette. The world seemed to close in on her. The cars in the clotted traffic jams forty stories below seemed not to move at all. Less than a week ago my life was orderly, satisfying, and secure she told herself. Now I'm broke and alone in Mexico City.

The tears of loneliness welled in her eyes, but she blinked them back and took another deep pull on another cigarette. A combination of nicotine, champagne, anxiety, fear, fatigue, and anger flowed over her until she had to turn away from the glass wall. She refilled her champagne flute from the fresh bottle of Cristal champagne. Cassy lifted off the silver cover of a tray in the center of the cart and discovered another perfect quadrangular pyramid of strawberries floating in the tan creamy sauce.

She then pulled the table next to the low cushioned sofa so that she could reach the berries and stretched her legs out on the sofa. Kicking her pumps to the floor she propped her feet on the end of the sofa and lay back, still within reach of her champagne glass and the strawberries.

"What am I doing here?" she asked again into the empty room. You have no real alternatives, she thought to herself. No job. No income. No assets. An eight-year-old son. A mortgaged home. You have no other choice. She rolled over on the soft leather sofa and refilled her champagne glass at the same time popping a cream-covered strawberry into her mouth. When she rolled back onto the sofa she felt a woozy rush to her head. For sure, her headache was better. Her mind wandered. Cassy drained off the remainder of her third glass of champagne and lit another cigarette.

By now her cheeks were flushed. The room seemed to spin in front of her. Cassy felt her eyes sliding downward. The late afternoon sky was already a dark, smoky haze. Just a few minutes' nap, she thought, and ground her cigarette into the ashtray on the rolling cart.

⸺

Two hours later the antique telephone on the table next to the sofa chimed softly. After the eleventh chime, Cassy groped for the phone. "Dr. Baldwin," Cassy said reflexively as a greeting to what her sleeping mind presumed to be a medical call.

For several seconds she could not comprehend her unfamiliar surroundings. She rocked her feet off the sofa, struggled to a sitting position, and felt dizzy as she came upright. An eerie glow of faint diffuse light fell through the windows shadowing the darkened room. Her watch indicated seven-thirty, but her mind couldn't make out whether it was morning or evening or even where she was.

"Buenas noches." Tenoch's voice entered her groggy mind through the telephone connection. "I hope that you have enjoyed your nap. Champagne, a long day, and a change of cities can make one sleepy."

"I'm much better now," Cassy said with a sudden awareness of where she was and what time it was. Then she saw that an unopened bottle of Cristal champagne stood in the silver ice container on the rolling cart beside the sofa. The ashtrays had been replaced with clean crystal ones. Fresh crystal flutes stood on the edge of the rolling table next to a perfect mound of untouched strawberries.

"Cassy?" Tenoch's voice intruded on her mind's rambling awakening thoughts. "Would nine o'clock still be convenient for dinner? We eat dinner much later than is the custom in the states."

"Yes, that will be fine."

"I have arranged for the two of us to eat at my home," Tenoch said.

There it was, Cassy thought. Does he intend to keep this visit on a professional basis? Cassy asked herself, but then just as quickly she put her question aside. "What shall I wear?" she asked, already looking forward to the evening with a mix of uncertainty and interest.

"You may find something suitable in your bedroom . . . you will be lovely in any of them. Maybe the red Escada will go nicely with the pearl necklace and earrings that I am sending over."

"You shouldn't . . . that's not necessary," Cassy said quickly, standing up and moving nervously, tethered by the length of the telephone cord. "No, I d–don't k–know . . . I–I haven't been in the b–bedroom."

She was certain now that Tenoch's interest in her went beyond a professional one. An Escada dress?

"It is my way of expressing my appreciation for your visit to Mexico City. Consider it a gift," Tenoch said smoothly.

"I couldn't."

"Consider it your consulting fee then."

"No . . . I shouldn't," Cassy said.

"Then perhaps you will wear it as a special consideration for me," Tenoch said.

"I will see you at nine." Cassy hesitated. "In the red dress," she added as she hung up the receiver and smiled.

The door to the kitchen of the suite clicked open, and Rosa, the suite

matron, stood at attention in the opening. "Buenas noches. Did you enjoy your nap?" the matron asked. She walked into the room carrying an
elaborate foil-wrapped box in one hand and a cream-colored envelope in
the other.

"Señor Tenoch asked that I present these to you when you awoke," she
said, handing her the gift box and the envelope.

Inside the box Cassy found a leather jewel case containing a single
strand of perfectly graduated pearls and a pair of matching Mikimoto
pearl drop earrings. "They're beautiful," she said, touching the shiny opalescent surfaces of the row of pearls. She stepped into the guest bathroom
just off the main living area, pulled the necklace around her neck, and
slipped the wire hanger of the pearl earrings through her earlobes.

"You are beautiful," Rosa said in Spanish and offered the envelope to
Cassy. Tearing away the cream-colored flap with its embossed T, Cassy
read Tenoch's flourishing script, 'Cassy, I look forward to dinner with
you this evening.'

"Gracias," Cassy said to Rosa and quickly slipped off the pearls, returning them to the leather case. There's no reason I can't wear these pearls
tonight, Cassy thought.

"May I assist you," Rosa said, breaking into Cassy's mental struggle
with Tenoch's extravagant gestures.

"Assist me with what?" Cassy asked.

"Preparation for your evening. Prepare your bath. Help you dress."

"That's not necessary," Cassy said. "I'll manage just fine."

"Allow me, please," Rosa said in a pleading way.

"Oh, very well, Rosa." The woman beamed and hurried up the stairwell to the master suite. Before following, Cassy filled a crystal flute with
the champagne and ate three more strawberries that she plucked from the
pyramid. As she walked up the stairs, she asked herself why not enjoy a
nice dinner with an attractive, hospitable man? You deserve it after this
past week.

The outer walls of the guest suite were floor to ceiling glass. For the
barest moment Cassy felt suspended on an open ledge high above Mexico City. The glass wall illusion caused her to hesitate before stepping further into the room. A flash of acrophobia gripped her. She circled the inner edge of the room until she reached the huge dressing area opening
off the bedroom.

Inside the walk-in closet in the dressing room, she found her two tailored business outfits, pressed and hung carefully. Beside them were three
designer dresses. One was the red Escada that Tenoch had mentioned—a
sheer silk fitted bodice and a dramatically low decolletage matched by the
shortness of the slim skirt.

Positioned beneath each of the three designer dresses was a pair of high heeled shoes matching the dresses. Cassy bent down to pick up one of the red shoes that matched the Escada dress. The long tapering heel of the soft understated leather shoe was a perfect match for the red dress.

She tried to remember an occasion when she had worn the extreme high heels. Not this past year she knew. Her only male companion for dinner had been Alex, and usually it was pizza for dinner, almost always at home. A big night out was a Pizza Hut evening.

She opened the dressing table drawer beneath the mirror to find her underwear and stockings perfectly arranged. An assortment of silk lingerie, still in the Victoria's Secret packages, all in her favorite style and size, were aligned with the underwear she had brought with her. *Is this what Trent tried to warn me about when he said 'Be careful'?* The sound of running water from the bathroom broke into her thoughts.

When Cassy opened the bathroom door, she was greeted by a fluff of bubbles that covered the surface of the water in the tub, which was elevated from the black marble floor. A glass column surrounded the marble tub and extended to a skylight that filtered bluish green vaporous light. She set the champagne flute on the edge of the tub.

Rosa turned expectantly to Cassy. "May I assist you in your bath?"

"No, please. I need to be alone."

She nodded politely and said, "I will be available just outside." Dimming the lights, the matron closed the door behind her.

Cassy peeled off her camisole and dropped her skirt to the floor of the dressing room. Moments later she slid slowly into the warm scented water. Floating off the bottom of the tub, she felt weightless as she stretched to her full length. The tub was large enough for three people. The warmth melted her anxieties away as steam filled the enclosed glass column all the way to the ceiling. Flickering faintly in the haziness, the brightest stars of the early evening shone through the round skylight.

After nearly half an hour Cassy stood up. The frothy soap bubbles dripped from her chin and shoulders. She adjusted the nozzles of the steam shower. Under the tepid jets she felt her skin tighten as she scrubbed. The leisurely shower revived her. Cassy stepped from the glass enclosed column and wrapped a towel about her head. The fluffy white terry cloth robe from the warming coil dried her skin and brought a flush to her face.

When she opened the door into the bedroom suite, Rosa stood by the side of the door. "May I give you a manicure and a pedicure?"

"No, that will be all now, Rosa." She felt invigorated after the shower, ready for the evening.

"Sí, Señora," Rosa said. Again she seemed disappointed by Cassy's refusal. "Alberto is in the hallway whenever you are ready for Señor Tenoch." Rosa turned to leave. The woman's simple remark puzzled Cassy and gave her the feeling that this bubble bath and dressing ritual was a well-practiced routine for Tenoch's parade of glamorous women that Kevin Knowland described.

"Wait, Rosa," Cassy said suddenly. Why not? she asked herself. It's been a year since I had a professional manicure. She reconsidered. "Can you give me a manicure?"

Rosa beamed and nodded. "Sí, Señora. Also a pedicure if you wish."

"Why not?" Cassy said. For most of the next hour Rosa expertly prepared and painted her nails a blood red tint to match the Escada dress. When Rosa had finished, Cassy stood before the dressing room mirror, drying and styling her thick wavy hair with a blow dryer until she was satisfied with the look of the back and sides of her hair. A touch of moisturizer and lipstick to match her nails completed her makeup. Her long eyelashes and thick brows needed no accentuation.

She then opened the drawer of the dressing room cabinet. Her hand hesitated a moment above the unopened Victoria Secret lingerie packages. She looked toward the Escada dress, hanging in the closet, before picking up the new package of shimmering red high-cut brief bikini panties and matching red lace bra with a deep decolletage that would hide below the low-cut dress.

Cassy dropped the terry robe onto the bed and stepped into the panties and bra. The cocktail dress fit perfectly and hugged the trim curves of her long torso, made even longer by the matching red high heel shoes. She then laid the pearl necklace on her bare skin and fitted the pearl earrings into the pierced points of her ear lobes. Finally she touched her neck and chest just above the decollete with the French perfume she found on the dressing table. The pleasurable smell exploded around her. She looked at her image in the mirror. A feeling of self-satisfaction at her striking appearance brought a smile to the lips of her mirror's image.

When she opened the main door of the hotel suite, Alberto stepped forward from where he had been standing opposite the doorway. "This way, Señora," he said, pointing toward an open private elevator door. The car dropped directly to a private entrance at the side of the hotel. Cassy stepped into a Mercedes S-500 sedan that sat in front of the door.

The dark surface of the Paseo de la Reforma glistened under the rain. For an instant the city was washed clean. Along the Paseo, the major boulevard cutting diagonally across Mexico City, the cars followed each other as if joined at the bumper. At each corner, swarms of street vendors selling everything from candy bars to window fans, car stereos to medicinal herbs, approached the car. The tinted glass of the Mercedes shielded

Cassy invisibly from the hurly-burly of street life. Children, some no more than Alex's age, teemed around her car, hawking postcards and kitchen plates.

Alberto braked the car to a quick stop at the red light in the center lane of an intersection a few blocks from the hotel. In the lane adjacent to Cassy's seat in the right rear of the Mercedes, the acne-scarred profile of a taxi driver concentrating on the traffic signal caught her eye. Cassy studied the young man's face barely three feet beyond the tinted window of the Mercedes. The taxi driver appeared to be a teenager despite the bushy mustache, and his passenger in the rear of the late model black Honda sedan appeared to be an American businessman.

The light changed and the traffic flow through the intersection reversed itself. Cassy's eyes were distracted from the Honda taxi at the next intersection by a young man performing flaming torch tricks, spewing kerosene in a geyser of flame from his lips.

As the Mercedes neared Tenoch's building, anxiety grew in Cassy in a classic approach-avoidance conflict—the closer she approached the meeting with Tenoch the more anxious she became about seeing him again. She remembered the same sort of anxiety as a teenager when her father drove her to the school parties—the closer to the party, the more anxiety she felt. She could not turn back then and could not now.

Alberto parked the car in the underground garage and ushered her a few steps into another waiting private elevator. Cassy's ears popped as the car shot upward over sixty floors to Tenoch's penthouse mansion. The door of the private elevator opened and Tenoch, dressed in a black dinner jacket, stood in the foyer waiting to greet her entrance. His smile reassured Cassy. She felt beautiful under his gaze. "You are lovely, Cassy. The red dress is perfect for you," he said and quickly touched her right cheek with his lips. His masculine fragrance immediately reminded her of their first encounter in the Metropolitan Emergency Room.

"Thank you," Cassy said, finding herself enjoying the lingering touch of her hand in his soft palm.

"May I offer you something to drink? Perhaps more Cristal champagne?" Tenoch asked.

"Champagne would be nice," she said.

Tenoch nodded to Alberto who remained standing silently by the foyer door. Moments later Alberto reappeared with a flute of champagne and a wide crystal glass filled with ice and clear liquid. "Only water or tea for me. I cannot allow my tongue to be loosened by alcohol. I know too many secrets," Tenoch said.

"That's a pity," Cassy said, sipping the champagne and studying him over the rim of her glass. His age was indeterminate. Cassy figured he must be close to fifty years old although his lean muscular body was that of a man twenty years younger. Despite Cassy's three-inch heels which pushed her height close to six feet, she still looked upward to meet his eyes.

He brought his water-filled crystal glass to the rim of her champagne flute. The black obsidian stone in the gold ring on his index finger reflected the light of the glowing chandelier globe overhead, mutating the black gem into an eyeball set in a gold mounting. "To our common destiny," he said. Cassy could not pull her eyes away from the gemstone as Tenoch raised the water glass to his lips.

"My ring pleases you?" Tenoch extended his index finger toward Cassy. The reflection of the chandelier's glow appeared like the dancing highlights of a living eye in the burnished stone. "The obsidian is from the eye of a stone jaguar from the ancient city of Teotihuacan."

"I remember visiting those old pyramid ruins north of the city when I was a teenager," Cassy said. She could not hold her fingers back from touching the highly polished surface of the gemstone in the ring. The warmth of the stone startled her, and she quickly withdrew her finger from its sleek black surface.

"We will visit there tomorrow afternoon," Tenoch said. "It is the place where Aztec men became gods." Before Cassy could respond, Tenoch said, "Come, I must show you my city."

Tenoch took her by the hand to lead her through the cavernous living room with its vaulted ceiling reaching two stories. An elegantly set table for two was again centered under the chandelier globe in the exact center of the room.

They circled the wide staircase that rose splendidly to the second floor balcony that overlooked the grand salon like a theater proscenium. Beneath the overhang of the balcony, Tenoch pulled open a sliding panel in the glass wall. They stepped onto an open patio that wrapped the sides of the building. The city below stretched to the hazy skyline in the far distance. Moving strands of traffic streamed like lava flows from the center of the city, leaving a smoky trail that fogged the city.

The haze blocked all but the brightest stars. As Cassy looked up into the dark night, she caught a glimpse of the nose of the helicopter that peeked over the edge of the rooftop landing pad. Two satellite communication dishes hung over the rooftop of the building but were discreetly concealed behind planters containing green shrubs and flowers. No building came within two hundred feet of the top of his skyscraper.

"It's spectacular," Cassy said, pulling back from the railing of the patio. "The whole city is beneath us."

"Yes, my dear. That is as it should be," Tenoch said, his dark face shimmering in the eerie, flickering light of the rooftop swimming pool that joined the walkway at the corner of the rooftop patio. Cassy's eyes, blurred by the glowing swimming pool light, were trapped in the darkness of his eyes. The warm, sooty wind, sixty floors above the city, swirled about them.

"You and I stand above Mexico City . . . the ancient city of Tenochtitlan . . . the city of Tenoch." Cassy's freshly styled hair seemed to stand on end as if charged with static electricity. The distorted hollow sound of his voice jolted through her. A discomforting prescience about this mysterious man flashed past. Just as quickly the feeling was gone when Tenoch gently retrieved her hand and graciously guided her back into the grand salon. "Let us return to the salon and enjoy our dinner." The gold chandelier globe dimmed, darkening the room into a golden glow, when they entered the vaulted room.

The meal, served on gold plates with matching gold utensils, was much to Cassy's surprise not a Mexican menu but a succession of small French courses. A kir royale champagne cocktail sparkled over a perfect raspberry in the bottom of a fluted glass at the edge of the gold plate. Thick fennel soup followed by a shrimp salad with mushrooms was tastier than any appetizer she could ever remember. For an instant she wondered whether Alex was eating pizza or tamales for dinner in Dallas. Immediately this thought was erased by the main course of noisettes of lamb that melted in her mouth.

By the last morsel of the lamb and her third glass of wine, a different one for each course, Cassy had mellowed into a pleasant relaxed mood, more comfortable than she could remember being in a long time. Especially more tranquil since the Saturday of the Marquez incident. She noticed that Tenoch did not drink any of the wines poured for him, his full glass being removed after each course.

Tenoch asked, "Would you like a cigarette?"

Cassy flushed and paused. "Yes, I would. I can't seem to stay away from them, especially this past week."

"Alberto," Tenoch said, snapping his fingers and holding his first two fingers up in a cigarette fashion. Instantly Alberto produced a fresh package of Marlboro Lights and opened it, extending one from the open end to her. Cassy inhaled deeply after Alberto lit it with a flourish from a gold lighter. She leaned back in the soft luxury of the leather chair. Her problems in Dallas did not seem so terrible after all.

"Tenoch, I feel as though I should explain my behavior at lunch on Wednesday. Perhaps I was rude and. . . ." She paused. "I'm sorry."

"Apology is not necessary," Tenoch said, waving his hand as if flicking away a troublesome insect. "Now we must enjoy the special entertainment I have arranged for you."

Alberto carried two cups of heavy aromatic Mexican coffee to the side of the room and positioned two oversized leather sofa chairs to face the wide expanse of the grand salon. Three waiters cleared the room quickly, removing the dining table. The dark hardwood floor glistened under the glare of spotlights that flashed from hidden points in the ceiling. The ring of lights created a stage out of the grand salon. Cassy felt as if she had been magically transported to the first row of the Palacio de Bellas Artes, the spectacular national theater in Mexico City. The room dimmed into near total darkness like the lowering of houselights before the opening of a stage curtain.

Tenoch's soft fingers touched her forearm lightly. "I hope you enjoy the performance. The dancers are from the Ballet Folklorico de Mexico," he said. The lively music from a dozen mariachi guitars, violins, and trumpets erupted around the perimeter of the lighted circle in the middle of the room. For the next hour Cassy was transported to her mother's world of interpretive dance. The troupe of dancers weaved the history of Mexico through their choreographic interpretations in a performance designed for her.

The intensely sensual adagio Deer Dance of the final act, depicting the struggle of life and death, drained Cassy as the lithe male dancer beautifully transmuted himself into a graceful deer. The grace and power of life was embodied in his acrobatic ballet moves until his character of the deer ended the performance in a tragic violent death. The salon crashed into silent darkness for several moments. For that time, all Cassy could see were the distant lights of Mexico City through a smoky haze. Tenoch's powerful unseen presence next to her alerted all of Cassy's senses.

When the gold globe chandelier softly relighted the room into a dim ambience, Cassy leaned toward Tenoch and rested her hand on his forearm. "Tenoch, that was wonderful. I've never felt the emotion of the dance more, even when Mother was dancing. I was more part of the performance tonight than if I had been dancing. It was wonderful . . . such a rare treat."

"It was my pleasure," Tenoch said, taking her hand in his. "Your mother was a great Aztec."

Cassy considered his cryptic comment. Perhaps it was his complete lack of predictability that fascinated her. "Maybe a nightcap or another cigarette," Cassy heard him say as he smiled widely around his perfect, even teeth.

"You've been so kind all day. It has been a long and full one for me,"

Cassy said as she looked at her watch. "My goodness, it's one o'clock. I really must get some sleep," she said and leaned forward to touch her lips to his cheek. "I will see you in the morning. Thanks again for a wonderful day and evening," she said and squeezed his forearm.

———

In the rear of Tenoch's Mercedes as it slipped in and out of the early morning traffic on the rain-slicked streets, Cassy smiled to herself in the darkness. He is a nice man. And yes, I'm attracted to him she conceded. I've never met another man like him—intelligent, successful, handsome, unpredictable, gracious. Tenoch and I are different, but in many ways we are alike Cassy thought. We may see things differently—probably a cultural difference—but one trait is absolutely identical—we both crave success. He has done so incredibly well, coming from nothing to where he is now—at the top of Mexico City—and he seems genuinely interested in helping me.

Alberto stopped the car at the private entrance of the hotel. He instantly was at the rear door, opening it for her before she had a chance to reach for the door handle. As his arm came forward to help her out of the car, a shoulder holster holding a blue-steeled pistol partially hidden by his coat lapel became visible to her.

———

Juan Torres lowered the driver's window of the black Honda sedan to relieve the humidity and the cigarette smoke from the interior of his uncle's taxi. For the past forty-five minutes he had sat in the turismo, gradually moving up into fifth place in the line of waiting taxis outside the hotel. Smoke from his cigarette wafted out the open window, mixing with the light rain in the midnight darkness.

Juan counted his pesos under the dashboard map light. It had not been a rewarding night. His fares would just cover the rental expense of the sedan he owed his uncle. Maybe thirty-five pesos in tips would be his profit for the eight hours but still better than what he would have made that night trying to sell the hand-tooled leather purses on the street corner of the Paseo de la Reforma, particularly in the rain.

A tapping on the passenger window startled Juan. He quickly folded the pesos, stuffing the wad on the car seat between his legs. Juan lowered the window opposite him. Alberto's face appeared in the window. "Amigo, are you for hire?"

"Sí, Señor, but I must wait my turn. There are four cars waiting for passengers from the hotel in front of me."

"I do not wish a taxi. My employer is looking for a good driver. A chauffeur. Are you a good driver?"

"Is the pay good?" Juan asked, nodding his response to Alberto.

"More than you can make driving this taxi."

"Yes. . . ," Juan hesitated and then flipped the door lock. Alberto slipped into the front seat, shaking the water from his umbrella, folding it outside the car before pulling it into the front seat beside with him.

"My employer is a wealthy businessman who requires a driver for his Mercedes."

"Who is your boss man?"

"I cannot tell you until we have done a security check on you, and my employer has interviewed you."

"What's the pay?"

"Three hundred pesos a night . . . twelve-hour shift . . . seven days a week."

"I'm interested," Juan said quickly, a grin transforming his cautious face. "When do I begin?"

"Not so fast. You have to be checked out and interviewed. Can you meet my employer Monday?"

"Sure. When?"

"Meet me here at the taxi stand . . . Monday, three in the afternoon," Alberto said, opening the car door and unfolding his umbrella. As he stepped from the car, Alberto turned and dropped three one hundred peso bills on the front seat. "Here's a night's pay for your time tonight. Adios."

The car door shut quietly behind Alberto, and he disappeared toward the Camino Real hotel.

TWENTY-ONE

T HE HEAVY drapes blocked the morning brightness except for a half inch of sunlight that slowly moved across the silk bed sheets until it touched Cassy's eye. She squinted open her left eye. Then both eyes opened cautiously in the dim bedroom of the hotel suite. It was one of those wild disorienting moments whenever she emerged from a deep undisturbed sleep. The few moments of confusion were invariably necessary for her to summon herself back into real time—to erase her bewildered senses.

Sleep had been a thoughtless void for the past seven hours. Now the memories of the evening with Tenoch filled her head—the touch of his hand around hers—his gentle graciousness—his underlying mystery that fascinated her—the delicious leisurely dinner—the powerful sensuality of the male dancer performing the Deer Dance—the subliminal sexuality of the entire evening—the mellow feeling lingering on the return ride to the hotel—and the final jarring appearance of the pistol in Alberto's shoulder holster.

As she slowly aroused in the murky bedroom Cassy realized that she was wearing emerald green silk lounging pajamas. She pulled herself up against the headboard and promptly slipped back, the satin sheets and silk pajamas slipping without friction against each other like greased plates. For a moment as her fingers explored the silky folds of her pajamas she couldn't remember changing out of the red Escada.

Then Cassy recalled the moment at the open drawer of the dressing table in her hotel suite. The new package of emerald green silk pajamas sat next to her SMU T-shirt that she usually wore for sleeping. She had pondered the choice as if accepting Tenoch's gift of silk lounging pajamas took on a sexual significance, well beyond a simple gift. Finally Cassy concluded that she was judging Tenoch when no judgment of his motives should be made. Why not? she asked herself. He has been a gentleman and gracious host. The silk pajamas are no different than the Escada dress. The memory flashed of herself standing in front of the dressing mirror and turning like a model, enjoying the softness of the emerald green silk against her bare skin.

She lingered in bed, pampered by the lush silk fabric as she moved her arms and legs slowly in the silk cocoon of the pajamas. Several minutes later, she left the bed to open the drapes and noticed two dozen red roses in a silver vase on the table by the window.

She pressed the drapery control button filling the bedroom with dif-fused light as the drapes swished open. Morning smoke and haze mired the city. The street traffic and buildings were barely visible through a gray haze that obscured the horizon. The rising sun blurred itself into a pres-ence of light rather than a discrete sun disc in the sky. The day would be an exact duplicate of yesterday.

Propped against the silver vase of roses, a white heavy parchment card embossed with a T stood on its open fold. Cassy read the bold flowing Spanish script. 'My dear Cassy, last evening was a special moment. You are more beautiful than obsidian.' A flourishing 'T' filled the corner of the card.

On her bedside table a pair of highly polished obsidian stone earrings, as brilliant as ebony diamonds, rested in a circle of a necklace made of graduated polished obsidian stones. Light sparkled from each stone. The miniature reflection of Cassy's face changed in the polished smooth bril-liance of the surface of each stone as she rolled the perfect stones in her fingers.

Impulsively she slipped the earring hoops through her ear lobes and clasped the gold chain holding the obsidian necklace about her slender neck and walked to the mirror. She smiled at her appearance. The black stones fit the base of her slender neck snugly and sat perfectly in each ear lobe. As she watched her mirror's image a realization struck her hard. She felt a hollow sensation drop in her stomach—someone had entered her bedroom while she slept.

The roses and the jewelry were not in the room last night when she had turned off the light. Someone had crept past her while she slept. Cassy shuddered—the flowers—the note—the jewelry—all left while she was asleep in bed. An enlarging anger obliterated any sensual pleasure from the touch of the black stones. Cassy quickly removed the necklace and earrings and stabbed her finger at the attendant call button on her bedside table.

Rosa immediately appeared at the door of the bedroom. "Buenos días, Señora," she said cheerily.

"Rosa, who was in my room last night while I was asleep?"

"I was. Early this morning. I brought your presents from Señor Tenoch. They are so beautiful."

"Rosa," Cassy said, summoning a sternness into her voice but knowing that Rosa simply followed Tenoch's commands like everyone else around him. "Never enter my room again while I am asleep."

"Sí, Señora. I am sorry," Rosa said, wringing her hands. "Señor Tenoch wanted the presents to be there when you awakened."

"I appreciate them, but do not ever enter my room while I am asleep."

"Sí Señora. May I bring your breakfast now?" The maid continued to wring her hands nervously. Cassy nodded, her anger already deflating.

Moments later, Rosa reappeared in the bedroom pushing a serving cart. She poured the freshly squeezed orange juice and then vanished from the bedroom as quickly as she had appeared.

Cassy sat on the bed again and took a long swallow from the freshly squeezed orange juice before idly scanning the headlines of the *La Prensa* and the *Excelsior* newspapers. She poured a cup of the Mexican coffee into a delicate bone china cup and flipped the front page of the newspaper over. Just below the crease was a picture of two men and a woman surrounded by a dozen white-coated personnel. A helicopter sat in the background. Not until she read the headline below the picture did she realize that the newspaper article described her visit to the Instituto de Medico the day before. Then she recognized Tenoch, Garcia, and herself in the front page picture taken upon their arrival at the Instituto.

The heading, 'Instituto de Medico to Establish International Organ Transplant Program,' glared at her. And just below, the subheading read: 'Mexico City native to head Instituto.' The lengthy article, continuing on the third page, described Cassy as a 'Mexico City native'—'educated in Mexico City and the United States'—'internationally renowned surgeon'—'brilliant and talented physician'—'virtuoso technical skills'.

"My god, this story reads like I have a publicist," Cassy said aloud. She reread the opening paragraph.

Dr. Raul Garcia, Medical Director of the Institute de Medico, announced yesterday that Dr. Cassandra Baldwin of Dallas, Texas has accepted the position of Surgeon-in-Chief. "All of Mexico can be proud of our heritage today. Dr. Baldwin, a Mexico City native, will establish Mexico City among the elite of transplantation centers in the world," Dr. Garcia said following Dr. Baldwin's afternoon visit to the medical facility. During her visit to the medical institution, Dr. Baldwin facilitated the procurement of a donor heart for transplantation from a twenty-seven-year-old man who had died earlier in the morning. The heart was transported to Dallas, Texas where it was transplanted.

Cassy sipped the coffee, shaking her head slowly while she read to the end of the article. In the final paragraph the reporter quoted Cassy, "This international organ sharing program will benefit all the citizens of Mexico as we share today's miracles of organ transplantation technology. Working together we will give the gift of life to many."

"What in the hell is this?" Cassy asked. "I've not even accepted the job, and the damn newspaper is already quoting me with words I never said." At that moment as if in response to her spoken word, the telephone chimed.

"Good morning, Cassy. I hope you slept well," Tenoch said as soon as she lifted the receiver.

"Yes, thank you. I did sleep well," Cassy said, her voice chilly. "But I'm not so well after reading this morning's newspapers."

"Yes, I can understand how you might be disturbed," Tenoch said pleasantly. "The reporters were instructed to run that particular article on Monday. I'm afraid it was a communication problem."

"I see," Cassy said, not wanting her anger to resolve so easily. "I want there to be no misunderstanding between us. I have made absolutely no commitments to you beyond this exploratory visit."

"Certainly. But I am confident that by the end of our weekend visit, you will accept my challenge . . . and your opportunity."

"Perhaps, but nothing is decided yet," Cassy said even though she knew that in truth she had decided last night to accept the position.

"Did you like the obsidian?" Tenoch asked, changing the subject as if her pique was of little consequence.

Cassy absently picked up the obsidian necklace, touching the stones and twisting the strand around her fingers like worry beads. "They're lovely."

"Obsidian is such a beautiful gemstone," Tenoch said. "The Aztecs were masters at working with these delicate volcanic stones."

"They're like black diamonds," Cassy said. "Absolutely gorgeous."

"I hope that you will consider them for our dinner this evening. They would complement the black Chanel dress very nicely."

There it is again, Cassy thought. The controlling personality. She responded to the veiled demand that she wear the black dress by gentle evasiveness but knowing she would wear it. "Let me think about it," she said.

"You would be lovely in black. The evening will be a traditional fiesta for you with the mayor of Mexico City, the United States Ambassador, a few of my business associates, and Dr. Garcia. I will plan to formally announce your acceptance of the directorship then."

"I must have time . . . ," Cassy interrupted.

"Surely, take the rest of the day," Tenoch said. "Let's enjoy ourselves today. As I promised, I will take you to Teotihuacan."

"I believe we should have some serious discussions about the position before we spend the day looking at some ancient pyramids."

"What is there to discuss, Cassy?" Tenoch asked. "Tell me what you desire. It is yours."

"I need your assurance, very specifically, on several things. We must discuss each of them."

"Would noon be convenient for me to pick you up?" Tenoch asked. Cassy agreed to the time, realizing that Tenoch's mind had moved on.

As Cassy replaced the receiver on the bedside telephone, the two obsidian earrings on the nightstand glistened at her like a cat's black eyes in the morning light. No sooner than her hand had left the receiver, the phone chimed again. The male telephone operator said, "Dr. Baldwin, a Lt. Kevin Knowland left a message for you to call him as soon as possible. May I connect you?"

Cassy lit her first Marlboro of the day, propped herself against the satin pillow in the bed, and reread the news article as she sipped at her coffee. While she read, she thought that maybe the position with Tenoch could be the opportunity that she and Alex needed. Living in Mexico City would be a welcome retreat from Dallas. Alex's mood swings, withdrawn periods, and stuttering were improving, but the past year had been tough for both of them. She must not allow the Marquez problems to set his progress back. Maybe time and distance from Dallas would help both of them.

Ten minutes later, the phone chimed. Cassy picked it up immediately. Before Lt. Knowland could say hello, Cassy asked, "Kevin, what's going on in Dallas? My housekeeper said the television reporters and cameras were at my home last night."

"I'm sorry, Cassy. This Marquez case has gotten away from me. The damn thing has exploded since the district attorney involved himself."

"The DA? Why? What the hell has the DA got to do with me?" Cassy asked, her voice rising to a near shout.

"There are several possible suspects in the Marquez murder case. You're one of the DA's prime suspects," Kevin said quietly.

"Suspect . . . murder? Are you telling me that the DA thinks I threw Marquez out the hospital window?"

"He's not said much. I can tell he's thinking you must be involved somehow."

"Why me? For god's sake, what connection do I have with Marquez except that I pronounced him dead when he wasn't . . . or was?"

"The DA is curious why you suddenly flew off to Mexico. Looks as if you are running. After all you were the doctor who said he was dead when he wasn't."

"Who else is the DA suspicious about? Maybe he thinks the tooth fairy poisoned Marquez?"

"Nobody's talking about a poisoning. I brought up your ideas with the DA about Marquez being poisoned. He wasn't impressed. The DA thinks you fled the country because you're scared. It won't look good if you don't return to the United States quickly. I called to urge you to fly home today. Somehow the DA discovered you had dinner at my home Thursday evening."

"Does the DA think I would run off and leave my son in Dallas?" Cassy asked sarcastically. "You inform Mr. DA that I'm in Mexico City on business. Looking for a job as you well know. I will be home tomorrow as planned."

"It doesn't look good that you went to Mexico the morning after I questioned you. The chief has been all over me about not filing a formal report about my contact with a potential murder suspect."

"You questioned me? We had shrimp and stir fries . . . that's all."

"I've had to file a formal report on you . . . for your own protection after what the Metro nurse said about you."

"Which nurse?" Cassy said, shaking her head.

"The ICU charge nurse . . . I believe her name is Joan."

"That's Joan Markison."

"Right," Kevin said quickly. "That's her name."

"Joannie called Dr. Simmons the evening I went back to the hospital to see Marquez . . . to let him know that I was interviewing Marquez."

"Well, she's now saying that Marquez started talking about someone trying to kill him right after you left his ICU cubicle."

"And let me guess. Walter Simmons called the DA," Cassy said.

"Right on target," Kevin said. "How did you know?"

"Simmons and I have our differences . . . professionally." She wound the telephone cord around her arm and paced the main floor of the suite. "Godamn it. I cannot believe this," Cassy said. "Don't I have any friends at Metro?"

"There's something else," Kevin said, pausing. "Dr. Simmons told the DA that there have been some recent irregularities in your narcotics prescription writing at the Metro. Pharmacies in the Highland Park and University Park areas have three of your prescriptions, each for a hundred Demerol tablets."

"I know that. This is insane. Someone is forging my name to prescriptions."

"You'll be able to tell your version to the narcotics investigators when you get back."

"I think I might just stay in Mexico City," Cassy said wearily.

"That's a bad idea," Kevin said. "Don't even say that as a joke."

"Why should I come back to Dallas? Sounds as if I don't have any friends left there."

"You need to get back up here to Dallas to protect Alex. Your exhusband is not being very supportive."

"What has my wonderful ex-husband been doing for me now?"

"He's questioning your fitness as a mother. His lawyer plans to file a motion next week to change the custody arrangements for Alex, charging that you are an unfit mother."

"That bastard. Let him try to take my son from me. I'll kill him."

"I wouldn't use those words, Cassy," Kevin said gently.

"I suppose you're right. I'm sure Scott is playing the role of wronged husband and dutiful father. He'll probably even pick up some votes from divorced fathers."

"I'll help in any way I can," Kevin said. "Right now, you're going to need a lawyer . . . and you should get back here as soon as you can."

"I understand," Cassy said. She felt a numbness overtake her. "Thanks for your call." She hung up the receiver without hearing his goodbye.

Cassy sat on the bed and pulled her long legs up under her lotus style and tried to sort through the information that Kevin had just told her. For sure, she now realized that the Marquez incident wouldn't simply fade away. Despite Trent's advice, remaining silent and ignoring the case was not feasible. If she did, it would swallow her. Not until she identified the reasons for Marquez's death and resurrection would she ever have peace in her—or Alex's—life.

Rosa entered unnoticed into the bedroom and startled Cassy out of her musing. "May I be of assistance, Señora?"

"No, that's not necessary."

"Alberto wishes me to remind you that Señor Tenoch will be here at noon."

Cassy sat in the steam shower letting its warm wet comfort quiet her jangled nerves until the skin of her fingers wrinkled and puckered. For a long time she considered leaving that afternoon to go back to Dallas and take Alex away—to where she didn't know—just away. Finally she forced her will to impose a loose rein, at least for the rest of the day. She would not cut and run.

By noon she had dressed in khaki walking shorts, Nike jogging shoes, and a blue sleeveless chambray twill shirt for the afternoon excursion to Teotihuacan. Large silver hoop earrings nestled against her neck.

Rosa answered the suite's door chime to let in Tenoch. He was dressed in a long-sleeved white silk shirt and matching white pants. He entered regally into the reception area of the suite with familiar ease. Taking her right hand, he kissed her cheek. "You seem a bit tense," he said. Her moist hand quivered in his.

"It's not been a good morning for me. I just talked with a friend in Dallas. The Marquez death is now being investigated as a murder, and I'm a suspect."

"I will take care of this nonsense so that we can enjoy our day to-gether." Tenoch turned to Alberto and said, "Get Haygood." Less than a minute later Alberto passed the portable phone he carried in the briefcase to Tenoch. "Please resolve Dr. Baldwin's problems. Speak to the District Attorney and get word to Dr. Baldwin's ex-husband. Do it now." Tenoch hung up the receiver and turned to Cassy, smiling. "There will be no more problems for you in Dallas."

"How . . . what? One phone call and my problems are gone?"

"I take care of my friends," he said, smiling and pulling Cassy toward the door of the suite.

"Who is Haygood?"

"A lawyer I retain. His legal staff will take care of this situation."

Cassy laughed and snapped her fingers. "Just like that! My problems vanish," she said. A grateful affection rose in Cassy. She now understood how Tenoch inspired loyalty in those around him. His charisma went be-yond charm and grace to the essence of power and the ability of power to accomplish his wishes.

TWENTY-TWO

MOMENTS LATER the helicopter carrying Tenoch, Cassy, and Alberto lifted off the rooftop helipad. The haze had risen to about five thousand feet, giving the city a freshness and clarity that Cassy remembered from her early years before pollution had choked the city. The helicopter thrummed the thick air when it looped over Chapultepec Park, the vast green park near the heart of Mexico City.

Saturday had brought families to the park. Swarms of people covered the walking trails and circled the edges of the bluish-green circles of man-made lakes that dotted the open green space. The chopper swooped up over the National Museum of History, and Cassy felt her stomach protest. The pilot swept low over the gray stone castle on the highest point of the park, sitting like a European castle above a sea of green. Just beyond the castle, the helicopter skimmed low and slowed as it reached the rise of a hilly section of palatial homes. Cassy looked puzzled as she felt the aircraft slow, then hover.

"Look out your window," Tenoch said over the roar of the rotors.

Just beneath the right side of the helicopter, Cassy recognized the high white stucco walls that enclosed the grounds of a mansion. "How did you know?" she asked excitedly as she looked down at the orange-tiled roof. She felt a throat-tightening lump form as she recognized the house in which she'd grown up.

Tenoch's teasing smile transformed his face into a playful companion rather than a wealthy businessman. "The pilot has taken several photographs. You will have a souvenir picture of your old Mexico City home. You will be able to show Alex where you lived when you were his age."

"Thank you," Cassy said. She touched the back of his hand. "You are the most thoughtful person. . . ." The aircraft suddenly rose and turned north into the smoky haze. Moving splashes of colored cars and tiny dots of people in the streets and sidewalks flecked the city.

Huts and low-lying cardboard shacks carpeted the rolling hillsides just ahead of the helicopter. Several minutes later the chopper slowly descended. The downdraft beat the hard dusty surface of the parched hillside into a whirlwind of grit and sand mixed with flying fragments of litter. A swarm of children raced in and out of the artificial dust storm, like rats scurrying at the sound of a footstep. The chopper hung in the air, its deafening roar drawing the adults out of their huts. They stared up at the helicopter, so close above them that its shadow turned their afternoon dark, like a solar eclipse.

Inside one of the hundreds of dirt floor huts just below the hovering chopper, Juan Torres lying on a thin sheet blinked awake from his afternoon siesta on the dirt floor of his family's hut. His first night in the taxi had finished at dawn.

"Juan, wake up," Jaquita shouted from the corner of the one-room shanty. The downdraft of the chopper's blades blew hot wind through the open door of the hut. The two Torres' infants screamed at the unrelenting noise. Their mother hugged one on her hip and cradled the other infant in her arms, trying to insert a twisted wet rag into the child's mouth.

"What the hell? Policía!" Juan leaped from the floor and grabbed an eight-inch hunting knife from behind a plywood panel that formed the outside wall of the sunbaked hut. Hiding the knife beneath his shirt, Juan joined dozens of peasants standing immobile in between their huts, gaping at the churning, roaring alien presence above. The children, emboldened by the presence of the adults, began throwing rocks at the helicopter, widely missing the belly of the chopper in their meager lobs.

Cassy leaned to the side of the window, stunned by the abject poverty stretching across the mountainsides like a human mud slide. The clumps of men and women stared at the sky, shielding their faces from the noonday sun. The downwind of the rotor blades churned all the litter into a tornado that rattled the paper, scrap wood, and mud village.

"Why are we stopping here?" Cassy asked, shouting above the rotor noise at Tenoch even though he was seated close to her in the six passenger compartment of the Bell helicopter.

They were low enough that Cassy could see the upturned faces of the peasants. For an instant Cassy thought that she recognized the acne-marked face of one of the young Hispanic men staring directly at her. His bulky moustache framed his open mouth. His eyes locked with hers for a split second before he was gone out of her line of vision as the chopper continued to rotate slowly over the shantytown.

Cassy drew back in the seat and stared out the window of the cabin, overwhelmed by the impoverished crowd of uplifted faces.

"Below is where I grew up . . . one of the lost cities that are everywhere around Mexico City. Thousands of children roam the streets of these camps in gangs. I was one of them." The pleasant expression on his face was now replaced with an aloof grimness.

"You came from that?" Cassy asked, pointing below to the huts covering the low hillside like an overgrown jungle as far as she could see.

"After the fire at the orphanage, I lived here," Tenoch said. "Only a few survive the tyranny of poverty. Many of these children you see will simply disappear."

"Disappear where?"

"Who knows? The families are often happy with one less mouth at the table. Who cares? The police are not much interested. No one is. The missing person is rarely even reported. No one searched for me when I left this hillside. These are animals . . . eating, breeding, and dying."

"But they are human beings," Cassy said.

"No. They are animals just like I was an animal when I lived here. You cannot understand until you have lived among them." His stare fixed her. "Have you ever killed to survive? Have you ever felt the cold sting of the winter night, the suffocating heat, the hollow hunger in your belly? Have you ever emptied your bowels and bladder into the street? Death is a reward for these unfortunates," Tenoch said.

Cassy sat, stunned into silence. "But you escaped. Look where you are today."

"Yes. It was my destiny," Tenoch said. His eyes hardened as if chiseled and polished from obsidian. No deeper could she peer into the depths of her obsidian necklace gemstones than she could see into his eyes.

He turned his head away and nodded to Alberto who then spoke in muffled tones into the telephone mounted on the cabin wall. The helicopter immediately flew upward. The cabin was silent except for the throb of the rotor blades as they rose quickly beyond the hillside.

Sometime later, it could have been five minutes or half an hour. Cassy was unsure. Time blurred for her after Tenoch's commentary about life in the lost city. The aircraft began to descend, finally settling into a flat valley bordered by low mountain peaks. Gnarled, stunted trees huddled low, nearly lifeless, under the broiling heat of the unprotected sun in the cloudless sky. Two massive pyramids rose preternaturally from the floor of this parched valley.

"My people are here. This is where I came from," Tenoch said the moment the helicopter touched down in a flat open area, brown and barren, east of the Pyramid of the Sun. The enormous, umber, quadrangular-tiered pyramid reached for the sky as if pushed up by some alien force from within the earth.

When Cassy stepped from the helicopter door onto the hot baked ground, the enormity of the pyramid rising from the flat floor of the valley gripped her with a foreboding, irrational sense of fear. The hot clear air of the barren valley took her breath as if she had opened the door to a roaring furnace. She stared at the monstrous symmetry of this ancient presence rising out of the valley floor as if it held her by some cosmic force. She finally was able to pull her gaze from the pyramid. Her breath came in short rapid spurts. Droplets of perspiration immediately formed on her face. The Pyramid of the Sun dominated her with its brooding presence.

A swarm of Mexican and foreign tourists circled the helicopter, held back by a cordon of uniformed security guards stretching a circle of heavy rope about the chopper. The crowd between the helicopter and the massive pyramid parted when a white open-top golf cart driven by a senior ranking uniformed guard rolled directly to the door of the chopper.

"Señor Tenoch. We are again honored by your visit," the driver said, tipping his billed cap when he got out of the golf cart. "As you directed, the Pyramid of the Sun has been closed since midmorning. It awaits your presence."

Tenoch nodded and climbed into the rear seat of the electric golf cart, bidding Cassy onto the cushion in the seat next to him. Alberto dressed in his usual blue suit and conservative tie took the front passenger seat. Without a word, the driver rolled the golf cart around the pyramid and onto a wide asphalt and pebbled esplanade toward the companion pyramid, the Pyramid of the Moon, nearly a mile away over the parched land. The flat valley floor surrounded by the distant mountains shimmered heat waves. Cassy felt herself drenched in sweat before the cart had gone a third of the way along the ancient avenue. Crumbling stone compartments that had served as the living quarters for an ancient civilization lined the roadway like relics of row houses.

"My people knew the relationship of the moon and the sun with the earth," Tenoch said, speaking for the second time since the chopper had lifted away from the hillside hovels. "These two pyramids are perfectly aligned with astronomical symmetry." The intensity of the sun fazed her, and she didn't pursue his vague generality. The cloudless crystal sky in contrast to the smoky haze of the city offered no filter to the burning sun. Its heat rays seemed to penetrate into Cassy's head like x-rays.

"This is the Valley of the Dead." Tenoch's gaze swept the entire valley to the distant volcanic mountain ridges. He peered intently into the distance as if seeing things other men could not. "This place is sacred . . . it is where Aztecs become gods." Tenoch gestured with a wave of his forearm for the cart to stop. A beatific smile transformed his face. Blissful and serene, he stepped out of the golf cart and turned to help Cassy out. His soft hand was cool and dry. Cassy felt herself pulled gently from the rear seat. Cassy's mouth was dry. Her teeth were rough and gritty from the invisible fine dust that coated her perspiring body like an ochre patina.

The hot pebbles embedded in the asphalt sizzled through her jogging shoes as if they were thin sandals. Walking beside Tenoch and trying to match his long purposeful strides, a woozy light-headed feeling slammed into her. Her mind muddled under the heat. She had no concept of how much time had passed or how far she and Tenoch had walked along the roadway. Cassy tried to focus on her feet. She watched the toes of her jogging shoes pass each other, back and forth, and struggled to keep pace with Tenoch. Her vision shimmered like heat waves rising vaporously off the broiling macadam.

The pungent odor of sizzling meat mixed with smells of a cooking fire floated into Cassy's nose. A stomach sickness revisited her. Instinctively she looked up, searching for the source of the odor. The crumbling apartment relics lining the asphalt boulevard of the Avenue of the Dead now appeared rehabilitated as pristine flat-roofed, stone apartments and shops under the blazing sun, unchanged from when they were built, a millennium ago.

Wiping the sweat from her forehead, she stopped in the center of the street. Her eyes stung and teared. She squeezed them shut for a moment, unconsciously protecting them from the searing heat. When she reopened her eyes, the Avenue appeared filled with hundreds of brown-skinned men, women, and children spilling from what had been ruins but now appeared in her mind as apartment complexes, artisans studios, and merchant shops filled with pottery jars overflowing with grains and corn.

Again she looked to her immediate right to see the individual dwellings filled with all types of potters and stone cutters. The brown muscular men were mostly unclothed except for white cloth ropes folded above their waists and groins. The women wore identical white smocks that varied only by the colorful designs along the edge of the skirts. Naked brown children ran in hide-and-seek among the workers. Cassy grabbed Tenoch's hand, but the images persisted. Her sweaty hand clung to his cool dry palm.

"The spirits of our prior incarnations are strongest here. Do not fight the spirits." He turned to walk up the Avenue of the Dead, pulling Cassy along toward the Pyramid of the Sun.

Cassy blinked again. She pulled her hand back from Tenoch to wipe her wet face against her blue denim shirt, stained with sweat. She looked again. The Avenue had become deserted and abandoned once again.

"This is where I was transformed . . . ," she heard Tenoch say. Cassy shook her head and pulled away, walking toward the crumbling stone and mortar steps of an ancient home relic that bordered the boulevard.

Sitting on the steps, she rested her head on her arms folded across her knees and tried to reorder her confused thinking and throw off the dizziness that consumed her sense of balance. When she reopened her eyes, she was again back in a teeming market place formed by three of the restored stone buildings along the Avenue. Artisans crafting arrowheads and obsidian knives worked next to families fashioning jewelry from the black and green obsidian.

The buzz of a strange language skipped around her. She could understand none of the words. Squeezing her eyes closed against the vision, she struggled to concentrate. Was this real? Was this an hallucination? A swirling red gauze floated in front of her eyes. Where had she seen those colors? Then she tried to raise her head off her arms and knew with certainty: she was paralyzed.

"Cassy, Cassy, are you well?" Tenoch said, standing before her. A restrained anxiety rippled his voice.

"I must be too hot," Cassy said, unable to raise her head off her arms. The sun heated her scalp. She did finally manage with great effort to look up into the face of Tenoch. In Cassy's distorted field of vision the blazing orb of the afternoon sun replaced Tenoch's head. Cassy closed her eyes, and her head fell back on her knees. The rumbling sounds of a strange language and the clattering of hammers against stone blotted out Tenoch's voice. The odor of cooking meat filled Cassy's nose again until she retched. She closed her eyes and prayed she would faint.

"Bring water for Dr. Baldwin," Tenoch called across the shimmering boulevard to Alberto who stood beside the golf cart parked on the ancient avenue. Quickly Alberto trotted across the hard-surfaced boulevard to the crumbling stone steps carrying a liter bottle of Evian water from the cart's ice chest.

She sat slumped forward on the steps. Tenoch touched Cassy's arm. When she looked up, all she could see was ghostly blue sunlight filtered through the sparkling clear water of the Evian bottle Alberto held directly in front of her face. Cassy fumbled at the bottle. With Alberto's help she brought it to her parched dry mouth and drank half the bottle in big swallows. Immediately the coolness began to revive Cassy.

The rumbling noises of the market place in her mind faded into the hot wind that whipped down the Avenue of the Dead. When she pulled her lips away, Cassy looked up again at Tenoch. The sun had moved on. His dark angular face was backlit, haloing his head. She looked around, trying to reorient herself. The relics of the disintegrated dwellings sat dead as they had been for over a thousand years.

"I'm sorry. I guess it's the heat and altitude," Cassy said and wiped away the gloss of perspiration from her forehead and upper lip. She managed a brief smile. "I'll be all right." Cassy lifted the bottle to her lips and drained off the rest of the liter. Gesturing to Alberto to bring another bottle from the golf cart, Tenoch sat next to her. His white silk shirt was dry and unruffled.

When Alberto returned with the second bottle of water, Cassy's mind had cleared almost completely. Tenoch dismissed Alberto who returned to stand in the sun by the golf cart. Cassy stood up unsteadily. "I apologize for acting so strange . . . I was hallucinating . . . seeing the Avenue of the Dead as it must have been hundreds of years ago . . . the people, the activity. It was so real."

Cassy took a long drink of water from the second bottle to avoid Tenoch's studied look. "The spirits are real. You were in touch with your own spirit," Tenoch said quietly.

Cassy shook her head. "No. I had an hallucination. I've experienced one before. When I was sedated right after Alex was born. I thought the doctors and nurses were monsters trying to kill Alex and me."

"The spirits are strongest here," Tenoch said. "You were not hallucinating."

Her head pounded. She felt weak and unsteady. Again she sipped at the water and studied Tenoch standing in front of her, dazzling in his dry white silk blouse, not a drop of sweat on his face.

"We must go to the top of the Pyramid of the Sun together for you to feel the true power of the Spirits of Teotihuacan."

"That's not a good idea," Cassy said even though she had cooled off in the narrow shade of the steps of the relic. "I don't feel very well," she said, hoping that Tenoch would not persist.

"Come," Tenoch said and tugged her toward the golf cart. "You will come." Her gait wobbled in the few steps to the golf cart. By the time the cart reached the base of the pyramid, her face was dry. The freshening wind cleared her swimming head.

"We must go to the top," Tenoch said and took Cassy by the hand as two uniformed guards led them through a crowd of tourists held back by the guards. The pyramid soared in front of Tenoch and Cassy. They stood alone in the courtyard of the manmade adobe mountain.

"Alberto, stay here. Allow no one near my pyramid." Tenoch pulled Cassy by the hand to the base of the steeply inclined steps leading up to the flattened top of the quadrangular pyramid.

Cassy followed Tenoch onto the first of the two hundred fifty stone and mortar steps. At each of five tiers that formed the pyramid, Tenoch stopped and surveyed the arid brown land extending like a table top to the distant mountain ridge between Teotihuacan and Mexico City. His face grew calm and peaceful the higher they climbed.

By the time they reached the flat square of the top of the pyramid, Cassy's head swam again. Her calves ached. Her pulse raced. Sweat glistened on her face and back. Her blue denim shirt was black with sweat.

Tenoch stood quietly on the truncated top of the pyramid with his eyes closed, breathing slowly and easily. His face was smooth, dry, and serene. Not a drop of sweat stained his clothes or his face. "This was my temple," Tenoch said, spreading his arms out from his side and twisting his body slowly back and forth as he turned a full circle.

Cassy sat on the low parapet surrounding the horizontal top of the pyramid. The sun burned into every pore. Cassy felt so lightheaded and woozy that she was certain that she was going to pass out. Dropping her head down onto her bare thighs, she breathed deeply. The hot air singed her mouth and throat, but the extra few deep breaths cleared her head.

Carefully raising her eyes, she saw Tenoch revolving slowly in the center of the square top of the pyramid. His eyes were unfocused. His arms stretched out as if he were crucified on an invisible cross that rotated slowly around the center of the flat top of the pyramid. Oh, no! Cassy moaned over and over in her head. Her head fell back onto her knees. When Cassy raised her head again, Tenoch's body had stopped twisting. He stood motionless, his face upturned into the bright sun. His black eyes stared unblinking into the white-hot brilliance of the sun high in the cloudless sky.

"The sun is the source of all life on earth," Tenoch said, reaching out his arms wide again, still staring directly into the radiant unfiltered sun. "From the sun I receive life and to the sun I will return man's energy. From the four quadrants of the universe, the sun will be adored." His dark skin glowed, translucent and dry. He stood rigid as a crucifix.

"Tenoch," Cassy called to him from where she sat slumped on the parapet. He did not waver and did not respond to his name. His dark eyes gaped wide at the sun.

"Tenoch," Cassy called out again. The shout died in the hot wind. Her mind cleared enough to make the diagnosis of a heat stroke—delirium, dry skin, staggering, confusion.

Cassy knew she had only a few minutes to get Tenoch cooled off and down from the pyramid. If he stayed in the heat, he would likely die on top of the pyramid. She pushed herself up from the edge of the flat square top and hobbled toward Tenoch until she reached his outstretched arm. "Tenoch, me entiende usted? Do you understand me?" Cassy shouted. He did not flinch. His eyes remained wide and staring skyward. There was no reaction when Cassy pinched the tight muscles of his rigid arm. "Tenoch," Cassy shouted. No response. She touched his face. It was hot and dry as a stone in the sun. "Tenoch, do you hear me?"

"Tenoch and the Aztecs are one . . . yesterday, today and tomorrow," he said in a deep sepulchral voice. His arms still stretched outward as if impaled on a cross. "I giveth the sun to drink." Tenoch slowly lowered his arms to his side, closing his eyes and prostrating himself until his forehead touched the blistering hot stone surface of the pyramid.

"Tenoch," Cassy shouted. She bent down over him. "Tenoch, talk to me."

"I am Tenoch, Supreme Aztec," he said in the same funereal tone as he lifted his head up off the stone floor to gaze upward at the sun.

Cassy put her arms into his armpits and wrestled him upward from his prostrate position. "Talk to me. Talk to me," Cassy shouted. Her head spun in waves of vertigo. Tenoch sat quietly in the center of the square. His face was hot and dry. There was no perspiration on his white silk shirt anywhere. Cassy quickly palpated his carotid pulse at the angle of his jaw—slow steady and full—not the rapid, weak pulse of a person with a heat stroke.

For a moment, Cassy left Tenoch sitting upright, ran to the edge of the top of the pyramid, and waved to Alberto standing beside the golf cart at the base of the pyramid. She made a gesture of drinking and could see that Alberto spotted her gestures through his binoculars and understood her request for water.

Moments later, Alberto, sweat dripping from his face, appeared at the top step carrying two bottles of Evian water. "Señor Tenoch is not well," Cassy said. "He's had a heat stroke. We must get him down off the pyramid."

Suddenly Tenoch's eyes blinked open. He said, "My Cassy, do not be concerned. My spirit left this incarnation momentarily but now has returned. The Sun commanded my presence. I am fine. I have now returned."

"Alberto, give me the water," Cassy said, grabbing one of the chilled bottles water from Alberto. Tenoch drank deeply from the bottle when Cassy brought it to his lips, emptying half the bottle.

"Get a stretcher and four men up here quick," Cassy screamed at Alberto. "We must carry him down from here and get him cooled off quick. He's having a heat stroke and will die if we don't hurry."

"Sí, Señora," Alberto said, panicky, and raced toward the steps of the pyramid.

"Cold towels. More water. Get your men up here. We've got to carry him down quick and get him out of the sun," Cassy shouted after Alberto as he jumped down the steps of the pyramid.

Tenoch shook his head and stood upright, steady and smiling, as if he had awakened from a brief nap. "Do not be concerned."

"Tenoch, we must go down," Cassy said, pleading.

"Do not be concerned," Tenoch repeated, standing comfortably in front of her. He took both her hands and looked intently at her. In his slow hollow voice, Tenoch said, "The fifth Sun has commanded me to continue this incarnation. I nourish the sun with life's precious liquid. As long as the world endures, the Aztec will never perish."

"Sit back down," Cassy said. "You're not making sense. You're having a heat stroke."

"You are not a believer."

"Believer of what?" Cassy's confusion and frustration creased her face. "You're talking out of your mind."

"I am Tenoch. Huitzilopochtli made into flesh," he said, blinking quickly for the first time against the brightness of the sun. Cassy dropped his hands and stood on her tiptoes to peer into his eyes. The darkness of his eyes constricted the opening of the pupil into a pinhole. With her fingertips, Cassy located Tenoch's carotid pulse—it was still strong, slow, and full.

"Que pasa? What's wrong, Tenoch?" Cassy asked, confused by her rudimentary physical examination that revealed nothing abnormal. Nothing made sense—if Tenoch were having a heat stroke, why wasn't his pulse weak and thready? It was almost as if his body did not recognize the heat. His skin was warm and dry. None of her clinical findings gave any indication of a heat stroke. But still, Tenoch was talking out of his mind.

"Tenoch, take it easy. Siéntese, por favor. Come sit by me," she said, pulling him down beside her near the parapet. "We must go down now. Vámonos."

After a few moments, they stood up together. Cassy led him slowly down the steep stone steps, his hand in hers. His gait was firm. His balance and bearing had the athletic certainty of coordinated muscular strength. By the time they reached the first of the five tiers of the pyramid, Alberto met them with cold towels and more bottles of water. Four khaki-clad guards carrying a canvas stretcher followed Alberto up the steps.

"We need to get Señor Tenoch where it's cool," Cassy said to the five men.

"No, I am fine," Tenoch said, waving away their concern.

"Give me a wet towel, Alberto," Cassy said. The bodyguard looked uncertainly to Tenoch who smiled and nodded.

Cassy wiped Tenoch's face with the moist cool cloth. "Drink this," Cassy said, handing him the Evian water. "Doctor's orders."

Tenoch drank from the bottle, again nearly half without taking the bottle from his lips.

"You got a little too hot up on the top. You were incoherent," Cassy said. "Not making a lot of sense. I'm worried about you. We should have you checked out. Your doctor might. . . ."

"All is well," Tenoch said in his conversational voice and continued on down the steps. When they reached the plaza in front of the pyramid, Cassy and Tenoch settled in the golf cart.

Minutes later, the helicopter blades whipped up a storm of dust and sand as the chopper carrying Tenoch, Cassy and Alberto lifted off the sunbaked Teotihuacan valley floor and reentered the smoky haze that hung over Mexico City like a gray afternoon blanket.

TWENTY-THREE

T HE TINTED TWO-story windows of Tenoch's penthouse filtered the late afternoon sunlight into an ethereal green. The cool dry air chilled Cassy as she stepped through the double door held wide by Alberto. The clean smell of the cathedral-like salon was so crisp that Cassy could taste it. Her perspiration-soaked blue denim blouse plastered her skin like a cold wet compress.

"Are you okay?" Cassy asked. "I was afraid you were having a heat stroke on the pyramid." Tenoch's blousy, white silk shirt hung loose and dry. He stood beside her, as neatly groomed and fresh as if he had just dressed.

"I'm fine," he said, smiling. "But you're a wilted flower."

"I feel like one, moldy and gritty," she said and sat with a sigh into the embrace of the soft leather sofa that was part of the grouping around the low stone table. Chiseled bas relief figures decorated its sloping sides.

"Would you like to shower and change clothes?"

Cassy hesitated at the delicious thought of a cool shower. "No, I couldn't," she said. "I should go back to the hotel."

"Don't be absurd," Tenoch said. "Take Señora to the guest room," he commanded the Mexican maid who stood attentively at the side of the room. With a helpless gesture of her hands, Cassy pushed herself up from the sofa. Tenoch's soft hand took hers and lifted her to a standing position next to him.

"While you're having a cool shower, I'll have my special blend of tea brewed. Then we can talk about your position at the Instituto de Medico."

"A cool shower ought to revive me. A glass of iced tea would be wonderful," Cassy said, shaking the soggy cotton shirt away from her chest.

"You'll find something that will fit you in the closet," Tenoch called after Cassy. She followed the maid up the grand staircase. As soon as they reached the balcony overlooking the immense salon, the maid pointed to one of the pairs of massive, wooden doors. The doors were separated by a twelve-foot circular stone replica of the Aztec sun god calendar highlighted by light beams from ceiling recesses. "This is the guest room," the maid said, opening the heavy door.

Tinted glass walls on two sides of the enormous guest room surrounded a canopied king-size bed and gave Cassy the same woozy feeling she experienced in the bedroom of her hotel suite. The floor-to-ceiling glass expanse appeared continuous with the sky beyond and momentarily disoriented her when she looked at the distant horizon.

When Cassy entered the bath suite, the maid with a slight bow in Cassy's direction opened the double doors of a closet so that Cassy could inspect a dozen designer dresses, ranging from casual to evening clothes. Then the maid left Cassy, discretely closing the door to the enormous bath suite.

Escadas, Armanis, Guccis—all hung perfectly. Cassy flipped through the rack and noticed that each dress was her size. And the matching high heel shoes were all her size as well. Just like the array of clothes at the hotel, only more. "This man knows more about me and my taste in clothes than my husband ever did," Cassy said aloud.

She dropped her sweat-soaked walking shorts to the floor and wiggled the wet blouse over her head. Cassy stepped into the oversized shower and stood under the surrounding spray from a dozen jets. Quickly the shower filled with steam, clouding the glass. After switching to a cool shower, she used a sponge scrub and the fragrantly scented French soap she found in the shower. Afterwards she toweled dry and patted her damp wavy hair softly into place.

Then Cassy selected an oversized white raw silk tunic from the closet. She looked for a designer label and found none, realizing that the casual short blouse-dress had been tailored to her measurements. Matching handmade white huarache sandals completed the outfit. Every item fit perfectly.

Hanging from a jewelry tree on the counter top were gold loop earrings and a gold chain necklace. She slipped them on. Satisfied with her mirror's image, Cassy looked for the sweat-soaked clothes that she had dropped on the floor before the shower, but they had disappeared.

The grand room was deserted when Cassy walked down the marble staircase into the living area. Tenoch appeared in his office doorway beneath the staircase. He greeted her with a large crystal goblet filled with ice and a dark clear tea. Mint sprigs and lemon wedges decorated the rim of the quart-size crystal glass. Condensed droplets of moisture hung on the sides of the glass and imprinted her fingers as she held the glass.

"You are beautiful in white," Tenoch said. "In any color," he added as his eyes lingered over her.

"Thank you," Cassy said, feeling her face suddenly pumped with blood. Over the rim of the iced tea glass she appraised Tenoch. His masculinity set all her senses on alert. Cassy caught the scent of his signature cologne. Then without her willing it, her medically trained mind took over and noted that Tenoch showed no outward sign of heat stroke. She quickly assessed his demeanor, speech cadence, and affect, satisfying herself that he was well.

"You really worried me on the pyramid. Some of what you said up there didn't make sense. You were delirious. It was so hot on top of the pyramid I thought I was dying," Cassy said, taking two more swallows of the icy cold tea.

"I was not delirious," he said. "But now you understand the power of the Spirits of Teotihuacan." Cassy looked at his black eyes, unsure of his words. She sipped on the pleasingly stout tea, letting it roll in her mouth before swallowing and then relishing the pleasant aftertaste.

Cassy reached for his forearm and said, "I just didn't want anything to happen to you." Cassy sipped the tea again. Its tart sweetness hung in her mouth. Tenoch said nothing as the two watched each other in the waning light of the afternoon. In that moment she understood the devotion, almost slavish loyalty that his staff showed to him. It was a reciprocal loyalty, Cassy told herself. Tenoch in his own way was loyal and protective of those he trusted. A kindness seemed to underlie his protective exterior, like the sweetness of a nut behind its hard shell, Cassy thought.

Moving quickly to refocus her thinking, Cassy changed the conversation abruptly. When she heard herself say, "Your tea is incredibly delicious," she felt foolish. And if that were not enough she added, "I would like to take some of your tea home with me." A flush colored her face. She felt like a school girl on a date—exuberant, lighthearted. It has been too long—she heard her emotions intruding again.

"I brew it myself. It's a special tea that is blended for me," he said. He refilled her glass from a crystal pitcher that sat on the low stone table. "To our Aztec forebears and to this day." He lifted his glass in a toast, touching the rim of her crystal glass with his.

Cassy sipped the tea again. The more she tasted, the more she wanted. Its crisp delicate tart taste left a lingering pleasant taste like the finish of a fine wine. "Where do you find this tea?"

"An old woman in the Mercado de Sonora market blends it for me."

The icy cold liquid on her tongue washed its coolness into her throat. The fleeting headache of a slushy iced drink wrinkled her forehead until the sensation passed. The lingering mint taste laid on her tongue. A pleasant rush of relaxation flowed through her.

She was mesmerized by the drink. "This tea is fantastic," Cassy said. She held the glass under her nose letting the minty aroma from the surface float up to her face.

"The old tea lady won't tell her trade secrets. I have reason to believe the leaves are brought into Mexico from Guatemala and Korea."

"Does she also read the tea leaves and tell the future?" Cassy asked as she swallowed deeply from her crystal glass.

"There is no need. The past and the future are predetermined."

"Not everyone would agree with you," Cassy said, a light frivolous tone in her voice.

"Not everyone is an Aztec like you and me," Tenoch replied simply.

The smoggy haze of Mexico City blurred the skyline beyond the windows giving a hazy monochrome to the sky behind Tenoch. Cassy watched Tenoch's profile bathed against light which filtered through the tinted windows. A rapturous blush enclosed her as she watched his thin lips moving. Her mind heard the sounds from his mouth but could not internalize their meaning.

"Yes, I see," Cassy said, realizing that she did not understand what she was agreeing with. She heard the sounds of his voice but could not decipher his words. The timbre of his voice fascinated her. Her eyes focused on the up and down motion of his voice box in his neck as he spoke. He seemed to draw her thoughts into him as if he were vacuuming her mind. The movement of his lips pulled her into his mouth. She could see his lips moving, but the sound of his voice was distant and indistinct.

His eyes, barely blinking, were black pools in the fading backlight of the windows of the grand salon. "You are lovely in the white blouse," she heard him say. The extra long tunic fell around her mid-thigh. Her skin had darkened already with the last few days of exposure to the sun. Cassy now managed to decode a few of his words, "lovely . . . selected . . . you."

What is going on with me? she asked herself. The discombobulation of her mind was not at all frightening to Cassy. On the contrary, she felt her senses alive and pleasurable with a euphoria that excluded all recent unpleasantnesses. Her mind wound into a slow motion sequence punctuated with bursts of staccato sound from Tenoch's voice.

Tenoch leaned against the back of the sofa. His body pressed comfortably into the soft black leather cushion. Cassy sipped at the tea. Her mouth was dry and tight despite its wetness. With every sip, her throat became more parched. She leaned forward trying to concentrate on his lips. Her entire focus was on how his lips would feel when they touched hers.

"Are you all right, Cassy?" Tenoch asked. He leaned forward to take the iced tea glass from her hand. Cassy tensed as his fingers closed around hers on the glass. Gently he took the glass from her hand and placed it on the ceremonial stone table in front of them.

Shaking her head, Cassy was able to refocus her mind on Tenoch's face long enough to answer. "I'm fine. Just a little distracted, I guess."

"Maybe a little tired from the afternoon on the pyramid?" Tenoch asked.

"No, I'm fine," she said, shaking her head, trying to clear her mind. What is happening? This man has aroused me, and he only touched my finger. I feel like a teenager, she thought. Sure, it's been three years since I—but Tenoch only touched my finger, and he set me on fire.

"Are you sure? Would you like to lie down?" Tenoch asked, smiling. Sure I would like to lie down, thought Cassy—in your bed. She giggled aloud at the thought. It was a flashing moment of fantasy as Cassy pictured Tenoch in bed next to her. What kind of lover would he be? Gentle, rough, slow, quick? She felt her entire body flushing under the silk tunic. Her palms moistened. Her mouth dried. She drank again from another glass of tea until the clear ice cubes rattled in the empty glass. Cassy looked back at Tenoch to find his dark eyes focused on her.

What is he saying? Cassy asked herself. Her thoughts were preoccupied with the thought of Tenoch's body pressing against her. What is happening to me? she wanted to know. She felt impelled by an unaccountable urgency to be next to him. The room behind them dimmed quickly into a dusky darkness as the late afternoon sun fell behind the thick gauze of smog covering the city. Cassy slid onto the leather sofa next to him.

"You're not having tea?" Cassy asked. Tenoch shook his head and smiled wryly. "I'll share yours." She leaned her body toward him and placed the rim of the glass on his lips. Her hand under his chin erupted with prickly moisture when her fingers brushed the skin of his face.

Her need to touch him became overpowering. What is happening to me? Why am I so worked up? She recognized the clear signals from her body: her moist palms, the dry mouth, the pounding of her rapid pulse in her neck, the aching fullness in her lower abdomen, the subtle awareness of her groin. What has this man done to provoke my feelings?

Cassy smoothed the soft white tunic blouse, trying to will her erect nipples away. Their twin impressions on the tunic were obvious. Her face was flushed as if she had been running. "I'm sorry, Tenoch," Cassy said. "I-I . . . something is happening . . . I-I d-don't feel right." Her voice quivered. Her eyes blurred. Her tongue thickened as she tried to articulate her words distinctly. She again reached for the tea and sipped deeply, fighting back her impulses to grab him. Her breathing became short and quick, giving her a sense of breathlessness.

The exuberance of her sexual urgings went beyond anything that Cassy had ever felt. The fullness in her lower abdomen and pelvis approached a real aching. She was so aroused she could barely control herself. Is it because it has been three years? Or is it because this man before me is the most exciting, most attractive, most mysterious man I have ever encountered? she asked herself.

Again Tenoch's mouth moved, but Cassy could not understand his words. An occasional word filtered into Cassy: "transplantation—donors—hearts." The movement of his lips mesmerized her. All she could think about was whether his lips would be soft, firm, or open when he kissed her.

The aching pressure in her lower abdomen caused her to lean her upper body toward Tenoch to ease the fullness. Her giddiness became replaced with butterflies. Then a sick feeling came into her stomach. The intensity and urgency pulled her toward Tenoch.

Her eyes trailed uncontrollably to Tenoch's groin, searching for any arousal reciprocal to her excitement. His eyes remained focused on her. When she looked up he moved his hand along the back of the cushion. She desperately wished for his touch. The tightness in her throat and her dry mouth caused her to finish off the third glass of tea. Tenoch's face appeared to rush toward her, blooming in an enormous increase in size. Cassy shook her head trying to clear the distorted visual images and held the glass of tea to her flushed cheek, feeling its chilly moisture on her hot face. When she reopened her eyes, Tenoch's face and body had dwindled away in the distance. The sound of his voice trailed after the phantasmagoric apparition.

She squeezed her eyes closed briefly and reopened them. Tenoch sat quietly next to her, his smiling lips moving easily. But his words blurred in her mind. She leaned close to him, trying to decipher the gibberish of words. The scent of his cologne rushed over her. Her bare knee touched his thigh when she leaned forward. A discharge of lightning connected her knee to the hard muscle of his thigh, fusing her to him. She was unable to pull her knee away. His energy passed into her through their touched legs.

Her left hand crept along of the sofa until she found his right arm casually cocked on the back of the leather cushion. Her slender index finger traced the back of his hand in concentric circles. The aching fullness in her groin and pelvis became a moist presence. She rearranged her legs, still keeping her bare knee pressed against his thigh. He took her hand from the back of the sofa and intertwined her fingers into his.

The movement of his lips synchronized with his voice. Her rational mind heard him say, "At the dinner party tonight, I will announce your acceptance of the position of Surgeon-in-Chief. . . ."

"But . . . ," Cassy said and tried to lean back. His hand held her and caressed the undersurface of her forearm. Her heart pounded. A sheen of perspiration flushed her face. Cassy felt as if her skin were electrically charged under his soft hand. Her hand reached beyond her control to touch the angle of his jaw and caressed the firm facial muscle just in front of his ear. Her urgency to have him quickened until she could barely remain seated on the sofa.

"Perhaps? I'm not so sure," Cassy said, her voice thick. She sipped her tea, swallowing a full mouthful of the cold liquid trying to moisten her dried mouth. She looked up, and his eyes captured her again. She felt her desire explode within her. The rushing roar of blood pumping through her body replaced all sound. She moved her upper body toward him. Her bare leg now lay against the length of his thigh. At that moment, Alberto opened the office door at the end of the grand salon.

"Excuse me, Señor Tenoch, it is the Dallas lawyer, Mr. Haygood, on the telephone. He is insisting that he speak to you immediately." Tenoch glared over Cassy's shoulder at the intrusion.

Tenoch leaned forward to touch the speakerphone on the corner of the stone table in front of them. Cassy fell back against the sofa when Tenoch's leg pulled away from her. A moment of reprieve rushed through her. Her rapid shallow breaths rocked her against the sofa cushion. The waterhammer of her heartbeat pounded her head into a throbbing headache.

"Yes?" Tenoch asked, looking malevolently at the speakerphone.

"I'm sorry, sir. It's gone beyond a quick fix," Haygood's warm voice came through the speakerphone.

"Why?" Tenoch asked, his voice hard.

"I'm still working on her problems, but the bell has already rung for Dr. Baldwin in Dallas."

"You'll need to translate your Texas expressions," Tenoch said flatly. "Just what do you mean by the bell ringing?"

Cassy stiffened and slipped off the sofa to stand at the window, looking back at Tenoch on the sofa, the hazy dusk at her back. Her breathing slowed. But her pulse still raced. What just happened to me? she asked as she felt her composure slowly returning. I was as aroused as I've ever been, and he just held my hand. For god's sake, get a grip on yourself.

"It's the goddamn DA's office," the twangy voice on the speakerphone said. "He's like a dog that has sniffed out a coon. He's been barking all day long about Dr. Baldwin and Marquez. That's not all the trouble . . . today the honorable Scott Spence, the fair-headed boy of Texas politics and maybe our next governor, has been stumping for new laws about declaration of death in the emergency rooms of Texas. I'm having hell trying to put a lid on this thing. There's more problems. The DA has been on every local television station talking about Marquez's death and his suspicion that somebody killed him. Dr. Baldwin could even be arrested when she comes back to Dallas. That's not all. Demerol prescriptions with Dr. Baldwin's signature having been popping up all over Dallas. Your lady's got a plateful of trouble."

"You have until Monday morning to resolve this matter, or I will," Tenoch said coldly and snapped off the speakerphone.

The conversation knocked Cassy off the peak of her euphoria. In those brief moments of the telephone exchange she had free fallen into an abyss of depression. She hugged her arms to her sides and paced the length of the glass wall, unable to look in Tenoch's direction. The fine moisture that had moments ago steamed from her neck and chest was now a chilly wrapper to her skin. The ends of her dark hair glistened with wetness. The skin of her forearms and legs puckered as she fought off a shaking chill.

A premonition rolled over her. A dread of events unknown shuddered her until a shaking chill rattled her body. Even though Tenoch was only a few feet away, Cassy felt more alone at that moment than she had ever felt. "I need to go to Dallas tonight. My son needs me now," Cassy said. Her words tumbled out on top of each other as she continued to pace in front of the glass wall. "I'm sorry. I'll take a commercial flight home tonight." Tenoch slipped off the sofa and intercepted her as she turned at the end of the room. He pulled her toward him. His closeness warmed her until her chill passed.

Cassy stood quiet, saying nothing. Her mind jumbled into thought fragments. The sexual attraction to Tenoch had withered into nothingness. She turned dazed in his arms.

"There is nothing you can do tonight in Dallas." He led her back toward the sofa. "I will take care of your problems Monday morning. Do not concern yourself."

"I've got to go home."

He offered her a full glass of iced tea that he poured from the crystal pitcher. Cassy shook her head. "I'm so tired," Cassy said and sat on the edge of the sofa, sipping at the fresh glass of tea.

"Perhaps a siesta before the dinner in your honor tonight?" Tenoch asked. With a slight move of his index finger he gestured toward the shadows at the far end of the room. The maid instantly appeared.

"Prepare the guest suite for Señora Baldwin," Tenoch said to the maid. "You should rest."

Cassy stood up, realizing how overtired she was. She leaned against Tenoch and kissed his cheek lightly.

"Thank you, Tenoch. I appreciate your understanding," Cassy said, whispering in his ear. "A nap is maybe what I need. I really don't feel well right now." Her breasts pushed against him. She felt the twinge of her sexuality again.

"Señora, your room is ready," the maid said, snapping Cassy back to reality. Cassy followed the maid up the staircase. The heavy blinds cast the room into darkness except for an aisle of lamplight at the head of the bed. The silk sheets had been turned down under the tapestried canopy of the king-size bed.

"Señora, I just need to lie down," Cassy protested. "I don't want to go to bed."

"Por favor, Señora," the maid said, guiding Cassy to the edge of the bed where she settled unsteadily on the edge. Cassy drank another half glass of iced tea from a goblet the maid placed on the bedside table. Her pounding heartbeat quieted a bit. Her skin still glowed with perspiration. The heavy fatigue overtook her. I can't think clearly, she told herself. She did not protest when the maid slipped the tunic over her head and settled a white silk chemise over her bare shoulders.

An unbearable weariness replaced the chilled feeling as Cassy crawled between the gold satin sheets. Her last waking image before sleep overtook her was of Tenoch, standing rigid and cataleptic, staring into the sun from the top of the pyramid. Time slowed into nothingness. Cassy floated as if she were drifting on a river raft, unable to see the shore. Her horizontal body swung gently from side to side in a constant vertiginous whirl.

———

"Señora. Señora!" The maid's piercing voice dragged Cassy to the shore of her subconsciousness. She felt the maid touch her shoulder as if she had bumped into a hard rock cliff at the edge of the river. The darkened bedroom dislocated her senses. Her head throbbed as the ceiling of the strange room spun dizzyingly above her. She pulled herself upright on both hands. The silk chemise slipped against the sleek gold satin sheets. What happened? Did I have too much to drink? Her mind refocused itself under the drumming in her skull. Where am I? she asked herself, looking into the brown face of the Hispanic maid hovering at the bedside.

"Señora, it is seven-thirty. Dinner is at nine o'clock. Señor Tenoch has told me to assist you."

"I'm not sure . . . ," Cassy said, rubbing her eyes and stretching her neck from side to side and trying to lock her mind onto the present. "Where's my son?"

"He's in Dallas," the maid said. "You remember? You are in Mexico City. At the home of Señor Tenoch."

Cassy twisted her bare feet to the floor, tentatively finding the plush carpet. The flood of memory spilled back into her mind. Oh, my god, she thought, remembering the overwhelming sexual fantasy that she had with Tenoch just before she went to sleep. Or was it a fantasy? Then her anxieties about her son rushed back into her.

"I need to talk to my son," Cassy said, reaching for the bedside phone. "I want to speak to my son," she told the male operator.

Moments later, Alex was on the line. "Hi, Mom. Trent's taking me to the baseball game tomorrow afternoon."

There was an unopened box of Marlboros on the bedside table. She pulled a cigarette from the pack. The maid stepped forward to light it as Cassy asked Alex about his day.

"Are you coming home tomorrow?" Alex asked.

"Yes. I'll be there," she said. There was an uncomfortable lull in the conversation. Cassy could not fill the gap. Alex again did not seem to be in a talkative mood. Finally Cassy said, "You have the phone number here. Have a great time at the Rangers' game. I love you."

Cassy replaced the receiver and inhaled deeply from the cigarette. The fuzzy feeling had not cleared completely. The dull fatigue pressed into her.

The maid reappeared with a pitcher of tea and ice. Cassy smiled and nodded in response to the maid's gesture at the cold pitcher. The tart taste of the tea washed away the lingering constricting tightness of her throat.

Cassy closed the bathroom suite door behind her and let the silk gown drop to the floor. After a cool shower, she stepped before the dresser. A fresh glass of iced tea stood on the dressing table. The obsidian necklace and earrings lay on a white silk cloth on the dresser top. Cassy found her luggage from her hotel suite had been unpacked and her two bags placed on the closet shelf. She spotted the black silk Chanel dress hanging among the dozen designer cocktail dresses. She remembered his words— 'You will look nice in black'. Her headache had disappeared, replaced by an excited anticipation of the evening.

For the next hour Cassy dressed leisurely. The formfitting black dress accentuated her slender waist. The bodice of the dress hugged her breasts. Narrow crossover straps exposed her golden tan back. Black sheer hose and thin high-heeled black pumps showed off her long legs. The mid-thigh length dress flattered her tawny skin. The fragrance of the expensive French perfume at the base of her neck brought a smile to her lips. The last touch was the obsidian necklace and earrings. She felt better than she had in a week.

TWENTY-FOUR

A T THE TOP of the sweeping staircase in front of the Aztec stone calendar, Cassy stopped to look over the grand salon of Tenoch's penthouse. Immediately below her an elongated dining room table glittered with gold, crystal, and china under the globe chandelier. In the center of the long table, set for nineteen, flickering candlelight from ornate gold candelabras danced highlights off the three crystal glasses in front of each place setting. A grand piano floated a soft romantic melody upward to Cassy from the far corner of the grand salon.

Tenoch, a cordless telephone at his ear, stood at the window wall that spanned the two floors of the grand salon. The twinkling lights of the darkened city below silhouetted his broad shoulders. As Cassy smoothly descended the steps of the broad black marble staircase, Tenoch watched her graceful reflection in the glass window wall. Their eyes met each other in the mirrored reflection of the glass. Turning from the window toward her, Tenoch snapped the phone closed. He reached out to catch her hand as she neared him. He brushed a light kiss to her cheek.

"You are beautiful in black, or any color," he whispered into her ear. The lingering scent of his cheek intoxicated her. Her palms moistened. Her face flushed. He laced his fingers with hers.

"I love the dress on you," he said, holding her at arms length like a couturier so that he could study her carefully. "The obsidian necklace and earrings are perfect for you."

"Gracias," Cassy said quietly, pleased by his admiring appraisal.

"My guests should be here soon," Tenoch said as they walked about the lavish table centered in the salon.

The maid appeared with a gold tray and two crystal glasses, one with tea and one with sparkling water.

"To our Aztec destiny," Tenoch said, touching the rim of Cassy's glass with his glass. The ping of the crystal touching was lost in the swelling of the piano melody as the piano player smiled broadly at them. At that moment the double door at the far end of the grand salon opened. A balding, rotund man, trailed by a matron in a long white evening gown, stepped off the elevator.

Tenoch wrapped his hand possessively on Cassy's bare low back beneath the crossover straps and guided her toward the couple who moved into the grand salon. His warm soft hand felt reassuring and comforting against her bare skin. The older couple stood stiffly as Tenoch closed on them like an approaching bulldozer.

"Buenas noches, Pablo," Tenoch said, shaking the formally attired man's hand vigorously. "Your presence with your lovely wife honors me," Tenoch said in rapid fire Spanish and bussed the reticent woman, standing a respectful step behind her husband.

Turning to Cassy, Tenoch said, "I present Señor Pablo Menendez, the Mayor of Mexico City." Cassy put out her right hand to shake the florid-faced man's hand. He bowed formally, kissing the back of her hand.

"You bring beauty, dignity, and honor to our city," the mayor said, still holding her hand as he returned upright. The plump matron smiled and nodded her head deeply. "Señor Tenoch has told us of his plans to bring the miracle of heart transplantation to the citizens of Mexico," Menendez said. "If I, or Mexico City, can provide you anything . . . anything at all . . . let me know. It shall be yours."

"Usted es muy amable. You are most gracious," Cassy said and thought what a difference her reception would have been at a Dallas dinner party that evening.

The elevator door opened again. Dr. Raul Garcia and his wife similarly dignified and gowned as the other woman stood just behind him. Tenoch guided Cassy toward the Garcias, moving away from the Menendez couple.

"Cassy, welcome home to Mexico," Garcia said and pumped her hand vigorously, then introduced his wife to Tenoch and Cassy. The woman nodded shyly. At that moment, Alberto appeared at Tenoch's side and whispered in his ear. A grim expression replaced Tenoch's bonhomie.

"Cassy, if you will excuse me for a moment, there is a telephone call I must take," Tenoch said and then smiled, the ever-gracious host, to the Garcias. Tenoch and Alberto disappeared into Tenoch's office beneath the overhanging balcony of the upstairs bedroom suites.

"How is our recipient doing in Dallas?" Dr. Garcia asked after Tenoch had gone.

"She's doing very well," Cassy said. "Trent told me just before I left Dallas that his daughter would be discharged from the hospital Monday."

"Dr. Hendricks' daughter?" Dr. Garcia asked, a baffled look changing his face. "Has she been sick?'

"Of course. A week ago tonight, Trent was here in Mexico City, retrieving a donor heart from a young girl who was injured in a car accident. I performed the heart transplant for his daughter Sunday morning."

"I'm sorry, I did not realize."

"I believe your signature is on the death certificate," Cassy said.

"No entiendo. There must be some misunderstanding," Dr. Garcia said, his English breaking down.

Before Cassy could respond, the muted thwop-thwop of an approaching helicopter vibrated the room. The nose light of the helicopter bathed the penthouse suite in a white incandescence. The aircraft enlarged like a rushing locomotive until it leaped upward to land on the rooftop heliport. The lighted Aztec sun calendar logo blazed on the door of the chopper as it disappeared over the edge of the rooftop.

Just then the elevator in the foyer opened releasing four more couples. The four middle-aged Hispanic men were dressed in finely tailored tuxedos. But it was the jewelry on the women that staggered Cassy. Even at the Dallas charity balls she had attended with Scott, she had never seen diamonds so large and numerous. At the same moment Tenoch reentered the grand salon from his office.

"My friends," Tenoch said, his voice booming in the open room like a cannonade. "Welcome." He swam into the crowd with the polished ease of a concierge, shaking hands all around and kissing the women. With the whole room's attention focused on Tenoch, he turned to Cassy wrapping his arm around her waist, his palm resting protectively on her bare back. Cassy let herself be eased toward Tenoch until their bodies pressed against each other. The touch of his hard physique stirred her again. "May I present my guest of honor, Dr. Cassandra Marta Baldwin?" Tenoch said to the group gathered about him.

Just then, the foyer door opened and disgorged tuxedoed Trent Hendricks and Walter Simmons. Hanging onto Walter Simmons' arm like a folded umbrella tucked neatly at his side and all but forgotten was Joan Markison, the ICU nurse from the Metro Hospital. The neckline of her strapless minidress plunged to reveal more than it concealed. Simmons leaned into her as he swaggered into the room in the stiff-legged stride of a drunk struggling for control. Cassy was so startled by the appearance of

Trent and Simmons that she was unable to do more than nod a greeting. Cassy eased back from Tenoch, and she took a step forward to meet Trent. "What are you doing here in Mexico City?" she asked, overcoming her momentary speechlessness.

Ignoring her question, Trent reached for her hand and pulled Cassy away from Tenoch to kiss her cheek. "My god. You look wonderful in that black dress and the black jewelry," he said, grinning like a smitten teenager.

"She is as lovely as she is talented," Tenoch said. He returned his open palm to her bare back and drew her close to him again.

"What are you doing here?" Cassy repeated as she stood next to Tenoch.

"Heather is doing so well that I could slip away for the evening. Thanks to Tenoch's jet, coming to Mexico City for dinner is like driving over to Ft. Worth." He grinned at Tenoch and shook his hand vigorously.

"Aren't you and Alex still going to the Rangers' game tomorrow afternoon?" Cassy asked.

"Sure. Walter and I will be headed back to Dallas tonight as soon as the party for you breaks up."

"Good evening, Cassy." Walter Simmons lurched up. He shook Cassy's hand politely and swayed against Joan Markison. "Is s'nice t'see you dressed up, Cassy. Nice dress," he slurred. The mixed odors of bourbon, cigarettes, and the heavy scent of Georgio Red slapped her nose. He leered at Cassy, his eyes drifting downward over the swell of her breasts into the deep decolletage of her black dress.

"Walter, what a surprise," Cassy said cooly. "You should introduce your friend to Señor Tenoch."

Walter Simmons interrupted Cassy's cold look at Joan Markison by drunkenly pulling Joan forward directly in front of Tenoch. "Oh yeah, Señor Tenoch, meet Joannie, she's my new Nursing Director of the ICU at the Metro Hospital." Tenoch nodded formally and politely shook the nurse's hand.

As soon as Tenoch released Joan's hand, Simmons said to Joan, "Babe, go get me another double bourbon, rocks, no water." He shoved her away without looking at her. As gracefully as she could manage, the woman unwrapped herself from Simmons and walked quickly away. Her hips swayed beneath the tightly fitted red velvet dress.

"I brought Trent and Walter down from Dallas so that we could discuss the logistics of my organ procurement concept," Tenoch said to Cassy. "We have much to discuss. The four of us can talk after dinner."

"The donor heart we procured yesterday is functioning nicely," Trent said to Cassy. "It was terribly fortunate that you were in Mexico City to procure the heart. I'm sure my patient would be dead without it." Trent turned to Tenoch and said, "The family is most grateful."

"Very good. Before you leave, we will discuss how the family can express their gratitude tangibly," Tenoch said, looking over the heads of the two men toward the foyer of the grand salon. "I see that the United States Ambassador to Mexico has just arrived. Cassy, come let me introduce you." Tenoch guided her across the room with his palm flat against her bare back.

"Looks like your friend, Dr. Baldwin, is fucking Tenoch," Walter Simmons whispered as he leaned over next to Trent. A crystal glass filled with bourbon rested in one hand and Simmons' other hand draped around the nurse's shoulders, bared by her strapless dress.

"Jesus Christ, Walter, get your mind out of the bedroom. I know that might not be possible but try to think about something other than sex for once."

Simmons pulled away from Markison who clung to him to whisper to Trent. "Tenoch has bought himself a playmate," Simmons said, laughing and coughing at the same time.

"Is that all that is important to you, Walter? Sex and money?"

Simmons roared with laughter and finished the bourbon. "No, my friend . . . just the money. I can always buy the women."

"Jesus, Walter. Give me a break."

"Admit it," Simmons said. "Your good lady doctor has the hots for Tenoch. Your little sweetheart doctor friend is putting out for Tenoch. Everyone else in this room can see that . . . even if you won't admit it."

Trent said nothing.

"I can always tell when a woman is fucking the man she's with," Simmons continued and drank half of another bourbon in a single swallow. "Give me two minutes around a woman . . . I can tell." Trent looked at Simmons skeptically. "Hell, man. Look at the way Tenoch has his hand on Cassy's back . . . the way she damn near falls into him. Just imagine what she and Tenoch will be like tonight, coupling up after we're headed back to Dallas."

"And I can always tell when you're drunk, Walter." Trent said, a hard edge sharpening his voice.

"What you need, my friend, is another drink," Simmons said, waving at one of the tuxedoed Hispanic waiters patrolling the room. "Bring my friend a double Jack Daniels on the rocks."

Trent looked across the room as Tenoch guided Cassy through the small group gathered at the end of the great room. His hand remained low and possessive on Cassy's bare back. They greeted the American ambassador and his wife, a distinguished pair, whose light skin and gray hair stood out in the group, the odd couple among the dark-skinned, black-haired men and women.

After drinking his double bourbon quickly, Trent weaved through the cluster of guests chattering in rapid Spanish. Expressive hands fluttered in the air about them. He dodged the conversational bunchings until he stopped abruptly next to Cassy. Trent's hand tightened on her forearm, pulling her away from Tenoch. "I need to speak to you a moment," he whispered. His warm breath filled her face with bourbon fumes.

"Now?" she asked as casually as she could manage. Trent nodded grimly toward the opposite end of the room. She felt his grip tighten even more.

"Excuse me," Cassy said to Tenoch. "Trent and I need to visit a few minutes about his daughter's surgical treatment."

"Certainly, my dear," Tenoch said. "You and Trent have your medical conference. Then I will announce dinner."

Once away from the group, Trent turned to face her, his back to the glass wall. His clenched jaw muscle twitched in the shadows of the room's edge. His eyes fixed her in a stony stare.

"What's the matter, Trent?" Cassy asked, apprehension filling her with fear that Trent was close to exploding.

"Don't get caught up with Tenoch," Trent said. His words ran over each other. "He's too smooth. You'll only be hurt."

"I'm a big girl," Cassy said. "And I don't need you to look out for me." She immediately wanted to grab the words back.

"If you're involved with Tenoch, believe me, you need someone to look out for you."

"I'm not involved with Tenoch, if it's any of your business," Cassy said and again regretted her words.

"Where did you spend the night last night?" Trent asked, his teeth grinding under his tight jaw muscles, his lips drawn into a tight frown.

Cassy felt herself stiffen in surprise. After a pause to control her rage, she said, "It's none of your damn business where I sleep . . . or with whom I sleep. But for the record, I spent the night in the Presidential Suite at the Camino Real Hotel."

Trent's face colored in a full flush. His mouth opened. He started to speak. Then he shrugged as if in resignation. "I'm sorry, Cass. It's just that I can't stand to see you . . . or Alex . . . get hurt."

"Maybe I'm a better judge of what's best for me and for my son," she said.

"Don't . . . Cassy . . . don't." Trent could not articulate any other words.

"We should return to the party," Cassy said, forcing a lightness in her voice, trying to cover her exasperation.

"No, just a minute," Trent said, gripping her forearm again.

"Let go, Trent. Don't make a scene here, please. You've had too much to drink."

"All right, have it your way," Trent said angrily. "Just remember Ana Ruiz."

"Who? What are you talking about?" Cassy turned back around, her curiosity overcoming her fury.

"Just remember the name, Ana Ruiz. That's all you need to know."

"Ana Ruiz? What the hell are you telling me?" Cassy asked, keeping her voice low.

"Ana Ruiz is all I can tell you," Trent said. "Be careful."

"The hell with you," Cassy said and abruptly turned away from him toward the group in the center of the room. Trent slouched in the shadow near the window, staring after her. Tenoch looked past the American ambassador, and his eyes engaged Cassy's as she approached him.

Tenoch slipped his arm easily around her waist again. "I'm sorry, Tenoch," Cassy said, "Trent needs a lot of support right now. He's been under a lot of strain with his daughter this week . . . and he's had a bit too much bourbon tonight."

"I've never seen Trent like this," Tenoch said, shrugged indifferently and apparently dismissed the incident. "I must introduce you to the wealthiest man in Mexico." He gently pushed her into the cocktail crowd that had congregated in the end of the grand salon. The piano player continued the soft anonymous songs from the other side of the room until all sounds blended into one low rumble.

Several minutes later, Cassy stood in a circle of businessmen, chatting comfortably with an older man whom Tenoch had introduced to her as the wealthiest man of all Mexico. The grandfatherly man had laughed heartily at Tenoch's introduction and denied in Spanish that he was the wealthiest man in Mexico because Tenoch was by far the richest of all men in Mexico. Cassy found herself under the spell of this charming patriarch when Walter Simmons waddled toward the group, his stiff, broad-based gait even more unsteady without Joan Markison's support.

Tenoch's arm pulled Cassy in close to him as they bantered with the elder Mexican. Simmons, unnoticed by either Tenoch or Cassy, whispered in her ear. Cassy jumped at the sound of his gravel voice. "Don't fuck with me, Cassy," he hissed in her ear so quietly despite his drunkenness that no one but Cassy heard the threat. She stood motionless for a moment, her anger taking her breath. "Even if you are humping Tenoch, don't ever threaten me again."

Her brown eyes glared at Simmons. Her lips pressed together in a taut line. "You are the most disgusting, despicable man I have ever met."

"Cassy, what . . . you," Tenoch said, recognizing then that Cassy had turned her head away. He looked past her to see Walter Simmons. "Walter, my friend. I know you cannot stay away from my beautiful guest. But where is your lovely lady friend who came with you?"

"It's always my pleasure to see Cassandra," Simmons said, his words soft and obsequious. "I was expressing my hope that she will accept this wonderful opportunity in Mexico City that you are offering her."

Tenoch pulled Cassy possessively toward him with his arm curled about her waist. "I believe I can count on Cassy."

At that moment Alberto materialized at Tenoch's side and whispered in his ear. Tenoch nodded. Alberto faded back into the room, again becoming part of the furnishings and trappings of Tenoch's lifestyle. The piano music melted quietly. The room's lighting system refocused itself on Tenoch. A chime from the concealed room speakers quieted the conversation.

"My friends . . . join me for dinner in honor of my special guest, Dr. Cassandra Marta Baldwin, premier heart surgeon of the Estados Unidos." His baritone voice rang through the room with command authority. He took a step back from Cassy and clapped. Immediately Cassy found herself ringed by the group, clapping and smiling.

Her face blushed under the recent tan that had deepened her natural skin tones. She stood, tall and erect, accepting the applause with the grace and beauty of a princess, embarrassed by the attention but pleased at the same time. She met the warmth of Tenoch's smile and took his extended hand as he reached to guide her to the table. Her smile faded slightly when she caught the drawn sullen look of Trent, standing at the edge of the crowd.

Tenoch seated Cassy to his immediate right at the end of the long table. He took the honored end position at the table. The Mayor of Mexico City sat at the opposite end of the table. The nineteen guests, Trent being the only unaccompanied person, were mixed together along the sides of the twenty-four foot table in order dictated by place cards beside each lavish china service.

As soon as everyone was seated, tuxedoed waiters efficiently filled fluted glasses with Cristal champagne. Tenoch rose from his chair and stood at his place, momentarily waiting for the dinner guests to look toward him. Cassy found herself acutely aware of his tall, well-muscled body standing just to her left. His dinner jacket hung exactly from his wide shoulders. His confidence and self-assured manner filled the huge room, quieting the murmuring of conversation about the table. All eyes around the table focused on Tenoch. He acknowledged each guest with momentary locking of gazes until he had touched the eyes of every guest.

His black eyes glowed in a halo of white and danced in the flickering candlelight from the ancient gold candelabras.

"Before we begin this evening, I want us to remember our compadre, Jeorg Marquez," Tenoch said solemnly. "His spirit is with us tonight. Jeorg has left this incarnation, but he is not forgotten. Our spirits move together beyond this world, as they have since the beginning. I honor Jeorg. It is to our spirits that I lift my glass." Tenoch lifted his glass high above his head before sipping lightly. The table followed his example. When the group finished sipping the champagne, Tenoch stood quietly with his head bowed a moment before sitting down. The conversational murmuring discreetly returned to the table.

Cassy reached her left hand under the corner of the table, resting her slender fingers gently on his wrist, teasing the soft black hair on the back of his right hand. She leaned forward from her seat across the corner of the table to whisper to him. "I know how much he meant to you." Her look lingered in his eyes. She felt a rush of excitement and a quickening of her pulse.

"We are one together," Tenoch said as he bent toward her. Cassy felt her euphoria from earlier in the day beginning to revive.

The team of waiters efficiently placed crystal stemmed goblets filled with shaved ice mounded under a ringlet of giant prawns in front of each person. Cassy finished drinking her second glass of iced tea. Immediately the empty crystal glass was replaced with a full one. The delicate sweet taste of the shrimp reminded Cassy that she had not eaten since that morning. She was ravenous. After the second cold shrimp, the same queasy feeling that had begun at the Teotihuacan ruins recurred but not severe enough to interfere with the pleasurable euphoria enveloping her.

With another peeled shrimp at her lips, Cassy's foot accidentally brushed Tenoch's leg beneath the table. An intense shiver of physical attraction prickled the skin of her entire leg. Her hand hesitated a moment with the shrimp at her mouth. She felt herself drawn into Tenoch's presence in the same manner that his nearness had aroused her in the afternoon. Carefully replacing the shrimp on the ice, she took two more deep swallows of the iced tea, hoping to calm her rolling stomach. Her mouth again felt like a parchment tube despite the pleasing aftertaste of the tea. Her pulse trip-hammered her neck. Her breath stuck in her throat when her foot again caught Tenoch's muscular calf beneath the corner of the table. This time she did not withdraw. His dark and unflinching eyes looked across at her, acknowledging the touch of her foot. The shoe dropped off her foot. She stroked his upper calf with the arch of her foot.

She tried to relax, but the excitement of his touch tensed her body. She blinked, trying to refocus the blurring of her vision. The sharp profile of his face blurred into a double image. She swallowed several more gulps of tea, trying to quell the churning that was growing in her insides. Her face flushed crimson on both cheeks. She touched the edge of the table for balance as the room wavered before her. Her foot remained firmly pressed into Tenoch's calf. The conversations flurrying about her grew into a rushing roar. Tenoch's lips moved but she heard no words, only a babble of noise.

Her stockinged foot caressed Tenoch's calf and inched upward to his thigh. His eyes constricted so tightly that it was impossible to see into them. She saw only darkness where his eyes were. Her mind raced in a collage of blurred colors while her stomach churned.

"Are you all right?" Tenoch asked. His voice echoed as he leaned toward her and rested his hand on her knee below her short dress. The light touch of his fingers shot a warm tingling bolt into her pelvis. "Cassy, are you all right?" Tenoch repeated. "Que pasa? What is the matter?"

Cassy stared at him, a dazed and bewildered look on her face. When Tenoch turned toward her, his knees parted. Cassy's stockinged foot rode up the inner aspect of his thigh toward his groin. The room began to spin before her, blurring the faces of the people around her out of focus. Tenoch's voice echoed itself into gibberish.

"More tea," she heard him say when he leaned across the corner of the table to whisper into her ear. His warm breath fanned her ear. Cassy could barely stay seated she was so aroused. 'More tea?' were the only words she understood. She drank deeply from the full glass of tea.

Momentarily her vision cleared. The whirling kaleidoscope of the room snapped into an abrupt sharp focus. She felt herself consumed in alternating waves of fatigue and nausea and exquisite sexual awareness. She froze, her mind motionless. Then she began trembling visibly. She swallowed a spoonful of cold tomato soup that the waiter placed in front of her, hoping to force away the queasy feeling. Bending her head low, she whispered to Tenoch, "Sorry. . . must be excused. I am sick. Estoy enfermo." Her tongue was thick and full, interfering with her words.

"Of course," Tenoch said, gallantly pushing his chair backward. As Cassy pushed herself up from the table, her knees buckled, collapsing her back into her chair. Her hands grabbed at the edge of the table for support. The room wobbled before her eyes. The roaring whir in her head deafened her. She tried to swallow to clear her seared mouth. All motion in the room slowed to a dream quality. The room and its sounds telescoped into the distance. Her last conscious impression was the sensation of floating. In some remote recess of her mind, she heard Tenoch's voice anxiously calling her name. "Cassy? Cassy?" And then she slid out of her chair, coming to rest under the table like a limp rag doll. Cassy heard Tenoch's full authoritative command. "Send for Dr. Gonzalez."

From a farther distance, Cassy recognized Trent's voice, harsh, rough, and large. "Get the hell away from her. Stand back."

Cassy's eyes flickered into a flat, unseeing stare. Her first visual perception was a circle of bent heads, leaning forward over her. In the center of the circle of faces, the great gold globe chandelier swung before her from the vaulted ceiling of the salon, two stories above the floor that she lay on. Under her neck, a hand lift her head. Then she heard Tenoch's voice again. "Cassy, I will move you upstairs. The doctor is on his way." He spoke soothingly and touched her cheek gently, sweeping a strand of her dark wet hair off her damp forehead.

When her eyes opened again, they fastened onto Trent's face. His reddish gray eyebrows drew together. Her mind began to assimilate words. "For chrissake, Tenoch. I'm a doctor. Move aside so that I can take a look at her."

"You're a surgeon," Tenoch replied. "I've called my medical doctor. He'll be here in a moment."

Trent ignored Tenoch, jostling him aside. He reached for Cassy's neck, palpating her rapid, weak carotid pulse with his fingers. "How do you feel, Cass?"

Her eyes refocused on him. She seemed to consider the question before answering. "Woozy. Head hurts. Thirsty. Embarrassed," she said, not able to string words into sentences.

"You need a quiet place," Trent said.

"Upstairs," Tenoch said, asserting his authority as he stood towering above Trent who knelt beside Cassy. "Carry her upstairs." Trent picked Cassy up, cradling her in his arms like a tired, sleepy infant and swept her easily up the staircase.

"Continue with your meal. Dr. Hendricks and I will see to Dr. Baldwin," Tenoch called over his shoulder as he followed Trent up the staircase.

The maid stood at attention at the opened double doors into the guest suite. Trent laid Cassy onto the bed. The closed draperies shut the city out of the dark room. A dim amber bedside lamp glowed the room into murky shadows. Cassy's eyes stayed closed as if asleep.

"Get her out of this dress," Trent said.

"Sí, Señor," the maid said. "I will take care of Señora." She closed the wooden double door behind Tenoch and Trent, leaving the two men standing on the central part of the balcony between the guest suite and Tenoch's bedroom suite. The conversational din mixed with piano melodies rose in waves to the balcony.

"What is your diagnosis?" Tenoch asked.

"Syncope due to dehydration . . . maybe a food allergy . . . perhaps the turista . . . bacterial gastroenteritis. Could be anything. Was she well earlier in the day?" Trent asked, holding the balcony rail as if afraid to let go.

"Late in the afternoon she complained of fatigue and weakness. We spent the afternoon at the pyramids at Teotihuacan. She was thirsty and became exhausted while we were there."

Beyond the dining table at the far end of the cathedral-shaped room, Alberto greeted a middle-aged man carrying a black doctor's bag as large as a suitcase. The doctor, stoop-shouldered in a black business suit, craned his neck upward in the direction of the balcony. He nodded his head when Tenoch raised a hand in a casual familiar greeting. At that moment, the maid opened the guest suite door and motioned to Trent to come in.

Cassy lay in the satin-sheeted bed, a moist gold terry cloth on her forehead. Color had returned to her face. A scoop-necked, black chemise nightgown hung loosely off the ends of her shoulders.

"Feeling better?" Trent asked.

"I'm so sorry. I just don't know what came over me. I've never felt that way before." Cassy's voice was hardly more than a whisper.

"We ought to get you back to Dallas for a full medical check up."

"I'm better already," Cassy said. "Anyway, I'm going home tomorrow. When are you going back to Dallas?

"Tonight. Remember I told you. Tenoch's jet brought us down. We're going back to Dallas right after the dinner party. There's room for you on the plane."

"I'm not so certain that I wouldn't throw up all the way back . . . especially if I had to sit next to Walter Simmons for two hours." Cassy managed a faint smile. "I'll be a lot better tomorrow after a night's sleep. Will you see Alex the first thing tomorrow morning for me?"

"Sure. Remember, I told you that Alex and I are going to the Rangers' baseball game."

"Oh, yeah. Now I remember." Cassy shook her head. Her eyes rimmed with tears. "Something's wrong with me. I can't seem to keep everything straight in my mind."

"There's nothing wrong with you that a good night's sleep won't cure," Trent said. "You'll be well in the morning. Alex and I will bring dinner home after the game for the three of us." He leaned over and kissed her cheek just below the edge of the moist wash cloth that covered her forehead.

The suite door clicked open. Tenoch and the Hispanic doctor entered.

After the doctor introduced himself, Trent and Tenoch were once again excused to the balcony overlooking the grand room.

"She's much better already," Trent said. "Probably dehydration and too much sun this afternoon."

"Very well," Tenoch said. "While Dr. Gonzalez is with her, I will return to my guests." Tenoch glided smoothly down the staircase, reentering the salon and drawing the attention of all the guests. Standing at the end of the table, he said, "Dr. Baldwin will be fine. Nothing more serious than dehydration and the effects of too much Mexico sunshine. She asked me to express her regrets, and Cassy wishes that we proceed with our dinner. Dr. Gonzalez predicts a quick and complete recovery by the morning. Enjoy your meal."

Trent's jaws clenched and his hands wrung the brass rail of the balcony. His face was a flushed mask as he stared down at the top of Tenoch's head. His black luxuriant hair glistened in a light focused at the head of the table. "Why can't the son of a bitch just tell it straight out for once, rather than embellishing everything he touches," Trent muttered to himself.

A few minutes later, Dr. Gonzalez stepped back onto the balcony, closing the guest suite door behind him. He turned to Trent and in a comfortable command of English said, "I've drawn blood for routine hemograms, blood chemistries, and cultures." He paused a beat. "I can't be certain of a diagnosis. Fatigue and dehydration could be the explanation. Her condition could be far more serious. I advised her to go to the hospital tonight, but she refused."

"I'm not surprised," Trent said. "She hates to see doctors."

"She did agree to remain here in Tenoch's suite tonight. I've left a sedative and an anti-emetic for her nausea. She should drink as much liquid as possible. I will check on her in the morning. Of course, I'm available during the night." Dr. Gonzalez shifted the oversized leather bag to his left hand and extended his right hand to Trent. "She asked that you come back in to see her now."

"Thank you, Doctor," Trent said. "I'll see that she gets checked over when she gets back home." Dr. Gonzales left the balcony, avoiding the dinner table as he circled the edge of the room.

As Trent watched the doctor leave, Tenoch's resonant voice again carried up to the balcony. "My friends, I have an exciting announcement that Dr. Baldwin planned to make at this time. Just moments ago she asked me to read her message to you." Tenoch opened a crisp, expensive-looking sheet of stationery and began reading from it. "It is with great pleasure and anticipation that I accept the challenge and the opportunity to create in Mexico City the world's foremost organ transplant center. Tenoch's generosity and vision will make heart transplantation a feasible method of treatment for rich and poor alike in all of Mexico. My son and I will return to Mexico City, the city of my heritage, by June thirtieth to take up this historic opportunity that Tenoch has created. This evening marks the beginning of our journey to an international program in transplant medicine, a model of co-operation that the world's governments can emulate." Tenoch reached forward for his crystal glass of Evian water. "I toast Mexico . . . and Dr. Baldwin." The men around the table stood with their glasses raised.

Walter Simmons rose to his feet, visibly weaving as he raised his wine glass, "Hear, hear," he said slurring the words into one. "I propose a toast to Mexico's Aztec son . . . a philanthropist, a humanitarian, a noble man, and my friend. He sits with the gods . . . Tenoch. We are in his land . . . Tenochtitlan . . . Tenoch and Mexico are one." Simmons' words were startlingly clear and crisply articulated. A thunderous applause erupted from everyone in the room including Alberto and the workers. Tenoch nodded once, holding his head bent forward accepting the applause.

The fingers of Trent's large square hands remained coiled tightly around the brass railing. His fingers blanched white with pressure as the roar of applause rolled up the stairwell. His jaw tightened and the muscles at the corners of his eyes twitched. His eyes narrowed as he glared at the back of Tenoch's head.

"That bastard," Trent said and turned to lean against the balcony wall, his back resting against the twelve-foot stone disc replica of the Aztec sun god stone. He shook his head as if trying to control the furies within himself. After a moment he twisted the knob of the door to the guest suite, knocking as he entered the room.

Cassy leaned back in the bed, her shoulders against the headboard. The telephone cradled her ear. The black chemise night dress exposed her neck and upper chest. A lace ruffle fell low across her breasts.

"Señora, please excuse Dr. Hendricks and me," Cassy said. The maid nodded and disappeared through the suite door.

"I'm glad you're better. You looked like you might not make it when I carried you up here," Trent said.

"I wondered how I got up here. . . in a nightgown."

"The maid undressed you," Trent said, smiling easily. "You still have your virtue."

Cassy laughed quietly and folded her knees beneath her, drawing the satin sheet across them like a drum head. She reached her purse on the nightstand and fished a cigarette from the open package in the purse. After lighting the cigarette, she filled her lungs with a full breath of smoke.

"I'm pleased you've recovered enough to want to kill yourself with cigarettes." Trent said with stern sarcasm.

"Cigarettes are the least of my concerns," Cassy said, taking another deep breath of smoke. "I've too many immediate problems." She leaned across to the bedside table to fill a glass with the cold tea from the insulated pitcher the maid left. "You should try Tenoch's tea. It's wonderful. Take a sip."

"No, thanks," Trent said and then added, "I want to be the first to congratulate you on accepting the Mexico City job."

Her expression sobered with eyebrows raised inquisitively. "I've not decided yet," Cassy said and swallowed several gulps of tea.

"That's not what Tenoch told the group at the dinner table. Your good friend just announced to the beautiful people of Mexico City that you've accepted the position. He even read your acceptance letter."

"That's absurd," Cassy said. "I didn't write any acceptance letter."

"Are you sure it's absurd, Cassy?" Trent asked quietly. "Tenoch told the dinner party that you and Alex will be living here in Mexico City by June thirtieth."

"What in the hell is with that man?" Cassy asked, sucking deeply on the cigarette.

"I was about to ask you the same question. The way you and he were glued together this evening made me wonder whether something might be going on between you two."

"He is an attractive, gracious, successful man, but I have not accepted his offer."

"Walter Simmons was right then with his opinion," Trent persisted.

"What did that drunken fool say about me now?"

"Simmons thinks that Tenoch has only one reason to bring you to Mexico City, and it has nothing to do with organ transplants or heart surgery."

"I don't give a damn what Walter Simmons thinks," Cassy said.

"Why are you here in Mexico City? In Tenoch's apartment? In his bed?"

"Go ahead and say it. You think I slept with Tenoch last night."

Trent looked at her and said nothing for several moments. Then softly he said. "It's your choice, Cass. Be careful."

"Well thanks for your faith in my moral character. Why don't you just leave. We don't have anything more to say to each other. Leave." Cassy turned her head away and blotted the moisture out of her eyes.

"Perhaps that's the best way," he said. He rose slowly from the edge of the bed. A scowl tightened his mouth. He turned back to her before opening the door to the balcony. "Remember the name I told you this evening."

"What?"

"Remember Ana Ruiz."

"Just the name. Is that all I get? Is this a riddle?" Cassy said sarcastically.

"Just remember Ana Ruiz. You may need to know the name," he said. Then he was gone.

TWENTY-FIVE

"ANA RUIZ," Cassy said to the empty bedroom as soon as she heard the door latch click behind Trent. "Who the hell is she?" Trent has never played riddles with me before, she told herself. What's he telling me? Why doesn't he come right out with it?

She lay for a long time in the dim bedroom, unable to put down her growing anxiety. The room closed in around her. Sleep would not come. She thrashed about between the satin sheets. Her black silk chemise slipped over her perspiring body as if her skin were oiled.

Finally, she pulled herself up in the bed and from the gold pitcher on the bedside table she filled a crystal glass full with ice and tea. She then lit a cigarette, leaned against the heavy carved wood headboard, drinking half the glass of tea at once. Still the claustrophobic feeling would not leave. Fiddling with the remote control keypad next to the bedside telephone, she stabbed at the control buttons until the window drapery parted like a stage curtain revealing the hazy sky glowing with radiant light from the city below. Moving tendrils of traffic coiled like fluorescent vines beneath the haze lying low over the city.

In the semidarkness Cassy was nearly invisible as she padded in her bare feet and short black chemise across the room and stood in the angle of the glass walls. The sky wrapped around her and floated her from the room into the dark hazy horizon. The minutes stretched into an hour as she stood in the same spot, sipping the cold tea. Her queasiness subsided, replaced by a jittery anxiety.

Turning back from the window, she hesitated at the bedside before picking up the tan and yellow capsule that Dr. Gonzalez had left. She knew that sleep might never come this night. Since Saturday night she had slept poorly, waking several times each night, her mind filled with bizarre, uncoordinated, multicolor dream patterns like a changing mosaic of lights and colors. Cassy quickly slipped it onto her tongue and with the remainder of the iced tea washed it down. She just wanted a good night's sleep to erase her anxieties for a few hours.

She carefully made her way around the bed in the dim room lighted only by the soft filtered light radiating upward from the city. The faint gleam of the moon's sliver was barely visible in the haze. She hit the button, closing the drapes and plunging the room back into absolute blackness. As she settled between the sheets, a heavy weariness quickly overtook her. Despite the sleepiness produced by the sedative, Cassy lay with her eyes open, her ears straining at the almost imperceptible rumbling of the penthouse.

Eventually the total darkness of the room overwhelmed her with an ill defined apprehension. She rolled over in the bed groping for the drapery control. The draperies swept apart once again. The city opened before her. The room was painted into a soft crepuscular film by the lights of the city sixty stories below reflected back down from a hazy cloud deck.

Her mouth was as dry as it was on the Avenue of the Dead that afternoon. Pulling herself up in bed, Cassy took the gold pitcher of tea in both hands and held it to her lips, drinking slowly and steadily until the ice cubes clattered hollowly in the bottom of the pitcher. Cassy kicked away the top sheet and spread her arms and legs wide on the king-size bed, willing sleep to overtake her. Her body slid back and forth on the slick surface of the sheets until her arms and legs wearied of the movement. Her breathing became slow and regular as sleep mercifully overtook her conscious uneasiness.

Mind pictures flashed in front of her like a jumbled dream sequence of holograms. Visual scraps gyrated through her head—the angular jaw line of Tenoch—his thin lips moving soundlessly—the rotund naked body of Jeorg Marquez on the ER gurney—Trent Hendricks' large hands gracefully tying a surgeon's knot—Alex pitching a baseball across their glistening blue pool—Charlie retrieving the baseball in his powerful jaws— Alex sleeping peacefully in his bunk bed—Kevin Knowland's intense blue eyes appraising her across a plate of shrimp and stir fried vegetables—Gracie's turbaned head turning to show her terror-filled eyes.

Overlying the staccato dream images, Cassy's mind became aware of Gracie's voice singing the words *Amazing Grace, How sweet the sound*. Cassy strained to distinguish the words—*Amazing Grace*. An organ dirge boomed on each of the syllables. But what were the words again? Gracie's voice had changed the words of the old hymn. Now Cassy heard *Ana Ruiz. How sweet the name.* Cassy listened again to her dream sounds; *Ana Ruiz*. . . . She was sure that was the name Gracie had sung to the soaring syllables of the spiritual—*Amazing Grace, Ana Ruiz.* Her voice continued with the melody and words of the song but now clearly substituting the syllables of *Ana Ruiz* for the syllables of *Amazing Grace.*

She jolted upright in the bed, her eyes wide, her hair damp, and the gown clammy against her skin like wet canvas. The satin sheet was imprinted with her sweaty silhouette. "Who in the hell is Ana Ruiz?" Cassy asked the empty room. A chill rattled her body and puckered her skin.

"Good god," Cassy said, sighing deeply and rubbing perspiration from her face with the edge of the sheet. In the dim room she gulped the dregs of icy water and tea from the gold pitcher. She reached into the gold pitcher and pulled out an ice cube, sucking its coldness into her mouth. A moment later she rubbed the ice over her face trying to cool off the blazing heat in her cheeks.

Cassy walked about the dim room, hoping to quiet her pounding pulse and to cool her flaming skin. The black short chemise gown clung to her like spandex. The wet silk chilled her skin even more. She pulled the gown over her head, tossing it on the bedside table. Then Cassy slipped back onto a dry area of the king-size bed and pulled the satin sheet over her shivering body.

The drifting dreams returned as she sank back to a disturbed sleep. The flashing holograms were as real as if she were awake—Alex lay anesthetized on an operating table—a cold flaccid donor heart rested in Cassy's latex-gloved hands—Tenoch's rigid cruciform body stood motionless on the top of the Pyramid of the Sun—Alex's naked body reappeared lying on the operating table.

Again Cassy heard a woman's voice singing the old hymn, *Amazing Grace.* Gracie's voice built to a crescendo. Alex's holographic image blurred into whiteness when Gracie's voice reached for each of the syllables of the words . . . *Amazing Grace.* Only then did Cassy realize that the words, as before, were not *Amazing Grace*, but were now clearly sung as *Ana Ruiz.* Over and over in her mind she heard *Ana Ruiz, Ana Ruiz, Ana Ruiz,* as if a recording had stuck on the name, playing it continually.

Stop! Cassy screamed but no sound came from her mouth. She willed the sounds in her head to cease but Gracie's voice continued singing the name *Ana Ruiz* to the chords of *Amazing Grace.*

The blurred whiteness faded into Alex lying naked and anesthetized on the operating table. Cassy could see herself walking toward her son as a surgeon approaches an operating table.

When she reached the table, green surgical drapes instantaneously

surrounded Alex's body except for an opening in the drapes exposing her
son's chest. *Alex!* she screamed in her mind, but all was quiet except for
the sound of Gracie's voice flowing with the organ dirge *Ana Ruiz*. She
grabbed the sides of the operating table. When she looked at the surgical
field outlined by the surgical drapes, a gaping midline incision suddenly
appeared in her son's chest. Blood oozed from the cut edges, soiling the
sheets a dark brown.

No! No! Cassy yelled inside her mind and raised her hands toward the
incision. Her arms moved as if under water. Slowly and with tremendous
effort her fingers touched the edge of the bleeding incision. Her eyes
searched the depth of the gaping incision in her son's breastbone. The incision became a black hole. Cassy pushed her face close to Alex's chest
until her nose nearly touched her child's breast. Then she screamed. Her
mouth froze in horror. Alex's heart was gone—torn from his chest—the
remaining ragged stubs of the arteries and veins dripped blood into the
dark void where his heart had beat.

Cassy bolted upright in bed. "God!" she screamed into the empty darkened bedroom. The sound ripped the stillness of the room. Then there
was nothing. Sweat bathed her face. Her heart beat pounded her temples
with pulsating pain.

"My god," Cassy cried, rubbing her hands against her face. "It was so
real." She stood up and walked across the room, standing in her sweat-
soaked bikini panties before the panoramic window. Grabbing a cigarette
from the bedside table, she returned to the window and smoked it quickly.
With each deep drag, the embers of the cigarette glowed a red dot reflection on the window and briefly illuminated her facial image on the glass.
Finally the heat of the cigarette touched her finger, and she stubbed it
into the tray on the bedside table.

"I've got to cool off. I'm burning up," Cassy said aloud and turned
from the window. Her appearance reflected in the lighted dressing room
mirror startled her. Her dark hair lay wet and black in a heap on the side
of her head. Bags of fatigue hung under her eyes. "My god, you look awful," Cassy told her mirror's image.

Stepping out of her panties and into the shower, she let the cold water
run down her neck and back. She turned her body slowly in the coolness
of the shower until she felt the heat of her body dissipate. Her racing
pulse slowed to a trot. The pounding in her temples softened to a gentle
thud with each pulse.

Cassy groped beyond the fogged glass door for the giant turkish towel
on the brass wall rack. After toweling dry and brushing her wet hair in
place, she stepped out of the shower and tucked the towel around her
torso. At that moment she noticed a gold pitcher and a clean crystal gob-

let resting on the marble counter top. She couldn't remember whether the pitcher and glass were there when she stepped into the shower. Had to be there, I just didn't see it, she assured herself.

She poured a full glass of tea, allowing several ice cubes from the pitcher to drop into the wide crystal glass. The tea refreshed her mouth, instantly cleansing the staleness away. The pleasurable rush to her face and head brought a smile to her lips. She carried the glass and pitcher into the bedroom where she extracted a Marlboro from her clutch purse. The flare of her lighter left a momentary red glare in her vision. She pulled deeply on the cigarette and drank the rest of the glass of tea while she sat on the edge of the bed in the dark room.

After stubbing out the cigarette, Cassy stood up allowing the turkish towel to drop away. The satin sheets caressed her as she moved her nude body between them. She recognized her own sensual arousal as she drifted languidly between wakefulness and sleep. In her mind the terrifying staccato holographic dreams were replaced by a pleasant drifting sensation as if she were floating naked on a raft on a warm summer's evening. She rode the undulating soft cushion, her body rising with sexual urgency. The full achy feeling in her lower abdomen built uncomfortably, begging her for release. The satin sheet brushed her breasts and teased her nipples upright.

Her eyes popped open in the dim shadows of the room. What was the sound? her waking mind asked. Blending into the darkness of the city beyond the apex of the glass wall, Tenoch's image stood, tall and muscled, in a black silk shirt and matching pants. Was he real or was he yet another one of her holographic nightmares come to visit? she asked herself.

"Hello," she called, not at all frightened by the specter. The satin sheet fell away to her waist when she propped herself on her elbows. Cassy pulled the sheet back up around her neck. Tenoch's image was gone when she looked back to the glass corner of the room.

"My god, I'm hallucinating," Cassy said into the darkness. Sliding out from under the sheets, she walked naked around to the foot of the bed, peering into the angled glass corner of the room. Cassy paced the length of the window to assure herself that Tenoch was not there. Disappointed, she returned to the bedside and poured another full glass of tea from the pitcher.

Back in bed, she leaned against the headboard and pulled the satin sheet up around her. With both hands around the frosty crystal glass, she sipped at the tea, relishing its icy tingling sweetness on the tip of her tongue. A quivering raced throughout her. She fidgeted her legs back and forth between the slippery sheets. She hugged the satin pillow against her body and bit her lip against a sexual urgency that she could not control. Her skin seemed electric. The fine hairs on her forearm stood up. The fullness in her lower abdomen intensified into a dull persistent hurting. She pulled the pillow tighter, pressing it against her lower abdomen. A vague sense of moistness permeated her thighs and groin as her legs continued their aimless restless movements. Her sexual urge was overpowering.

Her mind projected Tenoch's face back onto the dark glass wall. She walked again to the murky window to search for Tenoch but only saw the distant horizon of Mexico City merging into the night sky. Glimmering lights floated in the haze over the city as far as she could see. The city below slept.

She poured the remainder of the melted ice and tea into the crystal glass. The room grew smaller, and the stifling hot stillness closed in on her. "I've got to get out of here . . . some fresh air," she said to the empty dim room.

In the dressing room she found her walking shorts and blouse that she had worn in the afternoon, both hanging in the closet, freshly washed and neatly pressed. In a growing anxiety to escape the room, she began breathing rapidly and jerked the khaki shorts and blue denim blouse on.

The ornate brass knob of the double door of the guest suite clicked softly under Cassy's hand. She opened the door just wide enough to slip through onto the balcony above the grand salon. The cavernous room spread silent and dark before her as if the lights in an empty church were extinguished. The tan stone Aztec calendar replica mounted on the balcony wall behind her radiated a muted light from its carved surface. Shadows from the reflected light of the giant stone disc cloaked the grand salon as Cassy crept quietly down the staircase.

The marble stairs were silent under her bare feet. At the last step she held the brass post and swung onto the dark hardwood floor. The room was so quiet that Cassy could hear the rushing noise of blood flowing into her head. Looking behind her, she saw the entry to Tenoch's office. The wide open door pulled her, and she eased herself into the empty office. Tenoch's presence filled the silent room as surely as if he sat in the high-backed, throne-like leather chair in front of the windows forming the three sides of the room.

A frieze of red lighted numbers along the back wall behind his desk displayed the time at major cities around the world. The rosy glow of the digital time-clock display thrust the room into a spectral crimson light. The Mexico City digital time displayed 2:47. Cassy wandered aimlessly, touching the table tops, the furniture edges, the chair backs, and traced her fingers along the length of Tenoch's carved stone desk. When she rounded the edge of the gigantic desk top, she stepped onto the raised marble platform holding the desk and the throne-like chair.

Even though the room was cool, the same suffocation that awakened her in the guest suite flushed her face and quickened her breathing. Her fingertips tingled with the pricks of thousands of needles. Slowly she sank into Tenoch's chair. His pleasurable smell enveloped her as if he had embraced her. For a moment she luxuriated in the chair, her mind filling with the image of Tenoch's body under her as if she were sitting in his lap. The longer she sat in the chair, the smaller the room became. The three glass walls were silently collapsing on her.

She pushed herself off the chair, her rapid shallow breathing commanding her to find fresh night air. She slowly backed out of the office and tested the door to the outside patio where she and Tenoch had stood the night before. The door latch opened with a noise that resounded like a hammer pounding an anvil in the grand salon.

The concrete walkway was rough under her bare feet. The night air filled her lungs with a searing inhalation. Immediately the suffocating feeling cleared. A metallic taste dulled her tongue until she no longer tasted the acrid air.

At the convergence of the balconies at the end of the building beyond the panoramic window of Tenoch's office, a T-shaped rooftop swimming pool shimmered soft aquamarine light above the water as if a vaporous hood hung over the pool. The low lying haze and clouds descended on the city below in a fog, diffusing the city's lights upward, and gave Cassy the feeling that she was alone in the center of a cloud. The fluffing wind freshened her face when she moved around the lighted pool. Beyond the end of the balcony, the darkness of Chapultepec Park below was a black lake in the middle of the city.

The pool water drew her near like an insect to brightness. She eased herself to the concrete lip of the pool's edge, dangling her feet in the cool water and letting the water exhilarate her feet and calves. Her toenails sparkled like underwater rubies. The night closed around her. The shimmering light from the pool surface painted her face softly in a bluish hue. Cassy lit a cigarette and sat for a long time, smoking several cigarettes, one after the other, as her feet and legs danced in the water.

Her thoughts relentlessly returned to the sensuality Tenoch had rekindled in her. She felt the aching fullness grab at her lower abdomen again. Her nipples tented the soft fabric of the blouse. Her pulse pounded in her throat as the fantasy of Tenoch's lovemaking expanded in her mind.

Cassy reached into the water and splashed her face, trying to douse her fantasy. The water was cool with the freshness of a mountain stream, unlike the chlorinated water in her home pool. "I've got to get in the water and cool off, or I'm going to explode out of my skin." Swimming nude in a rooftop pool in the middle of the night in Mexico City seemed so natural and appropriate that her rational mind did not object at all. A nude swim seemed perfectly befitting her weekend visit to Mexico City.

Looking around the rooftop to be certain that no one was there, Cassy swung her legs out of the pool. She wiggled out of the walking shorts and pulled the blouse over her head. Naked she slipped into the cool water, feeling it enclose coolly around her feverish body. In a slow breast stroke, she pulled her body through the length of the pool, smoothly reversing into a back stroke at the end of the pool. The glittering stars studded the black sky. Above the horizon the moon's sliver danced with the cloud puffs. The coolness of the water calmed her racing mind and slowed her pounding pulse. But her sexual urgency did not subside completely.

Swimming her slow graceful strokes, her mouth curved up into a smile. A quiet contentment settled in her for the first time since last Saturday night. Her equanimity slowly returned as she floated contentedly on her back in the cool water.

While her hands sculled the water, Cassy became aware of another sentient presence nearby. She either heard or saw movement on the rooftop or picked up a subliminal sense. Perhaps a more primitive biologic warning system reacted in her. Cassy knew for certain that another person was on the rooftop and that she was being watched. It was not fear but a curiosity that filled her mind. She floated in the center of the pool, treading water and listening, absolutely certain that a human presence had intruded into her aerie. For quite a long time she floated, fanning the water, listening but hearing nothing. She waited. The sensation of floating in the water under the black sky with her arms outstretched, her back arched to maintain her flotation, created an out-of-body experience. She hovered over the city like a bird circling its rooftop nest.

Resuming her breaststroke, she was still certain that someone was watching her. As she stroked in the direction of Tenoch's office, she glimpsed inside the shadow of the glass wall a faint outline of a man, his form immobile and uncertain. Cassy swam the length of the pool and looked up at the glass windows facing her. The shadowy image was no longer visible.

When she reached the other end of the pool and tucked her head to begin her returning breaststroke, she saw Tenoch standing at the edge of the pool. A silk robe covered his bare shoulders and silk pajama bottoms covered his legs. Cassy glided slowly through the water, her tanned naked body silhouetted against the alabaster plaster of the pool's bottom. Her mind drifted as she swam toward Tenoch, not distinguishing dream from

reality, wondering whether Tenoch's image was yet another of her holographic hallucinations.

The rush of water about her body stilled when she stopped her stroke
at the edge of the pool and clung to the concrete lip of the pool to stare
up at Tenoch's image, standing quiet and unmoving, in the shadows. Her
eyes searched his face, half hidden in the dimness, trying to lock onto his
eyes. There were no eyes in the face of the man-size figure. Black holes
haloed in white appeared where his eyes should have been.

Tenoch's resonant baritone voice broke through her trance. "Couldn't
sleep?" His voice was easy and casual as if a nude night swim by his house
guest was a customary night ritual.

"I was hot and kept waking up," Cassy said, drawing herself through
the water toward him, magnetically attracted by his presence. When she
reached the edge of the pool in front of him, she pulled her arms over the
coping of the pool's edge, letting her long slender body float behind her.

"I brought you some more tea," he said. He kneeled beside her and
placed a large gold goblet filled with crushed ice and tea on the lip of
the pool. She pulled herself to a standing position in the water, her feet
barely touching the bottom of the pool, and drank quickly from the tea,
feeling its pleasant rush course throughout her body. A euphoria swept
over her. His robe dropped away from his muscular hairless chest.

The pool light played upon his face. Cassy could see his lips moving,
but she heard nothing. She drank from the gold goblet, trying to arrest
the arousal she felt so quickly in Tenoch's presence. Her legs floated off
the bottom of the pool until her body stretched out in the water held up
by her natural buoyancy. She slowly kicked her legs outward to relieve
the full feeling mounting in her groin.

"Why don't you join me?" she asked.

Tenoch stepped out of his pajamas. Cassy was riveted by his powerful
physique. Her mind spun. Her vision blurred. She blinked and looked up
again. Tenoch was not there. She slapped her face against the water's surface. "I'm hallucinating," she said aloud. Then she saw the gold goblet
and knew that her mind had not betrayed her. She brought the chilled
tumbler to her lips and drank until the goblet was empty. The tart dregs
of tea leaves puckered her lips.

The underwater pressure moved against her leg. She turned from the
edge of the pool, looking for the source of movement in the water.
Tenoch's long torso stretched into a slow easy crawl stroke. His naked
body barely broke the surface of the water as his powerful arms and legs
sliced through the surface.

Cassy breaststroked herself into the long length of the T-shaped pool,
slowly pulling along in the lap lane next to Tenoch. Her paced strokes

did not match the piston-like overhand crawl stroke that propelled him. Each swam the pool in a silent pas de deux. On the fourth or fifth lap they passed each other in the center of the pool, swimming in opposite directions. Her foot brushed his hard muscled thigh. Her entire leg felt as if a high tension wire had dragged across her foot. Immediately her swimming stokes ceased. Cassy floated, like a stunned swimmer, toward the edge of the pool until her head rested against the concrete coping. Her body lay spread in the water tethered to the pool's edge by the back of her head. Her wet hair plastered her head. Tenoch slowed his crawl stroke and pushed through the water toward Cassy in a slow motion breaststroke, his wet black hair matted above his half-submerged face.

Their eyes locked together just above the shimmering bluish green surface of the pool. His hand caught hers and pulled her upright against the hard flatness of his body. The buoyancy of her legs floated them upward until they encircled his waist. Her ankles locked together behind his back, and the two floated together without a word. Her mind filled with a mist of pleasure.

His hands moved firmly down her bare back holding her against him. His urgency pressed against her. Her body trembled in its arousal. His hands laced together in the small of her back. His forward movement in the water nudged her against the vertical wall of the pool bringing her body full against the muscular tautness of his chest and abdomen, pressed between the side of the pool and his firm body.

Eventually Tenoch slipped her legs from his waist. The two stood in water that rose to Cassy's chin. He pulled her gently by the hand toward the concrete steps at the shallow end of the pool where the pool merged into the crossbar of the T-configured pool. At the top of the pool steps, he wrapped an oversized terry towel emblazoned with a golden T around his waist and hips.

Holding his outstretched hand, Cassy emerged from the water and stepped into another terry towel he held for her. She slowly turned until it wrapped about her, covering her breasts and hanging to her thighs. "Come," he said, a command not a request. Cassy followed Tenoch as he walked into the penthouse and up the marble staircase. The Aztec stone calendar glowed at the top of the stairs as if it were radiating light rather than reflecting the spotlights focused on it.

Tenoch guided her into his bedroom suite, a larger version of the guest suite with a more expansive panorama through its glass walls. Candles flickered at the bedside, the only light in the room except for the ambient light from the sky above and the faint reflected light from the city below. A subtle odor of incense floated through the room.

At the bedside Tenoch lifted a frosty gold pitcher and filled two crystal glasses with a liquid that appeared dark as ink in the dim room. Then he dropped ice cubes from a crystal bowl into each glass.

"To us," he said, touching her glass and sipping gently at the surface of the liquid. Cassy looked into his shadowy face, seeking his eyes as she brought the crystal glass to her mouth. The glass was half empty before she pulled it away. The tingling thrill of the icy tea exploded in her mouth, a more powerful rush than she ever remembered. Immediately her heart jolted. Her pulse quickened. Her body felt heavy, warm, and wet beyond the moisture of the pool.

Blood surged and flushed her entire body. His closeness overpowered her. The unfulfilled sensuality that had been building in her for years burst forth. Still seeking his eyes, she stepped toward him in the murky shadows. His hand found the tucked edge of the terry towel and spun her slowly out of its wrapping until she stood naked before him. Without looking away, she flicked the towel from around his waist, letting it fall to the floor. He pulled her gently to him. She was exquisitely aware of each point where his body pressed hers.

He guided her in the flickering darkness to the bed and gently lowered her onto it. His lips found hers. His soft hands explored her body. Instinctively her body arched upward with his touch as she yielded to the tracings of his fingers.

Her lips parted, and he explored her mouth with his tongue. His passion quickly reached its peak and hung there undiminished while his body expertly sustained her again and again until she lay drained, consumed by an afterfeeling of desire and ultimate satisfaction. Sleep came suddenly and completely for Cassy.

TWENTY-SIX

T HE POUNDING in her forehead pulled Cassy from a dreamless
sleep. As she surfaced from the depths of her unconsciousness,
the throbbing made her afraid to open her eyes, certain that any
light would burst her brain. She squinted into the dusky room and carefully raised her lids. The morning sun peeked at the edges of the brocaded drapes blocking the windows. A muskiness filled the bedroom. She
swept her hands across the slick sheets, trying to orient herself but unable
to recognize the touch of the fabric. The bed beside her was empty. She
pulled the rumpled sheets over her naked body. Opening her eyes completely, she tried to inspect the dimly lighted room. The canopy over the
bed boxed her in and closed around her.

My god! What happened to me last night? she asked herself. Then the
mental images coalesced in her mind. She felt Tenoch's vivid imprint
on her. Her lips tingled, her throat parched, and her skin prickled. Her
pounding head fuzzed her thinking.

An impersonal decorator's touch imprinted the room. She might just as
well have been in a luxury hotel suite. No pictures, no mementos or personal items were displayed anywhere in the room. She slipped out of the
canopied bed pulling the sheet about her like a sarong and walked slowly
toward the bathroom, holding onto the edge of the bed for support.

As she approached the dressing area, Tenoch appeared in the doorway,
wearing only his pajama bottoms. Diffuse light from the open dressing
room door fell around him. In the half light of the room Tenoch slipped
his hands under her arms and locked her to him. Cassy tried to wiggle
away from him. "I must go now," she said stiffly.

"You look like you are not well, carina mía," Tenoch said.

"Please don't call me that. I'm not your lover," Cassy said. "I must go home." His embrace tightened on her body, holding her immobile like a squirming infant.

His eyes blackened into an opaque, impenetrable stare. "You will stay here until I release you," he said in a voice as hard as stone.

"No. I am leaving this morning," Cassy said, trying to force a casualness to her voice. She had seen that same wild-eyed, insensate expression in psychotic ER patients.

"Take a steam shower. You will feel much better," Tenoch said. "I will arrange our breakfast."

"What time is it?" Cassy asked, trying to reorient herself.

"Nine o'clock. The night passed quickly," he said, a wry smile showing his even white teeth.

Breathing the moist warm steam in the shower, Cassy's mind began to clear. The anxiety of the past week washed over her like the sudsy water, foamed now by the apprehension of Tenoch's commanding attitude. She replayed the night, over and over, searching for an explanation, only understanding that the night had aroused a possessiveness in Tenoch. After scrubbing herself vigorously and rinsing in the warm spray of the twelve jets arranged around her, she found a white terry robe and slipped into its lush soft fabric. She rubbed her fingers through her damp hair, stroking its dark wave to one side.

She stepped out of the bathroom certain that Tenoch must be waiting for her. Morning light filled the bedroom from the panoramic window wall looking beyond the city. Tenoch sat at a breakfast table rolled into the angled corner of the room formed by the glass walls. His silk robe fell open, exposing his chest. His silk pajama bottoms hung loosely on his flat abdomen.

"Carina mía, please join me," he said, appraising Cassy as she walked to the chair opposite him. Cassy ignored the Spanish endearment phrase, afraid to confront him again, and unconsciously pulled the terry robe around her neck.

"I've brewed some of my special tea mixture for you, hot and stronger than last night," Tenoch said, pouring from a long-spouted gold pot into bone china cups. "It has a special power, or so you might have noticed last night."

Cassy glanced at him across the rim of the steaming cup of dark hot tea and sipped several times, her tongue savoring the delicate tart flavor, enhanced by the heat. She felt the same euphoric rush, beginning in the center of her body and racing outward. Suddenly her headache was gone.

"What have you put in this tea?" she said, the warm glow suffusing her.

An ecstasy enveloped her. The sexual urgency of the night flooded back into her.

"It's the market woman's special blend of teas and herbs. It provides an interesting response, especially when hot," Tenoch said, sipping the steaming dark tea from his china cup.

Her sexuality swept over her. Overpowering sexual urges hammered at her: the facial flush, the pounding of her pulse, the warmth of her body. In that moment she understood the drug effect that the tea was having on her. The intensity of her desire for him was even stronger than the night before. The overwhelming sexual urge seized her reflexes just as it had during the night. She was powerless as Tenoch moved around the breakfast table to her. She stood to meet him, letting the terry robe drape open over her naked body.

He pulled her roughly to him, covering her lips with an insistent violent intensity. She returned his roughness with frightening savageness. The gentle urgency of their lovemaking of the night before was gone. They grappled at each other brutally, falling into the bed. An impatient culmination exploded their ferocious coupling. Tenoch fell away to Cassy's side. She lay consumed.

Her pulse raced, her head throbbed, her palms moistened, and her skin sheened with perspiration. Her breathing remained quick. Despite the savage climactic embrace, a sexual urgency still roiled in her. Cassy fought the gray mist that drifted in front of her eyes. Her heart pounded for a long time as she lay quietly, trying to calm the raging emotions of fear, anger, and defeat.

"You are good for me, carina mía." Tenoch opened his eyes and traced his fingers along her neck and lips. The touch of his fingers burned her skin. She rolled her head away, wanting to take him again despite the brutal sexuality moments before.

"It's impossible to resist me," Tenoch said. He rolled up on his elbow to look at her with his dark, baleful eyes. "I knew that our spirits found each other when I first saw you the night of Jeorg Marquez's death." His fingers returned to her neck, working their way to her breasts.

"I don't know what you're talking about," Cassy said coldly. "You've drugged me with something in that tea."

"You are mine, Cassy," Tenoch said. "You cannot resist me."

"This is all a terrible mistake," Cassy said. "I must leave for Dallas." She grabbed the robe from the floor.

Her euphoria, before and during the summit of her brief moment in Tenoch's bed, had given way to an anxious, depressed foreboding. The queasy feeling accelerated into nausea as she ran into the bathroom of the guest suite, retching bile and vomitus into the toilet. She had no idea how long she sat on the cold tile floor of the bathroom holding onto the edge of the commode, retching hot acid stomach contents into the toilet water. Apprehension devoured her.

Again in the shower, Cassy scrubbed herself violently with a soapy hand towel until her tan skin reddened. Quickly dressing in the same tailored tapestried fabric jacket and purple skirt she left Dallas in, she noticed that the dozen designer dresses including the black dress she wore Saturday evening hung in precise alignment in the dressing room closet, mocking her. Tears ran from her eyes.

Cassy found her cigarettes and tore the end completely off an unopened Marlboro package. Her hands trembled as she lit the cigarette. Hesitating for a moment with her hand on the telephone, she sat on the edge of the bed and lifted the receiver. The male telephone operator immediately answered. "This is Dr. Baldwin. Connect me to my home, please." The phone rang twice before Trent Hendricks answered.

"Oh God, thank you. Trent. I'm so glad you're there."

"I just came by to pick up Alex. Remember, he and I are going to the Rangers' game today."

"Is Alex all right?"

"Yes, he's fine."

Her voice broke into uncontrollable sobbing. Minutes later, Cassy was still unable to speak.

"What's the matter with you? Where are you?"

"I'm in Tenoch's guest bedroom. Everything's wrong, Trent. I've been such a fool."

"You sound awful. Are you still sick?"

"No. No. I got over that . . . but there's a bigger problem," Cassy said, her voice quivering as she tried to hold herself from breaking down completely.

"Tell me what's wrong."

"I'm coming home this morning," Cassy said, the vibrato lingering in her voice. "Will you meet the American Airlines flight to DFW?"

"Why isn't Tenoch flying you back on his airplane?"

"Because I won't let him," Cassy said. "I'm getting completely away from him." Her control was battered, and her voice broke.

"What the hell has Tenoch done to you?" Trent asked. "What is it, for chrissake? Tell me!" Trent shouted.

"Something happened between us last night," Cassy said quietly. "I'm not sure why."

"What are you telling me?" Trent asked, now subdued and quiet.

"For god's sake, Trent, must I draw you a picture?"

"Oh . . . ," Trent said. His voice sounded like air rushing from a balloon.

"It was something he put in my tea. . . ."

"What are you talking about? He drugged you?" Trent asked. "That's crazy talk."

"I don't know, Trent," Cassy said. "It was bizarre. I've never felt anything like that in my entire life." The line went silent. Cassy paused, waiting for Trent to respond. When he didn't, Cassy continued. "Now Tenoch believes he owns me and controls me."

"I know that Tenoch is obsessed with you," Trent said. "He's been stalking you since that Saturday night in the ER. I should have taken you home with me last night."

"I was too sick to go anywhere last night," Cassy said.

"Sounds as if you made an awfully fast recovery."

"All right, please, I'm sorry. I shouldn't have let it happen," Cassy said. "I'm asking for your help."

"Stay in Tenoch's guest room. Don't leave. I'll be there in less than three hours to get you out of there."

"Don't be ridiculous," Cassy said. "I can take care of myself."

"I'm not so sure."

"I think I know how to handle him," Cassy said.

"Don't be so naive to think you can handle Tenoch. I've got to get you out of there immediately," Trent said, his voice rising. "I'm going to call Tenoch myself."

"No. You stay in Dallas with Alex. I'll be home later today."

"Cass, listen carefully," Trent said. "Don't provoke him."

"I don't intend to confront him," Cassy said. "I just want out of here."

"If he gives you any trouble, tell him that you know all about Ana Ruiz."

"What good is that name?" Cassy asked. "Who is she?"

"You only need to know the name," Trent said. "I can't tell you more than that."

"If he gives you any trouble, tell him that I will go to the police about Ana Ruiz."

"For god's sake, Trent, tell me more." Cassy nervously shook another cigarette out of the package and spilled all of them on the floor. She reached down and picked up one, lighting it while shouldering the phone receiver to her ear.

"No. Just the name . . . Ana Ruiz. That's enough to get you home if you need it."

"All right then," Cassy sighed. "Tell Alex I love him. I'll call you from the airport to let you know what American Airlines flight I'll be on."

Cassy replaced the receiver and sat on the edge of the bed until she finished the cigarette. The sick feeling in her stomach nearly doubled her over. She tried to settle her foaming anxiety until she felt that she could make it down the stairwell. After several minutes, Cassy picked up her two bags and backed through the double door, pushing the heavy oak door open behind her.

"Are you going somewhere?" Tenoch asked. Cassy jumped at the sound of his pleasant baritone voice. Turning around, Cassy saw Tenoch standing casually in the open door of his bedroom suite. His canopied king-size bed neatly made with a silk bed cover treatment smirked at Cassy when her eyes flitted past Tenoch and into his bedroom. "I was planning lunch . . . just you and me . . . carina mía." He smiled widely, his dark skin vibrant against the whiteness of his silk shirt and pants.

"I must return home," Cassy said, trying to quiet her trembling hand as she pulled the guest room door closed behind her. "I will take an American Airlines flight to Dallas."

"I am not ready for you to leave." The smile left his face. His eyes sharpened into a fearsome stare.

"I really must go," Cassy said, picking up her two travel bags and moving toward the staircase.

"Come," he said. The word rang in her mind, the same word and tone that he used last night to command her to follow him from the swimming pool to his bedroom. She knew that she had no choice. "We have much to discuss."

"Very well then," Cassy said, trying to smile.

An indulgent smile replaced the dark taut lines of Tenoch's face. "Come to my office," he said, taking her by the hand. Cassy left her bags on the balcony and walked with Tenoch down the wide stairwell like a couple making a grand entrance into the salon.

—

In his regal office Tenoch leaned back comfortably in his massive throne-like leather chair behind his enormous stone desk. Cassy sat in a black leather barrel chair in front of the elevated marble platform holding Tenoch's desk. She was now convinced that Tenoch had been in the shadows when she had prowled his office last night, touching his desk and sitting in his chair.

As she watched Tenoch peer into the distant sky she was certain that he had been listening and watching her all weekend. Only then did she realize how stupid it was to call Trent this morning. Surely Tenoch had heard every word and then waited for her to leave the guest suite to intercept her on the balcony.

Cassy sat quietly while Tenoch stared at the distant jagged horizon. The morning air had cleared enough so that the distant ring of mountains cradling the city was visible. Impassively, engaged in his own world and apparently oblivious to Cassy's presence in the low chair before him, Tenoch was immobile, appearing catatonic. The digital time-pieces, displaying the time around the world, flashed the minutes past.

She tried to piece together the elements of Tenoch's psychotic behavior as she watched his malevolent stare: his bizarre thought processes—his mercurial personality changes alternating between the gracious and abusive personas—the eccentric behavior attributed to his wealth and status—his inhibited emotional expression—his intermittent withdrawal from reality.

Tenoch reeled his gaze back into the office and refocused his dark eyes on Cassy. His gaze burned into Cassy's eyes. She tried to match his look but was unable and averted her eyes.

"Both of us are powerless to avoid our destiny," Tenoch said, the first words he had spoken since leaving the bedroom with her. "It is your destiny to join me in Mexico City."

"Señor Tenoch," Cassy said, deliberately formalizing her conversation. "You are a visionary, but I must decline your kind and gracious invitation. My personal life requires me to be in Dallas. My destiny is there."

"You cannot deny me."

"I must return to my home and my son."

"You must accept your destiny."

"Please, Tenoch, I must leave," Cassy said and stood up at her chair.

"Tell me what you require. It is yours. You cannot resist me. I will not be denied," Tenoch said agreeably.

"You are most gracious and generous," Cassy said. "But I must leave now." She walked quickly toward the office door while Tenoch remained comfortably drawn back in his chair behind his desk.

Alberto blocked the doorway. "Come back, carina mía," Tenoch's voice called pleasantly. The endearing Spanish phrase hit her like a leather strap, raising an angry welt inside her. Her self-imposed mask dropped away.

"I will leave whenever I wish," Cassy said, her voice quivering with fury. She tried to squeeze between Alberto and the door jamb. Alberto edged his body against the door facing, closing off her exit. Alberto's face remained impassive.

"Sit down," Tenoch said, his voice gentle but slow-paced. "You will leave only when I say, and only if I grant you permission to leave."

Cassy walked back to the chair and sat defiantly like a child in front of the teacher's desk. "What do you want from me?"

"Perhaps you would like some iced tea?" Tenoch asked, his voice once again relaxed and soft. His fingers steepled in front of him.

"I am sorry for you if that tea mixture is the only way you can attract a woman," Cassy said, spitting her words at him. "You'll never interest me any other way."

"Our spirits have been together before, and we will remain together," Tenoch said slowly.

"My destiny is not here, I assure you. I'm leaving now, and I'll try to forget this weekend ever happened."

"You cannot betray our past and future destinies," Tenoch said, staring above her head off into the sky again.

Cassy sat stunned. She stumbled for a response, for a direction. What next? She remembered Trent's message from last night and again this morning. Ana Ruiz? How could the mention of the name harm her? "I know about Ana Ruiz," she blurted without further thought.

"Of course you do. The heart of Ana Ruiz beats inside the chest of Heather Hendricks."

"What?" Cassy said. "What?"

"Ana Ruiz's heart sustains the life of Heather Hendricks."

"Ana Ruiz was Heather's heart donor?" she asked. "The thirteen-year-old Mexico City girl who was in the accident?"

"Yes, carina mía," Tenoch said, rearing back in his chair, steepling his fingers again and smiling broadly.

"Who was Ana Ruiz?" Cassy asked, realizing she must plunge ahead with what Trent said was her only way out. "Why is she? What is she?" Cassy couldn't articulate her jumbled thoughts.

"A child of the Mexico City ghettos. You saw hundreds of them yesterday in the lost city," Tenoch said. "The disappearance of a single starving child was unnoticed."

"My god," Cassy said. "What are you telling me?"

"I provided the heart for Heather Hendricks so that Ana Ruiz might live in another incarnation," Tenoch said, his pleasant expression unchanged.

"Provided? You mean you killed Ana Ruiz to provide a donor heart for Heather Hendricks!"

"Hardly, carina mía," Tenoch said. "Ana Ruiz was living a death in the ghettos of Mexico City. She will find a greater reward in her next incarnation."

"You murdered Ana Ruiz! Does Trent know that you obtained Heather's heart donor this way?" Cassy asked.

"Of course, carina mía. He harvested the heart from Ruiz's body," Tenoch said.

Stunned senseless, her mind would barely comprehend what Tenoch had just revealed.

"Trent wanted the best available heart donor for his daughter. Would you not want the same for your son?" Tenoch asked. Cassy sat unable to move.

"Was Trent aware that you abducted Ana Ruiz for the heart?" Cassy asked quietly.

"Certainly, carina mía," Tenoch said. "He even made a substantial contribution to my foundation. The generous five hundred thousand dollars that he donated will go to support my work in the organ procurement program."

Cassy could not speak. Even if she could have sifted words from her rushing mind, her throat would not make sounds. Tenoch rested his arms on the massive desk. His expressionless eyes were cast like black ingots above his thin lips that twisted in a synthetic smile.

Finally Cassy breached the silence that enlarged the distance between them. "Half million dollars . . . Trent bought and harvested Ana Ruiz's heart. . . ." Her guttural groan finished off her sentence. She was spent— unable to say more. Her muscles, body, and mind petrified into stone.

"What is the value of a child? Would you not gladly pay a half million dollars for the life of Alex . . . if it were necessary for Alex to live."

Cassy sat motionless, staggered by his revelation and her dawning comprehension of cold-blooded, premeditated murder. Finally, in a quiet, meek voice, she asked, "What do you want of me?"

"Many motivations drive men," he said, pausing and added as an afterthought, "And women." He smiled down at Cassy who sat hunched forward in the chair, unable to move, hardly able to understand what she had heard. "I have made my fortune identifying those needs and motives and exploiting them."

"I don't understand what you are talking about."

"Your friend, Trent Hendricks, has shown me an unexploited market for the world's most precious commodity. . . life. You see, carina mía, death is an awful reality in the United States. Most Americans will give their life's possessions to avoid death. They will pay any price for an organ that they need to live even one additional day. The recipient is not interested in where the organ comes from as long as that organ gives him life. It is a perfect untapped market for the world's most precious commodity. . . life."

"Your black market for organs will never work," Cassy said.

He held up his hand, ordering her to be quiet. "Please, Cassy. Black market is an offensive word. I have simply applied the principles of free enterprise to meet a desperate shortage of transplantable organs necessary to save lives." Tenoch paused, his facial expression softening. "For my broker services in these transactions, you must concede that I do deserve compensation."

"You'll never succeed. . . ."

"Again, carina mía, you are quite wrong. I have been in this organ brokering business for years, supplying kidneys, corneas, and livers from my network throughout Mexico and Latin America for transplantation at my private hospitals in this country as well as in my own private facilities in Europe. It is truly a global network."

Tenoch sipped at his sparkling water, waiting for Cassy to respond. Cassy was unable to move, crushed to the chair.

"It was not until Trent perfected his revolutionary research work with the Hiberna solution that I had the technical ability to suspend and to preserve the donor of a heart for the few necessary hours while the appropriate medical and transportation . . . and financial . . . arrangements could be made with the recipients and their families. I am now prepared to add a new product to my program of donor procurement and organ supply. Not only can I offer kidneys, corneas, livers . . . but now I can provide hearts for transplantation anywhere in the world. It is the fulfillment of my Aztec destiny. Ana Ruiz was the first heart," Tenoch said. "The second heart was the donor you so willingly procured for Trent Hendricks on Friday at the Instituto de Medico."

"Oh, my god," Cassy said, slumping in her chair.

"The donor was suspended with the Hiberna mixture, just like Marquez and Ana Ruiz."

"Oh, my god. What have you done?"

"My heart program is ready, but I need your hands and your surgical skills." Tenoch gestured with a slight movement of his index finger, summoning Alberto to Cassy's side with the hand-tooled briefcase. In the same way he had displayed the open case's contents in Raul Garcia's office, Alberto showed Cassy five hundred thousand dollars in neat packets of one hundred dollar bills.

"It is yours," Tenoch said with a nod of his head toward the open case. "And, oh yes, on Monday I will resolve your unpleasant difficulties with the Dallas authorities. Money solves problems."

Cassy shook her head from side to side, slowly and uncontrollably. The sight of the money Alberto held in front of her melted into a bloody red pulp causing her to close her eyes against the horrifying image. When she reopened her eyes, it was to the sound of Tenoch's voice. "The money is yours."

Looking up at Tenoch, Cassy felt the room begin to move slowly about her. Her vertigo worsened when she looked away from his face, only to encounter the hazy sky beyond the curving glass walls of the office.

"Don't you see the potential market here, Cassy? It's a capitalist's dream. Control the supply of organs, and I control the market. The twenty-five thousand people in the United States awaiting donor organs . . . I can offer them life . . . at an appropriate fee."

"You mean by taking twenty-five thousand Ana Ruiz's from the poorest barrios of Mexico City to be sacrificial donors, you can sell life to those who can afford to buy an organ for transplant? You're sick," Cassy said.

"Not at all my dear. I am a capitalist and an Aztec. Our Aztec ancestors gave their life's blood to Huitzilopochtli so we all might live. It is no different for me to provide hearts so that the chosen may live today."

"Hasn't it occurred to you that some of the twenty-five thousand men and women and children you plan to pluck from the poorest hovels of Mexico City just might catch someone's attention by their disappearance?"

Tenoch shook his head. "Don't be absurd. I'm not greedy. A few at a time won't be missed and surely not from the poor neighborhoods where I lived and where you saw the terrible poverty yesterday."

"And what makes you think I would participate in this venture?" Her contempt for Tenoch lined her face.

"It is your destiny." Tenoch said. "A synchronicity of our destinies. You have no choice. You cannot resist your Aztec heritage. You cannot deny your Aztec destiny. For the thousands of people in the United States and around the world awaiting donor hearts . . . I give life."

"I hope you can get some help. You need a psychiatrist," Cassy said. "There is no way I will ever be part of this evil." Cassy's voice trailed off.

Tenoch sat motionless. His black eyes bored into her. After a long time, Cassy said quietly, "I would like your permission to leave."

"You cannot leave me," Tenoch said and signaled with a finger to Alberto. "You cannot reject our shared destiny."

Her anger conquered her fear. "To hell with you," Cassy screamed. She pushed Alberto against the desk. The briefcase clattered open at his feet, spilling the packets of hundred dollar bills onto the hardwood floor. The surprise of Cassy's sudden movement gave her a three-step advantage over Alberto until he recovered his balance enough to run after her. But his pursuit was unnecessary. Tenoch caught Cassy's arm as she ran for the door around the corner of his massive desk. Alberto grabbed her other arm and twisted it behind her back. The excruciating pain of the near dislocation of her shoulder immobilized her body.

The only sign of Tenoch's anger was the flat focus of his black eyes, opaque and hard as obsidian. "Take her to the guest room and stay with her." His voice was low, slow-paced and hollow as if disconnected and spoken through a long tube. "Prepare the plane for Dallas."

Alberto hurried Cassy from the office. Tenoch returned to his throne-like desk, reared back in the chair, and contemplated the smog blanket that lay over the city below the top of his building.

TWENTY-SEVEN

A DULL ROARING sound vibrated Cassy as her mind slowly became aware that she was alive. Her consciousness rose upward through a mist of jagged memories. She strained to visualize how long she had been unconscious or asleep. Minutes? hours? days? The last thing she remembered was Tenoch entering the guest suite—then Alberto dragging her to the bed and prying her mouth open while Tenoch stood in front of her. Where am I now? she asked herself.

Slowly every sense alerted until she was keenly aware, a state of accelerated consciousness. She felt a soft cushioned surface beneath her but could not move. Her eyelids would not open. She could see only the wavy red blackness of the interior of her eyelids. A great weight pinned her arms and legs into the soft surface. For an instant she thought an earthquake must have buried her under a mound of rubble like her dead parents in Mexico City.

The gentle motion rubbed the soft surface against the naked skin of her legs and back. Was it cotton? The smell was fresh soap. Why couldn't she move? Her arms and legs were leaden. Her eyelids felt sealed with glue. No muscle would move. She ordered her fingers to move. Nothing happened. She tried to breathe deeply. Her chest moved imperceptibly, reflexly and completely outside her conscious control. The haze in her mind cleared like a camera lens coming into focus.

Her supine body abruptly tilted to her right. She suddenly realized that she must be in an airplane, slowly descending. She tried to open her eyes again. Just a sliver of light squeezed through the eyelids to her retina. Her hearing was ultrasensitive. Faint voices trickled over the roar of jet engines. Was it Tenoch's baritone voice? A door latch clicked back. A rush of air fanned her face. At that moment the fragrance of Tenoch's cologne reached her. The faint rustle of silk fabric told her that Tenoch was near.

"Good evening, carina mía. I'm taking you to Dallas . . . not to your home just yet," he said. She felt his warm breath touch her ear as he whispered, "Our destiny draws us together. You cannot resist."

The fissure between her eyelids was a mere sliver. Cassy struggled to raise her eyebrow, hoping to drag her upper eyelid open a fraction more.

"I wish you could see yourself, carina mía. You are beautiful even near death," Tenoch said. The sheet fell away. Tenoch's soft hands raked her naked abdomen. "Even the best physician would mistake you for dead."

Repeatedly Cassy commanded her fingers to move until the pulp of her fingertips moved slightly against the surface. Yes, it is a cotton sheet, she thought. She continued to rub the soft fabric. Her fingers gouged ever so lightly into the soft mattress beneath her as Tenoch's hands stroked her breasts.

"You are coming out from under the effects of the Hiberna mixture," she heard Tenoch say pleasantly. "You can feel a small movement in your eyelid, can you not?" Tenoch asked in the tone of a kindly old family doctor.

Cassy willed her eyelids apart. Her lid hovered partly open. The brightness of the room seared her brain. After several moments her eyes were able to focus on the ceiling of the bedroom of Tenoch's airplane.

"It's time for another taste of Trent Hendricks' mixture, carina mía. We will be landing in Dallas soon. It would not be good for you to open your eyes or move when you are supposed to be dead as we proceed through Customs."

Cassy wiggled her toes slightly and concentrated on forcing her heels into the mattress, trying to roll away from Tenoch's hands. But her legs were not part of her. Her mind had become disconnected from her body's nervous circuits.

"Alberto, bring me her medication," Tenoch said. With his index finger and thumb, Tenoch pulled apart her left eyelid. The flash of brilliant light momentarily blinded her again, as if opening her eyes into bright sun.

"The tetrodotoxin in the Hiberna will subdue you for another four to six hours. Not to fear, it is quite safe in the correct dose ranges. Trent Hendricks has nicely worked out the dose-response parameters of the tetrodotoxin in his research laboratory."

Alberto handed Tenoch a box of miniature pharmaceutical vials neatly packaged in an aluminum container the size of a cigar box. Tenoch rolled one of the vials in his fingers and then flipped the rubber seal cap off the end of the glass tube.

Tenoch inserted his right index finger between her lips and slowly rolled his finger around her limp tongue. After removing his saliva-wet finger, he shook the tan granular powder onto the pad of his finger. The granules clung to his moist fingertip like brown sugar. Then pulling her slack lip and cheek aside, he painted the powder on his finger, coating the soft pink mucous membranes between her teeth and cheek.

Immediately a prickling sensation stung Cassy's face. Soon she could no longer wiggle her toes and fingers. Tenoch parted her left eyelid. The brilliant light scalded her sensitive retina once again. His face was close above her. His warm breath touched her ear as he spoke. "I control you, now and forever."

The paralysis overwhelmed her. She struggled to move a fingertip, to open her eyes, to scream. Nothing happened. It was as if the nerve circuits controlling her body had been closed off from her brain. Her mind was locked into her immobile unresponsive body. She screamed, but paralyzed and mute her terror was soundless. *Please* she tried to say to Tenoch. *Anything.* She knew he was nearby. The rustle of his silk shirt bellowed in her ears. *Stop* she screamed without a voice. *I'll do whatever you want* her mind pleaded. *Don't do it. Don't.* The silent screams in her mind obliterated her thoughts. The void overtook her again.

—

Some time later the abrupt contact of the plane's wheels on the Dallas airport runway jolted Cassy into semiconsciousness. She felt her body slide forward in the bed as the pilot braked the aircraft into its landing roll. The plane taxied for several minutes as her mind slipped in and out of its bizarre disorientation, not knowing where she was, unable to move. The exquisite sensitivity of her paralyzed body's five senses shrieked at her mind until it became so overcharged that it shut down again. She was plunged again under undulating red waves.

Later the bedroom door clicked. Cassy felt two muscular arms slide under her bare back. The hard hands lifted her gently onto a narrow cushion. Cool metal bars snapped up and held her naked hips. A wool blanket scraped her bare breasts and covered her head.

"Don't tuck the blanket so tight around her face," Tenoch's muffled voice said. "She looks dead, but she still needs some air."

Hard rough fingers turned her face to the side under the wool cover. A whiff of hot humid air caught her nostrils. Heat permeated the wool blanket, scorching her unprotected skin. Cassy felt herself being juggled, feet first, down a stairwell. The wool blanket smoldered as it transmitted heat into Cassy. Different voices mumbled as she felt herself placed on a hard surface.

Then the corner of the wool blanket covering her face whipped away. The Texas sun ignited her skin. Through her closed eyelids, the incandescence of the sun lighted her eyeballs.

The mumbled voices were now closer. She could make out a few of the words. "My condolences, Señor Tenoch . . . she was a beautiful woman." Then the wool blanket covered her face again. The voices muffled away. She felt herself lifted again. A car door thudded around her. She moved forward, head first. Oblivion fell on her mind once more.

Later the blanket came away from her face again. "Welcome home, Cassy," Tenoch said. "How easy it is for the dead to pass through Customs. You would have even been more lovely for the inspector if you had given me the time to select a lovely casket for you . . . like I did for Ana Ruiz." His whispered breath warmed her cheek. His hands cupped her breast under the rough wool blanket. *Please* her mind screamed but no sound came. *Anything* she pleaded silently. *Ask me for anything.* Her body remained absolutely still and flat despite constant commands from her mind. *Please let me leave* she cried in her mind.

"Rest, carina mía," he said quietly. His thin firm lips touched hers, and his tongue brushed her lips lightly. Her overloaded mind blacked into unconsciousness again.

When the oblivion receded, she perceived forward movement once more. Muted voices surrounded her. Still she could not make out the words. Unable to move or to speak, time lost its meaning. Then the darkness of her mind overtook her.

—

Her first conscious awareness was the cloying fragrance of flowers. Roses? Lilies? Cool air wafted onto her hot face. A touch of silk caressed her nude body. She tested her finger movements and found a twitch of her right index finger. Nothing else moved. Gradually her eyelids parted slightly, opening the fissure between the lids until she could make out the dimensions of a small windowless bedroom.

The tan stippled surface of the ceiling was like wet sand and blended seamlessly into a putty-colored textured wall covering. Her heavy eyelids sank back across her eyes, closing off her vision. Moments later, she struggled open both eyes, more fully this time. Her immobile neck limited her range of vision to the tan ceiling of the small square room.

"Good morning, my sleeping beauty," Tenoch said. Cassy with great effort rotated her neck toward the sound. Her fingers now flexed almost into a fist, allowing her to grasp a wad of silk sheet beneath her. Tenoch sat in a comfortable stuffed chair in the corner of the room. A china pot and cup rested on a small table at his side.

Cassy's eyes, barely visible between her droopy lids, peeked through the fissures to find Tenoch observing her like a scientist watching a laboratory experiment. Stacks of papers and computer reports were arranged in precise alignment on a low table in front of his chair. A brass reading lamp behind Tenoch's shoulder was the only light in the windowless room.

"I see the questions in your eyes . . . now that you are able to open them. You are in a slumber room of the Park Haven Funeral Home," Tenoch said and sipped hot tea from the delicate bone china tea cup. Her fist wadded the silk sheet beneath her into a firm ball. Her fingers and toes now wiggled freely. Her arms and legs were still leaden as if pinned to the bed sheets.

"It is ten o'clock on Monday morning. I trust you have rested well," Tenoch said. "Do I see another question in your eyes?" His tone was both gentle and patronizing.

"You are paralyzed. More precisely I suspended you in a lowered metabolic state with Trent's Hiberna mixture before we left Mexico City." Tenoch's voice reverberated through the room and into her mind. As if by some acoustical trick, his words echoed back and forth inside her skull. In silent agony she screamed. *Please. Let me live.*

"You must understand that your life is in my control. To live or to die."

Cassy opened her eyes wider and could see Tenoch twiddling the vial of tan granular powder identical to the vial she remembered from the guest suite just before she lost consciousness. The glass vial was her last conscious memory of Sunday afternoon.

"But before I will allow you to return to this incarnation, I must have your pledge that you accept our destiny together."

Cassy screamed *Yes.* Only a gurgling noise came from her throat.

"Was that a yes?" Tenoch asked and smiled pleasantly. "Blink your eyes if your response was yes." Panicky and terror-filled, Cassy blinked her eyelids several times as quickly as she could until muscle fatigue from the effects of the Hiberna-induced paralysis pulled her eyelids closed.

From the other side of the bed, Cassy heard Dr. Walter Simmons' hoarse whiskey voice. "Easy, Tenoch. She's a had a huge dose of Hiberna during the past eighteen hours. Lighten her up. Don't overdo the dose or you will kill her. For chrissake, Tenoch, let's not have another Marquez incident."

"I will handle her, Walter," Tenoch said. His harsh flat voice terrified Cassy.

Please, Walter. Do not confront him. Do not do anything to provoke him her mind screamed. But her throat muscles would only constrict enough to make a gurgling noise. She opened her eyes slowly to see Tenoch tumbling the glass vial of tan powder in his hands, rolling the powder in the tube like sand in an ancient hourglass.

Cassy quickly blinked her eyes twice. *Anything you want* she tried to say. Only rattling mucus sounded deep in her throat. *Just let me move, and I'll do anything you want.* Her tongue lay thick and immobile.

"Very well," Tenoch said. "I acknowledge your acceptance."

Tenoch held the vial in his fingers. "You will do as I wish . . . security and pleasure will be yours and Alex's. My destiny will be fulfilled."

Words would not come. *Please, Please* she pleaded soundlessly and blinked her eyes three more times. *Yes. Yes.* Tenoch replaced the glass vial in the aluminum case as if replacing a bullet into a cartridge case. Finally able to take a short breath, the stale air of the slumber room washed into her lungs and flooded her with relief. Her moist eyes glistened. Cassy blinked, a stream of tears rolling backward from the outer corners of her eyes.

"You will begin to emerge from this suspended animation state . . . much like the hibernating animal awakens after a long winter's sleep," Tenoch said pleasantly.

Cassy blinked her eyes several times quickly, squeezing the moisture from them. The tears rolled down her face to the sheet forming damp circles under her head. She could sense strength in her hands. *Thank you. Thank you. Please. Let me out of here.* No sounds came forth.

"You have already experienced the return of function of your eyelid muscles," Tenoch said. "Your hands, feet, and arms will soon return to your voluntary control."

Tenoch sipped from the china cup, stood up and walked toward the bed. Her eyes followed him, still too weak to move her head. Coming into her field of vision from the other side of the bed, Walter Simmons' puffy florid face appeared opposite Tenoch.

Simmons, dressed like a banker in a vested pinstripe suit, white pocket square, stiffly starched white shirt, and a red tie to match his florid face, nodded without changing his flat expression. He leaned over Cassy and whispered, "I trust that the past eighteen hours have taught you an important lesson. Do you understand what will happen if you fuck around with the heart donor program?" His rancid breath a few inches above Cassy's nose filled her with a sickening revulsion.

Cassy nodded slightly, hoping Simmons would move away before she vomited. He did, disappearing from her line of sight. Her weakened neck muscles could not move her head more than a few degrees to either side.

Tenoch bent over her and brushed his lips against hers. Her mouth felt as if it had been branded with a hot iron.

"If ever you interfere with my destiny . . . your son will be taken," Tenoch whispered.

Cassy blinked her eyes rapidly, hysterically. *No, No. Yes, Yes* her mind screamed.

"Very well," Tenoch said, standing full upright over the bed.

Cassy's eyes slid shut. Her heightened sense of hearing caught the sound of Tenoch's silk shirt rustling as he left. But he stopped a few feet away from the bedside. She heard him in his flat, terrorizing voice say, "My destiny will be done."

TWENTY-EIGHT

T HE LEAFY OAK trees shielding the front yard in front of
the Baldwin-Spence mansion in University Park drooped their
branches and staggered under the burden of another blistering
summer afternoon. The still air over Dallas held the heat of the day as if
an inverted convection chamber enclosed the city and baked its contents.

Tenoch's limousine rolled up to the wrought iron gate at the street entrance, its front bumper within inches of the upright bars. Alberto lowered the tinted driver's window and punched the five-digit security code,
C-A-S-S-Y, into the keypad of the brick security post. The steel wheels
screeched on the hot concrete as the halves of the gate slid apart.

The limousine rolled in a solitary stately procession up to the mansion,
easing to a dignified stop under the porte cochere. Behind the glass storm
door Charlie lunged in a crazed frenzy at the appearance of the long
black car. The dog's lips curled up ready for attack, baring his sharp teeth.
His paws banged and rattled the door. Charlie's growling rose menac-
ingly. He strained to crash through the glass storm door.

As soon as the limousine stopped, its rear door locks flipped open. Alberto jumped from the driver's side to hold the rear door open for Cassy.
Once outside the coolness of the limousine's interior, Cassy's headache
pulsed with her heartbeat. Scintillating light spots danced in her vision.
She shakily turned toward the front door, away from the brightness of the
afternoon light, squinting at the pain in her head. Her hair hung flattened
on her head like a skullcap. Charlie's growling changed into an excited
frenzy of barking as Cassy stumbled toward the door.

Cassy's jacket hung crumpled over her camisole-covered shoulders. She
had no idea where her bra and panties were. Her bare legs wobbled beneath her wrinkled skirt. Cassy walked unsteadily through the door, her
gait broad and jerky like a young colt. At the edge of the foyer she paused,
holding onto the coat tree.

"Where's Alex?" Cassy asked Lupita. The residual weakness from the
Hiberna suspension nearly collapsed Cassy as she tried to make her voice
heard above Charlie's barking.

"Señora," the housekeeper shouted. At the same time she snapped the
leash chain onto Charlie's neck and tried to quiet the dog's frantic snarl-
ing at Alberto beyond the glass door. "Where have you been?" Her tone
scolded Cassy.

Leaning against the wall, Cassy managed to raise her voice above a
whimper, "Where's Alex?"

"Dios mio, Señora. You are sick," Lupita said and dropped the leash
chain to reach out to steady Cassy. With his restraint gone, Charlie crashed
into the storm door. Alberto dropped Cassy's bags on the tiled driveway
and ran to the limo. The car raced down the driveway barely clearing the
swinging iron gates.

"Charlie," Cassy tried to shout. Her weakness collapsed her against the
foyer wall. "Lupita, take Charlie out of here," she croaked.

Lupita grabbed the leash chain and collared the dog.

"Mom!" Alex shouted as he ran down the staircase and hugged her.
"You said you'd be home yesterday."

"I had to stay an extra day," she managed to say, trying to hide the fear
from her voice. She released her grip on the brick foyer wall and held her
son tightly against her. After a few seconds he squirmed away. Tears of relief streamed her cheeks.

"What's the matter, Mom?" Alex asked. "Why are you crying?"

"I'm fine. Just glad to see you. I missed you," she said, biting at her lip.
She brushed the tears from her cheek.

"Dr. Hendricks said you ate some Mexican food that made you sick."

"I'm all right now, hon." She touched his dark hair and turned her face
to the front door so that Alex could not see her trembling chin. "Did you
go to the Rangers' game yesterday?" Cassy finally asked, her voice mostly
steady.

"Five to three, Rangers," Alex said. Cassy pulled her son close to her
again. She could not talk without her voice breaking.

"Did you hear me?" Alex asked. "Five to three." Cassy nodded and
held on to her son for support.

"Dr. Hendricks called three times. He wants you to call," Lupita said
in Spanish.

"Gracias," Cassy said in a way that dismissed Lupita. Then she asked Lupita as an afterthought, "Have you begun dinner for Alex?"

"I'll eat pizza," Alex broke in.

"No, Alex," Lupita said, turning her scowl onto Alex. "I will fix my tamales tonight."

"Fix the pizza," Cassy said.

The kitchen phone rang. Cassy shakily reached for the ringing phone. She stared Lupita down. "Fix the pizza . . . now!" Then she lifted the receiver. It was Trent.

His voice burst through the phone even before Cassy finished her hello. "Cass, where the hell have you been?"

"I just got home."

"You could have at least called me," Trent said.

"I would have if I could," Cassy said and turned her back to Alex and Lupita, trying to muffle her conversation.

"I'm sure you were very busy with Señor Tenoch," Trent said. "I didn't appreciate one bit hearing from Alberto that you decided to spend another night with Tenoch."

"We have a lot to discuss," Cassy said quietly. Her throbbing head now was exploding.

"You damn sure know we do," Trent sputtered. "I don't give a goddamn if you want to sleep with Tenoch, but for chrissake, give me a little respect . . . I'm not your babysitter for Alex."

"I was not sleeping with Tenoch last night," she said, whispering loudly into the telephone and slamming it into the telephone cradle. Cassy turned away from the cabinet to encounter the stunned faces of Lupita and Alex. Her son spun and ran from the room. Lupita shook her head and opened the Sub-Zero freezer, putting the open door between them like an instant frozen wall.

"Something is wrong with you, Señora," Lupita said over her shoulder. She shuffled through the frozen packages in the freezer.

"I'm fine. Just fix the damn pizza," she said and stumbled out of the kitchen.

In her bedroom Cassy stuffed her jacket, camisole, and skirt into a plastic garbage bag. Then she showered in a frenzy, trying to scrub away the weekend's memory. The warmth of the steam shrouded her and insulated her from the world. Finally, the hot water turned warm, then tepid, until she stood in the coolness of the flowing water as time stood still for her.

The weakness spread throughout her, pressing her back against the wet slick tile. Slowly she slipped to the floor of the shower. The cold shower stream pelted her skin, each jet separately magnified into a tattoo. Her mind grayed out in boiling clouds of rain pellets. Far in the distance of the churning gray cold rain, she heard Gracie wailing a keening version of *Amazing Grace*, rising to the words, *Ana Ruiz, How sweet the sound.* . . .

She had no idea how much time had passed when she finally opened her eyes into the cold torrents of the shower. She lay crumpled on the tile floor, the sounds of *Ana Ruiz* in Gracie's melodious voice echoing in her mind. Struggling up from the slippery wet tile, Cassy turned the shower knob, choking off the cold shower. The shower glistened with sheets of water. Cassy leaned her back against the cold tiles and steadied her body upright. She rubbed her eyes until red flashes appeared.

"What the hell is happening to me?" she asked out loud. Her hands palsied with a violent tremor. "For god's sake, I'm coming apart," she said, slipping her bare buttocks onto the wet triangular stool in the corner of the shower.

Finally she was able to gather enough strength to reach the dressing room and pull her blue terry cloth robe over her wet body. She ran her fingers through her wet hair, studying her face in the mirror. "My god, you look awful," Cassy said to her mirror's image. Her soaked hair, nearly black with moisture, limped around her face. Puffy eye pouches held up her reddened eyes. Cassy's fingers traced the outline of her lips, recalling the impression of Tenoch's lips on hers.

Reaching into the back of her dresser drawer, her hand came out with her cigarettes. Moments later she dragged a deep lungful of cigarette smoke, feeling the tension of her neck muscles ease. She took a last deep pull on the cigarette and walked, still in her bathrobe, up the staircase to Alex's bedroom.

"Alex," Cassy said. She gently tapped on the door. The room was silent except for screeching computer noises bursting from Alex's new computer baseball game. She knocked louder and twisted the doorknob, pushing the door open enough to admit her head. Her son's head appeared as a black cutout framed by the multicolored video images of the computer screen. "I'm sorry, Alex," she said, walking toward him in the dim room. His fingers flicked the mouse control of his Macintosh, expertly moving the baseball figures on the computer screen.

He ignored her. Cassy bunched the blue terry robe about her and pulled the captain's chair close to him. "I'm sorry, Alex. It's not the way you might think." Several minutes dragged by without a word between them. Alex's eyes never wandered from the computer screen.

"I'm sorry, Alex," Cassy repeated, covering his hand so that he could not move the computer mouse control. "Will you let me explain?" He pushed her hand away with his other hand, never letting loose of the mouse control.

Trent Hendricks' voice boomed up the staircase through Alex's open bedroom door and cracked the impasse.

"There's Trent," Cassy said, trying to put as much lightness in her voice as possible. She picked her hand up from his. "Let me go see what he wants." Uncertain that she could ever explain away the weekend to Alex, she tousled his hair in the affectionate way she always did and stepped into the upstairs hallway.

Trent, in scrub clothes, turned up the stairwell landing and bounded the additional steps to the upstairs foyer. "Cassy!" he shouted when he saw her standing outside Alex's room. "I came as soon as I finished up the day's OR schedule . . . are you all right?"

"Might I ask what you are doing here in my home?" she asked, her voice controlled beyond hardness. "I didn't invite you. Did it ever occur to you to ring the door chime?" A tremulousness rattled her controlled voice.

"I was worried about you. You didn't sound right." He paused. "I'm sorry," he said, turning his hands upward in supplication. "You don't understand how dangerous Tenoch can be."

"You think I don't know how dangerous that psychopath is? He damn near killed me. The son of a bitch poisoned me last night with some kind of neurotoxin that he says you gave him," Cassy hissed, pushing him on down the stairwell in front of her.

"Oh Jesus," Trent said, grabbing at the railing. She pushed him toward the front door. "He's gone over the fucking edge."

"What?" Cassy asked.

"I've known for a while that he comes and goes in and out of his own psychotic world. Most of the time he is perfectly rational and compensated. Then somehow and for no apparent reason, he thinks he's an Aztec god who's turned up in the late twentieth century to save the world," Trent said. Cassy stopped in the foyer dazed by Trent's confession.

"Why the hell didn't you tell me . . . or at least tell somebody . . . or get him some help . . . or call the goddamn police before he kills anybody else," Cassy shrieked. Her words streamed out in a waterfall of disjointed thoughts.

"I don't know . . . I wish," Trent stammered, shaking his head and looking at the floor, unable to return Cassy's withering stare. After many moments he was still unable to look at Cassy, but he continued. "His money and influence supported my research laboratory. I've made some important transplant discoveries . . . thanks to Tenoch's money."

"Most important, he sold you the heart for your daughter's transplant."

Trent looked up at Cassy. For the first time in her life she saw into another's soul. The agony and torment in Trent was a look into hell.

"I'm calling the police," Cassy said. She pushed Trent aside. "The bastard poisoned me, then threatened me and my son."

"Don't call the police," Trent said and pulled her after him into the family room. "You can't . . . he will know immediately."

"Are you planning to tell Tenoch?" Cassy jerked her arm away from his grasp.

"Can't you see what's happening?" Trent said. "Tenoch is a psychopath just as if he were a serial killer."

"I'm calling the police," Cassy said. She started toward the phone. "Right now."

"No, don't. He's too unstable," Trent said and grabbed her hand that held the phone.

"What are you trying to say?" Cassy asked, struggling to keep from screaming at him. Her flushed face streaked with tears. Her jaw trembled.

"He will kill you and Alex," Trent said.

"Why the hell do you think I'm calling the police? I know he's going to kill me. I know too much," she said. Her voice was shrill and brittle.

"The police can't do anything. They won't find anything. He's too slick," Trent said. "And if you cross him, he will destroy you . . . and Alex. He will kill Alex first just to watch you suffer."

"What can I do? Nothing? Is that what you're telling me? Do nothing? You've been telling me to do nothing all week long. Look where I am." Cassy stared at him. Trent shook his head and wiped his hand across his lips, swallowing dryly.

"Why is he after me?" Cassy asked. "You're not telling me everything."

"I could use a drink," Trent said.

"You know where the bourbon is," Cassy said. An overpowering weariness collapsed her onto the sofa in the family room.

In a few moments Trent returned from her ex-husband's study with a bottle of Jack Daniels whiskey. By the dark color of the whiskey in the glass he held in his trembling hand, Cassy guessed it to be undiluted bourbon. Trent sat down on the end of the sofa, his shoulders hunched forward. His head nodded over the tumbler of whiskey. For several minutes nothing was said. Finally Trent drained off the bourbon with one swallow. He refilled the glass nearly to the rim and gestured the bottle to Cassy in a way that asked whether she wanted a drink. Cassy shook her head.

They sat together for a long time in the family room as the late afternoon sun eased behind the cover of the elm trees. Control of her panic slowly returned in the quiet of her home. It was as if she had asked for the scalpel at the beginning of a surgical procedure. A resolute calmness settled the terror that had not left her since awakening in the bedroom of Tenoch's airplane.

Trent looked up, startled, when Cassy moved closer to him from the far end of the sofa. "I want to know everything you know about Tenoch," Cassy said quietly.

"Where do you want me to begin?" he said. His tongue lagged an instant behind his words so that each word slurred against the one behind it.

"Try at the beginning," Cassy said. "It was money, wasn't it? You've been taking money from Tenoch for how long?"

"It's not just the money, Cass. Let me freshen this drink," Trent said, obviously playing for time. Trent slowly refilled his crystal glass and again gestured to Cassy. "Sure you won't join me?" he said, waving the neck of the whiskey bottle at her.

Cassy shook her head and pressed him for more information like a police interrogator. In a brief flash she thought of Kevin Knowland sitting in a small plain interrogation room, listening patiently to a homicide suspect begin to tell his sordid story of killing another human being.

"When did you first meet Tenoch?" she asked as gently as she thought Kevin might.

"It was about four years ago."

"Where?" Cassy interrupted and immediately chided herself for stepping on Trent's beginning narrative.

"Walter Simmons introduced us at the Metro Hospital's annual Charity Renaissance Ball. You and Scott were there. Remember, it was the first year the Metro Hospital held the event at the Anatole Hotel," Trent said, slurring his words even more. "You know those events . . . the doctors and hospital administration getting in touch with influential Dallas citizens."

"Influential and wealthy," Cassy said. "The hospital administration is always on the hustle for wealthy donors to the hospital's fund-raising program." She knew that she would have to play into Trent's wandering attention. The cadence of Trent's speech slowed. He had finished his third drink in less than an hour. He waved the bottle at her, once again asking whether she wanted him to fill a glass for her.

"No thanks. And that's enough for you, too." She took the bottle from his hand and stuffed it between the deep cushions of the leather sofa. "What happened when you first met Tenoch?" she asked, a trace of impatience creeping into her voice.

"We hit it off pretty well at the dinner party that night. I remember that I was seated right next to him," Trent said. "He invited me for lunch at his home the following week. You know where we had lunch last week. It was a nice social visit. He quickly became interested in my cardiac transplantation research."

"What part of your research?"

"He has an extraordinary grasp of the heart's function and physiology. Tenoch's a most brilliant man," Trent said. "He's so smart, no wonder he's so goddamn rich."

Cassy forced a politeness in her voice and manner that she did not feel. She repeated her earlier question. "What part of your research was Tenoch particularly interested in?" she asked cautiously.

"Oh yeah. He was really enthusiastic about my research on organ preservation techniques for transplantation. Particularly my studies on suspending the metabolism of the donor prior to the transplantation of the heart into the recipient patient."

Trent looked vacantly beyond the family room patio doors to the glistening surface of the swimming pool. It was an uncomfortable pause, but Cassy held back, hoping that Trent had not drunk so much whiskey so quickly that he was going to pass out on her.

"You were telling me how much Tenoch was interested in your research. . . ."

"That's right. He and Alberto started coming to actually participate in my transplantation research experiments. Hands-on experience is how Tenoch described it. That's when I first became concerned."

"About what?"

"Tenoch's grip with reality. His first couple of visits to my research laboratory were nothing unusual. Then he wanted to scrub in and assist me on the heart transplants in the animal laboratory. When Tenoch held a transplanted calf's heart in his hands, he really became weird. Mumbling some crazy chant or something in Spanish."

"And you didn't think this behavior bizarre enough to discuss it with anyone?"

"For a million bucks a year, anybody can come into my lab and hold a calf's heart and mumble whatever they want to. You know how hard research money is to find these days. It's not like it was during the oil boom. The economy has squeezed all the money 'til there's hardly any left for research."

"A million dollars in cash?" Cassy asked. Her mouth remained open involuntarily. "What for?"

"That's what I asked. What am I supposed to do with all this cash? He said I could use it any way I wanted as long as it was for heart transplant research and as long as I didn't identify him as the source of the donation. He said he was plagued with requests for charitable donations. If I made a public announcement he would be overrun with people asking for donations, and I wouldn't ever receive another dollar from him for my laboratory research."

"What did you do with the cash?" Cassy asked.

"Do you realize how much space a million dollars in hundred dollar bills takes up? It's a hundred packets of a hundred one hundred dollar bills." Trent said, smiling at her with a foolish grin. "Does that make sense?" he asked.

"Yes," Cassy said, not even trying to create the absurd mental image of a million dollars in cash.

"How did you spend the cash?"

"The money was used in my experimental laboratory. I didn't tell anyone where the funds were coming from. I guess everyone assumed I was funding my own research. Do you realize how careful you have to be spending cash? The damn banks have all these government regulations requiring them to report cash transactions over ten thousand dollars. I sure as hell have opened a lot of nine thousand dollar bank accounts all over Texas in the past four years." He laughed and drank the rest of his whiskey.

Trent reached deep between the cushions for the bottle where Cassy had shoved it. Cassy took the whiskey bottle from his hands before he could pour another drink and slid it under her end of the sofa.

Something was still missing from the story, she knew. She had yet to close the circle of information that brought her to where Tenoch's involvement sprang. What was it? The thought niggled at her. She asked, "You've spent a million dollars of cash each year for four years on your organ preservation research?" Cassy shook her head in amazement.

"It's money well spent. I've made some real breakthroughs in donor preservation for transplantation. I've developed a new drug method for suspended animation using a mixture of tetrodotoxin. You know the puffer fish toxin. I've been able to induce a hibernating state in the experimental animal for periods of twenty-four hours," Trent replied defensively. "It's a safe method of lowering the metabolic rate. I can preserve a heart donor for a period of twenty-four hours with no deterioration in organ function." He looked into his empty glass, seeming to concentrate on his words. "Don't you see the implications of my discovery for surgery of all kinds? A prolonged interruption of circulation would allow extensive, unhurried surgery without the risk of bleeding . . . operations could be done that are beyond the reach of today's scalpels."

"Does Tenoch appreciate the importance and magnitude of your discovery?"

"Sure. I've been meeting him at his home in Dallas every month. Like you and I did last week. Tenoch even scrubbed in on some of our human heart transplant procedures at Metro Hospital when I first used the Hi-berna . . . that's what I call the mixture . . . Hiberna . . . you get it . . . ? Hiberna for hibernate . . . like an animal hibernating for the winter . . . we're able to mimic hibernation at our convenience." His attention span was drifting into foolish asides.

The information from Trent was painting an ugly portrait. Cassy could not yet see all its form or features. The colors and definition were still missing in the picture. She needed more. Trent was sprawled on the sofa. His head occasionally nodded over his green surgical scrub shirt. Cassy knew she had to keep prodding him.

"How does Tenoch know what you're doing in the research lab with his money?" Cassy asked.

"He didn't care," Trent said, hesitating. Cassy restrained herself until Trent continued, ". . . as long as he got to hold the heart."

"In the Metro operating room?" Cassy asked, unable to keep from questioning him. "On real patients?"

"Tenoch told me there would be no more research money unless he could scrub in and hold the human heart. That's the part he really liked," Trent said. "After the first time he scrubbed in the Metro OR, I had to tell him to ease up . . . that the nursing staff was complaining about his mumbling in Spanish when he held the donor heart in his hands."

"How did you justify to the nurses that Tenoch would scrub in on the transplant operations? Did they think that Tenoch was a surgeon?"

"Yes," Trent said. "I introduced him as Dr. Tenoch, a visiting surgeon from the Instituto de Medico in Mexico City."

"Isn't there something else you want to tell me?" Cassy asked as pleas-antly as she could manage. She had no idea what more Trent knew, but she wasn't through probing. She waited, letting the room fill with silence.

Trent hesitated. She was certain she hadn't retrieved all Trent's infor-mation yet. Cassy willed herself to be patient, knowing that if she inter-rupted with another specific question she might not get another chance.

"Gracie had nothing to do with any of this," Trent said softly, looking at the bottom of his whiskey glass.

Cassy felt as if she had been struck by a sniper's bullet. Trent's disclo-sure that Gracie was not involved was an obvious implication by his out-right denial. His totally unsuspected connection of Gracie rattled her for a moment. Before she could frame a question Trent said, "All Gracie did was point me to a source."

Cassy waited until Trent looked up at her through his rheumy red eyes. His face had transformed itself like Dorian Gray into an old man. Cassy knew that she would have to probe deeper. She wasn't yet through to the core of information that Trent possessed.

"Source of what?" Cassy asked, leaving the open-ended question hanging in the cool hush of the family room.

"The tetrodotoxin," Trent said, stopping and avoiding Cassy's eyes. Cassy waited him out until finally Trent said, "Gracie told us where to go in Haiti to find a bokor."

"What?" Cassy interrupted and immediately regretted breaking Trent's tenuous concentration.

"A voodoo priest . . . I found one in Haiti who has supplied me the unrefined raw materials that he has used in his zombie rituals. For cash. He's not at all interested in scientific research . . . money does the zombie priest very nicely. His zombie powders contain the tetrodotoxin." Trent looked into his empty glass before continuing. "I'll bet you thought I was just taking a lot of sailing vacations in the Caribbean. Those vacations were my trips to the source. I was bringing home the raw goods for my Hiberna mixture each trip."

"The tetrodotoxin is the biologically active compound?" Cassy asked.

"Yeah. But it's not that simple . . . four years and four million dollars later, I can tell you a lot about dosing, responses, necessary companion drugs, and appropriate pharmacologic buffers for the tetrodotoxin."

"But you've been using it in patients?"

"You bet. It works like a wonder . . . and I've applied for a new drug patent. It's going to make me a wealthy man."

There it was. Cassy knew then what had been niggling at her through-out the conversation. It was not Trent's scientific curiosity that propelled him to pursue the Hiberna solution—it was the money. But surely not, she thought. It doesn't make sense. Trent is financially comfortable. Why is he focused on the financial gain? He told me already that he had set up a trust fund to take care of Heather. Then she decided to try another open-ended question.

"Isn't there something else you want to tell me?" Cassy asked.

Trent shook his head. Cassy waited. Finally when she knew he would not volunteer any more information, Cassy asked, "When did you begin draining the cash out of Tenoch's donations to set up the trust fund for Heather?" It was a shot in the dark.

"How did you know?"

"You told me yourself about the trust fund for Heather. It was a guess." She waited for his response and was rewarded for her patience.

"The last couple of years when Heather became so sick, and especially after Marilyn died, I siphoned off two million dollars from the research money. It's in a special trust fund only to benefit Heather."

"So, you've been embezzling from Tenoch. Has he found out?"

"Yes. The man misses nothing . . . he has sources of information everywhere. He promised me that he would not make any complaints. I can still keep the money in Heather's trust fund if I would participate in his transplant organ procurement plan."

"You've left a lot unsaid," Cassy said. "Do you want to tell me all the story?"

"I can't . . . ," Trent said, standing up and walking to the window overlooking the patio and the pool. Cassy sat on the sofa watching his hunched back.

"Who is Ana Ruiz?" Cassy asked bluntly.

"Don't ask, please," he said. His voice reflected back off the window to Cassy. "Ana Ruiz died so that Heather could live."

"Tell me," Cassy said, her voice soft. She led him back to the sofa. "Start at the beginning." She knew what was coming, but she knew she must hear it from Trent.

"If it weren't for the Ruiz heart, Heather would be dead," Trent said. "I saw Heather dying. She nearly died several times during those months, waiting for a donor heart. It almost killed me, waiting and watching her die a little every day."

He paused, picking up the empty glass. "Go on," Cassy said. She reached under the sofa for the bottle and poured the glass full of whiskey for him.

"I couldn't go on living if I let Heather die. Each day she died a bit more. A part of me died with her. Month after month we waited for a donor heart. She was listed as a priority one for a donor heart in the United States, but nothing turned up."

"I understand," Cassy said, trying to imagine what she would do under any circumstance that Alex's life was jeopardized.

"A couple of weeks ago I almost lost Heather during one of her worst heart failure episodes," Trent said, slugging down half the glass of whiskey. "The next day I had to go for my weekly lunch with Tenoch. I mentioned my anxiety and frustration about not being able to find a donor heart for Heather to Tenoch."

"Why Tenoch? When you were so concerned about his bizarre behavior?"

"I don't know. I was desperate," Trent said. "I was asking everybody and anybody for help. Tenoch suggested we look for a donor heart in Mexico. He simply couldn't understand why the hospitals and transplant organizations in this country would not allow donor organs to be imported into this country from Mexico. He would not accept bureaucratic excuses to organ sharing across the border. Hell, he arranged an immediate compassionate exemption with the Mexican government for Heather so that I could look in Mexico for a donor. At his insistence the Metro

Hospital granted an exception for Heather so that we could bring a donor heart from a Mexican hospital if a donor ever became available in that country. Then you know the rest of the story," Trent said, stopping abruptly. But after pausing, he continued, "Ana Ruiz was the donor of Heather's heart. Tenoch found the kid."

"What do you mean by that . . . found the kid?"

"For god's sake, I swear . . . ," Trent said, his head pumping up and down. "She looked brain dead to me."

"Raul Garcia didn't know anything about a donor for Heather when I asked him about the donor procurement at the Instituto de Medico?"

"Of course not. The kid was brought directly to Dallas. She never was admitted to the Instituto."

"But her records are from the Instituto," Cassy said. "And you told me that you were in Mexico City harvesting the donor."

"I know, but I was across town at the Park Haven Funeral Home," Trent said. "I was trying to protect you. I didn't want you involved."

Cassy said nothing and waited for the silence in the room to force a response from Trent.

"Tenoch and I equipped the basement at Marquez's Park Haven Funeral Home as a complete operating room so that I could harvest the donors he would bring in from Mexico."

"How many hearts have you harvested at the funeral home?"

"Heather's is the only one. I'd do it again for her. But I swear that Mexican kid was dead," he said, his shoulders heaving in racking sobs.

"You removed Ana Ruiz's heart in the funeral home?"

"Yes. And I brought it to Metro Hospital straight from the funeral home."

"Who else is in on this?" Cassy asked coldly.

"Walter Simmons," Trent said. "Tenoch and Simmons go back a long way. Walter has been a partner in several of Tenoch's sweetheart business deals."

"Who certified the death of Ana Ruiz?"

"That was the problem Jeorg Marquez caused. On the Saturday afternoon that Ana Ruiz arrived at Marquez's funeral home, Jeorg Marquez tried to call off the organ harvest."

"Why?" Cassy asked.

"Marquez realized what Tenoch had done and figured out that the Instituto medical records were forged," Trent said. "But Cassy, I swear that the child looked brain-dead to me. So help me God!"

"You're not certain now?"

"Not after what happened to Marquez that Saturday night," Trent said. "I admit I was hardly objective in my evaluation. I didn't ask, and I really didn't look close. Ana Ruiz was the donor heart that would save my daughter's life. It was Heather's only chance. But I truly thought that the kid was brain-dead."

"Where did Tenoch find Ana Ruiz?"

"I didn't want to know . . . the day after Heather's transplant Tenoch told me. Ana Ruiz was a child from the slums of Mexico City. Tenoch snatched her, then drugged her with the tetrodotoxin, and flew her to Dallas in his 727. He brought her through U.S. Customs at the DFW airport in a casket directly to the Park Haven Funeral Home. But I didn't know what Tenoch had done until after I harvested the heart. I swear to God I didn't know!"

"He drugged Ana Ruiz just like he did me last night," Cassy said. She stood up abruptly. "I'm calling Lt. Knowland right now."

"No, you can't. What can you say? Nothing can be proved. Ruiz's body was cremated that night at the Park Haven Funeral Home. There's no trace of her. Tenoch is shrewd and manipulative. He will have covered all his tracks. The operating room at the Park Haven Funeral Home can be dismantled and shipped back to Mexico before you could get a search warrant."

"But . . . we can't. . . ."

"Listen to me. I'm in over my head. Tenoch has already warned you. You'll end up just like Jeorg Marquez . . . after he kills Alex."

"Why would he do this? It can't be for the money."

"No, it's not just the money. He'll make a fortune off this organ marketing scheme, but it's more than the money."

"Why?" Cassy asked. "What is it then?"

"Tenoch believes he's a reincarnated Aztec god requiring human sacrifices, just like the Aztecs did hundreds of years ago."

The two stared at each other until the ringing telephone broke the silence. After the fifth ring Cassy lifted the receiver. "Yes," she said blankly.

"I am Huitzilopochtli, the god of fire, air, water, and the sun." Cassy recognized Tenoch's voice even though his tone was flat, slow-paced, and disconnected. Her stomach rolled into her throat. For a moment the surging in her bowels almost left her.

"S-Señor T-Tenoch," Cassy said, stuttering her words like Alex.

"My nourishment and sustenance will come from you," Tenoch's menacing voice said. "You will honor me or tomorrow will not see the sun." The phone hummed like a bass string when the connection broke.

Her face drained of color. She dropped the phone as if it were electrified. "He's been listening to us."

"Tenoch has bugged the house," Trent said and moved toward her to pull her shaking body to him. "Let me fix us a drink."

The telephone rang again. Cassy looked at it, terror in her eyes. After the second ring, she started to pick up the phone. She pulled her hand back, unable to pick it up. On the fifth ring, Trent reached for the phone, but Cassy grabbed his hand.

"Don't answer it," Cassy said. The ringing stopped in mid-ring.

Moments later, Lupita's voice crackled through the intercom filling the room with her Spanish words. "Dr. Baldwin. It's Señor Tenoch."

Cassy flipped the speakerphone button. "Hello," she said, hesitating and her voice cracking.

"Good evening, Cassandra. Please give my regards to Trent." Tenoch's voice was now smooth and agreeable. "I trust you are much improved."

"Yes, I'm fine, thank you," Cassy said stiffly, staring toward the speakerphone receiver.

"A heart donor will be arriving tomorrow afternoon from Mexico City." Tenoch's nonchalant voice floated out of the speakerphone.

"Señor Tenoch," Cassy said quickly in a panicky voice. "We must discuss. . . ."

"There is nothing to discuss," Tenoch said pleasantly. "The procedure will go forth."

"I cannot do it," Cassy said.

"Yes, you will." The flat, slow-paced, menacing tone returned to his voice. Then the connection broke into ear-shattering silence.

Trent drained the whiskey from his glass. Cassy motioned him off the sofa and out the patio door. Outside she turned on the patio speakers, punching in her tape player. The sounds of Vivaldi filled the patio.

Cassy pulled Trent to the center of the patio and whispered in his ear. "He will kill us and Alex. We must do what he wants." Trent nodded, looking at her questioningly, his glazed eyes half hidden by his lagging lids.

"Now go home. I will talk to you tomorrow. No more whiskey tonight."

"What the hell are we going to do . . . ?" His alcohol-fogged mind could not complete the question.

"I don't know."

TWENTY-NINE

SCATTERED POOLS of landscaping light splashed Cassy's front yard beneath the trees and plantings of the sloping lawn. A whisper of hot wind rustled through the leaves, fanning but hardly cooling the trees dry roasted from the day's sun. Even though darkness was late coming in the summer of daylight savings time, it was murky under the porte cochere as Cassy watched the red rear lights of Trent's Mercedes weave erratically down the winding drive. His front wheels rutted the lawn adjacent to the driveway. She had tried to persuade Trent to call a cab rather than drive home with five glasses of straight bourbon whiskey in him. He refused with a nonchalant wave and staggered unsteadily to his car.

Cassy shook a cigarette from the pocket of her terry cloth robe and lit up as she sat on the raised brick flower bed along the edge of the tiled drive under the porte cochere. A plume of smoke wafted slowly away from her head in the hot night air. Her fear of Tenoch was palpable. She knew that she could do nothing without Tenoch knowing. He was inside her as if he had inoculated himself into her body and had overwhelmed her. She couldn't run. She couldn't call for help.

The burbling swish of the programmed lawn sprinkler whirled cascades of water in the flower beds. Cassy backed away from the spray of water and pitched the remnant of her cigarette in a glowing arc of embers toward a sprinkler head. The spray snuffed out the flare of the cigarette before it reached the flowers.

Cassy stretched her muscles in isometric contractions of her forearms.

Her only encouraging prospect of the whole evening was the progressive recovery of her muscle strength and co-ordination since Tenoch's limousine brought her back home a few hours before. At least whatever Tenoch dosed her with had left no lasting disability. But what reassurance was her recovery when she knew that Tenoch could kill Alex and her any moment?

After arming the intrusion security alarm, for a moment she stood inside the foyer listening to the familiar noises of the quiet house. The background sounds were usually a subliminal perception in her everyday living, but now each sound amplified itself as if the volume control of a hearing aid had been cranked up full. The whooshing of refrigerated air through the air conditioning ducts roared like a jet passing overhead. Muffled sounds, so inconsequential that her ear would have ignored them before this evening, clanged in her head. The synthetic sounds of Alex's computer games and the Spanish rumbling of Lupita's television tuned to the Mexico City satellite channel reverberated in her head.

When she entered her country kitchen through its high brick archway, Alex's dinner plate heaped with cold uneaten corn tamales greeted her like a wax display of tainted Mexican food. "Lupita, why can't you for once do what I ask?" Cassy asked the empty kitchen as she tossed the tamales into the roaring garbage disposal. "Would it be too much trouble to thaw a frozen pizza and cook it like I asked you?"

She refilled her glass with the Mondavi chardonnay from the open bottle in the refrigerator door. Cassy angrily jerked a frozen pizza and a carton of Blue Bell's chocolate ice cream from the freezer. Minutes later she pulled the bubbling cheese pizza from the microwave and topped a chocolate ice cream milk shake with aerosolized cream whip and a maraschino cherry.

Balancing the tray with the milk shake and pizza on her outstretched fingers and holding the wine glass in her other hand, she climbed the staircase and tapped on Alex's bedroom door. After several moments and no answer, Cassy set the tray on the floor and opened the door. Alex sat in the same position as earlier, his dark head backlighted against the video screen.

"How about pizza?" she asked. "And a milk shake?"

Alex turned from the screen and nodded. "Okay," he said without enthusiasm. Cassy eased the tray to the floor and folded her legs under her. Alex slid to the floor. The pizza separated them like a campfire. Alex took a triangular wedge of pizza and nimbly folded it lengthwise. The slice disappeared into his mouth in three bites. They ate in silence, sitting on the floor of his bedroom. Finally Cassy took the initiative.

"I'm sorry about this afternoon," Cassy said. "Trent said some things he shouldn't have. I spoke before I thought. I apologize that you saw me so angry."

Alex took another slice of pizza, carefully folded it lengthwise and chomped the end of the slice off. He looked at his mother and poised the rest of the pizza slice at his mouth. "Are we moving to Mexico City?"

"No. We're staying right here."

"Is Señor Tenoch going to be my stepdad?"

"No," Cassy said.

He brought the pizza into his mouth, seeming to say that he was satisfied. Cassy wondered whether his questions were truly answered. Or whether it was too unsettling for him to talk anymore this night.

They sat for a long time with their legs tucked under them until only dead embers of pizza crumbs separated them. The evening closed around them like the night on the prairie under a Texas sky. Neither said much more. It was as if they had reached across the campfire to touch each other and had singed their forearms in the heat of the flames. Unspoken communication passed across the pizza tray, each pulling back a bit from the glowing embers between them, afraid of being singed again.

They stayed together for a long time in Alex's room. At last with Alex in bed Cassy read aloud from *Huck Finn* until his long-lashed lids drooped. His breathing became slow and easy. For a time, she sat watching her son sleeping peacefully, his nearness soothing her anxiety but replacing it with a worried fear.

Standing in the doorway, she flipped off his room light and sensed more than saw the change in the rhythm of his breathing when his room suddenly darkened, lighted only by the flaring multicolored patterns from his computer video screen. Cassy slipped out of the room, closing the door behind her. The German shepherd banged at her knees. Across the hallway from Alex's room the muffled sound of a Spanish-speaking television program chattered on behind Lupita's closed door.

In the kitchen Cassy opened the patio door to let Charlie perform his nightly patrol of the yard. Exhaustion controlled her. Her weary body barely allowed her to pull the patio door closed as Charlie began his circuit of the grounds. The dog always ran two clockwise circuits around the house, sniffing the foundation plantings, barking at shadows, and finally urinating at the base of an elm tree in the far corner of the backyard. Precisely eight minutes after leaving the kitchen, Charlie invariably banged his paws against the patio door announcing his readiness to be back inside and declaring the yard safe.

With her wine glass refilled, Cassy settled in front of the television in the family room, her bare feet propped on the hassock, and clicked on the late news. Moments later the wine, the late hour, the fatigue, and the softness of the sofa soothed her to sleep.

Cassy did not know what woke her. Whether it was the screaming used car salesman on the television or the pain of her stiff neck. Slumped on the leather sofa, she rubbed her neck and face. A vague sense of uncertainty swept over Cassy. Her wine glass was empty on the floor beside the sofa. The smell of pizza lingered in the room. She slowly realized that Charlie had not pounded the patio door, wanting back in the house.

Opening the sliding glass door to the patio and the rear grounds, she shouted, "Charlie!" Cassy walked around the corner walkway where Charlie had cornered Gracie and whistled for him. That side of the house was quiet. She pushed through the creaking gate and turned the front corner of the house. The double front door stood locked and alarmed. The gate at the far end of the driveway completely barred the opening to the street.

She shouted again for the dog. The yard remained silent. The hot night wind slapped her face as she walked under the porte cochere. She called several more times for the dog and searched the front yard still lit by the landscape floodlights. Then Cassy went back to the front door and disarmed the intrusion alarm, keyed the door, and stepped back into the cool foyer. The voice of the news reporter on the late news gave her a momentary start. "Where in the hell is that damn dog," she said. She walked through the empty family room, turning off the television as she passed through, and opening the patio door again. The eerie quiet troubled her. Something was not right.

The hot humid outside air condensed into moisture on the cool plate glass of the family room. After Cassy pulled the glass door completely open, her eyes swept the yard and patio again. The exterior lights flooded the rear grounds.

She moved slowly through the patio door. Warning sirens screamed in her head. Charlie's confrontational behavior had occasionally brought him trouble with other dogs, but never more than he had been able to handle. But tonight was different, she somehow knew. Charlie had vanished.

She stepped onto the swimming pool's brick decking, still warm from the day's sun. The blue-green glow from the underwater pool lights reflected upward onto the overhanging leaves of the elm trees on the far side of the pool, giving each leaf a silvery undercoating. A dark shadow floated on the surface of the pool. At first it appeared to be a wet furry log just below the surface. She moved slowly to the pool's edge trying to make sense out of the dark object in the crystal clear shimmering water.

For a moment the image of Charlie floating unmoving with his head submerged in the pool would not register in her mind. The dog's image reached her brain, but her mind rejected the visual signal as too grotesque and awful to comprehend.

Then her mind suddenly accepted the horror of her dog floating lifeless in the pool. Cassy screamed into the night and jumped into the water. Her terry cloth robe fluffed up around her like a parachute when she hit the deep water. The wet cloth dragged her below the surface like a weighted vest. She kicked her bare feet off the bottom of the plastered pool surface, pushing herself upward to grab the dog. Her hands repeatedly slipped away. Charlie's wet fur greased her grip. In desperation she grabbed the dog's limp shaggy tail and towed him to the shallow water. Her feet bounced along the bottom of the pool until she stood in waist-high water. Charlie's lifeless eyes stared goggle-eyed at her.

Standing with her feet widely planted on the bottom of the pool with the limp dog's body in her arms, she hoisted Charlie partially over the concrete lip of the pool. But the dog's sodden weight pulled him back into the water. On the third attempt, she heaved the dog up the submerged concrete steps and pulled him onto the brick deck.

He lay dead still on his right side, water streaming from his mouth, his tongue blue and motionless. The leather collar choked the wet fur of his neck like a hangman's noose.

Laying her ear against his wet chest, Cassy heard nothing. The chest was quiet and still. No heart beat. With the heel of her right hand, she quickly pushed the dog's resilient rib cage inwards. In and out. Her arms bellowed the chest, forcing air into the dog and pumping out a squeezed beat from the arrested heart. With the first dozen pushes of her arms, foul chlorinated water spurted from Charlie's open mouth, pooling on the concrete surface in a blue-yellow stench.

"Lupita!" she screamed as loud as she could. Again and again she shouted for the maid, willing her voice into the closed window of the maid's second floor bedroom.

"Who? Why?" she shouted into the night. Tears rolled down her face. She knew the answer. Tenoch! A perverse symbol of his control over her. So intent on her massage of Charlie's chest, she did not realize that Alex, in his pajamas, and Lupita, in her polyester floral nightgown and robe, stood behind her, watching like bystanders at the scene of a street death—curious, horrified and fascinated by the quickness of death.

Cassy's arm movements became mechanical and unthinking as she pounded the dog's chest with her palms, frantically trying to squeeze life back into the animal. Her face dripped with sweat. Her eyes puffed nearly closed from crying. The wet robe hung like a body wrapping. She screamed again into the hot night, "Lupita!"

"Here I am, Señora," Lupita said quietly. Cassy looked up, seeing Lupita and Alex for the first time. The expression on Cassy's face was ugly and misshapened by the effort of her chest massage and by the fear that shrieked inside her.

Lupita put her hand on Cassy's shoulder, riding up and down with each squeeze of Charlie's chest. "He's dead, Señora," Lupita said. "El perro esta muerto."

"He killed him," Cassy said. She continued to pound the dog's chest, more in frustration than with any hope. "He killed him," she screamed and fell back on the deck holding her face in her wet hands.

Lupita pulled gently at Cassy's shoulders. "Let's go inside. You need to get dry." Slowly Cassy was able to control her sobbing and stood up. Her terry cloth robe hung like a drenched raincoat about her.

Alex disappeared in the house and returned immediately with a beach towel he draped over the dog's body. Cassy pulled her son close, hiding her face against his T-shirt pajamas. Tears streamed down his face. "Who killed Charlie, Mom?"

"I don't know," Cassy said, certain that Alex knew that she was lying. The three walked through the patio doors, not looking back at the towel-covered mound on the brick deck of the pool. The pool of green mucous water under Charlie's dead body stained the edges of the white towel that shrouded him.

When they were seated around the kitchen table, Cassy said, "I let him out an hour ago. Then I fell asleep." She continued her lies, wishing to protect her son from the horrifying reality that his dog had been brutally killed. She felt herself tremble. It had to be Tenoch's psychotic way of showing her that he controlled her and her family. But instead of telling that, she said, "Charlie must have chased the Williamsons' cat . . . he's been after him every time the cat appears in our yard. Charlie probably fell in the pool and then couldn't get out."

Suddenly and without warning Cassy jumped up from her chair and looked suspiciously at the telephone receiver, pulling at the cord, trying to tear the base plate of the phone off. "He can hear everything we say," she said in a frenzy.

Lupita looked at Cassy uncertainly as she pried at the receiver with a paring knife. Her eyes leaped about the kitchen and family room as her fear degenerated into panic.

"Lupita, lock all the doors and check all the windows. I'm going out to the back yard for a few minutes. Alex, you stay inside with Lupita," she said, her voice wild. Fear fueled her imagination, churning her abdomen with cramping waves. Cassy pulled her cellular telephone from the charger on her bedroom desk and looked through the cluttered desk drawer until she found Kevin Knowland's business card. He was her only chance. Running into the yard until she reached the shadows of an overhanging elm tree in the far corner of the yard, she dialed Kevin Knowland, reading the numbers in the radiated brightness from the yard's post lights, worried that Tenoch had even bugged her yard and could hear her every word.

Cassy sucked deep on a cigarette, shivering in the soaked terry robe despite the night heat. Kevin's voice was groggy but friendly. "Hello, Cassy. What? It's nearly midnight."

"Kevin, I'm in trouble. My dog was just killed. Tenoch's going to kill me. I've been poisoned," she said in a torrent of disconnected sentences like a hosing of cold water.

"Slow down, slow down. What happened?"

"He poisoned Charlie and drowned him. Tenoch poisoned me with the same drugs he used on Marquez."

"Cass, are you all right?" Knowland asked, now wide awake and alert.

"No, I'm not. I'm standing under an elm tree in my backyard, calling you on my cellular phone because my house and telephones are bugged. Tenoch can hear everything."

"How did Charlie die?" Kevin asked, ignoring the hysteria in Cassy's voice, refusing to acknowledge her paranoia.

"I found him floating in the swimming pool," Cassy said, slowing her words a bit. "I tried to resuscitate him, but it was too late."

"Maybe Charlie just fell in the pool and drowned," Kevin said sympathetically. "It could have been a terrible accident."

"You don't believe me!" Her voice again went shrill and high pitched. "Charlie was a good swimmer."

"Did you find any poison or anything that Charlie might have eaten?"

"No. But I know he was poisoned. . . ." Her voice broke. "I know Tenoch killed my dog. I'm sorry I ever bothered you . . . you don't believe what I'm telling you."

"Go back inside," Trent said. "Turn the security alarm on. I'll be there in fifteen minutes."

"Thank you, Kevin," she said, subdued. "I'm so scared." Flipping the phone closed in her hand, she skirted the pool and the shrouded dead dog, trying to keep her eyes away.

The air-conditioned chill of the house penetrated Cassy's wet robe, shivering her into a shaking chill. Lupita poured Cassy a mug of freshly brewed coffee and said, "Let's get you into some dry clothes."

After Cassy changed into a pair of shorts and her Texas Rangers' T-shirt, the three sat around the kitchen table. Alex sipped a hot chocolate, and Cassy held the steaming coffee mug under her nose. Her face was pinched into an angry frown.

"Who killed Charlie?" Lupita asked. Cassy shook her head, saying nothing with a gesture of her head. They sat in silence until the front gate intercom buzzed. Cassy jumped as if touched by an electric jolt and pressed the listen button of the front gate intercom. "Is that you, Kevin?" she asked.

"It's me." Cassy stabbed the remote gate switch and ran through the hallway, deactivating the intrusion alarm, releasing the dead bolts on the front door, and opening the double door just as Kevin's Chevrolet Blazer rolled to a stop.

"Jesus, you look awful," Kevin blurted as soon as he stepped out of his car. Cassy without thinking grabbed at him and pulled him to her. Her wet hair glistened in the shadows.

"My god, Cass. You're wet . . . were you in the pool with Charlie?"

Cassy nodded, holding him to her. "I'm so scared, Kevin. Tenoch is telling me that Alex is next. He will kill us both."

"Are you sure you're all right?" Kevin asked, looking at her skeptically.

Cassy pulled him into the foyer and quickly bolted the door behind Knowland. She motioned him to follow her into the hallway where she whispered in his ear. "Don't say anything yet. The house is bugged. He can hear everything we say."

"Cassy, are you all right?" Kevin asked, studying her under the hallway light.

"I'm fine," she said brusquely. "You check the house for bugs," she whispered. Cassy motioned him to follow her into the kitchen area. As soon as Lupita and Alex saw Kevin, Cassy gestured them quiet with an index finger on her lips. "Just check for bugs," she repeated her whispering into his ear. Kevin shrugged and left the three of them at the kitchen table.

Several minutes later, he returned to the kitchen and quickly disassembled the kitchen telephone. He shook his head. "I can't find any listening devices," he said in a normal conversational voice.

"Tenoch can still hear us," Cassy said, whispering into Kevin's ear. Lupita and Alex stared at Cassy, unable to hear her soft voice. "Tenoch poisoned me in Mexico City and brought me back to Dallas unconscious. The Customs people thought I was dead. Tenoch has set up an international conspiracy to black-market organs for transplantation."

"Cassy, hold on. You're not making sense. Do you realize what you're saying?" Kevin asked, disregarding her whispering.

"It's true. Tenoch will kill me and Alex," she whispered.

"Why? Can you prove it?" Kevin asked. "You've got nothing. Just a dead dog. I'm sorry, but what you're saying is not making a lot of sense."

Cassy pulled him out of the kitchen and into the hallway. "Did you bring your gun?"

"Yes," he said and patted his right hip beneath the blue blazer. "Don't you have the one I loaned you?"

"It's in my bedroom. Before I get it, I want you to go outside with me to make a telephone call. I'm afraid to be outside alone."

"Use the telephone inside the house then," Kevin said reasonably.

"No!" Cassy said, fidgeting and pulling at her T-shirt. "Tenoch can hear everything unless I use my cellular phone outside the house."

"Cassy, you've been under a lot of strain for the last week," Kevin said, trying to pull her close. Cassy resisted and pulled him through the family room and out the patio door.

In the night shadows of the elm tree in the far corner of the yard, she dialed Dr. Betty Freeman's house. "I'm calling Betty. I want her to do an autopsy on Charlie and also a toxicology screen on his blood."

Kevin reached for the telephone to take it from her. "Don't do it, Cass. Don't wake Betty up to tell her that your dog just drowned in your swimming pool. Calm down."

"He was poisoned! Betty can get the proof," she said, shaking visibly.

Kevin snapped the flip phone closed, catching her index finger in the fold up mechanism of the telephone's cover. "Wait, Cass. Just a minute. Get hold of yourself before calling Betty."

"Why?" She yanked the phone away and reopened it. The dial pad glowed and reflected a highlight into Cassy's dark eyes, made pitch black in the partial darkness under the overhanging elm. She punched in the prefix of Betty Freeman's number when Kevin wrenched the phone out of her hands.

"Stop!" Kevin said harshly. "It's the middle of the night . . . you can't even call your best friend and begin raving about someone poisoning your dog and trying to kill you and Alex. She'll think you have flipped out."

"I called you didn't I?"

"Well, yes," Kevin said and stopped. Cassy searched the darkness under the tree for Kevin's eyes until she found them in the dim light. After a moment he said, "That's different."

A male cricket in that end of the yard rubbed its wings together, chirping its nocturnal search for a mate. The thick hot night air hung stagnant under the elm tree. Cassy became aware of her rapid breathing. Her lips and fingers tingled. Her lips became numb. Consciously slowing her breathing, she felt the numbness of hyperventilation in her lips and fingers subside.

"I'm okay," she said. "I promise I won't tell Betty about my suspicions, but somehow I have to convince her to do the toxicology studies on Charlie. The toxicology results might be the evidence that you'll need."

"Maybe . . . ," Kevin said and slowly handed the cellular phone to her.

The phone rang a single time before Dr. Freeman's moist hoarseness coughed hello. Cassy explained for a minute.

"Oh shit, Cass, you want me to autopsy your dog at the coroner's laboratory because you think he's been poisoned with tetrodotoxin? Don't you think that you might be carrying this poisoning theory a little far?"

"Please. . . ." Cassy took in a deep breath and pulled the soggy package of Marlboros from the wet pocket of her robe. "I can't tell you everything right now, but if you'll do the autopsy and the toxicology tests, I'll tell you all as soon as I can. Trust me, Betty . . . please."

"All right. I'll run the toxicology and do an autopsy tomorrow on Charlie," Betty said matter-of-factly. "Stuff your dog's body in your refrigerator and bring it to the loading dock of the coroner's office in the morning. And for god's sake, don't tell anybody at the lab or anywhere else that you're bringing in your dead pet for me to do an autopsy. I'm going to have to call in some mighty big favors to slip this little veterinary project past the Chief Coroner."

"Is that really necessary?" Cassy asked. "I mean . . . to put Charlie in the refrigerator?"

"If you want me to do the autopsy, you're going to have to keep the body cold."

"All right," Cassy said and flipped the cellular telephone closed. Kevin's face was shadowed by an overhanging elm branch so that Cassy could not read his expression.

"Let's go inside," he said, taking her by the hand and leading her to the house in a direction that avoided Charlie's body. The silence of the rear grounds was broken only by the frying incineration of a hapless insect, flying into the electronic bug zapper at the far corner of the patio. Kevin closed and locked the patio door.

Cassy could not stand the silence any longer and said, "You don't believe me!"

"I've got to know more," Kevin said. "I know how you must feel about your dog, but I need more information. I'll begin looking for more tomorrow. But now it's time that you got some rest."

"I know what I know," Cassy said. "Killing Charlie is Tenoch's crazy way of sending a signal that he controls me. Tenoch is going to kill Alex and me."

"Cassy, easy . . . easy," Kevin said, reaching to take her trembling hands. "I'll stay here with you for the rest of the night."

"You think I'm obsessed with Tenoch?" Cassy asked. She couldn't turn off her words. Not even waiting for a response, she rushed on, the words spurting out. "He's going to kill me, I know." Kevin looked at her for several moments until Cassy wished that she could grab back the words. "Tenoch poisoned me on Sunday just like he poisoned Marquez and Charlie."

"You're stressed out," Kevin said. He pulled her in closer to him. "Should we have someone see you? Maybe you need a tranquilizer."

"Kevin, just say you don't believe me. Go ahead and tell me that I need to see a psychiatrist. You're like all the rest . . . you think I've gone over the edge."

"I'm only trying to help," he said and held her shaking body until she finally quieted down.

"I don't need a psychiatrist. I know what happened to me this weekend. Tenoch drugged me with the organ donor drugs that Trent Hendricks has discovered in his research lab," Cassy whispered in his ear before pushing him back. "I need a cigarette. Then I'll tell you the whole story so that you'll understand."

"We could go back outside," Kevin suggested.

After finding a rumpled package of cigarettes in her bedroom, she and Kevin went outside and sat on the grass at the rear of the grounds, hidden by the evergreen bushes and the vines curling up around and over the wall. Cassy smoked and talked. She told him everything about the weekend in Mexico City with the exception of her responses to the iced tea and what followed in Tenoch's bedroom. And she could not bring herself to say the name Ana Ruiz.

When Cassy had run out of words, they sat together like two adolescents on a summer night watching the starlit sky. Neither said a word. Finally Kevin let out his breath. "You need some rest." He stood up and took her hand, pulling her upright.

They retraced their steps toward the patio. Cassy saw the towel-draped body of Charlie across the glowing pool surface, and she turned her head into Kevin's shoulder. The heaving sobs convulsed her, tears of grief for Charlie but more of fear for Alex and herself.

Eventually Cassy was able to ask, "Would you take care of Charlie? Betty told me to keep Charlie refrigerated until in the morning. I'm just not up to putting him in the refrigerator."

"In your kitchen? A dead dog in your refrigerator?" Kevin asked, his face had become a horrified mask at the idea of the wet dog stuffed into her Sub-Zero refrigerator.

"No. No. We have an old spare refrigerator in the garage. It holds cokes and bottles of wine. That's all. Charlie should fit there."

—

Sleep was not restful when it eventually came for Cassy at three forty-five. She fidgeted in her sleep throughout the rest of the night until a light tapping at her bedroom door brought her slowly awake. The glowing red digits of the bedside clock read 8:20. Cassy threw aside the sheet, shook down the T-shirt around her waist, and edged the bedroom door open.

"Good morning." Kevin's voice came from around the partially open door. The rich aroma of freshly brewed coffee wafted into her bedroom. Kevin's hand holding a steaming mug of coffee reached through the crack in the door. She immediately pulled the door open and took the hot mug.

They exchanged appraising glances, Kevin seeing Cassy standing in the rumpled T-shirt sipping at the coffee mug held in both hands, Cassy seeing a stubble-faced man in a wrinkled denim shirt with a holstered nine millimeter pistol on his hip. Kevin smiled at her. "You look better this morning."

Without thinking, Cassy reached to touch his whiskered face. "Were you able to get any sleep at all on the sofa?"

"A little bit." He rubbed his unshaven face. "I must look gross."

"You're welcome to shower," Cassy said, nodding toward her dressing room.

"Thanks but no," Kevin said. "I'm going home to change clothes. I'll take your dog to Betty Freeman's on my way to the office."

"Thanks for everything," Cassy said, kissing him lightly on his lips.

"Glad to," Kevin said dismissively, seeming flustered by her gratefulness.

"Did Alex say anything about last night?" Cassy asked.

"No. Not a word. It's as if nothing happened." Kevin paused and continued. "You need to go be with your son. He's already in the kitchen. He and I had some toast and jelly earlier."

Kevin backed from the bedroom, and Cassy followed him into the hallway. "You need to call Dr. Walter Simmons," he said as an afterthought. "He called at seven this morning. Wanted me to wake you up right then."

"I must have been dead asleep not to hear the phone," Cassy said.

"I caught it on the first ring," Kevin said. "He wants you in his office tomorrow at ten. The federal drug agents will be there then."

Cassy shook her head, discouraged because she knew what was coming—a full scale investigation of her medication prescribing practices.

Kevin stopped at the arched doorway to the kitchen, "Anything I can help you with?"

"No, thanks," Cassy said, shrugging and smiling at the same time.

"Your housekeeper and Alex should stay in the house all day with the doors locked. I'll have a patrol car check on them."

"Now you believe me?"

"I believe your dog drowned. I believe Marquez died when he hit the concrete driveway in front of the Metro Hospital. That's about all I believe for sure."

"Well, I believe a lot more for sure," Cassy said.

"But all you can prove is that your dog is dead and Marquez is dead," Kevin said.

"I'll see what Betty Freeman says about my dog's cause of death. Maybe she'll be able to tell us something about Marquez's Saturday night toxicology report soon," Cassy said softly, reaching up to talk into Kevin's ear.

"Cassy. Stop it. You don't need to whisper. There are no listening bugs in this house. I checked last night."

"You should have them check on an Ana Ruiz. There should be a missing child report in Mexico City last week . . . about thirteen years old," Cassy said, whispering in his ear.

"What are you talking about? Who in the hell is Ana Ruiz?"

She put her finger to her lips and whispered again in his ear. "Ana Ruiz. You find out who she was, and you will know that I am not imagining all this."

"What does Ana Ruiz have to do with this?" Kevin asked in a normal conversational voice. Cassy quickly put her index finger up to his lips to quiet him. He continued in a whisper, "Why didn't you tell me about Ruiz last night?"

"I can't tell you. I just can't. She's the proof you need," Cassy whispered, leading him out of the front door.

"Cassy, you've got to tell me everything you know. I can't help you unless you come clean."

"That's all I can tell you right now," she said and closed the front door, leaving Kevin standing under the porte cochere, a bewildered frown on his face. Inside Cassy collapsed against the closed front door. Last night sitting in the yard with Kevin, she had intentionally left certain holes in her story—the iced tea, Tenoch's bedroom, and Ana Ruiz. Why had the name, Ana Ruiz, come out of her so quickly this morning? Cassy couldn't answer her own question.

With a mug of coffee, she slid into the chair opposite her son at the kitchen table. His concentration stayed on the sports page of the *Dallas Morning News*. "Alex, I'm sorry about Charlie." The boy didn't look up.

"T-That's a-all r-right, Mom," he stuttered. It was the first time that her son had stuttered in a conversation with her in months.

THIRTY

JAQUETA TORRES sat crosslegged on the dirt floor of the mud and
cardboard hovel on the hillside near Mexico City. Her two squawl-
ing infant daughters lay in cardboard box cribs in front of her. Little
air moved in the midday. Sweat rolled from the young woman's face
in the overheated room. A shaft of noon sun shone through the open
door onto the hardpacked dirt floor. With a fork Jaqueta mashed together
powdered milk, water, and mashed red beans to make a food paste.

Then she spooned the paste into her babies' mouths, first one then the
other. In the corner of the room stood a pink plaster bowl of water, a tat-
tered terry cloth rag hanging over its lip. After every few bites of the
brown paste she dipped the end of the rag into the water, wiping and
cooling each baby's face, letting each infant suckle the twisted end of the
moist rag. When the baby food paste was eaten, Jaqueta brought the
youngest child, five-month-old Maria, to her breast, letting her suckle at
her breast until it was her sixteen-month-old sister's turn to suckle the
other breast.

Jaqueta looked up to see her mother, a skeletal woman hunched forward like a crone. "Has Juan come back?" Jaqueta's mother asked, her
leathery wrinkled brown face scrunched into a perpetual frown.

"No, Mama."

"He's gone . . . just like they all do. Just like your papa did . . . go
north."

"No, Mama," Jaqueta said. "Juan wouldn't leave without me and the
girls. He's going to be a driver for a rich man. He went to see the man
this morning. Juan will earn enough to move all of us to a Mexico City

apartment with a real floor, running water, and a toilet. We won't have to carry our drinking water from the faucet. We won't have to use the ground for our toilet."

The mother shook her head and shuffled away toward another one-room burrow, a few steps away.

———

"Mom, what's wrong? Why are you crying?"

Red spider veins skeined the whites of Cassy's puffy eyes. "I'm fine," she said and turned away from the kitchen island. "You had lunch?" she finally asked, wiping her eyes on a dish towel. Alex shook his head. "I'm making us a real homemade pizza." Cassy arranged the cheese and pepperoni slices on the frozen pizza dough. Alex sat on the high bar stool next to the wood chopping block counter, watching.

"Why do I have to stay inside today?"

"It's what Lt. Knowland told us to do."

"Did somebody kill Charlie?" Alex asked.

"I don't know," Cassy said.

"Is that the reason you have Kevin's gun?"

"Yes. Now go wash up for dinner," Cassy said, hoping to divert her son's attention.

Less than an hour later the bubbling pizza filled the kitchen with smells of hot cheese. Cassy's fingers trembled in a fine tremor when she reached to take the pizza from the oven. The ring of the kitchen telephone startled her just as she lifted the flat aluminum tray out of the oven, causing her to bump her forearm against the hot oven grill. The burning pain on the undersurface of her forearm sent a fiery shock up her arm. She dropped the pizza pan back onto the oven rack.

"Hello!" Cassy shouted into the telephone. An angry red welt branded her forearm.

"Cassy, is that you?" a man's voice asked in Spanish. She stuck her forearm under the running cold water as she cradled the telephone receiver against her neck and shoulder.

"Sí."

"This is Raul. Are you all right? You don't sound like yourself," he asked.

"Hi, Raul," Cassy said. "No, I'm fine. I just burned my arm on the oven."

"I'm sorry, Cass," Raul said perfunctorily. The bewildered stunned look on Garcia's face as they stood under the gold domed chandelier in the Tenoch's grand salon flashed in Cassy's mind.

"It's about our conversation Saturday night."

"Yes, Raul, there is a problem," Cassy interrupted.

"Do you understand the extent of the problem?"

"I'm afraid I do . . . ," Cassy said softly. "I can't talk about it right now."

"We must talk."

"I can't . . . ," Cassy said. Cassy rubbed her forehead, trying to rub out the pounding headache that blurred her vision.

"Raul, I must call you back," she said quickly.

Raul persisted, his tone now stern and insistent. "I will expect to hear from you within the hour." He gave her the number of his cellular phone in Mexico City.

—

When Cassy hung up the kitchen phone, Raul Garcia, a thousand miles away, looked across the Mexico City restaurant table at his son, Roberto, thirty-two years younger than his father. The only physical difference between the two men was the younger Garcia's hairline had not yet receded into the smooth brown dome of his father's head. Both men's eyes wore the same heavy-lidded sadness coming with prolonged observation of human misery and suffering—the father as a physician and the son as an investigative reporter for a Mexico City newspaper.

"She will call back in less than an hour," Raul told his son.

—

Cassy sat with Alex at the kitchen table and together they finished off the pizza. Then she put the dishes in the sink. "I'll be out by the pool for a little while," she said to Alex.

Under the elm tree in the far corner of the yard Cassy punched the flip phone keypads for Raul's telephone number that she read from her scribbled notepaper. The phone rang a single time before Dr. Garcia answered. The connection was as clear as if Cassy had been calling into her home and not to a restaurant table in Mexico City.

"Cassy!" Raul snapped. "Are you aware of what situation you are involved in?"

"Oh, yes," Cassy said.

Raul Garcia exhaled across the thousand miles. "I know who Ana Ruiz was . . . a thirteen-year-old Mexican girl who vanished from her family in Mexico City the day before Heather Hendricks' heart transplant. There was no auto accident. She disappeared from the lost city. She was never a patient at the Instituto de Medico."

"I know about Ana Ruiz," Cassy said quietly.

The phone connection went silent. At last Dr. Garcia said, "I'm going to the police."

"You must not . . . Tenoch will kill you," Cassy said, walking behind the elm tree until the trunk hid her from the view of the house.

"Cassy, I've known you for many years. Never in a hundred years would I have thought you would be involved in these terrible things . . . kidnapping, murder, selling of organs. It saddens my heart to go to the authorities . . . after all you have done for our country . . . for the Mexican children."

"Wait . . . wait. Raul, you don't understand," Cassy broke in. "Believe me . . . please . . . I beg you. I'm not involved with Tenoch. Give me another day or two . . . let me talk to Tenoch some more. I can make him understand . . . he will stop this insanity."

"What about Ana Ruiz . . . her family? They deserve better. What will they learn about their daughter?"

"Be careful, Raul," she said. "Please . . . give me two more days. I promise you there will be no more heart donors like Ana Ruiz . . . I promise you."

"Cassy, I must step forward. This goes beyond Ana Ruiz," Garcia said. "For months my son has been telling me of news reports that he has been receiving at his newspaper of a black market in transplant donor organs in Mexico and South America." Raul paused and looked across the table at his son, the residue of their lunch being tidied away by the waiter while he refilled their coffee cups. Raul Garcia flipped through a manila folder containing an inch of newspaper clippings, handwritten notes, and typed reports. "I have my son's file in front of me."

"Mom, where are you?" Alex's voice shouted across the yard, interrupting Cassy's concentration. "Mr. Tenoch is on the telephone," Alex shouted. Cassy peeked around the tree trunk, still hiding her profile. Alex stood by the pool, looking around the acre of landscaped backyard, searching for his mother. "Mom," he shouted again.

"Raul, I must hang up. Tenoch is calling on the other line. I've got to talk to him. Trust me, please, Raul. Give me two days before you notify the police. Believe me, I'm not part of Tenoch's conspiracy . . . I never will be. Give me two days . . . just two days. I won't let him hurt anyone else."

"Cass, he might hurt you. If this is as bad as my son believes, Tenoch is behind all these reports of kidnapping and organ snatching."

"Please, just a little time. I'll get the evidence that you will need. If you don't let me get some hard proof, Tenoch will walk away from this untouched."

"If it were anyone but you, I wouldn't. Out of my great respect for you, I'll hold off two days. No later than Wednesday at noon I will go to the police."

"Thank you, Raul. I'll call you the minute I have what you need."

"Be careful, Cass," Raul said. Cassy snapped the flip phone closed and ran for the patio door. "Alex. Here I am. Don't hang up on Señor Tenoch," Cassy shouted across the yard as Alex disappeared into the family room.

She grabbed the kitchen phone. "Good afternoon, Cassy." Tenoch's pleasant voice filtered through the receiver. "The donor harvest will begin at Park Haven at seven p.m."

"You will procure the heart, and Trent will implant the heart at the Metro Hospital."

"I can't," Cassy said. She stood impaled by Tenoch's voice.

"You have no choice." Tenoch's voice, smooth and soft, eased through the phone. "The donor harvest will commence at seven o'clock."

Her face paled. Her hands trembled. Her voice cracked. "I will be there." The phone clicked in her ear.

—

Cassy carried her cellular phone back out to the patio. When she reached the far corner of the rear yard, she sat under the elm tree shielded from the late afternoon sun by its slumping branches. For a long time she brooded, smoking one cigarette after another, trying to sort through a plan for the evening. Finally she punched in Trent Hendricks' telephone number on the cellular phone. Trent's secretary connected her through immediately.

Her voice was wobbly and shaky. "The harvest is scheduled for seven. I don't know what to do. . . ."

Before Trent could respond a single explosive clap burst from the second floor of the house. Cassy stopped in midsentence, followed by silence. The birds in the elms stopped singing. Nothing. No sound.

"My god," Cassy screamed, dropping the telephone in the grass and running to the patio door. The aroma of melting cheese breezed past her in the kitchen. She ran into the hallway screaming, "Alex! Alex!", and leaped the staircase, two steps at a time. At the top, she paused for an instant, listening to the silence. Her panting brought a burning acrid odor of spent gunpowder to her nose.

Cassy burst into Alex's room. Her shoulder sent the door hard onto its stop. "Alex!" The room was empty and quiet. The smell of burnt gunpowder replaced the air in the room, suffocating her. The video monitor screen was a dark hole, imploded into thousands of shards, scattered like glass petals on the desk top. Kevin Knowland's pistol lay in the center of her son's rumpled bed.

"Alex!" Cassy screamed, spinning about the silent room looking for her son. The room blurred before her. She continued howling in a frenzy until she stumbled back into the hallway, shaking violently. "Alex! Alex!" she whimpered as she collapsed on the hallway floor. Her overloaded mind stopped, frozen like a jammed videocassette. She hunched forward on the floor. Slowly her son's voice pulled her to a hazy awareness.

"Mom, wake up . . . wake up!" Her son's worried voice called from a distant fog in her mind.

"Alex. Is that you?" Cassy asked, reaching to touch the blurred image of her son somewhere in the vicinity of his voice. Her fingers found his cheek. Like a blind person she reached both hands forward, tracing the features of his face. Gradually his blurred face focused before her eyes.

"I'm sorry, Mom." His eyes were swollen and wet, his long dark lashes sticking together. "I didn't think the gun was loaded."

Cassy couldn't say a word. The mixture of relief, anger, and happiness flooded her. She rocked back and forth with Alex held tight against her. They held onto each other until finally Cassy whispered in Alex's ear, "We're getting out of here."

"Where are we going?" Alex whispered.

"Shush," Cassy said, holding her index finger on his lips. "He can hear everything we say. We'll leave this evening."

"Where are we going?"

"I don't know. Just away from here."

Cassy pushed herself up from the hallway floor and walked into Alex's room. She picked the pistol off the bed and flipped the safety lever. The cartridge clip was still in place as she had left it. She placed the pistol, loaded and ready, in her pocket.

Trent's voice suddenly erupted through the house. "Cassy!" Fear shook his voice.

"We're up here," she said, leaning out Alex's bedroom door and calling downstairs.

"What the hell is going on?" Trent shouted. Relief deflated his trembling voice.

"An accident. No one hurt except Alex's computer screen."

At the top of the stairwell, Trent pulled Cassy into his arms, suddenly and impulsively. "Cass. What are we going to do?" he whispered.

She pulled back from him. "Let's go outside," she said softly into his ear.

Trent, looking ten years older than a week ago, followed her into the far corner of the grounds where Cassy found the cellular telephone in the grass. She flipped it closed and dropped it in her pants pocket.

"Alex and I are leaving. We've got to get away from him."

Trent looked at her, the late afternoon accentuating his flushed appearance. "He'll find you wherever you run. We have to go ahead with tonight's transplant. If you run now, you and Alex won't have a chance."

—

The waiter at the Laredo restaurant in the Polonco district of Mexico City discreetly presented the check and withdrew to the edge of the room while Raul Garcia and his son lingered over their coffee.

"Waiting is no good, Dad. I've seen these reports come across my desk for months . . . stolen corneas, missing kidneys, disappearing children. It all makes sense now. Tenoch has to be behind these reports."

"We must do nothing for two days, Roberto," the father said. "I promised Cassy. We must give her a chance."

"No, we must move forward now." The son reached for the check and flipped his American Express card onto the silver plate.

"Cassy asked for two days. She promised no more heart donors during that forty-eight hours. It's the best we can do. If we rush in now, we may lose the chance to get the evidence we need. He is a clever and powerful man. He can buy whoever he wants. We must be cautious."

THIRTY-ONE

A FLY CRAWLED slowly across the sleeping baby's face. Its spidery legs tracked in the dried bean paste crust around the infant's gaping mouth. Hot stale air in the one-room hut roasted the mother and two infants as they napped in a traditional siesta.

The sleeping infant rolled its head in the cardboard crib. The startled fly, the size of a bee, darted from the infant's face to land on the sleeping face of Jaqueta Torres. A dribble of spittle streamed from her lip, miring the insect's legs. She unconsciously flipped the fly away, and it flew out the open door into the suffocating hillside shantytown. Jaqueta's mother, a time-shriveled image of her daughter, ducked into the doorway.

"Jaqueta," she whispered. The two infants in the cardboard boxes stirred but did not awaken. Jaqueta's eyes blinked open. "Your husband home?"

"No, Mama," Jaqueta said, raising her head up and propping herself on an elbow.

"I told you. The men, they are alike. He has gone north to cross the border."

"Tomorrow, if he does not come, I will see Father Tulio."

"What good will a priest be? Who can blame the men?" the old woman asked, her voice waking both babies. The screaming of the infants reverberated in the closeness of the small room.

The manicured cemetery swept away from the gray marbled Park Haven Funeral Home at the center of a statuary community of Dallas generations past. The setting sun, the only visible movement among the acres of graves, cast lengthening shadows among the headstones. A squadron of matching gray hearses and limousines stood in the funeral home's deserted parking lot, ready to deliver newly dead citizens into this perpetual community, night and day.

Just before seven o'clock that evening Cassy pulled her Range Rover adjacent to the marbled building that served as the center of the cemetery, a reception hall for the recently dead. The dark green double doors of the marble mortuary stood half open and yielded easily to Cassy's touch, beckoning her in. Urns of lilies ringed the lobby. Wall sconces cast half cones of light up the walls. Directly behind the entry door and across the lobby, an archway led into a dark vaulted sanctuary. A geometric stained-glass mural framed the far wall of the church-like auditorium. Dark polished wood pews partially circled an empty black marble bier.

Cassy's rubber-soled jogging shoes squeaked across the empty lobby as she walked slowly toward the sanctuary. In the darkness of the sanctuary the faint chorus of *Amazing Grace* played in her mind. The sound of stone grating against stone from the far end of the lobby caused her to turn in time to see the wall panel sliding open.

"Hello, Cassandra." Tenoch's baritone voice echoed out of the black opening that had appeared in the marble wall. A raw shivering possessed her at the sound of his voice. Tenoch stepped across the threshold into the sanctuary. His dark skin and black hair contrasted sharply with the gleaming white cloth of his starched surgical scrub shirt and pants. His skin glistened as if oiled.

"Come. It is time," Tenoch said, extending his hand to Cassy and gently pulling her across the marble threshold into the dark passageway. The marble door slid closed behind her. Several steps down the dark corridor, another marble slab slid open. Guided by Tenoch's hand on her forearm, she followed him down marble steps to another closed marble door that opened the moment Tenoch reached it.

Cassy jerked back from Tenoch's hand, momentarily staggered by the large domed room, a precise copy of the cardiac surgical suite at the Metro Hospital. The terrazzo tile floor, an exact texture replicate of the Metro OR floor, glistened with light from four inverted aluminum cones focused on a surgical operating table in the center of the room. An anesthesia console, the vital sign video monitoring display, the overhead metal tubes for anesthetic gases and oxygen—all were painstaking duplicates of the Metro Hospital OR.

Tenoch stopped at the left side of a surgical table mounted on a hydraulic pedestal in the tile floor. A muscular Hispanic man lay serene and perfectly still on the operating table beneath a white sheet folded neatly back just below his broad shoulders. A paleness leeched color from the dark skin of his acne-scarred face. His bushy black moustache sagged above the man's slack, open mouth.

Tenoch spoke, but Cassy's mind could not find meaning for his words. Her concentration focused on the naked man lying on the operating table—trying to place him in her mind. Where or when had she seen him?

Cassy stared at the moustache—thick and exuberant, covering the young man's upper lip and drooping in a tapered curl at the corner of his open, O-shaped mouth. Cassy's subconscious mind began picking up the subliminal pieces. Perhaps it was the combination of the luxuriant ebony moustache combined with the youthful, acne-pocked face of the Hispanic teenager that hooked her subconscious memory, waiting to be triggered into her awareness. Suddenly the man's identity sprang forth into her consciousness—the taxi driver in Mexico City Friday evening when Alberto stopped the Mercedes at the traffic light on the Plaza de la Reforma just before she saw the Mexican street performer blowing flaming kerosene from his mouth. Yes! Yes! She was sure this man was the turismo driver carrying the American businessman passenger. She looked up at Tenoch to comprehend his last word, ". . . offering."

Cassy stood on the right side of the table staring across the still body of Juan Torres at Tenoch's flat black eyes. "Offering?" Cassy asked.

"Call him what you want," slurred Walter Simmons, seated at the head of the operating table in the usual position of the anesthesiologist. A surgeon's hood and mask covered his face like an executioner's hood. "You can call him a donor," Simmons said. "I'll call him a patient. Tenoch calls him an offering. Somebody else can call him a victim. Who the hell cares? It won't make any difference to Juan Torres." Simmons stood up from the stool and bumped against the sterile tray of surgical instruments on a sterile serving board at the foot of the operating table.

The odor of bourbon, cigarettes, and cologne radiated invisible waves from him. His closeness disgusted her. "Walter, you aren't in any condition to be anywhere but a bar," Cassy said, staring at his watery bloodshot eyes.

Simmons took one unsteady step toward her before Tenoch stepped between them. "Sit down, Walter," Tenoch said. "Your responsibility is to administer the Hiberna, nothing else." With a grunt Simmons collapsed heavily back on the metal stool.

The green phosphorescent line traced continuously on the video monitor screen above the surgical table, displaying the Hispanic man's flat-line electrocardiogram, broken by an occasional luminescent blip every eight to ten seconds. Tenoch turned to Cassy. "You may begin," he said, his voice calm and soothing as a priest at confession.

Cassy moved in close to the body and touched the shoulder of the young man. His supple shoulder muscles kneaded firmly under her finger tips. The expressionless immobile face of the man gave no hint of life.

"How did this man die?" she asked, standing back a couple of steps from the table. "There's no sign of injury."

"Massive cerebral hemorrhage," Walter Simmons said, pulling himself upright by the edge of the surgical table.

"I want to see the medical record," Cassy said.

"Of course." Tenoch nodded to Alberto who retrieved Tenoch's leather briefcase from the corner of the room. Alberto snapped open the case and withdrew an inch of papers bound neatly with a metal hasp. "It's all in there," Tenoch said cheerfully. "Every kind of documentation for the donor. Hospital records from the Instituto de Medico, Declaration of Brain Death, Consent Form. Whatever you should require."

Cassy flipped through the records. The typed summary in compressed medical terminology described the man on the table. A twenty-two-year-old Mexico City taxi driver.

Cassy flipped through the pages quickly, reading aloud from the chart. "Everything seems in order for this donor. CT scan shows a massive cerebral infarction. EEG is flat-lined with no electrical activity. Cardiovascular status is stable. Heart rhythm is slow sinus bradycardia with no myocardial injury pattern. Consent forms are signed by his mother. The diagnosis of brain death is certified by Dr. Garcia's signature. These records are perfect. Just like Ana Ruiz," Cassy said.

"Cassy, you are not to question the medical record," Dr. Simmons slurred. "These papers document the brain death of Juan Torres from Mexico City. Your job is to harvest the heart."

"I won't. This is crazy. I won't do it."

"Yes, you will, carina mía. It is your destiny," Tenoch said casually from his side of the table. Cassy looked fleetingly about the perimeter of the room. In each of the four corners of the domed operating room, young Hispanic men in gray surgical scrubs stood at attention. Surgical masks and hoods obscured their faces and heads except for identical pairs of deep unresponsive brown eyes. Each man's waistband held a holstered pistol.

"You will consecrate the Aztec gods," Tenoch said. His hard, hollow, slow-paced voice came from behind the surgical mask. A fearsome light had entered Tenoch's eyes, and Cassy saw a madness that filled her with terror. It was a look into Tenoch's soul, and she saw nothing there.

"You will do as I command . . . ," Tenoch said in the same hollow timbre, devoid of all humanity.

But Cassy could not do what he commanded. She knew that the man on the table was not dead. She would not be fooled a second time into declaring a patient dead when he was alive. She would not remove this man's heart. She could not.

"For god's sake, Cassy," Simmons said. "What more do you want? This Mexican is brain dead. The records prove he is legally dead."

"Then why am I in a funeral home harvesting this donor?" Cassy asked. "Why aren't we at the Metro Hospital harvesting this heart? I can't be a part of this."

"You will obey," Tenoch said. The deliberate, slow cadence of his voice made Cassy's heart jump, and she felt the jittery release of adrenaline. Cassy turned to look at Tenoch, standing across the table. His eyes had become black obsidian stones.

Simmons staggered around the head of the table, pulling Cassy a few feet to the side. "Christ, Cassy, don't cross Tenoch," Simmons whispered. "Of course the donor's alive. His metabolism has been suspended with Trent's Hiberna organ preservation mixture." Simmons pulled up a vial of tan powder from the lowest cabinet drawer in the anesthetic console and waved the vial of tan granulated powder in her face. "Harvest the goddamn heart, or Tenoch will use this Hiberna shit on you and your son. He's crazy. Don't get in his way or your son will be laid out on this operating table like this Mexican."

"Begin," Tenoch commanded. His hollow voice completely immobilized Cassy.

"I can't. I won't. The donor is not dead. His brain is alive. You've drugged him," Cassy stammered, retreating from the OR table and stumbling backward toward the door. "This man is still alive, just like me, just like Marquez, just like Ana Ruiz."

Tenoch nodded without changing the flat expression of his eyes. Instantly two of the young guards at the perimeter of the room leaped forward and jerked her back to the OR table.

Tenoch moved slowly around the table toward her and stretched his left hand out. The obsidian ring on his left index finger glistened in the glare of the four surgical lights. Alberto thrust an obsidian ceremonial Aztec knife into Tenoch's outstretched hand. "You give me no alternative, Cassandra," he said, now back in his normal, amiable conversational tone.

He moved further around the OR table, closer to her and stopped at her side. The obsidian knife handle spun in his hand as he raised his arm above his head. The knife hovered at the top of the arc of his arm. Sparkling green glints reflected off the blade's cobbled surface from the surgical lights. The two guards squeezed Cassy's arms holding her tightly at the table. Cassy screamed as Tenoch's arm began its descent.

His arm swung downward, plunging the Aztec obsidian blade up to its handle into the closed left eye of Juan Torres. The man's body remained motionless as dark venous blood oozed around the embedded handle. Clear gelatinous fluid from the punctured eyeball mixed with blood to flow over the left side of the man's face and pool on the green sheet beneath his head.

The room spun in a dizzying whir in front of Cassy, and she retched acid bile into her surgical mask. Vomit pooled in the pouch formed by the mask in front of her lips.

"You may now begin," Tenoch said. His voice was pleasant and smooth as a priest.

"Use the Aztec knife," Tenoch said. Alberto handed a towel-wrapped package to a surgical technician who unwrapped the sterile covering and placed an obsidian ceremonial knife on the sterile surgical tray.

Cassy jerked off the vomit-soaked surgical mask and tried to back away from the surgical table again. The guards grabbed her arms once more and pushed her forward. Simmons lurched around the end of the table.

Simmons stuck his face near Cassy's. The sour odor of her vomitus filled the mask that still hung around her neck. Simmon's rancid breath provoked another wave of nausea and retching from Cassy, doubling her over the table. Cassy's hands grabbed the edge of the operating table preventing her collapse onto the terrazo floor. Dribbles of vomit hit the floor.

"You bitch," Simmons hissed. "Do anything to screw up this deal, and you'll never see your little boy alive again. He'll be in the bottom of your goddamn swimming pool just like your fucking dog!"

"Leave me alone, Walter. Leave me alone," Cassy said, shaking violently. "I'm sick."

"I don't give a goddamn. Cut out the fucking heart!"

"Give me a couple of minutes . . . please . . . then I'll get it," she said looking at Tenoch.

"Certainly," Tenoch said, now in his pleasant conversational tone. "Has the donor's brain death satisfied you?" He threw back his head and laughed for a long moment. Then he stood calm and quiet at the side of the table, a blissful smile softening the harshness of his eyes.

Another wave of nausea rushed her stomach. Cassy ran from the room to the scrub sink alcove just as she vomited more hot yellowish green water into the surgical sink. A crushing weakness bore down on her. She was barely able to wash her face.

Cassy knew that she must go forward with the surgical procurement of the donor heart. There was no alternative. If she did not harvest the heart she knew Alex would be taken from her forever. He would vanish.

Cassy tied a fresh surgical mask on her face and scrubbed her arms and hands with a surgical brush. The obsidian knife remained embedded in the socket of the man's left eye, skewering Juan Torres' brain. For an absolute certainty, the Hispanic donor was now brain-dead. The long ceremonial knife had severed the man's brain stem.

Tenoch stood unmoved in the same location by the OR table, his eyes closed as if serenely meditating. A surgical mask and hood hid his face. Cassy slipped on a surgical gown and thrust her hands into the latex surgeon's gloves.

Tenoch opened his eyes and nodded benignly. He raised his hands as if in a sacerdotal blessing. "You may begin." His hollow voice resounded in the closed room. Cassy held her hand out, and the scrub technician slapped the sterile, ancient obsidian knife into her hand. Cassy then drew the blade downward in the midline of the donor's chest between his nipples, as she had done thousands of times for heart surgical procedures.

After sawing through the breast bone, Cassy's hands entered Torres' chest and dissected the beating heart with the ceremonial knife. Even though the irregular cobbled surface of the obsidian blade gave the appearance of a crude instrument, the keen edge of the knife performed as well as a modern surgical scalpel in dividing the tissues surrounding the man's heart to expose the organ. With deft motions of her fingers controlling the obsidian knife, Cassy severed the heart's blood vessel connections and pulled out the heart through the incision.

"Thus, he giveth the sun to drink," Tenoch said, taking Torres' heart from Cassy's hands. He held the heart high above him in his extended arms allowing the residual blood within the heart to dribble onto his white surgical clothes. "I accept the bounty of life." Then Tenoch returned the heart to Cassy's trembling hands.

The man has no reality base, Cassy realized. He's changing back and forth from delusion to reality. She now was certain that eventually he would kill Alex and her and rip their hearts out, just like all the others.

Mechanically turning back to the task of preparing the donor heart, she rinsed the surface and the interior of the heart with an iced saline solution before dropping it into a transparent plastic bag. Then she placed a second outer protective bag around the first bag and lastly positioned both drawstringed bags onto a bed of icy slush in an ordinary insulated

Igloo ice chest. Cassy shrugged off her surgical gown and ripped off the mask.

Simmons lifted the Igloo ice chest from the terrazzo floor and patted the side of the container and said to Tenoch, "Another five hundred thousand dollar heart."

In disgust Cassy turned back to the body on the table with the blade still embedded through the closed eyelid. The gaping incision in the man's chest scorned Cassy. She quickly slipped on another pair of latex surgical gloves to begin to close the incision with the care and dignity she used for a living patient.

"Forget the goddamn body," Simmons said gruffly. "My men will have it in the oven before the donor heart even reaches the hospital." He sat on the metal anesthesiologist's stool and studied Cassy through his red wet eyes. "Good work, Cass. Glad you're part of the team now." She continued to close the incision, ignoring him.

Moments later Tenoch reappeared in the operating room in a flowing black silk shirt and pants. "May I have a word with you, Walter," Tenoch said in his agreeable conversational voice. The two men huddled together just outside the OR in the surgical scrub alcove.

When they returned to the operating room, Tenoch gently placed his hands on both Cassy's shoulders and kissed her cheek. Whispering in her ear, he said, "Carina mía, our destiny is together."

After Tenoch and his entourage swept out of the OR with Alberto carrying the ice chest containing Torres' heart, Simmons grasped Cassy's arm, holding her at the door. "You stay with me," Simmons said gruffly.

⸻

In Jeorg Marquez's office at the funeral home, Cassy sat crumpled on the corner of the leather sofa, her feet and legs coiled under her. Her surgeon's mask dangled at her neck. A half cup of black coffee rested on the gleaming hardwood floor next to her hand that had dropped in exhaustion.

Simmons leaned over her, a glass of bourbon and ice in his hand. Cassy felt his rancid breath on her cheek. She waved him away and shook her head. "Don't even think of telling anyone about our donor procurement deal," Simmons said softly. For a moment she felt as if she would vomit on the oriental rug.

Cassy kept her eyes closed. "Let me give you some advice. Tenoch has the hots for you. If you'll just keep your mouth shut, life will be easy. All your problems will disappear."

Cassy listened to ice rattle in the glass and knew by the odor of cigarettes and whiskey that Simmons still stood over her. She kept her eyes squeezed shut. "Tenoch wanted me to keep you here until your mind was right," Simmons said. He drank half the bourbon in his glass in a gulp.

An armed guard in gray surgical scrub clothes stood impassively at the door. Simmons barked at the guard, "Get the fuck out of here." The guard hesitated. "Get out of here, or Tenoch will hear from me." The guard quickly disappeared from the office, pulling the door closed after him. Simmons walked back toward the sofa and looked down at Cassy. She lay limp and wilted with her eyes closed. He finished off his whiskey and bent over her.

"You liked fucking Tenoch Saturday night," Simmons said, his sour breath poured over Cassy's face. She opened her eyes to see Simmons leaning over her, undoing the drawstring of his scrub pants. "I'll give you something else to remember from this night."

Cassy struggled upright on her elbows. Simmons threw himself on top of her. She could not wiggle free of his weight. He slapped her cheek with his hand. Cassy thrust her leg upward between his straddled legs, kneeing him in the groin.

"Bitch," Simmons screamed, bunching the V of Cassy's gray scrub shirt in his left hand and repeatedly banging the side of her head with his open right hand. "Goddamn you," he screamed and pounded her head until it bobbed like a doll's head. She dropped into the grayness of unconsciousness.

Time had no meaning while she was in the void. The oblivion gave way to her recurring dream visions. The singing voice of Gracie floated in on the dark rolling sounds of *Amazing Grace*. Her unconsciousness thinned. *Ana Ruiz . . . How sweet she was . . . Once she was lost . . . now she is gone . . . Ana Ruiz.*

A chorus of children's voices swelled in her head. The blackness of her mind gave way to a dream hologram of a young boy, lying alone on an operating table in a marbled room. Cassy floated in the room, hovering over the table. Using her arms she swam through the air until she could see the boy's head sticking above the sheets. His dark tousled hair was identical to Alex's. The edge of the sheet was pulled up to the boy's hairline, and she could not make out his face.

A tall dark man in pressed white surgeon's scrubs reached his left hand to the sheet covering the boy. An obsidian stone gleamed on the man's index finger. His hand flicked the edge of the sheet off the child's head, exposing Alex's beautiful face, asleep on his favorite pillow. Cassy screamed and waved her arms slowly and languidly as if in water. Her throat screamed, but there was no sound except the overpowering *Ana Ruiz* sung by the children's choir inside her head. Slowly, slowly she swam her body toward the table.

When she was directly over her son's body, a metal surgical retractor

ratcheted open a vertical midline incision in Alex's chest. Cassy felt her
head pulled into the incision as though sucked into the vortex of a
whirlpool until she could see inside her son's chest. But there was no
heart where his beating heart should have been. Alex's heart was gone,
ripped from his chest. The gaping maw of the chest incision contained
only transected stubs of the great arteries and veins, spurting geysers of
blood. Then she fell headfirst into the void, disappearing into the incision
in her son's chest screaming *No. Alex. No, no, no . . .* into black oblivion.

"Dr. Baldwin, wake up, Dr. Baldwin." The Hispanic guard called her
gently but firmly. His hand shook her shoulder and rattled her against the
sofa in the Park Haven office. She blinked into the brightness of the
room. The light seared her eyes.

"Alex," she screamed, bolting upright on the sofa and looking into the
frightened eyes of the guard.

"Dr. Baldwin. Wake up. You're in the office," the guard said anxiously.

Cassy rubbed her eyes and looked at the blurred man in front of her.
The night images flashed back into her mind. Her fingers recalled the
tactile sensation of working deep inside Juan Torres' chest to remove his
heart. Terror seized her.

"My God," Cassy said, rubbing the side of her head where Simmons
had pounded her. "What happened?"

"Dr. Simmons was drunk. I came back in when you screamed. He was
hitting you."

"What time is it?" Cassy said sitting up. She heaved over the edge of
the sofa, trying to vomit but nothing erupted from her dry stomach. The
pain in her head was blinding.

"Midnight," the guard said.

"Oh my god. I've got to get home." She reached for the office telephone on the table beside the sofa and dialed her unlisted home telephone number. There was no answer. She dialed again and let it ring a
counted fifteen times. Still no answer.

THIRTY-TWO

THE SILENT winding streets of the exclusive University Park area of Dallas reflected the conservative habits of its residents, long asleep at one a.m. under the refrigerated chill of thousands of straining air conditioners. The trees spread their branches in the simmering darkness, relieved of the punishing sun. The lawn sprinkler had just completed its midnight circuit around Cassy's home, leaving the lawn glistening with a fine mist. The damp cedars close in to the house jiggled with water droplets after the spraying.

Cassy skidded the Range Rover around the corner of her driveway, stopping abreast of the brick post holding the security keypad. She rapidly punched the letters C-A-S-S-Y into the keypad and shouted at the intercom grill in the gate post. "Alex! Lupita!" There was no response.

The windows of the house sitting above the rise of the property cast long bright columns of light onto the wet sheen of the front lawn. Alex's second floor bedroom window shone like a lighthouse beacon.

The driveway gates slid slowly aside. Before the gates had opened enough to admit the Range Rover, Cassy shot the car through the partially open gates, scraping a crease down both side panels of the Range Rover. Cassy jumped from the car as it jerked to a stop.

The massive front doors were closed. The light of the burglar alarm on the door jamb winked green. Seeing the unarmed burglar alarm constricted Cassy's throat. Cramping pain tightened her abdomen. A rancid taste clung to Cassy's dry tongue. Lupita had never forgotten to arm the security system at night. Cassy fumbled with her key ring. When she stuck the door key into the lock, it swung open to her touch without turning the key. The foyer was empty and quiet.

"Alex!" she screamed. The interior was lighted as if it were early evening. Its stillness shrieked at her. Cassy listened and heard no sound except the distant whine of the air conditioner motors running constantly.

"Alex!" Cassy screamed again, uncertain whether to run upstairs to his room or to search downstairs. "Alex! Where are you?" There was still no sound except the rustle of air through the ductwork. Cassy moved slowly down the main hallway toward the kitchen and the family room.

All her senses became supercharged. The odor of feces smacked her nose when she reached the kitchen. A wave of nausea filled her throat. At the kitchen door Cassy stopped, struck motionless by the unimaginable horror on the floor of her kitchen. "Lupita!" she screamed. Slumped face down on the floor between the kitchen island and the refrigerator, Lupita's crumpled body hugged the brick floor. Her flowery polyester gown covered her face and head, falling above her feces-soiled white cotton underpants.

Cassy frantically circled the kitchen island. Kneeling in front of the body, she turned Lupita's bloated lifeless face up in both her hands. A garrote of sash cord, wound twice about her neck, indented the flesh below her chin into rolled folds. The woman's eyes and lips were so swollen that they appeared to erupt from her blue face. "Oh my god." Cassy's hands dropped Lupita's head. It fell to the brick floor with a thud.

"Alex! Alex!" she shouted, running from the kitchen. Fear chased her up the stairwell to her son's bedroom. The hardwood steps of the staircase screeched under her running shoes as she charged up the staircase. At the landing she shrieked, "Alex!" The rail post cracked as she swung into the hallway.

"Alex!" Her voice shot through the upstairs. Alex's closed bedroom door taunted her as she raced the length of the hallway. Her shoulder hit his door just as she twisted the knob. She fell through the door frame, stumbling across the middle of his room, landing in Alex's empty bed.

The rumpled sheets still had his smell, a scrubbed soapy freshness of his nighttime bath. The shattered video screen exposing the dark hollow interior of his computer monitor sat like a decomposed skeleton on his desk. Cassy huddled in her son's bed, wrapping herself into a fetal position and pulling his bedsheets about her, trying to draw her son's presence to her. An incoherent keening sound moaned from her throat. "Alex," she cried softly. Her mind retreated into its own private world.

For a long time, she lay curled in a tight ball, numb and unthinking, until the ringing of the telephone burst over the room like artillery cluster fragments. She grabbed at the telephone, knocking it to the floor. Cassy fumbled the receiver to her ear and listened, unable to make sounds come from her throat.

"Good morning, Cassy," Tenoch said in his smooth mellifluous voice. The pleasantness of his manner cramped her aching abdomen into intestinal spasms that doubled her chest to her knees. "What took you so long?"

"Where is Alex?" she cried, managing to make her words despite the cramping in her belly. She retched and swallowed the vomitus that welled in her throat and mouth.

"He's with me," Tenoch said indifferently.

"I want him back," she said, managing a soft whimper. "Please give him back. I'll do anything you want."

"That's much better," Tenoch said casually. "I must have your commitment and loyalty, now and forever into future destinies."

"Anything. Yes. Anything. Don't hurt him," Cassy said.

"Of course not, my dear, that will not be necessary now that you understand my power over you."

"I will do anything you want. Please, just don't hurt him."

"Would you like to speak to your son?" Tenoch asked.

"M-Mom," Alex's voice said. "H-Help . . . h-he's going to hurt me." Her son's voice cracked.

"Alex. Has Tenoch hurt you?" Cassy asked.

"N-No. C-Come g-get me. H-He's going to k-kill me."

"Everything's going to be all right, Alex. I'll take care of you," Cassy said, biting her lip in an effort to keep the sobbing from her voice.

"That's very noble, Cassy," Tenoch said. "I believe your son may have grasped the gravity of his situation. He's an intelligent child."

"I'll do anything . . . ," Cassy said, her voice now a whimpering prayer.

"M-Mom. I-I'm s-scared." Alex's choking voice broke in on Tenoch's speakerphone.

Hearing her son's voice, Cassy reached for the last of her inner reserves and controlled her voice enough to say, "Tenoch, tell me what you want. Anything. Anything. I will give you anything."

"Very good, Cassy," Tenoch said in his mellow baritone. "Alex and I are en route to Mexico City in my airplane. Carina mía, I want you and Dr. Hendricks in Mexico City in the morning. Be at the DFW airport at eight a.m. My Lear jet will bring you and Dr. Hendricks to join Alex and me in Mexico City."

"Please, don't hurt Alex," Cassy said.

"Of course not. Why would I want to do that?" Tenoch asked.

"Please. . . ."

"Your son is safe tonight," Tenoch said. "Provided you do as I command. Do not under any circumstances contact anyone but Trent Hendricks."

"Yes, Tenoch," Cassy said. "I will do exactly as you wish."

"Very well. You will see me tomorrow." The line clicked dead in her ear. Her intestinal cramping retched her forward over the side of her son's bed, yellow stomach contents dribbling from her mouth. The bilious vomit flowed over her face. Foamy yellow bubbles spewed onto the edge of the bed, dripping onto the carpet.

Cassy lay huddled in her son's bed. Time lost its meaning. The sour stench of her vomitus filled Alex's room. Her mind had disengaged, controlled by the retching impulses that seized her every few seconds. The telephone receiver screeched its pulsating disconnect siren into the pool that collected around the receiver. Cassy did not hear any sound. Her low guttural moaning filled her son's bedroom.

Finally she was able to slither off the bed. Unable to stand upright, she crawled to the bathroom door on her hands and knees. In her son's bathroom, she barely managed to get to the toilet. Eventually the cramping subsided so that she could cleanse herself.

Her mind, little by little, began to link random and uncoordinated thoughts into rational organized thinking. Her higher cerebral functions at last continued to the conclusion that if she did contact the police, Alex would disappear. Alex would simply cease to exist—like Ana Ruiz.

Cassy's fingers groped for the light switch, flooding her son's dressing mirror with a diffused light. Her image reflected in the bathroom mirror was not recognizable as Cassandra Marta Baldwin. A crazed, gaping woman stared back at her. Even though her mirror's image moved in synchrony with her movements, Cassy did not recognize the woman as herself. The dark hair on her mirror's image was matted, the puffy eyes circled in darkness, and the pale skin slack and wrinkled.

Cassy reached out to touch the surface of the mirror. The image's fingers met Cassy's fingertips at the surface. Cassy's fingers steepled the hands of her mirror's image. Slowly she moved her head, watching the head of her mirror's image move slowly in unison with her.

Standing immobilized in front of the mirror, Cassy observed as her mirror's image begin to move, now free and independent of Cassy's movements. The lips of the woman in the mirror moved as if speaking. What did that woman say? Cassy asked herself. Who is that woman? Cassy squinted close to the mirror's surface. The lips of her mirror's image moved again, independent of Cassy's lips. *"He must die."*

"What did you say?" Cassy asked her mirror's image.

Her image looked at her. Her image's lips moved when Cassy asked the question again. "What did you say?" Cassy reached to feel her own lips. They were pressed together in a scowl.

Her image's lips moved again. *"Tenoch must die,"* her image in the mirror said.

"What did you say?" Cassy asked again, quickly touching her own lips to see if they moved. Her image's face remained motionless, staring at Cassy.

"What?" Cassy asked, looking at the woman in the mirror, now still as a photograph.

Cassy grabbed the edge of the dressing lavatory and thrust her face at the mirror. Her image moved in unison with her.

"Tell me! What?" Cassy asked, staring transfixed at her frozen image in the mirror.

"Tenoch must die," her image said. Cassy touched her own lips. Her lips were motionless.

Cassy whispered at her image, "Who are you?"

The lips of the image moved. *"I am you. You are me,"* the lips of her image whispered back from the mirror. Cassy's teeth bit her motionless lower lip until a droplet of blood appeared. The lips of her mirror image moved into a smile. *"You are me, I am you."* There was no blood on her image's lips.

Cassy reached to the mirror to touch her image. The hand of her mirror's image met hers at the surface of the mirror. Heat sizzled through Cassy's fingers causing her to jerk back from the mirror.

"Do not be afraid," her image said and pulled back in a movement corresponding identically to Cassy's head and hand movements.

"Help me," Cassy said, gasping at her image.

"Tenoch is evil," her image said. Cassy's hand flew up to her still lips. She rolled her tongue over her lips and tasted her blood. Her image smiled at Cassy. Cassy's lips moved. She heard her own voice say, "He must die."

After several seconds, Cassy asked her image, "How?" Her eyes locked on the eyes of her mirror's image. Again her image's lips did not move. Cassy reached both hands to the mirror, watching her image's arms and hands rise to meet her finger tips at the mirror's surface. Warmth suffused through her fingers and filled her upper extremities. Her image's lips moved again while Cassy's lips remained pressed tightly together. Her image said, *"You must destroy Tenoch. He is evil."*

Cassy pushed her face to the mirror until her nose almost touched it. "Tell me what I must do?"

"Tenoch must die," her image said.

"How?" Cassy asked, again watching the lips of her image.

The lips of her image moved into a smile. *"You will know. I will be with you,"* her image said. *"You are me. I am you."* A warmth filled Cassy with purpose. She stood upright, dropping her hands from the mirror. Cassy moved now in perfect unison with her mirror's image.

Cassy shook her head and rubbed her eyes. She checked the mirror again. Her mirror's image moved once again in synchrony with her movements. The appearance of her image in the mirror slowly changed. Her eyes alerted. The puffy darkness beneath them faded. A knowing smile transformed her mirror's image reviving her facial tone, eliminating her pinched wrinkles, and lighting a fearsome resolution in the reflection of Cassy's eyes.

Cassy again leaned toward the mirror studying her reflected image. "Thank you," Cassy said to her image. Her image smiled. Its lips did not move when Cassy spoke. "Thank you," Cassy repeated. "I understand."

Cassy splashed water into her face and wiped the scum of vomitus from her face. She pulled herself upright and smoothed her surgical scrub tunic. She looked at her mirror's image one last time and smiled. The image smiled back in perfect mirror symmetry. Standing up, Cassy's face was at peace. An intensity hardened her expression.

Cassy switched off the bathroom light and crossed Alex's room, closing the hallway door behind her. Her mind was now clear and sharp, focused as it had not been in over a week. Her fatigue and uncertainty had vanished. It was a familiar feeling for Cassy, a mental and physical preparedness that always overtook her just prior to a surgical procedure. This confidence of purpose filled her with a calm certainty. She knew what was needed.

Cassy slowly walked down the staircase, holding onto the banister, her body held tall and erect. The stairs creaked under her light step. The sound echoed throughout the empty foyer like a sound chamber. The smell of death filled the kitchen. Cassy kneeled beside Lupita's body in the narrow space between the kitchen island and the refrigerator.

Her dead flesh had already begun to stiffen from rigor. Lupita's goggle-eyes stared at Cassy as she straightened out the twisted torso and folded Lupita's arms to the side of her body.

With two beach towels she retrieved from the utility room, Cassy covered the body. With a third towel, she padded the dead woman's head with a makeshift pillow. In an act of reverence, Cassy gently inserted the tip of a pair of kitchen shears under the two loops of sash cord encircling the dead woman's neck. "I am so sorry, Lupita. Please forgive me." Cassy's eyes flooded tears down her face.

Scissoring the blades against the rope, she sawed through the stout cording and brushed away the pieces of cord. Cassy's fingers massaged the corrugated ridges and abraded imprint in the swollen neck flesh. "Forgive me, Lupita," Cassy said, her face flat and expressionless as the dead woman's. Cassy said a silent Catholic prayer for Lupita and quickly made the sign of the cross. Her fingers pulled Lupita's eyelids closed. Then Cassy tucked the edges of the terry towel neatly around the body, covering it completely.

———

The grass in the yard still glistened from the midnight watering. Cassy leaned against the trunk of the elm in the far back corner of the property and called Trent Hendricks on her cellular telephone.

"Sorry to wake you up, Trent," she said calmly. "You and I are going to Mexico City at eight in the morning."

"I know. Tenoch called me right after our transplant last night. He said one of his wealthy Mexico City patrons has a ten million peso check to present to the organ procurement foundation. Tenoch also said the three of us needed to discuss our organ procurement procedures and protocols." Trent stopped and after a moment said, "Tenoch mentioned that there had been a misunderstanding on your part last night."

"Misunderstanding. . . ," Cassy screamed. "He's kidnapped Alex."

"Kidnapped! What are you talking about?"

"He's taken Alex. They're on his plane going to Mexico City," Cassy said. Words tumbled from her mouth as she paced the shadows under the elm tree.

"Slow down."

"Lupita's dead. Strangled."

"Are you all right?" Trent asked. "Are you sure Lupita's dead?"

"Yes, she's been strangled with a sash cord. She's lying on my kitchen floor."

"Jesus Christ! We've got to notify the police."

"No, Tenoch will kill Alex if we contact the police," Cassy said. "We've got to do exactly what he says. Tenoch will kill us all, if we don't. I saw him murder the heart donor last night."

"What?" Trent said.

"The donor was alive. The man was not brain-dead. He was just like Marquez. Walter Simmons was there. He admitted using your transplant drugs to suspend the donor, just like Marquez, Ana Ruiz, and me."

Trent said nothing.

"When I refused to harvest the heart, Tenoch killed the donor," Cassy said again. "He stabbed the man in the eye, right through the eyeball and into the man's brain with his goddamn Aztec knife."

The line was silent.

"Are you there, Trent?"

"I'm listening."

"He made me harvest the heart with his Aztec sacrificial knife."

"We've got to go to the police," Trent said.

"No. You will do as I say. Do not call the police. If you notify anyone I will come for you. I will kill you if Alex is hurt," Cassy said with an icy calm.

"Okay, Cass. Anything you say," Trent said, quickly comprehending the violent sincerity underlying her words.

"Be at DFW airport at the private terminal at eight."

Cassy pressed the END button on her cellular phone and closed the hinged phone like pressing a clam shell together. The trunk of the elm tree pressed against her back, almost as if it knowingly bent to support her from collapsing. Slowly Cassy slid to the grass. Her eyes closed, and her back pressed against the corrugated elm trunk.

Even though her body screamed with exhaustion and fatigue, her mind raced with renewed energy. The green leaves above her turned black in the darkness of the corner of the yard. The words of her mirror's image played over and over in her mind, forcing out all other thought. *You must destroy Tenoch. He is evil. I am you. You are me.*

Bit by bit, an algorithm developed in her mind. It was a familiar logic process, ingrained by her medical training. A stepwise analysis leading to a treatment plan. She used this thought process so often at the operating table that it was intuitive . . . a sequential logic process of multiple forked alternatives. If this—then this, a type of reasoning underlying all diagnosis and treatment. A syllogistic reasoned approach, but done quickly without conscious thought, like the movement of a pianist's fingers or a surgeon's hands. Her mind sorted through the thousands of approaches to Tenoch.

The night hours numbed Cassy as she sat under the elm, paralyzed with terror, plotting the matrix, an algorithmic plan, desperately wanting a failure-proof plan to regain her son. But knowing no plan was fail-safe against Tenoch.

Even as her mind tested several plans, she knew for certain that she was the only person who could save her son. She also knew for certain that if she sought help or told anyone, Alex would vanish. Tenoch would cleanse his connection to her and to his black market and in so doing, would punish her before he killed her. The unimaginable terror of Alex's fate, like Ana Ruiz, surfaced in Cassy's mind and would not leave. After a long time, she dozed into a merciful sleep void, freed for a brief time of the raging fear that immobilized her conscious mind and paralyzed her body.

When she awoke, the black sky had lightened, heralding the return of the sun. In that instant before her waking mind became refilled and over-burdened with the choking fear for her son, a plan of action appeared in her subconscious mind, generated in a diagrammatic, algorithmic design. Without further testing the merits or the logic of the plan, she picked up the cellular phone and called the information operator for the number of the Park Haven Funeral Home.

A relaxing peacefulness enclosed her. She now had a plan—her decision was made. The sound of the mirror image's voice refrained in her mind—*You will know. I will be with you.* The recorded voice of the information operator gave her the telephone number of the funeral home. She punched the digits into the glowing keypad of her cellular phone. The phone rang a single time. An older man's soft voice tinged with a Hispanic accent answered. Cassy gave the man a message.

Then she dialed Betty Freeman's home number. After several rings, Betty's voice croaked hello. "Sorry to bother you so early, but I need another favor. I'm leaving town early this morning."

"Where? What's happening?" Betty's voice, now alert and worried, asked.

"Too much has happened. I can't tell you everything now, but I will as soon as we get back."

"We? Is Alex going with you?"

Cassy hesitated a moment, hating that she must lie to her friend but knowing that she must not involve her in what she was preparing to do.

"Yes. Alex and I need some time together," Cassy said as she pulled herself upright and leaned against the tree trunk. "Would you call Kevin Knowland later today, around noon, and ask him to be sure that the patrol car checks on Lupita for me?"

"Patrol car? Cass, what is going on?"

"I can't say anymore right now. I promise I'll tell you everything within the next day or two. Please . . . have Kevin check on Lupita, but not before noon."

"Cass! What's . . . where are you going?"

"That's all I can tell you. Do this for me. You know I wouldn't ask you if it weren't important."

"Please, Cass. Wait. You don't sound right."

"I have to go now. I'll call you soon." Cassy snapped the flip-phone shut and lit a cigarette. Pulling deeply on the cigarette with each drag, she quickly smoked the Marlboro and crunched it under her running shoe.

Then she returned to the house, entering the kitchen through the patio door and stepping around Lupita's motionless, towel-draped body.
The mixed smells of death and feces filled the kitchen, but Cassy did not
notice as she walked through the kitchen to her bedroom to shower and
dress for the trip to Mexico City.

THIRTY-THREE

T HE DAWN'S aurora lit the stone grave markers and the eclectic assortment of monuments that lined the gentle curving driveways at the Park Haven cemetery. The distant chirping of the waking birds signaled the only life in this corner of Dallas. Cassy eased her Range Rover into a striped parking space in front of the funeral home, the same space she had used a few hours before for the donor harvest. The gray marbled walls of the mortuary and its long narrow tinted lancet windows glowed in the beginning light of the day.

An elderly Hispanic dressed in the somber uniform of a mortician held the heavy solid entry door open as Cassy hurried to the front entrance. "Good morning, Dr. Baldwin." His cheerless manner matched his black suit, white starched shirt, dark dot tie, and black wingtips. "I am Hector Chavez, Acting Director of the Park Haven Funeral Home."

"Buenos días, Señor Chavez," Cassy said, extending her hand in a vigorous Mexican business handshake. "Thank you for meeting me so early."

He returned her formal greeting but could not bring a smile to his lips. "We are honored to be of service," the man responded in Spanish.

"My inventory of the supplies and instruments should take no more than a half hour. As I mentioned in my telephone call, Señor Tenoch was not pleased with the performance of your staff during yesterday's harvest of the donor heart."

"My apologies to Señor Tenoch and to you," the mortician said, bowing his head. "I shall see that everything that you require is available. It is not often that we can bring life from death." Only then did a careful, obsequious smile part his lips.

"Several surgical instruments were not available when I needed them during yesterday's procurement," Cassy said coldly. The smile on the man's lips instantly turned into a worried frown.

"My most sincere regrets," the man said and beckoned with his head toward the end of the darkened reception lobby. Cassy followed the acting funeral director into a rectangular elevator, the approximate size of a casket, that opened behind a sliding marble panel. The car descended until the doors slid open directly into the operating suite where she had harvested the donor heart hours before. The déjà vu sensation caught her again.

The operating room had an air of readiness. The pedestaled operating table with the covering green sheets, precisely mitered, occupied the center of the room. Brushed aluminum surgical lights hung over the surgical table like aluminum umbrellas. The empty and darkened OR suite exploded with cones of light when the mortician's finger touched the wall switch beside the elevator door. Racks of stainless steel surgical instruments behind glass cabinet doors around the perimeter of the room gleamed like cutlery.

"This won't take long," Cassy said.

"As long as you wish, Doctora," the man said and followed her a respectful step behind. Cassy moved across the marble floor of the suite, her Armani pants suit flowing like silk around her long stride. She could not put down the awkwardness she felt at being in a surgical suite dressed in regular clothes rather than surgical scrubs, even if this OR was a counterfeit in the basement of a funeral home in North Dallas.

Cassy opened the first glass cabinet and pulled out a stainless pan containing dissecting scissors, metal incision retractors, hemostat clamps, and needle holders. After inspecting and counting the instruments, she jotted notes in her spiral notepad. The man followed her silently as she methodically worked her way around the perimeter of the room, checking all the instruments in each of the display cases. At the last glass cabinet, she studied her notes and then moved toward the anesthesia console parked at the head of the OR table.

"Now I need to check the pharmaceutical supplies in the anesthesia machine drawers." Bending over the front of the anesthesia console, Cassy opened each of the three drawers in the metal cabinet drawer, picking out glass medication vials and ampules of anesthetic drugs from the individual compartments. After scrutinizing each medication vial, Cassy jotted more notes in her notebook. After inspecting the contents of the third drawer, she turned back to the anesthesia machine to replace the last handful of glass vials in the lowest cabinet drawer, but her hand struck the corner of the anesthesia console. Glass vials clattered to the floor, scattering like marbles on the slick terrazzo surface.

"Oh my goodness," Cassy said, her voice high pitched and strained. Instantly, the mortician stooped forward, chasing the rolling ampules as they scattered in all directions across the terrazzo floor. As the man waddled about the OR, bent from the waist and grabbing at the fleeing vials, Cassy slipped four of the miniature rubber sealed vials into the pocket of her Armani jacket. The four sealed medication ampules labeled 'Dr. Hendricks' Hiberna Protocol' and each containing a tan, granular powder clinked lightly as she bent down to pick up the remaining vials from beneath the surgical table.

"Gracias, Señor Chaves," Cassy said and closed the lowest cabinet drawer of the anesthesia console. "I must hurry now for my meeting with Señor Tenoch." While the mortician walked Cassy across the reception lobby to the front door, the four cold glass vials of the Hiberna mixture rubbed together in her pocket like talismans.

———

The Lear jet waited on the glowing concrete tarmac in front of the executive jet terminal section of the DFW Airport. The Aztec sun god symbols on the body and tail of the plane sparkled in the rays of the morning sun. Cassy walked hurriedly across the tarmac. A three-foot-wide plush red carpet lay unfurled from the stairway of the jet. Alberto met her at the open door of the aircraft and took Cassy's overnight bag. He followed her into the cabin of the small jet and brought the door up after them, closing up the interior of the Lear jet like an upholstered aluminum can.

The shades on the plane's windows, shuttered against the morning heat, added to the closed-in feeling. The pair of passenger seats was separated by an aisle space narrower than a seat width. The low, rounded head clearance required Cassy to bend down as she slipped into the plushly upholstered leather front seat. Trent Hendricks sat glumly in the opposite seat and danced his fingers on the glove leather of the cushioned seat on the right side of the small cabin.

"For god's sake, Cass, you're half an hour late."

Cassy opened her hand with a dismissive twist of her wrist. "I had an errand early this morning."

"For chrissake, your kid has been snatched, and you're just as calm as a nun," Trent said. "I've been awake all night. I couldn't sleep after what you told me."

Cassy shook her head and held her index finger to her lips. Leaning across the narrow aisle between the two seats, Cassy whispered, "Be careful what you say. Tenoch can hear us."

Trent leaned forward in the seat with a resigned, defeated expression on his face and poured a bloody mary from the thermos on the bar of the bulkhead wall.

"It's a little early for vodka," Cassy said.

"I'll decide when I'm going to have a drink," he said and drank the bloody mary in three swallows. Trent leaned back in his seat twiddling the ice cubes in the empty glass. The Lear jet glided onto the end of the runway and paused momentarily as the pilot ticked off the last of his preflight check list before shoving the throttle full forward and rocketing the slender tube into the air.

The blast of the plane's jets stifled any attempt at conversation. Despite the roar of the engines, Trent leaned across the aisle space between the two seats and cupped his hand over Cassy's ear. The smell of the bloody mary rolled over her. Trent stumbled on his sentences. It was as if Trent couldn't make his mouth form the words. "I'm sorry. I had nothing to do with your being involved in this mess. Tenoch became obsessed with you. You leave him to me. I'll take care of him when we get to Mexico City."

"Leave him alone," Cassy said sternly. "I'll take care of him. I just want Alex back."

Trent reached across the narrow aisle, groping for Cassy's hand. "For chrissake, Cass. You're awful calm about this whole thing," Trent said, his voice thickened by the early morning vodka.

"No, I'm not calm," she said, angered by his drunkenness. She jerked away from his hand that had caught her elbow. "Tenoch just cut out my heart when he took Alex away from me last night."

"I'll talk to Tenoch as soon as we get there. I know how to handle him, man to man," Trent said and patted her knee.

Cassy turned toward Trent and pulled his face toward her so that she could whisper in his ear. "If you, or Tenoch, or anyone else, do anything that harms Alex, I will kill you." Trent stared at her unblinking brown eyes less than six inches from his face. "Did you not understand me?" Cassy asked calmly. "I will kill you, or anyone else who harms Alex." Trent could not return the stare of Cassy's brown eyes and pulled his head back. He poured himself another bloody mary from the insulated thermos.

The Aztec Lear jet leveled at its cruising altitude of thirty-seven thousand feet. "You don't understand what you are up against," he said, sipping at his fresh tomato juice cocktail. "Life is meaningless to Tenoch. Cross him, you're dead."

"I just want my son back and for him to leave us alone. I'll do whatever is necessary . . . to get my son back."

"Let me handle him," Trent said. "I know how his mind works. He's crazy. Delusional. Maybe a paranoid schizophrenic. Label him with whatever psychiatric diagnosis you want, he's a crazy bastard. Leave him to me. I'll get your son back for you."

A surge of intestinal cramping gripped her. Cassy fought back the primal urge of fear gripping her bowels. *Stop it!* Her mind screamed for her abdominal spasms to subside. Her anxiety was unbounded. Her fingers drained white under the pressure of her grip on the leather arms of the cushioned chair until the churning of her insides eased.

"I will get Alex back for you," Trent said, refilling his bloody mary glass and drinking half before taking it away from his lips.

Cassy leaned her head against the deep pillow cushion of the head rest and closed her eyes.

Control yourself! she commanded her body. The numbing monotonous whine of the jet engines followed the plane as it streaked through the crystalline and cloudless sky across the Rio Grande. A white vapor trail followed the jet's course south like a smoky rocket. The sun glinted into the cabin, and Cassy twisted the polarizing shade over the window obliterating the bright light. She kept her eyes closed, pretending sleep, so that Trent would not besiege her any longer with his threats to confront Tenoch in Mexico City.

A few minutes later Trent's mouth fell open. His head flopped over in a stupor. An alcoholic snore rolled out of his open mouth. With her hand in the pocket of her jacket she rolled the cold hard surface of the glass vials together, clicking them softly.

The overpowering anxiety from the early morning hours when she first discovered Alex missing seeped up again through her consciousness. An uncontrollable fear bubbled up and racked her intestines. Cassy opened her eyes and held her hand out to test her steadiness. The tremulous shaky movements of her fingers appalled her. Her breathing came in rapid short bursts. *Stop!* her mind commanded. She recognized the first symptoms of hyperventilation just as she had experienced at the Teotihuacan ruins—the rapid breathing, the quickening of her pulse, the tingling sensation of her lips, the fine sheen of perspiration on her forehead. Then, she was gasping for air.

Her emotional control was slipping away quickly. *Control yourself,* she screamed silently. But she could feel herself sliding into panicked disarray. "Help me." Her lips formed the words quietly. It was a prayer—to her God, to her mirror's image, to all gods. "I need your help," she said quietly. Gripping the arms of the seat, she thrust the seat backward until she was lounging with her legs and feet outstretched. Across the aisle, Trent snored on obliviously with his head slumped forward. A pool of saliva collected at the corner of his lax mouth.

The tedious whine of the jet engines whited out her conscious mind's flashing images. One, two—slowly—her rapid breathing slowed—in and out. Slowly. Regularly. The tightness of her fingers about the leather chair arms lessened. The cramping tension in the muscle groups of her legs ebbed. She felt a relaxation spreading upward throughout her body. A warm encircling cloud of white fog embraced her mind and touched her all over her body. Softly she floated as the relaxing ease unfolded in her, and she slept deeply and dreamlessly.

The screeching bump of the jet's tires against the hot Mexico City runway roused Cassy. She opened her eyes as the reverse jet thrusts slowed the plane into its landing roll. With her equanimity regained she felt the sense of purpose she knew she would need.

Before the jet had reached the end of its landing roll, Trent woke, looking about the small cabin wildeyed until his eyes slowed and fixed on the thermos bottle on the bulkhead shelf in front of him. He threw a handful of ice into a fresh crystal goblet. Filling the glass with vodka and the remaining dribble of tomato juice mixture from the thermos, he brought the glass shakily to his mouth.

"Don't you think you've had enough to drink?" Cassy asked gently. Trent sloughed off her comment and peered out the window, lost in his own turmoil. The plane taxied toward the Presidential air terminal. Behind a cyclone fence encircling the massive Presidential hanger, government officials and visiting dignitaries including Tenoch arrived and departed away from the hurly-burly of the main terminal across the primary runway of the Mexico City airport.

As soon as the plane stopped in front of the hangar, Cassy stood up, hunched over in the cylinder of the cabin. Alberto released the plane's door and lowered the steps to a red carpet runner on the tarmac. Tenoch's helicopter sat fifty yards away, its main rotors slowly turning like a moss green bug waving its articulated arms in the air.

Cassy descended the steps of the plane into scalding air that dried her eyes like a torch thrust in her face. The bitter metallic taste of the air stained her tongue. Before her feet touched the hot concrete tarmac, a pulsating pain settled in above each eyebrow.

"Buenos días, Dr. Baldwin," said a khaki-uniformed military man standing at the edge of the red runner carpet leading to the open door of Tenoch's limousine. "You have been cleared through Customs." The man scribbled a note on the inner pages of her passport. "Buenos días,

Dr. Hendricks," he then said to Trent who cautiously placed his feet on the steps of the lowered hatch of the jet. The officer scribbled into Trent's passport. Then he ushered both of them into the waiting limousine.

Across the blistering tarmac at the waiting helicopter, another khaki-uniformed soldier stood at the open cabin door of Tenoch's Bell helicopter and assisted Cassy and Trent into the passenger compartment. Just before the door closed, Alberto jumped into the chopper's cabin, taking the seat directly across from them.

The helicopter lifted directly up in a whirling storm of hot air and dusty downwash. Its nose pointed toward Tenoch's towering building in central Mexico City. The chopper rode the inversion layer of gray smoke and haze that covered the city. As soon as the helicopter entered this smoky layer, Tenoch's voice filled the small passenger compartment. "Welcome again to my city, Tenochtitlan, the land of Tenoch." Cassy looked at Trent. His vacant, bleary eyes were hidden in an alcoholic haze as thick as the smog overlying the city.

"Let me talk to my son," Cassy said, her voice calm and controlled.

"He's in my guest suite. Alex has not been very talkative this morning." Tenoch seemed to sense Cassy's fear despite her calm voice. "You have my honor that your son is not harmed." The threat was implicit. Cassy understood Tenoch's unstated meaning—not yet harmed.

THIRTY-FOUR

T HE PILOT dropped the helicopter into a gentle landing on the rooftop heliport of Tenoch's skyscraper. Moments later Cassy strode through the carved doors into Tenoch's grand salon. Trent trailed Cassy, hurrying after her like a child stumbling behind his mother, trying to keep pace with her quick long stride. Alberto followed both of them, a few steps behind Trent. The high vaulted salon bore no trace of Alex.

"Carina mía," Tenoch said effusively as Cassy approached under the archway into his office. "You are beautiful today." He pulled her to him and ceremoniously kissed her cheeks.

"Where is my son?" Cassy asked in Spanish. She modulated her accent to keep her voice nonthreatening and pleasant.

Tenoch ignored her question and turned a tight flat smile toward Trent. "Trent, I'm pleased you are here, also."

Trent took Tenoch's outstretched hand and shook it, pulling him forward at the same time. "Tenoch, this whole mess is fucking ridiculous," Trent said in a loud whisper. "You've pushed me too far by snatching Cassy's boy."

Tenoch studied Hendricks carefully. The alcoholic flush to Trent's puffed, ruddy face made it appear inflated and ready to explode. "Oh, my friend, I do have justification to bring Alex to my home as my guest. Cassy does not yet understand my power."

"That's enough," Cassy said, pushing herself between the two men. "Tenoch, please let me see my son."

"Certainly," Tenoch said. "He is in the guest room where you spent last weekend."

Cassy was already up the staircase before Tenoch finished the sentence. She shoved through the double doors into the dimly lit bedroom. The opaque drapery blocked out the midday sun. The cover on the bed mounded over a figure the size of Alex. After groping to turn on the bedside night lamp, she touched the figure under the coverlet. Her throat squeezed closed. Her eyes glazed with tears.

"Alex. It's me," Cassy said, touching his hunched back through the cover. "You're going to be all right." Slowly she pulled back the heavy bed cover. Alex's brown tousled hair fell down over his forehead. His expressionless face was an ashen mask. Huge frightened eyes dominated his pinched face. The knit collar of his Texas Rangers' T-shirt sagged against his thin neck.

"I'm so sorry," Cassy said, reaching to touch his cheek with her index and middle finger. She tenderly rubbed the softness of his face and brushed the tears from the corners of his eyes. Mother and son stared at each other, reaching for each other but not connecting across the abyss of fear and guilt that separated them.

Cassy could not ask the unaskable, one of the greatest fears a mother might have for an abducted child, short of death. The most specific query she could manage was, "Did Señor Tenoch touch you?" Alex's face did not register an understanding of the searching question. Gently she touched her lips to her son's cheek. "Did Tenoch hurt you?" Still no answer. Behind her mother's fear, Cassy's clinical mind wondered whether Alex had slipped into a catatonic, stuporous state of paralysis just like Marquez in the days after his Hiberna suspension. Had Tenoch administered the Hiberna mixture to Alex, inducing in him the same cataleptic state as Marquez? Or had the circuit breakers of Alex's mind simply shut down against overwhelming horrors?

Cassy slipped off her shoes and curled on the bed beside her son, cradling his head in the hollow of her right arm, and spooned his body against her. "I'm sorry, Alex," she said softly into his ear. "Can you forgive me?" Time passed without measure as they lay together—mother and child. Cassy hummed a lullaby that she had sung to him as a baby when she rocked him to sleep, again and again, slowly and softly. Alex remained motionless except for the pounding of his heart. His eyes were wide and fixed on a spot on the closed brocaded drapes.

A long time later Alex whispered, "M-Mom. I-I'm so scared."

"Did he hurt you?" Cassy asked. She had to know. Silence. Again Cassy asked, "Did Tenoch touch you?"

Alex slowly shook his head no. "I-I'm s-scared," he managed to say by forcing his head forward as if spitting out each word. "I-Is T-Tenoch g-going to k-kill us?" His speech was an engine that would not catch, sputtering but not igniting.

"No, No, No," Cassy said, repeating the word in rapid sequence. "No, No, No." She drew him tight against her, covering his body with hers and pulling the covers over them. They lay together for a very long time, neither saying a word, holding each other.

———

Directly below the guest suite the early afternoon sunlight suffused Tenoch's office into a celestial aquamarine cloud chamber. The chrome plating behind the elevated desk reflected the hazy sky like a mirror, bouncing the sky around the room through the tinted parabola of the glass wall. Tenoch leaned back in his throne-like black tufted leather chair behind the stone desk whose curves matched the two hundred seventy degree glass parabolic walls of the room.

Seated in a black leather barrel chair in front of the massive desk, Trent stared up at Tenoch who smiled benignly in return. The bewildered look on Trent's face was more than an alcohol-induced disorientation. The mirrored reflection of the blank sky on the chrome wall behind Tenoch disoriented everyone sitting before Tenoch's elevated desk.

"You've gone too far by snatching Cassy's kid," Trent said and swallowed half a glass of whiskey.

Tenoch's black eyes held Trent like a toreador facing down a bull in the center of a bullfighting ring. Moments passed as in the traditional standoff between bull and man. Neither Trent nor Tenoch spoke or moved their eyes in this impasse. At last Tenoch broke the deadlock.

"You do not understand," Tenoch said pleasantly. "Cassandra and I are intertwined in our destiny."

"Come on, Tenoch. Cut that Aztec crap. You're trying to bullshit an old Texas boy. The three of us have our own reasons for getting involved in these organ brokering deals. Walter Simmons is in it for the money . . . no big surprise. Me . . . you dragged me in the deal to get a heart for my daughter . . . you've got me. Why are you in the deal? I'm not sure . . . call yourself the leader if you want . . . you can even play at being a heart surgeon . . . handling human hearts during the transplants. I don't give a shit. I've always done what you wanted. Up to this point I got what I wanted . . . a heart for my daughter. But now you're threatening me, Cassy, and Alex with your mumbo jumbo Aztec bullshit." Trent's face flushed crimson, and his trembling hand shook the ice cubes in the crystal glass as he drank the rest of the bourbon.

"You desecrate my ancestry," Tenoch said amiably although his face and mouth hardened.

"Bullshit!" Trent slammed the glass onto a tan carved stone table beside the chair and moved forward on the cushion, causing Alberto to move in from the office doorway a few steps closer to the desk.

"Be quiet, you fool," Tenoch said in a throaty, slow-paced cadence, stressing each syllable. Tenoch's eyes were black impenetrable stones in his dark chiseled face. "You have no meaning in my Aztec destiny."

"Don't hand me your self-serving crap about Aztec destinies. You're in this deal for the money just like Walter. You've got expenses . . . this place cost you several million," Trent said looking around the room. "Your Dallas mansion . . . the airplanes . . . all the expensive toys. You're going to need the millions of fucking pesos you will get from brokering the Mexican donors for heart transplants."

Tenoch looked down on Trent as if a king beholding a prisoner before the throne. Trent squinted his watery eyes upward at the fuzzy image of Tenoch surrounded by the illusion of clouds on the mirrored back-drop.

The moment stretched silently between them like a charged electrical wire, measuring the life current of each. Tenoch broke the connection. His eyes blinked and wrinkled at the corners until his mouth smiled widely. He stood slowly behind the stone desk, reaching across the desk with his hand extended. Trent stood up reaching awkwardly at shoulder height across the surface of the elevated desk for Tenoch's hand. Tenoch shook Trent's hand passionately in a two-handed shake.

"Let me fix you another drink, my friend," Tenoch said congenially, but his flat black eyes were as lifeless as a grotesque Aztec stone carving at Teotihuacan.

Trent nodded and wandered aimlessly in front of the curved tinted windows looking over the swimming pool of the balcony patio. The amorphous, smoky haze of the sky flooded the room. Tenoch poured a crystal goblet full of whiskey and dropped in two ice cubes. For himself, he poured a glass of Evian water.

The two men returned to the pair of leather barrel chairs in front of the massive desk. Tenoch swiveled his chair to face the panorama of Mexico City below appearing as if painted on the tinted glass window.

"My friend, be not disturbed," Tenoch said pleasantly as he sipped his water. "We are as one. Confrontation will not serve any useful purpose between us."

"I'm willing to forget this ever happened," Trent said and took a large swallow of whiskey. "Cassy, Alex, and I will turn around and go back to Dallas. No hard feelings."

Tenoch studied the distance, letting Trent's request hang unacknowledged. The light from the window reflected in his black eyes until they
glowed in his smooth tan face.

"Do you know Huitzilopochtli?" Tenoch asked.

"Who the fuck is Huitzilopochtli?" Trent asked, slurring the syllables
of the Aztec god's name.

"Be not blasphemous, my friend," Tenoch said slowly and stiffly. "Hu-
tizilopochtli is the supreme Aztec god. It is Huitzilopochtli whose divine
intervention ensures that the sun returns each morning to light the day
and to nourish the world."

"For chrissake, Tenoch, this is the fucking twentieth century. Cortez
killed the goddamn Aztec civilization five hundred years ago."

"You are not an Aztec. You can never know the power of Huitzilopochtli," Tenoch said. He stared unblinking into the horizon. The
smoke funneling up from the city below like a burning pyre fogged the
incandescence of the sun into a blurred disc.

"That's enough, Tenoch. This is crazy. Count me out. We're leaving
now." Trent stood up in front of the low chair.

"You will remain," Tenoch said, not turning from his distant gaze. He
stared into the dispersed brightness of the midday sun as if entranced. Alberto moved to stand within arm's reach of Trent, pushing him back into
the chair.

"Huitzilopochtli requires a sacrificial presentation to preserve the sun's
presence," Tenoch said without taking his eyes away from the sun.

"Fuck your Huitzil—," Trent said, slurring the Aztec name unintelli-
gibly. Moving unsteadily out of the barrel chair, Trent staggered toward
the mirrored wall and the recessed liquor cabinet. Alberto followed him
around the desk, keeping himself positioned between Trent and Tenoch.
Trent refilled his bourbon glass, not bothering with ice. As he turned back
from the liquor cabinet, Alberto still stood between Trent and Tenoch in
the low chair in front of the desk.

"Excuse me, pard," Trent said, touching Alberto's forearm to nudge
him aside. When he lurched past Alberto, Trent stumbled, crashing into
Tenoch and flinging his glassful of bourbon over the front of Tenoch's
black silk shirt. The glass bounced off Tenoch's chest and exploded into a
thousand shards on the black hardwood floor.

"Infidel, do not touch my body." Tenoch snapped upright. "You have
defiled Huitzilopochtli!"

Tenoch looked down at Trent's prone unconscious body lying on the
highly polished hardwood floor. Three crystal glass shards impaled his
right cheek just below his eye, laying open an inch gash in his face and
drawing a stream of blood down his cheek. Trent lay unmoving, stunned

and drunk. Tenoch scowled, his dark eyes even blacker then the obsidian
stone in the ring on his finger. He lifted his huarache-sandaled foot and
placed it on Trent's head as if on a stepstool. The odor of bourbon from
Tenoch's soaked black silk shirt saturated the air. A calm beatific smile
softened Tenoch's face, as if a vision of pleasure had entered his mind.

"Prepare the honor for Huitzilopochtli," Tenoch said in his pleasing,
most gracious voice. Alberto nodded and quickly disappeared from the
office.

—

The thump of Trent's body crashing to the floor of Tenoch's majestic
office did not penetrate the soundproof guest suite directly above. Cassy
and Alex lay silently together in the canopied bed, mother holding her
child in a tight protective embrace.

Alex's breathing and his pounding pulse had slowed as Cassy cradled
him. He no longer cried, but his eyes stared at the single spot seen only
by his eyes on the brocaded curtain. After a long time Cassy lifted her
arm off Alex's chest and cupped his chin, turning his face to her. With
her lips an inch from his ear, she whispered, "I have a plan to get us out
of here. You're going to have to be strong and help me."

Alex looked at her, confused. Life ebbed back into his dull brown eyes.
He focused his eyes on his mother's—two perfectly matched pairs. Alex
nodded his head slowly, comprehension returning to his eyes.

"Let's go into the bathroom," Cassy whispered.

"I don't need to go to the bathroom." Alex pulled the covers up
around his neck again. With her index finger on her lip in a signal of silence, she led him through the dressing room, on into the bathroom, and
closed the door behind them. After turning the shower into a roaring
waterfall, she pulled him near her as she sat on the closed toilet lid. She
forced herself to concentrate on her son's face, only inches in front of
her. The moist steam polished their dark hair with coalesced droplets of
water.

"Señor Tenoch has a sickness of his mind that causes him to do strange
things, to see unusual things, and to act in crazy ways."

"Like bringing me to Mexico?" Alex asked solemnly.

"Yes. He is very dangerous, and the people who work for him will do
whatever he wants."

"The men hurt Lupita," Alex said simply.

"I know, hon," Cassy said, afraid to ask Alex how much he had seen of
her murder.

"Right now we must be nice to Señor Tenoch," Cassy said.

"Why do I have to be nice to him?" Alex asked.

"It's part of my plan to get us out of here," Cassy said without elaborating. The reality, Cassy admitted to herself, was that her plan was far from developed. Trent's drunkenness had disappointed her, and she knew that she could no longer count on him. She felt in her coat pocket for the four vials of the Hiberna medication and knew that it was her only weapon. But she had not figured a way to use the powder. She flashed on her image in the mirror. *You will find the way.*

"When are we going home?" Alex asked.

"Tonight. But you must help me," she said, taking both his shoulders in her hands. "Will you do that, my man?"

"Yes, Mom. What do you want me to do?" Alex asked, his speech clear and completely freed of the stutter.

"You'll have to pretend that Señor Tenoch invited us to stay as his guest in Mexico City. Play like it's a game. Pretend you're acting a part in the school play."

"Okay, Mom," he said firmly. Cassy knew he would play the role. "Is that all? Just play like everything's cool?" he asked.

"That's it. Just play up to Señor Tenoch as if he were the world's nicest man and so will I. It will be our secret plan. I'm going to tell Tenoch that you're not feeling well and should stay in the guest room. I'll tell him that you need to rest and to sleep."

"What will I eat?"

"Don't eat or drink anything that's brought into the room. Remember, you've been sick at your stomach."

"I-Is T-Tenoch going to poison me?" he asked, once again stuttering the first of the sentence before lining his words up smoothly.

"I don't think so," Cassy said. "We just can't take any chances. Now you hop in the shower."

Cassy returned to the enormous main room of the guest suite while Alex showered. She touched the switch on the bedside table, parting the drapes widely. The afternoon sun flooded the room through the tinted windows. Her hazy reflection peeked back at her from the tinted window. She thought back to the mirror's image in her dressing room and remembered the advice of the image—*Tenoch must be destroyed.* It was the only course available. She fingered the four glass vials of tan powder in her rumpled jacket pocket, trying to draw strength from them.

"Mom, where's my clean clothes?" Alex called from the bathroom. Cassy smiled at Alex's naked buttocks as he scooted through the dressing area into the walk-in closet where his clothes hung.

A discrete tapping through the thick door of the suite startled Cassy, and she crossed the room to open the door a crack.

"Carina mía, how have you found your son?" Tenoch asked solicitously. His flowing black silk shirt and linen pants bloused over his muscular body.

"He is fine," Cassy said, smiling and laughing. She reached up to kiss his cheek, allowing her open lips to linger a moment on the soft skin of his cheek. "I must apologize for being so abrupt when I first arrived, but I was anxious to see Alex. He's having a wonderful time. It's his first time in Mexico City. Please do come in," she said, opening the door wide.

With the door fully open, Cassy noticed the maid standing next to Tenoch and holding a German shepherd puppy against her white pinafored black uniform. The dog fit the crook of the woman's elbow and wiggled against her breast, pawing his oversized feet against the woman's dark uniform.

"Where did you get the puppy?" Cassy asked, her voice bubbling. "Or is he a she?" she asked, taking the pup from the maid.

"It's a he," the maid said in Spanish.

Just then Alex turned the corner into the living room. His face erupted into a grin. He ran to take the puppy from Cassy's arms.

"Maybe this dog will grow up to be as good as Charlie."

"Thank you, sir," Alex said. "What's his name?"

"He's yours to name."

"I'm going to name him Charlie Junior," Alex said quickly. Cassy leaned against Tenoch to kiss him on the cheek, once again intentionally lingering her open lips on his smooth cheek. "You're very kind."

"One more present for you, my young man," Tenoch said, returning to the foyer outside the suite. A moment later he returned carrying a portable computer the size and shape of a large notebook. "To replace your broken computer," Tenoch said. Kneeling to the floor, Tenoch placed the laptop computer beside Alex who sat crosslegged, cuddling the puppy in his lap.

"C-Cool! A M-Macintosh Powerbook!" Alex said, flipping the switch with one hand while scratching the dog's neck with his other hand.

"Wow, it's got all my software in it! Look, Mom. All these new games." Alex held the computer video display screen for her to see.

"Tenoch, you shouldn't have done that," she said, squeezing his arm and pulling him affectionately to her. She kissed his lips lightly and leaned into his chest. The image of Lupita's swollen face flicked past her consciousness, but quickly Cassy suppressed it.

"Splendid," Tenoch said in Spanish and then turned to Cassy. "Trent and I must visit Raul Garcia at the Instituto de Medico this afternoon." At the mention of Raul's name, fear gripped her heart and squeezed. She struggled to keep her face and body language excited and sensual even though Tenoch's world was closing around her. Had Tenoch somehow learned of her conversation with Raul? she worried.

"Do I need to go with you to the Instituto? Perhaps I should accompany you?"

"No, carina mía. Not today. We will have dinner when I return this evening."

Cassy noticed that he did not mention Trent's returning, but Tenoch kissed her lightly on the lips and was gone before she could ask about Trent. Cassy heard the dull metal on metal click of a bar lock sliding home on the outside of the door. After a few moments, she tested the door. It was locked. Picking up the phone, she heard nothing. The line was dead. They were prisoners in Tenoch's guest suite.

THIRTY-FIVE

THE TRANSPARENT air magnified the unfiltered sun searing
the flat brown plateau below. A jagged ridge of volcanic mountains separated the barren plain from Mexico City. The sun's blazing fireball touched the bluish red mountain rim, igniting the rugged
horizon into a fiery border with the dusky sky. Huddled clumps of sun
dried bushes dotted the arid, uncultivated surface of the plateau like lunar
boulders.

The daily firestorm of the sun in the sky over Teotihuacan, the vast
relic of an ancient Mexican city, was mercifully ebbing into the night. In
the center of this barren ground, two immense, quadrangular mounds of
olive-colored stone rose preternaturally like an incomplete alien eruption
of the earth's surface.

Tenoch's helicopter descended in its curved trajectory from Mexico
City to settle onto a rocky mesa adjacent to the larger of the twin pyramids. The hovering chopper fanned the gritty surface into a cloud of
brown dust, obscuring the helicopter in a bubble of flying grit as it touched
the flat, sunbaked surface. The flight from the rooftop of Tenoch's penthouse had taken Tenoch, Alberto, and Trent Hendricks twenty-two
minutes and more than a millennium to enter the ruins of this ancient
civilization.

Almost at the moment that the landing skids of the helicopter touched
the burnt ground, the sun extinguished itself completely below the distant mountain ridge. The last flickering rays of the sun doused themselves
into the black shadow of the colossal tiered pyramid. The dusk in the valley quickly deepened into dark shadows. With the sun gone, the valley

became dark as if the pyramid had drawn all the ambient light into it, causing night to appear abruptly. The Pyramid of the Sun dwarfed the chopper squatting before it like a desert spider.

The helicopter blades spun slowly to a stop. The chopper door popped open, and Trent stumbled out. The front of his wrinkled white shirt and tie were flecked with blood stains. Crusting blood caked his right cheek below a gaping laceration. "This ain't the fucking hospital," Trent said in a drunken slur as his feet hit the end of a carpet runner.

Trent squinted into the darkness toward the base of the mammoth Pyramid of the Sun less than fifty yards away down the patterned design of the carpet. He shook his head as if trying to clear his mind. While his eyes focused on the hard sloping surface of the pyramid, his bewildered expression reflected his mind's refusal to comprehend the spectacle between the door of the helicopter and the base of the pyramid.

At the open door of the chopper, four brown-skinned muscular men, none appearing more than twenty years old, stood on either side of the Aztec tapestried carpet runner that led to the shadowy base of the pyramid. The runner ended fifty yards beyond the chopper at a slit-like opening in the base of the Pyramid of the Sun. On either side of this concealed entrance to the pyramid's interior, the flames of two torches set into carved stone receptacles flickered in the dark. The young men resembled Aztec warriors, dressed in suede leather loin cloths and primitive moccasins. Each man's right hand held a feather-festooned wooden rod as tall as each and as thick as a wrist.

"This ain't the fucking hospital!" Trent shouted at the nearest man. "Take me to the ER." He turned around toward the helicopter door when Alberto jumped from the chopper just behind Trent, blocking his retreat from the greeting party. Trent weaved in the darkness, his head and body slowly turning from one to the other of the warriors. The horrifying spectacle was as if he had set foot into a time of ancient Mexico, hundreds of years ago.

"All of you are crazy! Get me out of here," Trent screamed. He turned to face Alberto who stood at the bottom of the steps of the helicopter. Alberto viciously and without warning shoved Trent toward the quartet of waiting warriors. Immediately the first warrior prodded Trent savagely in the chest with the end of his feathered wooden club.

"You crazy motherfucker!" Trent screamed in pain and pushed Alberto aside as he scrambled for the steps to the helicopter. At that instant, a blinding glare of light illuminated the interior of the helicopter. Tenoch stepped from the cabin doorway, clad in a suede breech cloth. His arms angled before him toward the Pyramid of the Sun. The brilliance of the interior light and the murky dusk outside threw Tenoch's body into a black silhouetted apparition.

"I am Huitzilopochtli, Supreme god of the Aztec." It was a hollow, slow-paced, disconnected voice echoing back from the sloping surface of the colossal tiered pyramid.

"Kneel before Huitzilopochtli," shouted Alberto and grabbed Trent's hand in a vise-like grasp, bending his fingers backward until Trent screaming in agony fell to the carpet. Tenoch stepped forward from the helicopter. A painted warrior held a cape of feathers and spotted jaguar skin up for Tenoch and draped the ceremonial cape over Tenoch's shoulders as if it were an overcoat. Tenoch stood silent, facing the dark shadow of the Pyramid of the Sun, as the warrior attendant adjusted the feathered cape, shrouding Tenoch's broad shoulders. Then the warrior placed a closely fitted feather cap on Tenoch's head concealing his ebony hair. With quick artistic strokes another warrior brushed bands of red, yellow, and green dyes on Tenoch's face and chest. Tenoch's eyes blazed from below the headdress like fiery beams.

With an elaborate drawn out movement, Tenoch raised his arms straight from his side. The multicolored feathers of the cape fluttered in the light of the helicopter's cabin. "I am Huitzilopochtli." The voice was sepulchral, not recognizable as Tenoch but more a mystical incantation. The words rolled slowly from his mouth, rising and falling, building to a crescendo as he repeated the chant, "I am Huitzilopochtli."

A rising cacophony of garbled Spanish erupted from the four warriors as they circled Trent, moving slowly and closing in on him until each of the warriors in the revolving circle was within a jab of their victim. Trent stood fixed to the carpet, following the movement of the circle of four warriors. A frenzied banging of the wooden clubs on the hard surface of the courtyard magnified the chant with its dysrhythmic accompaniment.

As the circle of warriors narrowed around him, Trent lunged between two of them, trying once again to reach the open cabin door of the helicopter. Alberto stiff-armed him back into the circle of four warriors with a backhand jab to Trent's cheek, bringing forth a gush of dark blood from the cut below his eye. As Trent fell back into the circle, the feathered club of one warrior struck the low part of Trent's back, sending him spread-eagled onto the tapestry runner in the center of the closing circle of warriors.

"You son of a bitch," Trent said, slurring his words as he lay face down, gasping for breath, on the carpet runner. Pulling himself up onto one knee, he lunged toward his tormentor as another warrior struck Trent's kneecap with the ornate battle club, throwing him face forward onto the carpet within the circle of four painted warriors. Trent's nose slammed into the hard baked ground, softened barely by the tapestry runner. An awful scraping crack declared the breaking of cartilage and bone. A steady stream of blood, black in the darkness of the flare light, ran from his nose and pooled beneath his face on the carpet.

Trent rolled over and looked up into the hideous painted faces of the warriors. "Stop. Please. No!" In response, the end of a wooden club immediately smashed into his ribs, cracking three of them like green sticks. Trent's terrified eyes darted in anguish around the closing circle of men. His swollen nose boiled blood down over his lips. Without warning, blood stained vomitus erupted from his mouth, spraying down the front of his dark suit and bloody white shirt.

Rolling his head away from the pool of bloody sour stomach contents that permeated the tapestry with a foul whiskey stench, Trent crawled down the tapestry and away from his tormentors, trying to reach the chopper. Scrabbling like a land crab, he ran into the sturdy naked legs of a warrior. Trent engaged the man's pitiless eyes. "Why?" Trent managed to scream. "Why?" His question was answered with a powerful jab from a warrior's club, punching him deep in the abdomen, curling him over and bringing on merciful unconsciousness.

Trent lay sprawled on the carpet, unmoving. Minutes later two of the muscular warriors grabbed him by each arm and lifted him between them, using their long wooden rod clubs inserted under his arm pits to hoist him upright. Trent's head wagged and bobbed back and forth, flinging sprays of blood from each nostril.

Alberto, now also in a suede loincloth and adorned with elaborate multicolor splashes of face and body paint, walked slowly toward Trent who hung slackly by his shoulders between the two warriors. Using a stone knife, Alberto slashed away Trent's Brooks Brothers suit and shirt and cut his boxer shorts away, leaving him naked and slumped on the rod between the two warriors.

The warriors hoisted Trent's unconscious body on the rod-like clubs and hauled him down the carpetway toward the Pyramid of the Sun. The two other warriors delivered measured jabs of their wood clubs to the muscle masses of Trent's arms, thighs, and calves.

At the slit-like entrance into the base of the pyramid, the two men carrying Trent shifted his body as if in a choreographed drill team maneuver and walked sideways through the slit, holding Trent suspended by his arms on the rod between them.

The warren of subterranean passages and crevices radiated through the central mass of the Pyramid of the Sun, lighted by occasional flaming sconces in the stone walls of the narrow passageways. Trent's trailing legs and feet dragged on the stones of the narrow passageways, abrading the front of his knees and feet into raw gouges, leaving a trail of blood and skin on the rough rocks of the pathway.

Ancient ocher paintings on the walls of the narrow stone passageways moved rhythmically as the torch lights passed over them. The macabre procession wound its way single file through the maze into a central domed chamber deep in the center of the pyramid.

The men dragged Trent to a tan round pedestal stone, the single floor fixture in the central burial chamber of the Pyramid. The sloping sides of the low hassock-size pedestal were adorned with bas relief petroglyphic carvings of grotesque humanoid creatures and serpents. Contorted animal-like human figures and manlike serpents in primitive frescoes also covered the roughened ceiling. The rose and ocher colors of these ceiling murals danced alive in the flickering yellow light of the torches.

The two warriors pulled the rod from under Trent's armpits, dropping his unconscious body on the stone pedestal. Alberto cut away the leather thongs binding Trent's wrists behind his back. Then the four warriors with another practiced choreographic move suspended Trent spread-eagled over the low stone pedestal. Each of the four warriors adjusted his pull on Trent's arms and legs so that Trent's body was suspended tense as a trampoline over the stone pedestal.

Caped in the jaguar skin, Tenoch walked deliberately toward the center of the room from out of a black slit crevice. Standing before the round stone, he resembled the feather-capped creatures in the wall carvings and paintings. The feathers of his head cap brushed the low arched ceiling. He stood with his feather-encased arms folded before him. With a barely perceptible movement of Tenoch's head, the four men pulling on Trent's extremities increased the tension so that he was quartered even more tightly over the stone pedestal.

Tenoch raised his arms upright, fanning the wings of feathers beneath each outstretched arm. His arms shook, vibrating the feathers over his arms. "I . . . am . . . Huitzilopochtli." His hollow voice echoed in the flickering light of the room. Taking his declaration as a signal, the four men suspending Trent's naked body lowered it carefully until Trent's back rested firmly on the flat surface of the stone's top.

Alberto confirmed the position of Trent's naked chest on the stone and gestured for the tension on each extremity to be increased, further tightening Trent's tense spread-eagled body. Then Alberto wrapped a thin long leather strap around Trent's head, holding it still as if enclosed in a leather bridle. Trent's eyes blinked open, apparently trying to focus on the low resonant vocal frequencies of Tenoch's voice with its grotesque cadence and menacing harshness.

"Huitzilopochtli will be honored," Tenoch said in the same ghastly low-frequency voice. At this command each of the warriors in the chamber dropped to his knees but pulled even harder on Trent's arms and legs.

"You will now honor Huitzilopochtli," Tenoch said. His head bowed, Alberto stepped forward, holding a thin stone tablet, the size and shape of a serving tray. On this black obsidian tray two dark green stone knives sculpted from volcanic obsidian glass shimmered in the flare of the torches in the chamber.

Tenoch shrugged the feathered shroud from his shoulders. His oiled body, muscular and dark, glistened in the torch light of the chamber. He pulled himself full upright, flexing and tightening his muscles. Tenoch walked slowly and regally to stand beside Alberto now holding Trent's head immobile in the leather bridle. Tenoch stood silently with his eyes focused on the ceiling mural of a feathered manlike figure dangling a snake from its mouth. The black obsidian stones used for the eyes of the mural's grotesque humanoid matched Tenoch's glistening black eyes.

As if anointing Trent, Tenoch laid his soft manicured fingers on the man's bound forehead. Trent's eyes flickered open at the touch. "You will honor Huitzilopochtli with your heart and the blood of your life." A horror of understanding filled Trent's eyes. He tried to shake his head, but the leather strapping held him motionless. Trent's aboriginal howl filled the chamber.

Alberto cinched the leather loop strap on Trent's writhing head and obliterated the scream caught in Trent's clinched jaws. Tenoch again turned his gaze upward to the figure of the feathered, bird-like man painted on the ceiling of the chamber. The portrait returned an unseeing stare through obsidian stone eyes. The bitter smell of the flaming torches crowded the air until the chamber was filled with a new and palpable air of expectation. Death was an imminent presence in the closeness of the subterranean tomb.

Tenoch lifted the obsidian knife from the stone tray as in an ancient ceremonial ritual. In a gracefully executed movement of his arms, Tenoch grasped the carved handle of the larger of the two knives, lifting it smoothly high above his head. The tip of the blade touched the painted birdlike figure on the domed ceiling. The light of the torches from the room glinted off the cobbled surface of the obsidian knife blade reflecting stars of green light onto the walls of the burial chamber like the inside of a kaleidoscope. Flare flames shot a translucent green through the thin sharp blade as Tenoch waved the ancient ceremonial knife high above his head.

Tenoch chanted his slow, booming cadence like rocking tumbrels carrying the condemned to the executioner. "I . . . am . . . Huitzilopochtli."

The pauses between the syllables of the Aztec god's name stretched the sound into an ominous pronouncement of execution.

Trent's eyes opened in horrified comprehension of his impending death to see the swift arc of Tenoch's hand carrying the obsidian knife moving downward toward his chest. Time languished. The hand of Tenoch drew with excruciating slowness a shimmering green stream as the obsidian knife blade slashed downward. The irregular surface of the dark green blade coruscated with flashes of the torches in its descending arc toward Trent. The penetration of the knife blade into Trent's chest echoed in the chamber like the sound of a punctured ripe melon. Trent's eyelids fluttered in a frenzy until they froze open as if the globes were about to burst from their sockets.

Tenoch's forearm muscles bulged under his dark oiled skin when he jerked the knife blade sharply upward toward Trent's left shoulder, cutting a precise opening in the chest from just below the nipple upward into Trent's left armpit. The soft tissue and muscle of the chest wall parted cleanly as if the edges of a cut melon had popped open. Alberto pulled the leather bridle around Trent's head to the left, directing Trent's line of vision so that his goggled-eyes focused on the handle of the obsidian knife embedded deep in his chest. Trent's neck strained as he struggled to breathe air into his left lung that collapsed away from the jagged sucking wound in his chest. Trent's jugular veins stood out like cables just below the skin of the neck.

The chanting stopped with the plunge of the knife. Tenoch pulled the long knife out of the chest and laid the obsidian knife on the tray. Droplets of blood tracked across Trent's abdomen following the path of the bloody knife. Using both hands, Tenoch grasped the upper and lower edges of the chest incision and pulled the wound edges forcibly apart. The cracking sound of fracturing ribs shot through the quiet chamber. The incision gaped widely exposing the pulsating heart, a muscular fist pumping and dancing beneath its tissue investments deep inside Trent's chest.

Tenoch took the second smaller obsidian blade that fit the palm of his left hand and plunged both bare hands into the gaping wound until the root of the heart was in his fingers. With his hands working together, he gathered the great arteries and veins of the heart in his right hand like a sheaf of blood-filled tubes. With his left hand Tenoch pointed the small stone knife blade upward towards the ceiling and repeated again in his slow fearsome cadence, "I am Huitzilopochtli." In response to the pain or to the eerie words from Tenoch, Trent's eyes opened one last time. He screamed silently his final and complete comprehension of his fate.

Tenoch's left hand, holding the smaller obsidian knife, disappeared alongside his right hand into the gaping bloody hole in Trent's chest. For a few seconds, both hands worked in unison, buried to his wrists in the incision. The only visible movement of Tenoch's body was the flexion of his forearms.

After nearly a minute, Tenoch flung his head backwards, setting the feathers of the hood quivering. He screamed at the ceiling mural. "Thus I receiveth the sun to drink." His words ricocheted around the circular chamber. The rumbling timbre of his pronouncement was obliterated by Trent's shrieking cry. Tenoch pulled his forearms upward delivering the severed pumping heart through the opening in Trent's chest.

Trent's heart pulsated and quivered in Tenoch's bloody hands as he raised the pumping heart above his head. Residual blood in the heart spurted in a bloody foam fountain from the eight cleanly transected orifices of the heart's major arteries and veins. The chest wound quickly filled with dark blood overflowing the edges and dripping onto the hard floor bathing Tenoch's bare feet in blood. Tenoch held the beating heart in both hands high above his head, letting the blood drip onto his face and bare chest. The warriors thrust their heads upward. At the tips of Tenoch's fingers, the pulsating heart nearly touched the grotesque bird-like figure painted on the ceiling of the chamber.

"I am the God of the Sun. The blood of life nourishes me," Tenoch shouted again in his awful cadence, turning the pulsating heart in his hands so that the spurting residual blood dribbled from the heart across his face. His tongue lapped away the blood as it fell on his lips.

"I am Huitzilopochtli," he said, now in a booming upbeat rhythm. Slowly he lowered the heart to his face. Tenoch kissed the pale red muscle of the heart. The beating of the heart faded in strength when the heart touched Tenoch's lips. He held the heart pressed to his lips until the beat of the heart stopped completely.

—

Cassy suddenly jumped upright on the bed in Tenoch's guest suite. "Oh my god," she screamed. Startled, Alex looked up from the floor of the guest suite and pushed the puppy out of his lap. He stumbled over his new Macintosh Powerbook computer as he ran to the canopied bed.

"Mom!" he said, shaking Cassy's shoulder. "Wake up. It's a bad dream."

Cassy rubbed her eyes. "I'm sorry, hon," she said, trying to remember the dream, but its overpowering images had already been repressed into the farthest recesses of her mind. Her hands trembled uncontrollably as she reached for Alex.

THIRTY-SIX

L ONG AFTER dusk the lights of central Mexico City below
Tenoch's penthouse twinkled under a dark hazy blanket of smog
that enveloped Tenoch's towering building. The approaching
Aztec helicopter bathed the top of the building in a beam of light that
bore through the gloomy smog to focus on the landing circle of the
rooftop. The passing brightness of the chopper illuminated the penthouse
bedroom. Cassy turned away from the helicopter's light on the panoramic
window and flopped on the bed.

Cassy's inner calm had progressively faded during the afternoon of im-
prisonment in the locked guest suite of Tenoch's Mexico City penthouse.
Lying under the canopied bed, she pulled a lungful of cigarette smoke as
deeply as possible, holding it and feeling the familiar rush of nicotine to
her head. At the peak of an inhalation, she focused on a corner of the
anxiety that had plagued her all afternoon.

It was Tenoch's comment as he left the suite that had jangled her all afternoon: 'I'll be back?' Tenoch had not said, 'We'll be back.' It was 'I'll
be back.' Was his use of 'I' understandable or was it a subtle mind game?
Or a signal to her that Trent would not be returning from the Instituto de
Medico, or wherever they had gone? But where had they gone?

Cassy pulled a last time on the cigarette and rolled over to stub out the
cigarette on the bedside table. She fell back and stared at the undersurface
of the brocaded canopy, knowing that she must reclaim her equanimity.
Unless she controlled her anxiety and dread, she would be unable to complete her plan to rid herself of Tenoch's control.

At that moment, a tapping at the heavy door interrupted her racing mind. The knock repeated itself politely. Rolling off the bed, Cassy padded the two dozen steps in her bare feet to the door. Alberto stood at the door, dressed carefully in a conservative blue business suit, white shirt, and striped tie. "Buenas tardes, Doctora. Señor Tenoch asks the pleasure of your company at dinner," Alberto said.

"It would be my greatest pleasure to dine with Señor Tenoch this evening," Cassy said, responding in fluent formal Spanish.

"Señor Tenoch would like for you to wear this outfit," Alberto said, holding a low-cut white silk blouse with long bouffant sleeves and a pleated long black silk skirt.

"Gracias, Alberto," Cassy said, taking the dress and holding it in front of her, kicking her bare tanned leg out gracefully to fan the pleats on the skirt over her leg. "Tenoch is a very kind man."

Alberto smiled graciously and asked, "What will your son require this evening?"

"Nothing, Alberto. Thank you," Cassy continued in Spanish. "My son is not feeling well right now. He's had terrible diarrhea all afternoon. Turista."

"Sí, Señora. A doctor can be obtained if you wish."

"No. He will be better tomorrow, I'm sure."

"Very well," Alberto said. "Tell your son I will be pleased to stay with him while you are dining with Señor Tenoch."

"That's not necessary. Alex will be in bed soon."

As she started to close the door, Cassy stuck her head through the doorway and asked as a seeming afterthought, "Will Dr. Hendricks be joining Señor Tenoch and me for dinner?"

"No, Señora."

Cassy paused an instant to control her voice. "Where is Dr. Hendricks anyway?" Cassy asked.

"I am not certain, Señora," Alberto said. "I believe the doctor has returned to Dallas."

The fear for Trent exploded within her. The most she could hope was that Trent was alive, but she knew that Trent was almost certainly dead—or suspended, awaiting use as an organ donor like Ruiz, Marquez, and Torres. The pain of realization struck her in the center of her abdomen—Tenoch could force Cassy to harvest Trent Hendricks' heart.

"Are you all right, Dr. Baldwin?" Alberto asked. "You do not look well."

"I'm fine." Cassy smiled and leaned against the door jamb. "Please tell Señor Tenoch I will look forward to his company tonight," she said, a smile frozen on her face.

Alberto bowed from the shoulders. "Muy bien."

Cassy closed the door and waved for Alex to follow her into the bathroom. With the noise of rushing water filling the room Cassy kneeled in front of him and whispered. "It's show time. If everything goes just right, we'll be back at home in the morning. Listen carefully. You must do exactly as I say." She told him what to expect for the next several hours.

"Okay, Mom," Alex said, his forehead wrinkling in attention.

"Don't leave this room tonight unless you're with me. You can watch TV or play with your new computer, but do not leave this room."

"Okay, Mom," Alex said. "When are we going home?"

"Later tonight, but don't say a word about it to anyone," Cassy said. "Now I've got to get dressed. I'm having dinner with Señor Tenoch." She kissed her son's cheek before standing up again.

After Alex had left the bathroom, she breathed deeply in the steam-filled room and pulled off her clothes, tossing them in a clump on the tile floor. She looked in the mirror but only saw her image that moved in perfect synchrony with her movements. Then she stepped into the shower.

After a long steaming shower, Cassy dressed in Tenoch's selection and spun herself in front of the full-length mirror in the dressing room. The whiteness of the long sleeve silk smock shimmered against the tawny skin of her chest. The low, open cut of the silk fabric reached into the cleft between her unfettered breasts. The silkiness of the fabric slid across her breasts, steepling the blouse above her erect nipples. It was the exact sensual effect that Cassy wanted to project at Tenoch. She knew that he would immediately notice. She would see to it that he did notice.

The pleated ebony skirt flowed from her hips to the midpoint of her tan calves, wrapping them in a soft, delicate pleated column. The laces of her black sandals crisscrossed her tan ankles and lower calves, completing a casually elegant effect. Her characteristic wave of dark chestnut hair hung across her right eye almost like a patch. Watching her mirror's image with satisfaction, she slipped the obsidian earrings into the pierces in each earlobe. The obsidian necklace centered on her creamy tan chest above the generous scoop of her white tunic.

Once again she turned to the mirror and looked intently at her face. Time and place vanished in her mind as she studied her facial image and tested her smile. The mirror's image smiled synchronously in return. Cassy watched in fascination. Her mirror's image frowned into a seriousness while Cassy still felt a smile on her lips. Then the lips of her mirror's image whispered, *"You're ready. Now is the time. Do not be afraid."*

Cassy blinked in astonishment. Her hands flew up to touch her still lips. Her mirror's image blinked in symmetry with Cassy. Yes, I am ready Cassy thought. The serious face of the mirror's image melted into a radiant smile that precisely matched her face.

Looking anxiously around the dressing room to be sure that the attendant had not slipped into the room, Cassy felt the hem of her skirt for the four hard glass vials of the Hiberna powder that she had hidden between the folds of fabric. She twisted them like a lucky charm.

Alex sat in the middle of the king-size bed when Cassy stepped through the dressing room door. "Wow, Mom. You're beautiful."

"Thank you, big guy," Cassy said. She kissed the top of his head.

"Remember what I told you about tonight?" she asked.

"I do," Alex said and returned his attention to the satellite broadcast of a Texas Rangers' game.

THIRTY-SEVEN

T HE CLICK OF the latch resounded through the empty dim salon
like a cell door slamming when Cassy shut the door of the guest
suite behind her. The musky fragrance of Tenoch's expensive signature cologne wafted like a smoke signal over the balcony rail of the
grand salon, announcing his presence somewhere in the palatial chamber.

Standing at the top of the sweeping staircase, she searched the murky
room below for Tenoch. The only light in the room, a luminescent haze,
flowed through the glass walls on either side of the vast cathedral-like
room. As she looked down from the balcony, thousands of opalescent
Tiffany chandelier panels glowed with a light that burst into a glowing fireball. The salon was enveloped by a sunlit brightness when Cassy
stepped onto the first step of the wide staircase. At that moment Cassy
caught sight of Tenoch in the leather sofa with his back to her.

"Good evening, my dear," Tenoch said without even turning his head.

His luxuriant black hair glistened with highlights reflected from the
crystals of the radiant chandelier globe. Tenoch's black silk shirt lay
open to the third button. A single ice cube floated in a crystal goblet of
sparkling water on the edge of the low carved stone table in front of the
sofa. Bas relief carvings of grisly misshapen humanoid figures on the sloping sides of the ceremonial stone table ogled Cassy as she descended the
stairway.

Cassy deliberately accentuated the movements of her hips and body,
not so much as to be a caricature but enough to be provocative. Tenoch
stared at her reflection in the glass wall directly in front of him, never
turning his head to look at her directly. Her image in the mirror of the

window wall appeared to be descending into the grand salon from a stairway into the clouds.

When her sandaled foot touched the gleaming dark hardwood floor, Tenoch stood up from the sofa, looking back and forth between her mirrored image in the glass wall and her. He finally turned to her. His thin lips smiled. She sauntered toward him, fixing his dark eyes with a smoldering gaze.

"You are beautiful, carina mía," Tenoch said. She reached her hands to him. The obsidian ring on his index finger gleamed like a shining third eye when he lifted her hand and pressed his lips to the back of her hand, lingering a moist caress of the backs of her fingers.

Tenoch pulled her forward and cupped her chin in his soft hand. His eyes met hers until he brought her lips softly to his. After a time that seemed forever to Cassy, he pulled away from her and whispered in her ear. "I have the special tea which you enjoyed with me the last time." He took her hand in his and guided her to the sofa.

Cassy folded her legs beneath her on the leather lounge and pulled the black pleated skirt above her tanned bare knees. A moment later Cassy rearranged her legs again so that her bare shin brushed the length of his thigh.

Reaching behind Cassy, Tenoch retrieved a remote control keypad. With the touch of his finger, the grand salon was plunged into shadows. The murky light from the chandelier globe produced a chiaroscuro of angles and ridges in Tenoch's face. The glass walls melted. The room became continuous with the dark hazy air hanging outside the penthouse.

Without looking away from Cassy's eyes, Tenoch touched the remote control keypad again. Instantly the pinafored maid appeared like a ghost out of the darkness carrying a gold tray with a crystal decanter of dark liquid and two crystal champagne flutes. Another maid materialized with a gold platter piled with a quadrangular pyramid mound of perfectly formed strawberries floating in a pool of tan crème fraîche.

Cassy leaned forward to pluck the topmost berry from the mound in a movement of her upper body that opened her scooped neckline to Tenoch. "Beautiful strawberries. My favorite!" she said. After burying the strawberry in the thick crème fraîche, she licked the sweet tangy sauce off the berry. The tip of her tongue sensuously rolled over the perfectly conical end of the berry. Tenoch's dark eyes followed the movements of her mouth and tongue as she sucked the sauce from the end of the berry. "I love them," she said and leaned forward to reach another berry, allowing her blouse to droop forward over her chest again. She lingered in that position for several moments as she seemingly hesitated over her decision about which berry to pluck from the mound.

"Strawberries stimulate all appetites," Tenoch said, reaching for a berry and dipping it in the thick creamy sauce. He bit the tip of the berry, chewing the fruit slowly.

"For every appetite?" Cassy asked, smiling as she looked into his eyes. His flat black eyes did not move from hers. Straining in the semidarkness, Cassy simply could not see inside Tenoch's inky eyes. With another berry, she repeated the dance of her tongue around the end of the berry, licking away the cream sauce.

"Yes, for all appetites, my dear," Tenoch said in Spanish.

"By all means, we must eat many of them," she said, dipping another berry into the cream and cupping her hand under it as she lifted the crème-dripping berry to his lips. "May I have some of your special tea?" she asked and rolled her body forward to press yet another cream-dipped strawberry to his lips.

"Yes, for both of us," he said. Cassy filled two crystal flutes with the sparkling dark tea. The side of the tapered glass immediately condensed with moisture from the frigid tea. Cassy folded her legs back under her, facing him. Her bare knee gently caressed the length of his thigh. "To our destiny," he said, lifting his crystal glass to touch the rim of her glass.

She held his eyes in hers. Even at the range of less than a foot, Cassy could not see into his opaque eyes. Perhaps I'm seeing all there is and nothing is behind his eyes, Cassy thought, as she lifted the tea to her lips.

The rush of exhilaration with the first sip of tea revived the euphoria that Cassy remembered from the weekend. The dose-response relationship of the tea and the euphoria is now so clear she thought. Why couldn't I have seen it at first? I was a fool. How could I not have connected my sexual responsiveness to the drinking of Tenoch's special tea mixture? It should have been obvious. Because I didn't want to make that connection, she answered. Her mind had simply denied the cause and effect—denied the tea as the cause. She had wanted to respond to this man, and she had wanted him to respond to her. It was a classic form of psychological denial that Saturday night, but tonight would be different she knew.

During her reverie after the first sip of tea, Tenoch's eyes had locked on her as if in a hypnotic trance. She saw Tenoch's lips moving. Cassy heard only his last few words. "Your son is not well?"

Tenoch reached for another strawberry. "Shall I have a nanny stay with him tonight?" The question implied far more than her son's welfare.

"No, that's not necessary. He's already in bed and will be asleep soon," Cassy said. "And I don't plan to disturb him all night." She was certain he understood her implied acceptance of his invitation for the night. She

drank the rest of the tea and rimmed the glass with her tongue as she
looked at him intently.

"Our fate together cannot be denied," he said, refilling her glass with
more of the iced tea mixture.

"I will not deny you." Cassy reached for his left hand and stroked the
obsidian stone in his gold ring.

Her body began to respond to the ingredients in the tea just as it had
on the weekend. Cassy observed her body's response like a detached, im-
partial research scientist. The warmth in her cheeks and face produced a
fine sheen of moisture on her forehead and at the base of her dark hair.
Her objective mind recorded, like an EKG monitor without emotion,
the acceleration in her heart beat. She noted the pounding pulse in her
chest, a sign of her rising blood pressure. By the end of the second glass
of tea, the dull pressure in her pelvis and groin rose like fog around her.
The intensity of her sexual urgency gnawed at her control.

Little by little, she moved her body closer into him letting the silk
blouse drop off her breasts. "I'm excited about being here in Mexico
City," she said, sighing heavily. Under any other circumstances she knew
her gestures would be theatrical and overstated. But this evening for her
purpose, her exaggerated emotions were quite appropriate and normal
appearing. Tenoch touched his finger to the remote control device. The
maid instantly appeared with another crystal decanter of tea and vanished
as quickly as she appeared.

"I am pleased that you insisted I come share our destiny," she whispered in his ear, letting her tongue flick his ear.

"Carina mía, do not be in a hurry," he said. "We have all night for each
other."

"I'm sorry," Cassy said. "Being near you does things to me." Tenoch
refilled her glass. Cassy sipped the tea. Warm sensual feelings flowed
through her body.

"I had a productive meeting with Trent at the Instituto de Medico this
afternoon," Tenoch said matter-of-factly. The skin on Cassy's neck shivered into goose flesh. She knew that Tenoch was exercising his control,
thrusting at her with the comment about Trent. She let it pass by. "The
organ procurement program is in full readiness. You shall remain in Mexico City."

"What about my life in Dallas?"

"It is past."

Cassy leaned forward to touch her lips to his. "I am yours," she whispered. As soon as she pulled her mouth away, Tenoch's lips moved again.
He smiled at her. She heard the sounds of his words, but her mind did

not decipher them. She felt herself drawn forward to him, her mind drawn into him through his lips.

Her scientist's mind recognized her body's responses. The powerful sensual urges, fueled by the aphrodisiac tea ingredients, fought to uncouple her control. She strained to rein in her body's swelling sexual impulses. The torment of her sexuality induced by Tenoch's tea shrieked. A mental flash of Alex countered her sexual urgency, and the cold grip of lucidity returned to her mind despite the burning responses within her body.

Tenoch was also becoming aroused by the pharmacology of the tea and also by Cassy's tantalizing. His dilated pupils, his riveting gaze, and his hands playing on her neck and dancing in the semicircle of her scoop-neck blouse told her that she was gaining control.

Cassy turned to him and clasped her body to his. He returned her kiss with surprising gentleness. Despite her renewed objectivity, Cassy felt a shiver of desire radiate through her. She touched her lips to his ear lobe and slid her hand up his inner thigh until she found the hardness beneath his silk pants. She felt his surge of breath as he sucked for air when she did not move her hand away from him.

He raised his mouth from hers and looked directly into her eyes. "Our incarnations have been together before and will always be." The cold hand of fear grabbed her. Cassy buried her face in the hollow of his neck and kissed the base of his neck. Her heartbeat detonated as she sensed the urgency of his drug-induced arousal.

Easy, easy, she cautioned herself. Cassy commanded herself not to lose control. She knew she must allow herself to be aroused in order to stimulate him even further. Her plan required these preliminaries, like a player's warm-up. It was a mind's edge between her body's desire and her self-imposed control that her plan demanded. Like an athlete, she could not lose that fine edge of mind control.

She searched his lips and explored his firm open mouth with her tongue.

"Come with me," she said, pulling away from him to stand in front of him. She picked up the gold platter of strawberries and leaned over him to kiss his mouth with an urgency and aggressiveness that belied her renewed inner calm.

"Let's go to your bedroom," she said, pushing her body against him. His tense rigidity pressed against her taut lower abdomen until she pulled away and led him up the stairs to his bedroom.

The two hundred forty degree glass parabolic bow formed by the three outside walls jutted his bedroom into the dark smoky haze shrouding the penthouse. Except for the flickering light of candles about the room, the only light was the moon filtering through the tinted glass. The canopied king-size bed was dwarfed in the huge glass room.

A gold tray filled with strawberries and crème fraîche sat on the bedside stand next to a gold decanter filled with tea. Cassy refilled two crystal flutes and turned to hand one to Tenoch.

They stared across the darkness at each other over the crystal glasses with a beamed intensity that could have lighted the room. Both drank the tea completely. Cassy set both glasses on the bedside table next to a flickering wax taper candle. She turned back to him in the wavering candlelight and slipped her arms under his silk shirt, pulling herself against him. With her chest molded to him, she breathed on his face and ground herself against him. She felt the moistness of her own arousal. His lips met hers. He regained control of their meeting. His hands searched for her in the darkness and caressed her neck and shoulders slipping his hands beneath her silk blouse.

Slowly she pulled back from him, tracing her fingers sensuously along his extended arms. Standing in front of him, she undid each of the buttons of his silk shirt, feeling for them in the flickering dimness. The black silk shirt fell away behind him onto the satin sheets of the canopied bed. His muscular chest glistened. Cassy traced the pattern of his pectoral muscles with the pads of her fingers, slowly outlining each areola and nipple. Control passed back to Cassy as her movements dominated Tenoch, much like the charmer before the cobra. Tenoch stood motionless as if spellbound.

While the fingers of her left hand traced circles around each of his nipples, her right hand groped in the darkness for the gold platter of strawberries. Coating a berry with the thick creamy sauce, she carried the succulent strawberry toward Tenoch's waiting mouth. The crème fraîche dripped a luscious trail across his chest and neck. She held the strawberry to his lips while his tongue licked away the creamy sauce from the finely stubbled surface of the strawberry. He then opened his mouth, nibbling away at the berry until her fingers were enclosed by his lips.

Cassy then brought her mouth over his neck and chest, licking away the crème fraîche that had dripped onto his skin. While he stood motionless, she continued to trace her lips over his neck and chest and felt his rapid intake of breath as her tongue grazed his nipples. She reached down to release his belt, and his silk pants dropped to the floor. He stood naked except for a suede loin cloth that barely contained its bulge. He was seemingly hypnotized. She teased and massaged every sensitive area of his body that she identified.

"Your destiny will be done," Cassy said as she knelt beside him. He stood quietly beside her, not reaching for her or reciprocating her touch.

Her head bowed before him as if a supplicant, and she rested her forehead on his bare knees. Her fingers treaded lightly along the muscles of his inner thigh. She gently pulled him downward until his knees bent. He sank slowly to the edge of the bed.

In the dim candlelight his black eyes were invisible dark cores in his face. He sat quiet and unmoving, ceding all control to her. Slowly she eased him flat onto the bed. Her hands and lips continued to mesmerize him until he lay motionless, a beatific smile on his face.

She leaned over him. Her tongue teased at his ear lobe. Finally she whispered into his ear, "I must prepare myself."

Cassy disappeared into the bathroom and closed the door securely behind her before turning on the light. The fluorescent brilliance stunned her darkness-accommodated eyes. She quickly squinted against the brightness and closed both eyes. Slowly her eyes reopened, one at a time, in the harsh light to look at her reflection in the mirror. Her cheeks and upper chest were flushed red with excitement.

She slipped the hoops of the obsidian earrings from her earlobes and unsnapped the obsidian necklace, carefully placing the earrings within the coil formed by the necklace on the black granite surface of the lavatory. She lifted the white silk blouse over her head and stepped out of the slim pleated black skirt. She stood before the full-length wall mirror, naked except for her black lace bikini panties. Her mirror's image stared at her. Cassy said to her mirror's image, "I am ready." Her mirror's image returned Cassy's serious, determined expression.

She hung the blouse and skirt over the brass towel rack and retrieved the four vials of Hiberna powder from the hem of the skirt. Twisting the rubber seals off each of the thimble-size glass containers she poured the tan powder into the palm of her hand and closed her fingers about the Hiberna mixture. The coarse granular powder of the four vials filled her palm. She felt as if she had grabbed a handful of brown sugar and not a fistful of a powerful deadly neurotoxin.

After flipping off the bathroom light, she opened the door into the flickering candlelight of the bedroom. Pausing until her eyes accommodated to the darkness, she was finally able to see Tenoch lying naked on the bed just as she had left him, a blissful smile on his lips.

As she quietly approached the bed in her bare feet, she could only see black voids where his eyes were located in his immobile head. For a moment Cassy stood at the bedside in her bikini panties, knowing now for certain the details of her plan and not regretting its necessity at all. Tenoch did not move.

Leaning over him, she pressed her lips against his and covered his mouth as the tips of the fingers of her left hand explored his neck and upper chest. She kept the balled fist of her right hand holding the Hi-berna tucked behind her back. Tenoch opened his eyes as her mouth found his. When Cassy finally lifted her lips off his, Tenoch said softly in Spanish, "Carina mía, come to me."

"It will be my honor to give you pleasure," Cassy said, whispering heavily as her tongue teased the ridges of his ear. "Allow me to offer a special treat." He slowly nodded his head in acceptance. The blissful smile stayed on his lips.

Standing upright, she moved her body slowly so that her buttocks were turned toward Tenoch. His view of her right hand was blocked by her pelvis when she dumped the tan granular powder into the crème fraîche and stirred the powder evenly in the creamy sauce with her index finger.

As she stirred the crème, she felt Tenoch's soft hand close around the back of her thigh and move upward. The gentle pressure of his warm, soft hand sent a shock wave up into her pelvis. The pressure in her lower abdomen became so intense that she was certain that her engorgement would rupture inside her.

Turning back toward him, she leaned over and covered his mouth with her lips, again tantalizing him with her tongue. As she moved her lips down to his neck, she brought her right index finger coated with the crème fraîche up to trace the outline of his thin lips. His tongue darted out to caress her fingertip and lick away the creamy sauce. His breath came in quick shallow bursts. She could hear the hammering of his heart beat beneath her left ear. She slowly pulled her right index finger back from his lips.

Cassy stood before him. He reached up to pull her back. Cassy was just beyond the reach of his hands, teasing him into further arousal. His black eyes focused on her. She knew that he would now follow her lead. Control was still hers. She had become the source of his pleasure. As he watched her, Cassy hooked her thumbs under the band of her bikini panties and rolled her hips sensuously. She wiggled the panties down her long legs and stepped out of them to stand naked before Tenoch.

Turning in a slow-motion, voluptuous pirouette before him, Cassy passed her right hand through the crème fraîche again. The cool, sticky sauce coated her index and middle fingers up to the knuckles. She curled two fingers into her palm and brought them dripping to Tenoch's mouth. His tongue licked the crème fraîche eagerly from her fingers and the palm of her hand.

With her other hand, she traced downward on his tense hairless ab-domen until her fingers slid under the slender suede leather strap of his loincloth. His lips sucked vigorously at Cassy's cream-coated index and

ring fingers. Her left hand found the clasp holding the loincloth and released the strap. His erection burst out of its suede leather restraint. In the
darkness Cassy smiled as she continued moving her lips around and over
his chest and upper abdomen, tantalizing him into a shivering frenzy. Cassy
was now more confident than ever that her plan might succeed.

When Tenoch had licked away the creamy sauce from her fingers,
Cassy rolled them again in the pool of crème fraîche and returned her
fingers to his waiting lips. Despite her steely determination, she found
her pulse racing. Tenoch's profound sensual arousal had ignited her own
biological responses.

Again and again she curled her cream-dripping fingers into her palm
and carried the sauce to his lips. A dribble of the sticky sweet sauce trailed
across the satin pillow case as Cassy moved her hand quickly back and
forth to the bedside platter. Each time she found his waiting mouth and
inserted both creamy fingers between his lips. All the time her left hand
enclosed his tense, engorged penis. His tongue licked hungrily at her
fingers. Her own urgency rolled up in crescendo waves as his arousal
intensified.

A rough urgency took hold of Tenoch. Both his hands seized her head,
pushing her toward his groin. No words were necessary. Cassy knew exactly what Tenoch demanded. Tenoch's sexual urgency would not be denied. His involuntary pelvic movements bumped Cassy's face as his hands
pushed her head downward.

With her head clutched in both his hands, his sexual command became
clear and insistent. He said nothing, but militant control changed his
mood—an aggressiveness had overcome his blissful acceptance of her
sexual tantalizing. She was no longer the sexual aggressor.

His underlying cruelness had been awakened by his induced sexual
urgencies. With her head caught helpless in the vise of his two hands,
Cassy's composure ripped apart. An overwhelming doubt exploded her
carefully designed plan. Stark fear gripped her tighter than Tenoch's hands.
Her rational mind flooded with self-doubt about her self-conceived plan
to escape Tenoch's madness.

Is the tan, granular powder really the tetrodotoxin? How do I know
the vials I stole from the Park Haven are really Hiberna? she asked herself. Maybe the powder I stole doesn't have the active ingredients to cause
paralysis. How long does it take for the tetrodotoxin to paralyze? How
could I be so stupid not to have checked to be absolutely sure the vials
contained the active drug?

His hands forced her left cheek against his rigid shaft. My god, she
worried in horror. What is happening? Tenoch should be paralyzed by

now! If the powder in the four vials did not contain the paralyzing tetro-dotoxin that Tenoch had used on Marquez, Ana Ruiz, and Juan Torres, she had failed. There was no contingency plan. No back up. She had been so sure, but now her rational mind was silent. Cassy was alone with Tenoch's unleashed power and unrepressed sexual urgency that she had purposefully aroused.

Once again she carried her cream-covered fingers to his mouth. He suck-led her fingers like a baby at his mother's nipple. Cassy held his erection with her left hand. A low moan of pleasure rattled from his mouth, vibrat-ing his tongue on her creamed index and middle fingers in his mouth. Then the tightness of his hands gripping her face lessened. His pumping pelvic gyrations slowed like a dying engine. For a moment, his erection maintained itself, but then gradually the swollen shaft wilted in her hand.

Cassy cautiously raised her head just as Tenoch's hands fell slackly to the side of his body. Was this the pharmacologic effect she had planned? Or was he just spent from a powerful orgasm? Cassy could not be certain. She moved her head slowly upward and looked into his black eyes, half hidden under drooping lids. His head drooped over his shoulder. She could read in his eyes his futile and frantic efforts to raise his extremities. His fingers tried to claw the sheet but were unable to grasp.

"I know that you can hear me," she said calmly, rolling from the bed and leaning over his face. Her naked torso angled over his upper body. "But you can't move. I have paralyzed you with Hiberna . . . just like you poisoned me, Marquez, Ana Ruiz, and Juan Torres, and who knows how many others."

Cassy sat down on the edge of the bed, crossed her naked legs, and placed her left hand on Tenoch's bare motionless chest. For several min-utes she sat in the quiet room, dimly aglow with the phosphorescence of the night sky beyond the wall of glass and the flickering candles within the room. Time blurred in Cassy's mind as her fingertips just below his left nipple monitored the gradual slowing of Tenoch's heartbeat until only an occasional thump of his heart muscle bumped his chest.

Pulling a burning candle close to his face, like an ophthalmologist ex-amining an eyeball, Cassy pulled apart Tenoch's eyelids, exposing the blackness of his dilated pupil set in its brilliant white scleral covering. The eye was as unmoving as if it were detached from the socket.

"You are evil," Cassy said. "Vicious. Without a conscience. You de-stroy everything around you," she said. The black pupillary opening in Tenoch's eyeball constricted in response to the candle flame Cassy held close. The light from the candle fluttered shadows across Cassy's face, turning her soft delicate features a hideous orange.

"How do you enjoy the paralysis of the Hiberna solution? You are in a suspended animation state from the tetrodotoxin powder I mixed with the crème fraîche you like so well. By all detectable signs you are dead just like Marquez." Cassy released his eyelids. They closed slowly like an oyster shell coming together.

With her right hand she wiped more of the adulterated crème fraîche onto her fingers. Pulling his lips away from his slack jaw, she carefully swabbed the poisonous cream sauce onto the pink mucous membrane of his inner cheek. Then, pinching his lips together, she rubbed his cheek to massage the crème fraîche into his gums and hasten the absorption of the neurotoxin into his blood stream.

For a long time, Cassy sat on the edge of the bed watching Tenoch, searching his naked body for any sign of movement. Several times she checked his pulse and could find none. Again she brought the candle flame close to his face, looking for any light reflex in his eye. There was none. Again she laid her left hand lightly just below his left nipple, feeling for any faint tap of a heartbeat. She could feel none.

After more time, Cassy was certain that Tenoch's life had passed into the clinical death phase, that metamorphosis into a netherworld just beyond life where all bodily functions essentially cease, a transient way station on the journey to irreversible brain death. For some, that clinical death pause might be extended for seconds, minutes, hours. Perhaps it is a zombie state . . . a state of temporary suspended animation. Trent Hendricks had discovered the pharmacologic means to extend the duration of the clinical death phase with his scientific titration of the dose of tetrodotoxin, and Cassy had built her plan of escape on Trent's discovery.

Much later, Cassy stood full upright at the bedside, her head grazing the heavy fabric of the canopy fringe. Her heart hammered away as she looked at the motionless, waxen figure lying before her. In an unwavering voice, she said, "I pray that you will find your own personal hell."

Cassy walked to the dressing room, her nakedness not a conscious awareness. When she turned into Tenoch's dark dressing room, the mirror above the lavatory shined with its own iridescence, lighting the dressing room with spectral beams of radiance. Cassy stopped cold. The mirror's glow backlighted itself. Her mirror's image appeared floating, blurred, and surreal.

"*He is evil,*" her mirror's image said. Cassy's hands flew to her lips. "*You are not finished,*" her mirror's image said. "*You have not yet destroyed the evil.*" Then her mirror's image faded into the dark opaque screen of the mirror.

A chill surged through Cassy, causing goose flesh over her bare arms and legs. Staring at the opaque mirror, Cassy could see only blackness.

No reflection whatsoever. The mirror was a black void. It was no longer a mirror that reflected. She searched the mirror, rubbing her fingertips across the slick dark flat surface. Slowly she comprehended the message from her mirror's image. Cassy was not yet finished with Tenoch.

THIRTY-EIGHT

THE NIGHT'S passage blurred in Cassy's mind. She had no idea how much time had gone by since she returned to Tenoch's bedside. Without turning on the bedside light she perched herself, still naked, on the edge of the bed and stared at the nude, motionless body that earlier had been so fearsome. Tenoch seemed smaller as he lay quiet and unmoving. His dark skin was dull against the gold glow of the satin sheets radiating the dim, flickering light from the dying candles.

Leaning under the canopied bed, she whispered in Tenoch's ear, "I know that you can hear me. You are suspended in the clinical death stage just like Marquez, Ana Ruiz, Juan Torres, and me. But I will not allow you to come back to life." Methodically, she dipped her fingers into the remaining droplets of cream sauce and swabbed the inside of his loose mouth, back and forth, time after time, until the platter was empty of the tetrodotoxin-adulterated crème fraîche. Cassy then leaned forward, placed her lips on his forehead in a kiss, and whispered in his ear, "Adios, carino mío."

In the wavering shadowlight, Cassy walked back to the dressing room, squinting into the brightness and momentarily shading her eyes from the mirror's light. The opaque black screen was once again a mirror. Her mirror's image looked back at her, in perfect symmetry, matching her every movement. Cassy leaned her face close to the polished reflective surface. She raised her eyebrows. Her image responded exactly. For several seconds Cassy studied her face in the mirror's reflection, testing her facial and lip movements. With each movement, her mirror's image responded exactly. Satisfied, she turned away from the mirror and into the shower.

Under the steaming rain of the twelve-jet shower, Cassy scrubbed her skin vigorously, washing away the smell and sensation of Tenoch's body. Out of the shower, she rubbed her body and face with the terry towel even more intensely. Again she checked the mirror and found that her mirror's image moved in absolute synchrony with her movements.

The candles smoldered in the darkness of the bedroom when Cassy walked naked back to Tenoch's bedside and examined him. She was unable to find any clinical signs of life. No respiration. No pulse. No movement. No reflexes. Tenoch's motionless body rested like a naked corpse on gold satin sheets.

The rumpled clothing dropped carelessly at the bedside, the champagne flutes, the crumbled mound of strawberries, the leather loincloth—all shouted 'orgy' at a moment's glance.

Cassy paced about the huge room following the glass curvature of the room overlooking the city. The next period of time collapsed on itself. Cassy was uncertain how long she stood at the window in a world of her own, staring without seeing into the smoky haze that eclipsed the city below and the sky above. Sometime later she turned from the window and glanced at Tenoch's body. It was unmoved and still as if he were asleep, quiet and peaceful. His lack of any movement betrayed any hint of life.

Back at the bedside, Cassy sat on the edge of the bed. After moving the burning candle to illuminate Tenoch's face, she again examined his eyes. The pupillary opening in each eye was a black dilated void, completely unresponsive to light. She lifted each arm by his wrist, releasing the arm and allowing it to fall limp to the bed. Then she picked up each leg by the ankle and dropped it, allowing them to fall heavily without muscular control onto the gold satin sheets.

A residue of unabsorbed crème fraîche remained in Tenoch's mouth. With a moist washcloth from the dressing room, Cassy meticulously cleansed away all the vestiges of sauce from Tenoch's mouth and lips. She carefully rinsed the washcloth she had used to wipe Tenoch's face. Then she heaved his limp body so that an arm and leg hung flaccid from the edge of the bed, appearing as if he had tried to get out of bed then fell back, half onto it. After tucking the four empty Hiberna vials back into the hem of her black pleated skirt, she dropped it crumpled to the floor at Tenoch's bedside.

Satisfied that Tenoch was totally immobilized and suspended by the tetrodotoxin of the Hiberna solution, Cassy walked to the massive double door of the suite and paused before opening it. She looked down at herself, aware of her nakedness for the first time that evening, and took a deep breath.

Throwing back the door of the suite so that it crashed against the door stop, she ran to the edge of the balcony at the stairwell opening. Cassy's scream shattered the silence of the dark grand salon below. "Help! Oh, God! Help!" she shrieked into the dark.

Moments later the grand salon burst into brightness as if under exploding incendiary flares from the gold chandelier globe in the lofty arched ceiling. Four khaki-uniformed guards, automatic rifles drawn, scattered like unleashed guard dogs through the doorway at the end of the room. The men hustled through the salon searching its corners, confused by the silence. Blinded by the brilliance of the chandelier globe, they were unable to see Cassy standing naked on the balcony.

Again Cassy screamed, "Help! Help me! For God's sake." She banged on the balcony balustrade. The guards stopped, gaping upward. Naked and screaming, Cassy swung her arms wildly, her breasts moving like an exotic club dancer on an elevated pedestal.

For the third time Cassy screamed into the huge room, finally galvanizing the men back into movement. They ran toward the stairwell as the maid rushed through the service entrance at the far end of the room. Cassy screamed again. "Help! Tenoch has had a heart attack."

The four guards hit the staircase in pairs, taking the steps two at a time. The maid scurried the length of the grand salon following the men up the staircase. Just as the guards raced past Cassy into the suite, Alberto lunged through the service entrance, pulling a pair of khaki pants up. His feet and chest were bare. His expression was bewildered and frantic.

"Madre de Dios," the maid screeched. She ran toward Tenoch's body in the dim room. One of the guards slapped the switchplate lighting the room with a harshness that magnified the horror of Tenoch's naked body sprawled half off the bed, swirled in the gold satin sheets.

The dark night sky beyond the glass window and the now bright interior of the room created a mirrored parabola of the room's windows, reflecting the people and movements in the suite as if on a curved movie screen. The maid touched Tenoch's expressionless face and immediately traced the sign of the cross on her chest, mumbling words that only she could understand. Spirals of smoke hung about the dying glow of the spent candles, permeating the room with a mixture of a sexual musk, expensive cologne and perfume, and the paraffined odor of a dozen dying wax candles.

Two of the guards pulled Tenoch's body back onto the bed and spread the gold sheets over his naked torso, gently placing his limp arms at his side. Even in apparent death Tenoch commanded the respect and fear of his followers and employees.

Cassy stood, appearing dazed, still naked. Gnawing the back of her hand, she stared at Tenoch as if she were stunned and disoriented. Sobbing sounds mewed from her lips and nose, but her eyes remained dry and clear. "He's had a heart attack . . . just as we . . . ," Cassy said. Her voice trailed into a moaning wail. Alberto wrapped a bath towel about her heaving shoulders.

"What should I do, Dr. Baldwin?" Alberto asked, his voice breaking. Cassy could read the strained lines of fear and panic in Alberto's face. "Is Tenoch dead?"

"I . . . I don't know," Cassy said, stuttering her words and pulling the huge towel about her to cover her body but not quite completely. She walked toward Tenoch's body. The two guards nervously fiddled with him, constantly readjusting the position of his arms and legs, and finally pulling the golden satin sheet up to his neck.

Finding Tenoch's limp forearm beneath the sheet, Cassy pressed her fingers on the flat surface of his wrist feeling for the radial pulse. There was none. Then her fingers searched for the carotid artery pulse at the angle of his jaw. Good, she thought. No detectable pulse. She peered in his eyes again, pulling apart the lids and exposing the widely dilated pupillary opening to the harsh bright light of the room. The black circular openings did not constrict when she held the eyelids open to the light of the room.

The maid nervously scampered about the room, clearing away the tea decanter and the crystal flutes, doing the only tasks she knew to perform. Balancing the gold tray on her other hand, she disappeared out the door.

Cassy straightened up, paused as if to compose herself, and shook her head. "It's bad. He may not be dead yet. We must get him to the Instituto de Medico. It's his only chance. Is the helicopter ready?"

Alberto grabbed the phone and shouted orders rapidly and turned back to Cassy. "Five minutes," he said and turned quickly to speak in Spanish to the two guards.

Two of the Hispanic guards grabbed Tenoch, one under his shoulders and the other at both legs, and trundled Tenoch's naked body out the door of the suite, down the staircase, and through the grand salon.

"Quickly. We must hurry," Cassy said. She pulled on her skirt and blouse while Alberto sat on the vacant bed, visibly shaken by the events of the last few minutes.

———

The square landing pad blazed under the focused beams of halogen lights that ringed the perimeter of the rooftop. The burnt orange wind sock flapped in the chaotic night winds swirling about the rooftop of Tenoch's penthouse as the two guards carried the limp body of Tenoch out of the elevator enclosure.

The Bell helicopter's engines' throaty rumble spun the main rotor blade slowly. The pilot looked anxiously out the side window at the hunched figures scurrying toward the open door of the waiting chopper. The pilot's instructions from Alberto during the frantic telephone call minutes before had been to prepare for an immediate 'hot loading'. A hurried nighttime departure with the helicopter's blades revolving even before Tenoch was seated in the passenger compartment was not at all unusual. Tenoch never waited in the chopper's cabin while the pilot completed his pre-flight check. Tonight was to be no different.

But the pilot was not prepared for the unnerving sight of the two guards carrying Tenoch's limp body suspended between them as the group ducked under the revolving blades. Anxiously he nudged the speed of the rotor revolutions up, whipping the air above the rooftop and vibrating the chopper.

Alberto jumped into the cabin of the helicopter. The two guards awkwardly handed Tenoch's naked body like a sack of potatoes into the passenger compartment. Alberto supervised the positioning of Tenoch, collapsed and accordioned, between the two guards on the front facing seat bench and cinched the seat belt tight around the body. Cassy, now dressed again in the white scoop-necked blouse and black pleated skirt, sat opposite them in the rear facing seats.

"Let's go," shouted Alberto into the pilot's intercom over the whine of the roaring engines. Alberto closed the cabin door, and the chopper lifted off the landing pad.

Tenoch drooped forward as the helicopter ascended and rotated to the south. His olive face blanched into a translucent tan. His eyelids remained closed. His black hair was dull and disarrayed as if life had already departed.

"He looks dead," Alberto said to Cassy, pulling Tenoch's chin up off his bare chest. Saliva drooled from the corner of Tenoch's slack mouth. Cassy could see flecks of the undissolved tan crème fraîche in the spittle. She reached across the cabin and wiped his mouth with the corner of the gold satin sheet that one of the guards had wadded over Tenoch's groin.

Cassy took Tenoch's wrist and felt for a pulse for nearly half a minute. "There's no radial pulse," she said. Feeling at the angle of his jaw, she finally said, "I can't find a carotid pulse either. He's gone into full cardiac arrest. Get Dr. Garcia on the airphone. We have to notify the ER to be ready for a major CPR effort when we land. It's Tenoch's only chance."

Alberto pulled the airborne telephone out of a wall cabinet and spoke in quick Spanish. Moments later he handed the telephone to Cassy. Without any preamble Cassy said, "Raul, I'm en route to the Emergency Room with Señor Tenoch in his helicopter. He's had a massive heart attack." She paused, looking at Tenoch's body and then to Alberto before she continued, "He's had a cardiac arrest. He will need full life support. We should be landing in five or ten minutes."

The pilot pulled the helicopter into a steeply arched trajectory toward the Instituto de Medico twelve miles away. When the pilot approached the landing square outside the ER, the helicopter hovered only a moment before the steel tubular landing sled of the helicopter banged the precise middle of the white concrete square, jarring the passengers and tossing Tenoch's body forward against the tight seatbelt.

A half dozen white-coated Hispanic men and women ran under the spinning blades as soon as the helicopter scraped to a standstill on the concrete surface. Tenoch's flaccid body was quickly lifted onto a waiting ER gurney. The team raced the cart across the concrete pathway into the ER. One of the white-coated attendants pushed, another pulled, and another pair ran along either side of the gurney. Cassy raced alongside the gurney with her hand on the side of the carrier, pulling herself along, hoping that her thin, black sandals didn't trip her. A khaki-clad guard, carrying an automatic rifle, ran in front of the hurtling gurney while the other trailed behind the stretcher.

"This is Señor Tenoch," Cassy said with authority as the gurney stopped at the triage area of the emergency room. "I am Dr. Cassandra Baldwin." The two young ER physicians, looking barely old enough to be medical school graduates, eyed her cautiously and then nodded to her as if acknowledging her position and authority.

A nurse quickly wrapped a canvas-covered blood pressure cuff about Tenoch's bare arm and with a handheld rubber bulb pumped up the rubber blood pressure cuff that encircled Tenoch's upper arm. Looking intently at the round dial of the pressure gauge, she released the pressure. She shook her head and grimaced before repeating the procedure three more times. Then the nurse announced solemnly what was clearly evident, "No blood pressure."

Another nurse quickly attached electrocardiogram leads to each extremity. A green phosphorescent dot immediately appeared on the video monitor screen. The green dot traced an unbroken line, as if a glowing wire had been stretched across the videoscreen. There were no blips or bumps in the luminescent flat line.

Tenoch's heart was in complete standstill.

One of the young doctors held the bell-shaped end of his stethoscope on Tenoch's chest just below the left nipple. He listened intently for a heartbeat for nearly a minute while the other ER physician lifted Tenoch's eyelids and peered into the eyeballs. Finally, the two physicians stood up from their crouched positions over the gurney. They both looked across Tenoch's naked body at Cassy and shook their heads. "I am sorry," the sober-faced young physician said in Spanish, "He's dead."

"This is Señor Tenoch," Cassy said, summoning up her most authoritative voice. Her Spanish phrasing and accent were nearly a perfect native tongue. "You must resuscitate him." The two physicians looked at each other and then at the guards holding the automatic rifles. Both of the physicians shrugged.

The somber expressions in their eyes needed no translation into English. It was the universal unspoken expression that physicians use to convey the grim reality of death without the spoken word. "It's no use, Dr. Baldwin," one of the ER doctors said. "He's dead. There's nothing more that can be done."

At that moment Alberto pulled the two Mexican doctors to the side of the room and in rapid street Spanish shouted at them. Their sweaty faces paled, and both heads nodded with a snap. The two men quickly returned to stand on either side of the gurney. "Sí, Doctora. As you wish, we will commence CPR," one physician said as he stepped onto a small metal platform stool beneath the gurney and began pressing his extended arms and flattened palms against Tenoch's breast bone, rhythmically compressing the ribcage and the heart within. The second physician adroitly inserted a laryngoscope flashlight into Tenoch's mouth and guided an endotracheal tube into Tenoch's windpipe, bringing oxygen into Tenoch's lungs. The two doctors worked in perfect concert, one inflating Tenoch's lungs with the breathing bag in between every fourth breast bone compression.

Cassy watched this death ritual—minute after minute, as the physician pumped Tenoch's chest with repetitive jabs. After nearly an hour of this intense and exhaustive effort, the two physicians looked inquiringly toward Cassy. An unspoken plea passed from the two men, silently communicating the message—'Dr. Baldwin, this is an exercise in futility. Señor Tenoch is dead'. Without a spoken word, the two doctors were seeking Cassy's permission to stop. The three physicians understood each other perfectly.

Without hesitation, Cassy shook her head. The acknowledged control of the resuscitation effort now rested completely with Cassy. Her plan that she had quickly designed in response to the words of her mirror's image required her to appear as if she were persisting beyond all reason to save Tenoch's life.

"You must not stop. This is Señor Tenoch," Cassy said. "Continue the closed chest massage." The sweat-stained doctor continued to pump his fist into Tenoch's breast bone each second, in time with the other ER physician's squeeze of the ventilating bag every four seconds. It was a four-to-one step—a death waltz in the ER of the Instituto de Medico.

Another fifteen minutes passed. Still no heartbeat could be reestablished. The phosphorescent dot on the video monitor remained a flat line. The doctors looked again at Cassy.

"We are doing no good," the ER doctor said in Spanish, his face wet and shining with sweat.

"This is Señor Tenoch. You will not stop," Cassy said irritably with as much anger as she could emote. "Where is Dr. Garcia? I called him over an hour ago." Cassy eased back from the table. "Why in the hell is he not here?" Her voice was harsh and loud. The two ER physicians kept their heads down and bent to their task of resuscitating Tenoch.

At that moment, the Medical Director of the Instituto de Medico burst into the treatment area. "Cassy. My apologies. I came as quickly as possible, but the street traffic is terrible," Dr. Garcia said. "How is Tenoch?" The doctor hurried to the left side of the gurney. He audibly wheezed when he saw Tenoch's apparently dead body, being pounded and rocked on the gurney by the vigorous CPR effort.

"Not good," Cassy said grimly. "He's not responding to the closed chest heart massage. I think that his chest must be opened. His heart must be massaged internally."

"Open chest heart massage won't be any more effective than the closed chest massage that you've been doing for over an hour," Garcia said. The ER physicians nodded their agreement quickly. The doctor compressing Tenoch's chest paused in his thumping on Tenoch's chest.

"Keep up the CPR," snapped Cassy. "You can't declare Tenoch dead."

The ER doctor, emboldened by the presence of the Medical Director in the ER triage area, lifted his hands off Tenoch's chest and stepped down off the metal platform.

"It is no good, Doctora," said the emergency physician who stood at Tenoch's head with the lung ventilating balloon in his hands. Both young physicians looked toward Garcia, silently seeking his reprieve from this forced CPR. With a grim, near irrational, expression on her face, Cassy shouted in Spanish, "Continue the closed chest massage."

"Cassy, with all due respect . . . ," Dr. Garcia said, stepping so close that no one else could hear. The two ER physicians resumed the CPR ritual, inflating Tenoch's lungs and pounding on Tenoch's flaccid chest. Dr. Garcia touched Cassy's hands that gripped the side of the gurney. "He's gone. We should stop the closed chest cardiac massage. We must give up. Tenoch is dead."

"No, I can't. I won't," Cassy said. "We must do more."

"There is nothing more to do. He is gone," Garcia said quietly.

"No. Tenoch can't be gone," Cassy said. Her voice cracked with an emotional tension that appeared as grief.

"It's no use. He is dead. I declare Señor Tenoch dead at . . . ," Dr. Garcia paused and looked at the wall clock, "at eleven forty-five p. m." The Medical Director pulled his hand back from Cassy's forearm and stepped away from the gurney. The two ER doctors and the nurses immediately stopped the resuscitation and also backed away from the gurney.

"His chest must be opened," Cassy screamed. "You cannot let him die without opening his chest. His chest must be opened and his heart massaged internally."

Dr. Garcia shrugged and turned to leave the triage area. "I'm no surgeon." The two ER doctors shook their heads in a gesture of sympathy to Cassy and said in Spanish. "We are sorry for your friend. We did all we could do."

"Get me the surgical instruments then," Cassy shouted. "If you won't open Tenoch's chest, I will. It's his only hope to live."

Dr. Garcia stopped abruptly in the doorway and turned back to face Cassy. The two ER doctors stumbled into him after his sudden stop. The three doctors faced Cassy across the triage room where she still stood next to Tenoch's body. Garcia, a profound sadness wearying his face, looked at Cassy. "Dr. Baldwin, Señor Tenoch died at eleven forty-five. I have declared him dead." The three physicians stood a moment longer, their eyes locked into Cassy's eyes. They turned away from her fierce stare, and then they departed.

Alberto and the two guards who had accompanied Tenoch on the helicopter ride stood mute at the edge of the room. The result of the physicians' argument was clear to everyone—Tenoch was dead if nothing more was done to save him, and Dr. Baldwin wanted more to be done. Suddenly Alberto left the ER triage area through the same door the three doctors had exited.

Seconds later Garcia and the two ER physicians reappeared through the same door followed by Alberto. Their stricken, ashen faces revealed a pure fear that had replaced their somber expressions of sympathy. The two ER physicians returned quickly to Tenoch's body and resumed the closed chest massage without saying a word. Seeing the CPR resumed, the nurses also returned to the gurney. After a moment's dumbfounded hesitation, they reattached the EKG electrodes and reinserted the intravenous fluids.

"You wish to perform internal cardiac massage?" Dr. Garcia asked Cassy formally but with deference.

"There is no alternative, Raul," Cassy said, intentionally using his first name and hoping to defuse the tension that she had ignited in the ER.

Dr. Garcia snapped at one of the ER nurses, "Obtain the surgical instruments for emergency thoracotomy." The nurse ran from the ER and less than a minute later reappeared, breathless, carrying a green cloth-wrapped bundle. She dropped the three-foot square package onto a stainless steel tray that was mounted on a rolling stand next to the gurney.

"Prep him, and I will open his chest," Cassy said. The three nurses worked quickly together, one painting Tenoch's chest with brown antiseptic fluid and draping sterile towels around the left breast, the other opening the sterile instrument bundle, and the third nurse assisting Cassy into a surgical gown and latex gloves. While these hurried preparations were underway, Alberto stood between Cassy and Tenoch's body, saying nothing but watching each movement of the three nurses. The gleaming stainless steel instruments were laid out in precise alignment on the surgical tray. Cassy leaned close to Alberto as she wiggled the surgical gown up onto her arms. "Alberto, what did you say to them?" Cassy whispered.

"I told the doctors to do as you said or they would not sleep at their homes ever again," Alberto said.

When the last of the green surgical drapes were in place, Cassy stepped to the left side of the table and picked up the surgeon's scalpel. In one slash, she laid open Tenoch's chest from the edge of the breast bone under the left nipple to just below his left arm pit. Cassy then inserted a stainless steel mechanical retractor and pried apart the ribs exposing the interior of Tenoch's chest. Tenoch's heart lay still and pulseless beneath the transparent canvas-like pericardial tissue investments. Cassy snipped away the pericardial tissue covering the motionless muscular heart and exposed the quiet, red muscle tethered by its great veins and arteries to the interior of Tenoch's chest.

Cassy wrapped her long slender fingers around the thick-walled heart, completely encircling the limp pulseless muscle and palmed the muscular ventricular chambers of Tenoch's heart. She methodically squeezed the heart every second like an udder, milking blood back into Tenoch's circulation, trying to revive his heart. With each squeeze, a green blip rose above the flat green baseline of the phosphorescent dot that traced across the heart monitor video screen.

"His heart has no life. It has no beat. It's a bag of blood," Cassy said as if dictating the report of her operative findings. "There are no contractions," Cassy continued, her face within inches of the bloody slash, peering into the dim depths of the chest incision. She opened her fingers exposing the fist-sized heart and retracted the tip of the bluish, cyanotic heart muscle up to the edge of the incision. "There is no life here," she said.

"Tenoch is finished," Dr. Garcia said.

"No, we must continue," Cassy said, shaking her head.

"As you wish, Dr. Baldwin," Dr. Garcia said, shrugging his shoulders. After a quick glance at Alberto, Dr. Garcia walked to the edge of the room and stood quietly.

The chest incision grasped Cassy's wrist as her gloved fingers rhythmically squeezed Tenoch's heart for several more minutes. She rolled her fingers from the tip of the heart to its base, gently but forcibly, pressing the blood in the hollow heart back into Tenoch's intrinsic circulation. Each squeeze mimicked the flaccid heart's own contractions.

The coolness of the tissues surrounding her left hand deep inside Tenoch's chest cavity startled Cassy as she compressed the heart. Already Tenoch was losing body heat. She glanced at the clock, looking for reassurance that Tenoch had irrevocably passed beyond clinical death. It's been two hours since he first collapsed in the bedroom and without any effective circulation during that time, surely he's beyond salvage, she thought. Despite the miracle of the suspended animation state induced by Trent's Hiberna solution, Tenoch must be dead, she assured herself. She smiled inwardly with relief at the conviction that the evil of Tenoch was destroyed.

Then an unimaginable terror leaped into her mind. Her own words came back to haunt her. Her mind flashed back to the first Saturday night and she heard herself say—'Let's call the time of death 19:45'. I thought Marquez was dead and he wasn't, she remembered with a cold shiver. Maybe Tenoch is not yet dead. Cassy then knew she must know beyond an utter certainty that Tenoch was dead.

"This heart is nothing but a bag of blood," Cassy repeated to the three doctors. She tipped the heart upward so that the doctors could see the bluish lifeless apex of the ventricular mass. "He's dead."

The two ER doctors and Dr. Garcia nodded in unison. "Let's call the time of death twelve fifty-eight a. m." Cassy said. She looked back at the wall clock and withdrew her blood-soaked left hand from the wound.

Cassy stood over the chest incision for a moment with her head bowed as if in a moment of silent prayer for a departed colleague and patient. When she looked up, the three doctors stared at her, their faces expressing a truly sad compassion for her. "Thank you for everything. I appreciate your assistance for Tenoch," she said softly.

"We are so sorry, Dr. Baldwin," Garcia said and touched her lightly through the sleeve of her surgical gown. The three staff doctors turned to leave the room. Then Cassy was alone with Tenoch's body.

The nurses busied themselves clearing away the blood-soaked instruments and detaching Tenoch's body from the vital sign monitoring equipment, intravenous tubing, and drainage tubes. Cassy returned to Tenoch's body and asked one of the ER nurses to find sutures for her so that she could close the gaping slash in the left side of Tenoch's chest. While the nurse was momentarily away from the triage area and unnoticed by the second nurse, Cassy slipped the scalpel into her palm and inserted her right hand into the chest incision.

Feeling through the gaping incision into the interior of Tenoch's chest, her experienced fingertips identified the anatomical landmarks at the base of Tenoch's heart. Within seconds her fingers searched for and found the major vascular connections of his heart.

While her eyes nervously scanned the room around her, in one nimble motion her index finger advanced the scalpel blade and severed the heart's venous connections completely. Immediately blood pooled from the severed vena cavae and pulmonary veins, flooding Tenoch's capacious chest cavity, exsanguinating Tenoch's body in less than a minute.

When the nurse returned with the sutures, Cassy quickly and efficiently closed the chest incision. Now she was satisfied to an utter certainty that Tenoch was destroyed.

THIRTY-NINE

THE TRIAGE area was a vacant stage after the theater audience
had departed. Tenoch's lifeless body lay naked on the gurney.
The neatly stitched surgical incision under Tenoch's left nipple
caught and reflected the still-focused surgical lights like a gleaming blue
coil holding the bloody cut edges together. A single nurse, like a stage
hand, moved slowly around the room, stuffing the detritus of the resuscitation effort—empty intravenous solution bags, blood-stained sheets, paper wrappings—into plastic bag hampers. Bloody stainless steel surgical
instruments overflowed a green plastic pail filled with sudsy disinfectant.
The audience had departed, the stage was empty, and Tenoch's body, like
a prop, was ignored, no longer a player.

In the surgical scrub sink alcove adjacent to the ER, Cassy scrubbed
her hands and wrists, trying to rub away the lingering sensation of Tenoch's
chest incision. The door to the scrub sink opened, and Raul Garcia
stepped into the small alcove.

"It's all over, Cassy," the Medical Director said. His relief was measured by his relaxed facial expression. "I never would have thought Tenoch
was at risk for a heart attack. He always was so healthy." Raul studied Cassy's
face as she rinsed the brown sudsy soap from her hands and forearms.

When she turned to face him, their eyes held each other for a moment.
Cassy at last said, "Perhaps it was his destiny."

"Or God's intervention," Raul said. He reached above the sink to pick
up a hand towel for Cassy's dripping wet hands and forearms.

"Perhaps . . . ," Cassy said staring into Raul's eyes until he turned away.
Then she asked, "Are you planning an autopsy?"

"I see no reason. The cause of death was an obvious heart attack. All of us saw Tenoch's lifeless heart. An autopsy would tell us nothing more than we already know." Raul paused and looked through the window of the small cubicle and stared at the naked lifeless body lying abandoned on the gurney. The precisely sutured curvilinear incision beneath the left breast was its only blemish. Raul turned back to face Cassy. A muted smile creased his lips. "Don't you agree?"

"Certainly. I see no reason for an autopsy," Cassy said, wondering how much Raul Garcia had managed to piece together.

"I will sign out the death certificate as a massive myocardial infarction," Raul said.

"Thank you, Raul," Cassy whispered, relieved that no sophisticated toxicologic testing would be done on Tenoch's body nor any autopsy inspection of the interior of Tenoch's chest which would have revealed the severed ends of the large veins of Tenoch's heart.

"It's time for you and Alex to go home," Garcia said, impulsively pulling Cassy to him in an affectionate hug. "Call me in a few weeks. The children of Mexico need you . . . and your skills. There will always be a place for you at the Instituto de Medico."

"Raul, I can't think of anything but going home. Maybe all that will change." Her voice choked. Raul released his fatherly embrace.

"I understand. . . ." Raul quickly kissed her cheek and started to leave but stopped a few steps away. He peered over his half-rim glasses at her and said, "I was wrong to question your CPR judgment for Tenoch. You made the right clinical judgment to perform the open chest heart massage." His restrained smile told her everything. Then he was gone before Cassy could say anything.

⸺

For several minutes Cassy stood in the alcove blotting her hands and arms with the green surgical towel and trying to collect her flashing thoughts. When Cassy pushed the cubicle door open, she confronted Alberto standing alone in the tiled corridor, slumped against the wall. A profound sadness weighted his body.

"I'm sorry," Cassy said, laying her hand on Alberto's forearm and gently squeezing it. "Tenoch is gone."

Alberto nodded his head, his lower lip quivered, and he looked away. Cassy said nothing while Alberto kept his head turned aside, obviously embarrassed by his own emotions.

"What am I going to do?" Alberto asked when he finally looked up at her from his slouch.

"It's time to go home to your family," Cassy said.

"Señor Tenoch was my only family," Alberto said. His voice broke. "He was a father to me." Alberto's eyes held Cassy with the same intensity as Tenoch's.

Only then did Cassy recognize that Alberto was more than just Tenoch's loyal disciple. He had become Tenoch's puppet, his free will completely replaced by the overpowering authority of Tenoch. Without his master, Alberto was unplugged, an emotional cripple, now that Tenoch was no longer available to command.

"I know it's hard to lose someone who meant so much to you," Cassy said, hating herself for the extraordinary deceit of expressing sympathy for Tenoch's death. She laid her hand in Alberto's hand. "We must go forward with Señor Tenoch's vision. Now it's time for us to go. Señor Tenoch would want you to take Alex and me back to Dallas," Cassy said gently but unequivocally. "Tell the pilots to prepare the Aztec plane." Her voice was clear, distinct, and authoritative.

The inky cloudless sky above the smoky haze extended endlessly into the reaches of deep space. Tenoch's 727 broke through the inversion layer of night haze above Mexico City and climbed upward into the carbon black sky on a northerly heading to Dallas.

In the bedroom cabin at the rear of the airplane, Cassy sat on the side of the bed watching Alex, tucked neatly under the gold satin sheets, sleep quietly. The German shepherd pup that Tenoch had presented to Alex lay cuddled under his right arm, partially covered by the sheets.

Since leaving Mexico City immediately after Tenoch's death, Cassy's tightly coiled anxiety had begun to unwind. Sitting by her son, knowing they would be home before sunrise, she felt her nervous apprehension replaced by a numbing fatigue that enveloped her.

A light tapping at the bedroom door intruded on Cassy's solitude, and Alberto's head peeked around the edge of the cabin door. "The pilot tells me we will land in Dallas at three forty-five," Alberto whispered looking at his gold Rolex watch. "May I arrange anything for you or your son?"

Cassy shook her head and smiled a thank you. He nodded and quietly closed the door, leaving Cassy alone again with her son. Cassy brought her fingers to Alex's face. The touch of his soft cheek charged her mind with love. After a long time watching her son, Cassy reached for her clutch purse and rummaged though it until she found Kevin Knowland's business card with his home telephone number scribbled on the back. Picking up the bedside telephone and lighting a Marlboro cigarette, she gave Kevin's unlisted telephone number to the airplane's communication operator. The familiar voice of Tenoch's telephone operator brought her the memory of that other trip to Mexico City in Tenoch's 727. How long had that been? Four days? It seemed four months or four years. The passage of time had become undefinable for Cassy. Her life had no milestones or time markers to guide her. What seemed moments later, but it could have been a minute or an hour, the connection clicked with the groggy voice of Lt. Kevin Knowland.

"Sorry to wake you," Cassy said.

"I was awake," Knowland said defensively, his voice filled with sleep. "Where are you?"

"Alex and I are on our way home."

"Where? What? It's two-thirty in the morning," Kevin said peevishly. "Where are you?"

"I'm calling from Tenoch's airplane."

"Everyone's been wondering where you are. I've been looking everywhere for you. You shouldn't have run off."

Her control shattered at the irritation that permeated Kevin's sleepy voice. Her words gushed forth. "Everyone's dead."

"What the hell are you talking about?" Kevin asked. "Are you all right?"

"No. I'm not all right!" Cassy said, her voice choking. "Tenoch had a heart attack and died two hours ago. Trent's gone. Tenoch killed him, I'm sure."

"Slow down," Kevin said. "Is Alex with you?"

"Yes. He's fine," Cassy said. She looked over her shoulder at her son sleeping soundly with the dog still curled in the crook of his elbow. "We'll be home in an hour." The horrifying image of Lupita's crumpled body, bloated face, and strangled neck on her kitchen floor burst onto the screen of her mind.

"Did you find Lupita's body?" Cassy asked. "She was dead on my kitchen floor when I left the house yesterday. Or was it today?" Her mind had fused the days together.

"No, Cassy," Kevin said. "I went to your house after Betty called yesterday morning. No one was there."

"Lupita was gone?" Cassy lit another cigarette and inhaled deeply.

"Yes. Her clothes were still in her room, but she was gone. No one was there."

"Tenoch took her. You'll never find the body. Just like Trent. The bodies are gone . . . cremated," she said, cupping her hand around the telephone to muffle her voice. Alex and the puppy slept on, not stirring.

"Cassy, you've been under a lot of stress. Do you need to see a doctor?"

"Lupita's dead. They're all dead," Cassy said. Her voice cracked in her throat and then rose stridently. Alex rolled over at the change in pitch of his mother's voice but did not wake.

"Have you tried to call Dr. Hendricks at his home?" Kevin asked gently.

"No, of course not. I know he's dead."

"How about Lupita? Have you tried to contact her?" Kevin asked.

"Why should I try to call her? I know she is dead. I cut the rope away from her neck . . . she was strangled," Cassy said angrily.

"Cassy . . . ," Kevin began but she cut him off.

"There's another dead one. Juan Torres. I saw Tenoch stab the man in the eyeball."

"When did all that happen?" Kevin asked patiently.

"Two days ago. Dr. Walter Simmons was there, the Medical Director of Metro Hospital. He's involved in Tenoch's scheme to sell organs for transplant . . . a heart sells for half a million dollars. It's all a black market to bring organs into the United States from Mexico City. Tenoch kidnapped his victims off the streets of Mexico City . . . Ana Ruiz." Cassy's words could not keep pace with her racing thoughts. "Did you look for a missing persons report on her in Mexico City like I told you?" Cassy rattled, her voice racing faster until her words and sentence fragments ended in a conversational explosion.

"No, Cassy," Kevin said soothingly.

"I know why Tenoch went after me and kidnapped Alex. To force me to be a part of the conspiracy. He was going to kill Alex if I didn't cooperate."

"Cassy, you need some rest. How can I help?"

"You might try believing me," she said.

"You need some professional help. I know a good psychiatrist. . . ." The phone connection clicked into a low humming noise in the lieutenant's hand.

Cassy replaced the telephone and slid fully clothed under the bed covers next to her son. The German shepherd puppy slept between them. The droning white noise of the aft jet turbines numbed her. But still she did not sleep. The horror of death overwhelmed her. Her body trembled causing the bed to shake like a massage bed in a cheap hotel.

Cassy stared at the ceiling of the compartment, trying to rein in her galloping memories. She closed her eyes, but the merciful oblivion of dreamless sleep would not come. If Kevin doesn't believe me, will anyone? Cassy asked herself.

The plane began its gradual descent out of the night sky toward DFW.

At the bottom of the mobile stairwell rolled up to meet the jetliner, two U.S. Customs officers stood quietly in the darkness of the deserted tarmac, looking up toward the fuselage door of the plane as it slid inward. Their drug-sniffing German shepherd dog, who could easily have been the father of the pup that Alex cradled in his arm, stood attentively between the two agents. The adult dog alerted itself like a soldier at attention the moment that Cassy and Alex stepped onto the staircase. The adult dog's wagging tail saluted the puppy. The drug-sniffing animal was far too well-trained and disciplined to bark a greeting to the puppy.

"Welcome home. Dr. Baldwin," the young Customs officer said, greeting Cassy and Alex with a casual touch to his forehead. They stepped off the staircase onto the tarmac. The concrete was warm under her sandals, a residual memory of the Texas sun. "The United States Ambassador to Mexico telephoned us that you and your son would be arriving and asked that we extend diplomatic courtesy to you and your son. Welcome home," the officer said, smiling as he looked at their passports under the beam of his flashlight.

Tenoch's black limousine, its darkly tinted windows concealing the interior, rolled across the tarmac and stopped at the end of the red carpet runner extending from the base of the aircraft staircase. My god! Tenoch's influence follows him even after his death, thought Cassy.

"Everything is in order for you and your son," the officer said, stamping the passport booklet with a small rubber stamp as he held it against the hood of the limousine.

Alberto stood by the open rear door of the limousine as Alex and Cassy walked toward him. "Alberto, my car is here at the airport. I left it in the parking lot."

"Do not concern yourself. It is time for you and your son to be home," Alberto said. "Your car will be delivered to your home."

After Cassy, Alex, and the dog settled into the plush leather cushions, Alberto closed the rear door and sat facing them on the jump seat of the limousine. Cassy's anxiety disappeared completely when she saw the familiar Texas highway signs. Rolling down the rear window for a moment, she breathed deeply the crisp warm air of the Dallas night.

The limo sped down the six-lane airport expressway, staying just below the speed limit. The sparse traffic at four a.m. blurred past the tinted windows. Fatigue crept over Cassy and no longer would be denied. She nodded into sleep.

Half an hour later the drumming of the tires on the pavement lane markers as the limousine changed lanes jostled her into drowsy wakefulness. "Where are we?" she asked in the dimness of the limo's rear compartment. Alex and the puppy nestled against her left side, sleeping peacefully.

"It won't be long," Alberto said agreeably from his comfortable seat across the carpeted footwell.

Cassy leaned forward to peer out the right window and quickly said, "We've just passed Preston Road. Tell the driver he's missed my turn."

"The driver has my directions," Alberto said. Although smiling, his face was transformed, angled and dark, into a beatific smile identical to Tenoch's wry upward twist of his mouth.

"This is not the way to my home," Cassy said, swiveling her head to look back through the rear window at the expressway traffic signs.

"We are not going to your home," Alberto said, pulling aside his coat flap to show her the butt of a nine millimeter pistol in a leather hip holster. His right hand closed about the grip and lifted it slightly before dropping it back into the leather scabbard. "You have an appointment at Park Haven."

FORTY

T HE STAINED-glass wall above the marble bier scattered shafts of
tinted light throughout the darkened sanctuary of the Park Haven
Funeral Home. The unearthly array of colors emanating from glass
panels of the cubist mural flashed over the empty pews. Sprays of drooping white lilies flanked the double door of the sanctuary. Cassy's leather
sandals, wet from her walk across the sprinkled moisture of the cemetery
grass, squeaked on the hard marble surface of the lobby as Alberto
nudged Alex and her through the open doors.

"Why did he take my dog?" Alex asked.

Cassy bent forward as they entered the carpeted chapel and whispered,
"The driver took your dog to a safe place."

"Why aren't we going home?" Alex asked.

"Shut up," Alberto said, punching Cassy in the back with the barrel of
his pistol. The curved rows of empty pews converged on a solid casket
size block of black textured marble. A single spotlight focused its soft
beam onto the marble block giving it a black luminescence. The multicolored rays from the lighted stained-glass mosaic cascaded in front of
Cassy and Alex as Alberto shoved them down the lushly carpeted aisle.

"Hello, Cassy," a raspy man's voice echoed from shadows at the base of
the stained-glass wall.

"Who's that man, Mom?" Alex asked as he squeezed his mother's
hand. They both looked around the dark sanctuary searching in the direction of the voice across the lighted bier.

"Walter?" Cassy called into the darkness. A dull thud, like the shudder
of a new car door closing, broke the quiet. A gray marble panel in the

side wall of the sanctuary slid open exposing a lighted stainless steel elevator car. At the same moment Dr. Walter Simmons, dressed in gray Metro Hospital surgical scrubs, stepped from the shadows. The multicolored lights painted his face in an impressionistic portrait.

"I am delighted you could join us," Simmons said as he walked toward the empty marble bier. The repulsive odor of whiskey, cigarettes, and men's cologne rolled over Cassy. When he reached the bier he bent over and put forward his hand to shake Alex's hand. "You are a big man to be out at this hour."

"W–Where's m-my d-dog?" Alex asked.

"Get this young man his dog," Simmons said to Alberto who had been standing in the dim shadows of the aisle behind Cassy and Alex. Alberto disappeared up the aisle and returned moments later to stand behind Cassy and Alex.

"Walter, why in the hell have you brought Alex and me here?" Cassy asked, not moving from her position by the marble bier.

"You must be exhausted by the traumatic events of the past few hours. Let's go to my office, and I will explain, my dear." Simmons motioned her toward the open elevator.

"Take us home, and I'll forget this side trip ever occurred," Cassy pleaded. "Please. . . ."

"I'm sorry, Cassy. It is not possible. In the words of the late Señor Tenoch, it's your destiny."

"Walter, I've reached my limit with you," Cassy said. Her voice was like steel. "Alex and I are leaving now." She pulled Alex from around the marble bier and took one step toward the aisle.

Simmons leaned across the flat marble surface of the bier, a ruthless metamorphosis changing his face. In a low grisly whisper, he said, "Get your ass in that elevator if you and your boy want to see the sun rise." The dark sanctuary was quiet as a crypt, but the crackling tension between them was nearly audible.

"Do what he says, Mom," Alex said, pulling at his mother's coat sleeve. His voice broke the impasse. Cassy allowed her son to pull her toward the elevator.

The door closed silently around the four of them. Its upward motion was barely perceptible until it opened again into a luxurious mahogany-paneled office suite. A massive wooden desk centered an expanse of glass that looked over the darkened cemetery stretching eastward on the sloping hillside.

"Please be comfortable," Simmons said, pointing toward the soft burgundy leather-cushioned sofa in the opposite corner of the room. "Alberto, fix me my usual . . . and not much water."

"Walter, it's five a.m. . . . I've not slept in two nights . . . can't we have this meeting some other time?" Cassy asked, holding her voice in check.

"You and I have a few things we need to discuss about our new relationship . . . now that Tenoch and Trent are gone," Simmons said, taking the bourbon and water filled glass from Alberto.

"What have you done with Trent?" Cassy broke into his rambling.

"Cassy, my dear, don't you know?" Simmons asked, laughing and coughing. "Your friend left his heart in Mexico City."

"Is that a sick joke?"

Simmons stopped and turned to her. "Not at all. I'm surprised that your lover Tenoch didn't tell you."

"Tell me, goddamn you. Where is Trent?" A surge of nausea grabbed her stomach. For a moment she did not understand Simmons' words when he continued.

"He's dead. Truly he left his heart in Mexico City. Tenoch ripped Trent's heart out in an Aztec ritual at Teotihuacan last night just like the Aztec human sacrifices hundreds of years ago. A virtuoso surgical performance if I ever heard of one."

"My god," Cassy said and felt the room begin to spin about her. The floor dropped from her feet. She clawed the air for support as she staggered to the leather sofa.

"Alberto, a glass of water," Simmons said. Several minutes later Cassy blinked her eyes as Alberto held her head up and offered the glass of water for her to sip. Slowly color returned to her cheeks. Cassy gradually righted herself on the office sofa, holding her head in her hands, crying quietly. Fear, anger, and frustration filled her.

Simmons led Alex, mute and terrified, over to the leather sofa beneath the expanse of windows overlooking the cemetery. Cassy sat on the sofa with her head bowed and cradled in her hands. Simmons stood in front of the boy. "Your mother's going to be just fine. Trust me. I'm a doctor." Alex's eyes darted between his mother's cradled head and Simmons' florid face.

Just at that moment Hector Chavez, the elderly mortuary director, stepped through the elevator door holding the German shepherd puppy. The pup squirmed out of the man's hands and ran toward Alex. The mortician immediately disappeared back into the elevator.

"Alberto, take the kid and the dog downstairs," Simmons said.

Alberto seized Alex's shoulder, pulling him toward the elevator. Cassy lunged off the sofa toward Alberto. "Leave him alone." Immediately Alberto's nine millimeter pistol appeared in his hand, drawn from his hip holster. Cassy froze.

"Don't make a fool of yourself, Cass, or you'll be a dead fool," Simmons said sharply.

"Don't hurt Alex," Cassy said. "Or I will kill you."

"Cassy, stop making those ridiculous threats," Simmons said, laughing himself into a wet cough. He turned back to Alberto. "Take the kid downstairs."

Cassy moved slowly toward her son, staring directly at the unwavering muzzle of Alberto's pistol. She leaned forward and pried Alberto's finger away from her son's shoulder. "That's not necessary."

Alberto backed away but still held the pistol aimed between Cassy's breasts.

Cassy kneeled in front of her son, pulled him close, and whispered in his ear, "Go with Alberto, and I'll be downstairs to get you soon."

"A-All r-right, Mom." Alex straightened up and walked past Alberto toward the elevator, carrying the puppy in both arms.

Cassy moved toward Alberto. He backed up a couple of paces. She stared at him over the barrel of the gun, still pointed at her. "If you hurt my son, I will kill you," she said coldly. Alberto looked at her for several moments and then abruptly dropped the aim of the gun. He followed Alex into the waiting elevator car. The door closed silently behind them.

"Bravo, Dr. Baldwin," Simmons said, clapping his hands and sitting down in the high wingbacked burgundy leather chair behind the massive desk. "You project your motherly love and concern quite nicely." The green shaded antique banker's lamp on the front of the desk reflected light up from the glassy surface of the desk top, creating shadows on Simmons' puffed and pasty face.

"Go to hell," Cassy said.

"Sit, please," Simmons said, motioning her to the chair in front of the desk. "In case you have any ideas about following your son. . . ." He pulled a nine millimeter pistol from the desk drawer and laid it on the corner of the desk next to a polished hardwood box.

From the hinged box Simmons withdrew an ornately carved twelve-inch ceremonial obsidian knife. "Of course you recognize this knife," Simmons said. The mental image of Tenoch plunging the pointed obsidian blade into Juan Torres' eyeball snapped into her mind like a colored slide in a projector.

"This is Tenoch's sacrificial knife used by the Aztec high priests to extract the hearts of their victims," Simmons said, chuckling as he twisted the knife in his hand. "Tenoch used it on Trent yesterday at Teotihuacan." Simmons tested the keenness of the edge with his thumb. "I do congratulate your finesse in dispatching Tenoch . . . the tetrodotoxin was an elegant touch."

"What are you talking about?"

"You murdered Tenoch," Simmons said quietly, balancing the tip of the obsidian knife in his palm. "Everyone else will believe that Tenoch died of a heart attack. You and I know the real cause of death, don't we?" Simmons asked, scratching his heavy right jowl with the tip of the blade. He finished the whiskey in a full swallow.

"I don't have any idea what you're talking about," Cassy said. "Dr. Garcia will sign out his death certificate as a fatal myocardial infarction."

"Cassy, I know that you were here at this mortuary just before you and Trent left for Mexico City yesterday morning. Hector called me as soon as you telephoned him that you were coming to inventory the OR supplies."

"So," Cassy said. "I was checking the surgical instruments inventory."

"Your little charade with the spilled medication vials was pathetic. Hector was amused that you thought you could steal four vials of Hiberna without being detected."

"Why didn't he stop me?"

"Because I told him not to interfere. It was obvious why you were here to steal the Hiberna. Remember, I showed you where the Hiberna vials were stored in the anesthesia console when you harvested Juan Torres' heart. When you stole the Hiberna, I knew what your little scheme with Tenoch would be."

"And you didn't try to stop me?" Cassy asked.

"Of course not. I wanted Tenoch out of the way. His psychosis jeopardized the organ brokering program," Simmons said slowly as his words began slurring from the alcohol.

"What do you want from me, Walter?" Cassy sighed and shifted forward in the chair.

"We have much to discuss, my dear Cassy," Simmons said, lifting himself slowly from the desk chair. He tucked the pistol under the waist band of his rumpled scrub pants and carried the ceremonial knife with him to a wet bar at the inside corner of the room. "May I fix you a drink?"

"No, thank you," Cassy said. Her eyes roved the room, searching for a way out.

Simmons filled the glass nearly full with the dark whiskey and splashed a few drops of water in the glass along with a single ice cube. He swizzled the drink with the tip of the blade of the obsidian knife, twisting the knife idly in his hand.

"Let's be comfortable, Cassy. Join me here on the sofa," Simmons said as he plopped onto the sofa, dropping into the middle of the long cushioned leather sofa.

"I'm comfortable here," Cassy said. moving her back against the chair.

"Come here." The harshness of demand rimed his moist voice.

There was no alternative. Cassy sluggishly left her chair, crossed the room, and sat down hugging the opposite arm of the sofa.

After taking another deep swallow of the whiskey, Simmons turned toward her and cocked his leg onto the sofa facing her. "I've known for at least three years that Tenoch was an outright psychotic. He was an intellectual giant and a creative genius too, but the bastard was crazy . . . he had this well developed delusion that he was an Aztec god . . . Huitzilopochtli."

"You knew all this time?"

"Of course. Tenoch was clever at concealing his delusions . . . only I was aware of his psychotic delusion that he was Huitzilopochtli. He was such a powerful personality that his staff, including that dumbshit Alberto, actually believed that Tenoch was the Aztec god reincarnated."

"And you did nothing to stop him or to get him treated?"

"Why should I? My organ marketing network played right into his delusions. . . ."

"What do you mean?"

"You don't think Tenoch conceived and organized all this international network of organ marketing himself?"

"You . . . you're the broker in all this?"

Simmons smiled, sipped his whiskey, and nodded. "When I realized Tenoch was crazy, wealthy, as well as having a legitimate Mexican import business, I knew that I had the makings of a Texas-size fortune in the organ marketing business. My god, Cassy, it's a fantastic opportunity. There are nearly thirty thousand people in the United States awaiting organs for transplantation . . . many ready, willing, and able to pay for whatever organ they need. So what if I make a fortune? I am fulfilling a social need for my fellow citizens."

"Aren't you overlooking the fact that your organ procurement and delivery system depends upon the murder of the organ donor?" Cassy asked. "You're no better than a serial killer."

"What is the dollar value that our society offers for a human life, Cassy? That question is answered every day by every government in the world. For chrissake, what are wars? Borders? It's all about the dollar value of human life."

"You are as sick as Tenoch," Cassy said, shifting on the sofa.

"I want you to be my partner in this enterprise. We would be good for each other," Simmons said.

"What are you saying?" Cassy asked, as she stared at the grotesque caricature that Walter Simmons' face had become.

"Cassy, my dear, you and I are both very much the same. How does the result of my organ procurement program differ from your poisoning Tenoch a few hours ago?" Simmons asked. "You made your own judgment about Tenoch and simply killed him."

"He self-destructed on his own insanity," Cassy said. "I will not be part of your cold-blooded scheme to murder poor Hispanics and sell their organs to the highest bidder."

"You have now come to a clear choice, Cassy. Either join me in this brokering enterprise, and we will prosper together. Or. . . ." He paused and looked down the length of the sofa at her. Simmons balanced the twelve-inch obsidian knife on his finger tips.

"Go to hell," Cassy said and stood up, taking two steps away from the sofa. "I'm leaving."

"No, you're not," he said, setting the whiskey glass and the obsidian knife onto the low table in front of the sofa. Reaching beneath the drawstring of his scrub pants for a nine millimeter pistol, he pulled it up to aim at her midtorso. Simmons' face disappeared into the darkness of the room as he shifted back on the sofa.

"I have no hesitation about killing you . . . and your son. Then my staff would cremate your bodies here in the mortuary. You and your son would simply vanish without a trace except for a few ashes that we'd toss out on the Northwest Highway during tomorrow's traffic. Either come with me, or I will kill you here," Simmons said. A wry smile wrinkled his mouth.

Cassy edged for the corner of the sofa, trying to judge how she might dive behind the adjacent chair. She had no choice. Cassy moved back on the sofa and turned to face him.

"So you're the broker behind this international organ program?" Cassy asked, reclining herself against the back of the sofa, giving a relaxed assured appearance.

"I appreciate your recognizing the symmetry of my concept . . . meeting society's health needs for a profit. My dear, you are fortunate to be involved in my grand design. It would be a pity to lose you." Simmons drained off the rest of the whiskey. "I need a heart surgeon I can always control. With you, I've got control . . . your son is my control. Alex will vanish if you ever cross me."

"You're a simple murderer . . . organs for sale," Cassy said angrily.

"And your friend, Trent Hendricks?" Simmons asked evenly. "I suppose his participation in the organ program is my responsibility?"

"His love of his daughter blinded him. Love as you've never known . . . all you've ever loved is yourself and money."

"It is a pity, Cassy. With your naive and unrepentant attitudes, you really give me no choice. . . ."

"You'll never get away with it," Cassy said. "Kevin Knowland knows about the organ black market."

"Knowland can never prove anything. You see, Cassy, we incinerate all the incriminating remains. My staff are Hispanics delighted to be out of the Mexico City slums. They will do as I say . . . always."

"You bastard," Cassy screamed.

"Such passion should not be squandered." Simmons smiled and leaned out of the shadows. The sky above the tree line beyond the dark cemetery had begun to lighten, heralding the return of the sun and filling the office with glimmering halos. He raised the obsidian knife and moved closer to her on the sofa, caressing her cheek and lips with the tip of the knife. "Take off your blouse," he said.

Cassy hesitated until he pressed the tip of the blade an eighth of an inch into the side of her neck, breaking the skin just beside the jugular vein. "You're going to give me exactly what you gave Tenoch," Simmons said, pulling the blade back. "And more." A driblet of blood coursed its way down her neck in a scarlet line between her breasts. "Now take off the fucking blouse."

Cassy yanked the blouse over her head. Her bare breasts thrust defiantly at him. Simmons caught himself with a quick inhaled breath. He waved the obsidian knife in a circle around each breast. "Off with the skirt."

Cassy hesitated.

"Don't make me hurt you," he said, drawing the tip of the knife across her breasts and touching each nipple with the tip of the blade.

Cassy turned and released her skirt's waist clasp. The black pleated cloth dropped to the floor in a circle around her feet. Simmons sat mesmerized, staring at Cassy's body. His eyes focused on her black lace bikini panties.

"Do you like what you see?" Cassy asked in a low husky voice. Speechless, Simmons held the knife blade closely in front of him in both hands. Cassy stepped out of the coil of the skirt and took two steps toward him, catching his right knee between her legs, rubbing her bare knees together along his right thigh. His mouth gaped, and his face flushed.

Leaning forward over him, she moved her breasts toward his face. Simmons pushed forward with his elbows to bring his upper body to meet her. The obsidian knife slid to the floor as he wrapped his arms about her buttocks, oblivious of everything except Cassy's swaying body in front of his face.

Cassy pushed him gently backward onto the length of the sofa with one hand while rotating her body on top of him. The two lay stretched together. Her hips rolled against his lower abdomen. His excitement grew beneath his thin cotton scrub pants. Cassy knew that she was in control. She swung her breasts up over his face. His open mouth followed their movements, trying to reach the nipple of each breast. The stench of Simmon's foul cigarette-whiskey breath gagged her, and she nearly vomited as her body swayed over him.

Gradually Cassy lowered her upper body on his and felt his mouth grab roughly at her nipple. Groping the floor beside the sofa, she found the obsidian blade that had fallen from Simmons' hands. His teeth closed on her nipple, shooting a fire of pain through her left breast.

"Easy, Walter," Cassy cooed. "Don't be so rough. Relax, let me help you." Cassy wiggled her pelvis and trailed her left hand down until her fingers closed around him. His involuntary pelvic thrusts rose to meet her hand. The fingers of her right hand coiled around the handle of the obsidian blade.

She slipped the fingers of her left hand under the drawstring of his cotton scrub pants, seeking his naked erection. Simmons groaned as her fingers touched him. Sweat dripped from his face. His eyes closed, his mouth opened, and he grunted with each respiration.

The instant the fingers of her left hand coiled around his bare erect penis, her right arm drew backwards. In a blinding arc she brought the obsidian knife blade forward into the rib interspace just below the left nipple, puncturing and lacerating the left ventricular chamber of his heart.

"Goddamn you!" Cassy screamed. She pulled the handle of the blade up hard with both hands, causing it to pivot upward, ripping the heart irreparably open. A flush of relief filled her.

The thrust was so sudden that Simmons' alcohol-befuddled eyes opened as his life drained out the slash in his heart. He was dead before a scream cleared his throat. Cassy released her fingers from the handle of the blade, leaving it embedded to the handle in his chest. A crimson stain enlarged on his gray cotton scrub shirt as Simmons' lifeless body crumpled backward against the cushions of the sofa. Cassy backed away from the sofa and stood looking down at the body. Simmons' eyes gaped wide, glazed, and lifeless.

Cassy stepped into the coiled circle of her skirt and pulled it up to her waist. She then tugged the white silk blouse over her head. Finally, she reached into Simmons' pocket and pulled the package of cigarettes out just before the blood-red stain reached the pocket of his scrub shirt.

Returning to Simmons' desk, she lit a cigarette and sat down in the wingback chair behind the desk. Smoke spilled slowly out of her mouth.

The glass wall above the sofa shimmered a faint crepuscular glow from the fading twilight. The horizon brightened beyond the cavalcade of tombstones that stretched to the edge of the sky. A frieze of umber and rose light announced the sun which hung just below the horizon. She felt nothing except the coolness of the room.

The pistol lay on the desk top, its barrel pointed toward her. Cassy bent forward in the chair and picked up the cold harsh pistol grip. After finishing another cigarette lit off the first, she checked the clip for a full load of bullets. Slipping the safety off, she sighted down the pistol barrel, aiming it between Simmons' glazed eyes, and held the gun motionless in her outstretched hands.

Cassy dropped her cigarette into the half-empty crystal whiskey decanter on the wet bar. The pungent odor of cigarette smoke trailed after her as she walked steadily to the waiting elevator car. Her right arm swung loosely at her side, the pistol in her hand moving in a tight pendulum arc.

FORTY-ONE

THE STAINLESS steel door of the elevator car closed with a hissing swoosh around Cassy like a hermetically sealed coffin. Her eyes stared forward blankly. As the car descended to the basement, the brushed steel of the car door extinguished her reflected image in its minute patterns. Her mind rolled over, trying to orient time. How long had she been under attack . . . forty-eight hours? Last week? Yesterday? Tuesday? Time blurred. What time was it? Night or morning? She had no idea. Her mind was fixed on her son. Nothing else mattered.

The car settled to a gentle stop. Cassy planted both legs on the PH crest etched in the center of the floor of the car. The nine millimeter pistol dangled loosely in her right hand. The seam of the elevator door parted slightly, flooding the closed space with commingled odors and fragrances of a hospital mixed with a mortuary—a cloying melange of antiseptics, embalming solutions, and the faint unmistakable sweet stench of decaying flesh. With the elevator doors completely apart, she stepped slowly across the threshold into a fluorescent brightness that momentarily blurred her vision.

The same déjà vu feeling took her into the Metropolitan Hospital Operating Room, stopping her at the threshold of the elevator, one foot in the car and one foot on the cool terrazzo tile. For a moment she could not move out of the elevator. Her mind tried to lock itself into appropriate time and space.

The pedestaled surgical table in the center of the room glowed under the converged surgical spotlights. Stainless steel surgical instruments in the glass cabinets gleamed like fine silver. The anesthesia machine with its space age conglomeration of control dials, digital computers, monitoring gauges, and anesthetic gas canisters stood at the head of the surgical table. All was in readiness for a surgical procedure. It was a comforting sight to her surgically trained mind.

Alex's voice broke through his mother's fleeting trance like a noon-day whistle. "Mom!" His shout ricocheted against the hard acoustics of the tiled floor of the empty operating room. With the German shepherd pup in his arms, Alex wiggled off the revolving anesthesiologist's metal stool where he sat at the head of the operating table. Trying to get to the floor, the dog worked his oversize paws furiously against Alex's Rangers' T-shirt.

"Stay right there," Alberto said and leaped from his perch on the oper-ating table. He grabbed Alex before he could move toward his mother. The puppy spilled from Alex's arms onto the tile floor in a tangle of yelp-ing paws and legs. The dog skittered across the gleaming terrazzo floor like a furry brown bowling ball. Alex tore away from Alberto's grasp and ran after the dog, catching the puppy as it slid on the waxed floor, land-ing behind the anesthesia machine.

Distracted by Alex's jerking away from his grasp, Alberto turned back toward the elevator door to focus again on Cassy. Her pistol was aimed with a defensive two-handed stance directly at him. Her arms were steady as if she held the gun in a firing brace. Cassy peered down the bar-rel sight like an emotionless target shooter.

"Wait, Dr. Baldwin. Don't," Alberto said, reflexively raising both hands palms outward and toward the ceiling. His right hand still held the pistol by the trigger guard. "Let's talk this over." His face drenched itself in sweat so quickly that it looked as if water had splashed at his face. Al-berto's eyes danced in fear around the room, looking for cover.

"It's all over, Alberto. Put the gun down," Cassy said, her voice devoid of feeling.

"Where's Dr. Simmons?" Alberto asked, crabbing a half step toward the bulky anesthesia console but still holding both hands above his head.

"Don't move," Cassy said. Alberto's white shirt was now ringed at the armpits with sweat. A smile of realization twisted his lips. He had moved a step without being shot. Another three steps and the anesthesia console would be an impenetrable barrier between Cassy and him. Alex and the puppy hiding behind the console would then be his hostages.

Cassy's pistol tracked Alberto's sideways move toward the cover of the anesthesia machine. Her feet, planted in the crouched wide-spaced stance, remained fused to the floor. Her gun barrel followed his sidestep. Still she did not fire.

"Stop," she repeated.

Another step sideways brought Alberto within two feet of the anesthesia machine. Alex's head peeped from behind the corner of the console.

"You're not going to shoot me," Alberto said, inching his feet sideways more quickly.

"Don't test me," Cassy said. Her voice was drained of all inflection.

"Mom! Mom!" Alex shouted. At that instant, the pup clawed its way out of Alex's arms and splay-legged its way on the icy slick polished floor of the operating room. Her son's voice cracked Cassy's concentration again. She glanced away from Alberto toward the direction of Alex's voice. It took a split second for her mind to comprehend the scene—the dog slipping erratically on the polished floor and her son's brown hair peeking above the edge of the anesthesia console.

Alberto, like a trained combat marksman, exploited this momentary lapse and whipped his pistol down from over his head and held it in a straight-armed aim at her. Cassy whirled her gun back around, but it was too late. Her initial advantage had turned into a classic standoff, the duelists separated by the width of the operating room. The two held each in their pistol sights, neither wavering as their eyes locked on each other like radar scanners searching for the slightest movement of a target. Time blurred for Cassy until finally her mind spoke for her, "Let's talk this over, Alberto. Lower your gun. I'll lower mine."

"Drop your gun, Dr. Baldwin. You can't shoot me. So don't make me kill you."

"I'll put my pistol down if you will . . . on the count of three," Cassy said. Alberto stood silent, glaring down the gunsight of his pistol. "One."

Alex still was shielded behind the metal cabinet base of the anesthesia machine. He pulled the whimpering pup close, protecting him under the console. He and the dog crouched behind the console, less than a lunge and a fraction of a second away from Alberto. Alex released the dog to sit on the tile floor. The pup relieved himself of a golden puddle of urine beside the anesthesia machine.

"I'm going to lower my gun," Cassy repeated.

Alberto held his pistol level directly at Cassy. The smug, wry smile that twisted the left side of his face relaxed, but the right side of his face remained flat, staring down the pistol sight at Cassy.

"You dumb bitch. Your kid is dead if you don't put down the fucking gun," Alberto said calmly. "I can take you with one shot," he said, staring at Cassy and looking for the physical impact of his taunt. "Then I will kill your son." Cassy's squint involuntarily tightened.

Alex reached his right arm around the top of the low cabinet of the anesthesia console, exploring its flat metal surface. Alex's fingers passed over the syringes and small vials of medication laid on the surface, tracing the outlines of the medication containers.

"Put the gun down, and I'll put mine down at the same time," Cassy said. "I'll tell the police that you saved Alex and me. You will be able to go back to Mexico City. Now let's both lower our guns."

"I'm taking you back to Mexico City with me. You and the kid are my insurance to get me out of the country."

"It's all over, Alberto. Don't end up like Tenoch and Simmons."

"Where's Dr. Simmons?" Alberto repeated his earlier question.

"He's still upstairs."

"You shot him?"

"Maybe," Cassy said.

"Goddamn it! Tell me!" Alberto said.

"He's dead."

Alberto frowned in incomprehension. "How?"

"With his own knife."

Unseen by Alberto, Alex's hand closed around a glass bottle of intra- venous fluid, the size of a baseball, on the surface of the anesthesia con- sole. His index and middle finger circled the neck of the bottle. His thumb hugged the base of it.

"You stabbed him?" Alberto asked in Spanish and moved around the OR table toward Cassy.

"Yes," she replied in Spanish, still holding her aim steady on Alberto.

"Give me the gun," Alberto said, slowly moving within a half dozen steps of Cassy. His back was now turned to the anesthesia console. Alex stood up behind the anesthesia machine, out of Alberto's line of vision, and readjusted his fingers around the unbreakable glass bottle.

Cassy stood stiff-armed with the pistol locked into the end of both arms as Alberto advanced on her another two steps. Her mind blurred as the barrel of Alberto's pistol bore down on her like an advancing missile. So focused on the barrel of Alberto's pistol, Cassy did not see her son step out from behind the anesthesia machine with the glass bottle in his hand.

"Drop the fucking gun," Alberto screamed again. His words reverber- ated around the circular room, accelerating in intensity as if in an echo chamber. Alberto's shout was a pitching signal. Alex reared back like a Rangers' pitcher and hurled the glass bottle at Alberto's head. The bottle spiraled and twisted in its trajectory, whizzing past Alberto's face like a Nolan Ryan fast ball, brushing his left ear.

Alberto reacted to the passing glass bottle like a dusted off batter, twist- ing and turning his body to face Alex. The glass bottle crashed into the surgical instrument display case, shattering the glass panel into a deafening clatter of glass shards. In that instant a shot exploded. The earsplitting discharge from Cassy's pistol magnified itself in the closed chamber of the operating room and stunned the three occupants with reverberating shock waves. The endless bang suspended time and blurred all perception for Cassy.

During this instant that seemed to stretch forever, Alberto's body rose from the polished terrazzo tile floor and floated lazily in midair. At the same time, a black buttonhole eerily materialized in the center of Alberto's white shirt. He seemed to hover suspended. A circular crimson stain soaked his shirt, widening about the blackened hole in the front of his chest.

Gradually, the rising and levitating of Alberto's body returned to a real-time sequence, and his lifeless body was flung abruptly backward like a cast off doll, sprawling with his arms outstretched against the length of the operating room table. The bloody circle on his shirt enlarged until droplets flowed in a continuous stream onto the green cotton sheeting of the operating room table.

Dropping the pistol to the floor, Cassy raced across the slick floor of the operating room and collapsed behind the anesthesia console, covering Alex and the dog, pulling them into the protective circle of her arms.

FORTY-TWO

THE WARM AIR blasted through the open driver's window of Kevin Knowland's Blazer and collided with the refrigerated chill of the interior as the car rolled up the long driveway to the Tudor house, easing to a stop under the porte cochere. Alex and the puppy lay tangled together on the back seat. Neither moved when Kevin opened the rear door.

Cassy crawled out of the right front passenger door. Her rumpled white silk blouse and black pleated skirt she had worn since Mexico City hung around her like a cassock. Exhaustion numbed her body. Fatigue fuzzed her mind. The fear and terror of the past forty-eight hours resonated inside her.

Kevin gently lifted the sleeping puppy from Alex's arms and handed him to Cassy. Then Kevin picked up Alex from the back seat and laid him easily across his left shoulder. His head rested against the curve of Kevin's neck. Alex momentarily opened his eyes and then fell back asleep. At the front door, Cassy punched in the intrusion alarm code and then looked helplessly at Kevin. "I've lost my door key."

Kevin rolled his hand around in his pocket and pulled out a brass key. "I still have the key you gave me last week."

Inside the foyer Cassy breathed deeply the clean filtered air. The house was silent except for the rustle of circulated air in the air conditioning ducts. She stood with her eyes closed, letting the home air cleanse her lungs of the impurities of the Mexico City smog. For a long moment her mind was in its own private world, the turmoil of her life since Marquez still roiling. Her whole life compressed itself into the past few days—

nothing before and nothing to come afterward. Into this turbulence of her mind, the aromatic smell of cooking pepperoni wisped.

At the same moment a moist raspy voice called her name from a far away corner of her mind. "Cassandra . . . is that you?" Was it her mother's voice calling her to breakfast? She shivered at the memory of her dead mother—seeing her mother's face as clearly in her mind as if she were beside her in the foyer. Her mind would not clear her mother's image.

Then the hoarse voice called again. "Cassandra Marta!" The woman's voice was so near that her words touched Cassy's face. She felt herself engulfed by a woman's arms. Relief flowed through those arms and into her, comforting her. Reality staggered back into her mind. Cassy opened her eyes to see the smiling face of Betty Freeman. Tears streamed from the inner corners of Betty's eyes down the thick skin of her broad face. Cassy hugged her friend fiercely.

"Cassy, I've been so worried . . . ever since you called. Nobody could find you."

"It's a long and awful story . . . ," Cassy said.

"Kevin told me what happened this morning at Park Haven," Betty said, still holding Cassy. "I'm so sorry for you and Alex." They held each other for a long time until Betty said, "Right now, let's get you something to eat. I've fixed Alex's favorite . . . pepperoni pizza."

"Betty, you are so thoughtful, but Alex needs to go to bed. It's been a long night. Give me a few minutes to get Alex situated, and I'll eat some pizza with you."

Upstairs in Alex's room Cassy pulled down the sheets. Kevin laid Alex, still sound asleep, into the lower bunk. Cassy nestled the dog in the crook of her son's arm. Then she straightened up and leaned against the rail of the upper bunk. Kevin stood silently at the end of Alex's bed. Cassy exchanged a look with Kevin's gentle blue eyes for a moment before saying, "Tell me it's over."

"It's all over," Kevin said, coming around the end of the bunk to touch her forearm. "And I owe you an apology." Cassy turned to look at him quizzically. "This morning the police surveillance team found the listening devices and electronic bugs that Tenoch had installed in your house. The microphones were the smallest and most sensitive available and were buried deep in the walls of every room. Tenoch heard everything you said."

"No apology necessary."

"Yes, there is. I didn't believe you when you said that Tenoch was listening to your every word. I apologize."

"Thanks for everything," Cassy said, standing quietly beside the bunk bed and looking down at her sleeping son. Her eyes moistened, and Kevin reached for her. She let him hold her close.

"You need some sleep, too," Kevin said, holding her by the shoulders as she pulled back.

"Not just yet," Cassy said. "I have to eat some of Betty's pizza . . . if she's kind enough to fix pizza at eight in the morning, then I'll eat a piece before I crash into bed."

The clean fragrance of dishwashing detergent, a floral scent like the inside of a florist shop, suffused the kitchen, mingling with the aroma of cooking pizza. The brick floor beside the kitchen counter glistened with a new coat of wax, and Cassy fought to prevent the mental image of Lupita's strangled and bloated face lying on this spot from entering the conscious screen of her mind as she walked over the polished floor. Betty quartered the steaming pizza and plopped the bubbling slices onto a serving plate as Cassy sat at the table. "I'll save a piece for Alex to have when he wakes up."

"Have you found Lupita?" Cassy asked Kevin as he slid into his chair beside her at the kitchen table. He shook his head slowly.

"I made some iced tea . . . it's that special fruit blend I found in your cabinet," Betty said. Cassy hesitated as she pulled her chair closer to the kitchen table. The offer of the glass of iced tea rushed back the conflicting emotions, the fear, the anxiety, her own self-doubts, and her guilt in a torrent. Sweat popped onto her forehead. She gasped for air. Holding onto the edge of the table, she fought for control.

"Cassy . . . are you all right?" Betty said as she laid the pizza at the center of the round table. "My mama would say that you look like you've just seen a ghost."

"No. I'm fine."

"How about the iced tea . . . ," Betty repeated.

"No, No . . . just water would be fine," Cassy said shuddering at the memory of a chilled crystal goblet, the moisture on the glass, and the sprigs of mint on the rim.

Cassy managed to pick up the hot pizza, nibbling at its edges but not tasting, while Betty and Kevin each finished their first piece. Finally, she shoved her plate to the center of the table, unable to keep the pizza before her any longer. The smell reprised the nausea from her weekend in Mexico City. The tightness of her throat and the dryness of her mouth choked her. She hated to admit it, but her body was demanding a cigarette.

"I guess this is as good a time as any to give you the toxicology report on Marquez and Charlie," Betty said. "Both were positive for tetrodotoxin."

"I guess it's just academic interest now, but at least I feel better that my mistaking Marquez for dead doesn't seem so dumb after all," Cassy said and reached for Betty's open package of Marlboros lying in the center of the kitchen table. Her hand stopped midway to the package. She pulled her fingers back without a cigarette and without a word slid from her chair. Kevin and Betty looked back and forth at each other, puzzled by Cassy's unexplained leave-taking from the table.

Stretching up on her tiptoes, she rummaged in the rear of the upper shelf of the cabinet above the sink until she had retrieved a carton of Marlboro cigarettes. As she pulled the carton off the shelf, two unopened packages fell out of the carton, landing in the disposal drain. Hesitating a fraction of a second over the spray nozzle, Cassy turned the cold water faucet on and flipped the garbage disposal switch. The garbage disposal roared alive, and she shoved the unopened cigarette packages into the growling black maw of the disposal, flushing the soggy packages away with the cold water spray.

"Cassy! What in the hell are you doing?" Betty shouted above the roar of the garbage disposal. "Those are perfectly good cigarettes."

"Not for me . . . they're part of my past."

At that moment the kitchen telephone rang. The three of them stared at the ringing phone as Cassy shut off the disposal—indecision hung suspended among them.

"Do you want me to get it?" Kevin finally asked. Cassy nodded slowly, afraid to answer and afraid not to. Kevin picked it up on the fifth ring. He listened a moment before turning to Cassy, his hand covering the telephone receiver.

"It's your ex-husband. He's heard on the morning news about the Park Haven incident. Do you want to talk to him?"

Cassy shrugged her hands and exhaled a long breath. "I'll take it in my bedroom."

The sun continued its rise, reflecting glints off the pool's surface into her bedroom when Cassy entered her room. Disordered piles of scribbled papers, unopened mail, computer printouts, and copies of medical articles cluttered Cassy's desktop. She collapsed slowly in the swiveling desk chair in front of the blank video screen of her computer and punched the telephone button under the blinking red light.

"Yes, Scott?" Her voice was flat.

"Is Alex all right?"

"He's fine. Sleeping in his room," Cassy said. "I'm fine, too." Her sarcasm flew right past her ex-husband.

"You shouldn't have taken my son with you to Mexico City," Scott Spence said abruptly. "No mother in her right mind would have subjected a son to the experience you just put my son through. You aren't fit to have custody of him."

"Are you through?" Cassy asked after several seconds. The restrained fury in her voice silenced Spence.

At last Cassy broke the hollow hum of the line that separated them farther than the miles across Dallas. "I did not take Alex to Mexico City. He was kidnapped by Señor Tenoch. I went to Mexico City to bring him home." There was a long pause between them that went on forever.

Cassy reclined the desk chair, resting her head against its back until she felt the tightness in her neck ease. "I understand that you plan to contest the custody arrangement for Alex, that you want custody of our son, claiming I am an unfit mother."

"Now, Cass. That was last week I said that . . . you know a week in politics can change everything . . . I'm still up five points in the polls."

"Stop it," Cassy said. She pushed her chairback upright in front of her desk and brushed aside the litter on her desktop. "Shut up and listen."

Again the telephone connection hissed into a distant hum as if charged with her electricity. "Never try to take Alex from me." The menacing tone in her voice ripped through the line. "Have I made myself clear?"

"Yes." His outburst doused, Scott Spence moved the conversation to safer ground, seeking to avoid any more conflict. "Cassy, you mentioned that you needed some money . . . now that you're no longer at the hospital . . . I've found a way to get you some of the money from our Cayman rainy day fund . . . it will be a loan from my. . . ." His words were nervously clipped, his sentences fragmented.

Cassy cradled the telephone at her shoulder and serenely leaned back against the chair lifting her bare feet to the edge of the desk and curling her toes over the flat edge of the desktop. The red nail paint on her toes from Rosa's pedicure was chipped and flecked. A smile danced on her lips.

"I'm glad you mentioned the Cayman treasure hoard, because it's another loose end that I need to take care of today."

"I will take care of your money problems . . . you'll get your share . . . your half . . . I promise."

"I don't want the money."

"If that's the way you want it to be. . . ."

"No, that's not the way I want it to be. I want you to set this tax due account straight with the IRS. Pay off the tax and the penalties and whatever else that we owe."

"Cass . . . I can't . . . the election . . . there won't be any money left after paying . . . I'll get killed in the polls if it ever becomes known I didn't pay my taxes!"

"Do it today." She laid the phone gently in the cradle and stretched lazily back in her desk chair that fit her body so comfortably. For the first time in what seemed forever she was at peace. The seconds ticked past into minutes. Maybe an hour passed. Cassy drifted half asleep, half awake in the chair, her feet propped over the edge of the desktop, until she felt a hand on her shoulder. When Cassy looked up, she found Kevin's blue eyes studying her as he stood quietly beside her chair.

"I have to be going now. Are you and Alex going to be all right?"

"I think so," Cassy said and paused. "Is there anything left for me to do with the police investigation?" Cassy asked, pulling herself full upright to stand in front of him, her eyes just below his.

"I'll need to take your formal statement for the homicide report. There won't be any Marquez investigation after Betty's report of the tetro-dotoxin results. No charges for Simmons' and Alberto's deaths either. That was clearly self-defense."

"What about the Mexico City end? Ana Ruiz, Juan Torres, and who knows how many other deaths Tenoch was responsible for in his organ market?"

"I've already checked. The Mexico City police have no missing person reports of Ana Ruiz or Juan Torres."

"What about Trent?" Cassy asked. She knew the answer but had to ask.

"He's vanished. Mexico City police have no report of anyone match-ing his description." He paused. "Dead or alive in Mexico City."

"The rest?"

"We really need to have a body or some evidence."

"You never will find any of them. Tenoch cremated their bodies," Cassy said. Hesitating a second, she asked, "Have you contacted Raul Garcia or his son?"

"Who?"

Cassy described her conversation with Raul and his son and told him of their plans to go to the police in Mexico City with the information they had about Ana Ruiz. "I want you to talk to Raul," Cassy said. She dialed the telephone number she found in her Rolodex.

Less than a minute later Raul Garcia was on the line. Cassy told him about Alberto and Simmons. "Raul, a good friend is with me here in Dallas. Lt. Kevin Knowland of the Dallas Police Department would like to hear exactly what you and your son told me." She listened a moment and then continued, "We must be certain that an organ black market like Tenoch set up never happens again . . . never!" Cassy handed the tele-phone to Kevin and motioned for him to sit in her chair. She left Kevin hunched over her desk with the telephone at his ear, scribbling notes onto a yellow legal tablet.

In the kitchen Betty piled the dishes and pizza pan in the sink while she chewed away on a slice of pepperoni pizza. "Where's Kevin?" Betty asked when Cassy appeared in the archway.

"In my bedroom talking to Dr. Garcia. Kevin will work with Raul and his son to follow up the investigation of Tenoch's black market in organs."

Betty lit up a Marlboro and offered the package to Cassy. "Do you want to tell me everything now or later?"

Shaking her head at the cigarettes, Cassy said, "I have one more person I need to call. Then I'll tell you everything."

Using the other telephone line, Cassy found Gracie at her daughter's house. As soon as Gracie was on the line she said, "Gracie, the evil is gone from the hospital." She listened for a moment. A smile replaced the frown that had creased her face for days. "You're very kind, Gracie. I'm sure I will be back at the Metro Hospital soon, too." Cassy listened again, now a broad grin came to her face. "That's where I plan to spend my time when I go back . . . in the heart surgery OR." Cassy listened again and then her smile faded into seriousness. "Gracie, I want you to help me locate the source of the powder that Dr. Hendricks found in Haiti. It's important that we learn more about it. He made an important scientific discovery for a new drug with your help. That discovery may be the good from all this evil." They said their goodbyes. Cassy looked up from the telephone at Betty, sitting at the kitchen table, the tip of a Marlboro burning close to her fingers, waiting expectantly.

"Let's go sit by the pool. I'll tell you the whole story," Cassy said.

At poolside Cassy edged her legs over the lip of the concrete coping, letting the water swish about her feet and legs. "Where shall I begin?"

From under the shaded overhang of the patio umbrella, Betty said, "At the beginning . . . who killed Marquez?"

"Tenoch. The Saturday night Marquez showed up in the Metro ER was to be the first heart transplant ever for Tenoch's organ black marketing scheme. Tenoch had been selling transplant organs out of Mexico for a long time, but never hearts. The technical necessities to preserve a donor in a state of suspended animation and to transplant the heart from that donor prevented him from expanding his market to include donor hearts. Until that Saturday night, Tenoch had prospered by selling organs that have a longer shelf life . . . like kidneys, corneas, and livers."

"You make an organ sound like a grocery store item for purchase."

"That's how Tenoch operated his organ market. Organs on demand."

"And where did he find his donors?"

"I'm not exactly sure yet . . . that's what Kevin, Raul and his son in Mexico City hope to find out. There is likely to be a trail that will lead to the poorest sections of Mexico City, throughout Central America, and maybe into South America. Raul's newspaper editor son has a file of unconfirmed reports about missing persons thought to have been abducted for their organs as far away as Guatemala, possibly even Europe."

"My god. I've read those newspaper and magazine articles. I always thought those reports of organ snatching were just hysteria or a reporter's overactive imagination," Betty said, lighting up again and putting on a pair of dark sunglasses all at the same time. "You still haven't told me why Tenoch overdosed Marquez with the tetrodotoxin."

"Marquez tried to block their plans for the first heart transplant. For months, years, Trent Hendricks had worked on perfecting a pharmacologic method of lowering the metabolism of a heart donor into a suspended animation state. And he found it with tetrodotoxin in a precise mix of other biologic agents."

"All supported by Tenoch's money?"

"Yes. So when Heather Hendricks needed a new heart and Trent couldn't find one in this country, he became desperate enough to use his discovery in whatever way necessary to find a heart for Heather. The plan to obtain a heart for his daughter came together on that Saturday night using Trent's surgical expertise, the Hiberna suspending agent, and Tenoch's underground network in Mexico City to abduct the organ donor . . . a thirteen-year-girl . . . Ana Ruiz."

"And nobody tried to stop the crazy bastard?"

"Marquez tried and was killed for his effort. Tenoch dosed him with tetrodotoxin that night when Marquez tried to call off the harvest of Ana Ruiz's heart."

"But Tenoch's dose of tetrodotoxin was not quite enough to suspend the good funeral home director forever."

"But enough to fool me into declaring Marquez dead."

"Then Tenoch completed the job on Marquez by having him tossed out the window," Betty said, lighting up another cigarette off the glowing stub of the one she held in her nicotine-stained fingers. "I still can't understand why he picked on you."

"I fulfilled some fantasy role in Tenoch's psychosis, as if our Aztec heritage had brought us together at this time and place in a divine destiny."

Betty blew her breath out in one long sigh, spilling smoke around her head like a wreath. "What an incredibly dangerous combination of psychosis and wealth."

Cassy lay back on the warm concrete decking, her feet still in the pool.

After a long while Cassy said, "Thanks for being here this morning. Will you stay here for the rest of the day while I sleep?"

"Sure, but you know you're safe here. The nightmare's all over."

"I'm not sure it will ever be over for Alex and me."

"Maybe never over. But surely a new beginning," Betty said.

At that moment the patio door slid back. The grating noise caused Betty and Cassy to turn toward the direction of the house. Kevin pulled the plate glass door closed behind him and walked toward them, holding the German shepherd pup in his arms.

"I just checked on Alex. Sound asleep. But this young pup is ready to meet the new day." He handed the dog to Cassy. She nuzzled him to her face.

Kevin kneeled beside Cassy and scratched the squirming puppy's ears. "Cass, I've got a lot of work to follow up on. From what I learned from Raul, we've just seen the tip of this organ black market. . . ."

"You're on the right track," Cassy said, pulling herself upright with one hand while still holding the dog in the other. "I'll bet you'll find that Tenoch has been operating his organ markets out of private hospitals in Mexico and Central America. It's the only way he could control both the supply of organs and the demand of desperate dying patients . . . away from scrutiny of the medical profession."

"I've got to get started. Are you all right now?"

"Yes," she said. "Betty is going stay with us today."

Kevin pecked Betty on her cheek. "You behave yourself today," he said and winked at her.

While Cassy walked Kevin through the house, Betty sat under the umbrella shade, a Marlboro in one hand and the wiggling puppy in her other hand.

In the foyer, Cassy leaned against Kevin as he opened the oak door. "Thank you for everything," she said and kissed him lightly on his lips. Kevin's fair complexion blushed a scarlet contrast to his blonde hair.

"I would like to see you again," he said flustered and awkwardly reached to touch her hand.

"Not right now. Too much has happened," Cassy said, gently touching his cheek with her fingertips. "Alex and I need some time together to get over all this."

"I'd enjoy cooking shrimp and stir-fries for you and Alex again . . . anytime," Kevin persisted.

"Maybe," she said, smiling and kissing his cheek. "Maybe for sure."